# KILLING THE BEE KING

Jaynie Royal

Regal House Publishing

Published by
Regal House Publishing, LLC
Raleigh, NC 27612

ISBN -13 (paperback): 9780991261208
ISBN -13 (hardcover): 9781646031634
ISBN -13 (epub): 9780991261215
Library of Congress Control Number: 2013921899

All efforts were made to determine the copyright holders and obtain their permissions in any circumstance where copyrighted material was used. The publisher apologizes if any errors were made during this process, or if any omissions occurred. If noted, please contact the publisher and all efforts will be made to incorporate permissions in future editions.

Interior and cover design by Lafayette & Greene
lafayetteandgreene.com
Original cover images © by Shutterstock/Chantal de Bruijne

Regal House Publishing, LLC
https://regalhousepublishing.com

Printed in the United States of America

To Jeff, Chi, Tal, Brax, and Max.
With love.

# Historical Background

England is precariously managed by Henry Addington, nominated to the prime ministership by his popular predecessor William Pitt who resigned in protest when King George III refused to support Catholic emancipation. Tensions are high as the Peace of Amiens—signed between Britain and France two years earlier after a decade of war—begin to break down. Addington institutes a naval blockade of the French coast as Napoleon gathers his forces at Boulogne, a formidable mass of soldiers and cannon designated the Armee d'Englaterre whose raison d'être is the wholesale invasion of England: "a nation of shopkeepers," Napoleon derisively claims, from whom they are separated by a "mere ditch." This *ditch*, however, is effectively defended by the mighty English navy, and French vessels find themselves confined to various harbors along the coast.

Convinced that if they can be "masters of the Channel for six hours," they will become "masters of the world," Napoleon develops a plan to combine the French fleet and lure the English from its vigil. He secretly offers a substantial payment to any English captain who can lead the French invasion fleet through the treacherous coastal waters of England, known as the Goodwin Sands.

The English populace is burdened by rising taxation to finance an increasingly unpopular war, and a series of poor harvests have resulted in grain shortages and bread riots. Popular societies advocating revolution are mushrooming up all over the English Isles, particularly in Ireland, which has long suffered under the tyranny of English domination. The Catholic majority in Ireland is poor and disenfranchised, and under the militant leadership of the United Irishmen is determined to win political freedom.

Napoleon Bonaparte has promised to provide military assistance if the Irish can demonstrate their own willingness to rise to the banner of revolution. At this critical moment of maximum peril, Britain is bereft of the European allies who once stood at her side in the former mighty coalitions against the Napoleonic tide. Russia is led by the youthful Alexander I whose father Paul I had been assassinated two years before. After costly campaigns against Napoleon, Paul I had abruptly sided with France: he sent an expeditionary Cossack force to attack English interests in India and established plans for a joint Russo-French naval assault on the English Isles. His son's emphatic pro-English policy led some to believe the English were responsible for the murder of Czar Paul I. Despite Alexander's condemnation of Napoleon as the "oppressor of Europe and the disturber of world's peace," there was little he could do to restore equilibrium. Prussia and Spain made peace with France, and Holland became the Batavian Republic, leaving Austria as Britain's only significant ally on the continent. When Napoleon's triumphs in Italy forced Austria to sue for peace, Britain stood completely isolated against the French juggernaut.

With Britain's meager army engaged in the maintenance of a wide-flung empire, the only defense between Napoleon's bristling army and the terrified English populace was the navy. The sailors of this inestimable navy, many of them Irish, were frequently pressed into service, ill-fed, underpaid, and primed for rebellion...

# Cast of Characters

**Wolfe Trant**: Owner of a linen factory; previously a bare-knuckle boxer with a history of political rebellion against England.

ENGLAND:

**King George III**: King of England, prone to bouts of madness that plunge the political world into chaos and encourage the formation of an opposition court around the Prince of Wales.

## The Torys

**William Pitt**: Lord Warden of the Cinque Ports, ex-prime minister, and leader of a clandestine spy ring operating out of Walmer Castle. Eloquent and popular with the people.

**Malcolm Dundas**: Pitt's undersecretary and closest friend.

**Lady Hester Stanhope**: Pitt's niece who resides with him at Walmer Castle.

**General John Moore**: General who fought in the Seven Years War and the War of American Independence. Pitt's military adviser and leader of the Walmer Volunteers.

**Henry Addington**: Prime minister of England, overwhelmed by the current challenges of office and the ominous threat of imminent French invasion.

**William Brunskill**: School friend of Pitt and warden of Newgate Prison.

## The Whigs

**Charles Fox**: Leader of the Whig opposition who seeks to curb Pitt's influence through moderate means.

**Henry Eden**: Young hothead of the Whig party who bristles under Fox's restrictions.

**Prince George**: King George III's son and heir to the throne. Self-indulgent and vain; eager to ascend the throne and reward those who cater to him.

**Duchess of Devonshire**: Popular society hostess who hosts political events to benefit her close friend Charles Fox.

## The United Irishmen

**Egan Trant**: Wolfe's brother; leader of the United Irishmen in London.

**Nick O'Connor**: Member of the United Irishmen; Egan Trant's right-hand man.

**Thomas Dildin**: Member of the United Irishmen in London.


## FRANCE:

**Napoleon Bonaparte**: Self-appointed emperor of the French, master military tactician, assembling an invasion force to conquer England.

**Charles Maurice de Talleyrand**: Napoleon's foreign minister, disillusioned with Napoleon's self-aggrandizing strategies; secretly conspiring with Pitt and the French Resistance.

**Casimir de Montrond**: Ex-aristocrat; Talleyrand's closest friend.

**Joseph Fouché**: Napoleon's commissioner of police.

**Chavert**: Fouché's second in command; chief inspector of police.

**Jeanne de Recamier (Primrose)**: Popular society hostess who operates clandestinely as one of the five leaders of the Resistance.

# Prologue

BOULOGNE, FRANCE
*November 22, 1803*

He wanted nothing more than to die, to fall, loose-limbed and grateful, into the pillowed softness of the snow-shrouded embankment. He rested a moment, sagging against the weathered bark of an ancient pine, hand pressed tightly to his side, dark blood seeping sullenly between his fingers. The musket ball had shattered upon impact, he knew, leaving a stippled array of wounds before lodging somewhere beneath his ribs. And it was from here, in the dark heat of ravaged flesh that the pain flared and intensified—as if a creature of fang and claw writhed within, desperately seeking escape from its imprisonment of bone. Life was now measured in moments, each breath a jagged agony. It would be so easily done—to simply fall to his knees in this quiet place, this clearing, this hushed enclosure of green slumbering beneath its burden of snow. The massive trunks of maritime pine, deeply fissured and sheathed in ice, rose like the columns of deserted cathedrals, their quiet stillness broken only by the occasional soft thud of snowfall released from a burdened bough and the whistling breath of the wind through the trees. High above, between their gnarled branches, he could see the darkening gray of a winter sky. As the shadows lengthened around him, the dying sun gilding the boughs in the last of its light, he felt the wetness of tears on his cheeks.

Yes, a good place to die.

As twilight gathered and thickened, a wild rabbit scampered into the edge of the clearing—a rapid blur of movement that abruptly stilled. Pink-veined ears cocked forward, nose twitching, it remained motionless, a pale smudge beneath the lengthening shadows of a lofty pine. Then, darting forward, it pawed at the icy crust. Bleached as it was of light and warmth, this terrain seemed the province of species owning the thickest of pelts. Indeed, the man who slumped on the fringes of this clearing, who watched the rabbit through blood-washed lids, had felt the chill most acutely. It had long since stolen all feeling from his feet and rendered his fingers unresponsive. The cold crept up through his boots, crawled through his sodden under-layers soaked with sweat and blood like some icy-fingered predator. He shivered as the body warmth of recent exertion left him, leaving a slowly freezing layer of wet undergarments against his clammy skin. While the cold presented danger enough to the uninjured traveler, this man welcomed the numbness, quite aware that the blood loss would accomplish what the chill would take longer to do.

The rabbit, unaware of this human intrusion, had unearthed a small clump of barrenwort beneath the snow, and its small body quivered momentarily, as if in delight of the anticipated feast. The man felt rather than saw the owl's arrival in the sudden cascade of dislodged snow and the whoosh of air propelled by the beat of powerful wings. It emerged from the landscape, as if conjured by the Great Pinetti himself, ghostly gray plumage flecked with white, yellow eyes unblinking within the feathered heart of its face. Then the bird swiftly lunged, the glint of outstretched talons visible beneath the snowy breast. Galvanized, the rabbit's powerful hind legs sprang into action as it leapt forward in a series of quick, erratic movements designed to evade and confuse. The owl, however, was not to be deterred. As its talons bit into the flanks of its prey, the rabbit screamed. The penetratingly shrill shriek echoed eerily through the forest and remained with the man long after the owl had disappeared into the dusky evening sky.

It would be easier for him, the man thought; simply a matter of welcoming sleep. He closed his eyes, and behind the red of his lids, amidst the sweet sap of pine, he smelled his own blood. The dogs, their barks shrill and excited in the crisp evening air, must have smelled it too. They were still some distance from him, and sound traveled rapidly in the mountains, but they would be here before long. Amid the pain, the deadening cold, and his yearning desire to sleep, he felt the weight of duty in the small oilskin wrapping that lodged within his coat pocket— his last mission, and a scrap of papers upon which a nation depended. Gritting his teeth, the man gathered himself around the steely resolve for which he had become renowned. Later there would be time to sleep. Now he must make the rendezvous, even if he had to claw a path through the snow trailing his innards behind him.

He had intended his departure to be a stealthy one, slipping out through the east gate, his ragged regimentals identical to the thousands of other fusiliers-of-the-line that crammed the military encampment at Boulogne-sur-Mer. Shot and pursued by an overzealous captain who had mistaken him for a deserter, his exit strategy had not exactly gone according to plan. But the years had lent him a certain resilience—being, as he was, an older agent who had grown white-whiskered in the service of his country, with a decade of field experience and a long list of successful operations. His inclination for unobtrusive travel had become almost instinctual, prompting him to avoid the ridge-lines and travel across ice and rock whenever possible in order to leave less evidence of his path. Denser vegetation or a swiftly moving stream would have been preferable—easier to throw off pursuers of either the human or canine variety. The lofty pine canopy, however, allowed little undergrowth, and the streams were caught and buried beneath layers of ice and snow. Ultimately his tracks had been impossible to conceal, his progress marked incontrovertibly by the deep furrow that formed in his wake and punctuated by dark drops of blood that appeared almost black in the fading light.

"Il est parti comme ça!" A voice echoed through the trees. *He went this way!* Shadowed pools of gray deepened to black as the pallid disc of the sun slipped toward the western horizon. He had perhaps five minutes of light left; it would be impossible to find the rendezvous in the dark. Assuming they had waited for him—he was at least an hour overdue.

The sweetish heave of nausea rose up in the back of his throat as he lunged forward, legs deadened weights beneath him, the musket wound a white-heated flame in his side. The trees gradually began to thin out, the maritime pine giving way to scrubby thickets of sea buckthorn and wild privet. Beyond was the meadow, bare and featureless beneath the soft drifts of snow, which then dropped forty feet in a craggy cliff to the ocean, and safety, below. He could hear the frenzied excitement of the dogs again, much closer now, and the shouts of the soldiers who accompanied them. Spheres of lantern-light appeared, illuminating in yellow, hazy spots the fringe of frozen pine fifty feet behind.

The dense clumps of buckthorn, some six feet in height, rose up before him like ice-shrouded specters, jagged branches tearing at his clothing and raking across his frozen skin. His peripheral vision shifted, darkened. The man stumbled and almost blacked out, the landscape slanting under him like the storm-tilted deck of a ship. As the darkness gradually receded and the world stabilized, he resumed his lurching path into the meadow. His legs, as far as he knew, were gone; he had long since ceased to feel them. The only indication that he was still moving forward was the gradual change in foliage; the blackthorn diminished in size toward the coast, and the meadow grasses, bowed beneath the snow, provided little in the way of concealment. His progress was easier, but the hazy light of the declining sun, without the shadowed retreats of the forest, highlighted his westward track and shrouded his figure in the last of its light: a clear target to the shooters who would soon appear in his wake. He was so close. Just another fifty feet to the path that wound down to the beach below, and the HMS *Redoubtable* that waited in the bay...

"Arrêtez!"

He could hear them close behind him, knew that they had their muskets aimed at his back, knew that there was very little hope. But he did not stop. He could not stop. To stop was to die, and he was not ready to give up. Not yet. His body, beginning an inexorable shut-down, was powered by the strength of his will alone. Gulping frozen air into his over-worked lungs, he felt peculiarly as if his entire being had washed away and all that remained was the thunderous beat of his own heart; that, and his indomitable determination to move forward, to keep moving forward.

"Arrêtez!"

An explosion sounded behind him, and a musket shell whistled past his left ear and landed with a soft thud in the snow. He wasn't going to make it, he realized dully. He had failed. Suddenly, in the growing darkness a shape appeared like an apparition ahead. "Down, man!" the figure shouted, raising a rifle to his head.

Without thinking, the man finally, with a sense of sublime gratitude, allowed his legs to collapse beneath him and fell forwards into the soft blanket of snow as a quick series of shots sounded above. Then more: four, five, six muskets firing. The muffled cry of the soldiers hit, the yelp of a wounded dog. Then quiet. He tried to roll over but found he was unable to move, the cold wet of snow in his mouth mingling with the metallic taste of blood. Then gentle hands turned him. "Is he alive?"

"Barely. Get him down to the boat."

English voices, English accents. They had come for him, he realized with relief. He raised an arm weakly. "Wait, Captain Blackwood?"

"Here," Blackwood answered, leaning down to hear his whispered words.

The man grasped the oilskin packet from his inside coat pocket, his hands sticky with congealing blood. With the last of his bodily reserves, he thrust the packet at the captain, his eyes communicating the urgency that his soundlessly working mouth, now filled with blood, could not. Finally, with the knowledge that the package had been safely delivered, the man allowed himself to succumb to unconsciousness.

# 1.

## WALMER CASTLE. DEAL, ENGLAND
*November 24, 1803*

In the predawn darkness the Channel was still and quiet. Coal-dark clouds pillowed over the black expanse of water which extended from the dunes of Calais to the salt-marshes of Kent. A loose flock of dark-bellied Brent geese, completing a cold migratory journey from northern Russia, appeared beneath the cloudbank and descended with guttural clucking and squawks to the flat shingle beach at Deal where tufts of sea astor and glasswort provided winter sustenance. Vessels moored off the Downs lay humped in silence, their stern-lights dull smudges in the gloom.

Above the anchored ships and the narrow streets of Deal, above the irregular patchwork of wood-and-brick houses, above the vast boat-yards, sat Walmer Castle, squat and robust like a disapproving dowager queen. Gray bricks streaked and textured with age (they had come from dismantled monasteries before Henry VIII's builders acquired them) formed an outer carapace ten feet thick with deeply sunken windows peering from shadowed recesses. These massive battlements had been made to support heavy guns that were now long gone; Walmer's days of battle and siege belonged to the distant past. At this present day, the castle had become rather old-fashioned and had been transformed from a military stronghold to the official residence of the Lord Warden of the Cinque Ports, the post being currently occupied by His Right Honorable William Pitt the Younger, who even now slumped in a leather armchair that had seen better days—as indeed had its current occupant.

Pitt's companion gazed bleakly across the Channel toward the coast of France. The thick-paned glass offered a distorted reflection of a rumpled linen waistcoat and one brawny hand sprinkled with fine ginger hairs, the owner of which leaned heavily against the casement as if his ability to maintain an upright stance without it remained in doubt. Behind him was a sparsely furnished but comfortable room with a threadbare Turkish rug covering the wood-paneled floor, a stone-brick fireplace, a narrow desk and chair, and a bookcase that sagged under its burden of leather-bound books. An upholstered sofa and two arm-chairs situated in front of the fireplace dominated the small space. The cracked leather and plush-but-faded carpet spoke of masculine comfort with little of the pretension that might attend the Lord Warden's room of choice.

"Are ye quite certain of his information, Will?" Malcolm Dundas asked, turning from the window. He gestured toward the desk where a small square of parchment lay open on its surface. The oilskin wrapper which had recently enclosed it lay discarded to one side, still stained with the blood of the man who had carried it.

"I am afraid there is little room for doubt, Mal. This agent was one of our very best." Pitt sighed wearily. It was late. Or early for those who might be accustomed to rising with the dawn, but these men had been awake all night.

"The thirteenth of December?" Dundas exhaled sharply. "That only gives us…"

"Nineteen days," Pitt supplied, rising stiffly to his feet. Crossing to the bookcase, he poured himself another glass of brandy from the decanter that occupied the top shelf. Loosening his cravat impatiently, Pitt raised his eyebrows in query, an empty glass raised in Dundas's direction.

William Pitt was a tall, angular man, all sharp edges and bony pro-trusions with prominent cheekbones and a sharply hooked nose. Dark hair, shot through with silver at his temples, was carelessly tied back in a ribbon; his countenance was pale, his cheeks flushed with fever or drink—it was often difficult to tell which. His expensive clothes were worn with casual disregard and often appeared as if he had slept in them overnight, as indeed sometimes he did. While his appearance tended toward negligence, it was his eyes that commanded the most at-tention. They were a curious shade of pale gray and seemed to contain all the energy and fire that his physical person lacked, as if his powerful intellect had been distilled to irises of silver that glowed with a molten inner heat.

"Aye, I think I'd better," Dundas replied to the unspoken question. Pitt poured a second and handed it to his friend.

Pitt gulped down the contents of his glass and slumped back in his chair. He was exhausted. It had been a tense few weeks. Actually, it had been a tense eight months since he had resigned as prime minister. What was supposed to have been a semi-retirement to the primarily ceremonial position of Lord Warden of the Cinque Ports had instead become an entrée into a world of espionage and subterfuge. Instead of playing the English prime minister on the world stage, Pitt had become the leader of an underground movement concerned with infiltration, subversion, and, if need be, assassination. The Black Hawks, financed by King George III himself, formed a highly secretive, closely guarded organization that was known to only a handful of men and whose base was located at Walmer Castle, where Pitt now made his home.

"We will have to move the timetable forward. There is no time to waste." Pitt leaned forward, ignoring the sharp pain in his belly. The doctors had prescribed gentle bitters with rhubarb and magnesia, but he just couldn't bring himself to swallow it.

"And Wolfe Trant?" Dundas asked skeptically. "How do ye know we can trust him?"

"I don't," Pitt said simply, rising to pour another drink. "But honestly, Mal, I don't know what other choice we have. I would rather take a chance on Trant than wait for Addington's solution." His lips twisted in derision.

Addington had turned out to be a blind fool, and the fact that Pitt himself had advocated his candidacy for prime minister was a constant plague to Pitt. While Addington's domestic agenda had accomplished little in the eight months he had been in office, it was his foreign policy—specifically, his inability to handle Napoleon Bonaparte who even now loomed ominously on the western coast of France, poised to invade English shores—that concerned Pitt.

"Our involvement would never be suspected. Wolfe Trant played a prominent role in the United Irishmen about ten years ago." Pitt turned to face Dundas, leaning one hip against the bookcase, his newly replenished glass in hand. "He was on our watch list, even targeted for retrieval and interrogation; needless to say, a fierce critic of English policy in Ireland and a focal point for Irish rebellion."

"Aye, I remember him." Dundas nodded. "He was a people's hero, led a rebel group at the Battle of New Ross, and then he just disappeared. 'Twas said he became a bare-knuckle boxer. About two years ago he turned up; bought a linen factory just outside of Dublin." Dundas tilted his head back and swallowed his brandy in several quick gulps, his throat working and knotted beneath fair, freckled skin. Pale blue eyes regarded Pitt wearily. "And he speaks French?"

"Yes. Not fluently, I understand, but enough to pass muster. He brings his linen in here to Deal every month, does business with Harding and Sons on Winch Street, so is intimately familiar with the Goodwin Sands."

"And his brother's position won't hurt us," Dundas replied with dubious satisfaction, obviously uncertain of the merits of the entire endeavor but simultaneously aware that some definitive action was required. While his instinct to trust Pitt's judgment was unerring and stalwart, he remained unconvinced of Wolfe Trant's ability to be similarly persuaded.

"Yes, that will be a fortunate relationship for us under the circumstances," Pitt mused. Egan Trant, Wolfe's brother, had been the London head of the United Irishmen for the past year, a subversive organization dedicated to liberating Ireland from the English yoke.

For a moment it was quiet in the room as Pitt and Dundas contemplated the situation in which they currently found themselves. The two men had been colleagues for several decades and had early discovered an instinctive affinity that both understood to be rare in politics, where the aspiring postured, agendas remained hidden, and relationships were prompted and defined by political expediency.

Despite an impoverished youth, Malcolm Dundas came from a proud clan; indeed, the Dundases were one of the oldest Scottish families in existence. When the whiskey streamed in his veins, and his memories of the Highlands became particularly poignant, Dundas would remind Pitt of his illustrious heritage: "Helias, son of Uctred, obtained a charter of the lands in Dundas in west Lothian in the reign of Malcolm IV in the twelfth century." Then he would clap one burly hand on Pitt's narrow shoulder and claim in triumphant, if slurred, tones: "Any prime minister can raise a man to the House of Lords, my friend, but it takes seven centuries of Scottish history to make a Dundas of Dundas!"

Georgian society was unimpressed. The Jacobite uprisings of 1745 and the English army's bloody victory at Culloden the following year remained fresh in English memories, and anti-Scots sentiment was rife. For Dundas, staunch friend and companion of Pitt, they deigned to make an exception. The snobbery, however, was just as prevalent but of a subtler sort. Other Scots seeking to clamber the slippery slope of high

society smoothed their distinctive Scottish brogue and anglicized their
rustic manners, concealing provincial origins beneath powdered wigs,
velvet, and lace. Malcolm Dundas wanted none of that. He deliberately
thickened his Scottish burr on those rare occasions he ventured forth
in society and, like Pitt, wore his own thick ginger hair in tangled profusion. Whether this stemmed from his own inclination or an instinct
to irritate was difficult to ascertain; Pitt, however, thoroughly enjoyed
both the process and the aftermath and cared little either way. Dundas
was blunt and short-tempered and had little time or appreciation for
affectation of any kind. In short, in society he was an irritable bear, his
belligerence only increased by his awareness of Pitt's quiet amusement
at his expense.

Despite their rational empathy, the two men could not have been
more opposite in physical appearance: Dundas was raw-boned, robust
and ruddy, and appeared as pink and healthy as his friend was pale and
sickly. His reluctant acceptance into Georgian society may have also
been influenced by his stature—not much taller than Pitt, he measured
twice the breadth, with a solidity of bone and muscle that disconcerted
many an aristocratic fop who was fool enough to cross his path.

"Mmph." Dundas broke the silence with a skeptical snort. "Do ye
really think this Wolfe Trant will help us?"

"Not us, perhaps, but Ireland certainly. I have studied his political
pamphlets, copies of his speeches. They were unquestionably inflam-
matory but also principled and pragmatic. As much as he hates the
English, I think he is a man who will do what he believes to be best for
his country, irrespective of how unpopular that decision may be."

"But they were written ten years ago. He sounds now like a changed
man."

"I am hoping a more reflective man, Mal," Pitt replied. "Our intelligence suggests that while Egan is pursuing Irish independence at all
costs, his brother is more cautious. Perhaps this prompted the estrange-
ment? Why else would he have cut ties and dropped out when he was
once a linchpin for political rebellion?"

Pitt set his empty glass on the table and sank back in his chair. For a
moment, both men were silent in the chilly stillness of the room. The
fire, deprived of human attention, had long since dwindled to ash, and
the sky beyond the window was dark and cold. It would be hours yet
before the pale warmth of the sun rose in the east. The men, however,

were oblivious to physical discomforts, which appeared of little consequence in view of the information they had just received: Napoleon was coming and they had less than twenty days to prepare.

"So," Pitt continued, with a tone of forced joviality. "It is just a matter of convincing Wolfe Trant that an alliance with us is the best possible opportunity to better the Irish situation." Pitt raised an eyebrow at his friend, his mouth curving in a ghost of a smile. "How the hell I'm going to do that I have no idea."

"Ye'll find a way," Dundas assured him.

"Let's hope you are right," Pitt mused, sipping his brandy in studied contemplation, a pensive frown forming between dark brows, his silvery gaze focused beyond room and companion. Dundas knew this look only too well. Conversation with Pitt invariably dwindled into silence, often abruptly so when the former prime minister became immersed in some introspective analysis; then, just as suddenly, Pitt would unexpectedly emerge from his reverie, often leaping to his feet as if the momentary respite had left him impatient for action. It seemed to happen more of late; Pitt had a lot on his mind, and Dundas had learned to bide his time in companionable silence—although he was unconvinced Pitt even recalled his presence. Once, Pitt had spent an hour in silent perusal of his empty brandy glass before abruptly continuing the conversation as if it had never been interrupted. This evening, however, Dundas had but only a minute to wait.

Pitt leaned forward in his chair, elbows resting on wrinkled trouser-legs, gaze earnestly holding Dundas's. "I am wholly convinced, Mal, that France is strong…even invincible at arm's length. But she is weakness itself if you can get to grapple with her internally."

Dundas took the topic change with the aplomb of one well-accustomed to Pitt's eccentricities. "I have no doubt yer right," he agreed. "Have ye had word from Cadoudal? Has he arrived in Paris? Did he make contact with Primrose?"

Dundas referred to the infamous Chouan rebel who, by virtue of his strong intelligence and personal charisma, had assumed a leadership role within the French Resistance. Napoleon had destroyed his base in northern France and forced Cadoudal into hiding. The Black Hawks provided him refuge, and now they had offered him an opportunity to return to France financed by English silver. There was an assassination plot afoot, and Pitt wanted to ensure it every chance of success.

"Yes, a cipher arrived from Primrose less than an hour ago. All is proceeding according to schedule. Now if we can get Trant into place…"

Pitt sighed wearily. He again sank back into his chair, suddenly exhausted, and rubbed his fingers across the closed lids of eyes that felt gritty and dry. He winced slightly as a muscle in his neck tightened and spasmed with pain—the price for spending the night in his chair.

"How long has it been since you slept?" Dundas asked, frowning.

Pitt shrugged. "I'll sleep on the way to London."

"Wolfe Trant is in Newgate Prison?" Dundas asked.

"Yes. Six weeks ago he was charged with assaulting a coal manufacturer in Sunderland. A minor incident that might have warranted a day or two of hard labor, but being an Irishman with a history of treason against the Crown… Well, he never stood a chance in English courts." Pitt bent his head toward each shoulder, exhaling in relief as the tightness in his neck eased with an audible crack.

A soft knock at the door preceded the arrival of a smartly dressed manservant carrying a silver tray.

"Just arrived by courier, sir," he murmured as Pitt broke the seal.

"Thank you, James." Rapidly scanning the note enclosed, Pitt rose to his feet. "Ready my carriage. I will be leaving for London directly."

"Very good, sir." James, already at the door, nodded before departing.

"What is it?" Dundas asked.

"It seems the situation has become a little more complicated."

"More complicated?" Dundas muttered with a snort. "Didna think that was possible."

"Yes, it seems that our friend Wolfe Trant killed a fellow prisoner and has been scheduled for execution."

"Are ye sure this Trant person is the right man for the job, Will?" Dundas asked doubtfully. "He sounds like a loose cannon, primed wi' grapeshot and topped by a rapidly burnin' fuse."

"We'll just have to make sure he's aimed at France," Pitt replied, grimly regarding his friend through bloodshot eyes. "There is no other man for the job. Believe me, Mal, he is our only hope."

"Nineteen days," Dundas mused. "It's going to be a damned close call, Will."

"Indeed." Pitt shrugged into the greatcoat held by James, who had long since perfected the art critical to every English butler: appearing silently upon demand as if materializing from the very wallpaper.

Pitt grasped Dundas' arm briefly and smiled. "See you in a few days, my friend." Then he was gone, footsteps echoing on the flagstones as the door closed behind him.

While Pitt exhibited a renewed sense of purpose and resolve, Dundas knew that his friend's weariness had not so much left him as it had been deliberately shouldered aside like an unwelcome guest he refused to indulge. Turning back to the darkened window, the silent Channel, and the French coast that lay beyond, Dundas's thoughts turned again to Napoleon, and he sent a fervent prayer skyward that his frail friend might persevere in the ordeal that was to come.

# 2.

The grubby hackney cab lurched through the ruts and hollows of rue St. Florentin, skating drunkenly as the wheels lost traction in the slush of refuse and debris that was channeled through the mud-caked street. The driver, howling obscenities at his plodding skin-and-bones nag, and the suck and squelch of wheels through the muck made Madame Louise de Caval feel rather ill. Bracing herself against the sweaty upholstery, she ardently hoped that the driver's repertoire would run dry before they arrived at Charles Maurice de Talleyrand's doorstep.

"Ay!" The driver thumped the rear of his seat with one meaty fist as the cab drew to a halting stop. Louise stepped gingerly down and tottering slightly in her new pattens—which elevated her shoes and hemline above street-level grime but made forward progress somewhat unsteady—lurched through the wrought-iron gate that defined the perimeter of Talleyrand's elegant property. The height of pattens seemed to increase in direct proportion to the burgeoning Parisian population and the detritus they produced that inevitably—via emptied chamber pots, horse droppings, or discarded rubbish—ended up in the streets. Despite the awkwardness, there was also the necessity to move quickly once one's feet were on the ground to avoid the spray and splatter of passing carriage wheels. Either way the pattens had to be mastered, Louise thought wryly, as she climbed the steps to Talleyrand's front door.

Admitted by his butler, Louise relieved herself of the unwanted pattens, shrugged off her outer woolen coat, and sighed with pleasurable anticipation of the warmth and comfort that awaited her each Wednesday evening at 18 rue de Florentin. Papered in pale yellow and illuminated by candlelight, the drawing room was enveloped in a soft cocoon of golden warmth. The underlying hum of conversation was interspersed with the tinkle of glasses, the sudden sprinkle of laughter, and the lilting melody of someone playing the pianoforte. The furniture, various sofas and armchairs, was fashioned of elaborately carved walnut, each piece gilded and upholstered in a rich buttery silk. Many of the chairs were occupied, and six tall windows cast a subdued light on elegant women in stiff brocade who flirted with their fans, and men in silken or velvet coats with white stockings and buckled shoes. Outside, the silvery-gray leaves of the beech trees shivered in the late afternoon chill.

These were the remnants of the proudest families of the aristocracy, the ones who had survived the terror of the Revolution and the turbulent years that followed; families with whom Talleyrand stubbornly maintained a friendship despite the disapproval of the emperor. The qualification for entrance to his Wednesday circle, however, was not restricted to birth or wealth but quite simply depended upon one's ability to talk; to do so well was considered one of the highest attributes a person could possess and was the one art in which all endeavored to excel. Students, politicians, and artists fortunate enough to be invited engaged in free and unfettered discussion upon every subject as they sampled what was generally acknowledged to be the finest gastronomical fare Paris had to offer.

The owner of the home, and Louise's host for the evening, was lounging nonchalantly on the sofa, exquisitely attired in a silk dress coat of soft gray, hair impeccably coiffed and powdered. Talleyrand had the manner and appearance of a true epicurean. His features had been described as imposingly noble by those who admired him and stoutly serpentine by those who did not. A certain heaviness of face and body was accentuated by his air of languid indolence. He did not sit so much as he lounged or sprawled, stretched out with what was almost a feline satisfaction, but somehow maintaining a refined poise and finesse that, for most people, might have been quite incongruous with such a posture. From this vantage point, he exhibited an air of quiet enjoyment, as if the life which ebbed and flowed around him were a light comedy being played out for his entertainment, as if it were all some grand joke to which he alone was privy. Heavy-lidded gray eyes swept the room with faint amusement; beneath them resided a nose aggressive in size but sculpted of contour and suggestive of a certain patrician elegance. His mouth, when not pursed in disapproval, was small but finely shaped with a sensually full lower lip. His face, however, was not one easily read; while those who surrounded him were expressive and animated—politics, literature, sex, and religion were all under discussion that evening and few had opinions that were less than passionate—Talleyrand's countenance was unchanging and impenetrable.

He rarely spoke, but when inclined to do so, would interject a single shrewd remark, brightening the discussion with a glittering spark, and then droop back into his demeanor of distinguished lethargy and detachment. Upon hearing a particularly witless comment, he would raise his lorgneurs to one eye and fix the individual within the eyeglass with a steady and immobile gaze before lowering the lens with an expression of fatigued disdain. It signified the coup de grâce. The man or woman in question subsequently found themselves idle on Wednesday evenings.

Louise, however, was a favorite. Talleyrand noticed her across the room and immediately rose to his feet. Limping stiffly over to her, he swept a deep, graceful bow, despite the relative immobility of his right leg which appeared slightly shorter than the other. While it pained Louise to see him thus inconvenienced, she knew better than to suggest he remain seated. Talleyrand was, if nothing else, a gentleman and an aristocrat to whom manners were elevated to the highest art form.

"Louise, ma chère, it is my deepest pleasure to see you here," he said in the grave and deep tone of voice that was so particularly his. "Please, do come and sit beside me." Talleyrand gestured toward the sofa, waiting for her to settle herself before resuming his own seat, stretching his right leg out before him.

"May I ask what Monsieur Carême has prepared for us this evening?" Louise asked with a smile, for she knew of the immense pride and interest Talleyrand took in the provision of his table. The talents of his chef had been brought to the notice of the emperor of Russia, and aristocratic gourmands across Europe vied with each other to secure his services. Despite these professional temptations, Carême remained steadfastly loyal to Talleyrand.

"We will begin with duck breast sautéed in butter and wine, topped with caramelized onions and goat cheese on a pastry crudité," Talleyrand informed her, as gravely as if he were speaking of political policy of the greatest importance. "Does that meet with your approval, madame?" he asked her, eyes gleaming with humor beneath heavy brows.

"Oh, indeed, monsieur!" Madame de Caval replied with a laugh. "I think I shall be able to force it down!"

"Louise!" Casimir de Montrond hailed her enthusiastically from across the room. "How lovely you look this evening."

The murmur of conversation ebbed, flowed, and stilled momentarily as women glanced enviously over fan or shoulder to see whom Montrond was addressing with such fervor. Casimir was a circle favorite and many had vied for the attention he was now bestowing with liberality upon Madame de Caval.

"Casimir," Louise replied with demure delight, a smile curving her lips, cheeks flushed to pinkness.

"I have a tale to tell," Casimir informed her in a dramatic whisper, teeth flashing whitely in a grin as he squeezed alongside her on the small sofa intended for two.

Casimir de Montrond, Talleyrand's closest friend—elegantly attired in a dark green coat that framed a sateen silk-embroidered waistcoat and cream breeches—was as debonair as the duke. But while Talleyrand, a child of the eighteenth-century, perpetuated the traditions of the Bourbon aristocracy in dress and powder, Montrond represented a visual model of current trends and fashions, which seemed overwhelmingly to be influenced by everything Roman or Greek. He wore his own hair clipped short with curls falling over his brow (a style popularized as le Brutus); his waistcoat and breeches were invariably of a lighter shade than the accompanying coat, a combination which sought to give the man's body the appearance of a marble statue.

Deep-set dark eyes, high cheekbones, and a relatively swarthy complexion suggested a Mediterranean heritage that Montrond mischievously claimed resulted from his great-grandfather's supposed infatuation with a Spanish mistress. Be that as it may, his lineage was an impressive one, his assets significant, his appearance generally acknowledged to be handsome, his demeanor personable, even charming. Grand dames thrust their pimpled progeny in his direction, and, with a surreptitious eye roll at Talleyrand, Montrond attempted pained civilities with all the good humor he could muster.

Louise, herself a widow of forty, was not quite immune to his charms. "A tale?" she asked eagerly, moving over to accommodate Montrond.

"Casimir, really," Talleyrand began in exasperation, rising from his seat. "I don't think Louise wants to hear—"

"On the contrary, my friend, I think Louise needs to hear this," Montrond interrupted with an air of feigned gravity. "In fact I think it might be of interest to the general party." Montrond rose to his feet, proclaiming loudly, "Mesdames et messieurs! Please favor me with your attention for one moment!" The surrounding conversations dwindled as heads turned in their direction. The pianoforte trailed off, and the room became quiet as Montrond took center stage. "Are any of you aware of the incident that took place at the privy council this morning?"

Talleyrand sighed in mock frustration. "I do not know why I invite you to these things," he muttered as he limped across to the hearth, turning his back to the guests who now clustered around the sofa eager to hear the latest court gossip.

"It was monstrous," Montrond declared with a dramatic shudder.

Talleyrand, who was half-leaning in a characteristically graceful and negligent attitude against the mantelpiece, snorted in irritation.

"It was, Charles—absolutely monstrous!" Montrond insisted vehemently.

"Well, what was monstrous?" Louise challenged impatiently, her fan fluttering in anxious agitation, her demand for information echoed by the general party:

"What happened, monsieur?"

"Did Napoleon finally proclaim his own divinity?"

Laughter rippled through the expectant crowd. The coronation ceremony, which anointed Napoleon emperor of the French, had been greeted with amused disdain among Parisian intellectuals. The political distance traveled from a socialist republic to an imperial dictatorship was lost on none of them.

"Divine?" another asked skeptically. "Or demonic?"

"Well, Napoleon's version, demonic or divine, leaves a great deal to be desired," a woman in green silk remarked tartly. "Do you mean to keep us forever in suspense, Monsieur de Montrond?"

"Of course. Forgive me, madame." Montrond swept her an apologetic bow. Like any good actor, he knew the fine art of relating a tale one teasing tidbit at a time until the audience stridently demanded immediate disclosure. And Napoleon Bonaparte always proved a source of diverting anecdotes. This was their way of minimizing his impact, lessening the fear, and reassuring themselves that when Napoleon proclaimed a general armistice with the aristocracy he actually meant it. Being in the habit of lively critical conversation that demanded reflective and analytical thought, few had actually succeeded in deluding themselves quite that much.

"As you are no doubt aware, Napoleon called a meeting of the privy council this morning," Montrond began as the room again fell to an expectant hush. "And of course his vice-grand elector, Charles Maurice de Talleyrand-Périgord, was present." He gestured dramatically toward Talleyrand, who was nonchalantly lighting his cheroot from the dying embers of the fire. "For a full half hour, he proceeded to upbraid and reprimand Charles, in words that became increasingly malevolent, until without interruption a steady flow of invective fairly *flew* from the emperor's lips. He called Charles a thief, a traitor, a coward!"

Muttered protests and gasps of dismay rippled through the assembled guests. Talleyrand, seemingly oblivious to the dramatic recitation that was taking place, had taken a seat by the fireplace, one leg thrown carelessly over the arm of the chair. He tilted his head back and blew three perfect circles of blue smoke into the still air.

"This tirade went on and on. Napoleon asserted, with great venom I might add, that Charles had never worthily performed a single duty, that he deceived anyone with whom he had ever dealt, that he didn't believe in God, that he would sell his own father for gain. Oh yes, indeed!" Montrond assured her as Louise shook her head in disbelief, eyes flashing in indignation. His performance had become a theatrical masterpiece with grandiose gestures and a dramatic delivery, and Talleyrand, amused despite himself, half-turned in his chair to watch the spectacle, puffing contentedly on his cheroot.

"You can imagine this, mesdames et messieurs," Montrond continued, his voice resonant, his audience raptly attentive. "Charles de Talleyrand stood impassively, his expression aloof, his manner completely unperturbed. And this enraged the emperor more than all else for he proceeded to lose all control. Fuming and spitting, his face scarlet with madness, he taunted Charles with his lameness, and shaking his fist in Charles' face he seemed to be at the point of striking him…"

Several women gasped in horror. "Mon dieu!"

"And finally, in what amounted to a shriek, the emperor informed the vice-grand elector that he was nothing but so much *dung in a silk stocking*!" Montrond finished exultantly, his eyes wide, his tone one of hushed horror. "But the best part was Charles de Talleyrand. Of all the ministers present, the only one unmoved by the outburst was the object

of the attack! His demeanor remained unchanged. No spark of color
appeared in his pale cheeks." Montrond crossed to where his friend was
lounging, placing one hand on Talleyrand's shoulder as he continued:
"Not a flicker of eyelash betrayed the fact that he was even conscious
of being addressed!" Montrond's dark face split in a wide grin. "Mesdames et messieurs, he was magnificent! And *then*, as he slowly limped
down the broad corridor, he turned to those who had witnessed his
ordeal and he said calmly, 'What a pity that such a great man should be
so ill-bred!'" Montrond laughed in delight.

"You listened to that?" Louise exclaimed heatedly, turning to Talleyrand, "and you didn't snatch up a chair, the tongs, the poker, or anything
and fall upon him?"

"Ah," replied Talleyrand gravely. "I did think of doing so, but I was
too lazy."

Later in the evening, after the guests, satiated in their appetite for both
food and conversation, had departed into the night, Talleyrand sat with
Montrond, idly thrusting the poker into the glowing embers of the fire.

"You are playing a very dangerous game, mon ami."

Talleyrand raised a quizzical eyebrow.

"Napoleon may have elevated you to a dukedom, made you prince
of Benevento, but how long do you think he will remain ignorant of
your activities on behalf of the Resistance or your collusion with the
English?"

"Hopefully, until it will no longer matter." Talleyrand leaned back
into his chair with a yawn, one elegantly manicured hand lazily tracing
circles in the velvet fabric of the armrest.

"I worry about you," Montrond persisted, leaning toward Talleyrand,
his elbows resting on his knees, dark brows drawn together in a frown.
"You openly defy Napoleon with these aristocratic gatherings, which
have not exactly made you popular with the people either. Mon dieu,
we have seen our share of toppled aristocrats. I have no wish to see you
share their fate. Look what happened to Mirabeau!"

"Ah, Mirabeau," Talleyrand murmured, a slight smile curving his
lips. He rested a glass of cognac on one silk-shod knee, admiring the
warm amber glow in the firelight. "I knew him, did you know that? He
was a great man, but he lacked the courage to be unpopular. In that
respect, I am more of a man than he. I abandon my reputation to all the
misunderstandings and insults of the mob," Talleyrand finished with a

dramatic flourish, raising the cognac to his lips. He swirled the liquor around in his mouth, eyes closed. "Eau-de-vie." The water of life. "You must try this cognac, Casimir. It is from the Borderies and has the most distinctive nutty aroma…mmm… most agreeable." Slouching back in his chair, glass raised in Montrond's direction, Talleyrand was the very picture of unruffled serenity.

"I am serious," Montrond persisted, waving away the proffered glass.

"So am I, mon ami. Deadly serious." Talleyrand's voice lost its lazy humor and acquired a sharp edge. His eyes caught and held Montrond's. "I am thought immoral and Machiavellian, but I am only calm and detached. I have never given evil counsel to Napoleon, but I will not share his fall. After shipwrecks, mon ami, there must be pilots to save the victims."

There was a moment's silence, the only sound the cracking and spitting of the dying fire as the blackened logs settled into their ashes.

"I have chosen my path, Casimir. If you feel this is not yours to follow, you need only say the word."

"You get lost on your way to Antonin Carême's pâtisserie on rue de la Paix! If you are the pilot for the French state, then God help us all," Montrond laughed affectionately. "No, you have need of me. Besides, what else is there for me to do? Since the Revolution life has been dull indeed. I will go to London as planned."

"When do you leave?"

"Tomorrow night I go to Bruges. I know of a merchant there who will ferry me across to Dover," Montrond replied.

Talleyrand arched an eyebrow. "A merchant? You mean a smuggler?"

Once every two weeks, Montrond unceremoniously dropped a bulging burlap sack inside Talleyrand's front door. Montrond never mentioned the gift, and Talleyrand graciously accepted it without compelling the awkwardness of a routine and repeated gratitude. The coarse-fibered sack, threadbare and often grimy in appearance, contained an item Talleyrand valued more than gold: coffee beans. And not just the watered-down dregs of the poor quality beans sold on the street corner, but the deeply roasted, glossy variety from Martinique that had been smuggled through the English blockade. The heady aroma, the richly potent taste of this coffee was a ritualistic delight to Talleyrand. He was a gourmand, and coffee had become less of a culinary indulgence than a highly anticipated necessity, one which was, however, increasingly impossible to fulfill. The English ships ferociously guarded French ports, stifling the once-thriving trade that had brought sugar, coffee, and tobacco to Paris. Sugar and tobacco could be purchased for an exorbitant price on the black market, smuggled overland from Amsterdam, or secreted in small trading boats through Marseille. But the kind of coffee Talleyrand preferred could not be found, except by Montrond it seemed, who took great delight in his nonchalant offering and the clandestine nature in which it arrived. Talleyrand would not dream of depriving him of that gratification.

"Smuggler?" Montrond raised his own eyebrows in mock surprise, the corner of his mouth quirking with amusement. "I do not, unfortunately, have any smugglers amongst my acquaintance, useful though that would be. A Belgian trawler actually. Will no doubt be an uncomfortable journey, and I will arrive smelling distinctly of fish."

"And you have my letter? To be delivered to William Pitt at Walmer Castle?"

Montrond patted his breast pocket. "Do not fear, Charles. I shall safely deliver your message if I have to leave bodies in my wake to do so."

Talleyrand smiled appreciatively. "This is why I like you, Casimir, because you are not overburdened with scruples."

"I like you, Charles, because you have no scruples at all," Montrond replied, with an answering grin.

# 3.

Newgate Prison was in its third reincarnation in the opening years of the nineteenth century. Despite the splendid façade, the graceful statues representing Peace, Plenty, Mercy, Justice, and Truth—precious little of which was found within the thick walls—it was a bleak and dismal place. The prison had been rebuilt after the Great Fire in 1666 and for a second time in 1770. The Gordon rioters had burned the prison to the ground in 1780, and, like a phoenix from the ashes, the notorious prison had risen again as a hovel for the condemned a few years later. It had been expanded both in size and fortification and squatted between St. Sepulcher's Church on the west and Old Bailey on the east. The main gate, replete with battlements and hexagonal towers, glowered over Newgate Street. Below the towers, set in a gloomy porch decorated with fetters and flanked by bricked windows that resembled nothing more than blinded eyes, was an enormous iron door. Above, the motto Venio Sicut Fur ("I come as a thief ") sternly addressed the new arrivals.

One of these, prisoner 51-A, had entered through these doors six weeks before. His name was not important, not to the keepers at least. In addition to shedding personal effects (although he paid a handsome sum for the privilege of retaining the shirt on his back and the boots on his feet), he was also forced to relinquish the very basic attribute of self-identification. Like the many that had gone before him and the many that would come after, his humanity was reduced to a number, a label.

Jack Manning, a corpulently built man with pale, squinty eyes and thinning gray hair painstakingly combed across a meaty dome, hated the prisoners. And unfortunately his position of employment, prison guard to cellblock A, meant he was perpetually associated with them. Manning had his eye on the warden's job: a cushy pad on the third floor, giving orders rather than submitting to them like a cowed dog afraid of being kicked. And the money, of course, was never far from his mind. A warden flexible in the finances could make a tidy sum at Newgate; bribes were a thriving trade.

But for now, he had to put up with these filthy wretches. Not for much longer though. Manning had plans. He had a way up and a way out. He grinned to himself, emptying his mouth of a fat wad of gray spittle. To Manning, the prisoners represented the dregs of society. It was not their crime that he objected to particularly, not being exactly law-abiding himself—it was being caught. For Manning, who imagined himself wily and cunning, stupidity deserved the harshest of fates. He reserved his greatest animosity, however, for prisoner 51-A.

51-A had arrived at Newgate in a lordly fashion: a tall, well-built man who seemed to possess all the advantages that the prison guard had been denied. The prisoner was rich, his clothes of fine linen, his cravat of the whitest lace Manning had ever seen, and he exhibited the proud bearing and manner of an aristocrat. While Manning had no love for the French, he had privately agreed that sending the pampered elite to the guillotine was the solution that should have been implemented in England. He would have gladly laid the chop on 51-A himself.

Arriving at the cell door, Manning opened the small latch and observed the prisoner sitting on the floor, dark head bowed, hands resting on crossed knees. The rusting manacles, heavy on his wrists, were secured to chains that snaked down to iron staples which bled rust into the gray flagstones. While 51-A had purchased a solitary cell when he first arrived at the prison—a dearly bought privacy which had lined Manning's pockets—his later attempts to acquire an "easement of the irons" had met with implacable hostility. 51-A had slipped him additional currency, or "rhino" as it was known to the inmates, to exchange these manacles for a lighter version that would have allowed him a greater freedom of movement. Manning had pocketed the money but refused to change the manacles. So 51-A had spent the last few days squatting on the floor like an animal with only a few feet of mobility before the chains constrained him. Manning's fleshy lips spread in a satisfied smirk. If he had provided 51-A with a private cell, he was damned if he would let him enjoy it.

The prisoner had not made any additional requests. In fact, for days he had said nothing at all, ever since that evening a week ago when he had killed a fellow prisoner. 51-A had been immediately placed in confinement; his execution, by special decree of the superintendent of prisons, scheduled for the following week.

"You! Up!" Manning spat as he opened the door. 51-A didn't move, his face concealed by a thick, tangled mat of dark hair. "I said get to your feet!" He kicked the prisoner viciously in the ribs, sending him sprawling back, the manacles savagely biting into his wrists as the chains constrained him. 51-A came slowly, stiffly, to his feet. He was a large man and had at least six inches on the rotund guard.

"Think you're a big man, dontcha?" Manning sneered, circling him like a feral hyena seeking a moment of weakness, an expression of vulnerability. He squinted from between pouchy lids, intent on his victim, searching for a chink in the armor. Manning was granted neither a tremor of fear nor a plea for mercy. In fact, the prisoner, towering over him, seemed altogether oblivious of his presence. Perhaps he needed reminding of who was in charge, Manning reckoned, feeling the heated rage rise in the back of his throat.

"Well, you ain't so very big anymore!" Bringing a truncheon from his belt, Manning brandished it in front of the prisoner. "Tomorrow you're gonna be worm food. My matey Wil is gonna stretch your neck!" Manning laughed, a low wheezing sound that emerged from deep in his fleshy belly. "But first I thought I'd have myself a bit o' fun." He drew back his truncheon and delivered a brutal blow to the side of the prisoner's face.

51-A staggered under the assault; his manacled hand came up to inspect the injury. The skin had been split down the cheekbone; blood in a warm sticky flow covered the side of his face. A sharp kick to the prisoner's knee sent him stumbling. Pressing his advantage, Manning rained a vicious series of truncheon blows to his shoulders and head until the man had collapsed forward, hands and head resting on the floor.

For a moment it was quiet in the cell. The only sound was the men's harsh breathing and the steady drip of blood that trickled down the prisoner's face to form a puddle on the gray flagstones.

"So who's the big man now, 51-A?" Manning leaned close to the prisoner's face, his lips wide in a triumphant sneer revealing teeth yellow with decay.

Suddenly, the prisoner brought his hands up and around, and in one swift movement circled the rusting chains around Manning's neck. He pulled them tightly until they bit into the fleshy gray skin. Manning clawed at his neck in an effort to loosen the chains, his mouth open and gasping, his eyes bulging from his skull.

"My *name* is Wolfe Trant," the prisoner growled. He pulled savagely on the chain. Manning's face, already swollen with the effort to breathe, began to turn blue, his tongue protruding from his slack mouth. "And if I'm to die tomorrow, what possible reason is there for me to let you live?"

# 4.

The three figures waited silently in the dark, oblivious to the normal nocturnal routine that occupied the rue de Malte after midnight. Several students were making their way raucously home from the café, arms draped around each other's necks. "Devant Naples, Nelson faisait un feu d'enfer!" They sang an off-key version of the street ballad that had been popularized after the disastrous English siege of Naples. Several prostitutes loitered under streetlights. A woman berated her husband for drunkenness, her voice strident and accusing through an open window. Cats screeched in a nearby alley, fighting over discarded bones from a café's rubbish heap. The three intently watched the street ahead. Waiting.

While the bustle and noise of human traffic continued unabated into the dark, the three spectators were united by their silent immobility. Their darkly clad figures formed a triangle. One, Pierre de Saint-Regent, was stationed in the rue Saint- Nicaise where it met rue de Malte. He crouched on a cart upon which sat, under an unremarkable brown blanket, a massive bomb filled with bits of iron. The second, François de Limeolan, waited across the street, positioned so that he had a view of rue de Malte as it wound toward the Opéra National de Paris. The third of this trio of conspirators, known only as Primrose, lingered just south of the intersection of rue de Malte and rue Saint-Nicaise, her face shadowed by the wide-brimmed cap that covered her head.

The sound of horses' feet clattering rhythmically on the cobblestone street and the rattling of wheels on the carriage that followed had a galvanizing effect on the three. François raced ahead, careful to keep in the shadows of the two-story buildings that crowded the narrow street. Then, arm upraised—a quick motion. Not the carriage for which they waited. The other two exhaled deeply, Pierre slumped against the wheel of the cart, their tension momentarily dissipated.

An hour went by. The three remained in watchful readiness at their respective posts. Just after one in the morning, as the moon was starting to sink into the western sky, they were rewarded for their perseverance. A carriage drawn by four white horses turned the corner up ahead. This time there was no doubt. Painted a dark blue and intricately embellished with golden frieze ornamentation, this dormeuse was as distinctive as its illustrious owner. Four lights, affixed to each upper corner of the bodywork, illuminated the top of the carriage, silhouetted the slouched figure of the driver, and cast a gleam across the sweating flanks of the horses. Door panels, emblazoned with the imperial arms, were lit to intermittent brilliancy by passing street lights, materializing from the street gloom in a flash of golden eagle and blood-red mantle. These doors were bullet-proof and fitted with locks and bolts; behind the windows heavy louvered blinds were operated by a spring. The three who waited in the dark knew all of this. They knew that a direct assault with muskets would be fruitless, that a detonation timed to explode as the carriage was passing by was the only feasible option.

What they had not been prepared for was the reckless speed at which the carriage hurtled through the narrow streets. The coachman had enjoyed numerous glasses of wine this cold November night and urged the horses forward with gleeful enthusiasm. At a frantic signal from François, Pierre lit the fuse before turning to sprint back down rue Saint-Nicaise, past startled onlookers still carousing at the Café d'Apollon. From her vantage point, Primrose observed the next few minutes as if in slow motion: the horse rearing forward, the cart and its ominous burden clattering wildly behind, the brown blanket flapping, the startled glance of the coachman, and then the explosion as the bomb detonated.

It lit up the night, sending tiles, timber, and debris raining through the sky on the bewildered bystanders who were temporarily shocked into immobility. The imperial coach was thrown to one side, the windows shattered and one of the horses killed. A dozen Chasseurs à Cheval of the Imperial Guard, who had closely attended the dormeuse behind, now surged forward to form a protective flank around the downed carriage. Napoleon had ordered the formation of this bodyguard coalition five years earlier after narrowly surviving an assassination attempt during the Italian Campaign. Now it proved useful.

Primrose waited tensely amid the screaming chaos to see if over three months of preparation had been successful. The carriage door flew open and a short figure in red military brocade emerged, enraged and bristling. Flying glass had cut his face and his dress coat was splattered with blood, but despite this superficial wound, the emperor of the French remained unharmed. They had failed. The bomb had exploded just after Napoleon's carriage had passed. The cavalry was starting to fan out from the downed coach, following the curt instructions issued by Napoleon before he departed on horseback surrounded by his military guard.

Primrose had to leave, and quickly. They had not been wholly inconspicuous, and once the general terror and confusion had abated, questions would be asked, fingers would be pointed. Hopefully, Pierre had managed to run clear of the detonation area. François was to retreat down rue Saint-Nicaise in the opposite direction taken by Pierre, and they were to rendezvous at Café Melian in an hour. The best disguise was none at all. Primrose pulled her cap lower over her brow and, assuming the jaunty air of a young man out on the town, entered into the throng that had gathered on rue de Malte.

She strode quickly, trying to swallow back the disappointment that soured the back of her throat. *Merde!* They had come so close. And all for naught, merely because the driver had happened to drink too much and drive too fast. Now the risk they all faced would be greater than ever. Napoleon would not rest until the perpetrators had been apprehended, and even if they were not discovered this time, the noose was inevitably drawing ever tighter around their necks. Joseph Fouché, commissioner of police, had spies everywhere. They infiltrated philosophical salons, loitered at coffeehouses, and mingled with factory workers, fomenting discontent and blaming it on Royalist and Jacobin radicals that these "'loyal" Parisians could help bring to justice. The Resistance could not be too careful. Paris was, now more than ever, a very dangerous place for those who opposed Napoleon.

Suddenly looking up, she caught a glimpse of a familiar face in the crowd: François, leaning against the balustrade of the Hotel de la Concorde, his face ashen. She hurried over to him, conscious of an officer of the Imperial Guard in his flamboyant green, red, and gold hussar-style uniform, a tall red plume bobbing authoritatively from his hat, making his way in their direction.

"You fool!" François hissed from between clenched teeth. "Get out of here!"

With dismay, Primrose realized he had a large piece of metal shrap-
nel protruding from his thigh—a piece of the undercarriage. The blood
spread in a scarlet stain around the makeshift bandage François had
yanked around his leg. The wound was largely concealed beneath his
voluminous cloak, but his face was alarmingly pale.

"Lean on me. Pretend to be drunk." She ignored his protests, and
positioning him against her body, his arm slung over her shoulder, they
began to make their way slowly through the milling crowd. Glancing
behind her, she saw the soldier raising an arm in her direction.

"You there! Stop!" he hollered.

"They know me," François managed, his face contorted with pain,
his leg trailing uselessly behind him. "I am already on Fouché's list—get
out of here while you still can."

"Just walk," Primrose muttered curtly, seeking a route through the
pressed cluster of bodies, his sagging weight heavy on her shoulder.
Abruptly, she was yanked from behind; the soldier grabbed her upper
arm and hauled her around. Somehow, Primrose kept a firm grip on
François as she stumbled.

"Heyyy!" she yelled in bewildered surprise. "Whatisttt...?" Slurring
her words and deepening her voice slightly, she could pass as a youth
who had imbibed a little too freely.

"When I tell you to stop, you stop. Do you understand?" The man
leaned close to her face, poking her sharply in the chest with his bayonet. The Chasseurs à Cheval were known as the "Favored Children,"
enjoying the power and privilege of being the emperor's favorites and
were, more often than not, quite willing to abuse and exploit that position. Primrose quickly became aware that the soldier was not suspicious
of them particularly. His chin sprouted the soft down of the very young
before it becomes stubble, and his complexion was fresh-faced and un-
lined. He was glancing at the crowd seeking approval, she realized. He
was a new recruit trying to make an impression. Well, she would oblige
him.

"Pardon, monsieur...oui, pardon..."she replied, her voice deliberately thick, weaving slightly on her feet. "We were just singing...and
then something happened?" she mumbled blearily, looking around her
in confusion. François was heavy on her arm, close to passing out from
the loss of blood. "Where did all these people come from?" Then,
brightening, as another thought occurred to her: "But we were singing...

you wanna hear our duet?" she asked the soldier, eyes heavy-lidded, teetering toward him unsteadily.

*Devant Naples*

*Nelson faisait un der d'enfer!*

*Mais ce jour...*

She sang loudly, nodding enthusiastically at the crowd who, having survived the explosion and feeling the need to celebrate the fact, joined in, one voice after another until the entire throng were singing in thunderous accord.

*là plus d'un ivrogne...*

The soldier waved them off in disgust. Primrose exhaled sharply in relief and, turning through the now festive crowd, struggled forward with François on her arm. A burly workman to her right, caught up in the fervent patriotism of the song, took François' other arm and placed it over his shoulders, obviously assuming the man was drunk and in need of assistance. He grinned at Primrose while belting out the rest of the song in his deep, surprisingly sonorous voice:

*Au lieu de vin, but l'eau de mer*

*Devant Naples!*

# 5.

## DRURY LANE. LONDON, ENGLAND
### *November 25, 1803*

Old London occupied the fringe of the city like an ulcerous growth, darkly swollen with a regular influx of rural immigrants seeking opportunity in the economic powerhouse of London town. New construction had shifted westward, away from the gloom of coal-smog that dulled the brick facades and dusted clothes and faces of pedestrians. The affluent in their airy townhouses with their handsome colonnades, the coffeehouses and gleaming storefronts that dotted wide tree-fringed streets—these had steadily and disdainfully removed themselves, leaving the squalidly squeezed tenements behind like poor relations none wished to acknowledge.

And so Old London became an outskirt suburb consisting of dilapidated-looking buildings with bulging leaded bay windows and great eaves shadowing ground floors, all enveloped by a labyrinthine network of narrow alleys and dusty back courts. Years of accumulated grime blackened their steep roofs and sagging walls. Many a tottering dwelling was reinforced by timber braces, propped between the walls of equally precarious neighbors, until one received the impression that if just one such strut was removed, the entire vicinity would crumble into a malodorous mound of damp and dirt. Other ancient buildings were entirely abandoned, unroofed and uninhabited, languishing in silent decrepitude until the moths and mice had eaten away any vestige of the original possessors, until documents of title had disintegrated into dust, until no living individual could be found either to claim the property or pay the maintenance.

These gloomy premises were now occupied by a motley variety of thieves, prostitutes, debtors, beggars, outlaws, and revolutionaries. While the laboring Irish numbered among all of these categories—many of whom crammed multi-family numbers into tiny tenements—it was the revolutionaries who held their meetings at the Green Dragon, 121

Drury Lane. Years ago, the number 121 had embellished a wooden sign that hung above the door, along with the painted green dragon that had given the tavern its name. In this present day, however, the rusted chain hung uselessly from the greasy iron post which remained bolted into the wall, the tavern now neither marked nor advertised—which suited its customers very well indeed.

The tavern, like the rest of Drury Lane, lay slightly below the high-water mark of the Thames, less than a mile away to the east. Ann Plowman, the intrepid owner of this establishment, had adroitly addressed the issue that plagued the neighborhood; boards, salvaged and stolen from other buildings, crisscrossed the dirt floor and provided a safe walking path from bar to tables when the sewage began to ooze up underfoot. Blackened walls enclosed the central room, stained by years of coal-smoke and illuminated by candles that guttered in waxy puddles. A stench of human waste, long unnoticed by the residents of Drury Lane, mingled with the strong aroma of yeasty hops and the heavy, fetid smell of unwashed bodies. A narrow bar occupied the length of the room, the wall behind festooned with the massive moldering leg bone that had been uncovered beneath the floor with the rise of the sewage tide decades before. The bone of the dragon. Beneath the bone, Ann commanded pride of place behind the bar; a beefy bulk of a woman with ice-gray hair and eyes like shards of flint.

It was late, and the thick throng of men, women, and children had come and gone, and for the most part, only tattered dregs were left— several old men who had come in "jes' fer a dram" earlier in the evening and now, slumped and recumbent, would leave by being bodily thrown from the front door when Ann closed shop. The table in the rear of the tavern was still occupied by three men, one of whom teetered on the happy edge of oblivion.

"Fuck 'em …" Thomas Dildin slurred, the ale pleasantly seeping into his bloodstream as he laid his head upon the table. He looked young and vulnerable, one cheek plumping out against the woodgrain, full mouth open in a low snore, lashes dark against pale freckled skin. Barely out of his teens, Dildin was, however, a veteran of the Irish wars and when awake, possessed that alert wariness reminiscent of seasoned soldiers. Like his countrymen, Dildin had a weakness for the fine stout brewed onsite behind the back walls of the Green Dragon. Having discharged his duty for the evening, Dildin was entitled, and indeed determined, to indulge. The two recruits he had brought along to the meeting that evening had been in a similar state of inebriation. Arthur Eagen and Finn McCourk, from poor Catholic families in County Cork, had committed to the cause with fervent approbation; they spent the rest of the night entwined in a knot of Irish laborers who occupied the far end of the bar, alternatively clapping each other on the back with jovial enthusiasm, or threatening a bleary-eyed physical reprisal. They had all dispersed an hour earlier in a singing, pummeling, struggling horde of legs and arms, ripped sleeves, bloody noses, and lost caps.

Captain John Spence of the HMS *Venture* and Nick O'Connor, however, were singularly sober. Spence wore a black cloth cap pulled low over his sun-darkened brow, his mouth tight beneath a sandy beard. His gaze studied the table marred by scratches, stains, and glass rings.

"So what're you thinking, John?" his companion asked, his tone deliberately casual, his fingers idly rubbing a grimy spot from the side of his glass. O'Connor was lanky and lean with a mop of unruly black hair and narrow eyes of hazel above a heavily freckled countenance. He wore the threadbare breeches and overcoat of a tradesman, his grubby cravat loose around his neck, his cap on the table beside him. O'Connor, feeling uncharacteristically tense and all too aware of how critical this next recruitment might be, surreptitiously wiped his palms on his breeches. Egan had given him the names of several individuals who would suit their needs, but Spence, due to his popularity with the sailors and his unwavering commitment to reform, was much the preferred candidate.

Captain Spence's command was a rarity in His Majesty's navy: one where, despite the pitiful pay that was regulated by the Admiralty, the food was wholesome and floggings rare. Spence treated his men with respect and received it back one hundred-fold. He deplored the conditions under which the sailors lived and worked and had sought reforms through conventional channels. These requests had been ignored or endlessly referred, and his own progress through the ranks noticeably stagnated.

"The petition was ignored?" O'Connor inquired, raising his frosty glass of ale to his mouth.

"Yes—yes, it was," Spence nodded with a sharp exhalation of breath. He had advised and assisted in the formulation of a petition that enumerated naval grievances; it had collected thousands of signatures before being submitted to the Admiral of the Fleet, Lord Howe. Again, no response.

"There'll be a mutiny, you know that?" O'Connor insisted. "A vast number of sailors in the English navy are Irish, not only pressed into service or sent there as a result of some petty political transgression, but now suffering under a repressive regime of low pay, abominable food, and arbitrary floggings. We'll rise, John. The question is, will you lead?"

For a moment Spence did not answer. "You do not know what you ask of me," he finally said, his face heavy with weariness, his ale warm and untouched before him.

"I ask you to act on your own convictions." O'Connor leaned forward on his elbows, his tone soft and intent between the resonant snores of Dildin who drooled on the table beside him.

"It may mean my very life," Spence replied quietly, his steady gaze holding O'Connor's.

"Aye, it may, as it does for us all. But how can a man live if not by his conviction of what is right? These men need you. Without your leadership and respectability there is no hope of reform; the sailors will be hung as traitors, you know that. With you acting as intermediary, however, with your solid service to the Crown..." O'Connor shrugged, raising one dark eyebrow. "Well, it just might have a chance."

"What might have a chance?" Spence leaned forward himself, pushing his ale aside with a deliberate motion. "You mean the insurrection in Ireland? Or the one planned in London? Or do you mean the landing of the French? I know what is going on, Nick, and it is a helluva lot more than just a naval mutiny."

O'Connor hesitated, schooling his features as best he could to conceal the shock he felt at Spence's words. The London plan had been one to which only he and Egan had been privy; although the broader agenda was one which might be readily apparent to any thinking man, and Spence certainly was that. A naval mutiny would paralyze the fleet, the only force keeping Napoleon's army in check, and the chaos that accompanied a French incursion would be a ripe time for Irish rebellion. Spence had been speculating, but that momentary hesitation on O'Connor's part served as confirmation.

"Bloody hell!" Spence exhaled sharply, leaning back in his chair.

Damn, O'Connor thought. His orders had been to bring Spence in,

not to confirm or convey any larger strategy the United Irishmen had
in place, but obviously Spence, working closely with Irish sailors and
already an advocate for reform on their behalf, had put two and two
together. There was still an opportunity here to secure Spence for the
cause—if he could establish a trust, if he could make him understand
the incredible opportunity that had presented itself here—an opportunity to enact the reforms the captain had so long desired.

Glancing around the dim interior, O'Connor spoke cautiously, his
voice a low undertone. "You're right. We're seeking redress for grievances beyond those of the sailors."

"At what cost? I understand you're chafing under the bit of English
domination, but I will not submit to a French one. You are pursuing
revolution. I want only parliamentary reform."

"Sometimes a revolution is the only way to bring about parliamentary reform," O'Connor responded quietly.

"I am not yet convinced of that. You advocate measures that enable
independence in your own country and ask me to pursue those that
compromise my own. If I lead my men and others in a mutiny, and the
blockade is compromised for even six hours it may enable the French
fleet to cross the Channel..." He held O'Connor's gaze as comprehension dawned across his own features. "But that is what you are planning,
isn't it? You are actually in league with Napoleon?" Captain Spence rose
abruptly to his feet, pulling the brim of his hat lower over his face. "I
am sorry, Nick, I cannot in good conscience support your venture."

Nick O'Connor, his face inscrutable, replied: "We just want to be
free."

"I understand." Spence hesitated for a moment, then leaned down,
one darkly calloused palm resting on the table, his mouth close to
O'Connor's ear, his voice hushed beneath the intermittent chatter of
late-night trade and the rhythmic snores of their table companion. "All
of England have Ol' Boney fixed squarely in their sights, with Nelson
in the Mediterranean, St. Vincent in the Channel, and Wilson in the
north. How is it you hope to get all of them to rise simultaneously?
You are going to do nothing but get yourself killed, lad. Or worse, find
out that Napoleon doesn't give a damn for Irish liberty and that you
are exchanging English authority for French tyranny." Straightening up,
Spence dropped several coins on the table. "It's a fool's errand you are
upon, Nick, but I will not betray you. You have my word as an officer."

"Thank you, John."

Whether Spence's word was sufficient to ensure his own safety was another matter, as both men were aware. That would be a decision Egan would make. It appeared the captain was willing to risk his life for his convictions after all, O'Connor mused, as he watched Spence's retreating figure. He would have to find another candidate. They could always rely on sailors within each unit, but to be effective it was essential the mutinies be a coordinated action, well-prepared and organized. It was crucial they have a point-man within the navy, someone trusted by the men who could engage the disaffected in the Channel fleets off Spithead and Portsmouth. And time was rapidly running out.

"C'mon then, Tom milad." O'Connor shifted one shoulder beneath Dildin's and hoisted him to his feet. Together the two made their way to the door. Ann, wiping the bar-top with a gray flannel cloth then tucking it beneath an equally soiled apron, caught O'Connor's eye and nodded briefly. An understanding had been reached, negotiated, and cemented with the frequent provision of silver. This bought them a discount on the local brew as well as the reservation of a particular table every Tuesday night, one situated in a back corner where one might be circumspect without advertising the fact. Even in the depths of Drury Lane, they were not entirely safe. They were dancing that delicate line between subversive secrecy and inclusive discretion. How could they be plotting a conspiracy if any Tuesday night deadbeat was invited to participate? Not that they were of course, but appearance was everything. The United Irishmen had been burned by English informants before and would not be so deceived again. The back room curtains were open; Ann had been instructed to inform any who asked that an open political meeting was taking place to register protest against the war. Grain prices were high. Bread riots were again prevalent. Anti-war sentiment was at an all-time high. Nothing unusual going on here. Or so the façade suggested.

Two years before, police had raided the Oakley Arms during a meeting of the United Irishmen, arresting all thirty involved. The great treason trials followed, and the combined testimony of government infiltrators and men who turned king's evidence to save their own lives convicted ten, all of whom were hanged and subsequently decapitated. The names of these men were now a call to arms: John Francis, James Wratten, Arthur Graham... The court transcript had described them as "laboring Irishmen of the lowest class," but now these men were martyrs, more influential in death than they had ever been in life. And the United Irishmen had learned the lesson well: subsequent actions were planned by the unit head (in this case Egan Trant) with each member given responsibility for a particular task without any knowledge of the intent of the broader whole.

The unit head was given considerable latitude in detecting and resolving "infiltration issues," which allowed Egan to pursue policies with little concern for casualties. Within the United Irishmen he was known as Bas, or death, a name spoken with awe or fear depending upon how closely that individual worked with him. The casualties were not restricted to English monarchists; Egan Trant had an uncanny ability to ferret out dissenting opinion—the owners of which were often found floating in the Thames or inexplicably murdered by a beggar in an obscure back alley. Nick O'Connor, Egan's unofficial right-hand man, was more trusted than most, a position for which O'Connor simultaneously felt gratitude and terror in approximately equal measure. Needless to say, he didn't sleep much. On those occasions where his fear urged a desperate flight into the Irish hillside until it was all over, he reminded himself of what he was fighting for and what, even with these sometimes distasteful means, they intended to accomplish. And more than anything he wanted to be a part of that. O'Connor wanted to be able to stand straight and tall on the day Ireland was finally liberated, knowing that he had helped make that happen.

# 6.

The dingy little man waited impatiently in the shadows of rue St. Martin. He was buttoned up in a faded black overcoat that had seen better days; a tattered hat sat squarely on a bony forehead, the rim casting deep shadows across his narrow face. Eyeballs glimmered piercingly in shadowed orbits. Thin lips and an aggressively sharp nose sat between flat gray cheeks of a greasy, unhealthy complexion. A cheap cigar was burning, forgotten, between stained fingers. His booted foot tapped out an aggravated staccato as he peered through the dim alley to the bustling thoroughfares on each side. His appearance was like many others in the faubourg Saint-Marceau, where cheap lodging houses squeezed themselves together in dreary profusion above muddy streets.

This man, however, attracted more attention than might be warranted by his unprepossessing appearance. His unwashed, slightly hunched-over figure was a familiar sight to many Parisians, one which was rendered sinister by his fearful reputation; most fell silent when Police Commissioner Joseph Fouché entered the room and breathed in relief when he left. The facts were ominous enough; in Lyon during the Revolution, Fouché had instituted a regime of swift and massive punishment, zealous in his pursuit of aristocratic heads. But this reputation had been further embellished by rumor. It was said that while parading the execution grounds on horseback, Fouché wore a pair of human ears dangling on either side of his hat, that he had personally operated the guillotine, severing twelve heads in five minutes. Stories spread of as many as sixty prisoners tied in a line and shot at with cannon; some said Fouché finished them off with his own bayonet. It was just the sort of macabre gossip that circulated around the police commissioner that Fouché himself did nothing to contradict. This notoriety isolated him, but he didn't mind. He preferred to work alone. In fact, he relished the apprehensive glances, the lowered voices, or the sudden silence that followed him in the street. It served to remind him of the power he wielded. He had one grimy finger on the pulse of Paris, and with just a little pressure, she would bend to his will. The time had come to apply it.

"Le Monsieur de Commissaire?" a voice wheezed. Germain de Lausain moved into the pool of yellowish light cast by the gas lamps. He was round like a tub, with an enormous stomach tightly encased in a brown linen vest and short, thick legs that stuck out from his torso like sausages. A thick brown beard covered his several chins in a surprisingly luxurious growth that curled and glistened in the light. Small eyes, almost lost in the plumpness of his face, gleamed above heavy ruddy cheeks. "I am honored to find such an illustrious personage in our humble faubourg."

"I am a busy man, Germain. What do you have for me?" Fouché growled impatiently. Twelve hours had already elapsed since the assassination attempt, and Napoleon was impatient for suspects. Germain had better provide a substantial lead or his days as police informant would come to an abrupt end. Fouché brought the neglected cigar to his lips, pulled deeply, and exhaled a stream of acrid blue smoke. "The attack on Napoleon's carriage last night..." Germain began in low dramatic tones, leaning toward Fouché in a conspiratorial manner. His husky voice wheezed as if smothered by the thick layer of fat that enveloped his chest. "I have discovered that it was the work of the French Resistance."

Fouché leveled a scornful glance at the police informant. "We are quite aware of that, Germain. I will need names if you want to be paid."

"Ah yes, of course, monsieur," Germain muttered, somewhat crestfallen. He shifted heavily on his feet, fleshy fingers twirling the coarse strands of his beard in a distracted manner.

He was playing for time. Fouché suppressed his irritation with an effort of will. Napoleon expected the conspirators to be apprehended within twenty-four hours, and while that did not bother the police commissioner—there were any number of ready "suspects" that could be rounded up off the streets—he disliked the idea that things happened in his city of which he was unaware. Fouché prided himself on being a step ahead of every plot or disturbance, but this particular bombing had taken him completely by surprise. Knowledge was power, and he was its most avid collector.

"There is a young man who lives in my lodging house," Germain whispered hoarsely. "Michel Desant, a cousin to Georges Cadoudal, who leads the uprisings in the Vendeé…"

"Yes, yes, I know of Cadoudal," Fouché interrupted. He had a thick file on Cadoudal, a Chouan assassin, who, his spies had informed him, had recently arrived back in France with pockets weighed down by English silver. An assassin financed by Pitt. Who else would they target but the emperor himself? That was another source of irritation to the police commissioner: that despite his extensive surveillance he had been unable to locate Cadoudal since his return to the continent.

"Anyway, he has a weakness for wine, which loosens his tongue," Germain continued in a confiding manner, covertly watching the commissioner's expression. It was the manner of all informants, Fouché knew, to play out the information, to give the police one suspect at a time, to maximize their own importance and multiply their payments. "Last night, he was boasting to me of his part in the attack on the emperor's carriage."

So Cadoudal was involved. This was hardly a surprise to Fouché. But where was he?

The vast majority of criminals possessed the fatal combination of smugness and sociability. They needed the camaraderie and approbation of their own kind and could not resist boasting of their exploits publicly. Like homing birds, both before and after a big operation, they headed for their habitual inns and taverns. And Fouché's agents were waiting, listening. The task of the police had been vastly facilitated by the unvarying habits of the Parisian criminals; they were as easy to find as a street singer on his usual beat on the Pont-Neuf. It was just a matter of knowing where and when. And there was very little Fouché didn't know. Cadoudal, however, was an exception. He was wily, unpredictable, discreet. He appeared and then was gone like a ghost in the night.

"And when does Desant meet with Cadoudal again?" Fouché demanded curtly. "I am unsure…" Germain hesitated, his expression calculating. "There were others with Desant though, three others who may also have taken part in the assassination attempt. They are perhaps all members of the Resistance. I took the liberty, at great risk of discovery, to follow them…" Germain wheezed, then paused, giving a gasp or two as his breath failed him.

"*May* have taken part? *Perhaps* members of the Resistance? Germain, you are wasting my time."

Fouché flung his still-smoldering cigar stub to the street and ground it viciously beneath his boot. He then turned and, like a crab, moved with rapid, scuttling steps toward rue St. Madeline from which the subdued rumble of carriage wheels and muted voices announced a brisk evening trade.

"Wait!" Germain cried out hoarsely.

Fouché did not pause, his shadow rising up on the brick walls like a specter, increasingly elongated as he approached the gas lamp, and then diminishing as he left its light.

"Primrose!" Germain blurted out desperately.

Fouché stopped in his tracks. He slowly turned, regarding Germain intently from beneath the rim of his hat. Germain, encouraged, hastened with waddling effort toward the waiting commissioner.

# 7.

## NEWGATE PRISON. LONDON, ENGLAND
### *November 25, 1803*

William Brunskill sighed in frustration. He hated his job. He hated the prison. Brunskill felt as if he were passing through the gates of hell every morning he stepped through the doors. The warden had the option of dwelling on the premises—a residential section comprised most of the third floor—but he shuddered at the prospect; he might as well be a prisoner himself. Brunskill had only been at the job two months and had learned enough to know how very little he would be able to change. The superintendent of prisons, his immediate superior, was smugly pious and ascribed to the belief that Newgate should provide its inmates with a foretaste of what, he was convinced, awaited them in the afterlife: a hell on earth. And in this, the superintendent could be rightly satisfied. Newgate was truly a hellish place.

And the keepers, Brunskill was starting to think, were appropriately devilish. Returning his gaze to Jack Manning, who slouched insolently before his desk, he asked evenly, "How was it that prisoner 51-A came to receive such a tremendous number of injuries?" Brunskill glanced down at the papers on his desk. The tiny, punctilious script of the doctor's notations lay in several sheets, underneath which resided the cream envelope that had arrived by courier less than an hour before—a letter from William Pitt. Brunskill and Pitt had been Cambridge schoolmates, friends long before Pitt began his meteoric rise in Parliament, but they had lost touch in the intervening years. Brunskill had not yet had time to read Pitt's epistle. The latest prison crisis had necessarily taken precedence. "Several broken ribs...stitches to his face...bruises that suggest he was repeatedly beaten with a truncheon. What do you know of this matter?"

"I was just defendin' myself, guv'nr. The prisoner tried to kill me, just like he did to that poor fella in the mess," Manning rasped defiantly. "Lookit what he did to my neck here!" The guard yanked aside the grimy collar of his uniform to reveal a hideously swollen neck, dark with the bruised imprint of chain links.

"Defending yourself ?" Brunskill said sternly, looking over his glasses at Manning. "The prisoner was *chained* to the ground."

Manning's mouth tightened in displeasure, his gaze dark with subdued resentment.

"This kind of activity will not occur under my supervision. Do you understand me, Mr. Manning?" Brunskill finished firmly. "Things may have been done differently in the past, but I am warden here now, and you will obey me or find yourself other employment." The warden had preferred the ready convenience of maintaining his inherited staff, having neither the time nor the inclination to re-hire and re-train. Manning, however, would be very soon to go.

"He's gonna die tomorrow anyhow," Manning grumbled under his breath.

"I beg your pardon, Mr. Manning, did you have something else you wished to say?" Brunskill demanded harshly, feeling the rising heat of anger and frustration. Manning was silent, his expression sullen. "You are dismissed," Brunskill said curtly.

After the guard had left, the door slamming behind him, Brunskill summoned his assistant, Charley, to the office. Charley was one of those people that seem to become part of the institution in which they are employed. He had been a fixture at Newgate longer than anyone cared to remember and had survived the various regimes by virtue of both his adaptability and his limitless knowledge about the building and its inmates.

"Sir." Charley arrived wearing the same threadbare green vest that Brunskill had seen him in every day for the past two months. Moist chestnut eyes drooped above flabby cheeks and a wide mouth wilted at the edges. Shrunken into skin that sagged around him in liver-spotted folds, it was as if gravity was gradually and inexorably pulling the man down.

"Charley, please sit down," Brunskill offered.

"Thank'ye, but I's fine, sir," Charley demurred with a respectful nod.

"I understand we have three dead men on our hands, including the one who was killed last week?" Brunskill asked, his tone one of weary resignation.

It was one of the many Newgate traditions that he found abhorrent:

if a prisoner was unable to pay the departure fee upon completion of his sentence, then he would be forced to remain until his relatives came up with the required sum. If, in the interim, he was unfortunate enough to succumb to gaol fever—as over half the population did in any given year—he would still remain incarcerated as a rotting corpse until his family could find the money to have it released. Two prisoners in the previous week had fallen to this unfortunate fate. And then, of course, there was the prisoner that 51-A had killed.

"Yessir, that'd be the right of it." Charley nodded again. He had been a part of Newgate life since his youth and had long since ceased to question policy. It was not right or wrong; it just was. As much as he respected the new warden, he was uneasy at the prospect of the upheaval which he seemed to portend.

"I want them gone. Call their next of kin and tell them the warden waives the required fee. If they remain unclaimed, call the morgue wagon and arrange to have them buried in pauper graves."

"But, sir—" Charley began in confusion.

"I will cover the cost personally," Brunskill interrupted. "I also want you to erect the gallows on Old Bailey Street. Put prisoner 51-A in the condemned hold tonight and prepare him for his execution tomorrow at dawn." The warden rubbed his eyes wearily.

"Yessir," Charley nodded gravely before turning to leave, shutting the door deferentially behind him.

His first execution. Brunskill was dreading it. Inmate 16-E had pulled a sharpened prison bar from beneath his tattered jacket and held the point to 51-A's throat. Apparently, he had wanted the Irishman's boots. 16-E had assumed this newcomer, this well-dressed novice to prison life, would be easy pickings. He had miscalculated. In a blur of movement, 51-A had spun on his heels, forcing the bar down and backwards as he did so. Unbalanced by this unexpected movement, 16-E had stumbled and fell, impaling himself on the sharpened point of his own weapon.

Privately, Brunskill was of the conviction that a rough justice had been done; 16-E had been a surly, vicious character with little in his prospect to suggest any possibility of reform. But the warden's superintendent had personally insisted that 51-A pay the ultimate penalty: an eye for an eye or some-such twaddle.

As personally repugnant as Brunskill found his current position, there was a certain prestige that came from successfully managing the most notorious prison in London. If he could persevere, effect some positive change without alienating his superiors, his future would be secured indeed. Musing on the vagaries of political appointments and the intransigence of the superintendent of prisons, his thoughts again turned to the letter that lay unopened on his desk. William Pitt—after all these years! What could Pitt possibly require of him? Breaking the wax seal, Brunskill scanned the contents of the letter with growing astonishment:

> Dear Mr. William Brunskill,
>
> It is with the greatest urgency that I renew our acquaintance these many years past. As you know, our country faces the greatest of perils in our renewed hostilities against France, and the request I make of you will be critical to the defensive effort. I understand an execution is imminently scheduled for one Mr. Wolfe Trant, an Irishman incarcerated some six weeks ago. I would have you delay execution and release the prisoner into my custody; currently I am procuring a royal dispensation to this effect. I will be at Newgate forthwith and must ask in the meantime that you keep this matter highly confidential; the security of our nation depends upon it.
>
> Ever sincerely and faithfully yours,
>
> W. Pitt

What could the former prime minister want with an insignificant Irish rebel? A confidential pardon issued from the king himself ? How bizarre!

Brunskill absently folded the letter as his gaze turned toward the only window and the empty courtyard that lay beyond. Gray and featureless on a chilly November evening, the sight usually depressed him. As the sun descended into the western sky and the thick stone walls cast the prison into the murky gloom of imminent twilight, Brunskill was thinking not of Newgate, however, but of the soft red brick of Pembroke College and the friendship that had been forged with the irrepressible young William Pitt.

He was remembering particularly an evening spent in Lincoln's Inn. Perhaps he recalled this evening so vividly because it was the night the Gordon Riots began and London burned for five consecutive days, or perhaps because it was then that he knew Pitt was destined for greatness.

Edward Gibbon, the renowned historian who was publishing the second and third volumes of his momentous *Decline and Fall of the Roman Empire*, had just concluded a splendid discourse to the general approval of the accumulated crowd. Gibbon had barely acknowledged the acclaim when a deep, clearly articulated voice was heard from the rear of the room, calmly and resolutely probing the accuracy of Gibbon's treatise and indeed the very pertinence of the principles that formed its foundation. Whenever Brunskill thought of Pitt, it was always that moment he remembered most vividly: the tall, ungainly, rather awkward-looking man who sat leisurely peeling an orange as he took on the cerebral luminary of the day without a qualm or a quiver. Despite his unassuming appearance, the few words he uttered provoked such admiration among the gathered crowd that Gibbon felt compelled to reassert his preeminence. A lively debate followed in which the genius of young Pitt triumphed over that of his senior, who, eventually, driven into a position from which he was unable to extricate himself, muttered an excuse and strode from the Inn in a seething fury.

Yes, Pitt was destined for great things; that was apparent even then. But as impressive as Pitt's ability and eloquence were, he was also a man of unfailing moral strength and certitude. Brunskill knew he could trust in him. If this Irishman was such a crucial component of national defense then the warden would find a way to be of assistance—even if he had to manufacture Wolfe's escape himself, Brunskill thought grimly.

# 8.

NEWGATE PRISON. LONDON, ENGLAND
*November 25, 1803*

The man slept; beneath turbulent lids, the man dreamed. In waking moments, he had somewhat succeeded in banishing remembrance of this battle, but at night he was vulnerable…

Tonight, again, Wolfe, in the company of eight or nine Irish rebels, advanced steadily down the steeply sloping streets of New Ross township. They were the first wave: penetrating the town from Three Bullet Gate in simultaneous action with Bagenal Harvey who, in command of five hundred insurgents, infiltrated Pillory Gate in the east. With the English somewhere in-between, armed with cannon, Wolfe thought sourly, gripping the wooden shaft of his pike more firmly.

"Misneach…" he muttered, whether to himself or his men he was uncertain, but an injunction to courage would surely benefit them all. Wolfe heard James McLafferty on his right mumbling the Lord's Prayer. "We haven't lost yet, lad," he urged, gripping McLafferty's shoulder in what he hoped was a reassuring gesture. James was barely seventeen. He should have been home with his mother. But here he was in the midst of hell about to meet his maker. Wolfe motioned forward, his pike outstretched before him, the iron spearhead one of nine bristling in layered formation.

They were near the town square, and the houses on each side of the narrow street were consumed by towering columns of fire that seethed and raged like some fearsome beast of voracious appetite. The roof and walls had collapsed, leaving charred frames that barely distinguished one residence from another. The road ahead, and to either side, was veiled by thick clouds of smoke and ash that stung their eyes and burned an acrid path in the back of their throats. The heat was ferocious. Wolfe felt the hairs on his arms crinkle and burn, his skin seared to painful intensity. Sweat darkened his tunic and breeches and ran in rivulets down his forehead; he could taste the salty tang on his lips as he wiped his face on the edge of his coat. It seemed as if the whole world burned. Perhaps the fires had been started by the English in an effort to distract and deter the Irish armies or by Harvey in an attempt to smoke out their adversaries. Not that it mattered much now.

When the battle began, it had seemed as if the earth slowed, as if every movement was protracted, every heartbeat an eternity. The English had surged into their unit from the left flank, emerging out of a smoke-obscured alley with a deadly volley of musket fire. Half of his unit had fallen by the time they had maneuvered their unwieldy pikes to the attack. James was among them. Wolfe, with a full-throated roar of fury, dropped his pike and threw himself into the melee with the short sword that hung at his side.

Later, he recollected the battle in a series of vividly visceral impressions—his feet slipping on the stones made slick by the blood of fellow Irishmen, eyes raw with smoke as New Ross burned around him. The flames in the still dark sky daubed the faces of the combatants in a demonic red and orange, their eyes glittering, teeth clenched with a mighty need: the inextinguishable longing to live and, for the tiny Irish contingent, the agonizing inevitability of death. But the one desire that superseded all others, that lent strength to their faltering numbers—what the English would later characterize with some bewilderment as a peculiar Irish madness—was the determination to die well.

Thrust and parry, the violent clash of steel, the heated rage that gave him strength beyond all endurance. Until that English soldier, the one that looked remarkably like James McLafferty who lay in a pool of blood behind him, charged from the rear. Wolfe had turned at the last minute; he saw him, the young red-haired English lad, who looked more frightened than victorious.

"Never ye mind, lad," Wolfe had murmured as he fell to his knees. The sword thrust had penetrated his side and glanced off his ribs. And there he lay in the dirt of Quay Street, his blood congealing beneath him, the burning houses disintegrating into piles of seething embers and fiery spits. He had been lucky, the doctor told him later; no major organs affected. Except his heart, Wolfe thought, that he had left behind him in New Ross, to be replaced by a hard ball of icy cynicism. Yes, his body had healed well enough, with only a ridged knot of twisted scar tissue marking the wound. While the battle had been fearful, it had only been a prelude to the hell that had followed...

Wolfe Trant woke with a shudder, feeling a phantom pain in his side, which was rapidly eclipsed by the brutal agony in his head. New Ross? He blearily tried to open his eyes, but his lashes were congealed and sticky, gummed together. A coppery taste filled the back of his mouth. Blood. "Never ye mind, lad," he muttered to himself, his body coiling into the fetal position in an involuntary response to the pain that stabbed through his head like shards of glass. "Never ye mind..."

Wolfe forced his mind to clear, to focus. He opened his eyes again; his right one offered a partial view of the stone floor, a coat of black grime covering the gray flagstones. The base of a wooden door. Moonlight filtered through the window in a yellowish haze, casting parallel shadows across the ground. Bars. Prison bars. Not New Ross, but Newgate.

He struggled to sit up, teeth clenched in agony, as his mind stubbornly imposed its will on his broken body. The pain in his head sent him reeling blindly until he reached out with one shaking hand to steady himself against the cool stone floor. Breathing heavily, he took stock of his injuries, examining his torso and face as far as the manacled chains would allow. One of his ribs was broken, his body battered and bruised, but it was the head injury that concerned him most. He could feel the sticky blood that congealed on his face and caked his lashes. It did not appear to be fresh or flowing, which was a good sign, but mentally, under the relentless shooting pain, he felt disorientated and confused.

Certainly, Wolfe had been beaten before. His bare-knuckled boxing career had begun as a scrappy ten-year-old. Timothy McFaddish had four years and fifty pounds on him, and it was not so much a fight as a sound drubbing. It was the first time, though certainly not the last, that Wolfe had tasted his own blood in the dirt. Uncle Ronan, at his sister's insistence, taught young Wolfe how to move, how to dance on the balls of his feet, how to feint a right hook and move in, almost simultaneously, with an uppercut that more often than not sent his opponents sprawling—a skill that had brought him from the farming village of Drumquin to the urban opportunities of Dublin. But that was in the ring, a long time ago now.

He was in prison. Newgate. But when he closed his eyes against the pain, it was not the cold stone floor he felt beneath him or the dank chill of the condemned cell, but the sticky puddle of his own blood in the dirt and the searing heat of his own personal hell. New Ross and the horror he had spent the last seven years trying to forget.

Vaguely, in the dim recesses of his mind, Wolfe recognized that it was not the flames of a small Irish town that enveloped him but the feverish heat of delirium. His past rose up before his lids: images red-washed in blood and guilt; men whose faces had been reduced to pulpy messes of splintered bone and jagged flesh; men he had beaten, and men who had beaten him. From Toulouse to St. Petersburg, the incessant rounds of fighting, the physical pain dulled by alcohol, his body increasingly marred by scars and contusions. Even in the heated confusion of fever, he acknowledged the irony: he had taken up boxing to forget the carnage, the humped profiles of the dead mounded like hillocks in the early dawn light. He had fled the slaughter only to inflict a different kind of butchery. A man defined by violence and painted in blood.

And when, hours later, he emerged from the delirium, chilled by fever-sweat and broken by pain, one thought gave him comfort. Despite the violence of his past memories, despite the blood and fists, despite the glassy-eyed stares of the dead that were etched in his brain, he was not a killer. He had yanked the chains around the guard's throat, his mind red-misted with pain, his body broken, and pulled with all the force of rage and fear amassed in a beaten man. But he had not killed Manning. He had relinquished the chains with trembling hands; the guard writhing and wheezing on the floor.

Bending to his ear, Wolfe had repeated, his voice a rasping whisper, "My name is Wolfe Trant." Then the darkness and merciful unconsciousness had claimed him and he remembered no more.

# 9.

## The Louvre. Paris, France
### *November 25, 1803*

Charles…Charles…" Adeläide repeated with exasperation. "Have you heard a word I've said?"

"Mmm? Apologies, ma chérie." Charles-Maurice de Talleyrand rubbed the bridge of his nose with long, pale fingers. His right leg throbbed. He had removed his shoe, something he rarely did except in the presence of those he truly trusted. It was not that he was embarrassed by the grotesquely distorted bones of his foot, but he could not abide the pity of strangers. And despite his sociability, despite the lavish feasts and entertainments, there were few who he regarded as true friends. Adeläide was one. There was something else too. The vulnerability, the nakedness, inherent in such an open display of deformity disconcerted him. He was a consummate politician, one who had mastered the art of conversational ambiguity, who, despite being involved in various labyrinths of intrigue, himself fulfilled no particular function. He served as an intermediary, acquainted with everybody, cognizant of everything, and held in his hands the end of every string. But Talleyrand's emotions were kept tightly sheathed behind his polite façade. He could not help feeling that baring his poor disfigured foot was tantamount to baring his soul.

"Your mind is elsewhere tonight," Adeläide murmured, moving toward him, her voluptuous figure silhouetted through her gossamer muslin peignoir.

The table was strewn with the remnants of their feast. The half-eaten carcass of a wild boar larded with foie gras sat in a congealing blood-red puddle of wine and grease. The discarded oyster shells glistened in the candlelight, still emitting a faint salty tang of the sea from where they had come. The tunny fish pâté from Toulon was a sadly squashed remnant of the artfully layered creation that had arrived with such pomp and circumstance an hour earlier. No matter. The ragged cluster who

waited outside in the cold didn't mind this. They would take it all, no
questions asked. The Parisian food dealers hovered in the lanes, alleys,
and backstreets, waiting to purchase the leftovers of aristocratic feasts.
A half-eaten croissant could be strategically trimmed and resold as brioche tidbits. A quail carcass would provide the basis of a tasty stew,
limp asparagus revived in a broth. And of course, Talleyrand's coffee
dregs were a highly sought-after prize. They could be watered down ten
times over and still provide a week's livelihood to the café latte girls that
loitered at every corner.

Adeläide de Flahaut lived in an apartment in the ancient palace of
the Louvre, surrounded by these newly sprung restaurants and cafés
that mushroomed across the Right Bank of the first arrondisement.
Her culinary leftovers—and there were many with her gourmand lover
in regular attendance—fatly padded her maidservant's already generous
wages. The apartment itself was a privilege that had been bequeathed to
her family over a decade before, Adeläide being a daughter of a former
mistress of Louis XV (not a fact she currently advertised). However,
with Napoleon's ambitious renovations well underway—the Louvre
was being transformed from a rather decrepit palace housing a motley
assortment of renounced aristocrats to a lavish art museum worthy of
the emperor's enlightened reign—she had been given a week to evacu-
ate the premises. Talleyrand had already secured her a chic apartment in
rue de Châteaudun; now there was just the inconvenience of the move.
But Adeläide was very much a creature of the moment.

"Perhaps I can bring you back to the present," Adeläide murmured,
a slow smile curving her red lips, dark hair falling across her eyes. She
hitched the sheer skirt of her peignoir up her legs and sat on his lap, one
plump, pale thigh straddling each side of him. Her dark eyes luminous
in the candlelight, her skin whitened with mercury, her cheeks flushed
with wine and rouge.

Later, Talleyrand lay in her bed as she lay sleeping beside him, her
mouth slack in sleep, burrowed beneath the quilted velvet coverlet
which rose and fell with gentle breath. Despite the pleasant exertion,
despite the heavy satisfaction of his body, his mind darted and probed
with persistent restlessness. He felt melancholy, he acknowledged with
some surprise. It was not an emotion he was familiar with. Talleyrand
was a pragmatic man who possessed an uncanny instinct into the nature
of others and had learned early how to manipulate them into doing

what he wanted, whether by force of reason or charm. He examined past events with an analytical eye and a view to utilizing his powerful personality to better effect.

The only period of his past for which he allowed himself any nostalgia was the time he had spent with his elderly grandmother, the Princess de Chalais, on her estates in Périgord. His lameness, in the opinion of his parents, had rendered him unfit to inherit any of his many hereditary titles—which were subsequently bestowed on his younger brother—so as a small child he had been banished to Périgord. It was in the aging grandeur of these rural estates that he encountered a period that was so soon to pass away and which had instilled in him an aristocratic bearing and an unfailing decorum that served him so distinctively in the years to come.

Certainly, his early teenage years had not been happy ones, he reflected. His parents had resolved upon a religious profession for their oldest son, unsuited as he was for military life, so he was abruptly removed from his grandmother's care and sent to the seminary of Saint Sulpice, where it was intended he would eventually take Orders. His whole nature, which was little inclined to spiritualism, rebelled against such a vocation. Despite the disapproval of his family, he abandoned the church for the glittering intellectualism of Paris. It was here that Talleyrand and his particular circle of friends had become distinguished for their irreverent wit and their sensual conquests. Talleyrand's intellect, however, demanded a type of fulfillment that could not be provided by idle pleasure alone; and so it was he discovered a passion for politics, one that stimulated both his cerebral appetite and, even more deeply, his unabashed yearning to restore to France some semblance of the rural dignity he had known in his youth. At the very least, peace for France. The rest would follow—or so he had always thought.

This had provided Talleyrand with a vocation, and he immersed himself in his work. From the first, in his political appointments—often positions in which a man could be forgiven for doing nothing and reprimanded for doing too much—Talleyrand succeeded in making a deep impression upon his colleagues. With his noble birth and influential connections, augmented by a powerful intelligence unburdened by scruples, Talleyrand rapidly achieved preeminence in the salon and a secure footing in the political arena.

His personality had little inclination to despondency, and Talleyrand had always anticipated the future with a confident expectation in his own ability to bring his plans to fruition. Napoleon Bonaparte, however, was proving intractable and Talleyrand feared for the fate of France. It was little surprise to him that the Peace of Amiens had failed. The treaty represented a temporary triumph as opposed to the permanent peace Talleyrand had been striving for—and how could the treaty be anything else when the terms were so disparaging to English commercial interests? He had been genuinely surprised Addington had signed the treaty at all.

Talleyrand sighed heavily and eased gently out of bed so as not to wake Adelaïde. There was little point in attempting to sleep. He knew from experience that his mental perambulations would last until the sky lightened in the east. He had a sudden urge to talk to Montrond. Hobbling to the chair, he pulled his flannel undershirt over his head and sat to put on his woolen socks and silk stockings. Mustard breeches were followed by a chambric linen shirt, a thin cravat of muslin, and a waistcoat of the same fabric as the breeches. His shoes were specially made for him, padded and enlarged underneath to accommodate his misshapen foot. A thick woolen overcoat and broad-brimmed black hat completed his ensemble. His coachman was waiting.

"Rue de Desay," Talleyrand informed him, settling back into the plush interior as the carriage clattered over the icy cobblestones. Montrond met him at the door.

Settled in by a roaring fire, cognac warming his belly, Talleyrand felt a little more at ease. "I apologize for calling so late, mon ami…" he began.

Montrond waved him off. "It is no matter," he demurred. "I am due to leave for Bruges in an hour. I am pleased to have seen you before I depart. I thought you were spending the night at Adelaïde's?"

"I was restless," Talleyrand replied carelessly, his long fingers tapping an unconscious rhythm on his thigh. Montrond waited. His friend was troubled, that much was clear. A man renowned for his languid detachment, he appeared tightly coiled and agitated. Talleyrand eased himself into a chair, then abruptly stood, his mouth grimacing in rare impatience as he lurched awkwardly to one side, his club foot folding beneath him. Regaining his footing, he commenced an ungainly gait across the room.

"I have endeavored, Casimir, to moderate Napoleon's ambitions."

When he began to speak, it was with a sharp tone, his words punctuated by an uncharacteristic jerkiness. "I have failed. I exerted all my influence against the resumption of hostilities. Again, I failed." Talleyrand paused, fixing Montrond with an icy glare, as if he were personally responsible for this litany of disappointments.

The decision to aid the English in the overthrow of Napoleon had been made at no small cost to Talleyrand's conscience, and only then after a long and pained deliberation. Montrond recognized his friend's need to reiterate those reasons and strengthen his own resolve. "The most difficult person you have to negotiate with is Napoleon himself," Montrond acknowledged sympathetically.

"That may be," Talleyrand muttered darkly as he resumed his ungainly perambulations across the room. "But the time has now come when the interests of France and those of her emperor have not only ceased to be identical but have become diametrically opposed. Napoleon never had *any* picture in his mind of Europe save as of one vast estate with himself as master and the various territories farmed out to his subordinate allies and relatives." Talleyrand's mouth twisted in pain as he sank abruptly into the chair, his fingers clenched around the carved armrests.

After a moment, he continued, his gray eyes dark with a subdued rage that had been building for years. "The problem, mon ami, is that while the French people are civilized, their sovereign is not," Talleyrand managed tightly. "The people have one desire—to have done with war and be allowed to enjoy the fruits of conquest. Instead, they are dragged as victims in the wake of his triumphal chariot to their own destruction! The failed assassination attempt on Napoleon last night is a case in point. The Resistance may be controlled by Royalist interests, but their determination to remove Napoleon from power is representative of the popular will."

"Are you having second thoughts?" Casimir asked quietly. Talleyrand knew without asking that Montrond referred to the upcoming voyage to Dover and the letter his friend carried in his breast pocket.

"No. If Napoleon succeeds in taking England, it will destabilize the entire European continent and inflame his territorial ambitions even further. We cannot allow that to happen." Talleyrand exhaled sharply and leaned back in his chair as if his tirade had exhausted him. Retrieving the cognac Casimir had poured for him, Talleyrand absently caressed the rim of the glass with long, pale fingers. When he spoke again it was with a renewed sense of composure. "I have already sent word to William Pitt of the emperor's covert probe seeking a pilot to guide the flotilla through the Goodwin Sands. It seems the former prime minister has found a suitable candidate. Your letter will provide further instructions to enable our meeting. I think it best that I introduce this spy to Napoleon myself."

There was a moment's companionable silence as the two men gazed reflectively into the flickering orange flames. Casimir hesitated. Talleyrand was in a rare mood. The two men had been friends for more than a decade, but Talleyrand's mocking civility often kept Casimir at a distance. His frank and open confidences this evening led Montrond to ask about something he had always wondered.

"All these occasions where the emperor has threatened to hang you or shoot you," Casimir began. "All these rumors that are circulating concerning your extracurricular activities, your sympathies with certain fallen aristocrats, myself included," he added with a grin. "How is it you have survived this long? Napoleon has executed men for much less."

Talleyrand smiled lazily, leaning back in his chair, legs stretched out to the warmth of the hearth. Whatever had unnerved him, whatever had disturbed his equanimity, it was evidently resolved. The languid poise for which he was so renowned had returned. Montrond's question amused him; his full lips parted to reveal gleaming white teeth and a deep chuckle escaped. "I am, to Napoleon, one of those grand dignitaries of the old nobility. My lineage and comportment are convenient accessories for a man who is seeking to legitimize his own imperial dynasty. He wants the support of the old nobility; he wants to reconcile the old France with the new, and for that, he needs me."

"Certainly there are less risky ways to seek legitimacy? Napoleon is an emotional man, easily and often enraged, and by *you*, it seems, most particularly."

"I do try," Talleyrand conceded dryly, with a gleam in his eyes.

"But there must be other more pliable aristocrats who would fulfill this function of associative legitimacy?" Montrond persisted thoughtfully, his dark countenance washed in the warm glow of reflected firelight.

"Ah yes, doubtless," Talleyrand acknowledged, with a wry smile. "Well, in the early days before the coup d'état of 18 Brumaire, Napoleon was little more than an awkward youth. Brilliant military strategist, certainly, but…" A languid gesture of one hand served as an elegant testimony to Napoleon's social shortcomings. "Certain insecurities have persisted over the years, particularly concerning his humble Corsican heritage. It suits his vanity, you see, that Charles-Maurice de Talleyrand-Perigord— peer, aristocrat, and confidante to kings—is at his service. Napoleon is also a creature of habit, and we have been conspiring together since the time of the Directory." Talleyrand swallowed a mouthful of cognac, regarding his friend through a heavy-lidded gaze. "To strike me down now, well, it would be like striking down a pillar of his own house, and the moment hardly seems well-appointed for internal reconstruction." A leisurely smile crossed his lips. "And as to my aristocratic friendships, Napoleon is willing to overlook a few dinner parties as long as there is no incontrovertible evidence of my betrayal. And there is none. Just gossip and innuendo. So he contents himself with public upbraidings and defamations. He calls me a traitor and threatens to shoot me. Really all quite amusing!"

# 10.

With dark head bowed over his knees, manacled arms limp at his side, Wolfe had every appearance of a broken, bleeding man waiting only to die. Newgate would very shortly accommodate him. After the brutal beating, Manning had been removed from the cellblock, and Wolfe's pre-execution care fell to Pally. The final meal had been removed, untouched, and Wolfe waited in the silence of the cell, listening to the midnight clang of the execution bell.

The bell would ring again in the morning, he knew, when the prison chaplain came to escort him into the Press yard where his leg irons would be removed and his wrists and arms tied. Then he would be led across the yard to the Lodge, out through the Debtor's Door and up a short flight of steps onto the gallows. He had heard them as the dusk faded into night, the sound of hammers and muttered curses as the portable gallows were erected just in front of the smoke-blackened prison. Wolfe's imminent execution had produced a bustle of activity. He could hear the hue and cry of excited voices as temporary benches were assembled. Houses opposite the prison entertained a brisk evening auction for prime window seats overlooking the gallows. The gleeful cackle of an elderly woman announced the victorious winner at seven pounds—not a bad take for ten minutes of viewing time.

Although Wolfe knew it would take more than ten minutes for him to die, the unknown winner would get her money's worth. Manning would take care of that. The prison guard had not attempted to hide his loathing for the Irish prisoner and had, in addition to the beating of the previous evening, endeavored for the last six weeks to maximize Wolfe's discomfort in numerous petty ways: adding cockroaches to his food dish, neglecting to empty his chamber pot, refusing to lighten his manacles despite Wolfe having paid amply for the privilege. And so it went on. Wolfe had closed in upon himself, ignoring Manning's taunts.

He thought of the Kerry slug that dotted the crevices and rocks of the coastal shores of Donegal Bay. When threatened, this smoky mollusk would curl up upon itself, retracting its head and tightening into a ball with only its hard, shield-like skin exposed. Wolfe had played with them as a boy, gently prodding them to provoke their immediate defensive response, and had eaten them roasted on a stick over the fire when all other food sources failed. He thought of the gray seas of Donegal Bay; he thought of the wild beauty of the cliffs of Slieve Leag; he thought of the humble Kerry slug; and he consigned Manning to another reality. Naturally enough, this seemed to provoke Manning more than anything else, which provided a rare source of satisfaction to Wolfe in his lamentable position.

A new type of gallows would be utilized the next morning, which also accounted for the bustling anticipation that took place beyond his cell walls. It incorporated a collapsible platform intended to break the neck and bring death more quickly. The relative speed with which prisoners were dispatched, however, depended upon the hangman making sure the rope was the right length. Very few got it right, even if they bothered to try. And Wolfe was sure the executioner, Manning's mate Will, would relish a painfully protracted process.

To distract himself from the evening's din and bustle that was taking place beyond his window, he sang, his husky baritone resonating softly in the dark cell:

*At a cottage door one winters' night*
*As the snow lay on the ground*
*Stood a youthful Irish soldier boy*
*To the mountains he was bound*
*His mother stood beside him saying*
*You'll win my boy don't fear*
*With loving arms around his waist*
*She tied his bandolier.*

He stopped abruptly as the concluding lines of the ballad flashed through his mind:

*Good-bye, God bless you mother dear*
*I'm dying a death so grand from*
*wounds received in action trying*
*to free my native land...*

No such grand end for him. He would die the ignominious death of a common thief: tongue protruding, eyes popping out of his head, and the body-snatchers lurking at the peripheries, poised to seize his corpse. Nothing dignified about it. At least his mother would not be around to witness it.

The ballad had been a favorite of hers. When Wolfe thought of his mother, as he often did, the haunting tune of this ballad always came to mind—that, and the fierce pride in her face when he left for Dublin that first time. He remembered the glint of unshed tears in her eyes, the warm touch of her gnarled fingers, the thick rope of gray hair that coiled at the nape of her neck, the lined face, always tired and careworn. She had seemed an old woman from birth, his mother. After his sister died, she stopped singing, and less than a year later she joined her daughter in the cold earth: another casualty of English oppression.

And then there was Egan. Perhaps *he* would oblige his dear departed mother with "a death so grand." Like Egan, she hadn't understood his abrupt departure for the continent, nor his decision to support himself in a trade she'd felt was a meaningless version of what he should have been doing: fighting for Ireland. Of course, they hadn't understood. How could they?

The bitterness remained, even after all these years. And sitting in the chilled silence of the condemned cell, waiting to die, every breath an agony, it was not his physical afflictions that wore him down, but the mental ones. Wolfe felt so tired.

He had been so certain in those days, so sure of himself and his opinions. His political responsibilities. He had declaimed and exhorted, urged and protested, his voice deep and compelling, his message always the same: rise up in rebellion, free Ireland from the yoke of English oppression. And the young men had followed him, listened to him, died for him.

What had been accomplished by all this hatred? Certainly, it had fueled the fires of revolution in Ireland, but to what end? The people lived and died as they always had—miserable and poor. The political youth wasted their energies and spent their lives in a futile struggle against a far more powerful oppressor. England seemed formidable. Unbreakable. All-powerful. The French never came, despite their promises. And the Irish were left to pay the price yet again. More blood in the streets. James McLafferty's blood. He felt sick thinking of his role in it all. The people called him a hero, but he knew better. Why couldn't he have died as so many better men had done?

Then, there was the factory at Carrickfergus, his self-imposed penance. After three years of struggle, he had turned a failing linen factory—crammed with a desperate workforce of grimy, half-starved men, women, and children—into a business that earned a modest profit which was divided equally between the workers.

And now he was imprisoned, his factory closed, its product confiscated, the workers sent home. It was the final punishment for daring to expect equality from the English: equality in politics, equality in trade. Without coal, his linen factory was as useless as wings on a piglet. Wolfe hadn't intended to punch that damned solicitor, but Mr. Tennant had been so smugly superior, so careless of the lives that would be devastated as a result of his breach of contract. Wolfe had been thinking of Kathleen, who had been recently widowed, and of how her three young children would fare if she lost her job at the loom. And a red-misted rage burned up from his belly, focused with lethal intensity on this powdered dandy, in his satin waistcoat and plush velvet coat, who had never missed a meal in his life—and suddenly, Tennant was lying on the ground with blood gushing from a broken nose. The police rapidly became involved, and Tennant saw to it that Wolfe's history of political rebellion became a focal point in the subsequent trial. This Irish madman obviously remained a threat to the English people. And so it went on. To an English jury, who had become accustomed to seeing ominous shadows at every turn, who daily expected the French hordes to land and slaughter them all, well, it did not take much to convince them that Wolfe, true to his name, was a predator and a menace and should be consigned to Newgate for a period of ten years.

Not that it mattered much now. It seemed Wolfe's unlucky encounter with prisoner 16-A would ensure he never left—except within the tight confines of a pine coffin, which had already been paid for. He would not be one of those left to rot and molder on the flagstone floor. Little matter that he had been targeted by 16-A; regardless of circumstances, he had defended himself a little too well. His size, his adept ability to move, and his uncanny capacity to locate his opponent's weakness and exploit it made it difficult for him to be perceived as a victim.

Shivering, he drew his tattered blanket closer around his shoulders. It crawled with lice, but he barely noticed anymore. The fleas and the lice were the only ones who led gluttonous lives in Newgate; they infested animal and human alike, conveyed from one end of the prison to another by scampering children encrusted with filth and clothed in rags. And, of course, there were the dogs, the pigs, and the poultry that ranged freely throughout the cellblocks, and the droppings they left behind. Most things that had bothered him upon his arrival were now unnoticed: the dirt, the lice, the smell, the food.

Quiet and alone with the pain that wracked his battered body, he sat in the ten-by-ten-foot stone cell. The bright moonlight marked out the passage of time in the shadow of prison bars that shifted slowly across the floor. The clamor of construction and trade had long since subsided. The raucous laughter of late-night revelers had dwindled as the moon rose and set across a cold black sky. Wolfe was left in silence, the only sound the rhythmic pounding of his own heartbeat, the blood throbbing painfully through his skull. Solitary confinement was disconcertingly quiet after the close quarters of cell life.

When he first arrived in Newgate, it had been the sounds that kept him awake: a cacophony reminiscent of a closely congregated, snuffling, snarling animal pack; a fetid mass of humanity where the hierarchy was established in blood and reiterated in violence. Exchanges were invariably boisterous, punctuated by howls and shrieks that he once found alarming but subsequently ignored. The inmates had a proclivity for murder—a quick thrust to the ribs with a splintered prison bar and the furtive acquisition of a wad of tobacco or a dingy blanket. A sharp cry in the night often meant one less to feed the next day. Incessant gambling relieved the dismal monotonousness, with play often charged by strident accusations and slurred threats, the participants well lubricated by the cheap gin brewed onsite. At night, the dim prison resounded with nasal gurgling snores, and the grunts of an inmate relieving himself with one of the prostitutes who plied her trade among society's dregs.

However, even then, it was the silence that Wolfe found most unnerving. You could always tell the prisoners who had given up, who seemed to sink into themselves. They stopped talking. What was the point? They lay motionless against the wall, hardly alive but yet not quite dead. The grime, the filth, seemed to sit heavier upon them, as if with each successive layer of grease the prison itself was reaching out to brand them, to own them, to swallow them whole. And now it would swallow him.

Squatting on the stone floor, head bowed in despondent surrender to an unjust fate—this was how Manning had found him the night before. Wolfe had relinquished all hope of a reprieve. He was ready to die, and as Manning's vicious blows rained down upon his head and shoulders, he'd felt gratitude—gratitude that this guard might spare him the indignity of a hanging, the spectacle of a sideshow. Perhaps that is why Wolfe eventually spared his life. But when Manning, with his fetid breath and smug arrogance, referred to him as 51-A that last time, something snapped. Wolfe's temper flared, provoked by the lifelong struggle to assert himself against all odds, to have the power of self-definition rather than submit to the labels of others. There were choices, still, on the brink on the gallows. He might hang, but he would not do so as 51-A. He was Wolfe Trant. He was an Irishman. He deserved to die as he had been born—with an identity.

# 11.

A scratching sounded on the other side of the door, and then a sharp insistent bark: Mutt. The dog roused Wolfe from his deep sleep. The execution, scheduled for that morning, had been delayed—for whichever reason Wolfe had not been informed. He had heard the angry complaints of the crowd that had gathered beyond his window in the early dawn, deprived of their anticipated spectacle. A doctor had stitched up his head wound and another on his arm and applied bandages, startlingly white against the grime that had become as much a part of him as his skin and hair. Despite the discomfort of his chains and the constant throbbing ache of his body, Wolfe, utterly exhausted by the mental effort required to face execution and then the flood of emotional relief at its postponement, slept deeply, head nodding over his knees. Until the dog woke him.

Mutt seemed to have adopted Wolfe since Trant's first day in Newgate. In the holding cell where new prisoners were brought upon arrival, Wolfe had been left among twenty or so others. He had seated himself on the ground, trying to reconcile himself to his situation and not having much success, when Mutt came and sat opposite. The dog was a rather pitiful looking creature, with bald patches of red skin amid fur so encrusted with dirt that it was difficult to distinguish its color. He was missing a leg but moved with a quick hobble that suggested he had long ago become accustomed to doing without it. He sat before Wolfe, head cocked to one side, long red tongue lolling from one side of his mouth, his eyes watchful but also slightly wary. Wolfe swore he was grinning.

"Well, then, what are you so happy about, Mutt?" he had asked the dog quietly. "You seem to be even worse off than me. At least I have all my legs." The dog gave Wolfe's hand a wet lick. Wolfe felt absurdly grateful for the small gesture of affection and shared the last of several crackers he found in his pocket with the dog. From then on, the two were friends, and Mutt could often be found scampering at Wolfe's heels.

"Hi there, Mutt," Wolfe called out softly to the dog on the other side of the door. "How're you doing?" Mutt whined again, scratching the base of the door with his paws, and then a soft thud sounded as he settled in on the other side to wait. The bells of St. Sepulchre began a doleful clanging. Wolfe cocked his ear to one side, listening attentively. It was time. "Hang on there, Mutt; I'll get us out of this."

Bending his head down toward his upper arm, Wolfe, in one savage movement, ripped the doctor's neat stitches away with his teeth and opened up a gash in his bicep that he had himself created the night before. Pain flared through his skull at the sudden movement, but Wolfe ignored it, biting into his own flesh until he came away with the prize he had been seeking: a small, insignificant buckle-spoke from the belt Manning had worn the night before. He could have stolen the keys, but those would have been immediately discovered and retrieved. The broken belt buckle, however, was easily overlooked in the ensuing excitement. And a more apt lock-picker was scarce to be found, Wolfe thought with grim satisfaction as he maneuvered himself out of his handcuffs.

Then, with brute strength, he twisted the small links in the chain binding his legs around until the center link snapped. Working rapidly, Wolfe drew each fetlock up the calves of his legs, securing each with his stockings to prevent them rattling. With the broken iron links from his leg chains, he then proceeded, standing in the hearth, to work at the crumbling masonry in the chimney.

After an hour's labor, the bells of St. Sepulchre sounding his progress and hastening his action, Wolfe had succeeded in creating a hole about three feet in diameter, his head throbbing in agonized concert with each scrape of the chain. Hauling himself painfully through the opening into musty darkness, Wolfe knew himself to be in the Red Room, directly above the condemned cell. A room where the Preston rebels had been kept seven years before, now as empty and stale as a seven years' absence would lead one to expect. The dim light of the street lamps illuminated the barred window and a small section of bricked ceiling, but the rest of the room was cast into deep shadow. Wolfe's attention was immediately focused on the stout door on the far side of the room—his way out. Even as he feverishly worked the belt spoke through the lock, fingers slippery with sweat, heart pounding with anxious fear, his mind was quietly calculating. It was just past two in the morning, which meant he had two hours until they would come for him. Two hours to flee across the shadowy rooftops.

"Mac an donais!" Wolfe cursed as the buckle slipped from his grasp. A faint ping announced its location somewhere to the left of him. He felt with his hands along the stone floor—nothing. The buckle was scarcely long enough to be of use anyway. Wolfe rested his forehead on the cool floor, his breath coming in harsh gasps as the pain escalated with excruciating intensity behind his left eye. And then he found he could not breathe at all but could only wait out the pain, digging splayed fingers into the flagstones until at last it began to subside, each wave slightly less painful than the one before. Until he found his breath again. Shakily rising to his feet, he reached out to support himself; and, in so doing, his fingers closed around a long nail embedded in the wall. Perhaps the luck of the Irish was with him after all.

The nail succeeded where the belt buckle failed, and before another ten minutes had passed he had left the Red Room to find himself in a small chapel. The light filtered in dimly from the open door behind him, but little of the room could be seen. Blindly reaching forward, Wolfe came across decorative ironworks that served to divide the congregation from the pulpit, and he wrenched a small spike from its companions. He located the door and felt the cool metal of the lock under his fingertips, the sleek smoothness of new brass. Wolfe spent twenty minutes working the nail through the lock without success and had just decided to use the spike to break through the wall and dislodge the bolt when the clock at St. Sepulchre's announced the third hour. He still had time.

Or so he thought. Even through the thick stone walls he heard the muffled shouts of a raised alarm: his escape had been discovered. Heedless of the noise, he struck the door lock with a fury born of desperation. Before he could cast his third blow, however, the door flew open. Four prison guards rushed forward, seizing him. They did not return him to the condemned cell, which by virtue of the gaping hole in the fireplace was now compromised, but hustled him directly to the warden's office where he was unceremoniously deposited to await the arrival of William Brunskill. The warden entered a few minutes later, clothes rumpled, eyes heavy with fatigue. Another who had been up all night.

"I understand you have had a busy night?" Brunskill asked him. Wolfe said nothing. Beyond the chapel lay the rooftops and freedom. If only he had had ten minutes more. The disappointment sat heavy on him. "You may leave us," the warden told the guards, his gaze lingering on the Irishman who stood opposite.

"But, sir, 51-A is dangerous," a guard protested.

"Go," Brunskill repeated impatiently. When the guards had withdrawn, the warden offered Wolfe a chair. Weak after his exertions, his head throbbing mercilessly, Wolfe sat. Brunskill leaned forward over his desk, arms carelessly scattering papers that littered its surface. "Do you know Mr. William Pitt?" he asked Wolfe intently, the candle glow glittering on the surface of his glasses.

Wolfe's head shot up in surprise.

"It seems the former prime minister knows of you," Brunskill continued, without waiting for Wolfe's reply. "I am to escort you to the Criminal Court within the hour. Fortunately, your escape attempt was unsuccessful or, apparently, there would have been a great deal more at stake than just my job." Left to ponder this perplexing statement, Wolfe was again released into the custody of the guards. The three followed the warden down a darkened hallway to a stout wooden door. Producing a large brass key from his pocket, Brunskill opened the door to reveal a narrow passageway enclosed by large masonry blocks.

"Sir! Mr. Brunskill, sir!" It was Charley who hastened down the hallway, his threadbare yellow robe flapping wildly about scrawny legs. "52-C has taken Pally hostage and is threatenin' to kill 'im!"

Brunskill sighed in irritation. Pally, along with Manning, was responsible for cellblock A. It seemed news of Wolfe's escape attempt had enlivened the prisoners. Apparently, Jack Sheppard's flight to freedom four years before had instigated a full-scale riot at Newgate, the mishandling of which had led to his predecessor's eventual removal. This situation needed to be addressed immediately before it got out of control. Given the importance attached to this prisoner, Brunskill would have preferred to escort him into Pitt's custody himself. The passageway, however, led directly to the Criminal Court where the former prime minister waited, and these guards were two he trusted more than most. Tim Fischer was young but honest, and Jacob Butler had been with the prison for many years.

"Very well," Brunskill said crisply. "Take him directly to the courtroom. Release him into the custody of William Pitt and none other. Do you understand?"

"Yessir," the older guard replied promptly.

As the warden and his assistant disappeared down the hallway, a shadow separated itself from the darkness of an alcove to their left.

"Gawd, Jack! Yer scairt the livin' shit outa me!" the older guard protested in agitated relief. "Why're creepin' up on us like that?"

"Let me take 'im to Pitt," Jack Manning rasped, his narrowed gaze fixed on the prisoner who stared impassively back.

"Oh, I dunno, Jack. The warden…"

Manning slipped the guard a thick wad of rhino. "I'll take 'im where he's supposed to go, and I won't touch 'im. I just wanna know what's goin' on. The warden'll be none the wiser. You owe me, Jacob."

Everyone owed Manning something, and Jacob was no exception. Jacob also knew that it didn't pay to make an enemy of him; Manning never forgot an injury and, being of a vengeful nature, would stop at nothing to see scores settled and retribution exacted. In truth, Jacob was afraid of him.

"All right then, Jack." Jacob stepped reluctantly back, then turned and hurried down the hallway, as if afraid of what he might be leaving behind.

"51-A," Manning spat derisively. Then, without warning, he punched Wolfe brutally in the stomach. The prisoner involuntarily doubled over as his breath left him. "That's for me neck," he hissed. "Now get goin'."

# 12.

The pain was back. William Pitt leaned forward over his knees, knuckles white and clenched over the edge of the chair, his breath coming in quick, agonized gasps. The pain twisted and curled in his belly like some writhing serpent, flared with white-hot intensity and then slowly, gradually, began to subside, leaving him pale and shaken. Heavy footsteps sounded in the hall. They must not know of his condition. Pitt rose with difficulty and, turning toward the window, leaned against the wall in a deliberately negligent fashion. Reaching into his black velvet coat, Pitt withdrew a small cotton handkerchief and with trembling hand pressed it to his mouth. Not so much blood today, he noted with grim satisfaction. The door opened behind him.

"Here, guv'nr," a young voice announced respectfully after a moment's silence. "The warden sent us with the prisoner."

"Thank you. Remove his shackles before you go," Pitt instructed, feeling his heart finally slow to a more moderate rate. Carefully, he returned the bloodied handkerchief to his inside pocket before turning to face the three men who had entered the room. He was immediately struck by the height of the prisoner; Wolfe, despite his darkly hunched posture, towered over the two guards who flanked him to either side. He could not see him well—only one small candle illuminated the room—but he could smell him. The pungent aroma of Newgate enveloped Wolfe like a cloud and was astonishingly strong in the small, enclosed room.

The younger guard hesitated, mumbling something under his breath as he shifted his feet. He cast a glance across to his companion, who chewed on the edge of a filthy fingernail.

"That will be all. You may go," Pitt repeated.

"We got our orders, guv'nr. Gotta stay while you talk to the prisoner," the older guard insisted obstinately, his voice a ragged wheeze.

Pitt sighed inwardly. A small man determined to abuse his small position of power. His declining health depleted his energy reserves without the addition of these tiresome exchanges. It was so damned unnecessary.

"Your name, sir?" he asked sharply.

"Manning, guv'nr, Jack Manning," the guard answered, his voice growing bolder, his stance one of careless indifference.

"Well, Mr. Jack Manning, it just so happens that I have a close, personal acquaintance with Mr. William Brunskill, whom, you will know, is the warden of Newgate Prison and therefore your immediate superior. When I inform him of your insubordination—well, the repercussions could be grave indeed. Men have been transported to penal colonies for less."

Pitt spoke pleasantly, but there was no mistaking the steel in his voice. Manning's eyes narrowed in dislike, his lip curling back from large yellowed teeth.

"Jack *Manning*, did you say?" Pitt continued with a deliberately thoughtful air. "It seems your reprehensible beating of this man saved his life. Mr. Brunskill requested a stay of execution until the prisoner was physically able to walk to the gallows unaided. It seems the superintendent of prisons can tolerate abuses within the prison system so long as they are not publicly advertised. But executions these days, as I am sure you are aware, are popular spectacles. Reformation of the prison system is all the rage. Newgate would come under scrutiny and insofar as you are concerned, Mr. Jack Manning, the penal colonies might be a kindly fate after all."

The guard reluctantly acquiesced, muttering under his breath as he fitted a large key to Trant's manacles and lifted the massive chains. From beneath his shaggy mane of matted hair, Wolfe winked at him, a mocking smile briefly crossing his lips. Manning's face flushed, his mouth working in silent rage as he stalked from the room, his companion scuttling close behind.

Pitt, still leaning against the window frame, his booted feet crossed at the ankles, examined Wolfe Trant with some interest. The sputtering candle on the table was the only source of illumination; it cast eerie shadows across this hulking mass of a man, highlighting a strongly hooked nose and the occasional gleam of his good eye and consigning the rest into darkness. Trant stood silently, a massive dark creature, his face largely obscured by a tangled growth of beard and hair, all of which appeared to be a matted repository for fleas. A bandage was wrapped tightly around his forehead, stained with dried blood, his eye beneath swollen closed, the purple and blue around the socket giving way to livid yellow at the base of his nose.

"You have been poorly treated in Newgate. I am sorry for that," Pitt began. "Please sit; have some water." He gestured toward a pewter jug on the table. Wolfe said nothing but stood silently before him like an immense injured bear. "I apologize for the lack of additional amenities," Pitt continued in a pleasant, conversational manner, undeterred by Trant's lack of response. "I had hoped to provide you with a meal in the dining room, but I understand it is still undergoing repairs."

The lavish dining room, which provided for the judges and their attendants, had been extravagantly furnished with mosaic decoration, mahogany furniture, Turkish carpets, and gilded mirrors. Elaborate meals, cooked in the kitchen on the ground floor and served with vintages from the wine vault, were available upon special request. Perhaps unsurprisingly, the dining room had been badly damaged during the Gordon Riots and was not as yet functioning in its usual capacity. And Pitt had other reasons for selecting this obscure clerk's office for their meeting, bare as it was of warmth or furniture.

Pitt moved to the table as he felt the nausea well up in the base of his belly. God, not now, he thought desperately. He felt that he was dying. The blasted physicians had poured bottles of physic down his throat and insisted that a week of the waters in Bath would cure what ailed him, but Pitt knew better. He had seen his father struck down while delivering a speech in Parliament, and he had determined much later on, suffering similar ailments, to go exactly the same way. Addington, currently prime minister, was tottering, his policies derided, his person humiliated. The populace was feeling the effect of renewed taxations to help finance the war effort against France. The Peace of Amiens had failed, and who else was there to blame but the man at the top?

The time was not only ripe, but Pitt felt instinctively that there wasn't much of it left. He had to move fast, and to do that he had to connect with Wolfe Trant, the former rebel who at one time, and perhaps still, was prepared to give his life in the struggle against the English. The future of England hung in the balance.

"I can arrange for your freedom," Pitt said quietly. "But I am going to need something in return." Still Wolfe said nothing, although Pitt saw his hands clench by his sides, wrists red and raw from the manacles. "I can return your lands in Ireland and reinstate the tax exemptions for your linen factory," he continued, seating himself gingerly at the table.

He felt himself instinctively at a disadvantage while Wolfe towered over him, but it seemed the only acceptable alternative to being violently ill. The rising nausea reached the back of his throat, caused a silent gag, and then obediently subsided to loiter ominously in his belly. Tame the savage beast, Pitt thought with some amusement, and that seemed to apply also to Wolfe Trant who stood hunched and taciturn before him. "I know the situation in Ireland is intolerable."

"What do *you* know of the situation in Ireland?" Wolfe finally spoke. His voice was a rasp, each word enunciated with precise, almost painful control. Pitt had the impression that he had not spoken for some time. "Do you toil in the fields till it is too dark to see? Do you live on potatoes from September till the following spring and then scrounge for wild berries and dandelions to survive the summer? Do you pay hearth, turf, and hay tax as well as tithes to support an administration and church that actively advocate interests contrary to your own? Do you do that now, Mr. Pitt?"

Wolfe moved forward, limping slightly, and placed his large hands on the table, leaning down in a menacing manner. The candlelight illuminated a fearsome visage: a gray bandage darkened with blood, beneath which a grotesquely swollen eye appeared in lurid shades of purple and blue. His good eye flashed, and his lip curled slightly as he spoke. His voice, tinged with an Irish brogue, was deep, rusty, and abrasive from lack of use; the bitterness, the venom, however, were clear.

"I can understand your anger, your distrust." Pitt leaned forward in his chair, nausea forgotten, as he moved to take advantage of this opportunity. At least Wolfe was talking.

"You've no bloody idea," Wolfe growled. He moved swiftly for such a large man; Pitt found himself unceremoniously hauled from his chair and thrust roughly up against the wall, a strong forearm across his throat. "I ought to kill you here and now."

"By all means, Mr. Trant," Pitt managed in a croaky whisper, feeling the suffocating pressure against his windpipe. "I am dying anyway. Certainly, this would be a quicker, less painful method. For me, that is. You, well, that is another story. I am still a popular man. You would probably be hung, drawn, and quartered for treason. What would happen to Ireland then? English views of Irish Catholicism would be confirmed; the opportunity to advance the cause of emancipation would be lost."

Wolfe's face was close to his own, his breath hot on his cheek, and for the first time Pitt could see him clearly. Beneath the thick knot of entangled hair and beard, he could see a pale, set face, strongly planed with high cheekbones and a wide mouth. Trant's nostrils flared with emotion; a trickle of blood ran unnoticed to his chin. His jaw was tightly clenched, his uninjured eye a narrow slit of hot blue fury; his fingers convulsed around the fabric of Pitt's coat. Pitt could see the battle being waged across Wolfe's face, the struggle to suppress a rage that had been building all his life, and he felt, with surprising calmness, that his end had come. He had tried at least. However, with great reluctance, hands trembling with emotion, Wolfe backed away. For a moment, there was silence between the two men as Wolfe struggled to recover his composure and Pitt sagged back against the wall, gingerly rubbing his neck.

"And you want to advance the cause of Catholic emancipation?" Wolfe asked with quiet intensity, his face set in lines of wary distrust. "And why would you do that, then?"

"Because I believe it is the only way to avoid civil war." Pitt moved unsteadily to his chair, wiping his brow with his handkerchief. "Every Irish crisis in the past nine years has been fed by demands for Catholic emancipation on the one hand and Protestant obstinacy on the other. If the Catholics were granted full rights of citizenship, including the right to sit in Parliament, the Protestants need not fear local Catholic insurrection in Ireland if the Irish representatives are seated at Westminster. And the Catholics need not fear Protestant oppression if the affairs of Ireland are subject to the votes of all MPs." Pitt held Wolfe's gaze. He spoke with a fervent intensity of his own; resolving the difficulties between immediate neighbors seemed to him an absolute imperative if war were ever to be successfully waged against France. And he had been formulating a plan for years. This was its last chance for success. "Basically, Mr. Trant, Ireland needs capital, and England needs security on her borders. Granting full rights to the Catholics in Ireland is the essential foundation of that process."

Wolfe did not respond. Pitt thought he swayed slightly on his feet. "Mr. Trant? Are you quite well? Can I call a doctor?" Pitt asked solicitously, rising from his chair. Wolfe turned to face him, his face pale and set, his jaw clenched tight, his eye dark with pain. Pitt recognized the symptoms only too well. "I do apologize; I should have called for one immediately. Would you like to sit down?"

"A doctor is not needed," Wolfe replied shortly in a strained voice, gingerly lowering himself into the chair opposite. A moment passed as Pitt occupied himself with uncharacteristic fastidiousness to the securing of a loose cuff. He was only too aware of the importance to a strong man of hiding his pain before his enemies. "Why should I trust you? The Catholics were to be liberated when the Act of Union was passed three years ago, but the English Parliament failed to ratify it. That was your doing I understand," Wolfe said gruffly.

"Mr. Trant," Pitt began, leaning forward in his seat. "You are an intelligent man. You understand the intricacies of politics, the necessity of support to pass any legislation. Unfortunately, the Catholic issue is a volatile one, and I will not deceive you, emancipation will take some time, perhaps even generations. It extends far beyond Church and Parliament. Catholicism, to the vast majority of English people, is synonymous with treachery and invasion, bloodshed and persecution. Any acceptance that Catholics could have the rights and privileges of other Englishmen constitutes pandering to the French, an alliance with the Jacobite sympathies that led to bloody revolution in France. Charles I, in company with the Scottish Catholics, brought the English to civil war. My point is that men have very long memories. The fight will be a difficult one, an exceedingly unpopular one, but I promise you I will devote myself to it."

Wolfe raised an eyebrow. "Well, to be sure, this is all very grand, Mr. Pitt, and while I appreciate the fresh air, what does all this have to do with me?"

Here it was. The moment of truth.

"I propose a partnership, Mr. Trant. As I said, I can arrange for your personal freedom and return your lands. I plan to aggressively advance not only the cause of Catholic emancipation in Ireland but also a radical liberalization of English-Irish trade which will, ultimately, I believe, address the overwhelming poverty in your country. And in return…"

In an adjacent room, Jack Manning pressed his ear against the wall, straining to hear the former prime minister's murmured words. The two rooms had only recently been one, but as the bureaucracy of Addington's government expanded, the need for additional clerical space had correspondingly increased. The wall was composed of a hastily erected barricade of flush-laid oak planking that served to provide privacy of sight if not sound.

What he heard astonished him, and when he departed less than an hour later, it was with the certain conviction that he would be warden before the year was out. This information was the kind that toppled governments, and he would make sure its worth was valued accordingly. Manning wet his lips in gleeful anticipation. Not only would he come away from this venture with more money and influence than he had ever dreamed of, but he would have the pleasure of exacting vengeance against the tall Irishman whom he hated with a broiling intensity. But he had to work fast. His sometime Whig-employers would pay handsomely for this juicy tidbit, but the usefulness of the information would diminish with each day that passed...

# 13.

The brougham clattered into St. Stephen's courtyard outside Westminster Palace just as the afternoon light was fading into the pearly gray of twilight. It had created quite a sensation as it emerged from Wilton Crescent with its glossy scarlet carriage emblazoned with the Sheffield family crest in embossed gold. The brougham, manufactured to the highest standard in Germany by Gabon Landau and Company, boasted a plush velvet interior and a folding leather roof; while it was becoming increasingly common among the European elite, few Englishmen or women had seen anything like it. Its owner and current occupant, Lord William Sheffield, was immensely proud of his newest acquisition and had every intention of putting it on display. Hence the magnificent white bays had taken a roundabout route to the Houses of Parliament: trotting sedately past St. James Palace Gardens, slowing to a walk in front of the bustling coffeehouses of Carlisle Street, meandering through the York Street shopping district, until they finally reached their destination just south of Trafalgar Square.

Lord Sheffield and his companion, Henry Eden, descended from the brougham, the former issuing curt instructions to coachmen who waited, stiff and uncomfortable in their elaborate red and gold livery. Eden, some thirty years younger than his colleague, had been already made impatient by the circuitous route and, almost before Sheffield had stepped to the ground, was striding through the large doors ahead.

"I say, Henry! Henry, wait for me." Lord Sheffield—as stoutly colorful as his companion was somber and lean—hurried after Eden. They made an unlikely duo. Lord Sheffield, an intimate confidante of the Prince of Wales, adhered to a similar regime of dressing, drinking, and womanizing to an excessive degree. Today, he sported a satin overcoat in baby blue (embroidered with tiny red rosettes that stretched tightly across his corpulent belly), crimson breeches, white stockings, and a profusion of expensive French lace at his throat. His face, round and florid beneath the elaborately curled and powdered wig, glistened with the unexpected exertion as he hurried after his young friend.

Eden, the political hot-head of the Whig party, paused in the foyer. He was dressed simply in black, a modest cravat framing a lean and sallow face. Eden's black eyes gleamed with impatience, his mouth tight with disapproval, his somber attire a deliberate criticism of his colleague's fashionable excess. "If you are quite ready, milord?" he asked mockingly. It irritated him, this pandering to a dandified fool. This particular fool, however, had risen to a position of some influence with the Prince of Wales, whose support for the Whig party would be of the utmost importance once the king died. And that was largely recognized to be imminent. Already, courtiers and politicians were scrambling for power, maneuvering and fawning around the prince, who would quickly and directly ascend to the throne when the madness finally consumed King George III.

The two men passed through St. Stephen's Porch into the bustle of the grand central hall. It was a magnificent structure, having served as the primary residence for the kings of England from the eleventh century until 1512, when Henry VIII abandoned it for Whitehall and it became the permanent home for the Houses of Parliament. Shops and stalls now took up residence along the three-hundred-foot length of the hall and sold wigs, pens, books, and other legal paraphernalia to the lawyers and politicians that thronged within. Several small coffee stands granted refreshments to those enjoying a respite from the sessions of the House or to wake up those who were about to commence speaking. From the ground, the roof appeared to be supported on the backs of hovering figures of angels carved into each hammer-beam that traversed the roof ninety feet above and provided the sole supports for the hall. Wall niches sheltered kingly predecessors and heraldic beasts carved in stone, frozen in silent perusal of the king's throne where now a flight of steps rose to the Central Lobby, a large octagonal hall that formed the centerpiece of the palace. Stout wooden doors led from there to the north, to the House of Commons, and south, to the House of Lords, both of which were currently in session.

Eden and Sheffield proceeded past the House of Commons, where they could hear the strident voices of their compatriots arguing Addington's latest legislation. Beyond the House were the offices of the Speaker and of the Sergeant-at-Arms as well as the various cubicles that housed ministers and officials of the Crown. It was at the door of one of these secluded back rooms that they paused, glanced around, and quickly slipped inside.

A small wooden table dominated the center of a room, which had at one time served as an antechamber to the Queen's Quarters. Now, however, it served the less illustrious purpose of a clerk's filing room with books and bound collections of paper filling the shelves that lined the walls. A narrow window overlooked an outdoor courtyard that appeared bleakly stark in the last month of fall. Two men were seated at the table. Eden recognized one as Charles Fox, the reigning voice of power and influence in the Whig Party and, indeed, one of its founders; the second was Lord Grenville.

"William, Henry, do come in," Fox drawled familiarly from his seat, gesturing toward the two remaining chairs. He was a large, meaty man, with a doughy rectangular face that spilled over in numerous chins into a finely wrought cravat. Auburn brows bristled like furry caterpillars over small glittering eyes and a surprisingly full mouth tugged upwards at the corners like a man ceaselessly amused by the world. This countenance was framed by a wild crop of ginger hair that hung in an unruly tail down his back. Unlike most dedicated Whigs, he opted to wear his own hair. Pitt, in the previous administration, had implemented a tax on hair-powder, which had almost extinguished a fashion already on the decline. The fervent aristocratic Whigs, Sheffield proud to count himself among them, continued to wear both wigs and hair-powder as a patriotic gesture, distinguishing themselves from the Tories they opposed as well as the Francophiles who still insisted on the virtues of the Revolution.

"Charlie!" Sheffield enthused, offering Fox a sweaty palm which the latter reluctantly took. "Quite a blustery day to be out, but bloody marvelous to have the opportunity to take the new carriage out for a spin, eh?" He grinned foolishly at Grenville.

Eden exhaled sharply and opened his mouth to issue a stinging retort. Fox interjected, sending a warning glance toward the younger man who flushed angrily at the implied reprimand. "Lord Sheffield, we are honored to number you among us. Your support, and that of His Royal Highness the Prince of Wales, is crucial to the success of the Whig party. I am afraid, however, that we have limited time for pleasantries; we have much to discuss and scarcely time in which to do it. The House will end its session within the hour, and we want our business completed before then. If you are attending the duchess of Devonshire's soirée tomorrow, I should be delighted to hear about your new conveyance."

Reluctantly Eden acknowledged to himself, the man was a charmer. Fox's personality formed the center of the Whig Party with others revolving around him like satellites around the sun. Sheffield beamed, sitting his ample rear down at Fox's right, wiping his damply florid face with an incongruously delicate lace kerchief.

"Anyway, gentlemen," Fox continued, "I have asked you here because I have recently received the most startling information from one of our sources at Newgate Prison regarding an Irish prisoner. It seems our Mr. Pitt has conspired not only to have him released but has offered Irish independence and Catholic emancipation into the bargain—"

"Catholic emancipation? Irish independence? Is Pitt quite mad?" Lord Grenville interrupted incredulously. He was another large man, squeezed into a green silk vest intended for one half his girth. Plump, pale fingers drummed restlessly on the table. The years of aristocratic over-indulgence had taken its toll on his voice as well as his person. The taking of tobacco had become a popular pastime among men of means, and this lord had rapidly acquired a taste for it. His extensive plantations in Barbados kept him amply supplied with tobacco, but it was his cattle interests in Ireland that were at risk with Pitt's infernal meddling.

"Mad or not, that man is a menace," Eden muttered darkly, brow clenched in resentment.

"If you will allow me to finish…" Fox continued, his voice deliberately calm. "Our illustrious former prime minister desires this Wolfe Trant to spy for him. To spy for England. To penetrate Napoleon's inner circle in order to determine the invasion point for the Grande Armée that is even now poised on the French coast to invade England."

"That is the most monstrous thing I have ever heard!" Grenville sputtered indignantly. Charles Fox did not answer immediately. Frowning, he looked out the window at the swirl of windswept leaves that rustled gently against the glass, and then, caught up in another gust, danced away, black against the fading gray of a dusky sky. The smooth, rounded limbs of the oak trees that lined the Criminal Court were bare now. Winter would be here soon. He wondered idly if Napoleon would occupy these very rooms before the first snowfall.

"Gentlemen, it is a very fine line we must tread," Fox began thoughtfully, his gaze still on the courtyard beyond the window. "Addington is increasingly unpopular, and presenting oneself in open opposition to Pitt is dangerous; he has always been well-loved by the people.

Particularly now that the Peace of Amiens has been such an abysmal failure and there have been no significant advances in the war against France. The English fleet is engaged in a perpetual blockade that exhausts our resources and diminishes morale, not only among the sailors themselves, but among the English people. Napoleon's invading army is growing in size every day, poised for attack. The people are losing faith in Addington. They are waiting for another spectacular victory, another Battle of the Nile, and I think they can very easily be persuaded that Pitt is the man who will give it to them."

"So what are you saying? That we do *nothing*? That we allow Pitt to send an Irishman to spy for the English?" Eden asked incredulously, dark eyes flashing, fists clenched on the table. "Trant? Not related to Egan Trant?"

"His brother."

"His *brother*?" Eden laughed scornfully, a harsh barking sound that had little humor in it. "The fanatical leader of the United Irishmen in London? This is a joke, right?"

"No, not a joke, Henry, but perhaps an opportunity," Fox replied.

"An opportunity for what? For whom? Ireland has been actively seeking French support for the past five years and would like nothing better than to see England crushed beneath Napoleon's heel! This Wolfe person would place his allegiance with Napoleon before trusting Pitt. Pitt didn't emancipate the Catholics after the Act of the Union as he pledged. Why would Wolfe Trant believe he would do it now? Of course this Irishman is going to betray us all! For God's sake!" Eden shoved his chair back from the table in disgust.

"Dangerous policies, indeed," Lord Grenville agreed, leaning forward in his chair, fat fists clenched on the tabletop. "Pitt has gone too far, Charles. Do you realize the repercussions if Pitt achieves Irish independence? And by some miracle he just might—you've heard him in the House. He has a silver tongue. If he could galvanize support for even a crazy scheme such as this...the equality of trade between Ireland and England would be catastrophic for our domestic industries. The Irish have cheaper labor and lower taxes. The competition would kill us."

"Gentlemen, gentlemen." Fox spread his palms in a placating gesture. "This is why we are here today, to define and unify our response. I agree, Henry, to trust a dissident Irishman with England's greatest vulnerabilities"—Fox shook his head in dismay—"is foolhardy indeed.

And Catholic emancipation? Even Pitt will not be able to persuade a majority in the House to pass that legislation. The king himself, is notoriously averse to emancipation, a whole bench of bishops are arrayed against him. No doubt many lords will be opposed from opinion and others from an inclination to follow the king. As long as George III is opposed, Pitt will never be able to force it through, and without emancipation, Irish independence is not possible. However, we must stop Wolfe Trant at all costs. I will not allow Pitt's foolishness to cost us our country."

"A pretty pickle indeed, gentlemen," Lord Sheffield contributed, assuming an air of what he hoped was suitable gravitas. He had caught snatches of the conversation, in between musings of whether the yellow silk pants he had ordered for that evening's entertainments showed his calves to advantage. But this interested him. An Irish spy commissioned by the former prime minister, no less! The prince woul d love this story. "And how will you stop this Irishman?"

"He must be killed," Eden stated vehemently.

"Easy there, my hot-hearted young friend," Fox cautioned. "Let us exhaust other more palatable options before we resort to murder, shall we? It looks rather nasty in the polls. Addington is going to be out on his ear before much longer, which will be followed by a period of political instability as the parties jockey for position and power. If we are to best Pitt, we must gain the trust of the people."

"And if this Wolfe fellow succeeds?" Eden bit out, his face dark and glowering with repressed emotion. "It could solidify Pitt's base. His popularity would skyrocket!"

Fox laughed, a deep rumbling sound that shook his rotund frame. It evolved into a gasping fit, until his entire body shook with mirth and tears squeezed themselves out of the corner of his eyes. "My dear fellow! Really! *Succeed,* this Irishman?" Fox managed between amused wheezes. "How do you think a linen manufacturer from Dublin is going to persuade Napoleon to disclose a secret so classified that he will not even reveal it to his highest ranking inner circle? Succeed? My dear Henry, I don't think we need worry ourselves about that." He chortled quietly to himself.

"Nevertheless, we must make sure Pitt does not gain ground in the House over this issue," Lord Grenville stated, thinking of his vested interests in Ireland.

"I will take care of that," Fox assured him authoritatively. "Now, I ask you gentlemen for your word that this affair go no further than this room; it is imperative, if our endeavor is to succeed, that we maintain the utmost secrecy." He rose to his feet, shaking hands with each man in turn.

"A word, Charles," Eden asked brusquely. "Lord Sheffield, please do not detain yourself on my account."

Missing the insolence of this less than subtle eviction, Lord Sheffield bowed deeply, extending his arm in a rather ridiculous flourish. "By all means, Henry. Charlie, a pleasure. See you at Duchess D.'s, William!" he exclaimed heartily with a parting wave as he disappeared through the door, slamming it behind him.

"You are relying upon *him* to keep this meeting secret?" Eden asked with barely concealed loathing. "That fop, that imbecile will be gabbing to the prince before the hour has passed, and the prince is hardly the soul of discretion. At his next drunken debauchery, he will be boasting of this plot, this intrigue. Before we know it, it will be general discussion amongst the ladies at Lady Spencer's tea circle."

"I hope so, my friend," Fox responded distractedly, tapping his chin with a plump forefinger, his freckled brow wrinkled with thought.

"Foxie, you sly one. What are you up to?" Grenville asked, an indulgent smile crossing his face.

"Once the prince becomes aware of the proceedings of this meeting and then, as you pointed out, Henry, the rest of society—well, I greatly fear that Pitt's reputation will be rather tarnished. Colluding with an Irishman. Perhaps, however inadvertently, facilitating the arrival of French troops on English soil. The hell it will raise with Protestants, not to mention the Josiah Wedgewood set. He has a great deal of influence, that fellow. Have you met him, William?"

"So this was all planned then?" Eden demanded in astonishment.

"'There are more things in heaven and earth, Horatio, than are dreamt of in your philosophy.'" Fox grinned, clapping Eden on the back. "This little society scandal could very well resolve the entire situation without any additional effort on our part. Don't you worry, my boy, the Whig party is in ascendancy. I can feel it in my bones. This is *our* time now."

# 14.

The carriage clattered through the northern gatehouse into the stone courtyard of Walmer Castle and a man descended, his short dress coat doing little to protect him from the gusts of wind that howled through the keep. Striding to the door, a man-servant ushered him inside, then admitted him into the library where Pitt had been impatiently awaiting his arrival.

"Mal! God, man, it is good to see you!" Pitt drew his friend into a warm embrace.

"'Tis good to see you too," Dundas replied, grasping Pitt tightly. "Ye look a little tired," he chided him gently as they drew apart.

"I have been *trying* to get him to rest, but he is so willful!" A pert voice announced Lady Hester Stanhope, who appeared at the far end of the room. "Hello, Mal," she greeted him with warm affection.

"Hester," Dundas responded with a fond smile.

"Well, come and sit, and we shall have some wine," Pitt declared, moving across to the deep leather chairs. The sky outside was a watery gray streaked with long wispy clouds. The wind gusted and howled around the castle, sending the clouds racing before it and whipping the Channel into a frenzy of whitecaps. The library, snugly insulated against the worst of the weather, was warmly inviting with a cheerful blaze crackling and spitting in the hearth. Pitt felt a rare moment of peaceful contentment as he propped his feet up on the footstool.

"Wolfe Trant?" Dundas asked.

"Resting upstairs. He will join us for dinner this evening," Pitt replied.

"An interesting man, that," Hester remarked.

"Do you approve of him, Hester?" Pitt asked, amused. Hester was a forthright young woman not inclined to mince her words or hold her tongue. Her sharp wit had pinioned numerous visitors regardless of rank or influence and had not infrequently put Pitt in the rather awkward position of making amends, smoothing the ruffled feathers of party affiliates made indignant by her treatment. Pitt supposed he should speak to her about it, but, truth be known, he found her retorts immensely entertaining. When her mother, his younger sister, had passed away, Hester refused to live with her eccentric and intolerant father (the third Earl of Stanhope) from whom Pitt was now also estranged. When he had offered his niece his home as her permanent abode, he had little notion of how much he would enjoy her company. Hester certainly was an enlivening presence in the long-established bachelor atmosphere to which he had become accustomed.

"Approval, sir, in my opinion, requires some degree of familiarity with a man's manner, with his views. I would not presume to grant any degree of endorsement in regards to Mr. Trant until I knew him better," Hester remarked primly. "Although, I can say his dog appeals to me," she added with a mischievous smile.

"Well, I do hope you will allow me some allies, my dear. Lord Mulgrave refuses to return to Walmer, and Castlereagh has learned of your nickname for him. His 'monotonous Lordship,' was it?" Pitt inquired with a smile, slouching happily into his chair.

"And Mulgrave? What keeps him from our illustrious company?" Dundas asked, pouring a glass of cherry brandy for each of them.

"The fork!" Pitt rolled his eyes in exaggerated horror. "Did you not tell him about the fork, Hester?"

"I did not see the need," Hester replied, smiling behind her wine glass.

"Lord Mulgrave arrived in time for breakfast last week and remarked that he had been given a broken fork. Hester here retorted: 'Have you not yet discovered that Mr. Pitt sometimes uses very slight and weak instruments to effect his ends?' Poor Mulgrave didn't know where to put himself," Pitt chuckled. Then he coughed. A spasm of pain wrenched through his belly; his face contorted momentarily until he managed to school his expression. He had forgotten for a moment—his ailment. Hester was instantly by his side, her face drawn in lines of worry and concern. "I am fine. Don't fuss," he managed weakly, waving her away.

"Are yer sure you shouldn't be in Bath, Will?" Dundas asked uneasily. Pitt looked drawn and pale. "The doctors said—"

"The doctors!" Pitt dismissed them contemptuously. "Mal, they would have me retire to the north a sickly invalid, and what good would that do anybody? Least of all me! I refuse to bow out, give in, and give up. There is too much at stake. Let me get some rest before dinner; I'll be all right." He rose slowly from his chair, Dundas moving quickly by his side to help him up the stairs. "Hester, you be nice to Wolfe Trant, do you hear me?" Pitt admonished his niece with mock severity. "I need that man," he finished softly to himself as he left the room.

*That man* was sleeping in an upstairs room; a dog with orange fur standing up in freshly washed tufts lay on his feet. Wolfe had bathed and shaved, marveling at the simple pleasure that entailed. Clean! Mutt seemed to enjoy being clean, too, despite his deep-seated suspicion of the entire process.

"Who ever knew you were quite so grand under all that dirt, eh?" Wolfe asked him, scratching the dog under the chin while Mutt whined in pleasure, his leg reflexively thumping against the bed.

Wolfe was less easily satisfied. The mirror presented the pale reflection of a man he hardly recognized. Dark hair was pulled neatly back into a short knot at the nape of his neck; his cheeks and chin were clean-shaven but pale beneath thick brows. A livid red scar pulled the skin tightly across his left cheekbone. His eye was still bruised and swollen but able, through a bloodshot retina, to see. The headaches, however, still plagued him. They would arrive with little warning, blossom in exquisite intensity behind his eyes, and send broad fingers of pain across his skull that left him stunned with their severity.

Despite his bath, Wolfe still felt contaminated by Newgate. He'd vigorously scrubbed himself until his skin was red and raw and yet felt the residual grime on his body. Finally, after the maidservants, with puzzled bewilderment, had filled and emptied three baths and brought enough beef pie and ale to feed four men, he lay down to rest for just a minute, Mutt at his feet. Two hours later, a knock at the door roused him from a deep slumber. Dundas was requesting his presence for dinner. Wolfe dressed in the clean clothes provided and felt himself to be living a dream.

They dined that night on simple but tasty fare: turtle soup followed by roast mutton stuffed with oysters. After the meal Hester retired for the night, and the men retreated to the adjacent library for brandy and coffee. Pitt settled into a well-worn red leather chair, while Dundas made himself comfortable on the adjacent couch. Wolfe stood at the window, Mutt prowling restlessly around his feet. The afternoon winds had brought evening storms. The panes streamed with rain, and the courtyard he looked down into lay wet and empty. The flickering flames of the gas-lamps behind him seemed to dissolve in a watery atmosphere. The sky was dark and foreboding, swollen black clouds barely visible in the fading light of dusk. Thunder grumbled discontentedly in the distance as a sudden streak of lightening spiked and flared, illuminating the base of a nearby cloudbank before sinking again into blackness.

The atmosphere within the room was as electric as that beyond the windows. Wolfe had agreed to consider Pitt's proposal but had yet to commit, while Dundas and Pitt waited with well-concealed anxiety to see what the evening would bring. The meal had passed in strained civility with Hester and Pitt engaging in deliberately casual conversation. Dundas waved away the soup and picked fastidiously at the mutton, his studied gaze often resting on Wolfe's bruised countenance. For his part, Wolfe ate with a barely restrained ferocity, answering questions put to him with monosyllabic abruptness.

"Why trust me, then? You've every reason not to," Wolfe asked brusquely, turning from the window. He stood intimidatingly tall in the low-ceilinged room. "I could arrive in France and betray your cause. We've been seeking a French alliance for years, now you're handing it to me on a silver platter."

Pitt was silent for a moment. He drew deeply on his cigar, before exhaling a fragrant blue cloud toward the ceiling. "I am dying, you know. I told you that, didn't I?" he remarked, as calmly as if he were commenting on the weather. "I have very little time. England has even less. Our agent infiltrated Napoleon's camp at Boulogne. He has over one hundred and sixty thousand armed men poised for an invasion that will most likely take place within the next eighteen days. By the time Addington realizes the gravity of the situation, our children will be learning French as their native tongue. He still believes diplomacy will prevail." Pitt snorted in disbelief. He stopped and turned to look intently at Wolfe. "I know the history of animosity between our people, but I trust you, Wolfe Trant. You know why?" Pitt leaned forward in his chair, cigar forgotten in his hand, his quicksilver gaze blazing with a fervent intensity. "Because regardless of our differences, you want what is best for your country. France has failed you twice, promising forces that either never materialized or that balked at the last moment, and each time you have suffered the consequences. Fulfill your promise to me, and you will have a powerful advocate at the highest level of English government. The real question here, Mr. Trant, is will you trust me?"

Wolfe did not answer straight away. His instinct was to respond to any English offering with contempt and suspicion. And he was a man who trusted his instinct. "The history you refer to, Mr. Pitt, with all due respect," he began in a scathing tone, "is one of deliberate and systematic destruction of Irish industry. When my grandfather, one among many, succeeded in establishing a thriving cattle trade, the English response was to forbid the import of Irish cattle into England, which destroyed the entire enterprise."

"Mr. Trant—" Pitt began with a conciliatory gesture.

"When the prospect of a thriving Irish wool trade threatened English interests," Wolfe insisted, his tone relentless, his expression forbidding, "you passed the act of 1699, prohibiting the export from Ireland of all goods made up or mixed with wool, except to England and Wales where they were subject to duties that made them completely unsalable."

"I do not dispute the unfortunate history that has transpired between our nations, Mr. Trant. Like you, I abhor it. I am not asking you to trust in English policies, nor am I asking you to forgive the atrocities of the past." Pitt paused a moment, his face tight and pale, his fingers convulsing around the glass in his hand. Dundas rose from the couch, but Pitt waved him off before continuing, his voice resolute if somewhat shaky. "I am asking you to put your trust in *me*."

"Trust an *Englishman*?" Wolfe laughed harshly. "You may just as well ask me to sprout wings and fly," he muttered darkly, turning back to the window.

Pitt sighed, rubbing the back of his neck in an attempt to alleviate the tightness that knotted there. Perhaps he had been too ambitious. It seemed as if the eloquent persuasion that had served him so well in the House was insufficient to overcome the longtime hatred that existed between the English and their Irish neighbors.

"So war and violence are the only options then, are they, lad?" Dundas retorted.

"Do you know what they say about the Irish in the London papers?" Wolfe demanded, his face white with fury as he turned to Dundas. "That we are a 'wild, reckless, and superstitious race consumed by clannish broils and a coarse idolatry, with a history characterized by an unbroken circle of bigotry and blood.'" Mutt, sensing Wolfe's tension, whined softly, tail between his legs. "No doubt this paternalistic attitude relieves the English of any humanitarian concerns they might have about allowing, even encouraging, via a systematic economic oppression, the Irish to starve. We are less than human after all, are we not?" Then, turning to Pitt, blue eyes blazing: "And that superior smugness, as if you were the proud products of a more enlightened civilization…mac an donais! I think you'd better return me to Newgate, Mr. Pitt. I have as little use for the English as they have for the Irish!" Wolfe stalked from the room, shoulders hunched, Mutt close at his heels.

"Well, that could ha' gone better," Dundas sighed, slouching back in his chair.

"Indeed," Pitt muttered, rubbing one hand across his brow. "Although, Mal, I would have been far more skeptical of a prompt endorsement. Don't forget our Mr. Trant has decades of hatred and bitterness to overcome; we cannot expect him to trust us overnight."

"We canna afford to give him much longer than that," Dundas reminded Pitt.

"He'll come around," Pitt replied. "We'll sic Hester on him."

Dundas laughed, and the simmering anger and tension of the previous few hours was broken. "Aye, well then, I almost feel sorry for the fella."

# 15.

She had never seen him before, but that was not unusual. The French Resistance was composed of a nebulous network of sections, each one engaged in isolated acts of sabotage and protest. Their defense lay in their relative anonymity. Jeanne worked with the same handful of members and while, unbeknown to most, she formed one of the Council of Five, the majority of the Resistance membership remained as obscure to her as it did to the secret police. Monsieur Emile Boutigny, well past his seventieth year, was frail in appearance, almost completely deaf, and obliged to lean heavily on his nephew's arm. He could not hear anything that was not shouted into his ear with an ear-trumpet, but Boutigny possessed a charming gaiety in spite of that. A shadow of a man with a shadow of a voice—he was the last person she would have expected to bear such a message.

"Monsieur Guébriant works for Fouché." Boutigny had leaned close to her ear, his voice dry and rasping like the rustle of dead leaves in autumn. Then he had smiled at her, a gentle curving of the lips accompanied by a vigorous nodding of his gray bewigged head, as if she had responded with some amusing tidbit. Jeanne had done nothing of the kind; she had been temporarily shocked into immobility, her gaze involuntarily seeking out Guébriant whose tall, lean figure could be seen conversing with a young artist at the far end of the room.

Typically messages, instructions, and plans were passed from one to another secreted in the wooden frame of a stretched canvas, or coded within the confines of a recently completed play or poem. These communications were never spoken aloud—one could never be certain who was listening. It was an indication of utmost urgency that this unwritten rule had now been broken. But Boutigny now revealed himself to be the perfect agent. His hearing difficulties required one side of the conversation to be shouted, which deflected the suspicion that might attend to more covert exchanges. Information, however, could only be transmitted, not exchanged or discussed; there was neither opportunity to verify nor any room for doubt.

"What did you think of Varnet's piece, Monsieur Boutigny?" Jeanne asked loudly into the flared mouth of his brass ear-trumpet. The unsigned oil painting propped above the fireplace had arrived from Italy, and Monsieur Varnet was convinced it was a Caravaggio.

His lips almost brushing her ear, the old man wheezed: "He has been under scrutiny for several weeks now after he was discovered to be trailing several members of the Resistance...has come into more francs than can be explained..."

Guébriant, Jeanne noted, was handsomely attired in a velvet brocade jacket, the cuffs decorated in embroidered gold thread. His boots looked new. "It has a sense of Caravaggio's dark drama," Jeanne hollered into Boutigny's ear trumpet as she gestured toward the canvas and the twisted torso of a crucified Christ that drew all eyes—all those here for art, she thought, as Guébriant's eyes caught hers across the room. He bent at the waist in an obsequious bow; she graciously inclined her own head in acknowledgment.

"He has a list in his pocket of half a dozen Resistance members. He meets with Fouché tonight. You must retrieve the paper—find out what he knows."

With Boutigny's breath warm against her neck, she shivered, suddenly cold in the heated room. "I entirely agree! It is a farce practiced upon poor Monsieur Varnet!" Jeanne concluded with a merry laugh. "Monsieur Boutigny, it is a pleasure! Bonsoir, mon ami." Then she kissed him on each weathered cheek, before moving away.

The first floor of her small apartment had been overrun by a motley assortment of artists, as was the custom on Monday evenings. These kinds of petit soupers, or little suppers, were nothing new in Paris, indeed they had been fashionable long before Louis XVI lounged on the throne. Artists were seldom invited to these gatherings; their manners were not always of the finest; their deportment tended toward the rough and brash. More frequently, they met in the cafés and cabarets or with the ladies of the theatre where they engaged their models, and left the elegant drawing rooms to literary experts with their polished phrases and witty epigrams.

Jeanne Recamier, however, was an avid admirer and collector of art, and the walls of her small home were covered with masterpieces by Boucher, van Loo, and Marivaux. On Monday nights, attracted by her bright gaiety of mind and warm-hearted benevolence, a number of renowned artists brought their latest oils, ink prints, and sketches, while patrons of the art brought acquisitions of uncertain origin for general scrutiny and provenance—as Varnet had done tonight. From the general tenor of the discussion around her as she moved toward Monsieur Guébriant, Jeanne gathered that Monsieur Varnet was to be disappointed in his aspirations of a Caravaggio.

"Too heavy a hand. Look how that paint is daubed on." Monsieur Marmonte frowned in disapproval, head bent toward his shorter companion. Jeanne smiled at her guests, fluttering her fingertips in a coquettish wave as her mind raced with strategies of intervention and persuasion. It was imperative that she learn not only who was on Guébriant's list, but also the extent of his knowledge and how he intended to act upon it. Privacy was essential. He must be lured elsewhere. Upstairs, perhaps. And if he would not talk—well, there was another way. Not the preferred method, but one she was prepared to pursue if need be. Merde! He was leaving! She could see him moving toward the hallway and the door beyond.

"Excuse-moi! The pastries! I almost forgot made particularly for us by Monsieur Dusson for this evening!" With a trilling laugh, Jeanne elbowed her way through the crowd. "Monsieur Guébriant! Monsieur Guébriant!" she shrieked, one pale arm waving frantically in his direction. Guébriant, already at the door, turned in surprise, his hand resting on the knob. "You are not leaving us already, monsieur?" Jeanne called in dismay as her forward momentum propelled her, seemingly inadvertently, into Guébriant's narrow chest. "Pardon, monsieur! Pardon!" she exclaimed with a laugh. "The wine is very good, is it not?"

Jeanne knew she presented a fetching picture. Her cheeks, no doubt, were flushed from the warmth of the room and the artfully applied rouge. Her piercing dark eyes—which she had often been told were her best feature—were fixed with flattering intensity on the man who even now hesitated on the threshold. Leaning forward just slightly, allowing him an involuntary glance down her décolletage, she touched his arm lightly. "Monsieur Guébriant, you *must* stay! I have a masterpiece upstairs of Jacques Louis-David of which I so hoped to have your opinion."

"I…madame…" Guébriant was flustered by her attentions. She was, after all, the winsome young widow made wealthy by her late-husband's estate, or at least that portion which he had successfully hidden from the revolutionary tribunal during the Red Terror, a detail the clever but poor artists were not above considering. And Monsieur Guébriant had proven himself an avid servant of the coin.

"I beg you, monsieur," Jeanne entreated, pressing fervently on his arm. "Just a quick glimpse before you go, je vous en prie!" There—she had begged him; certainly, he could not refuse her now? Jeanne was uncomfortably aware that their exchange was drawing some attention. While she was candidly open and warmly affectionate with those whom attended her Monday salon, this effusive display was indecorous even for her.

The split second in which Guébriant hesitated a moment longer seemed an eternity. How many other agents had infiltrated her salon? Fouché was as thorough as he was disreputable; no doubt several of the artists here this evening reported to him on a regular basis. They were poor after all. And one had to live to be able to paint. There was a lull in conversation, heads swiveled to glance curiously at the two locked in indecision at the door. Her heart pounded a frantic rhythm beneath her bodice, and her hands felt clammy on his sleeve. Whether it was the lure of the painting or the hostess, Jeanne was uncertain, but she was profoundly grateful when he murmured with a smile that of course he would be delighted to view her...ah...masterpiece.

Guébriant had attended her Monday salon before, several times. He was a tall yet slight man in his early thirties with stylishly pomaded curls and fashionable, if somewhat shabby, attire. Small, deeply set brown eyes spanned a hooked nose, below which pursed a tight rosebud of a mouth. Unusual for men in post-revolutionary France, he wore his face powdered, and a spot of rouge highlighted each sharp cheekbone. Whether this was part of his ritual toilette, a residual habit imparted from his illustrious father, or an attempt to conceal a complexion scarred by childhood exposure to smallpox, Jeanne couldn't say; and indeed, before tonight, it had barely occurred to her to wonder. Perhaps, it was because he had seemed the height of mediocrity, with little wit or talent to recommend himself, that she had been so surprised to hear of his extracurricular activities. He pronounced judgment with a pompous arrogance that endeared him to few, and when his opinion was not solicited—which indeed was most often the case—he proceeded to inflict it in high-pitched volubility with irritating frequency. Altogether a decidedly disagreeable personality, Jeanne had concluded. He had been more fortunate in his relations, however, and had been admitted to the Monday circle several weeks ago as the son of Antoine Watteau, the esteemed and prodigiously prolific pastoral painter whose work had been immensely popular fifty years before.

With a swish of her skirts, Jeanne led him upstairs as the general hum of conversation resumed in the rooms below. At the end of the hall, she opened a door into a comfortably furnished room softly illuminated by wax candles gleaming in silver sconces. A four-poster bed occupied the center of the room. One wall was lined with leather-bound books and the other dominated by a large brick fireplace. She could hear Guébriant's muffled footsteps on the carpet behind her. Gesturing toward the massive canvas that hung above the fireplace, Jeanne turned to face him. "What do you…?"

"Madame, indeed, I was most surprised to find your attentions bestowed upon me this evening." Guébriant advanced upon her with a rapidity she had not expected, his long pale fingers grasping her arms with an almost desperate intensity. "You are a pearl among women." He bent toward her, his small fleshy mouth grazing the long column of her neck, the cloying sweetness of his perfume mingling with the unpleasant odor of his unwashed body. So it was the hostess that had coaxed him above stairs, Jeanne mused grimly—all the better.

"Monsieur!" Jeanne protested playfully as she pushed him away with a coy smile. "Let us have some wine." She turned to the decanter that stood on a side table and poured a glass of burgundy for each of them. How could she find out what he knew without raising his suspicions? It was imperative that she retrieve the list. Was Guébriant a fervent Napoleonic agent or merely a loyal employee to those who paid? Jeanne suspected the latter. Her mind raced with possibilities as she passed him a glass, her fingers brushing his in a deliberately tantalizing manner. "I have to admit that I lured you up here under false pretenses," she murmured softly, looking away.

"Oh?" He raised a meticulously plucked eyebrow.

Retreating to the bed, she shivered slightly, biting her lip in a pretense of nerves. Guébriant closed the gap between them. This was one prize he was not prepared to relinquish easily. Jeanne inhaled sharply, hands twisting in her lap; then, in a tremulous tone, she continued. "I have recently been contacted by Chief Inspector Chavert. He is under the impression that several members of the French Resistance have infiltrated my salon. I can hardly believe it," Jeanne finished unsteadily, taking a gulp of wine.

Guébriant's gaze narrowed, fingers tightening imperceptibly on the stem of his glass. "And have they?"

"Well, at first I thought it a ridiculous notion," Jeanne confided, placing her own glass on the table. "But I have overheard some cryptic conversations…whispered and furtive. I heard the name of Primrose mentioned—"

"Primrose?" In an instant Guébriant had seated himself beside her, grabbing her shoulders in a punishing grip. "You must tell me everything. Who is Primrose?"

He shook her slightly. Primrose was the ultimate prize for police informants. The price on her head would enable a lavish lifestyle for ten years or more.

"Monsieur, please," Jeanne whimpered slightly, tears welling up in the corner of her eyes. "I am frightened. I do not wish to entangle myself with the secret police. My husband was guillotined…I used to be a countess," she sniffled pitifully, forcing a tremor into her voice. "I was hoping you could help me…you seem so capable…" Jeanne raised her large dark eyes, brilliant with tears, to his. She allowed her lip to tremble ever so slightly. Guébriant studied her thoughtfully, a muscle twitching spasmodically in the sunken cavity of his cheek. Jeanne could almost see the calculation taking place behind his eyes. Here was a vulnerable ex-aristocrat, desperate to avoid all contact with the police, who knew all manner of people, who was in a position to hear things. To know things.

"You did the right thing, confiding in me, madame," Guébriant reassured her. "I can protect you from the police."

"How could you possibly?" Jeanne cried fearfully, wringing her hands in agitation. Was she overplaying this? No, she thought; he seemed to relish her feminine fears.

"I am on intimate terms with Fouché himself," he replied with proud satisfaction, enjoying the look of astonishment in Jeanne's dark eyes.

"You are?" Jeanne gasped, hand flying to her mouth. So it was true. "Oh, merci, Monsieur Guébriant, merci! I am so grateful to you, I was so afraid." She shuddered theatrically.

"You must tell me everything, madame. That is the only way I can protect you. Did you discover the identity of Primrose?"

"No, no." Jeanne shook her head. "I just heard them mention her. There were no specifics."

"You need to discover the identity of Primrose, madame." Guébriant held her gaze with unblinking intensity. "This is the only way the police will let you alone. I know how they work. They are convinced that you are harboring members of the Resistance—"

"No!" Jeanne exclaimed, eyes wide with horror. "I assure you, monsieur, I am not!"

Guébriant raised one pale palm. "I believe you, madame, but the police are suspicious of everyone, as you know."

"But how will I discover such a thing, when the police themselves have been unable to?" Jeanne wailed into her handkerchief, shoulders shuddering with emotion.

"You might pay particular attention to Monsieur de Batts and Monsieur Canat."

Jeanne's head shot up, tears streaking her pale cheeks, mouth open in bewilderment. "They are members of the Resistance? They are downstairs, drinking wine…" She shook her head in stunned perplexity.

"I have been seeking the identity of Primrose for months now. I know her contacts. Sooner or later, she will make a mistake, and I will be there." Guébriant sat beside her on the bed, eyes glinting with a zealous fervor. "You help me, madame, and I will see that the police files on you are destroyed, that Fouché himself offers you immunity from implication."

Damn. Jeanne exhaled through clenched teeth. She couldn't let him leave. Guébriant was too vehement, too committed to be dissuaded. And, indeed, how could she even try without revealing herself ? This man was about to condemn half a dozen members of the French Resistance to death—perhaps not before torture induced them to reveal any others they knew, or even those they did not, in what would be a fruitless attempt to avoid further pain. They would be pleading for death before Fouché was through with them.

Her allegiance lay with the men who had spent the last decade fighting for a better France, risking their lives in a daily struggle to restore the monarchy. There was no doubt in her mind about this, but even so Jeanne felt the familiar nausea rise in the back of her throat, followed by the quickening fear that hammered in her chest. Resolutely ignoring her physical protests, Jeanne sniffled into her handkerchief, before raising glimmering eyes to Guébriant. "Oh, Monsieur Guébriant, thank you! You cannot know how panicked I had become."

Despite his scrawny frame and narrow chest, there was a surprising strength in his grip. If she was to overcome him with the knife in her waistband, she would require a position of maximum strength to his weakness. Her fear and nausea had subsided. Jeanne focused intently on the task at hand, assessing the situation with a heightened clarity that she had learned in the forests of the Vendée. Armand had taught her well.

"I know how you can thank me, madame," Guébriant replied fervently, pushing her back on to the bed, face leaning over her own, breath redolent with cheese and garlic. He traced a series of wet kisses across the swell of her breasts, groping with one hand beneath her skirts. Sighing in what she hoped was a breathless simulation of passion, Jeanne forced her body to limpness despite her growing desire to incapacitate him with a violently thrusting kneecap between his legs. To maximize her chance of success, Guébriant must be completely vulnerable. Surprise and speed. *Positional dominance wins fights*, Armand's voice repeated in her head.

"Ooooo, monsieur!" Jeanne giggled, as she wriggled out from beneath him. "Allow me," she finished huskily as she coaxed him back on the bed. And then, eyes dark with promise, she straddled him there, green skirts bunched up around stockinged legs. Jeanne leaned forward until her face was just above his own. His eyes were heavy-lidded with desire, mouth-rouge smudged across thin, pockmarked cheeks, curls askew. She could feel the reassuring hardness of the knife at her back and knew that very soon now the time would come to use it.

# 16.

Egan Trant shoved the limp body of the policeman over the gunwale and watched with satisfaction as it drifted under the pilings of the Canal Iron Works. Wearing the distinctive red woolen coat of the Thames River Police, Egan commandeered the oars of the galley and slipped silently through the murky gloom toward the West India Dock.

The police galleys were intended for a crew of four; by the time Egan neared his destination, his hands were slick with sweat, and his breath came short and quick in his throat. Drifting the last few yards, he rested at the oars, his quick gaze taking in the view. Despite himself, he was impressed. The spaciously elegant sugar warehouses formed a stately and imposing row. Beside them, massive round-bellied Indiamen berthed like sleeping beasts, their masts abruptly shortened by a thick mantle of yellowish fog. Gaslights, resembling colossal fireflies in the gloom, illuminated the sloped copper roofs of the warehouses, and timber wall cranes, fixed at attic- level, hung like giant, primordial crab claws. The West India Docks sprawled across sixty acres and accommo- dated over six hundred vessels—altogether, a monumental enterprise that illustrated the strength and grandiosity of the thriving West Indies trade and, for any who doubted it, an architectural manifestation of England's maritime power.

These were the import docks. They had been completed several months before and boasted an increased efficiency in turnaround time of twelve days to the forty of the previous year. The vessels would arrive from the West Indies, their barnacle-encrusted hulls wallowing wearily through the system of locks from the Thames into Blackwell Basin. Then they floated to the northern dock, where they would disgorge their precious cargoes of rum, sugar, coffee, and hardwoods before traversing the short distance to the export dock, where they would fill their bellies with fat rolls of woolen cloth, salted herring, and pungent hides. Less time meant more money for the gluttonous merchants who tripled their income with every load of "white gold" that arrived safely from the Caribbean. Sugar was a highly sought after commodity that few could afford and it composed the very lifeblood of West India trade. Profit margins were high, and the product itself fiercely protected, which was why Hardy had insisted on meeting him here.

"The second floor of warehouse number two. Two a.m.," Hardy had insisted; then he grinned, teeth broken and yellowed in a fleshy, sun-darkened face.

It was a test; Egan knew it, and Hardy knew it. The West India Docks were tightly secured and vigilantly scrutinized by river police and a cadre of guardsmen who occupied sentry boxes along the north quay. The entire complex was surrounded by an outer ditch and a thirty-foot-high brick wall. Hibbert Gate provided the only access but was manned twenty-four hours by three guards armed with muskets and swords. Persons unregistered with the West Indies Dock Company were prohibited; everyone else was patted down upon departure. Pilfering had provided a regular income for itinerant workers: a sorter at the East India Company warehouse had taken china home in the skirts of his coat; a tea-chest nailer had had a large piece of leather sewn into his waistband to accommodate tea leaves; a coffee cooper had carried samples in his knee-breeches and his hat; others had secreted their plunder in hidden pockets, bladders, and bags. Not anymore.

Despite the growing membership of the United Irishmen, Egan had been unable to penetrate Hibbert Gate security at such short notice. His only option then was a water-based approach, which meant he had the patrol guard to contend with. A force of approximately one hundred armed men worked in rotating shifts and provided a constant patrol of the dockage. When the berths were full, as was the case tonight, this already formidable force was reinforced by an additional fifty constables. So an encounter with a patrolman was, to some degree, inevitable, and Egan was prepared.

He had tied his boat off under the shadow of the white-brined hull of HMS *Magnitude* and nimbly climbed the ladder to the dock when a bulky figure approached him. "Peters? Still on the job, man? I thought—"

"No," Egan replied sternly. "Superintendent Surveyor Mathews. Empowered by the Crown and appointed by the customs and excise service to inspect the security of these premises. How many constables are on dock this evening?"

"Oh, I say…"

Egan could dimly make out the pale oval of the man's face, fleshy lips and wide, protruding eyes that caught and glimmered slightly in the gaslight. "Well? I haven't got all night, man!" he demanded in his best English accent. If a trace of the Irish escaped it was of little matter; a large number of his countrymen found employment at the docks or were pressed into service aboard the Indiamen. It would be unusual, though, for an Irishman to be promoted to such a degree.

The superintendent regulated numerous surveyors who each manned the police galleys in the company of three waterman constables. Fortunately for Egan, Superintendent Surveyor Mathews happened to be not dissimilar to him in general appearance: approximately six feet tall with dark hair. The superintendent was of heavier build where Egan was lanky, but that discrepancy was easily concealed beneath the heavy woolen coat. The timid Irish housemaid employed by Mathews in his Kingston townhouse had found the fever of Irish nationalism in Egan's arms. Pockmarked and bucktoothed, the scrawny maid had been quite overcome by Egan's attentions and readily agreed to fake the late-night summons. When her employer was discovered floating in the Thames the next morning, she would undoubtedly be discovered and condemned, but Egan did not concern himself with that. This was war, and casualties were an inevitable part of the process.

"About…forty-eight, I believe, sir…" the guard stammered.

"About?" Egan challenged in a frigid tone.

"I…I…am just a quay guard, sir…"the man said in a faltering voice.

Perfect, Egan thought to himself. This idiot was a quay guard, employed on a part-time basis only when the West India fleets were in the river, to be discharged when they had departed. A few weeks work every three months or so.

"Let me go find out, sir… I can ask the dock master—"

"Absolutely not!" Egan growled. "I intend to conduct an inspection of these premises and issue a report to the West India Board. To be effective, it is imperative that no one is aware of my presence. Do you understand? What is your name, man?"

"Ainsworth, sir. My name is John Ainsworth."

"Well, Mr. John Ainsworth, if any word of this leaks out I will hold you personally responsible. Now, go on then, get about your business."

"Yes, sir. Absolutely, sir." Ainsworth nodded furiously before scurrying off into the darkness.

Warehouse number two was situated directly ahead, the brick perimeter wall gleaming wetly behind it. This meeting was crucial. Captain Spence had met with an accident the night before, trampled by a runaway horse on Hartsborough Street, outside the Horseferry Pub that he was known to frequent. Tragic.

A replacement was imperative—one that had a similar ability to unite the seamen to a common cause. Egan was certain that the Irish sailors already recruited were sufficient to carry the day, but the presence of a leader, a captain, a man ordained and legitimized by the English Admiralty, would sway the uncertain. The Spence situation had been a lesson learned. The UI needed an Englishman, a charismatic leader respected by the men under his command. Not, however, a moral man, but rather one who might be persuaded by power and influence, by money and greed. And it seemed they had indeed found such an individual. Hardy was neither scrupulous nor principled, instead he was a creature Egan well understood: a man out to get what he could while he could but who also possessed a certain greasy charm.

The West India dock was a test. Did Egan Trant, the London leader of the United Irishmen, have the power and influence to infiltrate the security system? The exterior ditch, the massive walls, the sentry houses, and the river-police? The spiked iron frames that encased the windows? The thick, bolted wooden doors? Hardy had insisted upon meeting with Egan himself, no underling would do, at the most challenging location—bar the queen's personal bed quarters, and even there Egan had agents—for an outside infiltration. Hardy didn't know the United Irishmen, and he didn't know Egan.

It irked Egan that this insignificant wretch of a captain had elevated himself to such lofty heights that he presumed to command the leader of the UI with such imperiousness, but time was running out and Hardy, like it or not, was essential to success. Yes, as annoying as this evening's activities had proved to be, a deal would be struck. Ireland would be the beneficiary. Napoleon would come; the Irish at long last would be liberated, and Wolfe would finally understand.

Why did it matter so much? Egan wondered. He and Wolfe had always been so different. Wolfe was the older brother; Egan had always looked up to him, sought his opinion, and based his own upon the same. But in later years, he found Wolfe's cautious nature irritating, and the two brothers had an ideological parting of ways. Egan, full of the fervor of Irish nationalism, advocated a complete and bloody resistance to the English come what may. And come what may came indeed, in the form of New Ross. And the relationship between the two brothers had never been the same since. The political discord was augmented by an emotional distance that seemed impossible to bridge.

Admittedly, New Ross had been a disaster. The Irish rebels, despite horrific casualties, had managed to seize two-thirds of the town; that was, until the grim procession of English reinforcements arrived, by which time the little ammunition the rebels had was long gone. By noon, they had been driven from New Ross. When the pitiful remnants of their army reorganized and formed a camp at Sliabh Coillte, some five miles to the east, it became apparent that Wolfe was not among them. Egan assumed Wolfe had fallen in battle, but it was not until days later that he discovered his brother was still alive. Wolfe had never spoken of what had happened in the aftermath of New Ross, but stories circulated of all manner of atrocities.

In the months that followed, Wolfe became withdrawn, taciturn, impassively silent where once he had been roused to discussion. Finally, in what Egan perceived as the final betrayal, Wolfe not only abandoned his country, as well as their cause, but publicly spoke out against further military action; for that, Egan could never forgive him. How did he expect to win freedom for Ireland? With bouquets and pretty phrases? And now Wolfe was locked up in Newgate—what good was he to anybody? Egan supposed he should use his influence to spring him at some point, for his mother's sake, if nothing else, but he felt inclined to let his brother stew a bit first. Mayhap, time in prison would bring him to his senses. Egan felt the muscles in his shoulders tighten and lock. Damn Wolfe. He forced himself to relax. This meeting was too important to allow himself to become distracted.

Turning his key in the lock, Egan pushed open the heavy wooden door and stepped inside. The planked timbers underfoot were sticky with sugar that had spilled from their casks. This floor, Egan knew, stored two tiers of barreled "clayed" sugar, while the upper floors accommodated a single tier of the heavier hogsheads of muscovado sugar. The uppermost gallery held the lighter cargoes: coffee, cocoa, and cotton.

"So, you made it then, Mr. Trant." A gravelly voice emerged from the shadows as Egan stepped on to the third floor landing, the air fragrant with coffee. He could just make out the plump figure of Captain Hardy seated on a bulging burlap sack.

"Now, if ye've finished with your little games, perhaps we can get down to business?" Egan asked curtly.

"By all means." Hardy grinned, utterly unperturbed by Egan's hostility. "Did you bring the gold?"

Egan tossed a small sack on the ground. "Count it."

Hardy leaned over, seized the sack, and jostled it carefully in the palm of his hand—a man well-experienced with the weight and value of goods and gold. "Oh, I trust you, Mr. Trant. So, it's a naval mutiny you want then, is it? I think I might be able to help you with that."

"How precisely?" Egan demanded, his eyes glittering dangerously. "For the considerable trouble I've gone to acquire your services, I want to know exactly what you're able to do for us, Captain Hardy. And be warned, I'm not a man to be crossed."

Hardy inclined his head in apparent deference, his mouth twisting mockingly between flabby cheeks. "The Earl St. Vincent's fleet, which forms the primary mainstay of the Channel blockade, is due for re-victualing and repair in Southampton three days from now. Repairs are due to be completed within twenty-four hours with the ships returning to the Channel to relieve Commander Wilson's twenty ships-of-the-line. Not only will the repairs not be completed, requiring the fleet to extend their stay in harbor, but the sailors will mutiny, diverting soldiers from the capital to subdue it. How does that please you, Lord of the Irish?"

Egan leaned down until his gaze was level with the captain's. Swiftly, before Hardy could even register its existence, a knife had appeared in Egan's hand, and the sharp blade pressed under Hardy's fleshy jaw. "I am sure you've heard of Captain Spence's unfortunate demise? Trampled to death by a runaway horse, or so I understand. He was less than cooperative. But to be sure you will be a vast improvement, will ye not?"

Hardy's eyes widened and his mouth dropped open slightly. "I think you will be pleased indeed, Mr. Trant."

A slight quaver in his voice that was not there previously satisfied Egan that his point had been taken.

"See that I am, Captain Hardy. See that I am."

# 17.

With one hand, she reached behind her back for the small knife that nestled beneath her waistband. It was tiny enough to be easily concealed, but lethal enough to kill, providing she was precise and forceful. Jeanne could hear Armand's voice in her head: *Move quickly and do not hesitate. Work at close quarters and make sure you have the element of surprise.* She remembered vividly: the sun-dappled peace of the forest and the violent intensity of the man who was to train her.

"Here," he had said, his head tilted back, one finger pressing against the throbbing blue vein that pulsated beneath the pale skin of his neck. "It is the skin that offers the greatest resistance to the point of a blade. It is all about the sharpness of the tip and the speed of the lunge. Go for the throat. It is messy but certain." Jeanne knew this. She hadn't then, but since that time she had had to kill to survive—more times than she cared to remember. Each time the prospect of it produced a nauseated horror at the back of her throat that ended in a violent retching relief when the deed was done, and each time she fervently prayed there would be an alternative—but there rarely was.

Palming the knife in her right hand, she bent over Guébriant, ostensibly allowing him access to her breasts, which had spilled from their silk confines. Like other fashionable Parisians, Jeanne no longer wore the rigid stays and whalebone corsets that had become synonymous with the artificiality of the Bourbon monarchy.

"Oh, monsieur," she murmured huskily as he pinched and clawed at her breasts. Then, before another second had passed, the knife was at his throat, biting deep into the scrawny flesh of his pale neck. His eyes widened in shock as she leaned close, speaking softly but clearly. "I have my knife at your vital artery. If you attempt to move or if my hand slips, it will be your very life that spills away on this bed. Blink once if you understand." He blinked, his pale face a sudden sheen of sweat and makeup. "What have you told Fouché?" He stared at her, eyes small dark pools of fear and loathing, but said nothing. "Whom have you named?" she hissed, digging the point of the blade into his throat. A thin thread of blood traced an arc down his neck to drop crimson on the white coverlet.

"Just you," he snarled, and then with a sudden roll, the strength and speed of which surprised her, he twisted out from beneath her. His hand gripped hers in a battle for mastery of the knife. Then, with one fluid movement, their situations were reversed, and she was beneath him on the bed. His face, a surly mask of anger and desperation, hovered above her own; his teeth bared in physical effort as he tried to wrench the knife from her grasp. "Give it to me, you damned whore!" Guébriant muttered as he bent her wrist back with agonizing force. Wet drops of white sweat dripped on her face.

"Why did you do it?" she gasped as the pain seared through her arm. "Why would you betray your own people?"

"My own people?" he sneered, mouth curling in distaste. "What did my own people ever do for me? Fouché is going to see that I have the position and power I deserve…and if in the process it rids Paris of a few whores like you, then so much the better!"

There was a sinewy strength in his lanky body, and she knew if he managed to get the knife away from her there would be little hope of getting it back. She thrust her thumb upward with as much velocity as she could manage, connecting with the outside corner of his eye. When he momentarily released her wrist, his face convulsed in a tight grimace of pain, Jeanne stabbed upward with the knife toward his neck.

Lying beneath him, she witnessed it all with transfixed horror: Guébriant's shocked features, the throbbing arterial blood that spilled on to the white bedsheet and the bodice of her gown, the dainty pearl-handled knife that protruded gruesomely from his neck. Mon dieu, who ever knew the human body contained so much blood?

He was alive still. His blood-slippery hands reached for her. Twisting to one side, Jeanne yanked the knife from his flesh. Guébriant's fingers instinctively pressed to the side of his neck in an attempt to staunch the flow.

"You want to know the identity of Primrose?" she murmured, head bent to his ear. "I am. I am the one you have been seeking. I am Primrose." His eyes widened in shock, his mouth opened in a blood-frothed gasp. Moments later, he was on the floor, limbs flailing weakly, and then he was still, eyes glassy-wide, mouth slack.

Jeanne retrieved the paper from his coat pocket, and in the dim light, she rapidly scanned it. It was all there. Names even she had not known of. Eight in all; three of whom still chatted amiably downstairs, drinking wine and discussing the virtues of art under the Napoleonic Empire.

How long had she been gone? How long before she would be missed? Biting her lip, she realized she had to return to the salon and as quickly as possible. Summoning aide with an unnecessarily vicious yank of the bell-pull, Jeanne felt the rising heave of nausea and retched violently over the floor at her feet. Less than a minute later, the summons was answered, and two burly men slipped through the door.

They were a squat, muscular duo, bare forearms thick and darkly furred—men whose black gaze conveyed the intent to inflict severe bodily pain on any who displeased them. Few did, or few lived to tell about it. Armand had insisted they accompany her when she left the Vendée; for protection, he had said darkly. Karl and Pieter were twins, but beyond that Jeanne knew little of them. Pieter was close-mouthed and taciturn and stubbornly resisted all her efforts at civility, whereas his brother was a little more forthcoming. Whatever their social shortcomings, the Beauchamp twins were brusquely efficient. Jeanne knew, as she fled to the bedroom on the opposite side of the hall, that all traces of the macabre scene would disappear before the hour was out.

With a shaking hand, Jeanne scrubbed the blood from her face and chest, changed her gown, and repositioned her wig. She then daubed her pale cheeks with powder and reapplied lipstick that disturbingly resembled the scarlet of arterial blood.

Only ten minutes had elapsed since she had left Guébriant lying in a pool of blood; the briefest of time that could readily be explained away. But then, who had seen her at the door locked in pleading conversation with Guébriant? Who had seen them leave together for the upstairs boudoir? Her mind darting with plausible prevarications, Jeanne descended the stairs, teeth clenched in a wide smile. Below, in the candle-glow, she could see dark heads bent in conversation and hear the lilting murmur of voices and the occasional shout of laughter.

"Jeanne!" a young male voice hailed her enthusiastically. It was Monsieur Amiot, a rising young artist from the provinces who had thrown off the abbé 's gown and come to the city armed with only a brush and a meager store of assignats to make his fortune. "I was wondering where you had disappeared to!" Pausing on the stairs, she looked down into his eagerly upturned face. An automatic smile crossed her lips. Bounding up to her, Amiot grasped her arm. "How cold you are!" he exclaimed with startled concern. "Your hands are like ice!" Amiot drew her through the clustered throng to the warmth of the fireplace.

Varnet's luckless painting had been removed, and in the ivory-framed glass that adorned the space above the mantelpiece, Jeanne caught a glimpse of a striking face. The woman's complexion was pale, almost ashen, which accentuated the beauty of her piercing dark eyes. The strength suggested in wide cheekbones and a stubbornly jutting chin belied the delicacy of her narrow nose and small mouth. With a start, Jeanne realized it was her own reflection that had caught her attention. She had adopted the guises of so many different people over the past three years—had immersed herself within their communities, adopted their clothes, their accents, their bearing, their manners—so she could blend in, so she could survive. Her own visage was merely another in a parade of disguise and deception. Momentarily transfixed, she gazed at the elegant woman in the mirror, surprised by her apparent composure. Surely, she was a different being from the one who had just stabbed a man in the throat? Or the one who had raced breathless and scared through rue de Malte the night before after a failed assassination attempt?

Jeanne had memories of playacting when she was younger; she and Joachim had put on childish plays for their indulgent father. And then, when she was older, after an evening spent at the Comédie-Française or the opera, Jeanne would return to the house in rue Foutaine and entertain the household staff with a reproduction en caricature of the actors and actresses in their famous roles. This was a talent that had served her well. But now she often felt the parade of pretense was all that remained, and that Jeanne herself was merely a cover, a façade, a mask to hide the truth. Little wonder she felt so hollow.

"Jeanne, are you all right?" Amiot's youthful disquiet sounded in her ear.

*Reply!* Armand's voice, stern and sharp, sounded in her head. Yet she hesitated, wondering that Amiot didn't hear the wild thumping beat of her heart, see the sweat bead on her brow that even now she could feel trickle between her shoulder blades. *Get it together!* "I...I am quite all right," she managed with a determined smile. "Would you be a dear and get me a glass of wine?" Amiot's apprehensive glance before moving away told her that she had not yet sufficiently satisfied his concern.

"Jeanne, I have been looking for Monsieur Guébriant. Have you seen him?" The sharp voice of Madame de Stäel was followed by her equally aggressive figure. Germaine de Stäel's penetrating gaze pinioned Jeanne. "I have searched through these rooms twice! Mon dieu, where could he be hiding himself ?"

"I was in the kitchen...consulting with Abbé de Bernis," Jeanne murmured. "I have not seen him."

Germaine's plump cheeks pursed in dissatisfaction. "Humph," she snorted, exhaling in sharp irritation, before continuing with a petulant air: "It is a nuisance. He told me specifically he would introduce me to his publishing friend Gabón this evening. I had wanted to discuss my new book with him. You have read it, I trust?" Without waiting for Jeanne's response, Germaine dove into an animated discussion of the plot devices of *Delphine*; her large hands, ringed with stones and the glint of gold, fluttered in graceful accompaniment. Usually, Jeanne enjoyed the intellectual sparring, but tonight she felt unable to focus on conversation, to force the required cadence of normality to her voice. "...regardless of the reception, I have decided for Metz. Jeanne, are you listening?" Germaine demanded insistently, her mouth tight with irritation. "What is *wrong* with you?"

Jeanne had been looking over Germaine's shoulder, tracking the progress of Amiot who was returning with anxious haste to her side, an overflowing glass in his hand, wondering how she could possibly extricate herself from the remainder of the evening, when it happened. Germaine reached out and touched Jeanne's neck with cool fingers. They came away with a reddish smear. "What is this?" Germaine asked. "It looks like blood."

"Oh..." Jeanne gave an embarrassed laugh, hiding her suddenly trembling hands in the folds of her skirt. "I had to change my gown as well...a slight accident with the rag, you understand," she confided in hushed tones.

"Ah, say no more, ma chère." Germaine laid a commiserating hand on Jeanne's shoulder—one menstruating woman to another.

"I had better wash." Jeanne excused herself just as Amiot joined their circle, his face crestfallen at her departure. Germaine immediately relieved him of the wine he had brought for their hostess and began to interrogate the youth as to his opinion of the Louvre renovation.

"Eagles and bees and the letter N wreathed in victorious laurel, no less!" Germaine snorted loudly, referring to the symbols that had become emblematic of Napoleon's regime—symbols that were even now being chiseled into the ancient façade by his architects, Percier and Fontaine. Jeanne did not wait to hear Amiot's response, if, indeed, he had the opportunity to make one.

Jeanne reached down to steady herself, her fingers white around the cool rim of the porcelain basin, her chest rising and falling with agitated rapidity, quick and shallow. The green walls of the powder room whirled around her in a dizzying array of white and olive, descending into a kaleidoscope of gray and black at her peripheral vision—she was going to faint. Breathe, just breathe, she told herself. A hard, rising lump formed at the back of her throat, and she sagged against the wall, biting back a sob, fear and fury coursing through her shaking limbs in equal measure.

It wasn't just the encounter with Monsieur Guébriant that left her shuddering. Three years of suppressed emotion had been unleashed; her rising desperation fueled by the failure of the recent assassination attempt, and the escalating bickering that threatened the very unity of the Resistance. And always, in the shadowy recesses of her mind, was Joachim. The search for her brother, her twin. The enterprise had seemed a clear matter at first. With the lucid determination of the very young, which, indeed, she had been even after the guillotine claimed her new husband, she had ventured forth to the forests of the Vendée to recover her brother. Then, she had fallen in with Armand and discovered the truth about her brother. In the years since, her perspective seemed clouded, her vision less clear. And now this seething emotional mass from Pandora's box that refused to be contained. And it had to be, at all costs. The lives of others, as well as her own, depended upon it.

"Jeanne? Jeanne? Are you there, ma chère?" Amiot. Mon dieu, did the man never give up?

Jeanne Recamier turned with a start. "One moment, monsieur." Splashing her face with cold water, she critically examined her reflection in the mirror. Large dark eyes red-rimmed and besmeared with makeup, pale cheeks splotched with red that could hardly pass for rouge. What a mess. She wiped her eyes with damp tissue, dusted some rouge across her cheeks, and thickly reapplied kohl to her eyes to hide the evidence of tears. There. She could be accused of rouging with a heavy hand, which was entirely permissible, but not of having an emotional break-down in the toilette, which would draw unwanted attention and require an explanation which she was not prepared to give. Smoothing down the skirts of her green watered-silk gown and straightening the little hat that perched at a rakish angle on her head, she inhaled deeply, drawing the cold air through her nose. Then let it out in one whoosh of breath. She felt her breathing return to some semblance of normality.

Jeanne emerged from the powder room with a wide smile. "Pardon, monsieur," she replied brightly, her hands, still trembling slightly, white-clenched behind her back. "Did you find me some wine?"

"You do not wish to talk to me, madame." Amiot's face resembled nothing more than a woebegone puppy, his plump cheeks drawn in lines of sad despair. Jeanne sighed inwardly and stretched her mouth in what she hoped passed for a smile.

"No, indeed, monsieur," she demurred automatically.

# 18.

The storms had passed in the night, leaving a clear sky of freshly washed blue. The garden foliage dripped wetly, the early sun glimmering in each drop so the bushes and leaves twinkled and shone as if the stars had fallen in the night. The air was crisp and wintry and patches of frost lingered like fallen lace in the shadows. Wolfe, still edgy at the prospect of a closed door, had been outside since dawn. For a long while, he simply stood, inhaling deeply, like a drowning man granted reprieve; the cold air sharp in his lungs. Then, Wolfe ran: across the lawn, around the hedges, darting and racing, reveling in the freedom to move, the heated warmth of muscles working, and the physical beauty of a world he thought he would never see again. Mutt scampered, barking, at his heels. Real sleep—the kind that rests the body and nourishes the spirit—as well as a few hearty meals had restored both man and dog to sprightly good humor.

Mutt leapt, dashed, and bounded. He darted away to sniff at the base of a spotted laurel bush, snuffling and grunting in the wet dirt before prancing back to Wolfe, his nose muddy, his panting breath white puffs in the wintry chill. He dashed through and around Wolfe's feet, away and back in a tumult of orange fur and dripping tongue. "Well, then, Mutt, anyone would think you hadn't ever been outside…" Wolfe's voice trailed off as he realized the inadvertent truth of his statement. The animals bred in Newgate—unlike the prisoners they had not been brought in but had been grandfathered into that hellhole. "Mac an donais," Wolfe muttered, hunkering down to rub Mutt's flank, running one hand over his ear and ruffling the fur on his head. Mutt, ever appreciative of the attention, reciprocated with a wet lick on Wolfe's cheek. "'Tis a good life from here on, Mutt; that I can promise you."

Behind the kitchen garden, the two found a large rectangular patch of lawn framed by neatly clipped hedges of boxwood. Wolfe retrieved a small branch from beneath the canopy of an ancient yew. "Go, Mutt!"

Wolfe hurled the stick across the lawn and watched it land in a tangle of creeping juniper. Mutt raced after it, tail whipping back and forth in frenzied delight. In less than a blink of an eye he had returned, the stick a drooled gift at Wolfe's feet. Wolfe laughed, a deep and easy sound that felt good in his chest. The tight band that seemed to have restricted vital breath these past few months had loosened a bit.

"C'mere, Mutt," he growled, crouching down at eye level with the dog. Mutt, who seemed to have a deep appreciation for his master's newly found frivolity, grinned, tongue lolling wetly from one side of his mouth. Then, darting forward with astonishing agility for a three-legged beast, Mutt retrieved the stick and scampered backward, haunches high in the air, nose to the ground, tail an ecstatic blur of motion. "So that's how it is, eh?" Wolfe laughed again. "War it is then, me fine, furry friend." With a sudden lunge he reached for Mutt, who danced away, the stick dangling enticingly from his mouth.

"I think you need to rethink your strategy!" An amused voice drifted across the lawn. "I daresay you will never catch him that way."

Wolfe, still on his knees, glanced over his shoulder at Hester who, shading her eyes from the early morning sun, was observing them. He stiffened slightly. Regardless of the warm welcome that had been offered him at Walmer, despite the comfortable accommodations and the fine fare, he knew he was not a guest. He was merely a prisoner on probation, the judge waiting to see if he would agree to serve the formidable English will. However, this slip of a girl was hardly to blame. Wolfe forcibly relaxed. "Ay, well, I think you could be right there. But never fear, lass, cunning Irishman that I am, I have a master of a plan, don't you know." He grinned at her, his Irish brogue deliberately thickened.

"Really?" Hester demanded, hands on her hips, voice heavy with skepticism. "I am placing bets on the dog."

"Ye of little faith," Wolfe muttered under his breath, eying Mutt, who pranced just out of reach. With a dramatic groan, Wolfe clutched his chest and fell backward. Almost immediately, he felt a moist nose followed promptly by a long tongue, rough and wet on his cheek. With a roar of triumph, Wolfe threw his arms around Mutt's middle, rolling him over on to the ground. "You're a beastie and that's the truth of it," he murmured affectionately as he rubbed the dog's ears and scratched his belly. Mutt was scarcely recognizable as the neglected mongrel he had been only a few days before. His ribs were still uncomfortably

prominent and bald spots decorated his flanks, but his coat shone, and
Wolfe was certain he had never seen him prance in Newgate.

"Now that's hardly cricket!" Hester protested with a laugh.

"Sometimes we have to engage in roundabout methods to achieve
our aims," Wolfe replied, still smiling. He rose to his feet and came over
to where Hester stood on the stone path that wound its way through
the garden.

"And what exactly *are* your aims, Mr. Trant?" Hester asked him, tilting
her head back so she could look him directly in the eye. Hair the color
of caramel was tucked beneath a peaked bonnet; hazel eyes slanted up
at him above a slightly pug nose scattered with freckles. She wore a
jaunty dark-green spencer that descended from a high waist to drape
loosely around her cream wool skirts. It sported large brass buttons and
sharply delineated shoulders that gave her a vaguely military air that was,
apparently, quite the fashion. She was not a beautiful woman, but there
was a forthright honesty about her that Wolfe found appealing. And her
wry and witty humor was certainly entertaining.

Wolfe arched an eyebrow. "The way I see it, Lady Stanhope, my aims,
as you put it, are my own affair."

"My uncle is a good man, Mr. Trant," Hester insisted, her gaze holding his.

"I have no doubt you believe that to be true, Lady Stanhope," he
replied evenly.

"Oh, for God's sake, call me Hester," she countered, tossing her
head impatiently. "I keep thinking you are talking to my spinster aunt."

"Hester," Wolfe amended, his mouth curving in a smile. Mutt, having
capered around the lawn in a tail-chasing game comprehensible only to
the canine breed, finally collapsed at Wolfe's feet. "Worn you out finally,
have we, Mutt?" Wolfe asked with amusement.

"William Pitt is a man of integrity and honor. You can trust him,"
Hester maintained, a stubborn tilt to her chin. Wolfe paused, staring
into the young woman's eyes. He saw something in them—candor, conviction, and a fierce love—that he recognized, with a start, as a mirror
image of himself a decade ago. Back when things seemed simple; when
he had a family to love.

"I believe you," Wolfe said abruptly, a throbbing pain forming behind
his eyes. His headaches were intermittent now, which he was grateful
for, but when they arrived, often with little warning, they escalated into

a jagged agony that left him gasping. "It is just a question of where his loyalties lie. Mine are across the Irish Sea."

"Tea, Wolfe?" Dundas asked, dangling a delicate porcelain cup from one thick forefinger.

"Would you have any whiskey?"

Wolfe had excused himself after his exchange with Hester and re-treated to his room where he spent the subsequent hour with a cold towel on his forehead in an attempt to ease his misery. By dinnertime, the pain had diminished to a dull ache that throbbed deep within his skull. After dinner, he thought perhaps a draft might be just the thing to finish it off altogether.

"I have a mighty fine malt from a distillery in Strowan?" Dundas raised a ruddy eyebrow, a smile curving one corner of his mouth.

Wolfe grimaced. "I'd prefer Bushmills, if you have it."

"Aye, we have it," Dundas replied, with a grimace of his own. "If ye'd be preferrin' the Irish firebrand to the smooth silky finish of a Scotch malt, well, I'll nae be stoppin' ye." He shoved the teacup aside with a decisive flourish and proceeded to pour two generous portions of whiskey. Depositing a bottle of Bushmills and another of Strowan "Hosh" on the table, he handed Wolfe his glass and raised his own in toast. "The water o' life," Dundas said solemnly. Wolfe raised his glass, and both men gulped down the contents. Wolfe felt the whiskey's heat enter his veins and warm his belly and almost immediately he felt an easing of tension. The tautness of his shoulders relaxed; his arms felt less rigid. The conflict seemed to loom a little less when the good Irish fire ran through his blood.

Pitt and Hester were playing faro on the other side of the room, the only sound the occasional shout of protest mingled with laughter as the cards were revealed. The fire blazed companionably in the hearth while the wind roared outside. The couch was comfortable, and the roast beef sat pleasantly in his belly. For a moment, Wolfe felt something very close to contentment. Given the circumstances, a moment was all he could allow himself.

"Why do you stay in England?" he asked Dundas bluntly. "Do you not miss your own country? I mean after the Clearances…" Wolfe shook his head incredulously.

He referred to the infamous act of 1745 when all facets of High-land culture had been forbidden on pain of death, and most Scottish

Highlanders found themselves forced into the English army to serve in the wider empire. The remainder were dispossessed, or forcibly evicted, in what became notoriously known as the Highland Clearances.

"Ahhh," Dundas replied, ginger brows drawing low over his eyes. "Aye, not a verra pleasant time. And to answer yer question, I want nothing more than to return to Scotland. But I come from a village just south of Glasgow called Ayr. Born to a proud clan. The Dundases are one of the oldest, but times, as ye've pointed out, have changed. Me mam and da owned a farm; had six children squeezed into a two-bedroom cottage on a few poorly drained acres of the Clyde Valley. Barely livin'." He paused, gulped down a swallow of Hosh before proceeding. "I canna help them in Scotland, but here I can be of some use."

"Can you really?" Wolfe asked, regarding Dundas skeptically. "What change have you brought about, then?"

"Well, the Clearances were a horror, there is nae doubt of it. But think of it pragmatically rather than emotionally." Dundas lounged in his chair, whiskey resting on his midriff, his ice-blue gaze holding Wolfe's. "England emerged as the dominant colonial power in the world after the French and Indian War, ye ken. Defeated French aspirations in America as well as on the continent. Now, we can be as patriotic as ye like, but, at the end o' the day, England is a powerful foe. Ye can choose to be defiant till the blood runs through the streets and the young men are all buried. Or ye can be practical—"

"Is that what you told the children of the men that were forced into slavery by the English? That they should be pragmatic?" Wolfe answered heatedly.

"To move forward, ye have to let go of the past."

"We are defined by our past."

"Then I'd guess ye'd be doomed to repeat it." Dundas sighed heavily, placing his empty glass on the table in front of him.

"So you're truly content with the situation as it is, then? To be another colony in the English imperial crown?"

"Better than being wiped out, lad. I know ye dinna want to hear it, but the truth o' the matter is that Scotland has begun to flourish in a way that she never would have as an independent nation...no, wait!" Dundas protested as Wolfe opened his mouth to object. "The true strength for Ireland lies in an alliance rather than a bloody, and ultimately fruitless, opposition. And the dictations ye refer to..." Dundas shrugged. "Most of these were repealed by 1792, and ten years later, ye have the Scottish Renaissance." He replenished their glasses, grinning at Wolfe as if he, Dundas, were personally responsible for the scientific and economic advancements of Adam Smith, David Hume, and James Boswell. "Economically, Glasgow and Edinburgh are flourishing. Isna that what ye want for Ireland? Prosperity? Progress?" He leaned forward, elbows resting on his knees, his earnest gaze holding Wolfe's. "Believe me, lad, if there were disadvantages to Scottish interests, I'd be long gone." Dundas pursed his lips, contemplating. "And, of course, there is Will."

They both glanced across at Pitt and Hester, the two figures leaning forward over the table, silhouetted in flickering gold from the light of the fire.

"'When defeat is inevitable, it is wisest to yield,'" Pitt proclaimed grandly, rising from his chair in a languid stretch, the cards spread out before him.

"Impossible!" Hester protested, stabbing the recently overturned card with her forefinger. "The ace had already been dealt! You cheated! And Quintilian, by the way."

Dundas rolled his eyes. "Here they go," he mumbled good-humoredly under his breath. At Wolfe's inquiring glance, he explained. "They have this running battle, Will and Hester…have for as long as I have known them. Each seeks to outwit the other in a war of classical quotations. Best just to hunker down to avoid the crossfire." He promptly poured them another whiskey and, slouching lower in his seat, shot Wolfe a conspiratorial wink.

"'There are some defeats more triumphant than victory!'" Hester retaliated gleefully.

"Montaigne," Pitt replied, with an elaborate yawn.

"'Do thou restrain the haughty spirit in thy breast, for better far is gentle courtesy!'" Hester admonished him; her effort at severity undermined by escaping giggles.

"Homer, madame?" Pitt asked with one meticulously raised brow. Hester descended upon him, armed with a brocaded cushion she had snatched up from the couch. "Unbelievable…arrogant…swine!" she gasped between wallops.

"''Tis hard to fight with anger, but the prudent man keeps it under control,'" Pitt breathlessly advised her, arms protecting his face in a vain attempt to dodge the blows.

"Democritus!" Hester shrieked jubilantly.

"Lady Stanhope." Pitt saluted her as he sank into the chair with a wide grin. "You are a woman of inestimable talents."

Dundas's grin widened. "Wil is rather special."

"Is he now?" Wolfe muttered with some skepticism.

"He is," Dundas replied with certain affection. "And remember, me fine Irish lad, ye've an opportunity here. Dinna waste it. The past canna be changed, but the future is yet in yer power."

Later, as Wolfe lay restless, his chest beading in sweat despite the wintry temperatures that prevailed beyond the thick castle walls, he pondered on the evening's conversation. It was a difficult subject. Irish babes had been suckled on the bitterness and anger of an oppressed people, and, as each generation grew to adulthood, they took up arms against the economic, religious, and political tyranny that kept them poor and afflicted. But England was a formidable opponent with all the resources Ireland lacked, and it did not shrink from butchery. Wolfe had witnessed that much. It was customary, expected even. While he understood the pragmatic logic of Dundas's perspective, it was difficult to excise the emotion.

The fury was still there. It had just been tamped down for the past seven years. But where had it gotten him, after all? Alone with his grim memories of blood and death. And a feeling of futility and guilt that gnawed at him from the inside like an ever-ravenous beast.

There was a difference between peace and servitude. Which was Pitt offering? Peace was freedom in tranquility; servitude would be resisted not only by war but by death. Was this Ireland's destiny, then? Was there truly no hope of change? Just a few days before, he had been confined to Newgate, expecting to die within hours, disillusioned with the way he had led his life. Perhaps this was a second chance. Miraculously, hours from execution, he had been given a reprieve. And what could he do with it? Could he somehow make amends for the lives that had been lost in following his cause? Could Irish independence be furthered without bloodshed? A deal with the Devil? Did it matter? he asked himself sardonically. His choice now could have a decisive effect on the future of Ireland. English or French?

The French had failed them twice.

The English could not be trusted.

But perhaps William Pitt could be.

# 19.

Giltspur Street was a place to be avoided on Monday nights. From the relatively sheltered vantage point of a drapist's doorjamb, Nick O'Connor surveyed, with growing distaste, the path below. Giltspur twisted and writhed its way past the Green Man pub that marked the intersection with Flint. The thoroughfare was a sweaty, heaving mass of muscled flank, flaring nostrils, and rolling eyes. The resultant cacophony assaulted the senses: the bellowing of oxen, the bleating of sheep, the grunting and squealing of pigs. The screech and holler of butchers, apprentices, and drovers rose above the animal clamor, each bawling in their own particular effort to sell, buy, or—like O'Connor—find a path through.

The air, though chilly, steamed with animal heat; the ground beneath his feet a freshly manured muck. O'Connor edged past the quivering flank of a restless cow, narrowly avoiding being smeared by the greasy carcass of a newly slain sheep that was being hoisted on to a butcher's cart. Oxen, sheep, and pigs were all brought from the country to trade, barter, and sell, and here, in the narrow confines of Giltspur Street, deals were made and livestock were slaughtered. The butchers, whose establishments lined the roadway, would in turn convert the carcasses into the tidy ranks of T-bones and rib-eyes that tempted the haughty eyes of tidily dressed housemaids. Not that even servants of the gentry would step one neatly shod foot in the mire and muck of Giltspur Street on a Monday night, O'Connor reflected sourly as his right boot landed in the pungently soft leavings of some unnamed cow.

With relief, O'Connor finally turned on to Flint Lane. Tucked into the corner of Flint and Alby, a single lantern illuminated a green door. A sign swung above the establishment, depicting the head of a steer; the words Finney's Cookshop inscribed between the white horns. Finney's was crowded. The remnants of a dying fire glowed sullenly in the hearth, providing more coalsmoke than heat. The number of patrons accomplished what the fire did not: hackney coachmen, draymen, and footmen clustered together in convivial camaraderie. They crammed themselves around tables; bent over bowls of tripe, cowheel, or sausage; leaned against the walls; and propped themselves up against the counter behind which smoked carcasses hung from giant hooks. Their combined body heat mingled with the warm steam of boiled beef to produce a singular aroma that was not altogether unpleasant. Coal and pipe smoke hung in layers of blue and gray, stirred occasionally by the steady din of idle chat and chuckle that took place beneath.

Finney was waiting for O'Connor by the door. "Back 'ere," he muttered, pushing his way through the crowd with good-natured gruffness. "Watch out! Move over then, lads!"

The backdoor opened up into the cold room, distinguished from the front not only by the drop in temperature, but by the macabre stillness of its inhabitants. Massive slabs of meat hung from hooks, hardly recognizable as any particular kind of creature, shorn as they were of hide, head, and legs. The lamplight cast a warm glow on the red rope of muscle and sinew, the shadowed curve of ribcage, and the white gleam of bone. Cow and pig, O'Connor guessed from the size of them.

Egan Trant and Thomas Dildin were seated at a wooden table in the center of the room, their lean and somber faces rendered gaunt by the single candle that burned before them. Dildin, Finney, and O'Connor made up the triumvirate, the highest rank of the London cell, with Egan at its head. The theory was that the three would provide advisory council to Egan in the implementation of a policy previously determined by the UI command in Ireland. In practice, however, things operated quite differently.

"You're late," Egan muttered with a scowl, dark brows drawing fiercely over hooded eyes, hair slicked and gleaming against his head like the wing of a raven. A sharply cut nose dominated the center of a lean, sculpted face; his wide mouth compressed in a tight line of disapproval. It was his eyes, however, that riveted one's attention; they gleamed and silvered in shades of blue and gray like the dimpled surface of a deep and mysterious loch. Egan's gaze had a way of chilling one through to the core, but perhaps that was because O'Connor knew him so well. Shivering slightly, Nick took his seat at the table.

Nick had known the Trant brothers since childhood. They had lived on the other side of town—divided, however, by more than just geography. The Trants, according to Nick's Protestant father, were guilty of Catholicism as well as poverty—both afflictions which could have been adequately remedied by religious conversion; for God granted prosperity to those who devoted themselves to the Word. Despite his father's disapproval, and the occasional whipping intended as deterrent, the youthful Nick spent many a surreptitious hour in company with both Wolfe and Egan. The Trant brothers had always been indubitably charismatic. Both tall with coal-dark hair, Egan lean where Wolfe was solid; both possessed that aura of easy confidence and sharp intelligence that made them natural leaders of men. But beyond that superficial resemblance, they could not be more different than if they had been sculpted one of clay and the other of ice. O'Connor hadn't seen Wolfe for years, but he remembered the heat of his anger, the fiery passion of his convictions. Egan, however, operated with an icy precision and formidable control, secure in the indubitable righteousness of his path.

"Well, he's 'ere now; we can get on wi' it," Finney declared amiably as he seated himself next to Trant. Patrick Finney was a force of nature: a massive slab of pale freckled skin topped by a thatch of unruly reddish hair, and a stubbornly affable blue gaze the color of the Irish sky that dared you to be otherwise. Even Egan Trant softened somewhat under his influence, for which O'Connor was particularly grateful.

"Nick," Thomas Dildin nodded from his seat. "It's a nice place you've got here, Finney. A good stock o' meat."

"Aye, pilfered from the very best herds these were," Finney replied as he gestured toward the hanging carcasses, his face creased with pride.

"If we are quite done with the palavarin'," Egan interjected impatiently. "We do have work to do."

"Did you get a navy man?" O'Connor asked. Egan had found a replacement for Captain Spence, a contact in the navy who would incite rebellion. Who it was, O'Connor had no idea. After the failure with Spence, Egan was gathering plans and personnel close to his chest, scooping them in like a gambler's ill-gotten gains. He parceled out small nuggets of information individually as was required, jealously guarding the entire enterprise within the confines of his own mind. A fat tallow candle in a cracked ceramic dish sat squarely in the center of the table, illuminating a sturdy surface of wooden construction decorated with hatchet gouges and the dark brown of faded bloodstains. O'Connor folded his hands tightly in his lap.

"We did. Or so it seems," Egan muttered. "Cost us enough. He better be worth it. To be sure, Spence's accident will provide additional motivation," he smirked, lips twisting beneath the sharp apex of his nose. "Now that we have—"

The yellow flame wavered then flickered as the door to the cold room swung open. The men tensed; Finney rose to his feet, fists clenched on the tabletop. "Jayzys! What?" he bellowed in voice fit to scare the devil himself.

The pale, frightened face of the butcher's apprentice appeared around the edge of the door-frame. "They was wantin' more sausage, sir," he managed in a thin and wavering voice.

"Tell 'em to sod off ! Eat the bloody tripe!" Finney bawled as the apprentice scuttled out of view, the door slamming behind him. "I did tell him we weren't to be bothered," he murmured apologetically.

"All 'tis ready then, Tom?" Egan demanded, leaning forward in his chair, tapping the table restlessly with his fingertips.

"Aye, we are ready enough," Dildin replied laconically.

Ready *enough*? O'Connor thought. Ready enough? What the hell did that mean? He was uncomfortably aware of the meaty body of the pig swinging gently over his left shoulder, the steady drip of body fluids caught by the metal tub situated beneath. It could just as easily be a human cadaver minus the limbs. Just meat and bones, all destined for the same mortal end. Doubt threaded through him. Ready, were they? To be butchered by the English soldiers? For the streets of London to run red with Irish blood? But to admit any qualms to Egan…well, that constituted rebellion and heresy at the very least. For his task was a God-given one and anyone questioning his authority had a way of turning up face-down in the Thames or trampled beneath the deadly hooves of a whip-lashed horse. Captain Spence's death sat uneasily on his conscience. He had liked the man, and the cavalier way in which Egan disposed of loose ends hardly seemed in keeping with a higher cause.

O'Connor pulled his coat tighter around his torso. The cold room was indeed true to its name, and he felt a pang of envy for the warm camaraderie of those clustered in the cook-shop eating tripe, cowheel, and sausage. Instead, he was confined to the chilly carcass storage with a butcher and a madman. For of late, he worried as to where Egan was taking them. Certainly, he was dedicated. Perhaps too consistently unwilling to compromise or negotiate. Dogmatic. Hooks on the far wall displayed a gruesome array of cleavers, choppers, knives, and bone saws. Even the chosen meeting place seemed to prefigure the violence that was to come.

"When, Egan? When are we doin' this, then?" Dildin asked carelessly, lounging backward in his chair, hands threading through dark hair, his casual manner belied by the narrowed intensity of his gaze. Young Thomas had grown up fast.

"I will tell you when you need to know," Egan replied shortly.

"What are you sayin', Egan? Are we not to be trusted?" Dildin leaned forward, resting his threadbare coat sleeves on the table, pinning Egan in a dark stare.

"What I'm saying, you young eejit, is that the less people who know the date the better," Egan retorted icily. "Watch yourself, Tom."

"Or what?" Dildin challenged, rising to his feet, eyes flashing, freckles stark against the pale planes of his face. "Or what? Will you kill me, too, Egan?"

There was a momentary quiet as both men bristled, the uneasy hush broken only by the steady drip of animal juice.

"Now, lads," Finney cautioned, placing one beefy hand on Dildin's shoulder. "We are all on the same side, remember?" Ironically, he was the peacemaker; the man who knew how to take a whole carcass and break it down, how to quarter meat on the swing, how to hone his knives by listening to the blade's pitch sing on steel. The butcher who didn't like conflict. His quarry was already dead; inherently, there was no argument.

O'Connor cleared his throat. "Well, the timing couldn't be better. If there was ever a time for us to succeed, 'tis now. The naval mutiny will drop the government in its tracks, and we will seize control of London. How many do you think we'll need, Egan?"

"Fifteen hundred men to take London; fifty-thousand to hold it," Egan replied tersely. He was not one to forgive or forget. Thomas Dildin had been brash, O'Connor thought, but not unreasonable. Egan Trant had left a number of bodies in his wake, and not all of them on the other side of the fence. Despite himself, he admired Dildin's audacity. The lad would get himself killed, but he sure had nerve. "We need to step up recruitment in Irish neighborhoods. Nick, you're attending the meeting at Black House tomorrow night?" O'Connor nodded confirmation. "Green Dragon was the safe pub last week; this week 'tis Black House," Egan continued, pinioning each in turn with an icy blue gaze. "Nick will be there recruiting tomorrow, but the rest of you stay away. I will be laying low till the day of the battle, and the rest of you need to do the same. T'would do the cause little good to get yourself collared afore time. I'll be in touch wi' each of you in the next day or so and will let you know your own particular part to play."

"We need more men. Last count we've only eleven hundred," Finney contributed, his massive shadow looming darkly across the carcasses behind him, his freckled countenance warm in the candle glow. One would never have taken him for a revolutionary, O'Connor mused, a jovial pilferer of herds, yes—but not a steely killer of men.

But then war made strangers of them all.

"Nick? Where are the numbers, then?" Egan swiveled his gaze to Nick. "'Tis your responsibility to get that up. We need another four hundred at least."

"We've lost some English allies. They're worried that a naval mutiny will leave England defenseless and allow Napoleon to cross the Channel. Irish radicals are less conflicted," O'Connor finished dryly.

"Which is precisely the bloody point o' course, but not one the English need to know." Egan leaned forward on his arms. "You need to step up recruitment, Nick, and the pubs are the best place to start. Sleep at Black House if you have to. 'Tis a busy place, to be sure, and you'll have hundreds in and out over the next day or two. And brother will bring brother. Get one family member into the UI, and the rest will follow. You know how 'tis. Just get them in, Nick."

"And the sailors?" Dildin spoke up. "When will they rise, then?"

"Don't worry about the sailors, Tom. We got a man to take care of that. He'll make this mutiny about pay and food and whatever else the bloody sailors want. He'll separate the uprising from us. The Channel Fleet is a tinderbox as it is, just waiting for the match."

"I still think we should take the first step," Dildin insisted. "The government in Paris has betrayed the Revolution that brought it into power." And then more forcibly: "'Tis madness to wait till the French land!"

"With eleven hundred men, Tom?" Egan asked scathingly. "Enough to provide a temporary distraction, to be sure; but hardly long enough to do any good. Nay, we must wait. We cannot call for insurrection in

Ireland before the arrival of massive French military and munitions. Would you have another New Ross, Tom?"

"And would you have another Bantry Bay then, Egan?" Dildin retorted, referring to the French armies that had been promised to coincide with an Irish uprising that never quite made it ashore, leaving the Irish armies to be slaughtered by the English.

"You want to challenge my leadership here, Thomas? Do you think a pimple-faced boy from County Cork will inspire a nation, do you?" Egan rose menacingly to his feet, dark face glowering. "Just because you've killed a few Englishmen, don't think you can take me on." The moment of silence that followed bristled with tension.

Finney cleared his throat. "Well now, none of us would presume to fill your shoes, Egan, milad." He rested his massive hands on the table, palms wide and smooth, softened by animal fat and rendered powerful from the daily exercise of his trade.

"All's I'm saying is that the French have a history of letting us down," Dildin muttered.

"They'll come," Egan snapped impatiently. "Napoleon will land, and the English will be ground into submission. It will be a great day for Ireland, a great day indeed!"

# 20.

"I will maintain that no man was ever killed at two hundred yards with a common musket—at least not by the person who aimed at him," General John Moore stated emphatically, his dark eyes scanning the lean array of men who had assembled on the field before him. It was early in Shorncliffe Camp. The rim of the sun was just beginning to appear over the eastern horizon, sending pale fingers of light across the dew-wet fields. The men, however, had been up for hours, their dark clothes stained with sweat and grass, their breathing labored still. As the countdown to invasion had begun, so had their training intensified. That morning had started with a predawn operation: a covert assault on an established encampment. Wolfe had numbered among these men these past few days and slowly, with the punishing physical regime, felt his strength returning.

"Muskets are notoriously inaccurate weapons, and it is only the discipline of a large number of men firing them shoulder to shoulder, creating a veritable wall of lead, that makes them useful at anything over one hundred yards," Moore continued. Then, grasping the slender barrel of a rifle, he held it above his head, the metal gleaming in the early morning light. "This," he proclaimed, his voice deep and resonant even to Wolfe who stood at the back of the field, "is the means by which we will defeat the French. For those of you who do not know, this is a rifle rightly popularized by the American wars." Positioning the loaded gun at his shoulder, Moore sighted the center of the target then squeezed the trigger. A flash of light, a plume of smoke, and a hole appeared in the center of the target two hundred paces away.

Moore was the quintessential soldier: massively built with a perpetually grim expression on a swarthy face. He had seen active service in America, the Mediterranean, the Caribbean, the Netherlands, and Egypt, and had introduced a wide variety of unorthodox military procedures to the elite Black Hawk regiment. Moore's philosophy of warfare, developed in the forests of North America during the Seven Years' War, comprised what he called the Four Factors: speed, mobility, surprise, and accurate shooting. Unlike the rigid ranks of red, white, and gold that marched in obedient formation, Moore's men wore a signature green with black buttons. They attacked without warning and disappeared before the enemy could regroup. But it was the stories of the capture of Charleston and the campaigns of Cornwallis that circulated amongst his men. Moore had been present at twenty-four engagements, had two horses killed under him, was three times shipwrecked, and twice taken prisoner. The ridged scars that covered his arms, face, and torso, his quiet gaze, the confident ease with which he handled his weapon—these spoke more eloquently to his battle experience than any written endorsement could have done.

"As you see, there is a major improvement in terms of accuracy. A bullet fired from a rifled barrel acquires a spin that is far more accurate and will travel further than a bullet fired from a smooth barrel. At two hundred paces a rifle shot, fired by a trained man, would kill the target. Almost three times the range of the musket."

A low murmur of excitement rippled through the ranks. Many of them had seen action in Egypt and the Mediterranean, but only a handful had accompanied Moore to America and back, and it was from there that this weapon of war had come. "However," the general continued, "the rifle takes longer to load, and it is harder work ramming a bullet large enough to engage the rifled grooves down the barrel. In the full minute it takes to load the rifle, the musket could fire four to six shots, which is why Napoleon still uses the musket. He will have speed, but we will have accuracy. One shot, one kill."

The sense of urgency had increased almost overnight. The Addington administration had published the official decree of every citizen's responsibilities should the French land on English soil: all horses and carriages were to be relinquished to authorities; forests and villages were to be put to the torch; roads and canals destroyed; and cattle that could not be led inland were to be slaughtered.

Pitt had raised his eyebrows in disbelief. "So it does not seem that any resistance is planned, then? The retreat has begun before even the commencement of hostilities!" he finished with disgust, the paper crumpled to a ball in his hand. "The problem with Addington is that he is distrustful of large volunteer movements; he dismisses them as popular and unserviceable, preferring to expand the militia. Which, of course, is all very well if one has militia to expand upon! We need to mobilize the will of the people and create a sense of armed nationalism. Volunteers are economical, rapidly formed in times of crisis and, by definition, the kind of military service most congenial to the public." So in Deal, at least, under Pitt's eagle eye, a mass recruitment drive was underway. Hastily glued pamphlets fluttered from every pub door:

*Britons to arms! Of apathy Beware,*
*And to your Country be your dearest care!*
*Protect your Altars, Guard your monarch's throne...*

Volunteers had come forward. Not many, but some. And since there were insufficient funds to arm all the new conscripts, the government had distributed pikes. The Walmer Volunteers seemed undeterred and marched vigorously from six until eight in the morning, proudly brandishing their ancient rifles and rusty sabers and winking at the girls. They were followed by a scampering pack of dirty boys who formed their own brigade complete with a drum, pipe, and banners sewn by their mamas. They had procured small gunstocks into which they fixed mop sticks smeared with black lead to resemble real barrels. The leader of this ragtag parade was Captain Dr. Pickford, a fat little man who had squeezed himself into a scarlet coat trimmed in gold and strutted up and down Maine Street with a fussy step and a pompous demeanor. Personally, Wolfe thought the pack of dirty boys stood more of a chance against the French.

And, of course, that was part of the problem. The majority of the British army was still engaged in Egypt; the remainder was dispersed throughout the Caribbean, which left the old, the young, and the infirm behind to defend an impossibly extensive coastline. For one hundred and sixty thousand formidably determined men, commanded by battle-hardened officers, were poised just over the brief stretch of water that divided them from France. Unlike Captain Pickford's volunteers, these were seasoned veterans of campaigns with the Royal Army, as well as those of the Republic, and their officers were men who had earned their epaulettes at the point of the sword. Napoleon's generals and the men they commanded had become renowned for their military prowess in what was an almost mystical succession of victories against a long list of seemingly unconquerable foes. The French flotilla was concentrated at Boulogne, but the entire coast, from Antwerp in the north to the mouth of the Seine, bristled with iron and bronze. Little wonder the English were paralyzed with fear.

"Would you oblige us with a tale, Wolfe?" Hester asked, with a mischievous wrinkle to her nose as she settled her feet more comfortably beneath her on the armchair.

"A tale?"

"It is traditional in Ireland, is it not, that travelers are expected to entertain the host with a tale, in return for food and a night's lodging? And seeing as you have been with us for...what, several days now?" She glanced at Pitt, wrapped in a blanket and snugly ensconced in his red leather chair, who nodded in grave confirmation. "You are indebted to the length of a small book, I would imagine."

"Am I now?" Wolfe asked with a quiet smile. "Well, never let it be said I was an ungrateful guest."

Dundas, stockinged feet propped up on the table, lounged on the couch beside Wolfe. "A good Irish tale," the Scotsman agreed, wriggling his toes in the warmth of the fire. "Ah, but wait!" Grasping Wolfe's empty glass from the table, he poured a generous portion of whiskey and handed it to Wolfe. "Is túisce deoch ná scéal."

"I didn't know you knew Gaelic." Wolfe raised his eyebrows in surprise as he accepted the whiskey.

"Oh, just a wee bit 'ere and there," Dundas murmured as he settled back into his seat.

"What does it mean?" Hester demanded.

"A drink precedes a story," Wolfe translated for her. With a nod of thanks to Dundas, he began his tale, his voice deep and mellow in the lengthening shadows of the room. "In the ancient times, in Ireland, there was a man of the Fitzgeralds. He was called Gerald, but the Irish, that always had a great fondness for the family, called him Gearoidh Iarla or Earl Gerald. He had an impressive castle at Mullaghmast, and whenever the English government was striving to put some wrong on the country, he was always the man that stood up against it."

Hester snorted in a most unfeminine fashion, while Pitt choked on his brandy. This turned into a coughing fit, which drew Dundas and Hester from their seats in alarm. Hester urged a medicinal vial, which Pitt waved away, mouth buried in a handkerchief as the coughs wracked his thin frame. When it finally subsided, the former prime minister raised his pale face, eyes reddened, forehead a sheen of sweat, toward Wolfe. "Forgive my interruption. I was enjoying your tale immensely; please, do continue," he managed hoarsely, tucking the handkerchief into his pocket, but not before Wolfe saw the scarlet bloodstain.

Wolfe hesitated. "Perhaps a different story...there is one of the leprechaun of the Innishowen mountains I think you will enjoy."

"No," Pitt insisted, retrieving his glass from the table. "I would like to hear about Earl Gerald." He gulped down the remaining brandy in one convulsive swallow. A tinge of color reappeared in his cheeks.

Wolfe nodded in acquiescence. "As well as being a great leader in battle and very skillful at all weapons, he was well-practiced in the black arts and could change himself into whatever shape he pleased. His lady, the fair Kathleen O'Shea, knew of his gift and constantly pleaded with him to show her. But he refused, putting her off on some pretense or another. But she wouldn't be a woman if she hadn't perseverance." Wolfe winked at Hester. "And finally her entreaties to display his black arts wore him down, but he warned her that if she had the least anxiety while he was out of his natural form, he would never recover it till many generations of men were under the earth. So one lovely summer night, as they were sitting in their grand drawing room, he turned from her, muttering a few words, and before you could wink he was clean out 'o sight...and a pretty little finch was flitting about the room.

"Kathleen was entranced, as he flew hither and yon around the chamber, fluttered out and around the open window, and settled close upon her shoulder. Well, when bird and wife had been sufficiently delighted, he took one last flight into the garden but was soon rapidly upon his return, darting with trembling haste right into his lady's bosom. A fierce hawk tore through the window after him. Kathleen gave a piercing scream, affrighted to the very depths of her, though there was little need, for the wild bird came in like an arrow and smashed into the table with such force that the life was dashed outa him. She turned her gaze from the hawk's shuddering body to where she saw the finch a moment before, but neither finch nor Earl Gerald did she ever lay eyes on again..."

For a moment there was a silence, the crackle and spit of logs burning into their ashes the only sound in the quiet room. "What happened to him?" Hester asked, leaning forward, glass forgotten in her hand.

"Ah, well, legend has it that himself and his warriors are now sleeping

in a dark cave under the Rath of Mullaghmast. The Earl Gerald is seated at the head of a table that runs along the length of the cave, and his
troopers, clad in full armor, sit down along both sides, their heads resting on the table. Their horses, equipped with saddle and bridle, stand
behind their masters in stalls to each side…and when the day arrives,
the miller's son—that's born with six fingers on each hand—will blow
his trumpet, and the horses will stomp and whinny; the knights will
wake from their slumber, mount their steeds, and go forth into battle."

"With the English, I presume?" Pitt asked dryly, his composure quite
recovered.

"Who else?" Wolfe replied, mouth quirking in amusement. "Once
ever y seven years, Earl Gerald gallops round the Curragh of Kildare
on a white stallion, whose silver shoes were half an inch thick the time
he vanished. And when these shoes are worn as thin as a cat's ear, he'll
be returned to the society of living men, fight a mighty battle with the
English, and reign as king of Ireland for two-score years."

"And poor Kathleen never spied him on these jaunts around the
neighborhood?" Hester asked tartly.

"Well then, she was sewing and some such, as befits the wifely
station," Wolfe replied with a grin, as Hester scowled fiercely in his
direction.

"But some nights," Wolfe contined, "as happens once in every seven
years, while the earl is cantering around the Curragh, the cavern's entrance becomes visible to any one happening to pass by. Indeed, about
a hundred years ago, a horse-dealer that was late abroad and a bit drunk,
spied the lighted cavern and went in. The sight o' the men in armor,
resting so still on the table, the horses motionless behind them…well,
this cowed him a good deal, and he became sober. His hands began to
shake, and he let a bridle fall. The bit clattered to the ground, echoing
through the long cave, and one of the warriors seated near him lifted his
head and said in a deep, hoarse voice: 'Is it time yet?' The horse-dealer
had the wit to reply: 'Not yet, but soon will,' and the heavy helmet sunk
back down on the table. The man made the best of his way out, and I
never heard of any other one having got the same opportunity."

"Wolfe, you've discharged yer duty admirably!" Dundas stood. "So
much so that ye may be required to repeat the procedure again verra
soon. But I am off ta' bed meself."

Dundas patted Pitt's head as he passed the chair, wiggled his fingers affectionately at Hester, and was gone with a soft thud of the drawing room door.

"So are Irish and English to be forever at odds?" Pitt asked. His tone was deliberately casual, but with a thread of intensity that suggested he was asking something more. "Is that the primary import of your tale?"

He was asking, Hester knew, whether Wolfe was ready to commit to Pitt's cause, whether he could overcome his hatred of the English. Or whether all their efforts were, at last, for naught.

"There are two things Irish lads learn to master in their youth: storytelling and English-hating. Both of which we do very well, don't you know?" Wolfe grinned, his expression a curious combination of humor and ferocity. His words were languidly uttered but brought an underlying tension to the room. The thread of companionship, established in the past few days and strengthened by the cozy intimacy of a fireside story, became instantly taut and quivering, straining under the burden of all that had not been said.

"Oh, indeed," Pitt answered, rising from his chair in a deliberately languorous stretch. "You are most skilled in both departments."

"Thank you," Wolfe inclined his head slightly. "Although I feel compelled to add that neither requires much in the way of skill, both being much practiced and fairly effortless."

"*Both* worth the effort?" Pitt wondered idly. He decided on a more direct approach. "Have you thought anymore about my proposition to you, Wolfe? I understand your reluctance to trust me, but, to be perfectly blunt, we have quite run out of time." Pitt frowned slightly as he stood, his lanky frame erect, his cravat skewed and rumpled beneath the collar of his housecoat. "We have other options, certainly, and I need to know whether or not we need to act upon them." He paused, directing his silvery-bright gaze at Wolfe, intent and pinioning beneath dark brows.

"And back to Newgate with me?" Wolfe asked mockingly, gulping down the last of his brandy.

"If you decide not to work with us, then I will arrange to have you returned to Ireland, your lands restored, and a guarantee of future immunity from past transgressions. Providing, you continue to pursue your livelihood without taking up arms against the English, of course."

"Why would you do that? Run the risk of me interfering in your agenda?"

"Because it is your agenda, too, Wolfe. It is an Irish agenda as well as an English one. And I think you realize that, don't you?"

Wolfe did not answer straight away. Hester watched the exchange quietly. It was evident to them all that this was a crucial time. Either a trust would be developed here and England would be saved from French tyranny, or it would not. Pitt was compelling, but would it be enough to overcome an Irishman who had long nurtured a hatred and mistrust of the English?

"Coal," Wolfe said finally. A dull ache blossomed behind the scar on his left temple. He clenched his fists in the fabric of the couch.

"I beg your pardon?" Pitt asked.

"In order for the linen industry to survive in Ireland, we need coal," Wolfe managed in measured tones, the escalating pain cascading in waves across the back of his skull. "The handlooms are a relic of the past, but the new powerlooms rely upon steam power, which in turn requires coal. And, as you know, Ireland does not possess an indigenous supply. England does. I want the king's guarantee: stamped and sealed with all official documentation granting coal purchasing rights to Ireland. At market cost. We want to compete fairly, Mr. Pitt; it has been all we've ever wanted."

"Fair enough," Pitt nodded. "I will go to London and discuss it with His Majesty myself."

"Be warned, Mr. Pitt," Wolfe continued intently. "If Ireland has to choose between unconditional submission to England or a revolution with all the associated sufferings, they will prefer the dangers of rebellion to slavery every time."

"I understand, Mr. Trant." Pitt reached out, palm outstretched.

Wolfe hesitated, the muscle in his cheek tightening. Pitt's hand waited, his gaze intent and unwavering. Wolfe inhaled sharply, nostrils flaring, before reaching out to grasp Pitt's hand with his own. Hester exhaled in relief, not realizing she had been holding her breath. It seemed a truce had been established; how binding it was, remained to be seen. But these were men of honor, each in his own way, and they would not easily be compromised. They both believed in a higher cause, and as long as each believed his cause was being served, this union would hold. But the tides of passion were fierce. Wolfe's hatred was strong. As the three departed, each to his or her own bedchamber, Hester could not help but muse on the larger consequences should this particular tie unravel...

# 21.

The night grew over rue de Manot in lengthening shadows and pools that bulged in ever larger perimeters, as if the houses and storefronts were being slowly but inexorably swallowed by some darkly impenetrable beast. An icy wind howled down the narrow street, whipping before it derelict artifacts of daily trade and tearing the last of the brown leaves from the starkly bare elms. The Maison de Théâtre des Poissons Rouge had shuttered its door against the winter more than a half hour before, and the prosperously bourgeois crowd, eager to return to the warmth of home and hearth, had hastily dispersed to waiting carriages and cabs.

The drably dressed figure of a woman hurried through slush-filled streets, relinquishing her spot by the theatre doors where she had been attempting to sell cheap broadsheets and gossip rags for a half-centime to the exiting audience. She walked, as all of the Paris poor did at this time of year, in a curiously half-hunched scurrying motion intended, above all, to conserve what little body heat remained beneath thin, ragged attire. She tucked in upon herself: elbows tight against her torso, head bent down toward her chest, back and shoulders hunched and rounded against the cold. Her gaunt face was barely visible beneath the rim of a grubby bonnet, but when she passed under the occasional street lamp, the yellow light did her little favor. A sore, swollen and streaked with pus, festered on her right cheek. Eyes, set deep within a narrow face, were dark-rimmed with fatigue; her nose widely flat and marked with smallpox. A slash of a mouth appeared entirely lipless and parted, in her haste, to reveal teeth broken and yellowed with neglect and decay.

"Françoise! Françoise!"

Françoise stopped and turned, shifting her bag of broadsheets to the other arm. Her breath came in quick heated gasps in the cold air.

"Sell any?" Martin's pale face appeared beneath a soiled woolen shawl. He carried the accoutrements of a boot-cleaner: a basket filled with blacking, brushes and rags on his back, and a leather bag with odds and ends of shoes over one scrawny arm that shook with cold and consumption.

"One," Françoise replied wearily. With a thin hand, reddened with cold, she deposited two centimes in Martin's basket. "There's broth at Saint Marie's; call it a night." She hurried off, leaving an astonished Martin behind her.

Françoise had sold a broadsheet to an elegantly dressed man in gray. But it was not a broadsheet she had handed him from her basket, and he was not a customer of songs and gossip. The tattered paper had provided logistical instructions for the next meeting of the French Resistance. Extra precautions had been taken as they expected a guest of the highest rank. Monsieur de Batout would pass the letter on to Cadoudal, who would, in turn, coordinate matters with the remaining five.

Turning into rue de la Coutellerie, Françoise passed shuttered storefronts and wood-and-plaster houses, the streetlights here and there relieving the desolate boulevard in ruddy pools of light. She sensed more than saw the dark figure behind her—a prickling unease at the manner in which a shadow disassociated itself from a doorway, shifted and eased into the next gloomy hollow. It could be any manner of thief or pickpocket, any one of the many denizens of the Parisian underworld, but Françoise was familiar enough with their workings to know that she presented a highly unlikely target. From the toes of her scuffed and leaking clogs to the grimy bonnet that covered her gray stringy locks, she had little any pickpocket would covet.

One of Fouché's paid disciples? There were certainly no lack of them; they seemed to multiply with the cold, each seeking some lead that might line their pocket with coin.

Mentally retracing the evening in her mind, Françoise could not pinpoint anything out of the ordinary or any evidence that her cover had been blown. But coincidence or not, warranted or otherwise, Françoise, seller of broadsheets and gossip rags, had attracted attention—one identity that would have to be scrapped from the repertoire. Assuming she managed to evade her tail.

Scrupulously careful to maintain the same pace so not as to alert the figure behind her that he had been spotted, Françoise continued her silent scurry up the wet rise toward the intersection with rue Masant.

Suddenly darting into the street to her right, she almost collided with the wet whiskered nose of a gray mare.

"Au revoir…au revoir." The mare's owner, a thickset man in a blue greatcoat, face shadowed beneath a broad-rimmed hat, was taking his leave of a woman whose figure was silhouetted in a narrow sliver of firelight. The horse nickered impatiently, tossing her head and restlessly shifting her hooves, as the bitter wind whipped at her flanks and tugged at the cart that was harnessed behind. A heavy woolen cloth served to protect the cart's contents from rain and snow and was secured by a thick rope that linked through hooks secured in rough-hewn timber on each side.

Rapidly clambering over the rope, Françoise edged beneath a loose flap of blanket. Just as she had secured a cramped position between a wooden barrel, a rocking chair, and a burlap sack, she felt the shift of the cart as the driver took his seat and the jostling motion as the horse turned toward the left, down the road she had so recently ascended. Peering through a crack in the timbers, Françoise caught a glimpse of the man who had been following her. Having abandoned all pretense of stealth, he was running toward rue Masant, dark coat flapping behind him. As he passed under the yellow gleam of lamplight, she glimpsed dark hair and a pale cheek under the rim of a tricorn. The cart skidded slightly on the icy descent to rue de Manot, and Françoise could hear the driver cursing under his breath as he fought to control the horse on the slick roadway. Then they turned on to rue de la Coutellerie, and Françoise exhaled in relief and exhaustion.

She had evaded her tail, but she still had to get home. Working quickly, her frozen fingers stumbling over buttons, she yanked off her ragged coat and shuffled out of the soiled tunic underneath. In the clattering dimness, Françoise managed to divest herself of all her filthy over-clothes to reveal a blue woolen dress of considerably better repair than the broadsheet seller's attire. Beneath the gray flannel cloth in her basket, Françoise drew out a wig, a respectable chignon that replaced the gray, stringy locks she currently wore. The flannel, dampened by melted snow, served as a facecloth. The pus-filled infection and pock-marked nose came away in a smear of makeup, and Françoise presently became Juliette, a young woman of modest means seeking employment in one of the grander homes of the city.

She was tired and dozed for a moment, head lolling against the jolting barrel behind her, and, for a moment, she was back there...six years ago, when the back of a cart had once before provided refuge. Paris, then, had been a frightening place for an aristocrat and, suddenly bereft of husband and brother, Jeanne had fled the city crouched beneath fragrant bales of hay. Three years had elapsed before she saw the towers of Notre Dame again, and when she did, it was through eyes that did not seem her own, so much had she changed in the intervening time. So much had she learned in the forests of the Vendée...

# 22.

Jeanne found this land more by accident than endeavor. The hay cart took her as far as Rouen, where she emerged bedraggled, bewildered, and festooned with straw. A distant cousin had reluctantly sheltered her overnight—even a casual association with an aristocrat could mean an appointment with Madame la Guillotine—and then, pressing a handful of assignats in her palm (rendered largely useless by inflation), urged her onwards to Le Havre. Go to the coast, she was told. Avoiding the thoroughfares was paramount, for it was there the grisly roadside executions took place: the aristocrats initially, and then the counter-revolutionaries that targeted all those with suspected Jacobin ties, until finally it seemed little more than a frenzied rush of killing. It mattered little who you were or what you believed; if you were in the wrong place at the wrong time, you satisfied the bloodlust, temporarily assuaged the anger, until some other such unfortunate happened along. Brutal distinctions had been drawn between Citizen and Aristocrat, Patriot and Enemy, labels that would allow no human shades of gray. So she followed the sea, trudging hungry and desolate beneath the shadow of rugged cliffs by day and finding refuge by night in the shoreline of scrubby pine.

Even in later years, this remembered time remained a darkly shadowed one for Jeanne, with vividly visceral memories that she preferred not to dwell upon: the sour clenching heave of an empty belly; the light-headed dizziness and fatigue; the gritty rawness of eyes that seldom closed during long hours of darkness; nights that were plagued by the fit and start of trembling nerves, where every rustle and movement was a deliberate tread of a soldier's boots, his bayonet gleaming dully in the moonlight. When, despite her quickening fear, Jeanne finally slept, her rest was fitful and tormented. She dreamt of the Marquess de Listenay who had fled from her burning chateau with her young daughters, only to be apprehended and executed the following morning. Jeanne frequently awoke to the piercing sound of her own screams,

tears coursing down her cheeks, and the memory of the sickening thud
of bloody heads falling into the basket beneath the broad expanse of an
uncaring sky. Other such stories that did not trouble her sleep haunted
her daylight hours: Chevalier d'Ambly who had been strung up from a
lamp post, then decapitated with a penknife, his head paraded triumphantly through Paris on a pike. They had been only a few of the thousands who had perished at the hands of the Revolutionary Tribunal,
and whose grisly ends found their way in whispered confidence from
one ear to another. And so it was that the urban madness began to fuel
the rural fear that subsequently gripped the outskirts.

From Avranches, she turned south into the heart of the Vendée.
Everywhere, she encountered gaunt refugees pleading for bread or
information. Many men of the districts had already gone, seeking employment further afield in what seemed a vain attempt to buy bread at
an affordable price. Their wives and children followed ragtag behind,
no longer feeling safe in their humble cottages, each plagued with an
undefined fear that fire and slaughter were coming upon them like
the horsemen of the apocalypse. Rumors circulated of all manner of
atrocities: hordes of starving brigands falling like a swarm of locusts
on already nearly empty granaries, villages plundered, barns burnt, and
women and children slaughtered in their beds. She became one of these
refugees—thin, hungry, and desperately seeking news of her brother.

Jeanne traveled inland when the cliff projected out into the sea,
rendering further northward travel impossible. She followed remote
paths through deep deciduous woods, paralleled by slow rivers, sluggish
marshland, and small fields. And everywhere, in the drawn, pale faces
of the people, there was the terror, the dead living on in the somber
demeanor of the living. Small towns and villages with their gray stone
churches tucked in upon themselves and were suspicious of strangers;
everywhere, she was met with hostile glances and hurriedly slammed
shutters. Dark mutterings of suffering and death, whispered by twos or
threes in doorways, replaced the market conviviality of happier years.
Jeanne could hardly blame them. She knew only too well of the chaos
and ferocity which had descended upon Paris and which now found an
outlet in rural France. The nation seemed convulsed in a paroxysm of
madness where rational thought had no accommodation and innocence
no longer mattered.

A few took pity upon her, retaining enough humanity, despite the
terror of the times, to recognize a thinly forlorn young girl when they

saw one. To each, she asked the same question: had they seen her brother, had they seen Joachim?

It was in the shadowed back pew of the Church Saint-Léonard in Fougères where Armand finally found her. "The stained glass is beautiful, is it not?" The deeply grave voice came before she even realized someone had seated himself beside her. The man to whom it belonged was dark-haired and lean, with hooded eyes beneath brows so elegantly curved they seemed almost feminine. This delicacy of form was echoed in his thin but finely shaped lips that were all but concealed beneath a thick, black beard. He wore a coat of gray broadcloth buttoned to the chin, and from beneath the shadowed rim of a black cap he surveyed her with a seemingly casual air. "It is Lazarus, of course, returned from the dead. His tomb, apparently, was discovered in Cyprus in 890 AD, bearing the inscription 'Lazarus the friend of Christ.' The bones were stolen by the Crusaders in 1204 and brought back to France as booty of war from the Fourth Crusade. Of course, the villagers of Fougères believe they lie here, beneath the very chapel of Saint-Lèonard." His lips curved briefly in sardonic amusement.

Jeanne didn't know what to say. Her supply of assignats, the proceeds of hastily pawned jewelry, had been exhausted two days before. She had not eaten in as many days, and her stomach gripped and twisted in sour convulsions; her body, unaccustomed to the rigors of the road, ached and throbbed in every extremity. Her questions regarding Joachim had been met with blank stares or a quick, dismissive shake of the head. It seemed he had completely disappeared, and Jeanne was considering her options. Sitting in the back pew, the vault of the Sacred Heart shadowed by the fading sun, the windows lit to a deep brilliance of color, head drooping with weariness, she sat staring blankly ahead with numbed exhaustion.

"Some believe that France, like Lazarus, can rise from the dead. Your brother believed that." Armand's eyes, darkly piercing beneath their heavy lids, regarded her intently.

"My brother…?" Jeanne's voice reached her own ears through the thick fog of fatigue. "Joachim?" She twisted in her seat, eyes wide and imploring. "Joachim? Please, you must take me to him!"

"He is not with us any longer. But perhaps I can help you find him. Come." He gently took her trembling hands and helped her to her feet.

The Vendée Resistance had been brutally obliterated at Savenay the year before and the survivors, led and trained by the mysterious Armand, had gone underground. Her brother had spent the past year training with Armand, and then, during a mission to Paris to supply a contact with arms and information, he had gone missing. When he had not arrived at the pickup location at the appointed time, Armand had gone looking for him. Joachim had departed from Café Procope on foot at just past ten p.m. and simply walked off into the darkness. Every associate Armand had contacted in Paris came up blank. Jeanne felt with fervent conviction that Joachim was still alive and reasoned that when he reappeared he would contact Armand, so it was here, in the interim, that she made her home.

Jeanne spent the next three years among the Vendée Resistance. Without family, she had found one; without purpose, she had embraced the cause of the Vendée. Jeanne had been a countess; now she was a brigand. She learned how to survive in a new world, mastering the gutter slang of the Gascon and the Languedoc. The elite were easier for her to mimic—they came from a world with which she had once been intimately familiar—and the prancing dandy and the disdainful aristocrat were readily added to her repertoire. Having a natural talent for mimicry and inheriting her mother's vocal range, Jeanne found the process an easier one than might be expected. The vital importance of these skills would only become apparent to her later, when her proficiency in disguise and assimilation repeatedly saved her life. That, and her ability to kill. The art of killing had been Armand's forte, and he had taught her well; although it was a necessity that horrified her on every occasion and an ability she had been loath to master. After six months of grueling physical training in defense and attack, he had brought a prisoner before her, armed them both with knives and told her, quite simply, to kill or be killed. Yes, it was the lesson in killing that sat most starkly in the back of her mind.

Dense clumps of beech trees, surrounded by a perimeter of lofty hedges, provided a secluded grove in which to practice. In which to kill. A farmer recruited to the cause had happily relocated his field-stock at Armand's request. And it was here where Jeanne had been first instructed in methods of administering and defying death.

Jeanne's heart, stricken by anxiety beyond all ability to calm, beat the frantic rhythm of a runaway horse, drumming in her ears and threatening to burst forth from her chest. Her palms were slick with sweat, mouth dry with fear. *Kill him*, Armand had said, as calmly as if he were requesting eggs for breakfast. *Kill him. Him* stood opposite her now: a thin, gangly youth dressed in the bedraggled remnants of the Imperial Guard, knife hilt grasped firmly, blade glinting in the late afternoon light. *Kill him.* Why? Because he happened to be fighting on the other side? Because he was young enough and careless enough to be captured by the Vendean rebels while on a routine reconnaissance?

The prisoner grinned at her, his teeth blackened stumps, his eyes narrow slits of amusement; of course—one of Napoleon's own, undaunted by a mere girl. He would have no qualms about running her through if it meant his own survival. Jeanne felt her resolve harden. *Kill him.* Why? Ignoring the voice of reason that resonated in her head, the voice that had a place in the elegant drawing rooms of the French aristocracy but now was completely obsolete, she raised her own blade. Jeanne circled the prisoner warily. And so the battle had begun.

He was short and thin—weight-wise they were a fairly even match. *Shins. Eyes. Crotch. All points of vulnerability. Keep your distance. Engage the mind. Manage fear.* Armand's words ran through her mind in an abrupt staccato. The two circled each other, thrusting and parrying without any distinct advantage to either. The prisoner's cocky assurance gradually transformed into an irritable sourness at her unexpected skill with a blade, at her quick, light step that proved so elusive, and, in short, at her stubborn refusal to die. A lucky swipe opened up a gash across Jeanne's right shoulder which, in the adrenalin of fight, barely registered. She felt more than heard Armand's tension: the bunching of muscles, the tightening of mouth and eyes. "Come now," he whispered harshly under his breath.

Feigning weakness, she momentarily closed her eyes and slightly lowered her blade, as if overcome by the first blood drawn, as if finally exhausted by the physical and mental stress of battle. As she had hoped, the prisoner lunged forward with a stabbing motion which Jeanne neatly sidestepped, twisting to kick the side of his knee. The prisoner promptly crumpled to the ground with a howl of angry protest.

"Take the advantage!" Armand barked from the sidelines. Her opponent, momentarily vulnerable, lay before her. Quickly now...*what?* The jugular—pulsing blue with effort beneath pale neck skin? Hot blood gushing over her hands? Murder? She hesitated, giving her opponent the moment he needed to rise to his feet. His sly expression conveyed his conviction that she was unable to move in for the kill, that he had the battle in hand. She was a doe for the slaughter. And so the struggle continued; while Jeanne had been unable to kill him, she gave the prisoner no opportunity to take further advantage. She moved, not unlike a choreography of old, lightly and swiftly upon her feet, and the knowledge of her recent triumph—her ability to best him—lent Jeanne the confidence that increasingly bled from her opponent.

*Fight back in ways that give you the advantage.* There! A momentary gain of position: the prisoner, moving sluggishly now, presented his more vulnerable side as he attempted to bring his knife around to face her. Jeanne, dripping with sweat, exhaustion weighing down every limb, lunged. The prisoner, in a lucky swing, clumsily sideswiped, knocked the knife from her grasp, and sent her sprawling to the ground. Ignoring her fatigue, Jeanne twisted to one side and sprang to her feet, yanking a second knife from her waistband. The prisoner, half-turned in victory, was surprised by her quick movement. Jeanne brought the knife toward his throat, hesitated, and then he was upon her, and she was forcibly thrown to the ground with a strength that left her shuddering. Karl, her protector even then, had intervened, grabbing the prisoner around the neck with thick, beefy arms.

"Mon dieu!" Armand spat, his intonation heavy with equal measures of disgust and despair. He dismissed her recumbent form with a wave of his hand and strode off into the darkness of the surrounding forest. Staggering to her feet, Jeanne followed.

Armand sat by the fire that smoldered and glowed beneath a broad canopy of stars. Charles Armand Tuffin, Marquis de la Rouërie, also known in America as Colonel Armand, was a French cavalry officer who had served under the American flag during the War of Independence. Despite his promotion to brigadier general after the Battle of Yorktown, and the promise of a glorious military career in this newly established nation, Armand had elected to return to France.

Always alone, often on horseback, he presented a mysteriously aloof figure to the men that fervently followed him. A black cap covered his brow, shaded his eyes, and concealed his face; a thick, black beard obscured his lower features. Even among his own followers, there were scarcely a handful who could describe his countenance with any accuracy. Few were granted that physical proximity—it was an intimacy often reserved for those that were about to die. And so a sort of fervor grew up around his person: a hushed reverence that acknowledged, with each hard-won victory, the legend that was in the making. Jeanne, for reasons unfathomable to her, had been taken under his wing: whether because of Joachim, to whom she understood Armand had been close, or some other orchestrated plan in which she would play a part, she knew not. But she trusted him, and with each day that passed Jeanne felt less tormented, less frail, less alone; and for this, above all else, she was grateful.

Wincing, her body bruised, battered, and sore in every portion, she lowered herself gingerly to the ground next to him. The plaintive cry of a tawny owl sounded sharp and clear in the still evening air. The dying fire crackled and burned into hot white embers. "I will improve," Jeanne said quietly. "Have patience with me. I will work hard."

Armand turned to her, his dark face clenched and tight in the firelight. "Do you know what happened to the women after Savenay, Jeanne? They were either massacred or drowned at Pont-au-Baux...together with the old men and children." Jeanne looked away, but Armand was not finished. "We intercepted a letter from General Westermann to the Committee of Public Safety after the massacre at Savenay. The general wrote: 'There is no more Vendée. It died with its wives and its children by our free sabers. I have just buried it in the woods and the swamps of Savenay. According to the orders that you gave me, I crushed the children under the feet of the horses, massacred the women who will not give birth to any more brigands. I do not have a prisoner to reproach me. I have exterminated all. The roads are sown with corpses. At Savenay, brigands are arriving all the time claiming to surrender, and we are shooting them non-stop.'"

He paused, viciously jabbing at the fire with a blackened stick, sparks spitting into the dark night. For a moment there was silence, both contemplating the atrocities that had been committed in the name of political peace and national well-being. "Mercy is not a revolutionary sentiment, Jeanne," he continued quietly, his voice as deep and velvety as the night which surrounded them, his dark profile illuminated by the smoldering heat of the fire. "The war here is fought differently. We are fighting for more than just a king. To the Vendeans, this is a crusade for individual liberty and security in keeping with the Revolution's own declaration of the right to rebel against the violation of the rights of the people. And, you must remember, you are no longer a countess."

No longer a countess, and no longer a girl. Innocence was a virtue she could no longer afford. She had to become a killer of men. And so there in the star-dappled beauty of the Vendée, Jeanne died and Primrose was born.

# 23.

The social season of the English elite echoed the rhythm of Parliament; it began in late October with the commencement of a new session and concluded in June with summer recess. The two most popular evenings for social entertainment were Wednesday and Saturday, when Parliament had adjourned and the men's attendance could be assured. Lady Georgianna, the duchess of Devonshire, knew all these things. She was generally acknowledged to be the reigning queen of the ton, the ultra-fashionable set that resolved whether an opera was a success, an artist a genius, and what color would be favored that season. If there was one thing the ton had learned to expect from the duchess of Devonshire, it was the unexpected. The latest novelty that set the peers of the realm and their wives buzzing was the upcoming event: breakfast at Chiswick House. Breakfast! Unaccustomed to being up before noon, many of the ladies found it faintly horrifying that they were expected to be dressed and in attendance by ten in the morning. But nobody dared refuse the duchess of Devonshire, and, indeed, not to have been invited at all was, without doubt, the more appalling alternative.

Casimir de Montrond had been invited, much to his astonishment. The Revolution had not been popular in London—Napoleon even less so. Montrond, despite his impeccable lineage and obvious wealth, was a pragmatic man. In his mission for Talleyrand, he had been prepared to be snubbed, scorned, and even personally accosted. He was a Frenchman—that was enough in London these days, or so he had understood. So he was astounded, indeed, the very morning of his arrival in London, to receive at his hotel—where he had engaged a room only hours earlier—an invitation to breakfast with the duchess of Devonshire. He had an appointment at Walmer the following afternoon but saw no reason to disappoint a lady.

It was not that Casimir was unaccustomed to receiving invitations from aristocratic ladies—quite the contrary. He was tall, handsome, and wealthy with a ready wit. He was a gambler and a swordsman, well-versed and delighted to oblige in games of quince, lou, brag, whist, commerce, backgammon, faro, or any other game of chance current in elite salons and social circles. He possessed an impressive understanding of history, architecture, and politics, and was adept at both light-hearted sociability and somber intellectual discussion, as the occasion and audience warranted. All these attributes kept him in perpetual demand—across the Channel as well as in Paris, it seemed. Obviously, his reputation and appeal had overcome the haughty disdain most of English society maintained toward their French cousins.

"Chiswick House, your lordship," the driver announced from above as the carriage drew to a halt.

Montrond stepped down from his vehicle, tipped the driver, and, jauntily waving his cane, made his way through the elaborate wrought-iron gate, through the immaculately pruned boxwood hedges, to the gardens that stretched out to the stately elms that defined the property's perimeter. The tall narrow house, surrounded by five or six acres of landscaped terraces, was situated in one of the most desirable and central spots at 7 St. James Square. This elegant development, built in the late-seventeenth century, spanned the area between the old palace of St. James and the latest expansions north of Piccadilly, as new London's focus shifted from the City, the Strand, and Bloomsbury to the cleaner air of the west. Chiswick House was located on the northeast side of the Square, whose occupants included none other than the earls of Bathurst, Hardwick, Strafford, Dartmouth, the dukes of Leeds and Cleveland and a clutch of viscounts—the crème de la crème of English society.

A smartly dressed servant in green livery took Montrond's name. "Title, sir?" he respectfully inquired. Montrond shook his head. "Casimir de Montrond," the servant announced in ponderous tones to the general assembly that clustered in the central garden. Montrond doubted that many of the duchess' guests had had so brief an introduction. And, indeed, fifteen years earlier, his own titles would have impressed the most discerning aristocrat: cousin to Louis Jean Marie de Bourbon, duc de Penthièvre and, with the death of the duc's son, heirs to the title of comte de Toulouse, and marquise de Montespan. But that was before the fourth of August, 1789, when the National Constituent Assembly of the French Revolution abolished feudalism and all prerogatives and seigneurial rights of the Second Estate. And since then he had been simply Casimir. He did not mind—he had found the excessive privilege of his birth burdensome, the expectations immense, and the responsibilities overwhelming. Now that the properties and titles pursuant to his entitlement had been annexed by the recently made emperor of the French, Napoleon Bonaparte, he was liberated. He had his country estate in Toulouse, his apartment in the fashionable rue St. Chantereine, as well as the funds necessary to accommodate his lavish lifestyle. Casimir de Montrond had never been happier.

"Casimir de Montrond! How delightful of you to come! Allow me to introduce myself. I am Georgianna, duchess of Devonshire." A tall woman with a plump roundness that Montrond found immensely appealing extended her hand, which he gallantly kissed, bowing deeply at the waist. She wore a simple white robe with puckered sleeves and a pale pink ribbon tied beneath her breasts in a style Montrond recognized as one popularized by Marie Antoinette years earlier. Her blonde hair was gathered up in a large bouffant with fat ringlets curling around her neck and resting on her shoulders; a large straw hat with a profusion of white roses spilling over one wide brim completed her simple ensemble.

"Allow me to introduce you." She tucked her arm through his in a familiar fashion and led him toward the cluster of English elite that had gathered across the lawns. The gardens at Chiswick emulated the newly fashionable Italian style of landscape architecture, with terraced circles of lawn decorated with urns and defined by balustrades. These segmented gardens provided intimate enclosures for four or five guests, while rustic bridges and pathways wound their way around to more secluded ponds and shaded pergolas for those who wished for more private conversation.

The duchess introduced him to the earls of Leicester and Carlisle, the duke of Portland, and numerous other plump aristocrats and their satin-clad wives. The conversations whirled around him in a dizzying array of rumor and speculation, and while he did not recognize the names or the scandals in which the individuals were embroiled, the widened eyes, the smothered giggles, the stifled gasps—in short, the body language of gossip and intrigue—were familiar to any who had frequented a European court or a Parisian salon.

"Can you believe it, George? Lord Pembroke, earl, lord of the bed-chamber, major-general, possessed of *ten thousand pounds a year*, husband to one of the most beautiful creatures in England, father of an only son, owner of a great estate—quitting everything, resigning wife and world, and embarking for life in a packet-boat with a silly miss?"

"Apparently, on the day of their elopement, he dined privately in his dressing room, put on a sailor's habit and black wig that he had brought home with him in a bundle, and threatened the servants he would murder them if they mentioned it to his wife!"

"Did you attend the trial last week? Earl Ferrers…for shooting his own steward… can you imagine?"

"Did you hear about Lady Coventry? She is very ill, I understand… in hiding at Bristol. Her looks are quite, quite gone…"

"Did you know the queen gave Lady Bolingbroke a particularly fine enameled watch? I saw it myself…"

Montrond found himself perpetually engaged by English aristocrats eager to hear of the dismal fate which had befallen their French cousins. They wanted to hear that the Revolution was not to be rewarded, that there was nothing but famine and hardship for those who dared to overthrow the established monarchy. Perversely, despite his own fervent monarchism, Casimir found himself relating Napoleon's successes: his Napoleonic Code that was soon to be implemented, the universities he had founded, and the fine cuisine available in the newly established restaurants. For the most part, he was greeted by a disdainful sniff, a skeptically raised eyebrow, or an abrupt conversation change to mundane English topics of which he had little or no knowledge. After an hour, he wearied of the English aristocracy and sought a brief respite in a nearby thatch of trees.

The grove was dark compared to the bright sunshine of the terraces, the sun pale and dappled where it penetrated the thick canopy. A stream splashed and gurgled amid shady foliage, and a profusion of delicate fern fronds formed a rich tapestry of green shades. Clusters of pink cyclamens bloomed at the gnarled roots of the ancient oaks, and the large clumps of glossy barrenwort were starting to produce tiny yellow flowers. It was a pleasant spot, and Montrond was feeling the strain of conversing in English all morning. "Pour le moment," he muttered to himself, lying back on the grassy bank. He closed his eyes, hearing the faint sounds of the string quartet as they began another movement.

He must have dozed momentarily—the fatigue of the journey from Paris, his early start that morning—for he was awakened by a harsh whisper. Slowly, he became aware of two men on the other side of a shrub of golden yew talking in low, furtive tones. There was a hushed sense of urgency about their conversation, and once Montrond could make out what they were saying, he could understand why. "The risk is too great. He must be killed, I tell you. He will be in Paris next week... easier to do it there."

"And what of Fox?"

"He doesn't need to know."

"Don't you think he will find out?"

"He has grown old and complacent. How can he not see the need for quick, decisive action here? Who knows what this Irishman's intent really is? He is Egan Trant's brother, for God's sake! He will lead Ol' Boney right to our shores. Between Pitt and Fox, the country is led by fools!"

"Whom can we engage?"

"I already have someone in place—someone we can trust to do the job right... make it look like an accident. Paris is a dangerous place, volatile. It shouldn't be too difficult. Nevertheless, it must not get out. It would splinter the Whigs irreparably."

"Who?"

"L'Aigle. We used him in the Russian situation. He was the soul of discretion; nobody ever linked the Czar's death with us...very professional."

Montrond heard the rustle of leaves as the men departed. He sat up slowly, thinking about what he had heard. It seemed there might be an imperative to get to Walmer after all. The situation was a little more complicated than either he or Talleyrand had expected.

"Monsieur de Montrond! You are not leaving already? Monsieur?"

Montrond turned to find the duchess herself hurrying down the path after him; one hand grasped her hat that had come unpinned in her haste, her hair a disheveled halo about her head, her cheeks flushed with the exercise.

"Duchesse." Montrond gave her an elegant bow, smiling as he rose. "You are a most charming woman, so kind to have invited me. I am afraid I must leave, business awaits—more urgent than I had initially realized."

"Let me escort you to your carriage, monsieur." The duchess took his arm in that disarmingly informal manner that she had.

"Really, it is not necessary. I would not want you to neglect your other guests."

"It is necessary, monsieur." Glancing quickly around, the duchess pulled Montrond past a tall boxwood hedge where they could no longer be observed by the rest of the party. "I had hoped for a better opportunity... I don't know whether you are aware, but I have played the role of society hostess to the leaders of the Whig party for years, and I understand you are here to talk with Pitt..."

"Pitt? You do not mean the former English prime minister?" Montrond laughed. "Duchesse, mon dieu, someone has been teasing you! I am not a politician and have no interest in politics. I am merely a gentleman traveler, at your service." He bowed again, deeply and flawlessly.

Ignoring his polite deflection, the duchess continued: "The Whig party is willing to create a coalition government with Pitt, if an understanding can be reached with France."

"An understanding, Duchesse?"

"An agreement with Napoleon is not worth the paper it's printed on. If a treaty of cooperation can be agreed upon with his successor... Let us not mince words, monsieur; we do not have the time. If the rumors are true—that Pitt is secretly funneling money to the French Resistance, that he is actively supporting, financially and otherwise, attempts against Napoleon's life, and if he is successful in such an attempt, then the old Whig grandees, who have been hostile to Pitt these eighteen years past, will put aside any differences and support the creation of a coalition government, with Pitt taking a second term as prime minister."

"If what you say is true, and I am not saying that it is, why are you approaching me? Why not send a Whig representative directly to Pitt?"

"Because we want the French to know that if they succeed in overthrowing Napoleon, they will be allied with a strong coalition government in England. We will go to any lengths to overthrow Napoleon and defend England from invasion, in that the Whigs and the Tories are united. Also because the people I represent are ostensibly Addington supporters and if he does not fall as expected, they cannot be seen in open negotiation with the opposition."

"I see. Well, Duchesse, this is all très interessant. Certainly, if I do happen to see that illustrious personage, the former Prime Minister William Pitt, I will pass on your fascinating comments. Au revoir, Duchesse."

"Thank you, monsieur, for coming...and do not forget—"

"Duchesse, you may rely upon me." Montrond pressed her arm warmly before turning to the carriage that awaited him.

# 24.

The elegantly dressed man strode down the cobblestoned rue de la Citadelle; he followed the street over the ancient Roman bridge across the River Nive from the fifteenth-century Porte St. Jacques to the Porte d'Espagne. It amused him, this pretension to grandiosity. The town of Saint-Jean-Pied-de-Port, the capital of the tiny kingdom of Basse-Navarre that burrowed into the valley at the foothills of the Pyrenees, consisted primarily of this one street enclosed with sandstone walls. It had traditionally been a pivotal town on the Way of St. James, the medieval pilgrimage route to Santiago de Compostela that straddled the base of the Roncevaux Pass across the mountains into Spain. The routes from Paris, Vézelay, and Le Puy-en-Velay all met at Saint-Jean-Pied-de-Port, the pilgrims' final stop before the arduous mountain crossing.

The town was sleepier now; the pilgrims no longer came. L'Aigle preferred it that way. The anonymity was important to him, and there were fewer and fewer places where he could truly be at ease. He passed the crumbling Gothic church Notre-Dame-du-Bout-du-Pont and paused at a nondescript wooden door to an old house of pink and gray schist. He had chosen this house because, unlike the others on the row, it stood alone, divided from its neighbors on either side by a pedestrian path. It commanded a view up-river, where the Nive sluggishly wound its way from Bayonne, and down-river, to where it entered the Ossès Valley. The lower floor of the house consisted of thick sandstone walls; the upper possessed tall windows that opened to catch the summer breeze and a balcony that perched out over the river. The house could not be approached on any side without his being aware of it; the only entrances, other than the wooden door below, were the two windows on either side and the central balcony in front, all of which he had secured.

The old women who sat out under the porch eaves in the fading evening light, as regular as sunrise and sunset, had been born, raised, married, and, almost inevitably, would die in this town. They were the matriarchs of Saint-Jean-Pied-de-Port, and their eyes, though dimmed and rheumy with age, were watchful. L'Aigle did not mind this perpetual scrutiny; it protected him. Any untoward activity would immediately come to his attention, passed on from the wrinkled matriarchs through untold inhabitants of the town and eventually to the postman, who felt obliged to keep his important patron fully informed.

The local postman Jean de Vin, who also served as the town's grocer, knew the man as Monsieur de Vallete, a wealthy landowner from northern France who was seeking a quiet residence free from the tempestuous and often unfriendly politics of Paris and Napoleon Bonaparte. L'Aigle had secured the house several months ago and engaged Vin's sister as a housekeeper; the end result of which, rather annoyingly, produced perpetually effusive displays of gratitude from her brother.

L'Aigle unlocked the house and, more from habit than from any real concern, checked the thin silk-like strand of cotton that he had placed across the door- jamb. The housekeeper cleaned under his watchful gaze and kept him supplied with groceries while he was in residence, but otherwise the house was left unoccupied.

He was tired. The Madrid job had been more complicated than he had anticipated, and he was in need of a few days' rest. Upstairs, he sat heavily on the jacquard- embroidered bedspread. He had opened the balcony doors, and the cool northern breeze stirred the sluggish waters of the Nive, as if urging it to greater speed. Large terracotta pots on the balcony hosted his collection of les salads amères d'hiver, dutifully watered and weeded by his housekeeper. L'Aigle was rarely at home long enough to eat them, but the sight of the rubbery wine-dark leaves reminded him of his father. They had traveled in Italy together, when L'Aigle was young. A rare excursion. A "culinary adventure," as his father had described it. Four days of devoted paternal attention and a peak of childhood happiness amid a plateau of parental distraction. That was a time when only salads left a bitter taste in his mouth, years before the troubles began. A time when his future seemed calmly assured.

He was getting older, he acknowledged; it was time to retire. L'Aigle was tired of killing. His reflexes were not what they had once been, and each job seemed to exhaust him physically and mentally. More time was spent recovering from each assignment than it had taken to complete them. Eight years, and what had he achieved? Napoleon's decisive victories at Marengo and Hohenlinden had eroded the Austrian military and culminated in the humiliating surrender of the Treaty of Lunéville.

L'Aigle had attempted to stem the Napoleonic tide. He had initially selected specific targets due to their participation in the occupation and subsequent dismemberment of his country, and then for the atrocities that had been committed by the armies that remained behind. Then, as the French victories rolled in, he had targeted generals and government officials. It had been a cold and calculating agenda, designed to eliminate some and promote others who advocated returning the Austrian borders to their pre-Napoleonic state.

He had been scrupulously careful to cover his tracks, and his wealth and connections had enabled him to virtually disappear when and as he liked. Clients contacted him through a drop-point at a café in the Section des Invalides, the owner of which received a monthly stipend for his trouble and discretion.

Certainly, his reputation had become as intimidating as it was professional: he had ambassadors, generals, statesmen, even a czar to his credit, but he had little pride in these accomplishments. How many were there altogether? Eighteen, three of them women. Not many compared to other political agents active in continental Europe, but then he was not just a weapon for hire; he was a political assassin, and a particular one at that. Each and every target he had acquired—some of whom he had been paid generously to eliminate—had played a role in the destruction of the Holy Roman Empire, in the glory that should have been his heritage.

He should have targeted Napoleon Bonaparte to begin with, he thought bitterly. After all, wasn't Bonparte the one who had so effectively intimidated his uncle and begun this humiliating process? But the newly minted emperor was an extremely difficult target. He moved perpetually, in secrecy, and always under heavy guard. Besides, L'Aigle was too concerned with Austrian politics to allow himself to become distracted by French considerations, but any opportunity to thwart Napoleon was one he relished. And, he admitted to himself, he wanted to see the emperor fall. Death was too easy a fate for such a man; Napoleon's martyrdom a risk L'Aigle refused to run. He wanted to see the emperor cowed and in chains, disgraced and downtrodden. He wanted Napoleon to feel the pain of his own political demise.

A tentative rapping at the door roused him from his vengeful reverie. The housekeeper? He had only just returned from Spain and had not yet informed anyone of his return. Presumably, he had been sighted en route to his house on the Nive. The quiet indolence of this all-but-forgotten town belied the rapidity with which news was transmitted. It put Napoleon's new telegraph system to shame, L'Aigle thought wryly as he spied the rotund figure of Jean de Vin through a crevice in the porch floor. Not a flattering perspective: the shiny dome of a balding head caught the late evening light, beneath which protruded the wide girth of a man of healthy appetites.

L'Aigle descended the stairs and opened the door. "Monsieur de Vin." His tone combined just the right amount of polite cordiality with aristocratic reserve.

"Ah, Monsieur de Vallete. I heard you had arrived." Vin beamed to reveal a surprisingly fine set of incisors, his deep-set eyes almost disappearing in a generous mound of cheek. "We are so happy to welcome you back." He was dressed in his Sunday finery: a dark mustard dress-coat that had fit him a decade previously but now stretched across his middle and frayed at the sleeves, under which were a shirt and cravat— both an indeterminate shade of gray. Bottle-green breeches completed his wardrobe.

"What may I do for you, Monsieur de Vin?" Again, L'Aigle inwardly marveled at the haste that must have prompted Vin to his door; he could envision the red-faced exertions that must have accompanied the forcible insertion of body into suit—one much smaller than the other.

"On the contrary, monsieur, I am most happy to be of service to you…"

L'Aigle waited patiently through the ritual period of bowing and scraping, again treated to a view of sweat-sheened scalp. Finally, it became apparent that a letter had arrived for Monsieur de Vallete marked Urgent, and Vin had, naturally, hurried over, as soon as he was aware Vallete had returned, to deliver this document personally. "I do hope it is not bad tidings, monsieur," Vin declared, eyebrows raised in suggestive sympathy, his fatly florid face ready to assume any expression that might be suitable.

"Thank you, monsieur, for your trouble." L'Aigle deposited a gleaming coin in one sweaty palm, and, with a polite yet dismissive nod of his head, shut the door against the open-mouthed postman.

The letter had reached him via a circuitous route that he had set in place years before. The café owner who served as his Parisian drop-point would, upon receipt of client requests, forward them on to a shabby apartment in rue de l'Abbaye. The letters were subsequently collected by an elderly shopkeeper and sent, along with his own associated packages, to his sister in Ossès, a few miles northwest of Saint- Jean-Pied-de-Port. Thence they were directed to the prompt attention of Jean de Vin. This elaborate itinerary added a week or so to the interval between transmission and receipt but served to maintain and protect his anonymity—a consideration he valued above all others.

Ripping open the envelope, he discovered a copy of the Parisian Mercure. This paper, like others sold in the French capital, comprised primarily miscellaneous lists of advertisements. The remainder of the content was so severely censored that much that was compelling had little chance of getting into the papers at all; indeed, the Mercure had degenerated into such an insipid rag that, even in its third year of publication, it was the vogue to laugh at its absurdities and think it fit only for the parochial rustic who could not get much else to read—which was, of course, exactly the cover L'Aigle was assuming. Taking the paper inside, he sat at his desk, dipped his quill into a pot of ink and bent over the outspread pages. Using his usual number code, utilizing the first four advertisements, and selecting the letter that corresponded to the appropriate number, he decoded the first part of the message written in ink at the base of the paper: *Paris. Irish target. Wolfe Trant. 750. John.* A job in Paris. To kill an Irishman. He would have tossed the paper into the fire but for the offered payment. Seven hundred and fifty thousand pounds! A veritable king's ransom for ridding the world of one insignificant Irishman. Wolfe Trant. L'Aigle had never heard of him...or had he? Something about the name sounded familiar. Where had he heard it before?

Bending over the paper, L'Aigle completed the rest of the numerical translation. Apparently, this Wolfe Trant was providing Napoleon with the navigation routes for the invasion of England. The message was signed only John. The same signatory who had hired him in Russia to kill the czar: an Englishman of powerful means and influence who sought, yet again, to manipulate international intrigue to English benefit. It had suited L'Aigle's agenda to replace the maniacal Paul I with his more moderate son Alexander I, so he had been happy to oblige "John" in his initial request. The payment then had been as generous, not that L'Aigle needed the money. He was, however, a cautious man by nature and, having lost everything he valued most, the rapidly escalating personal fortune he had accumulated was of some comfort. The lesson he had learned earliest, as well as the one that had cost him the most, was that life was callously fickle and unpredictable. He sometimes wondered (his mother's fervent Catholicism surviving in fits and starts) whether God had given him over to the Devil—cast him out as Lucifer had been; a glorious destiny ground into ashes and dust. But this "John" interested him. And as much as English interests paralleled his own, he was happy to relieve them of their king's fortune. England served as a last bastion against Napoleonic ambition, and for the island nation to fall to the French tyrant…it was not to be borne. And if he could prevent such an eventuality by one simple job, well then, so be it. So much for his vacation. L'Aigle climbed the stairs, his mind already on Paris and the Irishman who awaited him there.

# 25.

It was a quiet morning. A light, fitful breeze softly stirred the pennants and flags of the ships moored below, sent wisps of cloud scudding leisurely across the oyster sky, and created small dimples and pits in the sea until it resembled a plate of finely hammered silver. The tumult of the previous night's gale had subsided, and Wolfe could almost see the coast of France that lay, shrouded in mist, twenty-five miles to the east.

The fishing community of Deal had always been of strategic importance. Situated on the English Channel, eight miles north of Dover, the castle and port of Deal overlooked the Downs, a naturally sheltered anchorage that served a variety of vessels. Four miles beyond the Downs, lay the notorious Goodwin Sands, a chalk seabed that not only shifted ominously but emerged from the sea with the ebbing tide; it required a skilled, and often locally experienced, pilot to negotiate these treacherous shallows.

Wolfe had been here before—many times. This was where, two years ago on a winter's night in January, he had almost lost the Isuelt on her maiden voyage out of Belfast. The Iseult and her crew had been caught in a blinding tumult of wind and spray as the gale-driven surf roared and lashed violently over the Sands. He could still recall the eerie sounds of the unseen bell-buoy and the ominous wash of shoal water heard through the murk of dense fog. The Isuelt had narrowly avoided being stranded. Once caught, the tides would sweep the sand from under the vessel's bow and stern to leave her supported only amidships. Wolfe had seen wrecks of other ships that had met this fate: keels snapped in two, jagged ends of vessels protruding from the surf, a lonely mast entangled with the tattered remnants of sail.

It had been six months since he had last negotiated his way through the Goodwin Sands, and even in that short time Deal had changed considerably. Numerous vessels crowded the anchorage, their masts thickly clustered against the ashen sky. He noticed at least twenty massive Indiamen bound for Bombay, Madras, or Calcutta; traders headed to the Baltic; and troopships for the Mediterranean that swung gently at anchor, awaiting a favorable wind to carry them down the Channel or across the North Sea.

Wolfe closed his eyes and turned his face up to the pale warmth of the early sun, breathing deeply the seaside tang of salt, tar, and fish.

For a moment, his mind turned to his childhood, and he was again wet and gasping in the shallows of Donegal Bay, dark head emerging like a seal from the depths, arms gathering the soft, thick strands of kelp. He spread the sea-grass, feathered and wet like the hair of a sidh, across the warm boulders and laid himself beside it, baring his young chest to the warm Irish wind. When the seaweed had dried to long, shriveled strips of dark, twisted rubber powdered white with salt, he stretched, yawned. Emptied as it was of water and volume, the kelp packed tightly into the twin burlap sacks he slung across his thin shoulders for the homeward journey. Wolfe had spent many years scrambling up the mica ridges of Dooish Mountain on his way to Donegal Bay, then staggering back under sacks of pungent oarweed harvested at low-tide, salt staining his clothes and crusting his lashes. He would deposit the sacks at his mother's feet, whereupon she would exclaim over the weight and size of them and the necessary strength of the man who had carried them so very far. Then, with the most dazzling of smiles, she would grasp him tightly in a hug so warm and completely enveloping that he thought he would die for the joy of it.

"Mo far darocha, ye've come back 'cross the mountain to me," she would say, cupping his cheek affectionately with one calloused palm. Far Darocha, after the Dark Man who served the fairy queen, renowned for the speed of his steed and his quietly indomitable will.

Like most of their neighbors, they grew potatoes. The dried kelp was mulched for garden fertilizer or burnt into potash sold to Nidden Mack, an itinerant trader who supplied Kinsale Glass in County Cork. And so the family was fed, at least until the hungry months. July and August loomed darkly on the Irish calendar, for that was when the previous year's crop became inedible and the current crop was not yet ready for harvest. If they were lucky, they might have enough saved to purchase oat or barley meal from price-gouging dealers. Otherwise, his mother resorted to begging along the roadside.

A trio of sailors roared out some boisterous Yankee sea chantey:
*Away Santy,*
*My dear Annie.*
*Oh, you New York girls,*
*Can't you dance the polka?*

Wolfe opened his eyes, and the hungry months receded. The clamor of the dock-front reasserted itself; the coastal brine of an Irish sea was replaced by that of an English one. The chains of harbor cranes, relieved of their weight, clattered as they were winched up again. Some captain bellowed orders through cupped hands, and empty barrels were rolled along the cobblestones with an echoing, drum-like sound.

The memories of his childhood did not sour him or haunt him as much as they hardened him; they served to sharpen his intention like the point of a spear. For now, he felt a renewed sense of purpose; as satisfying as the commercial success of the linen factory had been, the benefits were localized. For Wolfe, as for all Irish, it was the national oppression that most plagued him. His mother may not have suffered the horrific ordeal of the African slaves' transatlantic journey, or been chafed raw by iron manacles, but she was just as surely subjugated. Her English master was a little further away, across the Irish Sea, but one whose will could be just as easily imposed to deny religion, livelihood, shelter, sustenance, and thus life itself.

Perhaps, just perhaps, this could be a sea-change for Ireland, Wolfe reflected as he made his way through the bustling docks. But it would take time, and he had never been a patient man. Violent dramatic action tended to inspire a counter-response, and as long as each bloodied combatant eyed each other over his fists, the carnage would continue. And the Irish would always rise to the battle, regardless of their injuries, despite broken ribs and skin split to the bone; they would blink back the blood and grin as they crooked one finger in wicked invitation: *C'mon, ye bloody English—do yer worst!* And they had.

Wolfe negotiated his way through a crowd of flaxen-haired sailors chattering German and climbed the cobblestoned streets toward the castle that perched above the town. Deal Castle was a squat, square structure which had long since been transformed into a utilitarian watchtower with all eyes on France.

Wolfe made his way through the state rooms, crowded with burly, hardened men in the green uniform of the Cinque Ports Volunteers.

They were not the volunteers their uniforms proclaimed them to be, Wolfe knew; they were the military elite who composed Pitt's secret Black Hawk Force, trained at Shorncliff Camp near Walmer Castle in subversive warfare, espionage, and infiltration.

Pitt was leaning over a table, talking with Dundas and General Moore. "Montreuil, St. Omer and Bruges," Moore was saying, his thick finger stabbing at the map. "And then, of course, in addition to the main encampment at Boulogne, there are smaller corps stationed near the provincial towns of Arras, Amiens, Tournai, Meaux, and Compiègne. We think he is capable of mustering approximately one hundred sixty thousand soldiers. Sutton verified this for us."

"He was a good agent," Pitt agreed.

"Sutton indicated that the Liane River has been dredged and widened, and more than half a mile of quays built to accommodate one hundred gunboats and smaller landing craft. Preparations for invasion are escalating," Moore continued. "It is just a question of where Napoleon will land. Hopefully, something Mr. Trant can help us with."

"What seems most likely from a military perspective?" Wolfe asked, leaning over the map.

"Well, there isn't enough sheltered water on the Cornish coast, and Plymouth is well-defended. The Isle of Wight is obviously a dead-end for an invading force, even if it were successful," Pitt began thoughtfully. "Weymouth Bay is sheltered; the beach accessible. The beaches between Brighton and Folkestone are all at risk. The west side of Dungeness is vulnerable in an easterly wind, and the east side in a westerly."

"There are many beaches suitable for invasion along the east coast north of the Thames estuary," Moore added. "However, those would place Napoleon increasingly distant from London, which we have to assume is his primary objective." Pitt and Moore spoke with the weariness of men who had been over this subject a countless number of times.

"However," Pitt concluded, "given our intelligence that Napoleon is seeking a guide, a traitor I should say, who would be willing to pilot the French fleet through the Goodwin Sands to the Downs, we have to concentrate on that as our primary line of defense."

"Our own front door," Dundas mused. "Who would have thought?"

"It is the perfect location," Moore pointed out. "Once through the Goodwin Sands, you have the Downs, and the flat beaches from

Ramsgate to Walmer are ideal for the rapid and efficient deployment of cavalry and artillery."

"Of course, this assumes they can slip past the naval blockade," Pitt maintained. "Not something Napoleon has managed to do thus far. The ships-of-the-line are on a rotating repair and replenishment schedule that maintains a formidable presence in the Channel. Despite Napoleon's numbers, his fleet remains confined to port and his sailors largely inexperienced."

"And what, then, of the French fleet in the Mediterranean?" Wolfe asked. "Is there a chance they can slip past Gibraltar?"

Moore, leaning over the map, replied, "Intelligence tells us that the only real force in the Mediterranean consists of the eleven ships-of-the-line under Villeneuve in Toulon." His thick finger tapped the coast of France. "Vice-Admiral Horatio Nelson commands in the Mediterranean, and his sole purpose is to pin Villeneuve in, to keep him confined to southern France or Spain."

"Napoleon Bonaparte, as all of you are painfully aware, is a master tactician," Pitt interjected somberly. "It would be very unwise to underestimate him. At this stage, we will prepare our defenses based upon the assumption that Napoleon has a plan to evade the blockade that will prove successful. To adequately do this, further intelligence is critical. This is where Wolfe comes in."

"And if the information that Napoleon is seeking a guide through the Goodwin Sands is a ruse?" Wolfe asked.

"Well, then I guess you will be out of a job," Pitt replied grimly. "And God help the rest of us."

# 26.

The darkened sloop glided soundlessly toward the rugged cliffs of Normandy ten miles east of Dieppe. The half-moon cast the vessel in a pale blue light before retiring behind the thick cloudbank that scudded before a rising northeasterly wind. Close inspection would have revealed that the flags that snapped and writhed from her mast were the signature blue and yellow of the Compagnie Maritime Belge. Although, why a merchant trading company from Belgium was operating a vessel highly unsuitable for cargo transportation off the coast of Normandy in the darkness of night would have perplexed any given observer. For French troops, however, it would provide enough of a mystery to give pause to cannon fire. Belgium had recently been gathered to the French bosom, her vessels confiscated for the larger cause. Perhaps, this was a surreptitious foray ordered by the emperor himself to assess English ship positions? The ambiguity would be enough—at least, that is what Pitt hoped.

On a rising tide, the vessel closed the distance to the shore, and a light flickered briefly from the clifftops three hundred feet above the sea. Once, twice, three times. A small boat descended from the sloop to the dark swells. Black-clad seamen pulled on muffled oars, and a shadowed figure clambered ashore on the wet sands below an unobtrusive crevice in the cliffs. This route was well-known to smugglers. The deep fissure rose steeply in a narrow path that cut its way through the sandy soil to the fields above and emerged in a tangled profusion of scrubby holm oak. A knotted rope was lowered down the path, and Wolfe was assisted to the cliff-top by silent, burly men who were waiting above for him. One held a horse ready for him to ride. Nodding his thanks, Wolfe cantered through the darkness toward the safe-house at La Poterie, where he would collect his papers before traveling on to Paris.

Prior to leaving Walmer, Wolfe had been briefed by Jean Vierdieu, a French covert agent who served as an intermediary, carrying messages and information between the Resistance and Pitt's Black Hawk operatives. Vierdieu appeared just as he should have been—darkly intent. His black glossy hair descended to a jutting widow's peak that was mirrored by a sharply pointed jaw. Dark brows drew together in a perpetual frown, beneath which narrowed eyes were frigidly insistent, mouth tight and unsmiling. Wolfe had the distinct impression Vierdieu strongly disapproved of the man, the mission, or perhaps both. The briefing had been succinct.

"Your papers have been prepared and signed by Francois Ateuil, assistant to the minister of interior," Vierdieu had explained curtly in his impeccable English. "You will collect them here at La Poterie." A long, dark finger stabbed a map of coastal France that lay on the table.

"Is Monsieur Ateuil a member of the Resistance?" Wolfe had asked.

"That is of no concern to you," Vierdieu had replied brusquely. "The Resistance survives because of the anonymity of its members. All you need to know is that Monsieur Ateuil is important enough so that you should not be questioned too closely, but not so much so that it should be surprising you have procured his endorsement. You must be very careful never to lose your papers. Your French is acceptable, but your accent is…" Vierdieu's mouth tightened, corners descending in displeasure as if the mutilation of his native tongue was the final insult from which he could not recover. "Needless to say, you would never pass for a Parisian," he continued. "You are Jean Manot, a Belgian wine merchant from La Chapelle. There are other dangers, however. As a foreigner you will be under particular scrutiny, and as a traveler you will be watched even more closely."

"By whom?"

"Fouché's secret police, agents, informers, spies. They are everywhere. They see everything, and they report back to him. The agent that is discovered will be tortured and killed. I think you understand why I do not give you any information that is not vital to the success of your own mission?" Vierdieu asked, his tone flat, his dark eyes assessing Wolfe's face for a flash of dread or anxiety.

Wolfe bared his teeth in what passed for a smile, reflecting with some grim satisfaction that Vierdieu would not read anything akin to fear in his features. Wolfe had learned early to school his expression, to hide his emotions behind a rigidly implacable exterior. Despite having left that life behind, he was still a fighter, and everyone was the enemy. Don't let them see. Don't let them in. Don't let them know. Pain had become his friend. And he, too, was not afraid to die.

Vierdieu continued, his tone somewhat less terse. "There is a strict check on travelers. Even the most wretched peddler must have valid papers that are up to date. Ordinary Parisians who are putting up relatives visiting from the country are supposed to declare their guests to the commissiare. They don't, of course, but the checks are vigilant nonetheless. Lodging houses are particularly susceptible to raids. Just remember your cover."

In addition to his papers supplied by Vierdieu, Wolfe had other documents: letters procured by Pitt with associated credentials from the General Committee of Catholics, as well as the Catholics of Dublin, identifying him as a leader of the United Irishmen and their particular agent in the upcoming Irish-French collaboration. How Pitt acquired these seemingly authentic testimonials, Wolfe did not know, and knew better than to ask. The English government, or this shadowy form of it, was influential indeed.

Later in the evening, Wolfe retreated to his room, pain silvering through his skull in accordance with the beat of his pulse. The doctor had prescribed sedatives. Wolfe preferred brandy; and he had noticed a bottle beside his bed, courtesy of his host. So thoughtful, the English. In passing Pitt's office door, which stood slightly ajar, Wolfe overheard his conversation with Vierdieu:

"What do you hope to accomplish with this man?" Vierdieu's heated tone could be heard within. "Do you seriously imagine he will survive a week in Fouché's Paris?"

"I imagine not," Pitt replied, his tone as careless and nonchalant as Vierdieu's was impassioned and precise.

"What?" Vierdieu exclaimed in short surprise.

"I do not want him to be too convincing. Certainly, he will need to evade Fouché for a day or two until he can make contact with Talleyrand, and then with Napoleon. Wolfe Trant is perfect, Jean. He is an Irishman. He hates the English. That is who he is, and *that* is what Napoleon must see if we are to pull this off. Besides that, I have arranged for Primrose to keep an eye on him."

"Mon dieu!" Verdieu hissed, his voice tight with anger. "With respect, Monsieur Pitt, you go too far! This man could endanger everything we have accomplished in the past ten years!"

"With respect, Monsieur Vierdieu," Pitt replied, his tone measured and firm with a slight chill. "You do not know me well, so I will forgive your assumption that I would willfully jeopardize the cause to which I, too, have given a vast quantity of time, energy, and money—all of which are in desperately short supply."

A pause ensued in which Wolfe padded quietly to his room. There was a logic to Pitt's words. But behind the eloquence, behind the reason and rationale, Wolfe knew that ultimately he was expendable, bait with which to catch an emperor. But he would not go quietly and obediently; he was not a sheep to be prodded by English sticks. He would proceed with this agenda as long as it suited him, as long as it suited Irish interests. Pitt was merely another adversary in the arena against whom he needed to constantly keep up his guard. Wolfe leaned over the basin and splashed his face with water. In the mirror above, he saw the face of a stranger: a shaggy mane of hair, fiercely dark eyebrows, and skin drawn too tightly across pale features. The bruises had faded and finally disappeared, and now the still-livid scar that streaked across his right brow like a tart's lipstick was the only source of color. That and those blue eyes that stared back at him with the glittering intensity of a madman.

Muffling a curse, he reached for the bottle of brandy and took a deep swallow. He had an hour or two to numb the pain that knifed through his head with a severity that left him gasping. Wolfe prowled the small confines of his room, then paused at the shuttered window that overlooked a garden shrouded in shadow and gloom. The horizon was obscured by cloudbanks to the east, which boded well for his late-night infiltration into France. He was on edge, muscles tightly poised—a not unusual circumstance for Wolfe, who was restless by nature—a by-product, perhaps, of his life lived in the ring where attack could come from any quarter. He had a constant need for movement: foot tapping, fingers incessantly moving in an unconscious rhythm against his thigh, head swiveling, eyes narrowed and alert. Usually, he slept deeply, heavily immobile, as if exhausted by the physical strain of his waking hours.

Tonight, however, there was little hope of rest, despite the brandy. The pounding agony in his head would see to that. Mutt, sensing Wolfe's tension, kept him company. Every so often, the dog would whine anxiously, tail between his legs, head cocked to one side, as if seeking an explanation as to why the man so obstinately refused the comfort of a soft, warm bed. Mutt's tail wagged slightly when Wolfe's hand absently patted his head, but his master would not sleep that night.

# 27.

Montrond tapped the forward compartment of his hackney cab, signaling to the driver his readiness to move on. Rain lashed against the windowpane and drummed on the thick leather roof. Beyond, beneath a thick overhang of fog, he could see the heave and swell of waves crested by plumes of white spray. The Channel was a seething mass of dark water whipped to a frenzy by a wild southwesterly. He would not be sailing today.

"Merde," he muttered under his breath.

Water had started to darken the perimeter of the collapsible roof and drip in increasingly steady rivulets down the inside of the window. Montrond barely noticed; his clothes already hung around him in sodden discomfort.

He had departed from Walmer Castle half an hour before in order to rendezvous with the man who would take him across the Channel. However, the grizzled captain, warm and dry within his thick woolen sweater and oilskins, merely shook his head as Montrond, increasingly desperate and increasingly drenched opposite, pleaded his case. The man was not to be persuaded, and the rapidly escalating sums Montrond offered seemed to provoke nothing but an equally steady and growing disapproval.

Pitt, assessing the weather conditions with a practiced eye, had warned him the Channel was not to be crossed this day, but Montrond had felt he must make the attempt. Now, as the coachman returned him to his inn, he shivered in his chilly wraps and thought about his earlier meeting with Pitt. He had arrived at Walmer Castle directly from his lodgings in London, having stopped there briefly to gather his belongings after leaving the duchess' residence. Pitt had been seated at his office desk when Dundas had ushered him in. Montrond had steeled himself to present his customary polite façade, but the effort had been a strain to him. After exchanging the minimal customary pleasantries, the two men had settled down to business.

"Monsieur Pitt, I am concerned at the degree to which this agenda has become general knowledge throughout your government. As you are aware, Duc de Talleyrand has gone to great lengths to assist you in this matter with no little danger to his own person—" Montrond began heatedly.

"And I have the greatest appreciation of that fact," Pitt interjected. "The information you bring is most regrettable, but it changes nothing. It simply serves as an accelerant to our primary objective which, like yours, revolves around the removal of Napoleon from office. I assume you remain committed to this purpose?"

"My commitment to this purpose is not in question, Monsieur Pitt. Instead, I am concerned about the exposure of Duc de Talleyrand's association with your organization. Do you realize what that would mean for him? He has placed his trust in you, Monsieur Pitt; I advise you not to abuse it."

"Monsieur de Montrond, please..." Pitt began, raising a conciliatory palm. "I understand your concern, and please keep in mind that I take the health and well-being of Duc de Talleyrand as seriously as I do my own. I promised him the highest degree of discretion, and to that end his name has never been mentioned other than to Mal Dundas, whom I trust beyond all others. This conversation you overheard points to a conspiracy within the Whig party, one which targets Wolfe Trant. It has no association with Duc de Talleyrand."

The men were interrupted by an unobtrusive knock on the study door. It was Hester, bearing a tea tray and a tall glass of rose-colored liquid. She deposited the glass firmly before her uncle with a pointed glance. Pitt sighed heavily, acknowledging her with an exaggerated wince and a surprisingly brilliant smile. Hester, tray under one arm, frowned sternly at Pitt, then retreated, closing the door softly behind her.

"Supposedly, this concoction will cure me," Pitt told Montrond, as the former prime minister dubiously eyed the contents of his glass. "The doctors have diagnosed a diffuse form of gout, whatever the hell that means. I am looking at my legacy, Monsieur de Montrond. I am hoping for more time, but I am not counting on it. The only matter that concerns me, at this point in time, is an immediate cessation of hostilities with France and the return of a stable governing power to your country. I understand that is also Duc de Talleyrand's aim. My question to you, then, is this: do you feel that the duke would wish to continue in his endeavors regardless of this…complication? Or are you of the opinion that we should disregard his offer to facilitate a meeting between Wolfe and Napoleon?"

Montrond was taken aback. He had expected defensive excuses and evasions, interspersed with political promises for an impossibly pristine relationship with the future monarchical government of France. He had not expected the simple strength of Pitt's honesty, nor had he expected the power to himself decide the immediate course of action. However, he knew what Talleyrand's answer would be as well as if his friend lounged in the chair adjacent to his own.

"We proceed, Monsieur Pitt." Montrond reached inside his coat pocket and withdrew the sheaf of papers that he had carried across the Channel.

Yes, the meeting had progressed as Talleyrand had intended, with the rendezvous between the French foreign minister and the Irish spy detailed. However, Montrond could not help but feel a growing unease at the seemingly cavalier attitude Pitt had maintained toward the spy upon whose life an attempt was, even now, being manufactured. As the conversation had drawn to a close, Pitt had accompanied Montrond to a hackney cab waiting in the keep. Beneath the shelter of a broad black umbrella, Pitt had advised him to mention the assassination plot to no one other than the duke. "Are you going to tell Monsieur Trant?" Montrond asked as he climbed into the waiting cab. The driver above sat huddled in oilskins, his horse stoic beneath the lashing rain that darkened his flanks and ran in rivulets from his nose.

"Absolutely not," Pitt replied shortly, before nodding to the driver.

The wooden wheels of the cab splashed across the stones of the keep and down the road that wound toward the village of Deal. Pitt had sent instructions to a trustworthy captain who would return Montrond to Bruges at the earliest opportunity. "May not be until tomorrow," he had reflected, as the wind tugged at the umbrella and the rain fell in sheets.

Montrond, anxious to relay the events of the previous few days to Talleyrand and give him the opportunity to disengage from this entire enterprise before it was too late, proceeded to the appointed dock despite the increasing perilousness of the weather. But it was as Pitt had predicted. Montrond was Deal bound, at least for that night.

# 28.

## WALMER CASTLE. DEAL, ENGLAND
### *December 4, 1803*

*Dearest Mother, in case you heard an exaggerated account of my having been unwell, let me assure you I am well recovered from an attack brought on partly by a sudden change of weather and partly by a little over-exercise in shooting...*

Pitt put down his quill with a sigh. He was in the habit of writing often to his mother, whom he had not seen in several years, and did not want her alarmed by rumors of his ill-health. However, he was having difficulty concentrating on a letter that by necessity concerned itself with trivialities. His meeting with Montrond had disturbed him more than he had let on.

"Certainly, you can't tell Wolfe," Dundas had concurred. "What if he backs out?"

"Not an option we can accept at this point. Not with the Grande Armée breathing down our necks," Pitt agreed. "But I am not entirely comfortable with sending another man off to his death without any semblance of warning."

"You've contacted Primrose," Dundas reminded him. "She can provide some protection over the next few days. When does Wolfe meet with Talleyrand?"

"Thursday. Two days from today. Giving him just enough time to get to Paris; hopefully, meeting with Napoleon Friday or Saturday, with the whole business concluded by the end of the week. Which will give us a brief amount of time to arrange ourselves accordingly." There was a moment's silence as both men contemplated the logistics of what that entailed.

"Shit," Dundas exclaimed succinctly.

"Yes, my sentiments exactly," Pitt replied with a sharp exhalation. "Shit."

"We can muster our Cinque Port Volunteers, obviously, and have some confidence in their ability to perform, but..." Dundas left the rest unsaid. It was obvious to both men that Addington's preparations were wholly inadequate, that should Napoleon manage to cross the Channel, all would be lost, and there was precious little they could do about it.

"Right. Brandy?" Pitt poured a healthy dose for them both. "Ironic, isn't it?" He rested on the chair's edge, glass cradled between both hands, his voice a strained whisper in the quiet room. "Now that we have left Ireland in utter despair, after all this political manipulation, contrived economic ruin, religious discrimination…we will rely upon one of her rebel leaders, one who, at the Battle of New Ross, was intent on spilling English blood, to now provide our own salvation." Pitt laughed into his brandy, a hollow sound that had little humor in it. "And why should he not betray us at the first opportunity, Mal? Why should he not seek French military assistance against the neighbor that has so oppressed him for centuries? God, I believe I would."

Dundas, brow furrowed in thought, drew up a chair opposite Pitt's. "Fortunately for us, Wolfe is an intelligent man. Hopefully, he is basing his decisions not on the past, which would condemn us all to hell, but on the future and how Ireland is best served going forward. Remember, the history of the French in Ireland is as inglorious as that of the English; the French deserted the Irish at Bantry Bay. Napoleon is battling the entire European continent. How important, really, is the independence of Ireland to him?" Dundas shrugged.

"I hope you are right, Mal. I hope you are right," Pitt murmured fervently.

A discreet knock at the door preceded the arrival of James, a silver tray held between his white-gloved hands. "A letter just arrived for you, sir." His voice was a deeply modulated pitch, pleasing to the ear, his words precise but weighted with the somber gravity suited to one in the service of such an important man.

"Thank you, James." The butler silently withdrew as Pitt broke the seal with his forefinger and rapidly scanned the contents. "It's from Dragonfly."

Dragonfly was the codename for the mole buried within the London division of the United Irishmen. The past few years had been volatile ones, with a series of failed harvests prompting protest after protest as bread prices soared. This scarcity, combined with the heavy taxation required to finance an unpopular war and the ever-present fear of the French forces silently massing across the Channel, had resulted in the mushrooming of popular societies, some of which were intent on subverting the Addington administration, or utterly replacing it. Overstretched, undermanned, and increasingly erratic, Addington did little to either address these fears or quell the societies that promulgated them. Pitt, however, who had been active in intelligence gathering since leaving office, had various sources within many of these societies; ironically, none concerned him more than the activities of the United Irishmen, the very organization he was attempting to covertly utilize as a front for Wolfe Trant in Paris.

Dragonfly had alerted them several days before to an imminent uprising—the most ambitious of any undertaken in London—planned by the United Irishmen. This letter provided more information. "They are planning to provoke a naval mutiny," Pitt revealed in stunned disbelief. "Genius, really. The majority of the navy, many of them Irish, is pressed into service. And, on most of the vessels, conditions are deplorable. They're a powder keg awaiting the match."

"A mutiny would paralyze coastal defenses sufficiently to allow Napoleon to break the blockade and cross the Channel," Dundas replied, stunned. "When?"

"Dragonfly was unable to determine the exact date, but he anticipates, by the nature of the planning, that it will take place within the next two weeks, coinciding with Napoleon's invasion of England, which we believe is scheduled for nine days from now. So I think we can safely assume that is also the intended date for the mutiny." Pitt scanned the letter, brow furrowing. "He wants more money."

"How much can we trust this Dragonfly, do ye think?" Dundas asked.

"My impression is that his primary concern is surviving whatever comes and lining his pockets in the process. I have been dealing with him for the past year or so. His consistent demand is for regular, and increasingly exorbitant, payments, which, given his situation, is somewhat understandable. He would be summarily executed if Egan Trant found out, and the crime of collaborating with the English is beyond the pale insofar as his countrymen are concerned, as Wolfe has so pointedly reminded us." Pitt tossed the letter on the table and leaned back in his chair. "No, I get the feeling our friend Dragonfly is an economic opportunist, not an ideologue, which makes him more predictable. And his information, thus far, has proven correct."

"T'would seem likely that he is giving us wee tidbits here and there to keep the money coming."

"Exactly so," Pitt replied. "But he also knows that his usefulness ends with the Irish rebellion, given that is what we are most interested in. I will reply that this is the final opportunity for information exchange, and that our settlement upon him will be generous in direct proportion to the usefulness and magnitude of the intelligence that he provides."

"How do ye contact him?"

"Through the owner of a pub in Drury Lane. I will send a message to her, and she will see that it is passed on to Dragonfly."

"So accordin' to this letter, then, the United Irishmen are already in contact with Napoleon?"

"So it would seem." Pitt, retrieving the letter from the table, again read the last paragraph. "There is also a planned uprising in London. They have eleven hundred men and are attempting to recruit more. I imagine they will target the Houses of Parliament, possibly the Tower of London, even Buckingham Palace…"

Pitt moved to his desk and dipped his quill in the ink-pot, brow furrowed in thought. Retrieving a sheaf of paper from the drawer, he proceeded to write. "The king is currently in residence at Windsor which is more readily defended than Buckingham. However, we will need additional security in the city. I will also contact the Admiralty in regards to the maintenance schedule for our ships-of-the-line; we will want to ensure the process is expedited as much as possible with maximum security for those in dock."

"Can we not simply arrest the lot of 'em at their next meeting and put an end to it before it starts?"

"As tempting as that would be, we want Napoleon to believe that all is proceeding in favor of his invasion schedule." Pitt turned in his chair, his quill, poised in one hand, dripped ink unnoticed on to the rug under his feet. "Our only advantage here, Mal, is our awareness of Napoleon's agenda. If we lose that, we lose everything. No, we must allow the United Irishmen to proceed as if we were unaware of their intentions. We don't want to give Napoleon any reason to alter his plans. Let them have their uprising, Mal, but we will be ready for them." Turning back to his desk, Pitt completed his letters, and, a few minutes later, rising to his feet, he handed them to Dundas. "Here, have this delivered to Sir George Poole at the Royal Arsenal in Woolwich. And this to Sir William

Farrer at the Royal Military Academy at Sandhurst. I have asked them to send as many additional men to the capital as they can spare—not that there are many."

Dundas departed with the missives, and as the door closed behind him, Pitt, for a moment, allowed his eyes to close. His breath expelled in one sudden whoosh; his thin frame deflated into his seat like a purged balloon. The weight of national security sat heavily upon him, and, all of a sudden, he felt frail and elderly where only moments before he had been energetic and determined. The political pandemonium had taken its toll. Pitt, regardless of his current position, felt responsible for the life and livelihood of the English. Once prime minister, once sworn in, the oath of office lingered in the recesses of his mind, guided his actions, and prompted his conscience: "I do swear by Almighty God that I will well and truly serve our Sovereign King George the Third in the office of prime minister. I will do right to all manner of people after the laws and usages of the Realm, without fear or favor, affection or ill will."

*Do right to all manner of people.* A weighty injunction, indeed. And one Pitt was determined to uphold regardless of political upheaval and re-gardless of the cost to his own personal health, which was deteriorating markedly with each day that passed.

# 29.

"There, do you see?" Egan nodded toward the gloomy façade of Beth-nal Green workhouse. Its brick front towered above the dark tenements that leaned precariously on either side. "That's where James Duggin got the cramp jaw."

Duggin lived on in the collective Irish consciousness as the martyr of Spitalfields, hanged in the aftermath of the weavers' riots of 1769. "Cramp jaw" was one of many vivid euphemisms designed to reduce the fear of hanging, a fate with which the London Irish had profound familiarity. Despite his relatively brief domicile in London, O'Connor had heard all the hanging vernacular: one man had "danced a new jig without music," a victim of the "crack neck assembly" at Tyburn, his noose a "breath stopper;" and others that had danced "tuxt de ert and de skies."

He had left Ireland two years earlier, one among thousands seeking employment in the monstrous metropolis to the east. O'Connor was keenly aware of the desperation behind this migration; in Ireland he had seen laborers endeavoring to work at the spade but fainting for lack of food, an elderly man grazing grass like a beast, and a hungry infant sucking at the breast of a dead mother. Yes, they all knew what they were leaving behind. London could hardly be worse.

O'Connor recalled the drunken declaration of a dockworker the pre-vious night who stood, legs splayed and teetering, upon a table at Black House: "I proceeded on me way ta London, that greet and famous city, which may truly be said, like the Sea and the Gallows, to refuse none!"

London refused none indeed; the lowliest of trades needed their immigrant Irish workers. Men who were fortunate enough to find work became gang-labor workers, sailors, harvesters, canal-diggers, builders, and coal-heavers; their wives and their women became prostitutes, laun-dresses, scullions, and ballad singers. Many resorted to thievery on the side to make ends meet. Individually weak and pitiful, as a collective this labor had power and posed a considerable danger to authority, as Egan and O'Connor well knew. And it was here, in the silk-weaving district, in the restless parish of Spitalfields, where the rebellious Irish brooded. It was here that O'Connor would recruit the men he needed.

Bell Street was narrow and appeared even narrower in the pale light of an overcast afternoon, densely thronged as it was with the mass of humanity that bustled and hurried through it. The Rag Fair dominated the parish on Thursdays, with carts and stalls crowding the curbside. Brokers and sellers of old apparel and cast-off habiliments shared street-space with those seeking to upgrade a shirt or dispense with a finer pair of stockings for a ha'penny. Tattered trousers and shabby waistcoats, patched skirts and heel-worn boots jostled for room on crowded tables and well-used hooks. Cries of "old satin, old tafety, or velvet" mingled with the warm steam of potato cakes and hot pear.

"Why did you not want Tom along?" O'Connor asked. "His brother lives round the corner from here; he knows this parish well."

"I don't know that I entirely trust young Dildin. He's a little too inquisitive," Egan replied shortly. O'Connor mulled this information over with growing unease. Egan's morality was colored in black and white and tailored specifically to suit his own agenda. A slight suspicion in this time of tense preparation for what Egan termed "The Final Battle" might be all that was required to send young Dildin to an early grave.

"Sure, he's just young and arrogant, like we all were at his age," O'Connor replied, with a measure of forced joviality.

"Perhaps," Egan muttered noncommittally.

"Would ye want an old cloak, sir?" A pallid-faced vendor, with three hats on his head and a bundle of rapiers in his hand, positioned himself in Egan's path. "A hat? Or would ye be a fightin' man?" He brandished a rusty rapier, its blade veering alarmingly close to Egan's left cheek. Egan reached out and took hold of the man's wrist, gripping it with punishing force. The man yelped in surprise; his face contorted with pain as the rapier dropped to the ground with a clatter.

"I would be a fighting man," Egan growled. "So take heed and stay out of me way." He moved on, leaving the man on his knees scrambling for the hats that had fallen from his head.

"I wanted to take this opportunity to tell you what your own responsibility will be in the Final Battle," Egan resumed. "I've spoken wi'

Finney and Tom already, but your part will be to make sure the signal is sent to the rest of Ireland. As you know, Nick, you're my next man, and 'tis to you I entrust the most important duty. You'll infiltrate the Postal Service and prevent the stagecoaches carrying mail from leaving. United Irishmen in Bristol, Manchester, and Ireland have been instructed to consider the non-arrival of regularly scheduled mail coaches as the definitive order to begin the insurrection." He spoke quietly, his head close to O'Connor's ear. In the mingling shouts and cries of the multitude that surrounded them, all intent on their own specific business, the two men might as well have been in complete privacy for all the notice that was taken of them: a safe enough environment in which to discuss their particular arrangements.

"These coaches travel at 'bout nine miles per hour, stopping every ten miles or so to collect and deliver mail at inns and such. It takes 'em about sixteen hours to travel to Bristol and twenty-two to Manchester. When the coaches don't arrive on time, well'n then, the signal is sent. So you must take the Post Office afore the door locks at seven and hold it for at least three hours. That'll put the carriages two hours behind schedule. Finney will go with you; take what other men you need."

"And the insurrection in Bristol and Manchester, and here in London, will also coincide with the naval mutiny?"

"To be sure. Our strategy depends upon the uprisings taking place at the exact time the French appear on the coast. My naval man has made arrangements."

"And if we cannot recruit enough to take London?"

"The uprising will take place as planned." Egan's steely gaze sought O'Connor's. "'Tis up to you, Nick, to make it a successful one. Get the men we need, and we'll prevail."

The two men came to the front of the Freehold Porter Ale and Table Beer Brewery, a newly constructed brick-and-timber building occupying the corner of Bell and Frying Pan alley. A gleaming green sign hanging above the door boasted of "inexhaustible wells of very fine beer." It was an Irish bar, and from inside O'Connor could hear the bawling cacophony of a group already well in their cups.

"Don't let me down, Nick." And Egan was gone, lost amidst a swirl of dirty linen and rumbling carriages.

O'Connor pushed open the door and made his way into the smoky tavern. Despite the relatively pristine façade, the bar was populated by the usual motley assemblage who thronged and pressed, hollered and screeched. Together whores and thieves from Rosemary Lane and St. Giles, a company of idle sailors from Wapping, and the usual Irish laborers resolved themselves into clusters of threes, fours, or fives amidst the foul-smelling humidity that composed the pub's interior. Several bartenders were hard-pressed and harried, sweating beads of imbibed beer down grimy collars as they struggled to keep up with demand. Freehold Porter Ale and Table Beer Brewery, in the giddy enthusiasm of very recent establishment, had decided to open their doors with a week of ale on the cheap to entice and engage a regular clientele as well as to steal those from the French Maid tavern just around the corner. From the crunch and press of bodies it would seem they were successful indeed. After elbowing his way through to the bar for a pint, O'Connor made his way toward the unmistakable Irish contingent that gathered around a central table.

"James Leonard?" O'Connor addressed a cluster of brawny men who were raising tankards to a sloshing cheer.

"Who' d be askin', then?" a tall ginger-haired man spoke into the sudden silence.

"Nick O'Connor."

"Ah, Nick O'Connor, is it? Well then, sit yerself down! We've been waiting fer ye, haven't we, lads?"

# 30.

JARDIN DU LUXEMBOURG. PARIS, FRANCE
*December 4, 1803*

The carriage clattered down rue de Vaugirard, passing tall, narrow houses that squeezed against each other like beggars in a breadline. Threadbare washing, hung out to dry, flapped from long poles thrust from windows above. Within the carriage, L'Aigle leaned back against the padded leather seat and closed his eyes. There was little to interest him in the city through which he traveled, and he was tired. He was always tired these days. The nocturnal hours afforded him little rest; dark dreams plagued his sleep and lingered into the morning, leaving him tense and irritable.

He lifted the linen flap to look outside. The sight depressed him. The streets were dark and dismal. The late afternoon light gilded the roof-tops of the houses above but did not penetrate to the narrow streets that turned and twisted in a labyrinth below. A mud-bespattered priest announced himself with the doleful clanging of a hand-bell. Behind him, a hefty youth propelled a handcart, piled with bodies of the dead, through the squelching mud; one hand, unfeeling now, trailed along the cobblestones. Priest and youth were heading south to the paupers' grave in Clamart.

L'Aigle hated the city now. It had lost its romanticism, and he, for all his violent abilities, had deeply savored the refinements of the Paris of Louis XVI. While some things remained the same—shop windows were stocked with fine wines, liqueurs, turkeys stuffed with truffles, and pâté de foie gras—others were irrevocably changed. Gone were the liveries of the servants, gone were the arms upon the carriages and all vestiges of the proud Parisian lineages. It was no longer fashionable to be an aristocrat; the guillotine had seen to that. But to be wealthy, well, that was another thing, L'Aigle thought cynically. The nouveaux rich-es of Bonaparte's republican regime had restored some of the noble houses and palaces to their former magnificence. Others lay derelict or occupied by squatters—perpetual reminders of a glorious past that lay in ruins.

He was meeting his contact in the Jardin du Luxembourg at four. The carriage turned on to rue de Médicis before jolting to a halt by the large wrought-iron gates that opened up into the gardens, and the palace that lay beyond. Descending from the carriage, L'Aigle entered the gardens. The grounds were thronged with people. While the air was bitingly cold, the sky, darkening to the east as the sun slipped toward the opposite horizon, was relatively clear. The first stars were appearing as sharp pinpricks, and his breath blew out in plumes. While the Revolution had opened up the gardens to the public (prior to that time, they had been reserved for royalty), their continued maintenance had been neglected. The flower beds were choked by weeds, the lawns brown and patchy, and the central lake suffocated by algae. There's the Revolution for you, he thought derisively.

Circling the lake, L'Aigle sauntered past the statues of former French queens, past Saint Genevieve, the patroness of Paris, and headed toward the apple and pear orchards in the southwestern corner of the park. He was in no hurry. His contact would wait. Arriving at the orchard, he saw with some irritation that he would be the one waiting: his contact had not yet arrived.

A théâtre des marionettes had set up a stand nearby, and a trio of flickering gas lanterns illuminated a gaggle of children who sat, in open-mouthed absorption, watching a performance of *Guignol*. He had seen this performed before. Guignol and his friend Gnafron, silk weavers from Lyon, were perpetually hounded by the Gendarme Flageolet, who bore an uncanny resemblance to Fouché. Flageolet, dressed in black, was screaming shrilly at Guignol and beating him over the head with his truncheon. The children booed and hissed and then howled with laughter as Gnafron sneaked up behind Flageolet, yanking his dress coat up to reveal pink, frilly underwear beneath. Napoleon himself was not above lampooning, and the strutting corporal appeared in military dress as Flageolet's superior. In fact, Napoleon had appeared even more frequently and derisively in these puppet shows since he had made them illegal several months before. His regulation prohibiting performances seemed to result in an increased proliferation of shows and a renewed enthusiasm on the part of the audience. The illicit nature of the event added a thrill to what had previously been innocent entertainment.

Given the itinerant nature of these performances, lawbreakers were almost impossible to apprehend; puppeteers would set up shop in the middle of a marketplace, a central square, or in the gardens, and move on when they were done.

The show ended, as it always did, with Guignol and Gnafron thoroughly beating Flageolet with his own truncheon; this finale of violence was invariably accompanied by the enthusiastic approval of its young audience. A new generation of dissenters had been born. The puppeteer, a short stocky man in a black overcoat, took a cursory bow before turning to dismantle his stage. L'Aigle, glancing at his pocket watch with increasing irritation, had just about determined to leave when the puppeteer caught his gaze.

"The herrings are not so good this year," he remarked casually as he folded the stage curtains into his threadbare velvet bag.

"You must try the salted white herrings from Venice; they are excellent."

Point and counterpoint—the puppeteer was his contact.

The man passed him a book. "The details are as you see in the inside cover. The money will be deposited in the Banque Francaise, as is our usual custom. I must reiterate, monsieur, that this job is of the utmost importance. There must be no delay."

"Aren't they all?" L'Aigle responded dryly, opening the book.

# 31.

Wolfe slept deeply; the sharp rapping at the door did not rouse him. It was the rattling of the door handle and the insistent voices that finally penetrated the fog of his dreams. Wolfe blearily rubbed his eyes and swung his legs over the side of the bed, wincing slightly as the movement jolted his healing ribs. His head felt somewhat better at least, which was a small miracle considering how much wine he had consumed. The bottles scattered beside the bed reminded him. The boat trip the night before, the silent ride through the dark countryside to the outskirts of Paris—he didn't remember much of it. It was a trip made through a fog of splintering pain. Once in Paris, he'd bought enough wine to anesthetize himself. It seemed to have worked somewhat, as his agony had subsided into a dull throbbing ache, which was at least bearable.

Where was he? The threadbare coverlet of a murky olive and the peeling wallpaper with faded miniature roses offered no clues.

"Monsieur!"

Oh, yes, the Hotêl Céleste. A dingy lodging house in rue de Barrie. The previous few days came rushing back to him, bringing a sudden clarity to his mind. France. He was a spy. For the English! Galvanized now, he leapt to his feet, struggling into his breeches as the voices at the door became more aggressive.

"Monsieur Manot! Monsieur Manot! C'est la gendarmerie! Ouvrez la porte!"

The police! How had they found him? With a resounding crash, the door swung violently open and four men in the dark blue uniforms of the gendarme surged forward into his room in a flood of bristling authority. Madame Davall, the elderly woman who owned the lodging house, hovered inquisitively in the background. One of the gendarmes, a slender man with a long, thin face and small, squinty features, pushed

forward in an aggressive manner, brusquely identifying himself as Chief
Inspector Chavert. The man seemed a faded version of himself: his skin
was pale, almost translucent. Hair the color of pale wheat was greased
to a neat division in the center of his head, below which pale blue eyes
sat like small, round marbles in the lean column of his face. A small,
neatly clipped mustache nestled obediently beneath a long, angular nose.

"You are Monsieur Manot?" Chavert demanded belligerently, mouth
pursed in ready disapproval. Flicking his fingers, he gestured for his
man carrying the gas lamp to come forward until it included Wolfe in
the yellow circle of light.

"I am." Wolfe nodded, feeling the adrenalin begin to surge through
his body, his muscles tense. So it was over already. Not even a day in
Paris and his cover had been blown. He would end up rotting in a Parisian prison rather than an English one, and Pitt would have to find
himself another Irishman. Assuming he was captured, Wolfe thought
grimly. Remembering Newgate, he knew he would not allow that to
happen. But if he could bluff his way out, then there was a chance the
operation could still succeed. Perhaps they were questioning all Madame
Davall's lodgers; perhaps, he was not the target at all—just another late-
night unfortunate, a convenient stranger who would provide fodder for
Chavert's ambition.

Wolfe shifted one hand slightly to the right, surreptitiously feeling
under the thin mattress. The edge of the blade felt sharp against his
fingertips. It should even the odds up a little.

Chavert's men looked dull and inattentive. While they presented
large and bulky silhouettes in the light of the gas lamp, they were in-
dolent, mulling wearily about the room. One of them idly picked up a
book Wolfe had left on the table and began flicking through the pages.
Another sagged in the door frame, stifling a yawn. It had already been
a long night for Chavert's men. They were tired, and that would make
them careless. They were as indifferent to the outcome of the evening's
encounter as Chavert was vigilant. That would be their failure. One just
had to want it bad enough; and Wolfe always had.

"Papers, Monsieur Manot. Papers!"

"Of course," Wolfe muttered. Edging the knife out from under the
mattress and into the palm of his hand, he rose to his feet. Moving to
the foot of his bed, Wolfe dug around in the pocket of his coat for the
papers that identified him as a wine merchant from La Chapelle. He

handed them to Chavert with his right hand, keeping the knife concealed in his left. The pain was coming again. He could feel it escalating with relentless intensity behind his eyes, obliterating all thought and reason, except the growing conviction that his skull was about to explode.

"You are in Paris for what reason, monsieur?" Chavert asked, glancing through Wolfe's papers.

What was he supposed to say? What was his cover? Wolfe rubbed his forehead, trying to squeeze the pain away. He couldn't think, couldn't remember, his ability to focus undermined by the steel needles that pierced through his skull with white heat. "I advise that you cooperate with me, monsieur," Chavert barked impatiently, his small, round eyes bulging with irritation.

"I want to open a wine shop behind the Grève," Wolfe muttered, knuckles kneading his forehead, eyes closed. "I was forced to close my shop in La Chapelle. Many of the young men in our village are serving with the army. The rest have been devastated by the blood disease, their wives and children barely able to put bread on the table," he managed through clenched teeth. Wolfe looked up, eyes clouded by pain. Through the agony in his head, the thought occurred to him that he might inadvertently appear to be exactly whom he represented: a failed wine merchant, despondent over the loss of his business, drowning his sorrows and suffering the usual morning-after effects. He shrugged, in what he hoped was weary resignation. "Nobody buys wine anymore. What could I do? So I drank the few bottles I brought with me." Wolfe interjected a whining note into his voice, resuming a hunched-over position on the edge of the mattress in a deliberate attempt to portray an unthreatening, even pathetic, figure.

Was there a chance this was a coincidence? Verdieu had warned him that the French authorities were vigilant about checking papers, that midnight raids were not uncommon. The police frequently seized the opportunity to corner their quarry, defenseless and unaware. Was he the quarry? Or was this just part of a routine inspection?

"Yes, yes," Chavert dismissed his long-winded explanation with an impatient wave of one slender hand. "Your papers were signed by Monsieur Ateuil?" he demanded sternly, glancing up from the documents. Wolfe shrugged. The pain was beginning to ease. It had subsided to a dull, aching throb, one he could deal with. He breathed a little easier, unclenching his fists which had maintained a white-knuckled grip on the mattress edge, the small knife still concealed in the palm of his left hand. "Monsieur Ateuil was revealed as a traitor to the Imperial cause and was yesterday imprisoned in the Temple to await trial. All of his confirmations are suspect. You are going to have to come down to the Secretariat for questioning." Routine inspection or not, he was not going to the Secretariat. To be taken in for questioning was frequently, in post-Revolutionary Paris, a euphemism for the Temple Prison, or worse—assuming he even made it to the prison alive.

Leaping swiftly to his feet, he lunged at the gendarme nearest him. Wolfe caught a glimpse of his face, mouth dropped in surprise, before he plunged the knife into the man's neck, hot blood gushing over his hands. The guard slid to the floor, and Wolfe pivoted on his heel, fists instinctively coming up to protect his face as he turned to take on his remaining opponents. As Wolfe had anticipated they were slow to respond, and he had time to land one brutal right hook to the jaw of the man closest before they were upon him. The second gendarme slammed one meaty fist into Wolfe's side before he was able to twist around, kicking out with a powerful jab at his assailant's kneecap. The guard promptly sank to the floor with a groan of pain.

The other gendarme, meanwhile, had struggled to his feet, truncheon raised high, blood pouring from his nose, as he moved warily toward Wolfe. Moving lightly on the balls of his feet, Wolfe waited for the swing that came shortly after. His senses were heightened, as they always were during a fight, and as he ducked to avoid the truncheon blow, he caught sight of a movement in his peripheral vision. Almost before the gun registered, he had moved, throwing himself to one side as the pistol exploded with a flash of blinding light and deafening sound. The small room was momentarily filled with acrid plumes of billowing gunpowder. As it dissipated, Wolfe completed his roll and was back on the balls of his feet. The bullet lightly grazed his shoulder before landing in the belly of the guard who had not moved as quickly. Chavert, with unexpected rapidity, had tossed his pistol to the floor, realizing he would not have time to reload before Wolfe was upon him, and pulled a second from his waistband. It was a small, silver pistol, almost dainty in appearance, but as lethal as the first had been in such close quarters.

"Mon dieu! Mon dieu!" the guard shrieked in pain, writhing on the floor, hands clutching his stomach. Wolfe did not look at him but kept an intent gaze on the man with the pistol in his hand. The first gunshot had awoken the entire lodging house, and Wolfe could hear the pandemonium in the hallway as people rushed past his door.

Chavert backed slowly away, sparing neither a word nor a glance for his men who lay bloodied on the floor—one dead, one dying, and the other, desperately wanting to be neither, attempting to quiet his whimpers of shock and pain. Chavert's pale eyes narrowed in dislike; his lips curled in an angry snarl, his silver pistol held unwaveringly on Wolfe. His finger tightened around the trigger as Wolfe tensed in readiness.

Abruptly, the door was flung open, and several figures rushed through. Chavert glanced toward the door; his gaze was averted for a fraction of a second, but it provided all the distraction that Wolfe needed. He threw himself on Chavert, sending the slighter man reeling back, his head smashing forcefully against the wall before he slumped sideways, unconscious. The gun clattered to the floor beside him.

"Mon dieu, what the hell have you done?" a woman's voice demanded.

# 32.

HOTÊL CÉLESTE. PARIS, FRANCE

*December 4, 1803*

Glancing up from his crouched position on the floor, gun in hand,
Wolfe saw two solidly built men protectively flanking an equally robust
female figure who stood between them. Instinctively, not knowing if
these intruders were friend or foe, he rapidly sized them up, calculating
the best exit strategy: *determine their weakness, move swiftly, do not hesitate.*

The men appeared to be brothers, identical in both build and clothing. Hair, pulled back in tight queues, accentuated broadly flat faces
that shone, in the yellow gaslight, with perspiration. They were short
of stature but possessed the large barrel chests and thickly muscled
arms of blacksmiths. Their clothing consisted of faded black breeches
and dark gray linen shirts that, despite the cold, were rolled up to reveal
thick forearms carpeted with coarse, dark hair. The woman was tall
and wide. She wore a threadbare green coat, beneath which he could
see a cheap red dress stretched tautly across a round belly and large
pendulous breasts. The rim of a tattered black hat cast a shadow, which
obscured her eyes from his gaze. In the dim light, he could make out a
large, bulbous nose and a small yet full mouth. There was strength in
the set of her shoulders, in the way she stood with both feet squarely
planted forward. She stood like a fighter, he noted with some surprise.

*Target the woman*—the thought ran through his mind in a disconnected phrase. The men appeared strong and capable in a streetwise sense,
the sense that he had learned to respect the most. There were no rules
on the street; one had to be prepared for anything. The woman, despite
her size and strength, was their vulnerability. They were concerned with
her protection. He slowly rose to his feet, the gun hanging loosely from
one hand in a deceptively casual manner.

"Are you a complete idiot?" the woman demanded, striding forward
to crouch beside Chavert. She pressed two fingers to his neck, feeling
for a pulse. Wolfe swiftly moved forward, yanking her in front of him,

gun pressed against her ribcage. Her protectors rushed forward, then stopped as the woman raised her hand. "Do not fear, monsieur, we are with the French Resistance." The blacksmith twins shifted restlessly, itching to rush to the attack like feral dogs snarling at the leash.

"How do I know that you are not Chavert's agents?" Wolfe hissed in her ear, holding her close against him, finger tensed on the trigger. "You seem more than a bit concerned for his welfare."

"Pitt sent me," she replied in impeccable English. "You are Wolfe Trant, and I am here to assist you."

"How convenient for me," Wolfe growled. "Forgive me if I am a bit suspicious under the circumstances. I have no desire to return to prison." He edged toward the hallway, grabbed his satchel from beside the door and slung it across his shoulder, the woman held firmly in front of him, the men bristling with angry defiance.

"Any closer and she gets a bullet," Wolfe said deliberately, opening the door with one hand, his gaze locked on the men.

Moving backwards, pulling the woman along with him, he entered the hallway. Then, joining the crowd that thronged past, the gun against her back, the woman pushed in front, he moved quickly down the stairs to the front door and out into the Parisian night.

"You have nothing to fear from me," the woman gasped as they moved rapidly through the darkened streets.

Wolfe ignored her, passing dimly lit storefronts until they reached a narrow, fetid alley that did not presume to be named. Shoving her roughly up against the grimy brick wall, the gun to her temple, he said, "And how the hell do I know that, then?"

For the first time, he looked at her properly. Her face was surprisingly thin, given the bulk of her girth, and was dominated by a pair of impossibly large eyes above which arched darkly elegant brows. Her nose, unfortunately bulbous though it was and strangely chalky in appearance, sat above a small mouth. Her eyes, however, were mesmerizing: deep, dark velvet pools, framed by thick lashes that softened around the irises into molten gold.

"If you will unhand me, monsieur, I would be happy to prove it," she muttered in response.

Wolfe felt a searing pain as she shoved one knee into his groin. A small yet effective fist slammed across his wrist, sending the gun clattering to the ground. She made no move to retrieve the gun but crouched down beside Wolfe. "Pitt sent me," she repeated. "He wanted you to be protected."

"And this is how you protect me?" Wolfe rasped irritably. "I think I can manage better on me own." He rose painfully to his feet, leaning over until the pain subsided. He was annoyed with himself. The groin was an obvious place to protect—something fighters learned in their first year—and here he was so distracted by the passing beauty of a woman that he allowed himself to be disabled. He snatched the gun from the street, depositing it securely in the waist of his breeches, before turning to face her.

"Is that what you were doing back there? Managing?" she asked heatedly. "Do you think I *want* to be here? Exposing myself and my people to save some drunken Irishman on a killing spree?"

"Why *are* you here, then?" he asked brusquely.

"I *told* you," she replied, with growing irritation. "Pitt contacted me. He warned that you were in danger and asked that I watch out for you. He said your mission was vital to the interests of both of our organizations."

"Did he tell you what that mission was?"

"No," she replied shortly, her tone one of icy aggravation. "Why would he? I do not inform him of every stratagem employed by the Resistance but have no qualms about asking him for money to fund them. Quid pro quo. It was my turn to help him. I just didn't know it would be so damned difficult to do."

There was a moment's silence, broken by shouts and the clattering of carriage wheels in the street from which they had come. Wolfe moved toward the edge of the alley and peered cautiously around. He ducked back as several men in the starched blue military uniforms of the Parisian gendarmerie rushed past in a brougham, whipping the horses into a frenzy in their haste. Additional police agents followed on foot. They stopped just past the alley, apparently taking up a sentry post. Wolfe could hear them conversing in low tones. It seemed that Chavert had already summoned help, and the police had responded with what seemed unprecedented alacrity. Wolfe's mouth tightened in displeasure; he was hoping to have had a little more time.

"Look," the woman continued, in an obvious effort to quell her aggravation, "there is a house in Saint-Marceau where we can rest. You can dress and wash up." She glanced pointedly at his bare chest, and

Wolfe abruptly realized that in his haste to leave the lodging house he had neglected to grab a shirt or coat, which had been left hanging on the bedpost. He felt suddenly foolish. And cold. "And then you can get on with whatever it is you are doing here."

It seemed he had little choice. She had not reached for the gun when she had the opportunity. Was she smart or was she slow? Was she really what she seemed or was she biding her time to spring the trap? "How do you propose we get past the guards out there?" he asked finally

"Here, take this." She removed her green coat, revealing her widely ripe body beneath, and handed him her hat, exposing hair of wiry red that curled in rigid corkscrew curls around her face. Wolfe shrugged into the coat and pulled the hat down over his eyes. The sleeves were too short, and it would not close across his chest, but it was preferable to the alternative. "We can't do anything about your height. You might want to slump a little," she finished, her dark eyes glimmering in the dim light. She placed his arm across her shoulder and leaned heavily into him. He hunched over, holding the green coat together as best he could with one hand. "We go together," she said in low tones, moving toward the street beyond the alley.

They almost immediately encountered the three gendarmes who had been loitering across from the lodging house. The guards glanced curiously at the two locked together, and their gazes, sharp beneath their peaked hats, almost immediately slid away. Another whore and her client—nothing unusual in that.

"They are probably only looking for one man. Chavert barely got a look at me, and for all he knows I could have just been an inquisitive neighbor," she murmured under her breath. "Hey ya, watcha doin' later?" she called out to the policemen as they passed, her French suddenly guttural and heavily accented.

"Git on wi' ya!" the older policeman hollered irritably, waving her off. "Police business here!"

"Oooooo! Aren't we the fancy ones?" she cackled with hoarse amusement as they progressed past the lodging house, now a flurry of activity with gendarmes coming, going, and milling around the entrance.

# 33.

On rue Demarest, where the early dawn trade was in warm female bodies, the heavy-set woman walked languidly arm in arm with her companion, her wide bottom swaying provocatively in her tight red dress. She smiled seductively over her shoulder, fluttering her eyelashes coquettishly at the drunken catcalls that followed them down the street. "Bonsoir, mes chéris!" she called cheerfully in a rich Gascon accent, blowing a kiss toward the tottering trio that had just emerged from a café, their breath plumes of alcoholic vapor in the frosty morning air.

"Venez ici!" Come here! They called after her amidst masculine guffaws, tripping over each other's feet and cursing good-naturedly in the dark. "Combien?" How much?

"More than you can afford!" she replied tartly, moving more briskly.

The streets were dark and narrow here, with tall, tottering houses leaning over the street on either side. While gas lamps lit the way in the wealthier sections of the city, the rabbit warrens of Saint-Marceau, where the laboring poor lived, remained dark and gloomy. It was just past two in the morning, but the cafés still exuded the streaming light and drunken laughter of late-night crowds. Cafés elsewhere in the city were subject to a mandatory close-down at midnight, but those in Saint-Marceau prided themselves on flouting central authority.

It was the anniversary of some counter-revolutionary uprising, Primrose explained in a low voice, one in which the recent dead called out for vengeance. Murder rates tripled on these days. Scores were settled, sometimes decades after the alleged event. Saint-Marceau, being a semi-recognized zone of Paris rarely penetrated by the police, was particularly susceptible to these kinds of uprisings. An uneasy truce had been established between the inhabitants of Saint-Marceau and the gendarmes: the residents would not carry the banner of revolution beyond their streets in exchange for an immunity of sorts. The police still had their informants in Saint-Marceau, of course, but they tended to be moles of a deeper sort, those looking to make the big scoop. Integrate and ingratiate. Entrenched agents of this kind often spent years accumulating the information and pinpointing the participants, and then, when finally ready, they would pass it all on to a senior policeman who had deep pockets and the power to negotiate. These factors made Saint-Marceau both the safest and most dangerous place for a member of the French Resistance to hide.

Arriving at 52 rue Demarest, the woman rapped sharply on the door three times. It was opened by an elderly man in gray who, glancing anxiously down the street, hurriedly urged them inside. The interior was almost as dark as the street outside. A single candle illuminated a threadbare rug over a scarred wooden floor. Stairs disappeared into the darkness above.

"Primrose," the man spoke. His eyes filled with tears, and his gout-swollen hands patted the woman's arm. Already of small stature, but further hunched with age, the little man resembled nothing more than a wizened goblin, with coffee-colored skin pouched and wrinkled about a pair of bright brown eyes. For a startled moment, Wolfe was quite convinced a leprechaun had opened the door to them, and that if he withdrew his gaze but for a moment, the diminutive man, like his mythological Irish counterpart, would vanish into thin air. But their host remained, ushering them inside as he took the woman's arm in his own. "Primrose," he whispered again, with an almost reverent affection.

Primrose, of course! Wolfe vaguely remembered now: the conversation he had overheard between Pitt and Vierdieu. Pitt had mentioned contacting Primrose, the significance of which had been lost on him, given the blinding pain in his head at the time. But why the hell hadn't Pitt warned him? he thought irritably. Why arrange for a protector within the Resistance and then not tell him about it?

"Jacques," Primrose replied warmly. "Do you have a room?"

"Of course, of course. Follow me, please," Jacques replied shakily, wiping the tears from his eyes with his sleeve. "Forgive an old man his sentiment. It is not often a humble member of the Resistance is able to assist the renowned Primrose."

"We will not stay long, Jacques. Just time to rest and change. Thank you for your help." Primrose tucked her arm familiarly through the old man's, and together, heads bent close as they conversed in low tones, they ascended the stairs. Wolfe followed. They paused in the hallway before a wooden door. Jacques frowned in Wolfe's direction, muttering something to Primrose, who, glancing at Wolfe, shook her head and murmured a response.

With a doubtful expression on his weathered face, Jacques opened the door to them. The room was sparse but clean. Two narrow beds were lined up against the walls, each covered with faded, quilted blankets that probably used to be a cheerful yellow but were now decidedly mustard. A small table with a blue ceramic wash basin was positioned between them. The walls were bare, the shreds of wallpaper browned and curling at the perimeter. The only decorative item in the room consisted of a privacy screen that stood in one corner. Its glazed surface, now cracked and grimy with age, depicted a dirty pink flamingo standing in a pool of green water. Thick drapes hung over the only window. The room smelled musty, as if it had been long uninhabited—perhaps, since the last time Primrose had graced the premises, Wolfe thought cynically.

"What was that all about? In the hallway with the old man?"

"He was suggesting that you sleep downstairs."

"Downstairs?"

"Well, on the stairs to put it more accurately," she replied blithely as she moved behind the screen.

"Aye…well, thank you for the vote of confidence. You don't have to worry. While I may have the appearance of an Irish gangster, I'm a gentleman at heart." He touched one hand to his chest and bent forward in an attempted imitation of a courtly bow.

Primrose's head came out from around the screen, eyebrows raised in disbelief. Her lips twitched upwards in what may have been a smile. "Irish gangster? I would have thought Irish jester. You look ridiculous."

"Ridiculous, is it?" Wolfe looked down at himself: white stockings and black breeches, both rumpled and grimy from several days travel, topped by a woman's green overcoat that stretched tightly across his back and gaped open in the front. His chest and neck were covered, he realized with growing distaste, with the blood of the gendarme he had killed in his hotel room. "Aye, you'd be right." Wolfe discreetly sniffed one armpit. God, he reeked of sweat, stale wine, and, more disturbingly, the metallic tang of blood. "Any chance of a bath?"

"In the morning…" Her voice floated out from behind the screen. "Unless you want a cold one."

"I bathed in Loch Braden through the winter; a cold one would be fine." As bone-weary as Wolfe was, sleeping with another man's blood crusting on his chest was more than he could bear.

A sharp knock at the door announced Annette, a strapping woman whose peacock-blue dress stretched tight across at least two hundred pounds. Massive work-reddened hands held a tray of food. Above the cold roast fowl, fried carp, salad, and bread, Annette glowered at him. With her wild mane of steel-gray hair, hatchet nose and coal-black eyes, she undoubtedly possessed a daunting visage in the most frivolous of moods; now, in all her scorn, she was positively fearsome.

"Would there be any whiskey wi' that, by any chance?" Wolfe asked her in a smooth Irish brogue, his mouth curving in the sweetest of smiles. Annette snarled under her breath, darting black looks at Wolfe as she deposited the tray with a disapproving clatter. "I see she doesn't approve of my attire either," Wolfe muttered.

"Annette, could you bring a bath up for Monsieur Trant?" Primrose's voice came from behind the screen. There followed a grumbling vocal discourse as Annette's vast bulk retreated into the hallway, her supreme displeasure announced by a resounding slam to the door.

Wolfe shrugged out of the green coat and tossed it on the bed; the hat followed. He lay down on the lumpy mattress and closed his eyes. For a moment the room was quiet, with only the rustling of clothing and Wolfe's deep and steady breath. "Pitt didn't tell me about you," he said finally.

"So I figured. I guess we both assumed direct contact would not be necessary, that the Resistance could watch you covertly. Neither of us realized how much trouble you would get into, or how quickly."

"Trouble?" He raised himself up on one elbow and scowled in the direction of the screen. Her red dress was flung over the top, followed by a large black corset and several thick blankets. "The only trouble I got into was trustin' Monsieur Vierdieu's paperwork," Wolfe snapped heatedly.

"Yes, Monsieur Ateuil's arrest was regrettable," Primrose conceded, her bare feet visible beneath the base of the screen. Two small pillows dropped to the floor. What was she doing back there?

"Regrettable? To be sure, that's one word for it," he muttered darkly. "Do you mind if I go ahead and eat?"

"Of course," Primrose replied, emerging from behind the screen in a red Chinese silk robe. Gone were the wide, fleshy hips and the large breasts; in their place was a tall, angular woman with long, slender limbs. Reaching up, she removed the pins from her hair and tossed the brassy red wig to the bed. Beneath, her dark hair was cropped short about her skull. Wolfe dropped the bread he was holding to the floor. Blithely ignoring his obvious astonishment, she moved over to the small basin between the beds and bent over, immersing her face in the water. She scrubbed her nose, and then, much to Wolfe's bewilderment, portions of it began to break off and float in the water, which turned a milky white. The bulbous nose disappeared and was replaced by a long, narrow one dusted with freckles. "It is a type of plaster colored to match skin tone that is applied to the face while it's still wet. When dried, it attaches quite well to human skin. Well enough to pass inspection in candlelight," she explained, wiping her face dry with a hand towel. Primrose was now a tall, slender woman, with dark hair curling damply at her neck. Only the eyes and the mouth remained the same.

"Who *are* you?" Wolfe asked incredulously.

Before Primrose could reply, Annette arrived, in all her blustering venom, dragging a wooden tub; a scrawny boy, disheveled with sleep, was in tow behind her. Half an hour later, the chilly bath awaited him. Stripping off his breeches and yanking his stockings over his feet, Wolfe stepped into the tub, gingerly immersing himself in the icy water. He scrubbed himself raw with a thick slab of tallow soap. The water was gray by the time he finished, and he stood with a sharp exhalation of relief. Too late, he remembered his companion and glanced up in startled alarm. She was watching him with undisguised amusement.

"I don't think I have ever seen a man enjoy a bath more."

His cheeks colored slightly as he strode behind the screen. "I forgot about you," Wolfe said shortly, a note of apology in his voice.

"How flattering," Primrose remarked dryly. She was sitting cross-legged on the bed, a plate of salad and carp in her lap.

From behind the screen, Wolfe surveyed his grimy clothes in distaste, loath to wear them again. Just as he had decided to sleep as he was, etiquette and weather be damned, Annette arrived in surly disapproval with a clean change of clothes and a nightshirt. Her mouth was a scowling slash; her coal-black eyes flashed indignation.

"I think she's warming up to me," Wolfe remarked from behind the screen as he shrugged into the nightshirt.

"No, she isn't," Primrose replied. "She thinks you are a threat to me."

"A threat?" he snorted, rubbing the towel vigorously over his wet hair as he emerged from behind the screen. "Well, you fairly felled me in the alley as I recall…"

"A threat to our organization." Her half-eaten meal sat on the table between the beds, and she now lay beneath the quilt, propped up on one elbow. Her dark eyes watched him.

"Look, you helped me out in the hotel. I was *handling* the situation…" Primrose raised an eyebrow, and he held up a palm to ward off any further commentary. "I was handlin' the situation. I did what I had to do. Sure, I didn't like it any more than you did, but I sure as hell am not going back to prison. Least of all for a bloody Englishman!" He finished with more fervor than he had intended, his eyes flashing blue fire. Wolfe exhaled sharply through his nostrils. "You helped me past the gendarmes, gave me a place to rest me head and a bite to eat, and for that I thank you. But don't worry, I'll be gone with the sun, and your *organization* won't have to bother a thing about me. All right then?"

"I'm not worried, Monsieur Trant."

"Good." Wolfe sat on the edge of his bed as he reached for the food tray. She hadn't eaten much; most of the carp and fowl remained. The fish, lightly breaded and flavored with lemon, was delicious. He finished it in several bites.

"However," Primrose continued her gaze steady on his. "I think Annette is quite right. You are messy." She hesitated. "You attract… attention." There was no mistaking the archness of her tone, the invitation that curved her mouth, and the pointed glance at his crotch.

"Do I now?" He cocked his head to one side, regarding her intently. Did she mean what he thought she meant? There was only one way to find out. The food forgotten, he moved forward to where she lay, deliberately placing one large hand on either side of her blanketed form. Leaning down, dark hair falling in damp disarray over his forehead, he kissed her. Primrose reciprocated with a fierceness that surprised him: her tongue aggressively sought his own; her hands grasped his shoulders, pulling him closer; her body, naked beneath the quilt, arched up to meet his. Wolfe yanked the nightshirt over his head, cursing under his breath as the fabric caught and twisted. Then he was free of it, the nightshirt a crumpled pile on the floor.

With equal alacrity, he wrenched back the quilt, impatient to see her. Primrose's slender, pale limbs were edged in candlelight; her round breasts rose and fell with urgent breath. But she would not allow his gaze overlong; with unexpected strength, Primrose twisted with one knee, and Wolfe found himself lying on his back looking up at her. Reaching between them, she grasped the throbbing evidence of his own desire and gently lowered herself upon it, her moist heat encompassing him, gripping him, and moving around him in a leisurely circular motion. Despite his mounting pleasure, Wolfe had the unsettling sensation that

Primrose was orchestrating the event to her own particular timetable. It was not that she was giving freely of herself so much as she was freely helping herself to him. He was being taken.

Raising herself, Wolfe's gaze caught by her own, Primrose thrust down upon him with greater force. And then, as she bent over him, breasts grazing his damp chest, breath quick and hot on his ear, hair brushing his cheek, he thought no more about it. His eyes closed, and he could only feel the rising heat of pleasure to come. Another thrust, and her back arched beneath his hands. Primrose trembled around him, head tipping back, eyes squeezed tightly shut, her mouth gently parted to release a long soft moan. An instant later, Wolfe added a guttural groan to hers, his body clenching and spasming with the intense pleasure that convulsed through his body, from curling toes to fingers that tightened around her wrists.

Afterwards, she turned from him, settling back into the warmth of his chest. "Well, that was…unexpected, to be sure," he murmured against her ear, arms drawing her close against him.

"It is a cold night, monsieur," she replied softly, reaching out to nip the candle-flame between thumb and forefinger. "Best warmed by a stranger."

"A stranger? Why is that, then?" Wolfe felt oddly dismissed. He had been a hawkishly handsome youth with his fair share of giggling girls. Later, during the course of his travels throughout Europe—much of it remembered through the bleary fog of drink—there had been willing women enough. None that kept him long, but a few that tried. He was accustomed to the pursuit and subsequent leave-taking, but he was not entirely comfortable being the recipient of such a strategy.

She twisted to look at him; a thin band of moonlight fell across her cheek, her eyes a gleam in the dark. "Because, monsieur, there are no complications. No ties, no strings, no difficulties. Just the warmth of physical pleasure, yes?" Then, pillowing her cheek on one hand, she closed her eyes and almost instantly appeared to be sleeping, her breath deep and even.

"A Thighearna," Wolfe muttered in disbelief as he lay back on the pillow. "I think I've just been ravished." Closing his eyes, a broad smile crossed his lips. The warmth of a stranger, was it? "Madame, I'm happy to oblige," he whispered into the darkness before exhaustion claimed him, and he too slept.

# 34.

Police Commissioner Fouché leaned back in his chair, tapping one stubby finger restlessly on a black-clad thigh, thin lips pursed in thought. The grimy lead-paned window of the third floor office of the Secretariat de Gendarmie had been flung open; the brisk cold air of a Parisian winter swept through the room, rustling the long coat of Chief Inspector Chavert who stood to rigid attention before Fouché's desk. The desk itself, and every available space around it, was crammed with over-flowing folders, boxes, and books—each fat with secrets on spies, dissidents, writers, ministers, generals, and even, it was speculated, the emperor himself. A half-eaten bread roll lay discarded amidst letters and crumbs; a bottle of red wine left crimson rings on papers beneath.

An open box of cheap cigars was situated in the center of the table; the ground-out stubs of smoked ones decorated the window ledge. A particular cigarito-girl, who loitered at the south end of rue Buot, had secured a regular supply of cast-off butts of Justus van Maurik cigars. Manufactured in Valkenswaard, these expensive Dutch cigars were so prized that even the remnants of them, re-rolled and pasted under her deft fingers, made a fine smoke. It was the one indulgence Fouché allowed himself, and the provision of which, hastening back and forth to rue Buot, fell to Chavert.

Chavert, anxious to please, did what he could to make himself indispensable. He had seen many of the newly influential nobility or rising young officers made arrogant by early success fatally underestimate Fouché, sniffing disdainfully at his ill-fitting clothes, his greasy complexion, and his unimpressive figure. It was not a mistake they made twice. Fouché was nothing if not a survivor, and having survived—which was remarkable enough in view of the rapidity with which policies and regimes had been overturned in the previous two decades—he had an uncanny ability to rise to the top of the heap.

"And?" Fouché finally demanded, turning to cast a baleful stare at his subordinate, his dark, heavy-lidded eyes sunken in a fine web of wrinkled gray skin. "What happened next?"

"Well, I pretended to be unconscious, Commissioner, in order to be better able to gain intelligence..."

Fouché snorted in disbelief. He cherished few illusions, preferring grim reality with all of its dull imperfections and inconvenient truths. Chavert was a coward. That he had always known. The chief inspector's pretense served solely to avoid further conflict, to preserve life and limb; any overheard intelligence was entirely incidental. Fouché said nothing, however, wanting to hear the full story before he replied.

"A woman rushed in, said she was with the French Resistance. She had the voice and manner of an aristocrat, Commissioner." Chavert spat out the word aristocrat with all the fervent disgust appropriate in post-Revolutionary (but not so distant) Paris. His manner suggested that by lineage and accent alone this unknown woman deserved the worst possible fate.

Despite his apparent nonchalance, Fouché could feel his heartbeat accelerate, his breathing quicken, and the adrenalin rush through his veins like an elixir. At last! How long had he been chasing this tiresome woman through the streets of Paris? His Paris! She not only had the temerity to openly rebel against Napoleon's regime but to make a complete and utter fool of *him*. Most criminals were obvious, with little mystery or romance attached to their persons; they were merely brutal, often bestial, generally pathetic, and almost pitiable. Of course, when it came to reports written for his superiors, it served Fouché well to inflate the wily cunning of Parisian criminals, which in turn, naturally enough, augmented the merits of their captors.

With Primrose, however, there was little need of exaggeration. Like Cadoudal, she was a ghost in the night, appearing and disappearing, leaving chaos in her wake, until, like the rest of the Parisian population, he wasn't entirely sure she was real. A figment of the Resistance's imagination, created to stir the emotions of the populace, channel them to their own ends. A romantic fiction. But, Fouché admitted to himself, he had always known she was real. She was too clever to have been the invention of a group of men. She had been described by eyewitnesses as simultaneously short and tall, slender and heavy, brunette and blonde, a fishwife and a flower girl, an aristocrat and a duchess. Who was she really? No one seemed to know. The most dangerous thing about this woman, however, was not her actions as such, but her growing reputation. She had become a symbol for the restoration of the monarchy, the return of the Bourbon princes to France.

Parisians have short memories, Fouché reflected sourly. They had forgotten the extravagant excesses of Louis XVI and his Austrian queen. They dwelled only on current, short-lived dissatisfactions. While Napoleon had seemed the soldier destined to return stability and order to the chaos that France had become after the Directory, the optimism that accompanied the Consulate had faded with the emergence of the Empire. Famine and perpetual war had seen to that. The women had tired of sending their sons off to die in a foreign war, the point of which eluded them. Dark mutterings of discontent pervaded the more churlish Parisian districts, the very same that had served as points of ignition during the Revolution. Fouché was worried. He had burned all Royalist bridges years ago and would not survive the return of the princes. He must destroy Primrose and quash the hopes that had become associated with her.

Abruptly, his attention was recalled to the present by the chief inspector's subtle cough. "And what else did you learn?" he asked irritably, disliking Chavert's impertinence in demanding his attention before he was ready to bestow it.

"The one who killed my men, he is a spy for the English. His name is Wolfe Trant. The woman said that Pitt had sent her to protect him," Chavert disclosed with smug satisfaction.

"Wolfe Trant," Fouché repeated slowly, savoring the name in his mouth like a particularly fine vintage rarely sampled. Two birds with one stone. An English spy and a French one. They were obviously working together. He felt instinctively that something was brewing. Rumors had always abounded of English spies active in France. Some he had even spread himself when it was convenient: spies were purchasing large quantities of grain in an attempt to drive up the price or they were funneling funds to the French Resistance and assisting Chouan dissidents in the north. But this Wolfe Trant, he was here for some greater purpose. He was someone important enough for Primrose herself to come out of hiding to retrieve. Both had to be located and quickly. "Would you recognize this man if you saw him again?" he asked bluntly.

"Yes. He is very tall, dark hair...has a scar running down the side of his face, here." Chavert gestured across his right temple. "Yes, I would know that monster anywhere, Commissioner," he finished with a self-congratulatory air.

"And your men are in place at rue Foutaine?"

The informant Germain de Lausain had given him a street address used by Primrose: 27 rue Foutaine. The house was owned by Jeanne Recamier, a popular society hostess who had been widowed during the Revolution. Germain had intercepted a note intended for Desant directing him to Monsieur de Revert's, a popular bookseller in the Palais Royale. Germain, following his unsuspecting friend, had noted a casual exchange with a stout, drably dressed woman. Curiously, she appeared to have bought him a book, which he tucked under his arm before striding off across the square. Germain followed the woman to the address at 27 rue Foutaine and waited for several hours, but she did not reappear. Fouché had dismissed the information as trivial, expressing skepticism that this vagabond was the infamous Primrose, and managed to wave Germain off with a paltry sum. He had then promptly ordered Chavert to station agents at both the bookseller's and the Recamier house to watch and await further orders.

Fouché had infiltrated Recamier's Monday night salon with several informants and had received a message from another: a small-time operator by the name of Monsieur Guébriant, who had received intermittent payments for information that was both thin and, ultimately, useless. Guébriant had requested a meeting, confiding that he had in his possession a list of eight Resistance members—how much would the commissioner pay? Fouché had sent Chavert with strict instructions to acquire the supposed information without parting with a centime; this upstart needed to provide legitimate and compelling evidence if he wanted to be taken seriously. He hadn't even shown up, and Fouché had instantly dismissed him from his mind. Another fraud of an informant!

The others were just as useless. By the time he had sifted through their tiresomely verbose reports, Fouché came to the conclusion that Jeanne Recamier was like any other society hostess, at least within the confines of her Monday salon. She mingled and conversed with everyone, albeit with uncommon familiarity but that was all the rage these days: to achieve the complete antithesis of a stratified society. While Napoleon increasingly adopted the extravagance of a ruling class, his people still hungered for the social equality promised by the Revolution.

Or some such nonsense, he snorted. All in all, they had seen nothing, heard nothing helpful.

Was the woman at the bookseller's Primrose? She could have merely been a messenger, a go-between. There were numerous women active in the French Resistance, after all. Most, however, were from the working classes, and Primrose he suspected to be an aristocrat. So if this drably dressed woman at the booksellers was just another bourgeois member of the Resistance, what business did she have at the elegant home of one of Paris' most highly sought-after hostesses?

"Find out everything you can on this Recamier woman. I want an agent inside. Have Marie apply as a housemaid. Snatch one of their own if you have to. I want eyes and ears in that house, do you understand?" Fouché demanded.

"Yes, Commissioner."

"And your men, where are they stationed?"

"They have occupied the house opposite, are positioned at both ends of the street and at the rear of the house watching the back entrance. Nobody can get in or out without our seeing them," Chavert finished, his pale marble eyes gleaming, a slight smirk playing around his lips. He hesitated a moment before blurting out: "May I say you are brilliant at what you do, sir. You will be able to hand Primrose and this English spy over to Napoleon on a silver platter. Your future will be assured indeed." As will mine, Chavert thought with satisfaction.

Fouché took a large bite of his bread roll, carelessly filled his glass with wine and took a generous swig. "You are overconfident, Chavert," he told his chief inspector, chewing noisily as he spoke, bits of wine-soaked bread visible between large yellow teeth. "You want to rise to a position of power? Then there is one piece of advice I give to you." Fouché wiped the crumbs from his mouth with the back of one grimy sleeve. "Trust no one. You think Germain has given us Primrose on a silver platter? For the six francs I gave him? Come, come! A police informer is like a stagecoach, Chavert, which must leave every day, full or empty; if the informer knows nothing, he invents. This woman is probably nothing, a cog in the wheel. More than likely she will prove useless to us." He gulped down the half-glass of wine, rivulets running carelessly through the stubble of his flat, gray cheeks before blossoming like roses in the grubby cravat around his neck. "Germain will construct elaborate plots where most likely all that exists is an open and probably harmless association. He will make Machiavellian conspirators of simple and angry men. He will scent daggers where there are only kitchen knives and spoons."

"So what do we do?" Chavert asked, his posture a little less straight.

"We confirm the information, Chavert. If we want to catch a little bird, we don't hold up a cage with the door open and whistle for it. We widen the net. We use every available resource." Fouché picked up a thick stack of paper on his desk and waved it at his chief inspector. "Here it is, Chavert. This is the power of the empire right here." Fouché thrust the papers forward, his dark eyes gleaming. "This," he said intently, "is Paris. We have penetrated the minds of the people. Our agents listen in a hundred cafés, are present at every club and assembly, in public baths and laundry boats," Fouché counted them off on each dirty fingernail, his expression fanatical, "on the quais, on the terrace of the Tuileries, at markets, fairs, in queues at pastry shops, at hairdressers and billiard rooms, even at public lavatories! They listen, Chavert!" Spittle bubbled at the corner of his mouth. Fouché walked around his desk and stood next to his chief inspector. Yanking Chavert's ear painfully between two thick fingers, Fouché leaned close, his voice lowering to a gravelly whisper. "They listen, Chavert. And then do you know what they do?" Chavert bent accommodatingly to one side so the commissioner, half his height, was able to maintain a more comfortable grip on his earlobe. "They sit down in the back rooms in cabarets, and they write report after report on everything they heard. And those reports come to *me*. I am Paris, Chavert. I am the people," he whispered with measured intensity, his breath hot and fetid on Chavert's face. "And the Revolution has taught us what the people are capable of."

He released his hold on the chief inspector's ear and moved across to the window, gusts of wind ruffling the billowing sleeves of his shirt. The chief inspector was perfectly convinced that Fouché was the most powerful man in France, and keen to rise to the highest ranks on the commissioner's coat-tails, he strove to anticipate every thought and desire of his dingy little master.

There was some truth in Chavert's assessment. The paranoia of the Revolution and the repeated political purges under the Directory had created new police organizations on almost a monthly basis; each new institution reported variously to the minister of interior, the minister of war, and the administration of police. Fouché had inherited this veritable jungle of competing police departments and organizations that were devoted primarily to denouncing each other and sending their employers the sort of information they wished to hear. While Napoleon had created a new ministry that centralized the nation's gendarmes under the commissioner of police, enough confusion had survived to assure a wily individual in that position unparalleled power. And Joseph Fouché was indeed a cunning man. He used departmental jealousies to consolidate his own position and maintained a fanatical grip on the information flow that came through his office.

"But you are right in one thing, Chavert. The net is closing around our little bird. It is just a matter of time."

# 35.

Oui?" Madame Davall demanded warily, opening the door but a fraction, her solid frame blocking entrance to the elegantly dressed stranger who stood on the other side. She was feeling decidedly disagreeable this morning and not in the mood to play the gracious hostess, despite the obvious wealth of the man at the door. She had spent the morning on her hands and knees scrubbing the floor in room twenty-one. The gendarmes had removed the bodies but left the congealed puddles of dark blood. Madame Davall had opened the small window to the frosty December air and stripped the mattress, but the coppery smell of blood lingered in the room.

C'est la vie—what did one expect for a hundred livres a night? she thought irritably to herself. But what aggravated her more than the vigorous housework required this early in the morning was the stealthy departure of eight guests the night before. They had taken the opportunity, while Madame Davall was distracted by the gendarmes, to slip away into the dark without paying. And this gentleman didn't look like her usual clientele. This lodging house was not of the caliber suited for a gentleman; the beds were dirty, the décor mean, the hearths cold—even the cats were thin and hollow-eyed.

"Madame, I humbly beg your pardon for disturbing you at such an early hour," the stranger began, tucking his gray silk hat under his arm. "But it is a matter of grave urgency that I speak with you. May I come in?"

Madame Davall hesitated; her bulging gray eye scanned his figure suspiciously through the crack of the door-jamb. Beneath a swirling black greatcoat, she caught glimpses of the warmth of a steel-blue velvet waistcoat, black breeches, and impeccably pristine cream-colored stockings. Despite the rising wind that howled through the alley and played with his coat, the man's dark hair remained perfectly obedient, neatly brushed against a narrow head to form a small queue at his neck. His face, pale and lean, was dominated by widely set dark gray eyes, a thin aquiline nose, and a meticulously cut goatee that framed a thin-lipped mouth. Despite his impeccable manners, there was something cold about the man. His smile seemed to come reluctantly and with some effort, and while his lips moved in this strained manner, his eyes remained watchful and alert in a way that discomfited Madame Davall. She had known all manner of people and this man, regardless of his genteel appearance, made her blood run cold. Just as she had determined to shut the door on him, he spoke again, perhaps sensing her reluctance. "I will pay for information," he said pleasantly.

Pay would he? Well then, she could hardly turn her back on a fellow citizen in need. "Come in, if you must," she allowed ungraciously, turning her broad back to him as she returned to her labors at the kitchen table. Depositing her ample girth on the stool, she resumed peeling potatoes. Madame Davall was a bland, lumpy study in gray. A cotton cap, wrinkled and frayed around the edges, covered the coarse gray hairs that limply framed her round, doughy face. She stared at him fixedly with bulging eyes that never seemed to blink, her pallor as gloomy as her clothes. The only color in her rather featureless appearance was provided by spidery red veins that traced across the fleshy bridge of her nose, to disappear in tendrils across pouchy cheeks. Her thin mouth pursed in disapproval.

"Did you have a guest last night that looked something like this?" The stranger passed her a sketch of a man's face.

Madame Davall picked up the page with her stubby fingers and peered closely at it. "Eyesight ain't so good," she mumbled, glancing up at him significantly. Perhaps there was a way to compensate for last night's fiasco after all. The stranger deposited two silver coins on the table. "Oui, this was the man in twenty-one last night. Though he looked different; he'd been beaten up pretty bad. Had a scar here." Madame Davall gestured vaguely toward her forehead with one grimy fingernail. "Strange fellow," she continued, feeling more warmth for this stranger now that he had paid her the equivalent of a week's lodging. She wondered whether he could be persuaded to part with any more.

"He is in room twenty-one?" the stranger asked again, rising from the table.

"Ain't there no more," Madame Davall muttered. "The gendarmes came last night. They've been comin' round every other night, it seems, looking for workers without papers. It's these Lyonnaise who come to the city looking for handouts from the government that're meant for us Parisians." Madame Davall spat indignantly into the potatoes, glaring at the stranger as if he was personally responsible for this infiltration of unscrupulous peasants.

"Where did he go?" the stranger asked amiably, seemingly careless of her answer, his long, pale fingers absently rubbing the silk of his hat-band.

"Don't rightly know," Madame Davall replied, her eyes narrowing speculatively, tongue involuntarily licking thin lips as she contemplated additional silver coming her way. She was not disappointed. A third coin was dropped, rolled across the table in a tantalizing manner, and then fell with a satisfying clink against the other two.

"I will triple that if you can lead me to him," the stranger said intently.

Madame Davall's eyes shone with greed. "I can at that, monsieur," she said emphatically, her eagerness for the silver prompting her to agree to whatever might be required. Madame Davall had no idea where the man in room twenty-one had gone, but the woman he had left with looked familiar. Her son would know who she was and where to find her. He knew everyone in Paris.

"In an hour, shall we say, Madame Davall?" the stranger requested, his tone more of a demand than a petition. He rose and crossed to the door. "Until then, madame." He placed his hat back on his head, tipping it to her as he did so.

# 36.

She used to be a countess, did you know? A mariage de convenance, and why not? Beauty and youth on one side, blue blood and wealth on the other." The cook chopped garlic on a scarred wooden board, her knife a blur of motion beneath her hand.

"A countess?" breathed the housemaid, the bundled linens forgotten under one brawny arm.

"Oh yes!" The cook paused in her labors, looking out the lead-glass window at the lonely winter garden. The kitchen was situated at the back of the house over-looking the outdoor courtyard where Madame Recamier entertained in the summer months. Now, however, it was temporarily abandoned to the snow: the leafless trees were festooned in icicles, the fountain frozen, the statuary encased in a slick garment of ice. The cook, a thickset woman in her early fifties, had been with the Recamier family for several decades now and knew all there was to know. Jeanne Recamier was as fascinating and mysterious a creature to her household help as she was to the rest of Parisian society. "In fact, Madame Recamier descends from royalty herself, did you know?" the cook confided, glancing sidelong at the maid who hovered expectantly in the kitchen, mouth ajar, chores clearly forgotten. "Her father is the Duke of Bourbon; he had an affair with her mother, Marguerite Michelot. You are probably too young to have heard of her. She was a famous opera singer who died birthing twins. A girl and a boy. Jeanne and Joachim…such dear babes they were."

"What happened to them?" the maid whispered, eyes wide. This was better than the broadsheet tales sold for a centime on the Pont Neuf.

"Well, the duke bought this house for the children, made arrangements for them to be brought up with every advantage. Then, when Jeanne was thirteen he married her off to Count Crecy, a crusty old aristocrat in his sixties."

"And Joachim?"

"Ah, Joachim." The cook shook her head, mouth pursed in dismay. "Joachim became a wild youth, handsome as could be, but he fell in with a Jacobin crowd just before the Revolution and has been on the run ever since. He would stop in and see Madame Recamier… They were so close those two. But after the count was guillotined, Joachim never came again. It almost destroyed his sister."

The maid, utterly absorbed, sank to a stool, linens trailing unnoticed to the floor.

"And then Jeanne disappeared," the cook continued, enjoying the awed appreciation of her audience. "For three years!" She waved her knife in the maid's direction for emphasis before turning back to the carrots. "And then one day, she just walked right back through those doors, as easy as you please!"

"Where did she go?"

The cook shrugged vaguely. "No one knows. Some say she joined her father in England, others that she spent the years in Russia. When Napoleon issued amnesty for aristocrats, she came back with those two. Karl and Pieter." She dropped her voice to a hushed whisper full of portent and mystery.

"They scare me," the maid admitted with an involuntary shudder.

"Ladies!" Abbé de Bernis appeared in the kitchen, the door slamming behind him. "What smells so good, Madame Busot?" The dapper little abbé threw his damp coat over the kitchen chair and deposited his satchel on the table. He sniffed appreciatively, before nimbly snatching a small loaf from within cook's reach.

"Now…!" the cook warned, waving her knife threateningly in his direction. She was all bluster. The abbé, with his chubby face and sparkling good humor, was a popular fixture in the kitchen.

"You must be Marie, the new housemaid?" Abbé de Bernis reached out with both arms, grasping the maid's hands between his own. "It is a shame that Annette was so suddenly taken ill, but we are fortunate to have found so capable a replacement. Welcome! I am sure you will find this a most agreeable place of employment."

"I am sure I will, Abbé, thank you."

"What were you ladies talking about so earnestly when I came in just now?" Abbé de Bernis sat at the table and opened his satchel. He withdrew a handful of threadbare linen drawstring bags and began to divide a pile of francs between them.

"Oh, just telling our new housemaid about Madame Recamier," the cook replied, sliding her carrots and onions into the cast-iron pot bubbling on the stove.

"Ah!" Abbé de Bernis' dark brows rose in conspiratorial glee. "With all your usual dramatic exaggerations? Don't want to deprive the girl of a good tale," he chortled with good-humor as the cook turned to glare over her shoulder. "Now take all these stories with a grain of salt, my dear. Madame Recamier is a girl who has been through much hardship, as have we all."

"Madame Recamier travels a great deal, does she?" Marie asked. "I have noticed she is often not at the house. Where does she go?"

"Ah, yes," Abbé de Bernis replied, his thick fingers pulling a drawstring tightly and replacing the coin-filled bag in his satchel. "Well, I will tell you, my dear, if you promise to keep it between us. Do I have your word?"

Marie leaned forward on her stool in eager anticipation, hazel eyes wide in the freckled plains of her face. "Of course," she replied, head nodding vigorously.

"Despite Madame Busot's dramatic version of Madame Recamier's life, her only secret is her charitable works. Every month she has me tie up little bags of money for the poor. She pays the rent, you know, for various pensioners, destitute and friendless old women, retired servants and crippled workmen, all who would have starved long ago if not for her good and kind nature. While Madame Recamier insists that I disburse the money anonymously, she spends much time visiting these poor neglected people herself, taking baskets of food and clothing. She takes Karl and Pieter with her, of course, and often is away for days at a time. She is a desperately needed angel of mercy in these difficult times. It suits Parisian society to exaggerate events, to seek a mystery where none exists, and Madame Busot here is just as susceptible." The abbé grinned affectionately at the cook who harrumphed in response, turning her broad back to him.

"I'm goin' to need some more wood for the stove here, Marie. Could you fetch some for me?" Madame Busot announced briskly, stirring the pot which was starting to release a most fragrant aroma.

"Certainly." Marie slid from her stool and, wrapping a woolen shawl about her shoulders, disappeared through the back porch door to the wood pile that occupied one corner of the back garden.

Abbé de Bernais' cheerful countenance grew solemn as he watched her go.

"How did we do?" Madame Busot asked with breathless anxiety.

"Fine…fine," the abbé assured her. "Tell her everything that she would hear from other sources, and then deflect suspicion."

"I just can't believe that girl works for Fouché; she seems so sweet."

"It is fortunate that Annette managed to get word to Karl before the gendarmes took her in, otherwise we would have had little notion of Marie's true loyalties. Just remember, Madame Busot, Marie is an actress in Fouché's pay. Never forget that. Let's just make sure she is completely satisfied with our version of events. Annette's life, as well as our own, could very well depend upon it."

# 37.

## 32 RUE DU VERTBOIS. PARIS, FRANCE
### December 5, 1803

"Tiens, monsieur." The urchin pointed triumphantly at the red door across the street: 32 rue du Vertbois. It was nestled between a shuttered bakery, where a few stale baguettes could be seen propped up behind a grimy window, and a second-hand bookseller's, advertised by the sign "Librairie" which hung above the store. It had snowed during the day while he slept in the dim room at rue Demarest, and now the roofs groaned under their winter burden. The streets, however, were no longer white but had melted into clumps and trails of slush that gleamed yellow in the flickering gaslight. Wolfe pressed a coin into the little boy's palm, as tough and brown as a monkey's paw.

"Do you want to earn another?" he asked him in French.

"Oui, monsieur," the boy answered, stomping his feet in an attempt to keep warm. He wore a pair of man's boots and an oversized woolen shawl, beneath which Wolfe could see a pair of ragged knickerbockers. Wolfe shrugged out of his coat, placing it around the boy's narrow shoulders; it trailed to the ground, the hem dragging in the slush underfoot. The boy grinned, bunching his new possession up around his midriff to keep it dry. "Merci!"

"Can you whistle?" Wolfe asked him. The boy promptly put two dirty fingers in his mouth and gave a shrill, piercing whistle. "Very good." Wolfe grasped the boy by the shoulders, kneeling down in the street to look him in the eye. "Keep watch for me. Anyone comes to the door whilst I'm inside, you whistle. You see gendarmes coming, you whistle. Understand?"

"Oui, monsieur," the boy repeated eagerly.

Wolfe studied the red door opposite. All was quiet. At the end of the street, where rue du Vertbois intersected with rue de Turbigo, a café was still boisterous with a late-night crowd. Steam rose from the back kitchen, pungent with herbs, garlic, and sautéed butter. The doors opened, revealing the hazy gaslight glow of inebriated cordiality, a drunken chorus, a shriek of laughter—all abruptly stifled as the door slammed closed. The street, however, was empty. Well, almost empty. A figure wrapped in coarse, woolen cloth an indistinguishable shade of dark, back permanently bent like the curve of a sickle, was digging through the café's refuse heap. An assortment of glass bottles lined the ground beside him; a modest sufficiency could be made from reselling them to wine merchants. Wolfe stepped into the street and made his way over to the red door on the other side. It was open—just as Talleyrand had said it would be.

By the time he had awoken in that small room in rue Demarest, the shadows had lengthened and the day had dwindled into early evening. A tray of bread and cheese and a mug of ale sat on the other bed. A note had been propped up against the tray: *I would advise you, given recent events, to hasten your plans. You have not been exactly inconspicuous since your arrival in Paris.* It was not signed, just the quick sketch of a small flower: Primrose.

The room was chilly, and he dressed quickly. A warm overcoat had been added to his wardrobe, and he sent a mental thanks to Jacques, Primrose, or whomever else may have been responsible. Certainly, it was not Annette. The sight of his frozen corpse might be the only event that would coax a smile from her. Primrose was right, however; Fouché had been alerted to his presence in Paris and, since Trant had slept the day away, there was precious little time to be lost. The meeting with Talleyrand had been scheduled for the following day; the intervening time had been built in to account for weather and travel delays en route to Paris. As it turned out the interval had not been required, and now Wolfe could not wait. And so he had scrawled a note to Talleyrand, complete with the code Pitt had supplied him, and dispatched it off with a courier Jacques procured for the purpose. Within the hour, he had received a reply: an address in rue de Vertbois.

Wolfe entered a dim corridor and closed the door behind him. The house smelled abandoned. The walls were painted a dirty shade of peach that had begun to bubble and peel at the edges. The floor, buckled with moisture, was covered with a ragged, gray carpet that squelched disconcertingly underfoot. Ahead, lit by a flickering candle in a wall sconce, was a narrow corkscrew staircase that wound its way unsteadily up toward a higher floor.

"Up here, Mr. Trant." A voice drifted lazily down the stairwell. He followed it up to a narrow hallway. A single door at the end stood ajar; another candle flickered invitingly from within. The room, like those beneath, was bare of furniture except for a single rickety wooden chair and table. A scarred wooden floor mirrored a low soot-blackened ceiling, and the same unlikely shade of peeling peach covered the walls. A tallow candle sputtered in a waxy puddle on the mantelpiece and illuminated, in a warm flickering light, the elegantly dressed man who leaned casually against it. His immaculately powdered and bewigged head was cocked to one side in a quizzical manner; his heavy-lidded gaze, which was now examining Wolfe with frank appraisal, gleamed with intelligence and humor. In this dingy little room in a less respectable part of Paris, Talleyrand looked as if he were about to confer with the emperor. Gleaming leather shoes crossed nonchalantly at the ankles; creamy stockings defined muscular calves, and gray satin breeches and a matching coat gave off a lustrous sheen in the candlelight. An intricately embroidered vest, visible beneath the brocade of the coat, glimmered with gold thread. A dark woolen cloak had been flung carelessly over the chair, and a tall black hat sat on the table.

"So you are the Irish spy." Talleyrand raised an eyebrow, his mouth quirking in amusement, his voice deep and sonorous in the small room.

"Wolfe. My name is Wolfe Trant," Wolfe replied. "Thank you for meeting me at such short notice." He moved toward the window at the far end of the room. It was jammed in a half-open position, the lead glass obscured on the outside by a thick layer of begrimed frost. An icy draft whistled in the gap beneath. Below, Wolfe could see the wet cobblestones gleaming yellow in the gaslight. Across the street, where the narrow alley of rue Vaucanson emptied its slush of snow and dung into rue du Vertbois, he could make out the huddled figure of a small boy.

"Not at all," Talleyrand responded courteously. "I have been looking forward to making your acquaintance. I can only apologize for the rustic abode and lack of comfortable furnishings." He gestured vaguely at the dingy room. Talleyrand smiled, revealing strong white teeth that gleamed in the candle glow. The lack of amenities did not appear to disturb him in the least, and he seemed as languidly comfortable as if he were presiding over a state dinner in his own luxurious home on rue de Florentin. "It seems that you have run into some trouble since you arrived in Paris, monsieur?"

"So I have. Things have not exactly gone according to plan, to be sure," Wolfe replied grimly, thinking of the bloodied lodging house he had left the night before.

"In my experience, monsieur, they rarely do. But sometimes that can be the harbinger of, shall we say, more fortuitous opportunities?" Talleyrand began, digging with long, pale fingers into the small pockets of his vest. He retrieved a small ornately decorated silver snuff box, offered some to Wolfe, who declined, before proceeding to pinch a wad between thumb and forefinger. He raised it to his nostrils in one elegant gesture, sniffed delicately, and returned the box to his vest. "Napoleon has become skittish," Talleyrand began without further preamble. "Since the assassination attempt several nights ago, he has closeted himself away from all but his closest ministers and intends to depart for Boulogne before the end of the week."

"Did you tell him you'd found a pilot willing to guide his fleet through the Goodwin Sands?" Wolfe asked tightly. He had a sinking feeling that Pitt's plans to infiltrate Napoleon's inner circle were about to go awry, and with them, his own prospects to secure some kind of betterment for Ireland: coal at market price and Pitt's promise to pursue Catholic emancipation—the first of which would secure a ready competitiveness for all Irish merchants in the textile trade, the latter a long-term necessity for national stability. Wolfe felt instinctively that this was his opportunity to climb out of the abyss of self-recrimination and guilt that had been his life for the past seven years, a chance to make amends for the past. No one in Ireland would ever know of his involvement in a seemingly obscure chain of events that took place across the Channel. But he would know. And then, perhaps, he could live with himself after all.

"I did, monsieur," Talleyrand replied gravely. "He waved me off, saying plans had changed. He did not elaborate. I could not ask without arousing suspicions. Napoleon Bonaparte is an exceedingly private man. He retains a vast amount of strategy in his head, particularly if he is feeling threatened and uncertain of whom to trust."

"But he trusts you?" Wolfe pursued intently.

"It is difficult to say," Talleyrand answered. "I tend to say what I think, monsieur; a quality that Napoleon has little appreciation for, particularly if that opinion does not coincide with his own. There have been other factors, however, that have compromised this mission." He moved closer to Wolfe, his deep voice dropping to a confiding whisper. "There have been rumors in England that Pitt commissioned an Irishman to spy for him in Paris. Undoubtedly, Napoleon has his own spies in King George's court. Perhaps, it was this information that made him abandon the Goodwin Sands invasion plans. Perhaps, Monsieur Trant, he no longer trusts an Irishman." Talleyrand shrugged, a languid movement of his satin-clad shoulder.

"So we find another way," Wolfe insisted, pacing the length of the small room. "There must be papers, maps, plans…something that would tell us of his intentions. There must be preparations underway." He ignored the faint throbbing ache behind his eyes.

"Why is this so important to you, monsieur?" Talleyrand asked, lifting one immaculately groomed eyebrow in elegant surprise. "Would not the Irish be better served if the French succeeded in invading England? At the very least Ireland would be granted her independence. Why is it you have allied yourself with Pitt against your own countrymen?"

"I might ask the very same thing of you," Wolfe replied evenly.

"And well you might." Talleyrand's full lips curved in a sardonic smile.

There was a moment's silence as each man assessed the other. Wolfe sensed that Talleyrand had more information to divulge—the fortuitous opportunity that he had referred to earlier. But he needed a reason to trust Wolfe; a deeper sense of solidarity than was provided by the crumpled note that had instigated this meeting or by the machinations of Pitt that had brought them both together on this cold evening in Paris.

"The French haven't helped us," Wolfe began finally. "The Irish, I mean. They promised troops seven years ago, to arrive at Bantry Bay at dawn on the seventeenth of May. That was the plan. We were to join forces and march on Dublin." He closed his eyes for a moment, seeing the proud excitement of the boys in their ragged regimentals, brandishing sticks, pikes, and antique firearms. "I led the Irish brigade. We attacked the English stronghold at New Ross," he continued, his voice a husky whisper. "Brigade!" Wolfe laughed bitterly, his face contorted with grief and anger. "They were lads with sticks. And they were massacred because the French never came. So a week ago, I made a deal with the English devil. But you see, Duc de Talleyrand, I know this devil. We've been living next door to each other for thousands of years.

I know how his mind works, what he wants…what he fears. I do not expect him to watch my back. I expect him to stab me in it. But seven years ago, France was our ally, and they abandoned us to the worst possible fate. So now, I choose England. I choose the devil I know," Wolfe bit out, baring his teeth in what was almost a snarl. He turned toward the window restlessly, trying to get a grip on his emotions. It had been seven years, for God's sake. Would he never get past this?

"I am sorry," Talleyrand murmured softly from behind him. "There are many things I wish had been done differently." He sighed, a deep expulsion of air, before continuing, his tone regretful. "We have not always had the enlightened leaders one might wish for. The Directoire exécutif, in particular, was a bleak time. Barras was notoriously corrupt; he habitually disregarded the terms of the constitution and resolved to prolong the war as the best expedient for extending his own power."

He referred to the system of government, a Directory of five men who had come to power in France after the dissolution of the National Convention in 1795. They were the ones who had promised Ireland arms seven years ago and failed to deliver.

There was a moment's silence, then Talleyrand continued in his languorous fashion. "In a novel the author gives some intelligence and distinguished character to the principle personage; fate takes less trouble. Mediocrities play a part in great events simply because they happen to be there. Barras, Monsieur Trant, is a case in point."

"To be sure," Wolfe admitted, his fingers tapping out an agitated tempo against the window frame. The bottle scrounger made his way in a slow painful gait across the cobblestones, his sallow and wasted face briefly illuminated by the gleam of gaslight. No other sign of life. Even the café appeared to have closed its doors and extinguished its lights.

"We, in France, have also been subjected to the tyranny of an autocracy, one which allows no room for legitimate opposition." Talleyrand's voice was deep and fervent, and his expression, when Wolfe turned to face him, was one of passionate conviction. "The individual who sincerely believes that his country is suffering, and will continue to suffer as the result of bad policy, has to choose between becoming either a passive spectator of his country's ruin or taking steps to prevent it. This his enemies, of course, will denounce as disloyalty. When open opposition is rebellion, secret opposition becomes treason. Yet, I believe, Monsieur Trant, that there are circumstances in which such treason may become the duty of a patriot. Perhaps that is a path you have similarly chosen for yourself ?"

"Perhaps so," Wolfe conceded with a crooked smile, inclining his head in a gesture of respect and gratitude. Certainly a more palatable perspective. One, however, he doubted would be shared by his neighbors in Dublin. Spying for the English, regardless of circumstances, would constitute a hanging offence, his family name tainted in perpetuity. Egan would never forgive him; but then there was already a long list of accounts his brother could not forgive. What was one more? His name was already spotted with failure and death. He had nothing to lose and everything to gain. "So how can we help each other?" Wolfe asked intently, his tone determined.

"I may know of a way," Talleyrand replied, retrieving a small, tightly bound sheaf of papers from his coat pocket; with long pale fingers, he smoothed them out on the surface of the table, and both men bent over them.

Gaston was tired. He was hungry. The man had been in the apartment a long time now it seemed. Certainly, it would not matter if he slipped away for just a moment? The scent of roasting meat wafted across to him from the café at the end of the street. He knew a back way into the pantry there, a plank near the floor that had rotted through in the middle. If he was quick and quiet, he could grab something and get out before they even knew he had been there. But then if he missed the man he would not get his money. Opening his grubby fist, he again admired the gleaming silver piece. His stomach rumbled in irritable discontent. Just as he had decided to temporarily abandon his post, the succulent aroma of cooking having proved too alluring for his empty belly, Gaston was startled by a sudden clattering of horseshoes against cobblestones. The horses raced down rue du Vertbois and careered to a slippery stop in front of the red door. The gleam of silver buttons in the gaslight, the peaked hats, the blue short coats, and the sheen of black leather boots—Gaston knew this uniform well: the gendarmes.

Suddenly, the clatter and commotion of a detachment of cavalry sounded from the street below. A shrill whistle pierced the air. Talleyrand held the papers he and Trant had lately been scrutinizing over the candle flame, poised and calm as the flames curled around the roll. Once the papers had been thoroughly consumed, he tossed the blackened remnants in the fireplace and blew out the candle. Wolfe moved to the window as the room descended into darkness.

"A carriage," he muttered to Talleyrand who stood behind him. "And ten soldiers. Mac an donais! Tell me there's a back door to this place?" They could hear the muted shouts of men through the windowpane, a commander issuing orders, and the metallic clank of sabers as the men scurried to obey.

"I am afraid not," Talleyrand murmured complacently, shrugging on his coat. He might have been politely declining a second glass of wine. "The downstairs door is the only way in or out." And why the soldiers felt little need for stealth: they knew their quarry was cornered.

# 38.

RUE CHANTEREINE. PARIS, FRANCE
*December 5, 1803*

The house on rue Chantereine had an air of abandonment. The shutters hung drunkenly, the porch step had rotted through, and the front garden was largely obscured by an overgrown ficus tree whose roots had curved and twisted under the paving stones. It had once been elegant. Pretty Spanish tiles covered the birdbath that was now filled with dirt and moldering leaves; the porch was embellished with wrought-iron curlicues that were now tarnished by rust. It had been owned by Madame de la Croix, who had joined the émigrés in London seven years before. The house had been confiscated by Napoleon during his First Consularship but restored to the family the previous year in an attempt to win support for his regime. Madame de la Croix, unpersuaded by Napoleon's gesture, elected to remain in London. The house on rue Chantereine continued in a state of quiet decay. At least, that was the impression the casual passers-by received. In fact, the house had become one of numerous meeting places for the Paris Sector, and the first Tuesday of every fourth month (given prior confirmation) saw a steady but surreptitious arrival of lead members of the French Resistance.

Just past ten in the evening, as the pale December moon cast dancing shadows through the ficus leaves, a hefty figure made his way silently through the garden. He did not walk on the pathway but kept to the deep shadows of the perimeter. Reaching the side of the porch, he paused for a long minute, peering through the darkness, listening intently for anything out of the ordinary. Turning, he signaled quickly to another man still concealed within the shrubbery before proceeding up the stairs and disappearing around the side of the house. A few minutes later, he squeezed his vast bulk through the small cellar door to take a seat with the three others that awaited him in the dark room below.

"Charles, you are late," a voice grumbled. It was Michel Desant, his cousin, who lounged idly in the chair next to his. Dark hair receded from a high forehead. Spectacles perched on a long, narrow nose behind which deep-set dark eyes glinted. His cravat was disheveled, his frayed coat rumpled, and he was two days past a shave. Desant was a student at the Ecole Francaise and, like many other students in Imperial France, wore a deliberately disheveled appearance like a badge of honor. Priding himself on being an intellectual, he spent most of his time in the Café de Montaine drinking wine and vociferously debating what he called philosophical politics. Desant's recently published pamphlet, *Republicanism and the New France*, had been immediately confiscated by the ministry of police, with further distribution banned and all available copies seized. Despite such measures, the treatise enjoyed considerable notoriety; there remained some ambiguity, however, as to whether the popularity of this work derived from the philosophical acumen of its author or the alacrity with which it was condemned by authorities. A bottle of wine and a glass, both almost empty, sat on the table before him.

"I was inevitably detained," Cadoudal replied shortly, his voice deep and gravelly, as he lowered himself into a chair. He was a hefty man, broad of shoulder and wide of girth, with a long, white face that expanded at the base by the lack of a chin and a short, thick neck. Heavy-lidded brown eyes that regarded his colleagues with deceptive casualness capped a large, rounded knob of a nose, and a small, full mouth. Tufts of thick reddish hair emerged from beneath the hat on his head and streaked down either side of his face in carelessly maintained sideburns.

"You are here. That is all that matters," Jeanne Recamier interjected, anxious to diffuse the tension simmering in the room. She stood at the other side of the table, her figure encased in the signature breeches and short coat of the laboring workman.

"Is it?" General Charles Pichegru spoke wearily from one end of the table. He had once been a distinguished-looking man, however his recent eight-month imprisonment in a fortress in Guiana had added twenty years to his appearance. Below the frail forehead, sparsely covered in an unruly fringe of gray whisker, eyes with puffy lower lids stared from either side of a long, thin nose. His eyebrows, like the coarse hair that surrounded his dome, were untamed and sat high on his forehead, as if in perpetual astonishment. His mobile mouth followed suit, and, despite his unhappy tone, the corners quirked upwards in a parody of merriment. "I mean, what exactly have we accomplished to date?" He leaned forward, sharp elbows resting on the table, his military brocade just visible beneath the sober black broadcloth of his coat. "We have become petty murderers operating out of dark back-alleys. And I, for one, did not sign up for that."

"Well, what did you expect, General?" Cadoudal replied mockingly. "That Napoleon Bonaparte would gracefully yield? The tyrant has usurped the throne of France, and the blood will flow through the streets of Paris before he will give it up. We cannot depend upon the people to rise in support of the monarchy. They are sick of war, sick of food shortages, and afraid that any change will be for the worse."

"It takes a strong hand to govern a state. What did Louis XVI do for France?" The third gentleman entered the conversation. He was a short, stocky man, impeccably dressed in a dark blue coat, lapels decorated with an elaborate brocade of gold thread, a cravat tied firmly under his chin. Strong blunt features occupied a square head that sat atop a short, thick neck. His booted heel tapped restlessly under the table. "He emptied the coffers of France on wars in some savage land half way around the world while her people starved to death. Damned right the people will not support the return of the king—why should they?"

"So what are you proposing, General Moreau?" Desant drawled lazily, reaching his arms above him in a languid stretch. "That you are the strong hand that France so desperately needs?" He smiled slightly, as if at the absurdity of the suggestion.

General Moreau rose from the table, nostrils flaring like a bull about to charge, his body a tightly coiled band of muscle and sinew. "Certainly," he flung at Desant. "I command the Armée du Rhin and can summon the support and loyalty of the majority of the French troops. I have, as you know, tremendous popular approval. It is not the monarchy, necessarily, that the people want. They don't give a damn about Louis XVIII. Their lives are characterized by chaos and anarchy; they want a sense of normalcy. They hunger for order as well as bread. Scarred and haunted by the Terror, the people want stability, an end to these foreign wars of conquest, and a strong military to preserve and defend the natural boundaries of France. They know I can provide that." He spoke tightly between ground teeth, parting with each word as if they pained him.

There was a shocked silence before Desant clapped his hands

together in a mocking salute. "You should write a political pamphlet, General. You certainly have a command of the required rhétorique."

Moreau's lip drew back from his upper teeth in a snarl; glaring at Desant, he snapped, "How it was a self-important, drunken pig of a boy ever rose to eminence within the Resistance I will never know." His dark gaze swept the room in angry reprimand, his coat almost bristling with the force of his fury. Desant opened his mouth to issue a fiery retort but was preempted by Jeanne.

"General Moreau, are you withdrawing your support for the duke?" she asked, her words cautiously measured.

Cadoudal slammed a meaty fist on the table. "Merde! I should have known! The ultimate ambition for the ambitious man—the very throne of France!" He rose to his feet, face flushed with angry exertion. "It is over, then. All over!"

"I will support the Duke d'Enghien's claim to the throne on the condition that he proves worthy of the honor," Moreau replied curtly.

"And that assessment will be made by *you*?" Cadoudal boomed scornfully, shaking his head in disbelief. Pichegru rubbed his wrinkled brows with one gout-swollen hand, his mouth a worried smile. Desant appeared to be enjoying the spectacle, his booted feet resting casually on an adjacent chair.

"Gentlemen," Jeanne interrupted forcefully, moving to stand beside Moreau. "At the very least, we can meet with the duke. He is not only a prince of the blood with a legitimate claim to the throne, but he is also an intelligent man of integrity and honor. I trust General Moreau to be a similarly worthy man and am certain that he will be soon convinced of the duke's merits." Moreau nodded stiffly. Cadoudal roughly loosened the cravat at his throat, his breathing heavy, as he lowered his ponderous bulk back into his chair. Desant cheerfully poured himself another glass of wine, the liquid blood-red as it swirled around the rim of the glass. "He is outside?" Jeanne turned to Cadoudal.

"Yes, waiting for the signal that it is safe to come in," Cadoudal wheezed, wiping his glistening forehead with a sleeve of his coat. Jeanne moved to the door, and the men sat in stony silence. A moment later she returned, an elegantly dressed man emerging from the shadows behind her.

"Gentlemen, the duke and heir to the throne of France," she said simply.

# 39.

Germain de Lausain peered intently through the pantry door. He had been crouching in the musty cupboard for over an hour, and the physical discomfort had become excruciating. He was unable to stand upright but leaned back against the wall, legs uncomfortably bent beneath his massive bulk, arms splayed against each side, eyes fixed to the very slight opening afforded by the door. His lower back was a searing paroxysm of pain, his legs trembled with the unaccustomed exertion, and he had a desperate need to cough. Faint scuttlings, which he tried to ignore, sounded behind the floor skirtings. Rats. He hated them with an irrational shrieking fear that would embarrass a young girl. Germain refused to contemplate what he would do if one of them emerged within the pantry.

Had they left yet? he thought with increasing desperation. A thin crack of light flickered through the planks of the cellar's slanted wooden door. They were still there. Merde! he muttered to himself, feeling a cramp spasm across his right calf.

He had had the immense good fortune to secure his hiding place immediately after Desant's arrival (whose brooding egotism and the warm flush of wine had kept him oblivious to the fact that he had had a tail for the past two weeks). The dilapidated floorboards creaked and groaned with every movement, and Germain had to remain impossibly still if he were to remain undiscovered. An overpowering stench of urine emanated from the corner of the pantry where he had been forced to relieve himself an hour earlier, cringing and wincing in fear as the hot yellow stream splattered against the dusty boards.

But what a coup! In the midst of his physical misery, Germain could not help congratulating himself. For this he would demand a *fortune* in francs, and Fouché would have no choice but to pay. And he could leave this miserable, rat-infested city behind once and for all. His sister had a little cottage in Marseille; he had always wanted to visit the coast. He was damned sick of politics. Germain yearned, above all, for a peaceful existence. French society had changed with dizzying rapidity over the past twenty years and his attempts to keep up had exhausted his reserves and left him a broken and nervous man. His profession as a long-time police informant meant that he was perpetually tossed about by prevailing political winds. And they had blown from all directions over the past decade: radically Bourbon, then fervently Jacobin, and now resolutely Bonapartist. Was Napoleon on his way out, or would he maintain power for another ten years? Who was to say? Or if the Bourbons were successfully restored would his relationship with Fouché be his undoing? The price of guessing wrong about the next wind-change could very well cost him his life. Where should he place his loyalties? He sensed that the ground under his feet was not just likely to shake but drop right away…

His dismal thoughts were interrupted by the gentle thud of the cellar door as it swung to one side. The lean figure of a young man appeared, a workman by his appearance, briefly silhouetted by the gas-lamp below before the door was quickly replaced, the light extinguished as quickly as it had appeared. Germain's breath caught in his throat, eyes fixed to the pantry door, hands damp with sweat and fear, splayed across the side of the cupboard supporting his gasping bulk. He could hear the man move from the kitchen toward the front of the house.

Should he follow him? Germain wondered uncertainly before reluctantly dismissing the idea. As desperately as he wanted to leave the stifled confines of the pantry, Cadoudal was the primary object of interest. And what if he were to be discovered in the process of leaving? Germain knew it would be a protracted, painful process extricating himself; the burning pain in his knees assured him of that. Stealth would be next to impossible. Leaving before the Resistance had all departed was not a viable possibility. He could not move without alerting them to his presence, and if that happened—well, he did not delude himself that he would survive the night; he would be just another fat white corpse floating in the Seine with a swiftly efficient gash where his throat used to be.

A moment later, Germain was sending his humble thanks to the Almighty for a decision well made, for the young man had returned with a grander one. Again, he had a momentary glimpse of both figures as the cellar door opened to them and they were bathed in the gaslight. Beneath the voluminous great coat and black tricorn of the taller man, Germain caught the glimmer and sheen of silk. The man's face, turned toward the room below, was in shadow, but his hand, grasping the edge of the cellar door, was that of an aristocrat. Long, pale fingers adorned with several rings glinted gold in the dim light. And the other, the young man: his face was pale and set, and for a moment Germain hesitated— the eyes, the curve of mouth and jaw…was it a *woman*? Was *this* the infamous Primrose?

He had to be sure! Damned if he was going to leave without definitive proof after all that he had already suffered. Germain waited until the cellar door closed behind the two, then slowly, carefully, pushed open the pantry and with excruciating pain, tears prickling at the corners of his eyes, he eased his unwieldy bulk through. The low murmur of voices drifted from below. Germain's breath caught in his throat as the pantry door squeaked on its hinges, his kneecaps popped, and the floorboards creaked alarmingly underfoot. Fervently hoping the noises unheard, or dismissed as the sighs of an old house in a rising wind, Germain gently closed the pantry door. Moving as stealthily as he was able, his heart hammering in anxious fear, his knees, arms and back spasming in pain, Germain crouched with one ear to the cellar door.

Less than ten minutes later, he was staggering through the moon-dappled garden, torso drenched with sweat, breeches stinking of piss. Beneath the glossy beard, however, his lips stretched in a broad smile, his pain and discomfort utterly forgotten in his expectation of an imminent seaside retirement.

# 40.

Wolfe took up the chair and, with a grunt of effort, yanked the legs apart. It splintered under his grip, and he was left with a serviceable club. Not much, but better than nothing. He had his fists, but they would be of little use if these soldiers came in firing. "What about the window?" he asked Talleyrand urgently. "Can we not get out to the roof?"

"It's a little cold for that kind of activity, do you not think?" Talleyrand murmured from the window, gazing down at the activity of the soldiers in the street. "Besides," he said with a yawn, turning to Wolfe, "this vest was a gift from the czar of Russia; I would so hate to get it spoiled." Wolfe glanced at him incredulously. Was he out of his mind? "Do not worry yourself, my friend." Talleyrand's mouth curved in amusement. "It seems they did not want us after all." Wolfe moved to the grimy windowpane and glanced down at the wet street below. "I recognize the carriage," Talleyrand continued with unruffled smoothness. "It belongs to Monsieur Astartiste, the owner of the Hotel Apollion in the Palais Royale. He is, no doubt, taking his week's earnings home tonight, and, being a nervous sort, has hired a police detachment to see him safely to his destination. It appears his carriage wheel has broken right outside our door."

Wolfe exhaled in sharp relief, tossing the broken chair leg in the fireplace. "And here I was a spoiling for a fight." He shook his head regretfully, casting a rueful grin at Talleyrand who raised his eyebrows in mock commiseration.

"It will be a dull evening for us both, Monsieur Trant. Let us hope that your infiltration of the Tuileries will be as quiet." The clatter of carriage wheels on the cobblestones, and the gradually receding clamor of soldiers announced the successful completion of repairs in the street below. It was safe to leave.

"If all goes according to plan, I'll be in and out in no time at all."

"Tomorrow evening at the Tuileries then, Monsieur Trant," Talley-rand pulled his hat down over his eyes and drew his cloak close about him. "Good luck to you."

"And to yourself, Monsieur de Talleyrand. Thank you." Wolfe watched the foreign minister disappear down the dingy stairwell in a swirl of black cloak. He would give Talleyrand five minutes before he himself departed. Returning to the window, he could see Talleyrand climbing into a covered black carriage that rattled its way toward rue de Ventine. Wolfe glanced across the street. The boy was still there. He would double the promised payment, Wolfe thought. He had been a good lad. As he was turning from the window, he heard a second shrill whistle from across the street. Was someone else coming up? The police? Should he try to climb up to the roof ?

Heaving with effort, Wolfe managed to force the window pane apart sufficiently to climb through. But even as he did so, he could see that it would not be an option. The house was crumbling with rot and mildew, precariously supported, or so it seemed, by the similarly dilapidated buildings to either side. The bricks beyond the window were coated with grime and rendered slippery by a second layer of ice. A rusted drainpipe snaked its way up the brick facing toward the roof above, but it would not bear the weight of a man. The icy cobblestones lay a good thirty feet below. One way in, and one way out. With a prickle of unease, Wolfe turned from the window, retrieved the chair leg from the hearth and rapidly moved to the door.

L'Aigle moved cautiously into the house. He had been fortunate in tracking the target down so quickly. Madame Davall, as he had sur-mised, proved of little use. Her son had wasted an hour of his time before leading him to a plump scarlet-headed whore who had glanced uncomprehendingly from the sketch to his face, her expression vacuous, her voice a garbled stream of high-pitched consonants. A dead end. So he had gone back to his initial notes and the pages of information pro-vided by his English client. The clues were there. The target was to meet surreptitiously with Napoleon, to conduct a secret meeting whereby he would agree to guide the French fleet to English shores. He could not just arrive at the Tuileries and expect an audience with the emperor. The target needed the influence of a powerful man, a conduit who would act as intermediary. One who not only had access to Napoleon and was privy to the invasion plans but who was himself easily approached.

His client had suggested a possible affiliation with four candidates: Claude Francois De Menval, Napoleon's private secretary; Alexandre Berthier, minister of war; Dominique de Villepin, minister of the interior; or Charles Maurice de Talleyrand, foreign minister and, most recently, grand chamberlain and vice-elector of the empire. Since Berthier was currently overseeing troop movements in the Rhine Valley and Villepin was bedridden with edema, that left Menval and Talleyrand. Considering that the former spent much of his waking and sleeping time within the Tuileries and would be largely inaccessible to the target, Talleyrand seemed a more logical choice. And the contact would be made soon. The target's arrival had been advertised in blood; Wolfe Trant would need to proceed rapidly before Fouché's henchmen tracked him down.

A few hours after staking out Talleyrand's elegant house in rue St. Florentin, L'Aigle had been rewarded with a late-night, stealthy departure by a cloaked figure with a pronounced limp. Talleyrand. Either he was going to visit one of his mistresses or...? Climbing into a waiting hackney cab, the driver of which had been handsomely paid to wait upon L'Aigle's convenience, he followed the foreign minister's carriage down rue St. Florentin and around the bend. It clattered to a halt in a dismal part of Paris before a red door, the paint peeling and weathered in patches to a light gray. Not the luxurious abode to which Talleyrand's mistresses were accustomed.

L'Aigle wrinkled his nose in disgust. His polished Hessian boots sunk an inch into sodden gray carpet. The corridor was no less pungent than the street outside where rotting vegetable scraps, horse dung, and sour spirits stewed in icily stagnant puddles. Here, though, in the small house, it had a way of closing around his face, tendrils snaking their way up his nostrils, clinging to his skin, clothes, and hair. Kill Trant and get it over with. Making his way cautiously toward the darkened stairwell at the end of the hallway, L'Aigle brought his pistol up close to his face, pressing the steel barrel against his cheek. The cold metal, the acrid smell of gunpowder—now that was a smell he liked. He moved quickly, not wanting to meet his quarry on the winding stairwell where a tussle might prove unpredictable. Moving silently and rapidly up the damp stairs, which sagged underfoot, he had almost reached the top when his booted foot, expecting the solidity of a wooden surface beneath it, encountered—nothing.

L'Aigle lurched forward in surprise, leg dangling through the broken step, the rotted wood to either side crashing with a sodden thud to the carpeted floor below. Heaving himself up, one arm to each side of the stairwell, he managed to extricate his leg just as he felt the crushing blow of a wooden object to the back of his head. Reeling, but conscious, he drew back a step or two, bringing his pistol up to the shadowy figure that even now was bearing down on him. He fired. A brief explosion of light illuminated a billowing cloud of gunpowder.

*Had he got him?* The fleeting thought crossed L'Aigle's mind before Trant was upon him, the Irishman having hurled himself down the stairs with an almost manic momentum. L'Aigle felt his ribs crash against the stairs, the huge Irish demon lying atop him, seemingly similarly stunned. Before L'Aigle could raise himself to check, he heard splintering wood cracking beneath their combined weight. The stairs, already damp with mold and rot, had little chance of surviving this additional assault. With a shuddering, sodden groan, the wood disintegrated around them. Then, he was falling—not far, eight feet or so; but he felt his back slam against the floor with an agonizing force, the pain of impact taking his breath away. The limp body of his target covered his own, heavy and inert, pinning him down.

L'Aigle shifted slightly, pain shooting through his spine. But he could move. That was something at least. His pistol was nowhere to be seen. He turned his torso slightly to one side, trying to dislodge the body covering his own, grimacing with the effort, his back contorting in spasms of pain. The Irishman stirred. Merde! His knife! Feeling with his fingers, he grasped the steel point of the knife that lay snugly inside his left sleeve...

Wolfe felt the searing heat of a bullet lodged in his left shoulder and knew that he was still alive. He had fallen on the assassin. The body of the man lay beneath his own; the damp remnants of the broken staircase lay in splinters around them. Placing one palm on the floor, Wolfe raised himself slowly to his feet. The assassin lay unmoving. Wolfe reached down, intending to check the prone form for weapons, when, with lightening rapidity, the man rolled to one side, a glimmering steel blade appearing in his left hand. Holding the knife in front of him, the assassin slowly, painfully, got to his feet, his face dark in the shadowed hallway.

"Who are you?" Wolfe rasped hoarsely, his body tensed in a fighter's crouch, his fists instinctively clenched at his chin. "Who sent you?"

The assassin did not answer, his thin lips spread in a mirthless smile. Lunging, he thrust the slender blade viciously forward to where Wolfe's torso had been a fraction of a second before.

"You are fast, monsieur, for a man of your size," the assassin complimented him, his voice a husky whisper, his accent peculiar. Aristocratic, flawless French but tinged with something else. Without removing his gaze from that of his opponent, Wolfe reached behind him and, with brutal force, wrenched apart a sharply splintered segment of the stairwell that was hanging drunkenly in place. He wielded the wooden beam like a club. The assassin was tall and quick but relatively slender. If he could get within grappling distance, Wolfe was certain he could force him down. There was just the knife to consider.

The assassin feinted to the right and then, with surprising speed, stabbed to the left, catching the side of Wolfe's chest as he brought the beam around to bear with bludgeoning force. The assassin ducked, avoiding the blow, but failing to notice Wolfe's right foot which had kicked out sharply, colliding with his right knee and sending him sprawling to the ground.

"Monsieur?" The door at the end of the corridor stood ajar. A hand pushed it open, and the silhouette of a small boy in a large coat appeared. Both men glanced up, momentarily distracted by the intrusion. The boy hesitated, taking in the two men: one armed with a knife on the floor, the other gripping the beam; both breathing hard. "I've brought the gendarmes, monsieur, as you wanted. They're comin' now."

The assassin lurched to his feet, still brandishing the knife threateningly in front of him. "We are not finished, Monsieur Trant," he muttered. And then he was gone, bolting past the open-mouthed boy in the doorway and melting into the blackness of the night from where he had come.

"I didn't really get the gendarmes, monsieur. I just thought it might scare that fella away. Was he really trying to kill you?"

Wolfe handed the boy five silver francs. "You did fine, milad. Find me a carriage," he muttered. "And the rest," he grasped the boy's narrow shoulder, "is all yours."

# 41.

## Secretariat de Gendarmie. Paris, France
### December 6, 1803

It was cold in Fouché's office. The windows, as usual, were wide open to admit the frigid morning air. It had started to snow, and fat flakes, carried into the room on icy gusts, melted on the wooden floor. Fouché seemed impervious to all weather, hot or cold, and wore his threadbare black coat and breeches day after day. The only change seemed to be an added layer of grime that gradually accumulated, giving his clothes a greasy sheen. Probably waterproofed them, Chavert thought idly from his place across the desk.

"I have completed the report for the emperor as you requested, Commissioner." Chavert handed Fouché a sheet of paper, half of which was covered in a neatly penned report. Napoleon had grown impatient for culprits; Fouché would have to deliver some soon. With this in mind, he had instructed Chavert to draw up an account of the assassination attempt to submit to his superiors. Fouché glanced disdainfully at the paper in his hand. "Is that *all?*"

"Yes, Commissioner. I think all the pertinent facts are there."

Fouché, scanning the paper, snorted derisively, dark brows drawing across his forehead in a frown. "Attacked by Royalist conspirators," he muttered, running a dirty finger along the compact script, "and supported by hungry Parisians." Without reading any further, he crumpled up the paper and flung it across the table where it joined other discards scattered across the floor. "Have you learned nothing, Chavert?" he asked scathingly. "Fishwives and market porters employ the language of le rhétorique with more flair than you." Retrieving a thick sheaf of bound papers from his desk drawer, he flung them at the chief inspector. "Read that! My report on the rue de Violi riot last month."

Fouché rose from his chair, grinding the smoking remnants of his cigar into a corner of the windowsill with thick yellow fingers. "Volume is of the essence," he continued, pacing across the room behind Chavert, his tone one of impatient condescension. "What can be written in three

lines takes on more authority when spun out to three pages. To be effective and attract attention, you need to be long-winded. Never use plain
speech…the more adjectives the better." Fouché, his thin mouth pursed
in irritation, stopped beside Chavert. "And you suggest these desperate
acts are spurred on by *hungry* Parisians." He shook his head in dismay
at his subordinate's foolishness. "Hunger is an embarrassing topic for
the empire. These new aristocrats eat unusually well. You are ill-advised
to report literally what you see, and, mon dieu, don't draw too much
of a distinction between fat and thin. You should report instead that
people are basically good and loyal, even grateful." Fouché resumed his
pacing. His tone, thoughtful now, contained the self- congratulatory air
of a man who has perfected the art of maintaining harmony with his
superiors and keeping his underlings in check, all whilst maximizing his
own importance and influence.

"Report that the people are patient in adversity, that they know the
government is concerned with their ills and is actively seeking to alleviate their suffering, but that ex-terrorists, Royalists, Jacobins, et cetera are
seeking to undermine their loyalty to the empire and channel their anger and despair into political riots and assassination attempts." Fouché
turned to scowl in Chavert's direction. "Well? What are you waiting for?
Go write it up, you imbécile! And this time do it right!"

Chavert hurried to the door, but his exit was forestalled by the flur-
ried arrival of Germain de Lausain, his pouchy cheeks flushed with
heated excitement, his breath labored, his mouth a gasping O within the
curly nest of his beard. "I did it, Monsieur Commissioner!" he panted,
placing one meaty hand on each knee as he bent forward, struggling to
regain his breath.

"Chief Inspector, close the door!" Fouché ordered without taking
his gaze off Germain's shuddering form. "I hope for your sake the
information is astounding," Fouché remarked dryly, retrieving another
cigar from amidst the scattered papers on his desktop. "Because you
may very well have blown what little credibility you had as an informant
by coming here."

"Oh…no…Monsieur Commissioner! I was…exceedingly…care-
ful!" Germain managed between wheezes. "I came in the back way
and…"

"What is it, monsieur?" Fouché barked impatiently. Germain proceed
-ed to inform the police commissioner of how he had been following

Desant for the better part of a week and how the previous night Desant had taken a brougham to an abandoned house in rue Chantereine. Curious, Germain had slipped inside, hiding in a musty pantry of the dilapidated kitchen. Moments after securing his hiding place, a heavy tread announced the arrival of another. "Did you see him?" Fouché demanded, chewing on the end of his cigar.

"He was a large man, Monsieur Commissioner. I did not see much of him and only for a moment in the candlelight as he opened the cellar door. He had bushy hair, reddish in color, with sideburns that came down to here…" Germain gestured toward his jaw.

"Cadoudal!" Fouché murmured, his deep-set eyes gleaming triumphantly.

"Cadoudal!" Germain echoed, his head bobbing up and down in excited affirmation. "And there were others!" he continued gleefully, sensing his news was of tremendous interest to the commissioner of police. "I saw a woman! I thought she was a man; she was dressed as a man, but I am sure it was a woman. She left, and then she returned with the duke! I heard her refer to him as the duke!"

"A duke?" Fouché hissed. "*Which* duke, Germain? Do you know how many dukes there are?"

"A prince of the blood, Monsieur Commissioner…"

Primrose, Cadoudal, and a duke. A prince of the blood. This could only mean one thing. The French Resistance was preparing to make their final move. They were going to bring the Bourbons back! An heir to the French throne. "But who was it?"

Germain's face fell only slightly at this sharp interrogative. "I did not see his face, Monsieur Commissioner…"

There were five possibilities: the Ducs d'Orléans, de Condé, de Bourbon, d'Enghien, and de Conti—all princes of the blood, all bearing legitimate claim to the throne of France. Fouché sucked deeply on his cigar, feeling the pungent nicotine fill his lungs. Events were escalating. The momentum was building; he could feel it. Primrose and Wolfe Trant, now Cadoudal and a royal prince. But Napoleon Bonaparte had to be removed before the Royals could be restored. The previous assassination attempt had failed. They would make another, he knew, and soon.

"Germain. You have proved yourself useful after all. Continue to be so, and you will be further rewarded." Fouché paid him in coin and, with a negligent flick of his wrist, gestured toward the door. "Stay in Paris, monsieur. I may have need of you," he added curtly. Germain's face, reddened with the emotional exertion, was instantly crestfallen. After the informant had departed, the door firmly closed behind him, Fouché turned toward Chavert. "Still nothing from the Recamier house?" he demanded, thoughtfully scratching a stubbly cheek with one grimy fingernail.

"No, Commissioner. Marie is one of our best. She is listening and watching, but there has been little activity to report..."

"Madame Recamier?"

"Has not been seen for two days."

"Mmmm." Fouché sank into his chair and looked out the window. The rooftops of Paris stretched out beneath an arctic gray sky, the spires of Notre Dame almost obscured by the rising swirl of snow.

"A doctor has been to the house, perhaps that accounts for Madame Recamier's seclusion," Chavert offered cautiously.

"Perhaps," Fouché's tone was noncommittal, his gaze still on the wintry sky beyond a windowpane that was steadily accumulating a powdery mound of snow. "Marie can confirm this for us. She leaves for the market in an hour. Send someone to meet her and find out." And, in the direction of Chavert's retreating figure, added: "and inform me immediately, Chief Inspector."

"Madame Recamier," Fouché murmured to himself. He had long been convinced that Primrose was educated. A former aristocrat perhaps? "Madame Recamier," he repeated, almost lovingly, his tongue caressing the words. It was she. Fouché felt it almost instinctively. Madame Recamier used to be a countess. She hosted an art salon in her home every Monday, mingling with everyone of consequence and many of not. Marie had proved useless; if he wanted to apprehend the infamous Primrose, he would have to take care of every detail himself. And if he was wrong, if somehow Madame Recamier was an innocent dupe, she would still be required to explain her relationship to the old woman who had met with Desant at the booksellers. Shuffling to the door, Fouché opened it into the dim hallway outside his office. "Chief Inspector!" he bellowed. Chavert hastened from his own cubicle next door. "Send out a warrant for the arrest of Madame Recamier. Do it discreetly; I don't want her forewarned!"

# 42.

"When did she start?" Jeanne asked, peeling the grizzled gray beard from her chin as she lowered her bulky figure to the chair. While the tightly wrapped pillows and layers lent solidity to her size and obscured her shape, they were damned hot inside the heated bedchamber. The light sheen of sweat on her brow was not entirely due to her cumbersome costume; it seemed Fouché had managed to infiltrate her household staff.

"Three days ago," Karl replied steadily. "Do you want me to get rid of her?

"No, too risky." Jeanne removed the gray spectacles and scratched the middle of her forehead where the plaster attached to the skin.

"Careful, you still have to get out of here," Karl cautioned, kneeling down in front of her. With one thick forefinger, he gently pressed the plaster into place. The spectacles neatly hid the division, and makeup colored the wide fleshy nose to an identical skin tone. The artful application of kohl and dark powder, combined with strategic daubs of white face cosmetic, and a smooth gray wig gave her an appearance remarkably like the elderly Dr. Dumieu, who served as Madame Recamier's physician.

"Let's use this to our advantage." Jeanne could feel the sweat dampening her armpits and trickling down her back. "Are you certain she believes me ill?"

"We have told Marie you have a most contagious form of the pox. Fouché isn't paying her near enough to risk getting any closer to you."

"Nicely done. Might irreparably harm the charm of Madame Recamier's boudoir, but then who hasn't had the pox in Paris these days?" Jeanne gave a half smile. Mon dieu, she thought, she even referred to herself in third person. Jeanne hesitated before asking: "Monsieur Guébriant?"

"Taken care of."

Jeanne nodded grimly. She didn't need to know any more. "Will that produce difficulties for us?"

"I don't think so," Karl replied. "He didn't have many friends, other than those he owed money to, and they were disgruntled as it appeared he chose to replace his wardrobe rather than satisfy his debtors. We cleared out his apartment. People will assume he left Paris in order to evade his obligations."

"Fouché?"

"He won't find the body. We are hoping he will arrive at the same conclusions as everyone else, that he will assume the list of Resistance members was a bluff."

"Right." Jeanne sank back into her chair suddenly exhausted. The layers of wool, pillow, and rope felt inordinately heavy, and under the wig and thick makeup, she suddenly felt as if she were suffocating. Closing her eyes and forcing herself to breath evenly and deeply, she managed to suppress her momentary panic by force of will.

"Jeanne, are you all right?" Karl's concerned voice sounded in her ear.

"Yes…yes, I am fine…just a little tired." In truth, the meeting at rue Chantereine worried her. The generals had coalesced behind the duke; at least General Moreau had conceded that he seemed an acceptable candidate, but his black eyes gave nothing away. Was Georges Cadoudal right? Had General Moreau determined the Napoleonic Empire was best supplanted by his own military regime? Jeanne had confronted him after the meeting in an attempt to secure his support.

"General Moreau…"

"I will give you one week," he had said forcefully before she could say anything further. "One week to get rid of Napoleon and begin transitioning power to the duke." Jeanne exhaled in sharp relief. So he would support them. The Army of the Rhine would follow their general, and the duke would…

"If you are unable to accomplish this or if it becomes apparent that the Duke d'Enghien has not the caliber required to lead, then I will declare myself for France and urge the armies to support my candidacy." Moreau spoke with ferocious intent, his compact body taut and straining under the military brocade, his gaze compelling and powerful.

"It seems, General," Jeanne began heatedly, "somewhat arbitrary to require the complete change of political power within the period of seven days. Why not eight, or six? If the process is the right one, then it should be supported, whether it requires a week or a month."

"You mistake the matter, madame. It is not I who demand this; it is the people of France. There is no more time. Thousands of men desert the army every week; thousands more cut off the fingers of their right hands to avoid conscription. Napoleon has betrayed the very principles on which the Revolution was founded. He has established a new aristocratic order, granted royal titles out to his family, crowned himself emperor! What of the people, Madame Primrose? More time? More time, madame? I have no more time!" Moreau finished, his voice rising almost to a shout, his chest heaving in indignation, his dark eyes flashing heat and fire.

"I understand, General," Jeanne answered, placing a hand upon the general's arm. "A week."

General Moreau was indispensable to the effective transition of power. It was all very well to assassinate the emperor, but one had to prevent the country from falling into chaos and anarchy. The people needed to be reassured that a strong hand was governing the state, that the military was supportive, that France was safe, that governance was effective. Moreau commanded unparalleled popularity among the soldiers as well as the French populace. To maintain stability during transition, to command the crucial support of the army immediately after the assassination, Moreau's support was essential.

As she had walked briskly south from rue Chantereine, Jeanne soberly reviewed the events of the evening. The Resistance was fragmenting; she could feel it. Cadoudal was suspicious of Moreau's motives; Pichegru was questioning the strategy employed; Desant was a drunken sot who cared more about the impression than the difference he was making, and Moreau was becoming increasingly impatient with the lack of results. Jeanne couldn't blame him. Most of the time, she felt much the same way. But he had given her a week. Beyond that, the Resistance would have difficulty maintaining a united front anyway. A week to fashion a miracle.

"So how will we do it?" Jeanne mused, not realizing that she had spoken aloud until Karl responded.

"Do what?"

"Fashion a miracle," she replied grimly.

"A letter came." Karl handed her a cream envelope with *Madame*

*Recamier* written in graciously flowing script across the front. "It arrived on Monday, but we had no way of getting in touch with you. I presumed it to be some inconsequential social invitation." He shrugged.

Madame Recamier often received such overtures. As a popular society hostess, her advice, her thoughts, and most of all her presence were perpetually sought after by younger women seeking to make a name for themselves in society. Or by those older and more influential who were seeking reassurance that they were not forgotten or outdated. The popular were always in demand. And, for the moment, there were none more solicited than Madame Recamier. The vast majority of these requests ended up in the rubbish. Probably, this one would be no different.

"Not Madame Geoffrin again?" Jeanne sighed, tearing open the envelope with her forefinger. "Really, I just don't have time…" she stopped short. Her mouth fell open.

"Jeanne?" Karl asked.

"It is from the empress," Jeanne murmured absently, her eyes scanning the paper with renewed concentration. "She wants me to attend the assemblée tomorrow night at the Tuileries. Karl, this could be our chance!"

"With Napoleon in attendance?" Karl asked, sinking into the seat beside her.

"Yes," Jeanne replied, looking up at Karl with a gleam in her eyes. "Concealed weapon and close-quarter kill? Poison in the wine? We have one week, my friend. One week to take care of this situation, and I doubt there will be a better opportunity than the assemblée. Where else can Madame Recamier achieve close proximity to the emperor of the French?" Her lips curved in a slow smile.

"Poison," Karl answered thoughtfully. "That way you can administer the lethal dose and get out before you are suspected." Then his face clouded as he raised anxious eyes to her own. "But Fouché is watching the house. He suspects you. What if he has already communicated his suspicions to Napoleon? What if this is a trap? I don't like it." He shook his head in dismissal, mouth tight with disapproval.

Jeanne leaned forward, cupping his face in her hands. "Mon cher," she began earnestly. "Armand trained me for this. If we can save France, if we can finally achieve what we have been struggling for, what sacrifice is not warranted? I can do this, Karl. Help me, please."

Karl gazed at her, his own eyes suspiciously bright.

"You know I will do anything you ask of me, madame."

"Then we will need a poison. One that works fast."

"I can take care of that. Will you be at rue Demarest?"

Jeanne bit her lip. Wolfe would be gone, of course, fulfilling what-ever mission it was that Monsieur Pitt had assigned him. Nevertheless, spending two consecutive nights in one place was not something she did under ordinary circumstances. "What about rue Rivoli? Is the up-stairs apartment available?"

"No. It seems that Madame Arbour has found a tenant."

"Boulevard Saint Germaine?"

"Categorized as wavering."

"Rue de Chateau?"

"Seen with gendarmes last week." Karl shrugged, doubt flickering across his features.

"Well, Saint Marceau it is then. A safer place than most, perhaps, Karl," Jeanne decided. All of a sudden she craved a drink—a splash of whiskey, a swallow of wine, something that connected her intrinsically to the world. "Do we have any wine?" He poured her a glass from the decanter on the table and placed it in front of her. Jeanne rose, retrieved another glass, and poured one for Karl. "To France," she said solemnly before swallowing the contents down.

"To France," he echoed. "And what of Madame Recamier's pox?"

"Well, I suppose she is about to effect a most miraculous recov-ery—the wonders of Dr. Dumieu's medical prowess!" Karl frowned. Sensing his disapproval, Jeanne continued: "What choice do we have, Karl? I think Fouché relies upon Marie's report for final confirmation. He isn't a fool, and I doubt he will report to the emperor on hearsay. Particularly when the emperor's wife is somewhat influenced by the charming Madame Recamier, pox and all." She grinned at him. At his dubious expression, Jeanne reached out and grasped Karl's hand. "God willing, all this will be over in a few days and France will again belong to the people." Tears pricked the corners of her eyes, and she bit her lip to prevent it from trembling. "Whatever happens, Karl, thank you…for everything you have done."

"Be safe, Jeanne," Karl muttered fervently.

Jeanne retrieved the black medical bag from its place against the chair and grasped the doctor's silver-handled walking stick. "I suppose

the good doctor has visited the poxy patient long enough," she finished
with a tremulous laugh.

"Wait, your beard." Karl applied fresh face plaster from a small tub
in the doctor's bag and pressed the beard piece into place. It consisted
of carefully cut portions of fur from a Brewie Yorkie, a small dog with
short silky hair that closely resembled that of a human (a greasy-haired
human, granted, but that was also more common than not in Paris). It
was sufficient to pass inspection on the street anyway, which is all that
was intended.

"There! The spitting image of Dr. Dumieu!" Jeanne proclaimed
stiffly through the dog hair that obscured her mouth. "Mon dieu! I can't
wait to get out of this thing."

"We were concerned for you, my brother and I..." Karl began
suddenly as she turned toward the door. Unaccustomed as he was to
expressing emotion, his tone faltered, hands curling into fists at his
sides. "When that...that damned Irishman... took you at the hotel..."
The damned Irishman. The one Jeanne had left in bed at rue Demarest
earlier in the day. "We lost you in the crowd." Karl and Pieter blamed
themselves, she realized with dismay.

"I was fine; I am fine," Jeanne told him briskly. "I know Armand told
you to watch out for me, but I can take care of myself. I have been doing
it for many years now. He taught me well." Karl rose to his feet, arms
crossed across his chest, his expression one of stubborn skepticism.
"Except sometimes...as with Monsieur Guébriant, of course..." her
voice trailed off. From beneath the fur, she gave a half-smile, awkwardly
patting Karl's massive shoulder as she shuffled past, stick and bag in
hand.

# 43.

Jeanne opened the door to her room to discover Wolfe Trant stripped to the waist. "What the hell are you still doing here?" she demanded furiously. "I *knew* I should have just left you at the hotel...the moment I saw the mess you had gotten yourself into..."

"One I was quite capable of getting meself out of ! Believe me, this is not by choice," he snapped over his shoulder. Wolfe stood by the window, twisting sideways in the pale afternoon light as he bent to examine himself. The pale skin of his back was ridged and knotted with scars and contusions, his fingers red with blood. "I got into a bit o' trouble..." he began, then stopped short as he turned and took in her attire. Jeanne would have laughed if she hadn't been so angry. His expression was one of baffled bewilderment. "Well, the dead arose and appeared to Mary!" Wolfe muttered in a low undertone. Then, louder: "Who the hell are you supposed to be?"

"Doctor Dumieu," she replied, yanking the dog hair from her chin and tossing the spectacles on the bed.

"Just what I need, a doctor. Do ye have anything useful in that bag or 'tis it just for show?" He gestured, wincing with the movement, toward the medical case on the floor.

"What happened?" Jeanne crossed the room, divesting herself of coat, pillows, and blankets. She halted in front of him at the sight of the bullet wound in his shoulder and the laceration across his lower torso. "Merde."

"Right, merde."

Jeanne glanced over his shoulder at the broad expanse of his back. No exit wound. "Did you get the bullet out?"

"It's what I've been bloody tryin' to do for the past hour," Wolfe growled, his face white with pain.

"With *that*?" she glanced skeptically at the dull kitchen knife in his hand.

"Annette offered to help; I declined. She left me with that."

Without a word, Jeanne opened her medical bag and retrieved a small surgeon's scalpel. "Sit still," she instructed, placing one hand on the side of his arm and leaning in close to examine the jagged edges of the wound. Dark blood welled and spilled, trickling down his chest to form a dark stain on the waistband of his breeches. The puckered skin was angry and swollen around the site of the wound—no doubt from his repeated forays with the kitchen knife.

"Just get the damned bullet out, and I'll be on me way," he bit out savagely, eyes startlingly blue in a pale face. "I've been in scraps far worse than this."

"I believe you." Jeanne probed the wound with the point of her scalpel, feeling for the telltale hardness of a lodged bullet, her head bent close to Wolfe's shoulder. Wolfe grunted in agony, nostrils flaring, eyes closed against the pain.

"Are you sure you know what your doing?" he rasped irritably, without opening his eyes.

Jeanne's head snapped up, dark tendrils of hair curled with damp and perspiration beaded her brow. She wiped the back of one hand across her cheek, smearing blood and makeup into gruesome blotches of red and gray. Jeanne glared at him, brandishing the bloody scalpel in her hand. "If you want to try again with the kitchen knife, by all means, be my guest!"

"Have yer found the damned thing is what I want to know!" Wolfe snapped back, his Irish brogue thickening in his pain and irritation.

"I have. Just sit still, and let me get at it," Jeanne retorted, her eyes flashing with annoyance. "Are all Irishmen this difficult, or just you?"

"To be sure, lass, I'm the worst of the lot," he muttered.

"I figured as much," Jeanne murmured under her breath, eyes steady on her work, mouth pursed in concentration. "So who shot you?"

"Complicated story..." he began, then, as Jeanne's scalpel jabbed into his flesh with vicious force: "Argghhh! Jaaaaaaysus, Mary, and Joseph, woman, what are ye tryin' to do, kill me?"

Jeanne gently pried open his hand that was clenched, white-knuckled, over the edge of the bed and dropped a bloody bullet into his palm. "Hold this over the wound." She gave him a towel to staunch the blood-flow.

"You look awful," he said hoarsely.

"And you don't?" she retorted, wiping her face with the sleeve of her shirt. It came away in shades of bloody gray. Splashing her face with water, she rubbed soap across her cheeks, chin, and forehead with quick practiced movements, then she splashed once more and wiped the remnants clean with a second hand-towel.

"Where were you, dressed like that?" Wolfe asked nodding toward the costume debris that littered the floor. She did not reply immediately but turned away from him, digging in her medical bag for bandages and a small dark jar that she tossed on the bed behind him. "You can trust me, you know," he said quietly.

He had his mission; she had hers. But ultimately their goals were the same, the risks were the same, and it never hurt to have someone to watch your back. After the furor at Hotêl Céleste, however, he wasn't at all convinced that she would see him as anything other than a liability. And for all her willingness to accommodate Pitt, she had already dismissed him from both her bed and the safe house—he was just another stranger in the streets of Paris.

"I can't," she stated abruptly, turning to look at him. "It's nothing personal. There is just too much at stake."

"Well, you provided me with a fine meal, a warm bed, and now medical attention; the least I can do is return the favor. I hate to be indebted."

"Look, you seem like a nice man, dead bodies notwithstanding, but what I need more than anything right now is for you to go your own way. You do not exactly fit any category of Parisian. You are too tall, too aggressive, and too...too..."

"Handsome?" he suggested helpfully, with what he hoped was an engaging grin.

"Noticeable," Jeanne finished sternly. "That scar of yours is difficult to hide. Anyone with you is going to be just as conspicuous."

"I'm not suggesting you marry me," Wolfe replied sardonically. "A simple exchange of intelligence will do."

"My intelligence is perfectly adequate," she replied shortly. "Now this might sting a little."

"What's that?" he asked as she opened the jar to reveal a yellowish balm.

"Chloride of mercury. It will help prevent flesh-rot and promote healing."

"Flesh rot?" he muttered with a grimace. "Aye, well then, have at it." He winced as she smeared the concoction over the bullet-wound. Looping a long white bandage over her forearm, she pressed one end against the cotton compress and proceeded to wrap it tightly around his shoulder.

"For God's sake, you're a stubborn lass," Wolfe muttered, raising his arm so Jeanne could examine the slash on his torso. He grimaced as the movement aggravated his shoulder wound. "I met with Talleyrand earlier this evening. He's been secretly working with Pitt in an effort to restore the monarchy. There was a plan. Napoleon let it be known, among those who have no love for the English, that he was seeking a guide, a nautical pilot, who would chart a route for his invasion fleet through the Goodwin Sands. 'Twas assumed that Napoleon intended to land on the beaches of Deal. Pitt wanted to be sure. He sent me to pose as that guide." Jeanne, intent on swabbing his wound, said nothing, and her face gave nothing away. "Talleyrand was to introduce me," Wolfe continued, "validate my credentials as a disaffected English-hater. But someone in London leaked the mission. Napoleon changed his mind. The carriage bombing, the rumors of English agents in Paris…he is suspicious and hard to get to."

"But not impossible," Jeanne murmured as she gathered up the unused bandages.

"What are you planning?" Wolfe asked, eyes narrowing in suspicion.

"What are *you* planning?" She turned to face him.

"Well, I thought I'd knock on the door of the Tuileries and ask Ol' Boney ever so politely if I could rifle through his map room, sort through his military papers, that sort of thing." Jeanne said nothing, merely raised an eyebrow. "I'm going to infiltrate the Tuileries during the assemblée tomorrow night, find a way to Napoleon's map room, and determine the exact location of his intended invasion."

"Is that all?" Jeanne replied, with a derisive snort. "How do you expect to do that exactly?"

"So, are we trusting each other now?" he asked softly, head cocked to one side. And then, suddenly, as the thought occurred to him: "If it's so dangerous to return here, why are you back?"

"I need to hide out for another night. It was risky coming back here so soon, particularly with you still here, but I had no choice."

"Why?"

"Why do you need to know?"

He held his bare palms up in surrender. "Argh, woman, forget I asked. I just thought we might be able to help each other, is all." Wolfe rose to his feet, towering over her as he shrugged back into his bloodstained shirt. Retrieving his coat from the bed, he leaned down and kissed her briefly on the mouth. "Take care of yourself," he muttered softly before turning toward the door.

"Fouché knows who you are, knows you are in Paris. He even knows what you look like," Jeanne said. He paused, hand still on the door handle, then turned back to face her. "Chief Inspector Chavert in the hotel room," she replied to his unspoken question. "I was checking his pulse to make sure you had killed him. You didn't, and now we are both on the run... He is Fouché's stooge," Jeanne added impatiently at his look of incomprehension. "He has circulated a description of you and has infiltrated my house. I can only assume he knows who I am, or at least suspects."

"And who are you, then?" She hesitated a moment. He covered the ground between them in a moment and grasped her by her upper arms. "You've been living with the fear of betrayal, with the necessity of deception so long that you no longer know how to recognize an ally. If we're being hunted together, why should we not help each other survive? But first you have to trust me. Who are you?"

"My name is Jeanne. Jeanne Recamier."

# 44.

Andrea Palladio's neoclassical architecture, which characterized much of the new Parisian skyline during the later years of the Consulate, had taken scarce consideration of the comfort of their cooks. As in other kitchens built in the neoclassical style, the Napoleonic banquets were prepared under the Tuileries Palace, below the level of the street. In the early afternoon of a relentlessly cold December, the dim kitchen resembled a field of battle or a subterranean abattoir; it was dark, damp, and pungent with death.

The acrid aroma of burned feathers mingled with the sharp, metallic stench of blood and bile. The tiny puckered-pink bodies of quails, headless and tied, lay in tidy ranks on the workbench. Flayed baby rabbits obscured the central table, surrounded by plump regiments of plucked pigeons cross-hatched with bacon lard. The cocks' combs and testicles glistened like peeled grapes on the counter-top prepped for the nesle vol-au-vent. The tenderest of calves' udders had been simmered to a pulp in cream and were being pummeled through a sieve. Partridges were being plucked, washed, disemboweled, and stuffed by a small army of kitchen hands. Overseeing them were seven under-chefs, similarly attired in their signature white caps, buttoned short coats, and large aprons.

As the icy wind howled through the Place de la Revolution, ten feet below in the kitchen depths the fires were being stoked. A cubic meter of burning charcoal awaited the entrees; another massive pile smoldered in the ovens to heat the soups, sauces, and ragouts. A third next to the door was being prepped to receive the massive spits that would hold the sirloin, veal, fowl, and game.

The brawniest of kitchen hands, a newcomer, was a tall, burly man known to the others only as Monsieur Reynière. He had been given the task of pressing the raw flesh of two boneless chickens through mesh—an inordinately difficult task. He strained at his sieve, bloodied and sweating in the growing heat of the airless room, skidding slightly on a floor made slippery with melted ice and running with flour and seasonings, feathers and fat. A boy, wielding a broom twice his size, was industriously brushing them all into the sluice drain. Monsieur Reynière paused in his labors, wiping his dripping brow with the sleeve of his coat.

"Excuse moi, monsieur." Several workers squeezed past him, struggling under a massive block of wrapped ice.

They were going to the confectionery room, he knew, to keep the desserts and unbaked pastries chilled in the growing furnace of the subterranean kitchens. An hour or so later, he would be following their route. A narrow stone-paved hallway wound its way through the confectionery room, the pastry room, and ended in a flight of steps that led up to Joséphine Bonaparte's receiving rooms and the site of that evening's festivities. He had calculated exactly the amount of time required to get to the banquet hall and then estimated another fifteen minutes for obtaining entrance into Napoleon's map room.

Infiltrating the security of the palace as a newly acquired member of Antonin Carême's kitchen staff had been an inspired idea. While Carême had been less than enthusiastic, his loyalty to Talleyrand was unswerving, and Wolfe now found himself helping to prepare a succulent feast for the man he was attempting to undermine. His tasks had been carefully selected: fetching and carrying the massive haunches of raw meat, cauldrons for boiling water, and wood for stoking the flames beneath—all unskilled labor where his lack of kitchen experience would pass unnoticed.

Unskilled though the labor might be, it was heavy work, and his shoulder throbbed painfully with each new exertion. He could feel the blood begin to seep beneath the bandage. Wolfe returned his attention to his task, and the raw threads of translucent pink meat began to emerge in fat strands through the other side of the mesh. His mind, however, was reviewing his plan, which would have to be enacted with military precision and efficiency. And hopefully a little luck of the Irish would be on his side. Napoleon's apartments were on the north end of the Tuileries, just south of the Pavilion de Flore and directly above Joséphine's apartments on the ground floor, where even now the elaborate table was being prepared.

He had memorized the floor plan Talleyrand had provided.

Napoleon's apartments were constructed in sections. The outer offices consisted of the antechamber, the salon de service, and Napoleon's salon, from which one gained entrance to the inner sancta: the emperor's study, the map room, and beyond that Napoleon's bedroom and dressing room. Each ushered one into a space more private and more privileged than that before it, the inner offices protected by the layers of bureaucracy and officialdom that preceded them. Most officials, ministers, and foreign dignitaries passed through the outer offices without realizing the emperor's study and map room, the beating heart of the Napoleonic empire, lay just through the door.

"You might have twenty minutes, or you might have two hours," Talleyrand had instructed Wolfe as they had pored over the map of the Tuileries the night before. "Napoleon hates state dinners and avoids them whenever he can. Joséphine detests them in equal measure. So it will be a brief affair. The meal, of course, will be service à la française." At Wolfe's quizzical glance, Talleyrand had elaborated. "After the initial soup course, all the remaining dishes will be served simultaneously. Napoleon always eats fast and conceivably could be finished within fifteen minutes of being served." The foreign minister paced the small dingy room, tapping his chin thoughtfully with a pearl-handled lorgnette. "Joséphine might persuade him to a game of whist or backgammon after dinner, in which case you will have a little more time. If not, he will take his leave and typically retire to his study to work. You will need to have made your way downstairs by that time."

"Right," Wolfe nodded. "And what about guards?"

"Usually, a ceremonial detachment of twenty men are posted beneath the state apartments, but they will be redeployed to the surrounding grounds for the evening. Joséphine does not care for their presence during state dinners."

Moving to the table, Talleyrand ran one long, elegantly manicured finger across the map. "In each doorway leading into the emperor's private apartments, you will find a doorkeeper, an usher, or sometimes both. They will be unarmed, except for the doorkeeper in the stairwell by the antechamber here." He pointed at the curved stairwell depicted at the eastern end of the apartments. "He is supplied with a ceremonial halberd and sword, but I doubt he knows what to do with either. Other upstairs staff consists of several officers, pages, and servants who sleep at their posts, ready to be roused at a moment's notice if the emperor requires them. Roustam, Napoleon's mameluk, sleeps outside the emperor's door. And then there are the valet and the wardrobe assistant who sleep in closets nearby. But they will be taking their own evening meal in order to be back at their posts should Napoleon require them after his own."

Wolfe slipped through the door into the comparative cool of the confectionery room and gently closed the door behind him. The sweet scent of almond milk and the tang of citrus oil from the discarded pith of oranges lingered in the air. Marble slabs on either side of the room held the desserts while trays of broken ice beneath slowly melted into cool liquid pools. Blancmange in layers of orange and almond were setting on their icy pedestals. He passed an under-chef, so engrossed in piping the last of the creamy mocha filling into pastry baskets that he did not notice Reynière's passing.

Opening the door to the stairwell, Wolfe quickly shrugged out of his chef 's attire, stuffing it in the large-mouthed Etruscan jar that decorated the entrance. He could now hear the buzz of conversation from above, the rattle of dinnerware, the clinking of glasses, and the lilting tones of a string quartet. Moving silently and quickly up the stairs, he adjusted the blue coat of his footman's uniform, one amidst a rush of similarly dressed men groaning under heavy soup tureens and platters of bread rolls. Arriving at the top of the stairs, he kept moving purposefully forward. To his right was the arched doorway that opened into the reception room. Wolfe spared but a glance for the guests who congregated around the table, yet to be seated, still lingering over champagne and admiring Carême's centerpiece. Talleyrand was among them. The thought gave him some comfort. He had one ally amidst the enemy camp, not that it would matter much if he were caught.

Jeanne moved through a cluster of the elegantly dressed, her hand clutching her pelisse tightly; it contained a linen handkerchief scented with jasmine, a white lace fan, a bonbonière with bits of licorice, and a small porcelain box from Limoges. The last, a delicate container with gold ornamentation, was a gift for the empress—to add to the two hundred she had already collected. As with all her assumed identities, and this one felt merely another in a long succession, Jeanne had meticulously selected accessories that complemented her role. These Limoges boxes were frequently utilized by the nobility for the storage of pills, rouge, powders, snuff, diamonds, rings, gold, love letters, or precious tobacco. Jeanne's, however, contained a vial of cherry laurel water that, administered to the emperor's wine, could cause death in as little as thirty seconds. Assassinate the husband and present the box in which she had carried the poison as a gift to the wife: a thought that might have made Jeanne rather ill had the target been any other than Napoleon himself.

The assemblée room was luxuriously appointed with walls of Danish oak, carved, gilded, and covered in sumptuous Flandish tapestries. A U-shaped table, draped in crisp white, was laid with gleaming silverware and gold vermeil-edged flatware. Candles flickered from wall sconces, but the primary source of light was the crystal chandelier which hung like the sun above the center of the table. Below the chandelier, and the sight of all eyes, was the massive Italian gondola Carême had created entirely of marzipan and sugar, riding on an ocean of azure-tinted meringue.

Beyond the gondola, on the far side of the room, Jeanne could see the short figure of Napoleon holding court. He wore a dark blue dress-coat with gold epaulettes and a red sash beneath, the breast of which was decorated with the star of the Legion of Honor and the Iron Crown of Italy. He was visible to her in profile: dark hair swept carelessly back from his brow, large gray eyes wandering from his companion, mouth turned down in momentary displeasure. His figure, rigidly held, conveyed an impression of tightly coiled control and simmering tension beneath a thin veneer of social propriety. While he clearly understood the necessity for these events, he endured rather than enjoyed them. Joséphine, attired in a yellow gown that did little advantage to her sallow complexion, fidgeted to his left. A full glass of vin de Constance, glinting crimson in the candlelight, stood on the table behind the emperor. If she could get a little closer…

"Madame Recamier! I thought it was you!" Jeanne was intercepted by the rotund figure of Jean-Etienne Portalis. On occasion, Napoleon included an artist or two among the officials, ministers, and their wives who normally attended these events. Monsieur Portalis, dark hair coiled in greasy ringlets across his high forehead, began to earnestly explain why he believed the painting recently displayed at her salon was indisputably a Caravaggio. "In fact," he went on, licking thick lips with a wetly darting tongue, "I would be enormously indebted to you if you would ask Monsieur Varnet what he intended to do with the painting. Perhaps he would be willing to sell it to me?" Monsieur Portalis' face gleamed with sweaty avarice, his plump fingers convulsing around the delicate stem of his champagne glass.

"Well, I can certainly contact him for you."

Attuned as she was to Napoleon's movements, the murmur of conversation conducted across the table reached her ears:

"...regional disturbances in the Pas-de-Calais...machinations of English agents..."

"...some say the English seek allies to bring another coalition against us..."

"The English...the English!" Napoleon spat derisively, color suffusing his pale cheeks in blotched fury. "They will force me to fight for fifteen years or more. But if they arm, I shall arm too; if they fight, I shall fight! They think to destroy France; they shall never intimidate her!"

Jeanne wondered if the emperor realized his instinctive usage of I rather than the collective we. But he had always thought of the throne of France as a private aspiration, and his need to maintain himself there as a personal imperative rather than a national one. Joséphine had confided in her once that he perceived the continuance of war as a personal slight; the five or six families that shared the thrones of Europe had taken it badly that a Corsican seated himself at their table, and that if Napoleon desired to keep his seat so must he maintain it by force. She caught Joséphine's glance from across the room, accompanied by a tight-lipped smile that concealed teeth in an advanced state of decay. Jeanne, grateful for an excuse to move closer, returned it with one of her own.

"Madame Recamier! So good of you to come." Joséphine greeted her with a degree of warmth unusual to the occasion. The empress hated these gatherings, Jeanne knew, and, despite her elevated rank, had demonstrated a grateful partiality to Madame Recamier's favor and company. There was a coolness between the imperial couple, a deliberate half-turn in Napoleon's shoulder that bespoke an irritable avoidance, and a reciprocal anxious nervousness in his wife that lent credence to Jeanne's gathered intelligence regarding extra-marital affairs indulged in by both. Not that adultery was uncommon, or even frowned upon, in post-Revolutionary Paris; indeed, many after the Terror seemed to have flung all caution to the wind in a wild abandon of sexual largess. Women shivered in strategically dampened gowns, transparent in candle-light. Love was a physical act that celebrated vitality and a successful escape from the jealous clutches of Madame la Guillotine. The uncertainty of life and the remembrance of the recently dead lent a feverish urgency to all things. Jeanne found her thoughts drifting to Wolfe and the pleasure she had found with him.

Jeanne maintained a relentless guard against infiltration and exposure, a heightened awareness of every moment that left her drained and exhausted—*who am I? How should I move? How should I be?* There was a predetermined cover for every occasion and no time for Jeanne. But, however briefly, Wolfe had given her time. Time to momentarily lay down her weapons and relinquish her guard. And for that, for that ability to live in the moment and simply revel in being alive as so many others had done before her, she was immensely grateful. Jeanne wondered if he had any idea of the gift he had bestowed: the opportunity to be simply a woman who desired a man. What a luxury!

"Do you know the story of Laenas?" Napoleon's interrogative abruptly brought her mind from the bed at rue Demarest to the assemblée rooms, where she silently chastised herself for the distraction. That damned Irishman.

"Laenas, mon empereur?" The minister squirmed under the intensity of Napoleon's gaze. Joséphine sighed, a soft exhalation of breath that told Jeanne this was a story that had been told many times before. Catching the empress's gaze, Jeanne smiled, a slow conspiratorial gesture of exasperated camaraderie, of women together suffering the transgressions of arrogant men. Her connection with the empress had served the Resistance well, and Jeanne had every intention of fostering it. Even if it was the last time it might be required. Who knew indeed, what small consideration might end up saving a life—her own, or that of one she loved. Jeanne edged closer to the table where Napoleon's glass lay tantalizingly close.

"I do not know, mon empereur," the minister muttered fretfully, bowing his upper torso in anxious obsequiousness as he attempted to disengage himself from the immediate circle.

"Ah, you speak of the Syrian King Antiochus, do you not?" Duc de Talleyrand came to the minister's rescue, and Jeanne pretended an absorbed interest in Joséphine's description of a hybrid rose she had

acquired for Chateau de Malmaison. Talleyrand, who neither acknowledged her presence nor glanced her way, endeavored to engage Napoleon's bristling attention by shifting slightly to the left, as if perusing the
assembled guests with a weary eye. "About 170 B.C., I believe it was,"
he declared lazily, drawing Napoleon slightly away from the table and
the glass that glinted there. "King Antiochus attacked the Egyptians,
who, in turn, appealed to Rome for an army to repulse the invaders.
The Romans, their treasuries depleted by the Punic Wars, had no army
to deploy. Instead, Rome sent the elderly counsel Gaius Popillus Laenas
and his twelve assistants. When they came upon the great Syrian army,
King Antiochus demanded of Laenas, 'What are you doing in Egypt?'
And the Roman senator replied: 'Your Majesty, I believe the question
rather is: what are you doing in Egypt?' Antiochus demanded the senator move, but Laenas stood firm—"

"And Antiochus," Napoleon interrupted in a booming voice, eyes
glittering feverishly, "demanded: 'Who do you think you are? Behind
me stands an army of thirty thousand men!' And *what* do you think the
great Roman senator said to that?" The emperor pinioned Talleyrand
in a ferocious glare. The question, however, was a rhetorical one. Napoleon was embroiled in one of his infamous tirades, an emotional rant
that one had only to wait out.

Joséphine's mouth tightened; her voice trailed off; her very figure
seemed to wilt; her roses overcome, as it were, by the foreign policy
of ancient Romans. Jeanne murmured in her ear—she had a gift for
the empress: a little porcelain box from Limoges to add to Joséphine's
collection. Would she like to see it? Relieved to have an excuse to move
from the vicinity, Joséphine smiled politely and gestured for Jeanne to
follow her to the other side of the room where her women clustered in
supportive profusion. Leaning back against the table, as if momentarily
fatigued, Jeanne emptied the contents of her vial into Napoleon's glass
with one deft maneuver and then was away, following Joséphine's swaying skirts with an attentive smile.

She could hear Napoleon behind her: "The Roman senator said: 'Behind you stands only a visible and rather small army. Behind me stand
the invisible legions of Rome. In the name of the senate and the people
of Rome, I order you to go home!' As the king hesitated, Laenas took
his staff and drew a circle in the dirt around the king. When done, he
stated, 'Step out of the circle, King Antiochus, in any direction but east,

and you will answer with your kingdom and your life.' What happened? The king stepped out of the circle to the east and went home! Do you know why?"

Napoleon caught Talleyrand in a measuring stare, then proclaimed with triumphant exultation: "Because they were *afraid* of the power and reputation of Rome!" Then his voice, hushed and confiding, although still irate enough to be readily heard by Jeanne across the uneasily stilled room, came to a heated conclusion: "Just as these royal European families are afraid of Paris. I can only get them used to regarding me as their equal by keeping them in check. My empire will be destroyed if I cease being fearsome. I cannot afford to let anyone threaten me without striking out at them. Among *established* sovereigns, a war's only purpose is to dismember a province or take a city. But with me, it is always a question of my very existence as a monarch, of the existence of the whole empire!"

Talleyrand said nothing, just smiled slightly, the picture of courteous attentiveness. Napoleon's gaze narrowed. He was waiting for approval, Jeanne knew, an avowal of solidarity before the imperious European aristocracy. The implication, she mused, was that the French required wars and empire in order to confer legitimacy upon the emperor; that he was not safely on his throne unless he was mounted in the saddle at the head of the Grande Armée in a never-ending quest for validity and to serve as his own rationale for aggressive behavior.

"...it is always a question of my own existence as a monarch!" a voice belligerently proclaimed. Napoleon. Wolfe moved quickly onwards. Ahead, gleaming marble stairs wound their way up to the emperor's private apartments. To the right was a massive door, ornate and gilded, which led, he assumed, to Joséphine's quarters. Wolfe paused in midstride as a thought occurred to him. Hadn't Talleyrand briefly mentioned a staircase that connected the empress's quarters with those of her husband? If he could bypass the outer chambers and emerge in Napoleon's bedroom, which was directly adjacent to the map room, he would have only one or two men to contend with as opposed to the ten—however unarmed and sleepy they might be—that occupied the others. Slipping inside the door, Wolfe found himself in a small antechamber. The sole source of light in the room emerged from a half-open door on the opposite wall, spilling in a narrow strip across the carpeted floor. A second door, adjacent to the first, was closed. The walls were covered in Greco-Roman friezes; the rounded limbs of languid maidens shone palely in the muted light, their colorful robes falling in graceful, classical folds. Several formally upholstered white chairs and a central cabinet, ornately decorated with hieroglyphs, stood against the wall to the right.

Through the open door, Wolfe could hear the muted chatter and laughter of female voices. Eyes fixed on the open door, he moved silently through the carpeted room. Wolfe could now see the figures of three women bent in close conversation, skirts bunched under them as they sat on a narrow sofa bed under the window—Joséphine's ladies-in-waiting. Abruptly, a low throaty growl issued from a dark corner of the room. Wolfe turned to find himself confronted by a bristling pug, his wrinkled black lips lifted in a snarl, baring small, sharp teeth. The conversation stilled next door, and the narrow strip of bright light expanded and filled the room as the door was pushed open. A woman's silhouette appeared.

# 45.

L'Aigle winced as he shrugged his arms into the billowing sleeves of his shirt. Lurid bruises covered his torso and back in blossoming fingers of purple and blue and streaked around the swollen, reddened flesh of his thigh where he had fallen through the stairs. L'Aigle prided himself on his ability to disconnect, to remain detached and unperturbed, to execute a job dispassionately and efficiently. He had built his reputation upon it. But he felt he was losing his edge. The unfortunate encounter with the Irishman had taken its toll.

This man. He was familiar from somewhere. A faint memory nagged at the fringes of his mind. L'Aigle had seen him before, he was certain of it. Something about the way the target fought, the loose-limbed way he moved, almost dancing, lightly, on the balls of his feet. L'Aigle never referred to his quarry by name. He had learned early to depersonalize his actions, to keep his mind firmly fixed on his ultimate goal: the restoration of his political birthright. In his tired moments—and there seemed to be more of them as of late—the faces of those he had killed floated through his mind in quick succession, like a macabre series of oil paintings. When so haunted, L'Aigle thought of Napoleon, which served to quell any doubts he had about his chosen profession. Thousands upon thousands of men had perished under the Napoleonic regime, whether Frenchmen serving under the tyrant or Europeans defending their homes against him. The sacrifice of several dozen individuals—always men and women of political acumen and intelligence who had willfully chosen to ally themselves with Napoleon's oppressive policies—would, in the end, serve a noble purpose: to hasten the Corsican's downfall, bring back stability in Europe, and, above all, re-constitute the Austro-Hungarian Empire.

Yes, the Irishman would be one of his more challenging opponents, L'Aigle mused as he bent painfully to pull on his boots. Different targets presented different challenges. In many cases, however, the procedure was a simple one of surveillance and infiltration. He would locate the subject, shadow him or her for the course of days or weeks (as much time as was necessary to become familiar with their habits and routines) and assess their vulnerabilities. While bodyguards were accustomed to perceiving threats from the angry mob—the destitute, the denied, the downtrodden—L'Aigle's aristocratic bearing, impeccable presentation, and suave, persuasive manner deflected all suspicion. He became one opulently dressed among many at the theatre or restaurant, at the opera or the park. For who could readily distinguish one man from another in their elegant uniforms of hat, coat, and breeches? Once he had sufficiently infiltrated the target's general circle, he could maneuver to obtain personal proximity. There were a variety of methodologies that would serve for the subsequent assassination: close-contact stabbing, quieter smothering or strangulation, and an array of poisons such as the death cap mushroom pulverized into powder and dispensed in a drink.

The Irishman, however, was an anomaly. He was not the usual stationary target, and despite the corpses of the gendarmes that had announced his arrival in Paris and their encounter in the stairwell, he had been decidedly circumspect since. The Irishman was also a fighter, but of the brashly aggressive variety. L'Aigle's training, like others in the Austrian court, had been of the formal kind. Under the tutelage of Guiseppe Rondolo, he had excelled at classical fencing; hunting expeditions in the forested outskirts of Bavaria had familiarized him with the composite bow, hunting pistols, and the knife, of course, for close-quarter kills. Yes, he had been well-trained indeed, but in only conventional, aristocratic warfare. The Irishman fought a different kind of battle. He was a street-fighter who did not play by the rules. He was strong; he was fast; he was unpredictable and therefore dangerous. Grimacing slightly, L'Aigle shrugged into his long overcoat and pulled his hat low over his brow. It was time to hire some watchers.

Outside, the Hotel des Tournelles opened up into the bustling Les Halles market of the Marais. Despite the handsome brick façade, an imposing combination of arched galleries and ornate stonework, the hotel had, like many other grand buildings of the ancien régime, fallen into a state of shabby disrepair. The Marais used to be the most fashionable address in the realm, with a profusion of grand Louis XIV mansions amidst immaculately maintained landscaping; now, scarcely two centuries later, it had started a gradual descent into a slum, with dark narrow lanes that twisted and turned, flanked by tall narrow houses that teetered over the street like tipsy bystanders.

Turning into rue du Pont aux Choux (translated peculiarly as the Street of the Bridge of the Cabbages), L'Aigle made his way to the tavern of Chez Perruque. The interior was smoky and dim. Stretched cloth treated with turpentine covered small window panes and let in squares of afternoon light in a fading, mellow haze. The tavern smelled of unwashed bodies, spilled liqueur, cheap perfume, and unemptied chamber pots. Stumps of dripping candles flickered and pooled on upturned barrels. The chimney flue appeared to be a relic of Louis XIV's time; its wide vertical shaft had a persistent tendency to spew smoke that seeped out from the hearth in curls and tendrils to hang just below the ceiling in a pestilential cloud. Narrower and deeper hearths with curved chimney shafts had been in evidence in the better homes since the Regency and effectively heated entire rooms. Chez Perruque, however, in the dark streets of the Marais, had no such pretensions to grandeur.

It was a busy night, as L'Aigle had predicted it would be; the prevailing temperatures without had long served as an indicator of crowds within—as the former plummeted the latter increased with equal ferocity. Most of the customers were crammed around the hearth, which, due to its antiquated construction, served to toast those in close proximity, while the rest of the clientele, huddled in their surcoats, seemed resigned to the colder draughts of the outskirts. Several tables were occupied by gray-clad soldiers in boisterous appreciation of their cups. Workmen, in peaked caps and threadbare long-coats, milled around the narrow bar that extended the length of the room.

A large meaty man with brawny forearms and a wide, barrel chest sat in conspicuous solitude at a table under the window. A dark red tunic opened at his thick neck and was cinched at the waist with a black leather belt. The light from the window bathed him in a halo but did little to soften his demeanor. There was a grimness about him that was not entirely explained by his unyielding physicality. Beneath closely cropped silver hair, small eyes were coldly unblinking in a darkly weathered face, lips a compressed line in a heavy clenched jaw. Thick fingers curled menacingly around his mug, and a thin nub of skin protruded where his right ear should have been. The patrons of Chez Perruque glanced up as L'Aigle entered the room. There was a moment's silence as they took in the rich sheen of his leather boots, the thick warmth of his woolen overcoat, and the sumptuous gleam of satin beneath. When L'Aigle joined the silver-headed man who sat alone, they turned back with a murmur to their colleagues.

"I need some men," L'Aigle muttered, omitting the customary pleasantries that neither man desired.

Etienne was a gangster of sorts, one who specialized in hiring out muscle for any manner of jobs. Shrewd, dark eyes slid his way. "How many, and for what?" he replied gruffly, idly fingering the rim of his cup with one stubby finger.

"I will need a few watchers. Your best."

"Who?" Etienne was sparse with his words, as if each one parted from him with great reluctance. He was asking who the target was, L'Aigle knew. These two were well acquainted with each other. Etienne had been a soldier during the Revolution and the Directorate, had served under Napoleon during the siege of Toulon. But when, in a drunken brawl, Etienne had killed his superior officer, he had been sentenced to five years in the Temple Prison. He had escaped en route to the prison, killing the four guards who accompanied him. Recaptured a year later, he was sent to the galleys for life. Bribing the official overseeing his transport to Marseille, Etienne took advantage of the upheaval of the Terror to disappear. Now, he had re-emerged at the head of Paris's most notorious gang, involved in everything from black-market sales and smuggling to prostitution.

"Napoleon Bonaparte."

Etienne grinned slowly, his lips parting to reveal large yellowed teeth, the front two separated by a gap that gave him a distinctly hare-like appearance. "The target is working with Bonaparte," L'Aigle continued in a low murmur. "I have been unable to locate him, but I know at some point he will attempt to communicate with the emperor. I need your men to watch the Tuileries, the Place de Concorde, the Comédie-Française. Anywhere Napoleon frequents. I will provide you with a detailed description of the target, of course. He is tall, scarred, an Irishman who speaks French, but with a deplorable accent. He has also met with Duc de Talleyrand, who must also be monitored in case the target contacts him again. I want him located and that is all."

"It will be expensive," Etienne replied. "You will need many men for this."

"Of course." L'Aigle placed a small leather coin sack on the table. "Consider this a down payment."

# 46.

The lady-in-waiting moved into the dim antechamber, her shadow lengthened and monstrous against the far wall like the angel of death amidst the painted maidens. Wolfe pressed back into the shadowed corner. The woman had emerged from a brightly lit chamber; this one would appear darker to her than it did to him. If only she would not look around her too closely! He would have to silence her, leave her gagged and bound. He didn't want to think about the necessity of killing again. God knew, he had enough blood on his hands. But of course, there were the other two women as well…

"What is it, Fortune?" the woman murmured to the small dog in French, scooping him up under one arm. "Are you missing your mistress?" she cooed, scratching his silky ears as she returned to her companions. Fortune continued to growl, a low throaty rumble, as he stared fixedly in Wolfe's direction, but he allowed himself to be carried from the room. The lady-in-waiting shut the door behind her, and the room descended into darkness. Wolfe exhaled in quiet relief.

Turning the handle of the door behind him, he moved quickly into Joséphine's bedroom. It was a surprisingly small room dominated by a large bed shrouded in muslin. A massive gilded swan, stilled in mid-flight, its wings gracefully outstretched, glimmered above the canopy. A floral motif decorated pale walls; the furniture was light and delicate. A single candle burned in a bejeweled cup by the bed. Across the thick carpet, several tall doors concealed what appeared to be a wardrobe. The middle door opened to a narrow flight of stairs that wound up to the floor above. The stairs emerged in another bedchamber, this one unmistakably masculine. While the room itself was ornately decorated with Egyptian frescoes—supplemented by the emperor's monogram, N, and his emblem, the bee—it was sparsely furnished, austere even. A canopied bed stood solidly against the wall to his right, and a few embroidered chairs were awkwardly situated next to a sturdy chest of drawers. There were no personal possessions scattered about, no evidence that the room was occupied at all. Napoleon, like his army, was perpetually on the move. Talleyrand had mentioned that the emperor spent an average of only three months a year at the Tuileries, the longest he resided in any one location. His personal necessities were carried in a few small chests which moved with him from place to place. Perhaps this was why the room had an empty feel to it. A closed door in front of him led to the emperor's dressing room, and the one behind him opened into the map room.

Grasping the hilt of his knife, Wolfe withdrew it from the waistband of his breeches and moved soundlessly to the door. Gently turning the handle, he opened the door a fraction and could see the map room beyond. A large window constituted the wall to his right; the others were covered from floor to ceiling with bookcases and open cabinets, within which nested a countless number of rolled papers, files, and notebooks. A mahogany claw-footed table dominated the center of the room, its surface strewn with maps anchored by an equestrian bronze statue of Frederick the Great. A cluster of wrought-iron oil lamps hung suspended from the ceiling above the table, one of which was lit, its warm glow reflected in the glass windowpanes. The room was empty.

Slipping into the map room, Wolfe returned the knife to his breeches and moved to the table to examine the papers and documents. A large map of Europe was unfurled and dotted with pins that plotted the movement of troops all over the continent. Blue pins were positioned at Boulogne, Brest, Montreuil, St. Omer, and Bruges. Smaller yellow pins marked the smaller coastal provincial towns of Arras, Amiens, Tournai, Meaux, and Compiègne. A number of red pins, positioned in the Channel, represented, Wolfe assumed, Lord Cornwallis's English fleet. But where in England did Bonaparte intend to land? A circle had been penciled around the Downs, a question mark vivid over the Goodwin Sands. Brighton and Weymouth Bay were circled, as was a flat stretch of land just north of the Thames estuary, subsequently crossed out with the words *trop loin de Londres* scrawled underneath. Too far from London. Was Napoleon going to try for the Downs without the aid of a pilot? Or had he altered his destination? Was Brighton the target? Or Weymouth?

He needed more information. Turning to the cubbyholes behind him, Wolfe rapidly scanned the neatly printed labels beneath each one: Armée du Nord, Armée des Pyrenees, Armée du Rhin, and then Flotille Nationale—the invasion fleet at Boulogne. Pulling out the rolled papers, Wolfe spread them over the table. They consisted of maps of the harbor works at Boulogne and instructions for the dredging of the Liane River and the construction of quays. Dated three months previous, perhaps already completed. Sifting through the papers, Wolfe found detailed descriptions of the vessels of invasion—hundreds of them—along with instructions for additional requisitions from other regions of coastal France.

And then, a letter addressed to Napoleon, signed by Louis-René de Latouche-Tréville, the admiral of the fleet at Boulogne. Dated two weeks ago. Wolfe's book-French was rusty, but he gathered that the fleets under Admiral Villeneuve and Admiral Ganteaume were to join Tréville's force in Boulogne. Combined, they would form a formidable fifty-one ships-of-the-line that could then engage the English in the Channel. Overwhelming force! So *that* was it! The destination at that point didn't really matter. If the French could defeat the English at sea, England would lie open to them. They could land anywhere they pleased...

His train of thought was suddenly interrupted by a soft thud in the room next door. Slipping the papers into his coat pocket, Wolfe unscrewed the cover to the lamp and extinguished the wick between his thumb and forefinger. The room plunged into darkness. He crouched at one end of the table, poised to spring, heart beating in rapid counterpoint to his quickening breath, the hilt of his knife grasped firmly in one hand. The door from Napoleon's bedroom opened, and a figure appeared on the threshold.

# 47.

Holwood House, William Pitt's country residence, was a small white brick building. It was more minimal than elegant, and visitors, who were not well acquainted with Pitt, often expressed some surprise at its unpretentious simplicity. A carriage way, two rutted tracks barely visible beneath dirty frost, swept from Westerham Road in a circuitous route through a cluster of beech trees to the small wooden stoop that constituted the front entrance. A massive oak, limbs stark against a slate sky, dominated the front yard under which a stone slab bench collected the last dry, rustling leaves of the season. A pond, originally constructed to provide a water supply to the house, was now inhabited by rapidly breeding carp, whose shadowed orange forms moved and danced sinuously beneath a lid of ice. Clumps of late grass stood up in icy tufts, but there was little color in the garden now.

Seated on the bench overlooking the pond, Pitt didn't mind. He found a sense of rural tranquility that gave him much-needed peace. In fact, the neutrality of monochrome, the bland indistinctness of white and gray, the weary dullness of the evergreens, already drowsy beneath their thin mantle of ice, soothed him. He had left Walmer at Hester's insistence, and Dundas's unyielding concurrence, for the rural peace of Holwood House. Feeling drained by his increasing exertions in the House—the incessant visitors, ceaseless paperwork, and his unremitting supervision of coastal defenses—Pitt finally agreed to an overnight stay in the country en route to the capital. The visitors and paperwork seemed to find him regardless, traveling a little further but arriving on his doorstep just the same.

"Will!" Hester's voice called from the stoop. Turning toward the house, Pitt raised one hand in an acknowledging wave.

In the sitting room overlooking the garden and cheerfully warmed by a vigorous fire, Hester had placed a cup of tea and a plate of freshly baked scones. "I thought you might need a little refreshment." She proceeded to pour him a cup, adding milk, and stirring in sugar with a silver spoon.

"Ah, Hester, you are an angel." Pitt accepted the cup with an appreciative smile. The door flung open, and Dundas appeared. He strode into the room with his usual robust physicality and plopped himself in a chair opposite, grinning amiably. "And the peace is shattered," Pitt murmured ruefully. He took a sip of his tea and placed it back on the tray with an expression of amused resignation. Dundas leaned forward in his seat, fiddling absently with a small object in one brawny hand. Glancing sideways at Pitt, Dundas's brows drew down in a mock-fearsome scowl, his lips pursed in a pretense of anger.

"Do ye remember that time ye put jelly in my boots?" he demanded.

"Ah, yes, indeed," Pitt replied gravely. "Took three weeks to get the pink out of your stockings as I recall."

Hester smiled behind her teacup.

"And last winter, when ye tied a string to my toe in the night and jerked it about so sharply that I didna know if I was comin' or goin'?"

Pitt nodded sagely, attempting in vain to restrain a smile that twitched about his lips. "Quite a fit of bellowing. I do remember."

"Your account has come due, my friend." Dundas rose to his feet with a belligerent leer, waggling a small object between thumb and forefinger.

Pitt raised one eyebrow, his eyes silvery-bright with amused disbelief. "Burnt cork, is it?" he inquired. "What is it you intend to do with that?"

"Blacken your face with it!" Dundas roared, leaping across the table in one lithe movement. Pitt, with a rapidity unexpected even by him, slid off the chair and ducked around behind it, a wide grin creasing his face. Hester, shrieking with laughter, joined in the pursuit, another piece of cork held triumphantly aloft in one hand.

"Traitor! Thought you would lull me with tea, did you?" Pitt laughed.

A quick knock on the door announced the appearance of Anthony, the resident butler at 56 Westerham Road. Confronted by the chaotic hilarity of Dundas and Hester chasing the former prime minister around the couch, Anthony maintained his impassive demeanor. Clearing his throat loudly, he announced, "The Lords Castlereagh and Liverpool desire to see you on business, sir."

"Let them wait in the other room," Pitt gasped as he snatched up a cushion from the couch and pummeled Dundas, then ducked beneath Hester who was approaching from behind. They were, however, too many and too strong for him, and after ten minutes of fight Dundas and Hester managed to pin him down on the couch. With gusts of laughter, they proceeded to daub his face, when, with a look of pretended confidence in his own prowess, Pitt announced: "Stop! This will do. I could easily beat you both, but we must not keep those grandees waiting any longer."

"Right," Dundas replied with exaggerated deference. "But, of course." He bowed mockingly from the waist and disappeared into a neighboring water closet, re- emerging with a basin of water and towel. Hester proceeded to wash his face clean. His appearance thus put to order, the basin and towel were hidden behind the couch, and the lords ushered in.

Lord Liverpool, whose demeanor had provided much fodder for Hester's wit, was characteristically melancholy and nervous. Lord Castlereagh, an older man who had maintained the athleticism of youth, was a model of quiet grace and strength. Both inclined their heads and bent at the waist with obsequious respect. Dundas winked solemnly at Hester, and she pursed her lips sternly over her cup in an effort not to laugh. Hester and Dundas, ostentatiously sedate and serious on the couch, offered the lords, who sat opposite, tea which both declined. It was Pitt, however, who drew their admiring attention: his tall, ungainly figure seemed to expand to the ceiling, his head thrown back, mouth pursed in thought, his expression one of solemn deliberation. In an instant, he had become the great statesman, assuming his public mantle of conscientious somberness.

"Sir," Liverpool began, "we wanted to confer with you regarding our concerns for national safety. The threat, not from Napoleon, particularly, but the domestic troubles. As you know, there has been another poor harvest, and it seems—"

"The point, however," Castlereagh interrupted forcefully, "is that popular societies are forming in unprecedented numbers throughout Britain, each threatening to form their own national conventions. And of course, there are the rumors of French agents active in London and secret shipment of arms. As you know, there have been riots in many of Scotland's major cities."

"We are concerned," Liverpool concurred with a worried frown, "that with all the attention focused on Napoleon's fleet across the Channel…that the possibility of a local insurrection is not being adequately addressed—"

"There has been a wave of revolutions from America to France; why not now in England? We are concerned that the current prime minister," Castlereagh coughed delicately, "is perhaps unaware of the seriousness of the situation."

"We have both come…" Liverpool stammered, glancing at Castlereagh who nodded in earnest affirmation, "to request that you consider… that is, that you might—"

"Form an alternative administration," Castlereagh interjected, unable to endure his colleague's long-winded entreaty. He leaned forward, his gaze seeking Pitt's. "Take back the prime ministership. The country needs you!"

And so for some time they spoke. Pitt made, now and then, some short observations and finally: "Gentlemen, I understand your concerns," his voice grave, his expression duly somber. "Let me take these matters under consideration."

With an abrupt, stiff inclination of the body, he dismissed them. Then, as the door closed behind the lords of the House, he turned to Hester and Dundas with a laugh, caught up his cushion, and renewed the fight.

# 48.

"Damnation!" Frederick, the Prince of Wales, exclaimed in frustration, flinging the offending cravat to the floor. "Again!" he demanded of the valet. "And get it right this time!" The prince reclined in his chair as if he were being shaved, extending his thick, meaty neck for the valet to adjust the fourth cravat of the evening. Then the prince lowered his chin, ever so slowly, to allow the starched linen to wrinkle to perfection, to achieve that appearance of studied carelessness that was all the rage. If one wrinkle was too deep or too shallow, the cloth was thrown aside, and most evenings the valet was sent, shaking, from the ritual with an armload of tumbled white cloths: the failures.

The prince examined himself critically in the gilt-framed mirror that occupied a corner of his lavishly appointed dressing room. He was obese. His small brown eyes, nestled like raisins within the doughy plumpness of his face, glanced over his corpulent figure with a self-complacent approval. What a fine figure of a prince! His lush auburn hair was meticulously "wind-blown," cropped short except for a tumble of curls that spilled over his meaty forehead à la Titus. The prince had inherited his father's sharp, protruding nose, but the small, fleshy mouth beneath, artfully rouged, was completely his own. The double chins were obscured by the perfectly arranged cravat which draped carelessly over a satin embroidered waistcoat, detailed with tiny rosettes. Tan buckskin breeches stretched and strained across his wide, fleshy bottom. A dark blue coat, the collar fashionably high, silk stockings, and ornate silver-buckled shoes completed his apparel.

It was an important evening, and the prince wanted everything to be perfect. Carlton House was on display for the first time since undergoing extensive and exorbitantly expensive renovations. The Whigs would all be in attendance, and wine, promises, and personal attentions would not be spared to confirm their allegiance to Fox. Regiments, offices, preferments, and titles would all be dangled, serving to retain the wavering and lure the credulous and discontented.

Henry Eden alighted from the phaeton. Unlike others at the party, he was severely dressed in black broadcloth, his cravat limply tied five minutes before. He would have preferred a quiet brandy at The Green Man, but for a man ambitious in Whig-politics, scorning the invitation of the prince was foolhardy indeed, particularly on this grand occasion of the Carlton House unveiling. And then there was Grenville. The duke would be expecting him. More accurately, Grenville would be expecting an accounting of the funds diverted to ensure the assassination of a troublesome Irishman. He would be waiting, in all his plump pomposity, to hear of a sudden death in Paris and the concomitant satisfaction that Irish interests were, as always, secondary to English ones, that his landed estates in Ireland were safe from the legislative turbulence Pitt's plans seemed to portend. Eden had nothing to tell him.

L'Aigle had been worryingly silent. Wolfe Trant should have been disposed of by now. Certainly, the Irishman was a much easier target than the czar of Russia that this assassin had so effectively dispatched on their behalf. And there had been other jobs, other targets; L'Aigle's performance had always been exemplary, his notification of completion prompt. So why then, Eden worried, had he not yet received word? Storms had prevented Channel crossings the last day or so... Certainly, the deed was done, and notification of the fact was currently en route? At least that is what he would tell Grenville. He glanced up at Carlton house, brightly lit and magnificent under the yellow gleam of gas-lamps. The front of the house was peculiarly obscured by a colonnade of single pillars that, despite the entablature which rested upon them, supported nothing. Eden recalled a rhyme that had circulated the coffeehouses over the past month as the construction had neared completion.

*Dear little columns*
*All in a row*
*What do you do here?*
*Indeed we don't know.*

Behind the columns, the façade of the palace was composed of a central portico flanked by two wings. The portico consisted of six Corinthian columns, with details taken from the Temple of Jupiter Stator in the Forum at Rome—so Eden learned later from the occupant of the house. Above this, a tympanum was adorned with the prince's coat of arms. Sculpted gardens in the foreground were home to two massive stone statues that flanked either side of the grand portico, one of Alfred and the other Edward the Black Prince. The interior was as extravagant as Eden had been led to expect. He was ushered through a central hall, magnificently illuminated by a circular skylight richly embellished with painted glass. Arched doorways, above which cherubic figures lounged, opened up to adjacent rooms, and a spacious stairway wound elegantly to the second level. The party was being held in the Golden Drawing Room, where Eden entered to find the Prince of Wales already holding court.

The walls were adorned with statuary and paintings, and thick rugs covered the Italian marble floor. Writhing female figures in bronze supported gaslights that cast a flickering warmth over the profusion of gold and reds in the room. The chair of state, in which the prince was sitting, was of crimson velvet embroidered with gold. Eden had heard it cost upwards of five hundred pounds. Little wonder the heir apparent was drowning in debt. The prince looked flaccidly fat and carried that air of a half-worn rake that had spent his youth and his energies in excessive indulgence and was now paying the price.

"Your Highness." Eden bent at the waist, delivering the necessary obeisance to the prince, before moving across to a mahogany side table, inlaid with lustrous mother of pearl, to pour himself a cognac. The prince acknowledged his arrival with a regal inclination of his head, before resuming an animated conversation with the Earl of Egmont, who hovered attentively at his side. Eden was popular at Carlton House, he knew, not because of the flattering manner in which he spoke, but because he seldom spoke at all. The prince admired the timbre and resonance of his own voice and was immeasurably peeved with those who presumed to interrupt it. Those who were granted admission to the Carlton House circle rapidly learned the significance of being good listeners, or else subsequently came to lament the lack of that qualification. "Hear what you may, but keep your words to an absolute minimum," was the directive among the fawning devotees who surrounded the Prince Regent.

The Earl of Dodington glowered in the corner; his rival, Egmont, had the prince's ear. The shadowy court at Carlton House was the center of two hostile factions, each attempting to ingratiate themselves and their policies with the future king of England. And with the present king's latest bout of madness, the prince's ascension to the throne seemed imminent indeed. It was rumored that the prince had already established a list of those he would elevate to the peerage, those he would support as candidates in the government, as well as all the financial dispositions that would be adopted on the demise of his father.

Charles Fox arrived, plumply distinguished in a dark blue dress-coat.

"I wonder," the prince addressed Fox, careful to raise his voice so all in the room could hear and admire his subsequent witticism, "that you, who are so severe on kings, should be so complimentary to me."

"Your Highness," Fox replied, a wicked gleam in his eyes, "that is because I like the lion before his claws are full grown."

"Ah, well said indeed, sir!" the prince chortled in appreciation.

"How do you think we are doing?" Eden murmured anxiously to Fox as they stood together observing the arrival of the Whig grandees.

"Well, we have a majority in the House of Lords attending tonight." Fox gestured toward the Earls of Middlesex and Guildford, Lord John Sackville, and the Duke of Queensberry, just then handing off greatcoats to the hovering attendants. "Let's hope the prince will be able to entice them over to our perspective." Fox grinned.

"If he isn't too busy coordinating his future kingdom," Eden replied sourly, taking a deep gulp of the cognac. "Don't you think it is dangerous, blatantly courting the disfavor of the reigning king? He and the prince converse at dagger-point, barely bothering to conceal their mutual hatred. I know the king is mad, but who is to say he won't reign for another ten years in this fashion?"

"When the king is prepared to sacrifice the constitution to serve his own personal ambition then he is not worth supporting, Henry." Fox shrugged a hefty shoulder. "The prince is conducting himself as many a rebellious royal who has come before; generally all that scorn their father's ministers and measures during the course of their minority tend to adopt both when they come to the throne. It is our job, Henry, to make sure the son does a better job than his father." Clapping Eden on the shoulder, Fox left his side to mingle with the lords.

"I say, have you heard the most alarming bit of scandal?" the prince announced with dramatic pomposity, licking a smear of cream-filled brioche from the corner of his rouged mouth. A fat cat, Eden thought derisively. If this bombastic fool represented a political front to the party, at least there were capable men working behind the scenes. Fox was too conciliatory, too tentative in his approach, unable to make the hard decisions for fear of rupturing the Whig coalition. Perhaps a party-split was precisely what was required, Eden reflected, a splinter group that was prepared to engage in whatever ruthless means might be necessary to protect the realm.

An expectant hush fell over the crowd, as the prince had known it would. "It seems that the former Prime Minister William Pitt has commissioned an Irishman to spy for him in Paris!" Many of the Whigs had heard this report at the prince's soirée the previous day, but they dutifully murmured words of shocked disbelief.

"Do you think it is true?" the Earl of Guildford casually inquired of the two men who stood with him at the buffet table as he helped himself to a custard tart. "That Pitt sent an Irishman to infiltrate Napoleon's inner circle?"

"For what purpose exactly?" Lord Sackville asked dubiously.

"To determine the invasion point, or some such."

"How absurd," the Earl of Rochester, a shrewd, bright-eyed man in his early sixties, exclaimed skeptically. "How on earth would an unknown Irishman get the emperor of France to reveal such information to him?"

"It is all moot, gentlemen," Guildford interjected impatiently. "Napoleon would never be able to get past the blockade of English ships. We have them hemmed in, outmanned, and outgunned—they cannot even get their ships to sea! Look, I do not say the French cannot come; I only say they cannot come by sea!"

"And how else can they come, then?" the prince demanded, raising one finely plucked brow in practiced skepticism.

"My point exactly, Your Highness!" Guildford declared triumphantly, brandishing his smoking cigar.

"The threat is hardly contained to the continent," Fox noted thoughtfully as he squeezed his hefty bulk around the buffet, a china plate loaded with dainty cakes clasped in one meaty hand. "I understand the Irish are rumbling again. If Addington doesn't take matters into hand, we will have more than just the French to worry about."

There was a momentary silence. Guildford deposited his custard tart back on the table as if he found it suddenly indigestible. Fox licked his forefinger clean of fudge sauce before commencing on the strawberry tart.

"Do you think the rumor is true? About Pitt, I mean?" Sackville inquired, his florid face creased with concern.

"Oh, I think Pitt gets up to all kinds of nefarious activities at Walmer," Fox replied cheerfully as he selected a glass of brandy from a passing attendant.

"I have heard that Pitt intends to bring up the Catholic emancipation issue again," Guildford confided grimly.

"He'll never get it past the king."

"Perhaps. But how long will the king remain on the throne?" There was a momentary awkwardness when all remembered the presence of the king's son among them. The prince, however, bored with political intricacies beyond the socially scandalous, had turned with a sniff and was engaged in an animated conversation with Lord Sheffield at the other end of the room.

"The real question is, if Pitt can persuade the king to change his mind, how many lords will follow him? And will it be enough to push it through the House?"

"Good God! Have the Gordon Riots completely slipped his mind? Twenty years ago now, I realize, but the Protestant Association is still in existence and as vitriolic as ever. They marched on Parliament, destroyed the Bank of England and Newgate and Fleet Prisons, not to mention the home of the Lord Chief Justice, the Earl of Mansfield!"

"Napoleon will be Pitt's priority," Fox asserted thoughtfully. "He will not tackle such a thorny issue as Catholic emancipation until he is snugly back in Downing Street."

"That little Corsican upstart!" Sackville spat, lip curling in contempt.

"Say what you like about Napoleon, he is a military genius when it comes to terrestrial warfare. Of course we are terrified; we would be utterly foolish not to be. If Ol' Boney's forces got across the Channel..." Rochester shrugged. "With Addington at the helm?" He shook his white mane in a manner that suggested the utter futility of resistance.

There was an uncomfortable silence. They all knew Rochester was quite right in his assessment, but it hardly seemed cricket to voice it aloud.

"You sound as if you admire the man!" Sackville retorted incredulously.

Rochester nodded thoughtfully, pursing his lips. "I do indeed. Napoleon is a military strategist of the highest order."

"I say!"

"Downright treasonous!"

"Treasonous, is it?" Fox chortled. "These facts are undisputed. I think the real betrayal of one's country occurs when the peers of the realm persist in their self-indulgent oblivion. Sticking one's head in the sand is the euphemism I am searching for, I believe. Wouldn't you agree, Rochester?"

"Indeed, I would, Fox! Indeed, I would!" Rochester laughed, a quiet wheezing sound that shook his thin frame with merriment. At the relatively ancient age of sixty, Rochester considered himself obliged to create a few disturbances at every social engagement. Of all the men there, he had the least to profit by royal decrees, secure in a generous ancestral endowment and the gleeful immunity of old age. Fox enjoyed his company immensely. "In that, you and Pitt are united, are you not?"

"Perhaps so," Fox reluctantly acknowledged. "Our methods, however... Well, I believe mine have a little less madness to them!" He grinned companionably as he gestured for a second brandy.

"Ah, there you are, young Henry. I have been looking for you!" Lord Grenville's portly figure insinuated itself within the group, clapping one beefy hand in jovial camaraderie across Eden's narrow shoulders. "Come," he expounded, munching a cigar between large, yellowed teeth. "We have much to discuss..."

# 49.

The door eased open, and a dark figure moved noiselessly into the room. Wolfe, hidden behind the table, fingers white-clenched around his knife, body tense and poised, heartbeat quickening, frantically discarded one option after another. There was nothing but to fling himself forward, hoping the element of surprise would work in his favor. Despite the coolness of the room, he could feel the sweat trickle a meandering path between his shoulder blades. The wind rattled at the windowpanes and sent dark clouds scudding across the sky, intermittently revealing a luminous moon that sent shafts of pale light into the dim room. He heard a rustle of skirts. His eyes had adjusted to the darkness, and, surreptitiously peering around the table corner, he could make out a tall figure, the dark silk of her gown a lustrous gleam.

"Wolfe?" It was Jeanne.

"Jaysus! What are *you* doing here?" he exclaimed, rising from his crouched position, his breath exhaling in sharp relief.

"I came to kill an emperor," Jeanne replied grimly. "But a footman spilled his wine after I added the poison, and Napoleon did not pour another. Now they are eating, and he rarely drinks wine with his meal. So…" she shrugged, her face momentarily twisting in bitter disappointment. "We have been foiled again, it seems. But I came to find you, to tell you that we have been betrayed. Desant is in custody; Pichegru and Cadoudal were arrested this morning, and Moreau earlier this evening. The safe-house in Saint Marceau has been compromised. We have to get out of Paris. Tonight."

"You took a great risk in coming here'."

"My very life is a risk, monsieur. I gambled that Fouché would not inform Napoleon of our conspiracy until he had us in the Temple Prison. Otherwise, the chance of escape would leave him looking the fool. And he is anything but a fool. Which is why we need to leave. Now."

"I have what I came for," Wolfe replied.

A door in the adjacent salon room shut with a sudden thud, and the sound of heavy footfalls could be heard moving toward them across the wooden floor. Wolfe and Jeanne exchanged glances and with unspoken agreement moved through the open door to the emperor's quarters. Rapidly descending the stairwell to Joséphine's bedroom, they paused halfway as the low murmur of voices reached them from below.

"We can't get out this way," Wolfe whispered, turning back up the stairs. The door to the map room was now ajar, and glancing quickly through, Wolfe could see the back and upper torso of a man, a white turban covering his head, leaning over the map table. A loose green shirt and vest tucked into voluminous red pants, themselves gathered into yellow leather boots. It was the weapon that hung at his waist that immediately attracted Wolfe's attention—a curved scimitar. A leather sash, ornately decorated with a brass crescent and star motif, ran diagonally across his back holding a brace of pistols. The pommel of a second dagger lay snug against his other side. This must be the mameluk. Roustam, Napoleon's personal bodyguard. They were trapped in Napoleon's bedroom. Wolfe felt a tap on his arm. Jeanne was pointing at the muslin curtains that he noticed were billowing slightly in the rising wind. The window was open.

# 50.

Fouché leaned forward, his arms forming a protective cradle around his bottle of Burgundy, his booted feet tucked back under his chair. Seemingly oblivious of the café's evening business that bustled and flowed around him, he sat, brow furrowed, eyes half-closed, dark and heavy with thought.

The waiters and customers did not so much ignore Fouché, hunched in conspicuous solitude at the center table, as they warily skirted around him. Despite his regular occupancy of this table at this café, the staff and clientele still fell silent when Fouché's hunched-over figure entered the room and breathed in quiet relief when he left. This evening, however, he did not notice the sudden quiet, intent as he was reviewing the events of the day.

It had been a good day. Actually, it had been an astoundingly good day, but Fouché was not one given to excessive sentiment or undue complacency. Emotion was a weakness. It confused perspective, disrupted reason, and resulted in an increased susceptibility to the influence of other agents who invariably had an agenda of their own, however surreptitiously they applied it. And as to complacency—well, he was intimately familiar with his city and well-acquainted with her inhabitants.

Fouché often likened Parisian dissidents to sewer rats that thronged the sluggishly fetid labyrinth beneath the city streets. For the most part, their behavior was predictable. They were scavengers who fed on the dead and the vulnerable, but when they were cornered, backed up against the wall, when they were hissing with fear and anger, when they were trapped…well, *that* was when they were most dangerous. And two rats continued to elude him. Wolfe Trant and Primrose. Or should he call her Madame Recamier?

Gendarmes had stormed Madame Recamier's house, and despite Marie's testimony to her sickness, the lady of the house was not to be found. She was on the run. His suspicions were confirmed: undoubtedly Madame Recamier was Primrose. That knowledge alone proved a source of significant satisfaction.

Fumbling in the pocket of his coat, Fouché withdrew the last of his cheap cigars and inserted it in the corner of his mouth. He leaned forward to the flickering candlelight and, sucking in his gray cheeks, pulled the flame toward the cigar. He inhaled deeply, holding the acrid smoke in his lungs, feeling the heat scorch the back of his throat, before releasing a blue plume towards the ceiling.

He had every reason to be satisfied with the day's accomplishments. Michel Desant had been arrested the night before and, under interrogation, had revealed two addresses of Resistance safe-houses in the suburb of Chaillot. They had been raided early that morning and Pichegru and Cadoudal had been apprehended and taken to the Abbaye Prison. A warrant had been issued for the arrest of Moreau, whom Chavert was taking into custody even now. Desant had not yet given up the identity of the prince of the blood, the Royalist hope for the throne, but it would not be long. Desant was weak, and Fouché's methods of persuasion seldom failed to produce the desired response. Meanwhile, the guards on the gates of Paris had been strengthened, and detailed descriptions of both Trant and Recamier had been disseminated throughout the network of agents who were watching anyone with known links to Chouans and other dissidents. It was just a matter of time…

He had not yet informed Napoleon of his progress, despite an increased pressure to do so. Chavert's re-written report, marginally improved over the initial draft, lay on his desk. Experience had taught him not to reveal the plot until all the conspirators had been named and apprehended. It would do his reputation little good if he denounced Madame Recamier as the perpetrator and was then unable to apprehend her. Apparently, she was on friendly terms with the empress. No, he needed the woman in custody as well as definitive proof of her treason. A confession would suit the purpose admirably. Fouché, with his sinister reputation, had little difficulty in obtaining them.

Napoleon was convinced the attack on his carriage was borne of a Jacobin conspiracy rather than a Royalist one; Fouché had no desire to disillusion him just yet. Usually, it did not matter too much who had committed the crime; the principal concern was to produce credible culprits, the more the better, rather than pinpoint the actual conspirators.

Ordinary bystanders would do in a pinch; there were always a number of lamplighters or errand boys not wearing the badges required of outdoor trades or water-carriers whose papers were not completely in order.

His second concern was to establish the existence of organized leadership and prove the existence of a hidden bailleur de fonds, or mastermind. Who more obvious to fulfill this role than Primrose and Monsieur Trant? The former of whom had already been indicted by Desant, and the latter lent the conspiracy an exotic international element that Napoleon always found appealing. Then, of course, he would be obliged to produce a contrived plot, and the requisite hired muscle that had carried it out—their guilt ensured by the discovery of a certain sum of money that had been planted upon their person prior to arrest. Fouché knew the zeal and effectiveness of the police was measured by the number of arrests—better to produce one hundred as opposed to a meager ten.

A dark coat appeared in his vision. Glancing up, Fouché saw Chavert slide into the chair opposite. "Forgive the intrusion, Commissioner," he murmured. "But you said you wanted to be apprised of any new development? Denis Renault has been contacted by the Resistance to secure a safe-house."

# 51.

Having clambered through the window, Jeanne and Wolfe found themselves on a narrow ledge that extended along the front of the palace. It terminated at the Pavilion de Flore at the easternmost end of the structure, and disappeared into the central dome to the west. The weather had deteriorated rapidly, and their vision was almost immediately obscured by swirling snow and ice. Tall double windows flanked the ledge, interspersed with sculptured figures, their surroundings dense with Roman architectural motifs. Blinking against the driving sleet, Wolfe considered their dilemma.

They could edge past the windows of Napoleon's antechambers and hope one of them was open. However, in all probability, they would surprise an aide inside who would immediately sound the alarm, and doubtless most of the windows had been secured against the increasingly violent weather. Wolfe just hoped the curtains were drawn and that a slumbering attendant would not waken to see their sodden figures pressed against the windowpanes.

The Pavilion de Flore presented a more favorable alternative. It flanked and rose above the main Tuileries structure to the east. From this vantage point, Wolfe could make out decorative Corinthian columns set between recessed archways, above which sat a steeply pitched gable roof and several tall stone chimney pieces. The significant feature, however, to the two fugitives clinging to the side of the building, was the scaffolding that enshrouded the roof of the structure, as well as that which encased the Grande Galerie, which emanated from the Tuileries Palace toward the Louvre.

In the tradition of previous monarchs, Napoleon was leaving his own architectural mark on the palace façade, and it was currently under heavy construction. The roof of the Pavilion de Flore, the Grande Galerie, and the façade of the Cour Carrée were all sheathed in a thick web of scaffolding. If they could edge along to the pavilion, they could make their way across the roof of the Grande Galerie and descend the scaffolding into the central square of the Louvre.

"This way," Wolfe yelled, the driving sleet drenching his clothes and obscuring his vision, the ledge dangerously icy beneath his feet. "We need to make our way toward the pavilion. Do you see the scaffolding?"

The wind whipped and howled around them, snatching his words away even as he uttered them. Fortunately, the gusts blew in a westerly direction which served to push them toward the building rather than away from it. Jeanne nodded, hair plastered to her head, skirts a heavy, wet mass against her legs.

They edged cautiously along the platform, their frozen fingers seeking purchase in the etched masonry. They passed the first double window. The map room. The glass was already covered in a thin layer of frost and was icily slippery under their fingers. Inching their way past, bodies pressed against sculptured figures of ancient mythology—glacially elegant in their recessed niches, a quickly accumulating layer of snow and ice gathering in their crevices—their progress seemed both precarious and torturously slow.

They were just approaching the third window, the emperor's salon, when they heard a shout of alarm directly behind them. Startled, Jeanne almost lost her footing before Wolfe, with one hand gripping the protruding arm of Aphrodite, steadied her. Looking back, blinking against the relentless sleet that stabbed frozen needles against his face, he saw the mameluk climbing out the window of the map room, his red cape flapping in an agitated frenzy against his back. They had been spotted. Roustam began to move rapidly along the ledge after them.

"Go!" Wolfe yelled at Jeanne. She forced her frozen limbs to move. One step after another. The rain fell in streaks to the icy cobblestones fifty feet below. They sidled past Napoleon's service salon. The tiled roof of the Pavilion de Flore loomed just a foot or so above their heads, offering temporary shelter in the overhanging cornice.

Roustam, moving less cautiously than they, was only ten feet behind. Sheltering beneath the window molding of the service salon, he held a paper envelope between strong white teeth and emptied gunpowder into the barrel of his pistol.

The ledge widened here, forming a corner before becoming incorporated into a recessed arch that formed the side wall of the pavilion; it then traced a path around to the front façade. The scaffolding, covering the tiled roof, descended tantalizingly just below the edge of the cornice. The sleet ran in steady rivulets off the bamboo poles. In an hour, they would be icicles.

"We'll have to jump up and grab it!" Jeanne hollered. "Help me across." Wolfe jammed one foot against the ledge moulding under the last window and the other against the pavilion wall, his body straddling the precipice. He hoisted her across his torso and with a grunt of effort, the pain shooting through his shoulder, raised her sufficiently to grab the scaffolding and pull her arms through.

"Kick your legs up!" he yelled.

Jeanne struggled through her layers of wet linen and silk to comply. She managed to get her knees hooked through the bamboo pole, her dark dress flapping in a wide sodden arc beneath her, and then heaved herself up to grab the next pole half a foot above the first. In another moment, she was sitting upright, then, clambering to her feet, she disappeared over the roof edge.

Roustam rammed the bullet down the barrel of his gun and emptied gunpowder into the flintlock's pan with a shake of the envelope between his teeth. He steadily edged toward Wolfe, the flintlock hammer fully cocked and ready to fire.

Wolfe took a deep breath then lunged upwards, his body flying through the frigid air. He grasped the slick bamboo pole with both hands. A piercing pain streaked through his wounded shoulder, and he slipped…and dangled, one hand on the scaffolding, struggling to maintain his grip. He could see Jeanne's white face above, leaning anxiously over the edge. Wolfe hung helplessly as, several feet away, Roustam raised the gun.

# 52.

"Help yourself to more coffee, Casimir," Talleyrand yawned, leaning back in his chair, stretching his hands above his head in a languorous motion. "I am almost done here." Casimir raised one hand in casual decline but did not reply.

Talleyrand leaned forward again, scrawling instructions to his secretary in the margins. The marble-topped desk was strewn with papers, all densely covered in hastily scribbled, almost illegible handwriting, each terminating in Talleyrand's distinctively flourished signature. As he completed each letter, he stacked them carelessly to one side. André would reduce the roughly scrawled notes to correct diplomatic formality the next morning.

Casimir slouched in the brocaded chair by the fire, feet resting casually on the ottoman. The only sound in the room was the occasional spit and crackle of flames licking and curling hungrily around the dry logs and the scratch of quill against paper.

"So how did you find English society?" Talleyrand inquired idly, without looking up from his papers.

"It had its moments," Montrond replied. "I must admit I was quite taken with the duchess…but cannot say much for the society she keeps. I still cannot believe the English assassinated Czar Paul I." Montrond shook his head incredulously. "Obviously he was assassinated after all, and it must follow that someone was responsible. But to overhear those very people discussing it in the shrubbery! I tell you, Charles, I had no idea that the English were so…so…"

"Fanatical behind their stiff upper lips?" Talleyrand suggested, mouth curving in amusement as he glanced up at his friend. "There are extremists in all societies, my friend. Someone once told me that 'there is no place in a fanatic's head where reason can enter.'"

Montrond raised an eyebrow in query.

"Napoleon Bonaparte," Talleyrand informed him with mock solemnity.

"Ah, a man who has confronted the darkest parts of himself !" Montrond laughed, raising his glass. "To our emperor!"

"To our emperor, indeed." Talleyrand laid down his quill with a yawn. "And what of Pitt, what did you think of him?"

"Intelligent, certainly. Articulate. A bit on the stiff side. He didn't seem quite so well."

"It's the weather," Talleyrand replied solemnly, leaning back in his chair. "How would you feel living in a place of gray clouds and perpetual rain?"

"And women who are primly buttoned up. It was delightful to get back to the French girls in their sheer muslin and ample décolletage!" Montrond grinned wolfishly.

"Well," Talleyrand noted, his tone heavy with irony, "I suppose between the weather and the prim women, the English are able to apply themselves to innovations, as well as assassinations, with admirable fervor. Did you know an English company has invented hollow pens with metal nibs?" Talleyrand shook his head slightly in bemusement, before reluctantly picking up his quill again.

Casimir drained the last of his coffee, placed the empty cup on the table, and shifted slightly in his chair until his friend occupied the center of his vision. Talleyrand's quill continued to scratch across the paper, leaving a chaotic flow of letters and blots in its wake.

"But I fear I am loath to relinquish my quills. There is something delightfully natural about them, the way they fit in the hand, the way they bend under pressure. Did you know the strongest quills are those taken from living birds in the spring? From the five outer left wing feathers. The left wing is favored, you see, because the feathers curved outward and away when used by a right-handed writer."

Talleyrand sighed, finally laid his quill aside, and rose to his feet. "Are you aware, Casimir, that Europe has been at war now for more than *ten* years?" Talleyrand limped toward the spacious windows that lined the wall behind his desk. The smooth, bare limbs of the beech trees gleamed yellow in the gas-lamps. An equally yellow moon hung in a darkly sullen sky. "And in that time, there have been so many changes... both causes for which nations were fighting and sides upon which they fought. Enemies of one year become allies of the next. Alliances so rapidly formed have been dissolved with equal rapidity. Dynasties have been overthrown, new monarchs set up, old ones sent into exile, new kingdoms called into existence. Frontiers that had been unmoved for centuries have disappeared. What will become of all this chaos?" Turning back toward his friend, Talleyrand's lips curved in a rueful smile. "The world I know is slipping away, Casimir. I am starting to feel like an old relic myself."

"On the contrary, my friend, you incorporate the best of your era. You are suave, courteous, and, may I say, as exquisite in your dress as in your conversation. And *most* impressively, you manage to overcome, by force of your charm, every woman in France!" Montrond grinned, raising an imaginary hat in Talleyrand's direction.

"Ah yes, well there is *that*," Talleyrand replied drolly, with a smile of his own.

The men were interrupted by a discreet knock at the door, and a manservant in sleekly elegant livery announced in a solemn tone: "Police Commissioner Fouché."

The men had time for a startled exchange of glances before the grim figure of Fouché was ushered into the room. He stood for a moment, hunched within his greasy overcoat like a crow in shiny plumage. A cigar hung limply from the corner of his mouth, the ash dropping carelessly on the Persian carpet beneath him.

The manservant, hovering impotently behind Fouché, uttered a murmur of distress at the sight; his gloved hands fidgeted anxiously, as if wondering how to whip the carpet out from under the commissioner's feet without him being aware of it—much like the trick street magicians performed with tablecloths fully laden with dishes. Talleyrand languidly waved him away.

"Please, Commissioner Fouché, come in. What a pleasant surprise."

"Somehow, Monsieur de Talleyrand, I doubt that," Fouché replied irritably. If he was at all uncomfortable in these sumptuous surroundings, he gave no sign. He glared at Talleyrand, then at Montrond, his heavy brow bunching in wrinkles above deeply set eyes. "I have Desant, Cadoudal, Pichegru, and Moreau in custody," he barked without any further preamble, acrid puffs of blue smoke issuing out from between yellowed teeth. "What do you know of their conspiracy to place a Bourbon prince on the throne of France?"

"Would you care to have a seat? Can I take your coat?" Talleyrand offered soliticiously, as determined to be elaborately courteous as Fouché was rude.

"Do not mock me, monsieur!" Fouché growled, sucking energetically on his cigar.

"Forgive me, Commissioner; certainly, that is not my intention. However, I am afraid that I can be of little use to your investigation. I am shocked to hear that Moreau and Pichegru have betrayed the empire. As to the Bourbon conspiracy...well, I understood the Royalists were responsible for the attempted assassination of the emperor last week?" He shrugged one silk-clad shoulder, leaning nonchalantly against the pale gold wallpaper, arms crossed over his chest as he regarded Fouché impassively from beneath heavy lids.

Montrond, for his part, was enjoying the performance. Talleyrand was as smoothly sophisticated in appearance and conversation as Fouché was brutal in manner and ill-kempt in dress. Talleyrand was an ex-bishop consorting openly with numerous mistresses while Fouché was an ex-terrorist, the faithful husband to a dour wife. To Talleyrand, politics comprised the settlement of dynastic disputes or international debate conducted in a ballroom or across the dinner table; to Fouché, the same word invoked street corner assassinations planned by masked conspirators in darkly secluded cellars. A distinct stench enveloped the police commissioner like a miasma. Montrond, wrinkling his nose in distaste, marveled at Talleyrand's ability to maintain perfect composure without the slightest breach of etiquette. The duke was scrupulously polite but maintained his characteristically cool reserve. He did not seem to notice the steady mound of ash accumulating on his lush carpet. If he did, he gave no indication of it.

"I will get right to the point, monsieur," Fouché began, chewing vigorously on the end of his increasingly ragged cigar.

"By all means, Commissioner," Talleyrand inclined his head deferentially, unruffled by Fouché's scathing use of *monsieur*—the commissioner deliberately ignoring Talleyrand's recent elevation to the dukedom and the title bestowed upon him by the emperor.

"I have reason to believe that you are involved in this plot and perhaps even that you are concealing the two remaining *conspirateurs*," Fouché's eyes narrowed suspiciously, glancing around the room as if expecting them to be discovered cowering behind the sofa.

Talleyrand threw his head back and laughed, a deep infectious chuckle that reverberated through his chest and brought a smile to Casimir's lips. "A *conspirateur*? Ah, Commissioner," he managed at last, with unconstrained amusement. "Now, if you do not mind my asking, what evidence do you have implicating me in this nefarious plot to enthrone the Bourbons?" Talleyrand asked, wiping tears of mirth from his eyes, a smile still lurking about his lips.

"I have evidence for all manner of crimes against the empire, Monsieur de Talleyrand," Fouché retorted menacingly, stabbing one thick, grimy finger in the duke's direction.

Talleyrand raised an eyebrow in skeptical acknowledgment. "Well, by all means, you are welcome to return when you have the papers for my arrest. Until then…" He discreetly yanked a bell-pull that formed part of a decorative curtain behind him. The door opened almost immediately and the manservant appeared in all his starched impassivity. "You will forgive me, Commissioner, but I have an evening menu to attend to." He inclined his head slightly in dismissal. Fouché glowered, munching furiously on his cigar as he stalked from the room. The door slammed behind him, causing the delicate blue chinaware to rattle and waver on its stands.

"He is a powerful man, Charles. You had best not antagonize him," Casimir warned.

"Oh, I have every intention of antagonizing him, Casimir," Talleyrand replied grimly. "But I do not intend to underestimate him."

"How much do you think he knows?" Montrond asked.

"I am quite certain Fouché has infiltrated the Resistance. There is a mole deep enough and powerful enough within their ranks to have succeeded in breaking apart the leadership at the highest levels. I have made contact only with Primrose and Monsieur Trant. I think our friend Fouché is hoping to beat the bushes. He is seeking to confirm what he already suspects."

"So what do we do?" Montrond asked.

Talleyrand smiled slowly and limped over to the chair in front of the fire. Easing himself into a comfortable slouch, he replied: "We do what I do best, my dear Casimir—absolutely nothing."

# 53.

Roustam bared his teeth in a grin that was almost feral, his forefinger squeezing the trigger as Wolfe hung helplessly in the blinding sleet and rain. There was an audible click and...nothing. Roustam glanced down at his pistol in fury. The powder was wet and unable to ignite. Wolfe, teeth clenched against the searing pain in his shoulder, pulled himself up toward the bar, simultaneously reaching up with his other hand. Then, when his handhold was secure, he kicked out with his feet in one fluid movement, catching the mameluk's wrist and sending the pistol clattering to the cobblestones below. Roustam, with a cry of rage, reached for Wolfe's legs, narrowly missing them and almost lurching from the ledge in the process.

Wolfe, with a grunt of effort, heaved his body up to the bar, his bunched muscles screaming in protest, his shoulder a fiery spasm of pain. Jeanne was waiting for him on the scaffolding, her face white and pinched with cold. She grabbed his coat and helped haul him up and over the edge. He lay for a moment, leaning forward against the sloped roof, his arms wrapped around the sturdily lashed bamboo frame, his body shaking with the effort of his exertions.

They were perched like highly nested eagles in the rooftop of Paris. While the descending cloudbank and the dark swirl of sleet and snow largely obscured their vision, the prominent sloping roof-line of the long, narrow Tuileries building was sporadically visible to their left, its ornately carved façade brilliantly lit by sheltered gaslight. Window-glow from the Grande Galerie spilled patches across the rippled black body of the Seine to their right. The domed roof that capped the Galerie above stretched out into the darkness.

Wolfe turned awkwardly on the scaffolding, his body facing outwards. Jeanne's drenched figure edged toward him, treading gingerly on the slippery bars. "If we c... crawl...that way," she yelled at Wolfe, indicating to her right with a nod of her head, "we can drop to the Grande Galerie...get across to the Louvre...then climb down the scaffolding." Her words came in fits and starts, her body shuddering violently with cold. Shrugging out of his coat, he placed it around her shaking shoulders, helping her insert one arm at a time before laying his body flat next to hers.

Directly below them, where the last bars of scaffolding dripped wetly to the cobblestones two stories below and where they had lately climbed, Wolfe saw a tanned hand of the mameluk. Then the second. Then, a moment later, his dark visage, black eyes gleaming beneath the pale turban, white teeth bared in a growl of physical strain. A bushy black mustache covered his upper lip, glistening with droplets of rain that streamed down his face and darkened his robes.

"Let's go!" Wolfe hollered, sleet stinging his face in icy pricks. They clambered over the scaffolding, the gusting wind shrieking across the slanted roof of the pavilion like a scorned and demented Fury. In his peripheral vision, Wolfe could see Roustam haul himself up to the roof-top and clamber to his feet. Damn. Wolfe had his knife but didn't trust his ability to throw it hard enough and accurately enough in these wild gusts. Better to save it for close encounters. Roustam had two other pistols, Wolfe remembered, but it would be difficult, if not impossible, to load them under these circumstances, particularly when trying to protect the powder from the rain. That left him with a scimitar—also a close-quarter weapon.

Wolfe and Jeanne had reached the other side of the pavilion, and the rounded roof of the Grande Galerie loomed approximately ten feet below. Jeanne dropped her legs over the edge and, holding the scaf-folding tight, allowed her body to drop until she was dangling over the Galerie. Then she let go, fell several feet, and almost slid off the curved roof before managing to get an elbow around the scaffolding. Wolfe, wasting no time, leapt over the edge, falling with a thump before rolling and grabbing at a slick bamboo bar with one hand. Wincing slightly, he yanked himself up, and he and Jeanne began clambering along the rooftop toward the Louvre.

# 54.

## TUILERIES PALACE. PARIS, FRANCE
*December 6, 1803*

The domed roof of the Grande Galerie, encased in bamboo scaffolding, stretched out before Jeanne and Wolfe like the bony carcass of a giant river serpent which had hauled itself from the black Seine to die upon its shores. The roof extended for nine hundred feet or so before it united with the Louvre, the point of which was utterly obscured by the darkness of the night. The sky was a thick, heaving pitch, unrelieved by moon or stars, but illuminated in all its grand ferocity with the occasional lightening that flared and lit the dark underbelly of roiling cloudbanks. The rising wind shrieked in their ears and whipped Jeanne's dress into a flapping frenzy about her legs. They moved forward at a cautious crouch, keeping their bodies low to the rooftop for fear a sudden squall could send them skidding over the edge. The bamboo poles, each festooned with thickly clustered icicles on their undersides, crossed the rooftop in a grid at approximately one foot intervals.

Wolfe and Jeanne were just passing the first skylight, consisting of multiple panes of slick leaded glass that were already dusted with a layer of snow, when they heard the thud of the mameluk hitting the roof behind them. The skylights emitted a dim glow from the Grande Galerie beneath, providing a weak sphere of dim perception within which pelted yellowish bullets of snow and sleet. Beyond this, beyond the treacherous curve of icy roof, was an impenetrable darkness with death waiting on the icy cobblestones far below. Further down the Galerie, toward the Louvre, Wolfe could see the second skylight. This one, however, had yet to be completed, and the faint glimmer from below illuminated the billowing canvas of a temporary cover. It had come loose, tethered at only two corners, and twisted and whipped in the wind like the ragged sail of a boat lost at sea. Roustam was only minutes away.

"Over there!" Wolfe hollered, gripping her arm with one hand, his mouth close to her ear. "Make for the skylight. Maybe there is a way down into the gallery. Go ahead; I'll be right behind you!"

Jeanne's face was taut and pale in the dim light, skin stretched tight across her cheekbones, eyes dark and shadowed, teeth a chilled clitter-clatter between bluish lips. "I s…stand w…with… you," she cried back, the words fractured by the cold that had iced her skin and frozen her bones to near immobility. Her body was convulsed by violent trembling, and Wolfe knew she needed immediate shelter and warmth.

"And what use will it be, then, if both of us die?" he demanded harshly, his grip tightening on her arm, dark hair whipping about his face. "It'll all be for nothin', don't you see?" Wolfe leaned forward, pressed his lips hard against her frozen ones. "Now, go!" She hesitated a moment longer, her dark gaze holding his blue one, doubt and uncertainty flickering through her features. "Or ye'll freeze to death, and how will I carry you out then? You're too stiff and cold to be any good to me, and if you're here I can't focus on the fight fer worry of protecting you. For God's sake, lass, *go!*" His Irish brogue came thick and strong, as it always did in times of tension and fear. She leaned forward and kissed him again, a brief quick touch of their lips, and then she turned and stumbled from the circle of light, her body stiff and clumsy with cold.

Turning back toward the Pavilion de Flore, blinking through the blinding sleet and snow, Wolfe had but a moment to prepare for battle. Reaching down, he knotted a loose end of the rope that secured the scaffolding around his right ankle. Then he steadied himself on the slick roof, one ankle braced against each inside edge of the bamboo poles, the knife gripped tightly in his right hand.

It was then that Roustam appeared out of the darkness, his robes wet and heavy with snow and sleet, his dark face clenched with grim intent. The glint of a blade, a scimitar, appeared in his right hand. A leather belt crossed his chest, with pocketed inserts from which three small hilts projected—throwing daggers. Roustam had been forced to discard his pistols, rendered useless in the wet weather, and the strength of the wind should make throwing difficult. As that thought passed fleetingly through Wolfe's mind, the wind died down, and the pool of light that encompassed the two men became eerily quiet. The stinging, blinding snow and sleet now became small flakes that swirled gently around them, dusting their shoulders and melting into their hair.

For a moment, the air between them charged with the electric potential of battle about to begin, the two men regarded each other silently, each assessing the other, each all too aware that only one would survive the engagement. The numbness of Trant's fingers, the icy vertical drop just yards from his feet, the heated throb of his shoulder, Pitt and Ireland, Jeanne and Fouché—they all dropped away, and the man opposite him magnified within Wolfe's sensory perception. His entire world consisted of his opponent's physical presence: the set of Roustam's shoulders, the position of his legs, and above all, the nuance of his expression.

Then, moving forward at a deliberate pace, Roustam deftly whirled the scimitar in wide sweeping arcs, the blade a blur of steel singing through the icy air. Wolfe crouched in readiness, holding the knife before him. It was a fairly pitiful weapon against the long curved blade that Roustam wielded with such dexterity, but it was the only one he had. Fear and intimidation served as Roustam's primary weapons, and overconfidence was his weakness. Wolfe knew that in order to exploit this vulnerability, he must encourage the mameluk's expectation of a battle speedily dispatched against a vastly inferior opponent. Wolfe was, after all, relatively unarmed and weakened from a previous shoulder wound. He exhaled through clenched teeth, lowering his right arm momentarily, as a deliberate wince tightened his features. A scarlet stain had spread through the gray linen of his shirt. Wolfe took a step back.

And all the fury and guilt that Wolfe had carried within him coalesced and distilled into a volatile energy source that would either sustain him or be his undoing. It had always been this way before a fight—if he could channel the rage, control it, use it, master it, he would emerge victorious; if he allowed it to consume him, blind him, he would find himself face down on the cobblestones in a puddle of blood. And then none of it would matter anymore anyway.

Sensing Wolfe's weakness, Roustam lunged, thrusting the scimitar forward toward Wolfe's torso. The movement brought him close to Wolfe, who ducked to avoid the weapon, then twisted, his unsecured foot sliding precariously across the rounded roof. He drove his arm forward, delivering a quick, sharp blow to Roustam's jaw with the heel of his palm. Roustam staggered under the unexpected assault and, reeling backwards, feet sliding desperately beneath him, lurched over toward the side of the roof. Grasping the scaffolding, he slowly regained his footing, dislodging a cascade of snow to the courtyard far below. The scimitar had gone. Wolfe had seen it skitter across the rooftop and disappear into the dark.

The mameluk approached Wolfe a little more warily, planting his booted feet cautiously within the bamboo grid. Wolfe waited for him, conserving his strength and maintaining a strong balanced stance. He was exhausted, the knife a leaden weight in his hand. Wolfe knew that in order for him to survive this confrontation it had to be resolved rapidly.

Abruptly, his hand a blur of motion, Roustam had withdrawn a blade from his chest strap and hurled it at Wolfe, who had barely registered its appearance before it was upon him. He had been expecting the knife, but his reactions were dulled by cold and fatigue. Wolfe had scarcely time to shift his head to one side as the small dagger flew past his cheek. A second followed the first with inconceivable rapidity, and Wolfe felt a dull pain in his right arm as he lurched forward, a roar of fury erupting in his throat. He lunged in a maniacal leap off the bamboo cross-piece, glimpsing Roustam's look of startled surprise before his head connected with the mameluk's torso and sent him flying backwards.

Grappling for control of Wolfe's knife, his own last blade inaccessible between their chests, Roustam utilized their momentum to powerful effect, and Wolfe found himself on his back painfully braced by the bamboo grid with the mameluk above. Dark eyes gleamed with cool self-assurance; his mouth curved in a glacial smile. Roustam reached for the last blade in his chest strap.

As he did so, Wolfe reached up and grabbed the leather strap with one fist, swung his legs across the roof and in a scissoring motion unbalanced the mameluk. In one quick movement, Wolfe was on his feet, using his powerful build and close-quarter strength to seize Roustam around the middle, landing a forceful blow to his ribs.

The mameluk, dangerously close to the roof's edge, stumbled and staggered; his booted feet caught the bamboo bars and sent him reeling backwards. Grabbing Wolfe's tunic with one dark hand, he teetered and then fell, pulling Wolfe over the edge with him. A sickening dull thud announced Roustam's death on the cobblestones below, while Wolfe, his left ankle still secured to the grid above, dangled upside down alongside the upper windows of the Grande Galerie.

For a moment, he hung thus: arms limp over his head, gulping in frosty mouthfuls of air, waiting for the hammering of his heart to ease.

"Wolfe?" It was Jeanne. Twisting his body upwards, Wolfe grabbed the rope and, with a grunt, hauled himself up on to the roof. He found himself facing the business end of a makeshift bamboo weapon, the broken end a jagged spear-point aimed at his chest.

"Grand," Wolfe gasped, nodding approvingly as he struggled to his feet.

"N...next t...time...give me a chance to use it," Jeanne stammered, with a pitiful attempt at a smile. Together, they traversed the remaining length of the Grande Galerie and slowly, painfully, made their way down the scaffolding that covered the ornately carved façade of the Louvre.

# 55.

## Blackman Street. London, England
### *December 6, 1803*

"Here, here!" Malcolm Dundas waved his arm frantically in the dim yellow gaslight of Blackman Street. "Damned cabbies," he muttered under his breath, casting an anxious glance at Pitt who had shrunk into the collar of his coat like a turtle withdrawing into his shell. They had arrived from Holwood House that morning and spent a harried afternoon in meetings with various lords of the realm, many of whom urged Pitt to take up direct opposition to Addington. A note had arrived from Charles Fox requesting a meeting the following day. The serenity of Holwood, the frivolity that had momentarily smoothed his brow and brought a lightness to his heart, had ebbed and dissipated as their coach had approached the city. Responsibilities were resumed; the mantle of leadership, ever-weighty in the absence of effective administration, was taken upon his shoulders until, like Atlas, Pitt seemed bowed and bent beneath the world.

Darkly sullen clouds obscured the sky and sat low and swollen over the spires of Westminster, as if weighed down by their winter burden of snow and sleet. They were soon to be relieved of it as the first fat flakes began to swirl lazily from the sky, buffeted playfully by the rising wind before landing, in all their lacy white delicacy, on the men's thick woolen coats and melting into nothing but damp patches.

After the "Irish Scandal" that had blazoned across the top of every cheap broadsheet in the East Side, Pitt felt himself not only obliged to accept Fox's proposal to meet but even to suggest an earlier appointment. Hounded for a statement, Pitt had finally expressed an amused incredulity at the transparent ploys of the opposition to impugn his candidacy: "You would think at the very least they would have come up with something a little more plausible than this fabrication of fairytales! An Irishman, was it?" he enquired of the reporter with a chuckle. Privately, he was devastated. Certainly, this was a plan Napoleon had now promptly abandoned, and with the intelligence he had received from

Montrond regarding a hired assassin… God knew if Wolfe was even alive. There were other issues—now made even more urgent by the demise of the Irish agenda. And so it was to Fox's he went.

And despite his concern for his friend's health, Dundas understood his determination to attend—something Pitt himself had referred to in the last Commons debate about setting aside rivalries in a time of national extremity. If there was a chance that a strong coalition government could be formed on the tottering remnants of Addington's administration, if Fox, Grenville, and the prince could be wooed…

"Here!" Dundas hollered. The swirling snow stung his cheeks into pinkness as the wind began to rise. Finally! A round-bellied horse veered in their direction, cantering placidly through the snow-strewn streets, his breath warm plumes in the frosty air.

"What'll it be, gu'vnr?" the driver gruffly asked, his face a pale blur swaddled beneath his dark overcoat and hat.

"Holland House!" Dundas replied, shouting above the rising wind that howled and rattled its way around the black carriage. Once inside, William Pitt sank back into the leather upholstery and closed his eyes, his face ashen. "Remind me why we're doin' this," Dundas grumbled.

Pitt opened one eye. "We are extending the olive branch, Mal. Setting aside rivalries in a time of national extremity, remember?"

"Yes, and that went down verra well in Parliament last week, Will, but really how do ye propose to do that? Ye know full well the king would never accept a government with Charles Fox in it; he blames him for the prince's bad habits. And the Whigs wilna even consider an administration without him."

"Perhaps more can be done," Pitt responded wearily. "If the nation of England is to survive Napoleon, we must have a strong unified government. I need to make the king understand that. We have to exhaust all options."

"The only thing you're exhausting, my friend, is yerself," Dundas replied. "You need to declare open opposition to Addington. Form your own administration just as Lords Castlereagh and Liverpool have asked of you. Regardless of the rumors and intrigue, you've never been more popular."

"I *supported* Addington, Mal. I placed him in office. I persuaded Flemming and Defries to become a part of his government, against their own wishes, so that the Whigs would not entirely dominate legislation.

So how can I now turn against them?" Pitt sighed heavily, kneading his brow with the thumb and forefinger of his right hand. "I will come to government, but the call to do so must come from within the existing administration and with the ready agreement of the Crown."

"And if it doesna come?" Dundas demanded impatiently.

"It will."

"God, you're a stubborn bastard." Pitt gave his friend a crooked smile. "You know what your problem is, Will? You're too honorable to be a politician," Dundas exclaimed, folding his arms across his chest and regarding his friend with some disgust. "You conduct your political career according to the honor and integrity which govern your private life. You place yerself above party politics; you run election campaigns based on character and actually mean every word you say. You're immensely popular because people feel they can trust ye. You dinna want to be seen graspin' for power after relinquishin' office. You dinna want to withdraw support from an administration you've initiated. But don't ye get it, you stupid wee laddie?" He leaned forward, elbows on his knees, eyes beseeching, tone urgent. "It isn't about you anymore; greater issues are at stake."

"Don't you think I know that?" Pitt replied evenly. "Do you think I am fortifying the coastline and training a volunteer army for my own amusement?"

"My point is that character, or honor, or integrity, whatever ye want to call it, obliges you to serve your country and to take charge when others canna cope. And Addington canna cope. You know that. What was it you said in Parliament last week? That France has attained new and extraordinary energies. That we ought to meet them with at least equal, not inferior, activity and energies? And what has Addington done to protect our nation from France? Nothing! You have to step in before it's too late."

"'I realize, Mal, that rapid, and probably drastic, action is required. You just have to let me do it my way. If we are going to form an alternative administration, strident opposition will make it damn near impossible to effect change in time to do us any good. We have to at least see if we can form a strong and comprehensive government."

"Meaning?" Dundas demanded.

"One which includes Charles Fox."

# 56.

## HOLLAND HOUSE. LONDON, ENGLAND
### *December 6, 1803*

Although scarcely two miles from London with its smoke, its din, and its crowded thoroughfares, Holland House and its immediate environment suggested an aura of rural solitude. Nestled beneath the arching canopy of giant oaks, leafless now in the winter, the house was surrounded by green meadows and overgrown sloping lawns. The building itself wore a rather dilapidated air and the crumbling masonry implied that its time of grandeur had passed. But like an aging dowager queen, the house retained an elegance in the steep-roofed turrets and carved stonework that made up its weathered exterior.

This pastoral peace was lost on Pitt and Dundas, jolting along the Kensington Road which circled the property to the north. They were still embroiled in heated political discussion.

"I surrender!" Pitt raised his hands in mock defeat. "So what would you have me do? Charge Downing Street and bodily oust Addington from the establishment?"

"That'd be a good start," Dundas grumbled.

"I will make you a promise," Pitt said, suddenly solemn, as the carriage clattered to a stop in front of Holland House. "If we are unable to form an alliance with Fox, I will seek counsel with the king…" Dundas opened his mouth as if to voice a protest, only to be silenced by his friend's raised finger. "And I will actively pursue the immediate formation of an alternative administration." Dundas raised an eyebrow. Pitt sighed in acquiescence. "And I will bring the motion forward in the House of Lords. Are you satisfied now?"

"Indeed, I am," he replied happily, grinning at Pitt as the two men alighted from the carriage.

They were greeted by a manservant, stiff with either protocol or cold, who ushered them into the foyer. The long, narrow room spanned the entire width of the house and was flanked by a wide staircase that swept up each wall to a walkway above.

The rotund figure of Charles Fox was descending the one on the right. "My dear friends!" he boomed jovially.

He appeared all belly to the men who waited beneath him; indeed, his abdomen preceded him down the stairs, tightly encased in a red velvet vest that wobbled to a rhythm independent of its owner. Reaching the landing, however, Fox with his heavy, ruddy cheeks and forest of disheveled ginger hair, stood several inches shorter than his visitors.

"Thank you so much for coming." Fox shook each man vigorously by the hand, his eyes gleaming with intelligent good humor, before suggesting they adjourn to the library.

The library was a remarkable room that had doubtless been converted from its previous use as a greenhouse or observatory for it was walled almost entirely in glass. The only solid construction apparent in the room was the wall through which they had entered, which contained a large fireplace surrounded by faded remnants of frescoes. Tall mahogany bookcases extended across one glass wall, their shelves groaning under an unruly assortment of books, pamphlets, and notebooks that were stacked, jammed, and wedged into every available space.

"They were supposed to represent the Aldobrandini Marriage," Fox remarked as he noticed Pitt's interest in the chimney frescoes. "Commissioned, in fact, by the first Earl of Holland for a ball to celebrate the wedding of Prince Charles and Henrietta Maria of France. The ball, for some unexplained reason, never came off." Fox's voice dropped to a husky whisper as he settled his hefty bulk into a massive leather chair before the fireplace. "This library is now said to be tenanted by the solitary ghost of its first lord, who, according to tradition, issues forth at midnight from behind a secret door with his head in his hand." Fox chuckled, eyes shining, plump cheeks wobbling with mirth, thick lips spreading wide in a childlike grin. "I do like that story. But gentlemen, forgive me. You did not come all the way out here to listen to ghost stories. Please sit." He gestured toward two chairs opposite.

"Thank you, Charles, for this opportunity," Pitt began. "Please know how much I appreciate your efforts. The administration, quite simply, cannot afford to be divided at a time of imminent national peril."

"Yes, quite," Fox replied, soberly now. "Speaking of national peril, I understand that you have sent an Irish spy into Paris to determine Napoleon's landing point for his invasion fleet?"

Pitt said nothing for a moment. He knew Fox to be a wily adversary and knew that he formed the heart and soul of the Whig party, knew that he conquered friends and foes alike by force of charm. Nevertheless, Pitt was momentarily taken aback by the quick transition from childlike mirth to astute political insinuations. "What an incredible idea! Please don't tell me that you of all people are lending such credence to the gossip of penny-rags and scandal-sheets!" Pitt exclaimed with a snort of derision. "I can assure you, Charles, that there is no such plan afoot." He realized with grim regret that this was in fact the truth. Wolfe was dead for all he knew, executed in a Parisian alley by an assassin with a smoking pistol. Pitt had little hope for further intelligence from that quarter. Fox raised a bushy orange eyebrow in skeptical disbelief. "The issue at hand, however," Pitt continued, leaning forward with grave intensity, "is Addington's failure and the formation of an alternative administration. I am willing to resume the reins of government, but I want the support of both the current government and the Crown. We need to move very quickly to contain the French threat." He hesitated a moment, wondering how much he should trust Fox. "We do not know where Napoleon is going to deploy his troops. Intelligence gathered, in association with the French Resistance, has been unable to pinpoint the location of invasion. Every day that goes by, Napoleon's fleet grows in size. We have to act now, or we will find that England will be governed by a military regime from across the Channel." Fox leaned back in his chair, his gaze thoughtful, thick hands resting on his round belly. "This is not about you or me. Whigs or Tories. This is about England."

"The people want Pitt at the helm, Charles," Dundas interjected. "You know that. The issue was raised in the House of Commons only last week. The question is whether he will do so with or without you."

"Gentlemen," Fox replied at last. "I am not unaware of the gravity of the situation. I have no more desire to see the Little Corporal strutting on English soil than you. You realize, I am sure, that the king will never consent to an administration if I am a part of it." Pitt knew he referred to the long history of animosity that existed between the two men. Prompted by the Royal Marriage Act of 1770 and the associated stipulation requiring royal consent for noblemen under twenty-five seeking to marry, Fox had denounced the king from the House of Commons podium. He decried, with resounding force and enthusiasm, that the king and the establishment were more of a threat to the constitution and individual liberties than the radical politics that were even then

being implemented across the Channel in France. George III had neither forgiven nor forgotten. The Prince of Wales, invariably enamored
with whatever or whomever caused his father most distress, embraced
both Charles Fox and the political Whigs.

Pitt knew, from personal experience, how implacable the king could
be. "You are probably right," Pitt conceded. "But you have accomplished more for the Whig party since leaving the administration. You
exert a powerful influence whether you are in government or not."

"I'll tell you what I will do," Fox said. "I will announce a general
retirement from active politics, which should prevent any friction with
the king. At the same time, I will urge members of my own party to join
your coalition government."

"Brilliant, Charles," Dundas exclaimed, his face lighting up. "This is
exactly what we need."

Fox raised his shaggy eyebrows as he replied, his plump hand patting his round belly affectionately. "I have always been afraid that my
natural idleness would, in the end, get the better of what little ambition
I had." With a grunt of effort, he hoisted himself from the chair. Pitt
and Dundas followed suit. "Although, there is just one thing I want
from you," Fox remarked, almost as an afterthought. Pitt and Dundas
paused. "Drop Ireland," Fox said, his voice soft but resolved.

"I can't do that," Pitt said bluntly, turning toward the fireplace. He
knew this was coming, knew there would be a price he was unwilling
to pay.

"Will." Dundas rose too, walking over to the fireplace where Pitt was
leaning with both arms against the mantelpiece. "Let's think about this
at least," he urged him, his voice low in Pitt's ear. "The infiltration has
failed; the Irish agenda has busted wide open. We've heard nothing from
Wolfe. He's probably dead. I am not sayin' we forget about Ireland, but
the Irish, at this point in time, are not poised with a massive army about
to invade. Like it or not, the French are the concern right now. Let's take
care of Napoleon, safeguard England, and then we can turn our attention back to Ireland. Catholic emancipation and Irish independence are
volatile, divisive issues. If we are tryin' to form a coalition government
with a broad base of support, this is not the time to insist that tenant
farmers in Dublin should be able to worship the Virgin Mary." Pitt
sighed, looking down into the charred remains of yesterday's fire. "I'm
not sayin' drop it…just postpone it," Dundas finished gently.

# 57.

Kneeling before the fireplace, Wolfe poked the embers, blowing gently in an attempt to coax a flame from ash-fringed logs. He added a thick branch of knotted pine. One curling tongue licked and caught, the splintered edge smoking as the fire again flared into life. The shabby room was one of many in the grim boarding house of Maison Boucher tucked between bustling rue Saint-Honoré to the north and rue de Rivoli to the south. An additional franc bought them a fireplace, a bowl of hot broth, and a generous hunk of day-old bread.

Jeanne's dark head barely protruded from the blankets, her huddled form shivering violently. Wolfe scooped her up and brought her before the fire, holding her close against the warmth of his chest and wrapping the blankets around them both.

"We…need to go…" she whispered shakily, her words halting as her icy limbs shuddered and trembled with cold. "We have to get…out… of Paris. My contact can…help us…"

"And we will. But not tonight. You're hardly fit to wander through the snow. We'll locate your contact tomorrow. Tonight, just thaw out." Jeanne opened her mouth to protest, but Wolfe shook his head. "Tomorrow, ye stubborn lass. What use are you to anyone dead of cold in the gutter?" he murmured, his tone one of quiet amusement. Wolfe proceeded to gently rub warmth back into the shivering woman. He started with her hands, moving his calloused fingers rhythmically across the fleshy underside of her palm and smoothing his thumb across her numb white fingers, gently encouraging blood flow.

Gradually, despite herself, Jeanne relaxed into the warmth of his chest and the hypnotic movement of his hands. She could not recall the last time she had been taken care of in this way, and, knowing Wolfe's intractable will, understood that regardless of argument they would not be leaving the boarding house until morning. Despite circumstances, despite the inexorable fear that constricted her chest when she allowed herself to contemplate the logistical difficulties of her current situation—the whys and wherefores of getting out of Paris, eluding Fouché, and still somehow managing to orchestrate the crumbling remnants of the Resistance—she felt curiously calm and detached. And it was as she was drifting off to sleep, Wolfe's heartbeat a strong repetitive thud under her ear, her body finally restored to tingling warmth, that she drowsily realized that she had allowed Wolfe a degree of intimacy never conceded to any other man. She had allowed him to take care of her, momentarily relinquishing her fierce independence. For Jeanne, this release was far more intimate than the physical act of sex. She had utterly let down every intellectual guard, every barrier; was vulnerable in a way she had not allowed herself to be since she was a girl. And so she slept the deep sleep of the young and the innocent in that shabby room on rue de l'Echelle.

"You're going to freeze in that thing. And I just got you warm again," Wolfe remarked disapprovingly, taking in her shivering figure clad in the empire-waist gown of sheer muslin, made popular by Joséphine earlier in the season. A light fitted jacket was her only concession to the winter snows that piled up in soft drifts outside the door. "Why not be warm bourgeois rather than frozen aristocrats?"

"Because bourgeois do not frequent Frascati's," Jeanne replied pertly. "And Denis, the owner of the establishment, is my contact. Here, let me help you with that." Wolfe was peering into a polished pewter mirror as he attempted, with irritable futility, to tie his cravat. With deft fingers she tied a loose knot and tucked the folds neatly within the confines of his collar.

They had exchanged their clothes, along with a handful of francs, at a second-hand rag merchant's across the street from the boarding house—one torn, bloodstained footman's uniform and a sodden, be-grimed lady's evening gown—for less conspicuous attire. The clothes merchant impassively tucked their garments under his table, as if he routinely received such curious assemblages. In return, he provided them with a high-waisted gown of pale butter for Jeanne—complete with delicate green embroidery and matching yellow bonnet—and full leather boots, tan breeches, shirt, cravat, and a black surcoat for Wolfe.

Wolfe was exhausted. The physical effort of the previous night had re-opened his shoulder wound and strained the muscles of his back so that every turn of his torso caused an involuntary wince. Wolfe was also ravenous. He hoped to God they served breakfast at this fancy establishment.

Frascati's was everything Jeanne had intimated and more. The proprietor had purchased adjoining houses and demolished the wall that divided them. Tapestries and mirrors decorated the walls and defined the perimeter of a single spacious room that accommodated the latest mania for dancing as well as the need to see and be seen. This was a rendezvous for idle gossips, conversationalists, and wits, and despite the early hour, the café was already bustling with the early crowd of coffee drinkers. The elegantly dressed couple that occupied the corner table appeared no different than any other; no more weary than other revelers that had caroused through the night at the brothels and gaming rooms for which the Palais Royale was so renowned—an aristocratic fatigue that would be amply addressed by a large cup of Frascati's horribly expensive coffee.

Wolfe demolished a plate of eggs, while Jeanne gratefully cradled a second steaming coffee between long, slender fingers.

"Where's your contact?" he asked, taking a gulp of coffee.

"He'll be here," Jeanne replied. She spoke quietly in a refined accent that closely resembled her own, leaning toward him, her hand resting on his arm as a lover might do—one of many on the streets of Paris that morning.

He had to admit that she knew her trade. She had an uncanny ability to melt in with a crowd. It wasn't so much her appearance that allowed her to do so—although he now had a new appreciation for the transformative power of artfully applied plaster and makeup—but her voice, expressions, mannerisms, the way her body moved and the way she held herself. Jeanne had explained to him, as they settled in the back of a carriage en route to the Palais Royale, that it was all about becoming what was expected.

"This city," Jeanne gestured out the window, "is the heart of France, and everyone at one point or another comes through Paris looking for work, food, customers, or wanting to hide. And each and every one of them is defined by their dress and their manner. Solemn professors in black robes, lawyers in their scarlet ones, boisterous prostitutes in tight gowns, uniformed soldiers and ragged beggars. The little details are often what matter the most. The smell, for instance—tanners stinking of urine and butchers of blood; or the bleeding gums of those suffering from scurvy; the missing teeth of women worn out by pregnancies. These are the little things that create the cover, that make the façade real. The police look for anomalies, people and situations that are out of the ordinary. If you become ordinary, you escape notice. And everybody has their specific characteristics, something that makes them inexplicably belong. Sometimes, it is merely a matter of location. Look there, see that water-carrier?"

Wolfe saw a man in a frayed black tunic deftly maneuvering his way through the crowd; a pole, slung over his shoulders, supported a bucket on either end. "He is from Auvergnat. And he is selling water here because one block south, and downstream of the Seine, dyers pour their residual dye off the end of the Pelletier quay. The Gêvres quay, further downstream, is always contaminated by pestilence. So here, he can sell his water, advertising its purity, for two sous a load without having to haul it further than absolutely necessary."

"So this man a hundred yards south of his current position would be suspicious?"

"That, or a swindler. Either way, he will draw attention, from skeptical customers or from a gendarme who has nothing better to do. When assuming a cover, you must become invisible by being so familiar, so right there and then, that you are no longer seen. The eye skims over you, like waves against the shore that the seaside residents no longer hear. Or there, look!" A slightly disheveled dandy in white stockings and a braided coat—returning home after a night's debauchery at the Palais Royale—was attempting to cross rue de Rivoli, running along the filthy street on the tips of his toes. Overhead gutters swollen with melted snow dripped on his taffeta parasol. Upon reaching the street corner, he called stridently for a shoeblack who proceeded to wipe clean the street-acquired grime. "It is all about having the right costume in the right place and demonstrating the expected behavior. 'All the world's a stage, and all the men and women merely players: they have their exits and their entrances.'"

"'And one man in his time plays many parts...'" Wolfe completed the Shakespearean quotation with a smile.

Now, Jeanne played a member of the privileged elite—a comtesse, perhaps, who recently purchased a title from the emperor to accompany her newfound riches, riches borne of speculation on the assignat after the Revolution or the land of aristocrats that had gone cheaply after the Terror. She glanced idly around the room with the studied boredom of the fashionably rich, stifling a yawn with one delicate glove-clad hand.

The tables were snugly positioned around the perimeter of the room with barely space enough for an occupied chair to fit underneath. Denis did it on purpose, Jeanne knew. Facilitated contact, he claimed. And, after all, wasn't that why they were all here? It enabled a flirtatious exchange after an "accidental" nudge to the chair, or the purchase of ices for the young ladies in apology for treading on the hems of their gowns. This relative proximity also meant that conversations swirled around them like eddies and currents in a fast-flowing river of banter and pomposity.

"Taste the wines of the Romanée, Saint-Vivant, Cîteaux, and Graves—both red and white—and insist on Tokay if you meet it," a dandy in blue satin pronounced at the table to their left. "In my opinion, it is the greatest wine in the world, and only the masters of the world should drink it."

Two pale Englishmen, conspicuous in their woolen broadcloth, were discussing the French performance of *Othello* that had aired at the Théâtre Feydeau the previous night:

"What did you think of it?"

"Abysmal. You?"

"Agreed. The Moor whined abominably, and they softened the villainy of Iago's character…"

"And saved the life of Desdemona!"

"Mmmmm…a happy ending for Othello, who would have thought?"

"Did you read the brochure? The postscript explaining the altered version? I have it here." A rustle of papers. "Here: 'The humanity of the French nation and their morality would be shocked by such exhibitions.'"

"Don't you admire a nation who can guillotine sixty people a day for months—men, women and children—and cannot bear the catastrophe of a dramatic exhibition?"

"Where is he?" Wolfe had finished his eggs, drained his coffee, and sat, fingers drumming restlessly on his thigh. Despite his weariness, he felt restless. Paranoid. He scanned the bustling crowd with a narrowed gaze. While the jostle of people might offer a comforting anonymity,

Wolfe knew it also worked against him. Fouché's agents could be any-where: casually sauntering past with an ice in one hand, lounging by the gilt-edged mirrors where the elegant couple at the corner table could be easily viewed without suspicion. Or the assassin for that matter.

"I don't like it here," Wolfe growled. "Too many people."

"Don't worry; I see him." Jeanne casually inclined her head toward a thick-bodied man who was threading his way through the crowd toward their table. His dark hair was immaculately tousled around somewhat protuberant ears; his eyes, small and unblinking above a moist rosebud of a mouth, darted restlessly across the room as if ceaselessly calcu-lating expenditure and income. A sheen of sweat glistened upon his brow and darkened white armpits to gray. A thick canvas apron strained across his paunch, a wooden tray secured under one meaty arm.

"Bonjour! May I interest you in some patisseries this morning? To go with another coffee, perhaps?" Denis asked, without looking at them, as he busied himself removing their dishes.

"Perhaps just one more," Jeanne murmured with a sigh. "Do you have the ones with chocolate inside?"

"Alas, madame! Sugar is so hard to come by these days. We only have plain brioche. Or perhaps preserved fruit might be to your liking?"

"How disappointing! I suppose a plain brioche will have to do." Jeanne pouted slightly. "One more thing, Monsieur Renault." She laid her gloved hand on his arm. "I was wondering where you purchased that magnificent chandelier? I am desperate to have one just like it for my chateaux in Montmartre."

Renault started slightly in surprise; his hands stilled on the dishes, his gaze flying involuntarily to her face. She smiled slightly and nodded her head. "Ah…yes…" he muttered awkwardly, struggling to regain his composure. "It was purchased from an antique dealer here in the Palais Royale. Let me see if I can find out the details for you." His hands trembled slightly as he completed the loading of his tray.

Ten minutes later, they left Frascati's, paper bag in hand, and emerged into the great central square of the Palais Royale which, despite the early hour, hummed and teemed with its characteristic lively frivolity. A colonnaded piazza at each end of the square was crammed with booksellers, jewelers, milliners, coffeehouses, and gaming rooms. Cof-feehouses were already bustling, and shopkeepers, opening their doors for the day, were scraping ice from pavements and arranging displays to entice the morning crowd. They found a bench in front of the leaded glass window of Bourret et Fils, suppliers of fine gourmet delicacies, where a massive salted Bayonne ham vied for space between cooked tongue from Vierzon and sauerkraut from Strasbourg. Breaking open the brioche, Jeanne retrieved a slender slip of paper with an address: rue des Mauvais Garçons, Number 32.

"Come, Monsieur Trant." She smiled as she tucked her arm through his. "Unfortunately, this comtesse appears to have lost her fortune as quickly as she acquired it. Time to change the gown for rags."

"Who's at number 32 rue des Mauvais Garçons, then?" Wolfe asked.

"An old friend," Jeanne replied, squeezing his arm.

# 58.

## Place d'Enfer. Paris, France
*December 7, 1803*

The storm of the previous night had receded, leaving a sky still sullenly gloomy and a dark horizon to the south where thunder grumbled and growled as it lingered, stalled, and gathered. In the Place d'Enfer, however, the slick film of gray ice that covered rooftops and doorways did nothing to deter the vigorous activity that was characteristic of the weekly hay market. It had begun an hour earlier, in the predawn chill, when the first wagons, mounded high with feed, clattered through the iron gates; frozen puddles of stagnant ooze cracked and sprayed beneath the wheels as they jolted and lurched through the dips and hollows of the street.

By the time L'Aigle had arrived, the square was squeezed to capacity with carts spilling hay, coarse sacks of oats, baskets of barley, and stacked bales of alfalfa and red clover. Fragrant bundles of cool-season species of timothy, smooth bromegrass, tall fescue, and redtop grasses extended from the gates of Raspail in the east to the Barrière d'Enfer in the west. The Parisian merchants, as if in defiance of the brooding sky that proclaimed bitter winter, thronged through the lush meadows of Place d'Enfer, examining the hay for weeds, blister beetles, alfalfa weevils, mold, and dust. They rubbed the straw between thickly calloused fingers, brought it to their noses and deeply inhaled the scent of it; they chewed a portion between worn mealy teeth—the better to critically evaluate stem thickness, leafiness, and maturity of heads.

The sellers, for the most part, conceded in the hard-driven negotiations that took place over barrel and basket. It had been a rough year for the farmers. A wet fall and an early winter meant that much of the hay had been cut and stored in damp conditions which made it susceptible to mold and mildew. Buyers bought low, hoping they in turn could sell the hay before the mold became obvious to those with less discerning noses. And so the hay was measured out in musty fork-loads and weighed by the tonnage in massive iron scales.

Etienne's meaty silver-shorn head, rising above his immediate neighbors, was readily identifiable, and L'Aigle made his way through the throng to where Etienne was completing his purchase.

Hay was the coarse gold in a city that teemed with horses, L'Aigle reflected, pondering not only the thousands of hackney cabs that relied upon horsepower but the carts and wagons of the farmer, the merchant, and the housewives. Sleek Andalusians trotted proudly before the gilded broughams of the wealthy, while broken-down nags constituted the sole possession of the poorer sort. Horse trains of ten to twelve animals tied together at their flanks cantered through cobblestone streets to assemble at Saint-Victor or the horse market in rue Saint-Honoré. Horses crowded the thoroughfares. Every alleyway was dotted with their steaming droppings; every street housed a stable or two; and all these horses required sustenance. Feeding the animal force during winter was increasingly a challenge, and Etienne had, several years previously, shrewdly recognized the profit potential inherent in the massive purchase of hay early in the season. He would hoard it until stored supplies within the city were scarce and then sell for four times the purchase price to the houses of those who could afford to maintain horses—upon which enterprise he appeared to be currently engaged. Money changed hands, and Etienne left the farmer with explicit delivery instructions before turning to greet L'Aigle.

"Bad year for hay," Etienne remarked with his characteristic gruffness. "I will buy oats and barley instead. But you did not come to talk of horse feed." He grinned, baring large yellow teeth that conveyed an impression of ferocity rather than amiability. "Come." He slapped L'Aigle on the shoulder as the two men made their way through the hay market to the eating house advertised by the macabre designation La maison de la Tombe Issoire. It occupied half a stone structure fronted by wide Romanesque arches, beneath which empty tables, flaked in frozen rust, shivered in the empty portico. Brawny tradesmen with straw-dusted hair thronged the interior, devouring the house special of capon au gros sel fished out of the every-ready pot that boiled over the hearth.

The other side of the establishment served a more sinister purpose and provided the unlikely name for the convivial enterprise that neighbored it. It was here that a narrow spiral staircase descended into the long-abandoned stone-mining tunnels of Fosse-aux-Lions, previously the haunt of rag-pickers, but now a repository for the bones of the

dead. Many an inebriated individual had mistaken the respective entrances—the one to the right being that of the infamous catacombs, the
Barrière d'Enfer, or the Gates of Hell—and while the proprietor of the
eating house may have lost the occasional customer to dark wanderings
among the bones, the tourist trade that had already been generated by
their proximity more than compensated him.

The two men by the window, their features washed in the watery
gray light of a dreary morning, were indifferent to the constant thread
of black-clad priests and bone-laden wagons that traveled like a line
of marching ants around the edge of the haymarket and disappeared
through the Barrière d'Enfer. Over burgundy wine, Etienne told L'Aigle they had located the target. One of his watchers, stationed at the
Tuileries the previous night, had watched, aghast, as the very Irishman
they were seeking climbed down the façade of the Louvre and melted
into the crowd that had gathered in the rue de Rivoli.

"Are you quite certain it was him?"

Etienne nodded assent, a downward thrust of his massive chin.
L'Aigle knew better than to question him further. Their business relationship, although not without its difficulties, had proceeded smoothly
for the past four years to their mutual benefit. As terse and prickly as
Etienne could be, he managed his various dealings with the impressive
precision of a military operation. His tutelage had been under the inter-
nationally recognized master of battle strategy and tactics—Napoleon
himself—and one that he currently employed, ironically enough, to
subvert the very legal code that the emperor was attempting to put into
place. Etienne's men numbered less than fifty, but each one was hand-
picked for his finely honed skills and unswerving loyalty. They were paid
well, and with any number clamoring to take their place, these men were
relentless in their efforts to please and assiduous in the performance
of their duties. If Etienne's man said he had seen the target scaling the
Louvre, then L'Aigle believed implicitly it must be so.

It just didn't make sense. Wolfe's clandestine appointment with Talleyrand confirmed what the English agent had told him: that Wolfe
was in Paris to conclude an alliance with Napoleon, to betray England
and bring the French emperor to the Irish cause. It seemed logical that
Talleyrand had been the preliminary contact who would then set up
the meeting with the emperor himself. But if Wolfe Trant's purpose at
the Tuileries was to make contact with Napoleon, why would he end

up outside climbing forty feet above the rue de Rivoli in an ice storm? What was going on?

"Where did he go?"

"He was with a woman. My man followed them to a lodging house and then the following morning to Frascati's in the Palais Royale before losing them in a carriage heading east along rue Saint-Michel."

"Frascati's. Owned by Denis Renault." L'Aigle absently stroked his elegant goatee with one long finger, his expression thoughtful. Renault was a double agent who worked for the Resistance and confided in Fouché. A dangerous game. The Resistance had been known to unflinchingly execute those who betrayed them—a blade drawn across the neck, a body dropped in the Seine.

Renault was either very greedy or very stupid, both or either of which would suit L'Aigle nicely.

# 59.

The southern end of rue de la Loi, where it abutted the sluggish brown waters of the Seine, was occupied by several small tanneries that reeked of decaying flesh and urine. Further northwards, the brick-laid street wound and twisted its way through decrepit house-fronts to emerge, at the rue du Musée intersection, with the broader boulevard of rue Fliette. At this more salubrious end of the street, the gray limestone buildings offered the most elegant Parisian fashions behind gleaming glass.

A throng of afternoon shoppers milled and meandered, their hemlines inevitably fringed with mud, their conversation peppered with the rattle of wagon wheels and the occasional bawl and holler of cab drivers. Window displays beckoned, with hatters, haberdashers, and milliners exhibiting broad straw hats and bonnets decorated with flowers, feathers and gauze, bolts of rich-sheened silk and velvet, and arrays of buttons, linens, and ribbons.

Gerard Bouilly shuffled unsteadily forwards, the shoemaker's bench strapped across his chest. Strips of recently cured leather dangled from his rope belt, and several wooden lasts click-clacked together across his back. The pungent aroma of piss enveloped him like a pestilential cloud and may have accompanied him from the tanneries where he had procured his cast-off strips, or more likely he had wet himself, a common occurrence for him when under the influence.

He stopped before an elegant shoe shop where a pretty wrought-iron sign hung outside the glass-paned door and advertised the business of Theot et Fils. The window was occupied by several pairs of ladies' leather boots, neatly stitched in red and blue, tied with satin ribbons, and embellished with embroidered rosettes. Conspicuous at this end of the street, but utterly at home at the other, Bouilly positioned his bottle more securely under one arm and raised his gnarled fist, swollen and distorted by gout, to push his way inside. The door, opening so abruptly that Bouilly staggered back, revealed a smartly dressed woman, her features tight with annoyance and scorn.

"Get away from here, Bouilly!" she hissed. "I told you, I don't need your shoes! I buy my products from shoemakers who actually fill their orders on time and are not spending their leather advance on drink. Get going before I call the gendarmes!"

Bouilly stood a moment, swaying slightly on his feet, his expression registering open-mouthed surprise rapidly followed by anger as comprehension dawned. "Yoush...bought...shoes!" Bouilly began vehemently, stabbing a thick dirty finger in the woman's direction. Then, shaking his head, as if to clear the confusion that misted and clouded there, he upturned the bottle into his mouth, staggering backwards as he attempted to hold Madame Theot within his field of vision. "I am a Vainqueur de la Bastille!" Bouilly shouted.

The crowd slowed and ebbed around his stumbling form, watching in silence as his eyes, red-rimmed and bloodshot, rolled up. He tottered unsteadily, the cobblestones rocking precariously beneath his booted feet, and crumpled to the ground. There he lay in an undignified sprawl, spittle gathering at the corner of his slack mouth, his bottle of wine glugging cheap burgundy into the dirt beside him.

The conversation of the shopping crowd resumed its steady hum as they stepped daintily around his prone figure. The afternoon's entertainment was done. A darkly cloaked figure separated himself from the bustle and approached Madame Theot.

"This is Gerard Bouilly?" Fouché asked her, sharply nudging the man's prostrate snoring form with the point of his scuffed boot.

"Oui, monsieur," Madame Theot replied.

Fouché knew his type. He had lived through the Great Revolution, survived the Counter-Revolution, and, during the comparative stability of the Consulate, returned to his previous profession as a shoemaker. Times were hard, however, and he nourished a memory of militancy, remembering a time, not so very long ago, when the people of the streets mattered. When they had risen up and formed an army. When they had overthrown a king! Vive le République! And now? Now, he made shoes with scraps of worn leather that nobody could afford to buy. An old man with an empty belly hankering after Brave Times. Times that seemed all the braver when remembered under very hard ones.

"Every Tuesday," Madame Theot muttered, pursing her lips in disapproval as she drew her delicate woolen shawl closer around her narrow shoulders. "He comes and tries to sell me his shoes. Boasts of the Septembriseurs. Bah!" She spat disdainfully in the direction of the shoemakers prostrate snoring form. "I think he wants to bring back the Terror!" Her thickly rouged lip drew back from blackened stumps of teeth in a gesture of contempt. She waved one hand dismissively before turning back into the shop, the door coming to a close behind her.

"Get up," Fouché growled, nudging him sharply with the toe of his boot.

Bouilly blearily opened his eyes, swollen and splotched with red. "Qui sont vous?" he managed, his voice broken with age and hampered by drink.

"I am the commissioner of police," Fouché replied imperiously, yanking the old man to his feet. Several feet further, past a bookseller where tables of dusty volumes could be seen through a propped open door, the Café de Babette occupied the corner of rue de la Loi and rue d'Esay.

Jerking Bouilly inside, Fouché was greeted by a thick-set man in a green apron who opened his mouth to irritably eject the two disreputable-looking men who had just entered, then closed it just as rapidly upon realizing the identity of the man cloaked in black.

"Get me a private room. And bring some water and wine," Fouché told the man curtly. A small side room fulfilled Fouché's requirements, and several chairs and bottles were hurriedly deposited by the proprietor.

Bouilly, finally released from Fouché's grasp, slumped into the chair, eyes closed, mumbling something incoherently under his breath. Fouché threw a glass of water at Bouilly's face. He spluttered and moaned, raising one gnarled hand up as if to defend himself against further watery onslaught. A straggled mess of gray hair hung in wiry profusion about a shriveled bony face; small bloodshot eyes narrowed against the late afternoon sun that slanted through the window. His mouth, a dark cavernous slash in a stubbled chin, opened and closed in confusion. His teeth, like Madame Theot's, were a feature of the past—gone with the glory days of the Revolution. Instead, when he opened his mouth he emitted the scent of pungent decay like the exhalation of the dead.

Bouilly raised one trembling hand to his face and rubbed his eyes with a grubby fist; water droplets glistened in the crevices and ran in grimy rivulets down his neck.

"You were a member of the Septembriseurs?" Fouché asked him sharply, taking the seat opposite.

Bouilly must not be coerced or cornered. His imagined remembrances of a heroic past might persuade him at an inconvenient time to rebel against an oppressive authority. In order to be truly useful, he had to be encouraged in his belief that his role in the upcoming capture and arrests was a glorious one. An opportunity to feel important again as well as line his pockets with coin, and avoid the Temple. Yes, Bouilly would be grateful indeed. Bouilly's reddened eyes widened and struggled to focus on Fouché for the first time.

"I also count myself among their number," Fouché confided conspiratorially, pouring a glass of wine for each of them before leaning back to light a cigar. He watched his prey squirm between heavy-lidded eyes. Good. He was afraid.

The Septembriseurs were a mob that had become legendary for the storming of the Bastille and the subsequent September massacres that had taken place within its thick stone walls. Decades later, the term had become synonymous with bourgeois politics and the power of the people—a concept that was increasingly prevalent in popular memory during these times of repression and dearth. For others, however, particularly those who now enjoyed a degree of comfortable security, the Septembriseurs represented the madness of the masses, the threat of anarchy, and the chaos that came with mob rule. One had to be cautious when, where, and with whom one made a confession of partisanship with such an infamous organization.

"I remember you," Fouché confided casually, blowing a thick stream of smoke into Bouilly's face.

"You do?" Bouilly mumbled in astonishment.

Of course, Bouilly had had nothing to do with the storming of the Bastille, Fouché thought in derision. No doubt he had spent the day cowering in his workshop or in a drunken stupor on the floor. Just as the members of a foiled riot will deny their involvement (producing bystanders to affirm that they had never left their workplace), everyone wants to have participated in an event that has acquired immediate historical respectability. Possibly, Bouilly had seen the whole thing through a wine-shop window in the faubourg or near the Grève and later was able to persuade himself, and his neighbors, that he could not have missed such an occasion to distinguish himself. It was awkward to have been within yards of a great Revolution.

Yes, thought Fouché, with a sneer of revulsion. This beast was perfect. He had evoked Bouilly's bourgeois patriotism, and now to apply the pressure. "I understand you have been detained several times without your work papers, Monsieur Bouilly? You know you can be sent to the Temple Prison for such a crime?"

Bouilly, greedily gulping down his wine, sputtered and choked, wiping one grimy hand across his chin; "I have lost them, monsieur... Commissioner," he whined, abruptly sobered at the thought of imprisonment in the notorious Temple Prison; not many lived to complete their sentences.

"Would you like a chance to redeem your crimes and be useful to the empire once again?" Fouché asked sternly. At Bouilly's pathetic eagerness to comply, the commissioner of police leaned forward to instruct the rapidly sobering shoemaker on exactly what was expected of him.

Later, leaving Café de Babette, Fouché felt a warm satisfaction with the afternoon's events. Chavert and his battery of gendarmes were scouring the city with a physical description of the suspects; Fouché doubted their effectiveness and suspected their bumbling attempts would do more to alert Wolfe and Primrose than enable their apprehension, but he thought Chavert might inadvertently provide a useful diversion.

Fouché had personally visited Denis Renault, who had served as a double agent for six months and had done little, in Fouché's opinion, to merit the fifty francs he pocketed a month—until now. The expenditure was, finally, paying off. He knew exactly where Primrose and Wolfe were going; Bouilly would do his bit, and finally this chase would be over.

# 60.

"Mon dieu, imbécile! Do you know nothing?" Denis Renault roared, his carefully tousled mane quivering in indignation. "The ices must be firm! What do you call this slush, eh?" He flung the wooden spoon at the offending under-chef and stalked from the kitchen. Renault was worried—and it wasn't about the ices. He had been happily depositing fifty francs a month as a police informant, unbeknownst to the French Resistance who occasionally also employed him as a go-between. He had collected his subsidy for the past six months without incident and had hoped to go on doing so.

Frascati's was less financially sound than it might have appeared from the crowded dining room. The cost of sugar had risen astronomically in the past year—if, indeed, it was available at all—and while Renault had systematically cut out the chocolate pastries, the custard tarts, and the sugared flans for which Frascati's had become famous, the crème ices constituted the very foundation of his enterprise. Their recipe and process of manufacture were closely guarded secrets and the reason the nobility flocked to his café from as far-afield as Montmartre and Passy. And while the cost of production had soared, so had Renault's penchant for a red-headed courtesan in La Salle Rouge across the street—one of the more infamous dames du Palais Royale. Even now, his knees weakened when he thought of her. But she was expensive: one hundred francs a night.

But Frascati's, like other coffeehouses in the city, had become a magnet for the sheltering poor as well as the idle rich; they arrived at seven a.m. when the doors opened and lingered over a single coffee until closing time at eleven p.m. Coffee had been found to suppress the appetite, which was useful when there was little food to be had and even less money with which to procure it. In his efforts to establish an "elite clientele," Renault had employed a hefty soldier from Normandy, rendered unfit for military service due to the loss of his right hand, to discreetly evict these languishing indigents. Needless to say, Renault was a man in debt. He needed the money and had become quite accustomed to receiving it without any undue inconvenience on his part.

That is, until today.

Renault had been contacted by the Resistance early that morning. His usual contact had arrived for coffee, but instead of slipping him money in a folded newspaper as was their custom, he had said he was looking for a hotel, a special hotel. Was there one Renault could recommend? Renault, mouth dropping open in surprise, had stood dumbly for a moment before the contact impatiently reiterated his question—the trigger. Renault was to disclose the current safe-house, which would then be scouted in advance by the Resistance. Special precautions were in place. To protect whom?

"Ah, of course…of course…monsieur," Renault finally replied, a forced smile crossing his small pink lips. "There is the hotel on rue des Mauvais Garçons…number 32. A lovely establishment. I think you will find it quite comfortable." He had rattled off the first name on the list of safe-houses given to him by the Resistance six months before.

He had been instructed to maintain contact with sympathizers to the cause, updating the names and addresses so that he always maintained an accurate list of accommodation should it become necessary. He had not bothered. Instead, he had memorized the first name and address on the list—rue des Mauvais Garçons, number 32, Monsieur Rumigny—and reasoned that he would use that particular contact as required and memorize a second after the first had already been utilized.

According to protocol, a second visitor would arrive asking about the chandelier. In due course, an elegantly dressed woman accompanied by a tall man, somewhat fearsome in appearance with a long, jagged scar across the side of his forehead, did just that. Could this be *Primrose*? He fervently hoped not. Just as things had started to improve for him! Now he was embroiled in this mess.

He was one of the few Parisians who did not have a son, brother, or father on the military front and was grateful that the bloodshed was taking place across the border. Sugar was hard to come by, granted, which presented numerous difficulties for a man in his profession. But compared to the Revolutionary years and the fear and uncertainty of the White Terror, which had rendered any profitable business venture—any that did not deal in murder and vengeance—impossible, life had improved. It was far from perfect, but it was better. Until this!

But if these unwelcome visitors were not enough (he was still somewhat shaken from the morning's encounter) he had had a third visitor that morning—who did not buy a single crème ice as it happened—none other than Police Commissioner Fouché himself!—wanting to know the address he had given to the Resistance less than an hour before.

Flustered, and readily intimidated by Fouché's imperious curtness as well as his terrifying reputation, Renault had babbled the information as quickly as it was asked of him. Fouché had departed satisfied, leaving an increasingly anxious proprietor in his wake.

What would happen when the Resistance discovered he was betraying them? For certainly they would when the conspirateur—whomever she was—encountered Police Commissioner Fouché. Renault was frantically wondering whether he should leave Paris for a few weeks—perhaps the salty air of Normandy?—when Guillaume, the head waiter of section two, informed him that a gentleman wished to see him.

Mon dieu! Renault located the aforesaid gentleman at table four—patrician, certainly, the thin, ascetic face of a disciplined man, dark eyes and thin lips, an elegantly shaped goatee. Renault's belly clenched in acidic discomfort; fear fluttered in his breast like a winged bird desperately seeking escape...*run...run...run.* The words ran through his mind like a disconnected phrase, and before he was even aware of his own actions, he had gone.

Knocking down a surprised kitchen boy, he exited through the rear door into a dark back-alley. He hurried toward rue de Malamasy, pushing past a peddler hawking rabbit skins, the man so overloaded with furry pelts that they completely obscured his face and torso.

"Heeyyy!" the peddler cried out as he lost several skins from the top of his pile.

Renault did not hear him, skidding to a halt as he noticed the tall gentleman waiting for him just ahead where the alley opened up into a broader thoroughfare. Desperately twisting around, he collided with the hulking chest of another who barred his way.

"Denis Renault?" the elegant gentleman asked him, a grim smile crossing his lips.

# 61.

## LES HALLES. PARIS, FRANCE
### *December 7, 1803*

The market of Les Halles was bustling. Wooden stalls of varying size and construction clustered in long rows paralleling rue Rambuteau, which defined the square to the north. Just as the tables, heavily laden with a variety of produce, vied for space, so did their vendors compete in gustily advertising their wares.

"Pomme frites!" bawled one, holding out a tray of fried potatoes.

"Fromage!" A red-clothed table sold a variety of Beaufort and Comté cheeses produced from the summer milk of alpine cows; cheeses from Montreuil and Vicennes were displayed freshly curdled and drained in little woven wicker baskets. Plump fish rested on beds of ice, their scales glistening in the evening sun. Winter vegetables, which made up the diet of most of the city's population, were in abundant display. Onions and garlic hung in thick long braids; parsnips and leeks formed stacked rows of yellow and green; woven baskets were piled high with small onions; and strands of dried bush beans hung from knotted vines.

Between these rows swarmed a multitude of Parisians, a dense throng that flowed in a river of jostling elbows and bobbing heads. It surged more swiftly in the middle of the aisles, borne on by those shoppers who had completed their purchases and were struggling impatiently toward the exits, and then slowed on the periphery, where the indecisive and speculative lingered.

A couple paused to examine a selection of dried meats. There was nothing remarkable about them. Like many Les Halles patrons, they were clad in layers of threadbare brown, serviceable for this year but probably fated for the rag heap by the following. A grimy woolen shawl crossed tightly across the woman's torso and tucked beneath an equally dingy apron. A dark bonnet of indeterminate shade hid her hair and shaded most of her features. The man at her side was equally nondescript in a brown coat that stretched and pulled across broad shoulders and frayed a little higher on the wrist. A tattered black vest buttoned over a gray shirt and breeches, worn at the knees, tucked into black boots. The only unusual attribute of the two was the man's height; despite a slumping posture, he towered above the crowd that milled around them.

"Achetez votre viande!" the stocky man behind the table hollered. Massive carcasses of pink-fleshed pig, covered in thick crusts of salt, molasses, and saltpeter, hung from large, rusty hooks, while thin slices of cured beef and mutton covered the table. A small child waved cheap newsprint over the meat to keep the flies away.

"I'll 'ave these ones 'ere," the woman rasped, her voice the bronchial wheeze of one in the later stages of consumption. She passed over a few coins with a trembling hand and received a wrapped packet of salami in return, which she deposited in her basket. The man guided her forward, one arm protectively around her shoulders as she shuffled through the crowd, her breath a labored pant in the raw evening air. They passed a stall where a robust woman, yellow scarf wrapped around her sweaty head, bent over a hot pan flipping crepes with a wooden spatula. Abruptly, Wolfe pulled Jeanne to a stop. A stout man to their rear collided with Wolfe's back.

"Que faites-vous?" he bawled irritably, gesturing rudely as to what he thought of people who halted the flow in mid-stream. Wolfe ignored him, yanking Jeanne over to a nearby stall that featured neat rows of fat gourds and pumpkins. Necklaces of dried apple and pear hung like strips of leather at the sides and back of the stall, almost obscuring the rosy-cheeked face of the young woman who beamed at them from behind the table.

"Gendarmes," Wolfe whispered fiercely in Jeanne's ear as he leaned over the vegetables.

"The fruit will keep for years," the woman explained loudly, obviously encouraged by their deep interest in her produce. "Then you can moisten them in cider or milk." Mercifully, she was then distracted by another potential customer who had paused to inspect the ridged orange skin of a pumpkin.

Out of the corner of her eye, Jeanne could see three gendarmes pushing their way authoritatively through the crowd. Had they been seen? Jeanne didn't think so. But they were looking for someone; their heads swiveled, eyes scanning the crowd. Scarcely twenty feet away.

Thrusting a coin into the surprised woman's hand, Jeanne ducked under the table and crawled out into the adjacent aisle of traffic. Strident curses accompanied her arrival as several shoppers tripped over her kneeling form.

"Excusez-moi," she murmured automatically as she rose to her feet, swiveling around to glance at the aisle over. Had they been seen?

"Next time, pick a taller table," Wolfe muttered, squeezing his tall frame past the surprised vendor's green skirts.

Joining the traffic, Wolfe and Jeanne elbowed their way toward the exit. Heads down, they noticed the peaked caps of the gendarmes bobbing in the opposite direction. Emerging in front of the priory of Saint Martin-des-Champs, they crossed to rue de Réaumur, leaving the market district, and the gendarmes, behind them.

# 62.

## Rue des Mauvais Garçons. Paris, France
### *December 7, 1803*

Wolfe and Jeanne hurried through rue des Mauvais Garçons and stopped outside a wooden door with a glass-paned inset. A small plated panel below the glass contained two numbers in elegant script: thirty-two.

"Monsieur Legros de Rumigny?" Jeanne knocked on the door as Wolfe glanced down the street. The gendarmes were now entering rue des Mauvais Garçons from the market behind. They had not seen them, but it would not be long.

"C'mon," Wolfe muttered uneasily under his breath. The gendarmes split up: one moving toward them, looking down each side street, the other disappearing in the opposite direction, interrogating passersby in an authoritative manner. Jeanne rapped again, more insistently.

"Monsieur Rumigny!"

The dark shadow of a figure appeared through the glass window lit by flickering candle glow. "Who is it?" a thin, reedy voice called.

"Primrose," Jeanne replied in a low urgent tone. The door opened a fraction, and a sliver of a man peered suspiciously through. Wolfe, pushing his shoulder against the door, flung it open; the man inside fell back with a surprised gasp. Yanking Jeanne inside, Wolfe shut the door behind them.

"What is this?" Monsieur Legros de Rumigny demanded hoarsely, backing away slightly.

"Monsieur Rumigny, we were given your address as a safe-house."

Rumigny cut a lean and lanky figure, with a thick gray mane that gave him a vaguely leonine appearance—although apparently with little of the ferocity of that beast. Dark bristling eyebrows and a lush mustache ran across the width of his narrow face and stood in stark contrast to the paleness of his complexion. Limpid brown eyes, magnified behind thin wire spectacles, peered at Jeanne in the dim light of the foyer. A cravat, carelessly tied, and a misbuttoned housecoat produced an impression of a distracted man of mild manners.

Jeanne moved forward, reaching out to grasp Rumigny's hands with her own. "Have I changed that much in three years? Do you not remember me?" Without recourse to plaster and makeup, her face was merely strategically begrimed; her attire, posture, and assumed expressions represented the totality of her disguise. Jeanne herself was closer to the surface than she might have wished.

"Jeanne? Jeanne Recamier?" he gasped incredulously, drawing her into an enthusiastic embrace. "Can it really be you? After all this time!"

"Ouvrez la porte, c'est la gendarmerie!" A sharp rap sounded at the door. Rumigny started in fright.

"There's no time," Wolfe growled as the insistent pounding repeated.

"Ouvrez la porte!"

"Please, monsieur, tell them nothing. I will explain everything," Jeanne implored, pushing him toward the door before stepping with Wolfe into the recesses of the darkened room.

"We are looking for two very dangerous fugitives. A man and a woman. They entered this street just moments ago. Did you see them?" the gendarme demanded.

"Two fugitives, you say?" Rumigny repeated, adopting a vaguely confused air. "No, no…I heard nothing," he mumbled before closing the door with a sorrowful shake of his head, the picture of the conscientious citizen disappointed at being unable to assist the authorities. The gendarmes had already gone; Wolfe and Jeanne could hear them next door. "Jeanne!" Rumigny shook his head in wonder, tears glimmering behind the glinting glass of his spectacles. "I heard nothing of you, feared the worst. And now look, here you are! But…you are not… you cannot be…Primrose?" At Jeanne's quiet nod, Rumigny gasped in disbelief, a shaking hand rose to his mouth. "Mon dieu…mon dieu…I need a drink."

A dusty case of Bordeaux had been brought up from the cellar by Madeline, Rumigny's housekeeper, and the three settled into quiet comfort before a blazing hearth. The house, like others on the street, was tall and narrow with tiny rooms one above the other. This ground-floor space served as both a sitting room and a repository for a wide variety of paraphernalia. The walls, papered in red stripes that had faded into pink, supported wooden shelves cluttered with an assortment of jars, bottles, and tubes. Glass pots were filled with an intriguing assortment of brightly colored powders, pastes, and gels, and liquid vials gleamed blood red and mossy green in the warmth of the firelight. The handsome leather bindings of a single work L'Art de la Coëffure des Dames Françoises in thirty-nine volumes, occupied the bookshelf, sharing space with neatly stacked boxes, each labeled in a tiny slanted script. A variety of strange models, reminiscent of neglected children's toys, covered the mantelpiece above the hearth: a tall ship under tattered sail, a rusted birdcage, a waterfall frozen in mid-stream, its waters gray, the paint cracked with age.

A small window looked out into a tiny courtyard enclosed by tall stone walls. It was dark now, and the gas-lamp illuminated the lacy pattern of frost on the outside windowpane. If not for the thickly upholstered sofa—whose embroidered stitches had begun to fray—the cheerfully fading wallpaper, and the warmth of the worn Turkish carpet underfoot, it could have been an apothecary shop or a dark place of heathen magic.

Jeanne, Wolfe, and their host consumed a tasty partridge pie that Rumigny had sent his housekeeper to purchase from a nearby restaurant. The woman had arrived back, frozen with cold, the pie still steaming hot and fragrant from the oven. "These restaurants are the only product of the Revolution of which I approve," Rumigny had muttered between appreciative bites. "Liberté, égalité, fraternité!" he continued with a derisive flourish, pastry crumbs frosting his mustache, dark eyes flashing beneath heavy brows. "And what has it brought us? The Terror of the Counter-Revolution, continued political repression, and now a virtual dictatorship under a Corsican war-monger! But at least the Revolution got rid of the aristocrats, leaving their great chefs unemployed to open public restaurants, so, we, the humble people, have the opportunity to eat partridge pie!" he finished with a curious blend of bitter humor.

"It has been a difficult time for France," Jeanne said softly, laying her hand on Rumigny's arm. "So much has happened; so much has changed, and so quickly."

"Forgive me, ma chère," Rumigny declared with forced joviality. "It does little good to dwell on the miseries, now does it? You are alive; for that I am grateful." He patted her hand affectionately. Wolfe had consumed his portion of pie in several bites. Feeling somewhat constrained, confined, and cornered in the small room with few apparent exits, he restlessly wandered from window to doorway, gaze sweeping the darkness outside.

"This is a safe location," Jeanne assured him.

"I rather doubt there is such a place for us in Paris at the moment," Wolfe replied from the other room, his voice muffled by the intervening wall. "But I don't know that we have a choice." His massive silhouette reappeared in the doorway, having thoroughly examined and fastened the latches and locks of doors and windows in the adjacent kitchen.

"I have been a trusted member of the Resistance these past four years now..." Rumigny began stiffly, adjusting his spectacles with growing indignation as he attempted to rise out of his chair.

"Of course you have," Jeanne soothed him, with a glare in Wolfe's direction. "I would trust you with my life." And then, in a more confidential tone: "You must understand, Monsieur Rumigny, I have found Irishmen to be rather unrefined in their expression, this one in particular. But this situation worries us both. High-ranking members of the Resistance have been arrested; safe-houses have been penetrated; the city gates are heavily armed; and Fouché's innumerable agents, as well as the entire force of gendarmes it seems, are combing the city looking for us. Everyone is being watched." She sighed as she rose from the sofa, suddenly weary. "Perhaps you are right, Monsieur Trant. Perhaps we should leave now...under cover of darkness."

"Absolutely not!" Rumigny protested irritably. "The gendarmes are obviously searching the faubourg but do not know your precise location, or they would certainly have stormed the house. To go out now, while the gendarmes are still in the street, is madness. You must both stay here tonight, and I will find a way of getting you out of Paris tomorrow. I am not just a useless old man; you must have confidence in me, Jeanne." There was a moment's silence as each considered the situation.

"Monsieur Rumigny is right," Wolfe concluded as he returned to the fireplace, leaning with one hand on the mantelpiece. "The gendarmes haven't found us yet, which suggests they don't know exactly where to look. We stay here tonight and slip out before first light." Jeanne reluctantly nodded assent, refilling her glass with Bordeaux that gleamed ruby red in the firelight. "Now, I must ask you, monsieur," Wolfe asked in a deliberate attempt to lighten the atmosphere. "What're these?" He gestured toward the curiosities that graced the mantelpiece.

"Ah! I don't know why I keep them," Rumigny murmured. "They are from another life...but what a life it was, isn't that right, ma chère?" He directed a slightly mournful smile in Jeanne's direction. "Marie Antoinette wore that ship in her hair for the ball celebrating the birthday of Louis-Antoine, the Duke d'Enghien. And that was also your debut."

"My debut." Jeanne had resumed her seat at the couch end, feet tucked under her, a thick wool blanket around her shoulders. She had discarded her bonnet, and the fire-glow cast her finely boned features in a golden hue. "Mon dieu, I had forgotten all about that."

"Comtesse! How could you forget such an occasion?" Rumigny glared at her from his position across the table, his stockinged feet resting comfortably between the dark glass bottles. "Your hair that night," he continued wistfully, "was my masterpiece."

"Countess?" Wolfe interjected with a raised eyebrow.

"I gave up my titles years ago," Jeanne replied.

"Such a shame!" Rumigny snorted with laughter. "And after I worked so hard for you to acquire them!"

Jeanne laughed, a surprisingly deep chuckle that brought an answering smile to Wolfe's lips. It occurred to him that this was the first time he had heard her laugh. He liked the sound of it. "So you did, monsieur!" she affirmed, a wide grin revealing small white teeth, eyes shining in the firelight.

"You were suprême," Rumigny mused, eyes almost closed as he sprawled lower in his chair. "I remember being so proud. The Duke d'Enghien flouted convention and danced with you all night. We all supposed you would become his duchess before the year was out…but you have always been very close with the duke, have you not? Ah, we all kept such illustrious company back then, didn't we, ma chère?"

"Monsieur Rumigny," Jeanne elaborated, turning toward Wolfe who leaned against the wall beside the fire, "before the Revolution, was le meilleur coiffeur á Paris—the most magnificent hairdresser in Paris."

Rumigny smiled broadly, his glass of wine resting casually on his reclining stomach. "The birdcage," he reminded her with a chuckle.

"Mon dieu, the birdcage!" Jeanne leaned forward, hand over her mouth. "Don't tell me that…?" She glanced up at the birdcage rusting quietly over the mantelpiece.

"The same," Rumigny affirmed.

"He draped my hair over and around the birdcage," Jeanne explained to Wolfe, "and put a live canary inside."

"Which died an hour before the ball, do you remember?" Rumigny exclaimed. "I sent my boys out to find another at any price."

"That's right! I was *spring*…twigs, fruit, flowers, and that wretched bird that I was quite convinced was going to shit all over my head." She hooted with laughter over the rim of her wineglass, her usually solemn expression alive with mirth and merriment. "As it turned out, everyone else was spring too! We must have had several acres of shrubbery between us: vegetables, grass plots, bird's nests, and tulip beds!" Jeanne explained to Wolfe. "Monsieur Rumigny was furious."

"I am still furious," Rumigny insisted, his voice slurring slightly as he slumped further into his chair. "My assistant was leaking vital secrets as to how the most popular of aristocrats were styling their hair."

"A crime, was it?" Wolfe asked dryly as he stretched his long frame out in the chair.

"Oh, indeed, it was," Jeanne answered. "That was Monsieur Rumigny's prerogative." A resonant snore from the other side of the coffee table indicated that the gentleman in question had, at last, succumbed to the combined sedative of finely aged wine and fond memories of a shared past.

"Thumbscrews in the Bastille?" Wolfe inquired, his voice suitably grave.

"At the very least," Jeanne responded, with a warm smile. "It was an extremely serious offence. Monsieur Rumigny had a special recipe for his styling pomade. It was a highly kept secret then, but has since been published in his book. Beef lard and bear grease mixed in with a little hazelnut oil and essence of lemon." Wolfe grimaced good-humoredly. "He rubbed this mixture into my hair," Jeanne continued with a giggle, relishing Wolfe's expression of mock horror, "which stiffened it sufficiently so it could be draped over an egg-shaped wire frame about so high." She gestured two or three feet above her head. "And then, of course, the powder, and the decorations... what were the most popular ones that year?" Jeanne mused, screwing her face up in concentration. "Ah yes, there was the *drowned chicken, chest of drawers, mad dog,* and *sportsman in the bush,*" she concluded with a triumphant grin.

"Ah, now you're pullin' my leg, to be sure," Wolfe snorted, shaking his head in amused disbelief.

"No, indeed, monsieur, I would not joke about such a serious matter," Jeanne frowned at him, her lips quirking in an attempt to suppress the amusement that sparkled in her eyes.

"Must've been hell getting that stuff out," Wolfe mused, interested despite himself—this was a glimpse not only into the world of feminine toilette, of which he knew very little, but one of aristocratic extravagance and excess that he found difficult to even imagine.

"Oh no, Monsieur Trant! You did not take it out!" Jeanne shook her head in dismay. "You see, these hairstyles cost a small fortune. You had to keep them intact for a week or two, which meant you had to sleep sitting up. And of course, doorways and chandeliers posed a constant challenge. The smell left a little to be desired," she admitted with a shrug of one shoulder, "but in turn accelerated the production of French perfume, formulated specifically to mask the smell of rotting pomades!"

"Now that is truly foul." Wolfe wrinkled his nose in disgust.

"But the worst part, monsieur," Jeanne leaned forward in a confiding manner, "was that often when they cut these hairpieces open they would discover…apart from the smell which was, as you can imagine, quite putrid…living creatures nesting in the hair!" She laughed in delight at his expression of exaggerated distaste, and Wolfe was struck with how young, how innocent, she appeared. The lines between her eyes, grooved by years of worry and tension, were replaced by those that crinkled at the corners and the deeper ones that framed round cheeks when she laughed. Her eyes glowed. She melted into the chair with languid ease, long fingers caressing the stem of the wineglass, a smile playing about her lips. He felt tranquil for the first time in many months; the ordeal of the previous few days temporarily forgotten. And he felt lighter, as if an oppressive burden had been lifted, and hopeful, as if a future beckoned—one that might actually be worth living.

Tomorrow would bring its own concerns, but for the moment, there was a sense of peace. The pie had filled his belly with satisfying heartiness, the wine had warmed him, and now he had the pleasure of this woman's laugh—and it was a pleasure, he realized with some disconcertedness. It was the infectious deep kind of laugh that began as a low rumbling chuckle and cascaded into an irrepressible fit of giggles. He grinned despite himself. She was at ease too, he thought. Each of them had been living a life of self-imposed solitude: Jeanne in her various roles and disguises, necessarily wary of friends as well as strangers; and he, traveling from one fight to another, drinking his way across the continent in a blur of fists and blood. He had hauled himself out of it, become a manufacturer of fine linens no less. But Wolfe remained scarred by his past. He buried himself in work. He did not seek happiness in the company of others because deep down—in places he did not even recognize himself— he did not think he deserved it. But here and now, with Jeanne, he felt a sweet camaraderie. "What did Rumigny mean when he said he was responsible for your titles?"

"Well, the birdcage that night caught me a count. For a year, anyway."

Jeanne retreated back into the curve of the couch, eyes dark and shuttered, her amusement gone as swiftly as it had come. Wolfe instantly regretted the question. "He was one of the first to be guillotined. Then I went into hiding, changed my name, dropped my titles and all claims to the estates." She shivered slightly, drawing the blanket more closely around her shoulders. "I didn't feel as if any of it was mine anyway."

"And you became Primrose?" Wolfe prompted her. "How did that happen, then?"

"I was looking for my brother. For Joachim…" She broke off, turning to stare into the dying glow of embers in the hearth, her delicate profile illuminated and the rest of her face cast into shadow.

"Did you find him?" Wolfe asked gently.

"Not yet," she replied steadily, without looking at him, her eyes suspiciously bright in the firelight. "But I will."

"What happened?"

"He disappeared six years ago. Usually members of the Resistance who are captured are publicly executed. But there was no word of Joachim, no statement, no trial. It was as if he had never existed." She stated this factually without emotion. He recognized her defensive tactic, having frequently utilized a similar one himself—if she allowed herself to feel the pain of her loss, then she would have to recognize the truth of it, and she was not ready to do that. "You see, he had become involved with some dangerous people, Chouan rebels in the Vendeé. I went in search of those who knew him, thinking that perhaps he had been released, or had escaped, and Napoleon was too embarrassed to admit it. Why else this silence? I didn't find him, but I did find a cause. I became a fighter, a spy. I became Primrose." She shrugged, turning to face him. "I could see how much these people needed me. Well, not me particularly, but the myth I had created in Primrose. I showed them that Napoleon's regime was not invulnerable, that there was reason to hope."

"Do you believe your brother was arrested?" Wolfe asked. "If so, there would be papers, documents of some kind. 'Tis just a matter of accessing them."

"I intend to find out one way or another before I leave Paris," Jeanne answered. At his arched brow, she elaborated: "There are two men in Paris, one or both of whom know what happened to Joachim: Fouché and Bonaparte. The first hordes secrets and the second… Well, imperial decree can be silent as it is deadly. I have one last source to tap."

# 63.

"Just so I understand you," Pitt mused, looking up from his papers with an expression of amused skepticism at the American who sat across from him. "You have been conducting experiments in Brest with your... what do you call it?" He glanced down at the diagrams on his desk. "*Nautilus?* An iron ship that travels *under* the water?"

"That is correct," Robert Fulton replied confidently in his easy Virginian drawl. His self-assurance bordered on arrogance, but Pitt liked that about him. If the inventor were not supremely confident in the value and utility of his product, why should anyone else have faith in it? And, if the truth be told, Pitt had always found Americans to be refreshingly innovative and optimistic—something about the pioneering spirit, he supposed. But the conservatism of English naval traditions under the current Admiralty would pose an implacable resistance. This new-fangled underwater contraption had better work.

"So if the French weren't buying, why do you think we should?" Pitt asked, leaning back in his chair, his quicksilver eyes watchful, his graying hair brushed thick against the crown of his head.

"Because the French are short-sighted and hampered by their own conservatism. Because maintaining pre-eminence at sea is of much greater strategic importance to England than it is to France."

"True enough," Pitt conceded. "Your experiments in Brest, however, came to nothing. The French government, I understand, became disaffected with the entire undertaking when you failed to blow up the English ships patrolling the coast. Not that that disturbs *me*, of course." Pitt's mouth curved in a wry smile. "But if you failed to blow up English ships, why would I believe you can destroy French ones?"

"The specifications for the *Nautilus* still need work," Fulton admitted, "but I have other designs that I did not share with the French." He leaned forward, dark hair falling carelessly across his brow, eyes glowing with conviction. "Designs for underwater incendiary devices that can be deployed against the hulls of moored ships. I have tested them and would be delighted to give you a demonstration."

Pitt pursed his lips thoughtfully. If these devices did what Fulton claimed, it could make all the difference in their attack on Boulogne. And it seemed as if they had little choice in the matter now. While he had received word of the arrests of Pichegru, Cadoudal, and Moreau, as far as he was aware Wolfe and Primrose were still at large. He had no way of knowing whether the Irishman was alive or dead. Lacking intelligence of Napoleon's intended disembarkation point, England was going to have to take the battle to French shores and throw everything it had at Boulogne in a desperate attempt to destroy the flotilla before it could depart for the Channel.

"Let me pass these plans on to General Moore; we will let him review them, and then, if he thinks they are of use to us, we will schedule a demonstration. How quickly would you be able to have the devices ready?"

"Depending on the quantity you want, approximately a week."

"I'll be in touch," Pitt promised. Both men rose to their feet and were shaking hands when the door flung open with a crash, and Dundas rushed in. A piece of paper fluttered from his outstretched hand.

"You need to read this," he barked without preamble, seemingly oblivious of Fulton's presence in the room.

"Thank you, Mr. Fulton." Pitt nodded, waiting until the other man had departed, the door closing firmly behind him, before quickly scanning the letter.

The note was concise. It was from Talleyrand: *Following intelligence sent by request of your agent Wolfe Trant: Napoleon plans to unite entire French fleet in Boulogne for imminent invasion—embarkation point in England unknown. I intend to relay false orders via semaphore system sending Admiral Villeneuve to Cadiz instead, and thus divide the French fleet and delay invasion.*

Pitt sank into his chair, gratefully accepting the glass of brandy Dundas had poured for him.

"So that was his plan," the Scotsman mused. "Overwhelming odds. The French fleet together would total...what, fifty ships-of-the-line?"

"Fifty-one," Pitt replied. "Not inconceivable. You would have to get past Nelson, of course. Vincent's fleet is in Southampton for re-victualing and maintenance, which is taking longer than expected. They could slip through the blockade but would have to do so within the next six days…my God, Dundas."

"Indeed," Dundas agreed grimly.

"There is no time to lose." Pitt rose decisively to his feet, placing his still-full glass on the table. "Get Charles Fox in here. It was an extremist within the Whig party that hired this assassin; perhaps Fox might know who is responsible and can put a stop to it before it is too late. It seems Mr. Wolfe Trant has, again, risen from the dead to become a terribly important asset to the English government. Or at least to this covert part of it." Pitt grinned at Dundas. "And you know, Mal, I'm inordinately glad he is alive. I rather like the man."

"So do I, Will."

"And get these specifications to Moore to review. If he thinks it worthwhile, tell him to lead negotiations with Fulton to get these contraptions ready."

"Will do." Dundas nodded as he headed for the door with long strides.

"Oh, and, Mal, make sure Fulton understands he has less than seventy-two hours."

"I'll tell him," Dundas affirmed, his face set in lines of quiet determination.

Pitt retrieved his brandy from the table and moved toward the window. Ignoring the aching discomfort in his belly, he tossed the liquor down in one swift movement, relishing the fiery heat at the back of his throat. Through the thick leaded window, he could see the long stretch of water that disappeared in a misty horizon twenty-five miles to the east. Boulogne—where hundreds of thousands of hardened soldiers, veterans of brutal battles under distant suns, wanted nothing more than to obliterate all that was dear to him. Not without a fight, Pitt vowed. Not without a fight.

# 64.

## RUE DES MAUVAIS GARÇONS. PARIS, FRANCE
*December 7, 1803*

By all accounts, the dark-timbered lodging house that leaned precariously out over the cobblestones of rue des Mauvais Garçons was a dismal place. The ground floor served as the store for the resident wigmaker and owner of the establishment. The sagging timbers of the second supported the single room occupied by an impoverished family of four, and the tiny street side room on the third floor had very recently been vacated. The scrawny prostitute was even now hurrying through the cold streets, coins grasped tightly in her claw-like hand. One hundred francs! She had never seen the like and intended to fill her belly with the finest pork pie Monsieur Anglade had to offer at Café Perrault. And perhaps a tipple of brandy to keep her warm. All for the use of her grim garret room for the night! Would the foreign gentleman like to rent it from her for the week? she wondered.

The room was bleak indeed. It extended out over the street and consisted of little more than a barricaded closet. With price being defined by the lot size on which the building had been erected and income generated according to available living space, these houses were narrow and high. In the quest for paying lodgers, the owners had every incentive to divide the available space as much as was possible. As a result, these establishments were extended in every imaginable way, with additional floors erected in upper stories and carved out beneath the floor in subterranean basements. Rented rooms were created in recesses and annexes, linked by narrow staircases or ladders. Generally, the social condition of lodgers deteriorated the higher they climbed, with poverty being the general rule on the top floors, in attics, and garrets.

The prostitute's room was no exception. The bed consisted of a thin straw mattress covered with a rumpled sheet. A few cooking utensils sat on an overturned wooden crate, beside which resided a chamber pot—thankfully empty, L'Aigle noted. The room, shuttered against the cold, was imbued with the pungent scents of tallow candles, sex, and sweat, a greasy commingling of odors that left L'Aigle feeling distinctly nauseous. He ripped away the oiled paper that served as a barrier against the weather and felt instantly better. The room, dreary as it appeared, was absolutely perfect for his purposes: it looked out over number 32. The wooden door with its glass-paned inset sat squarely opposite.

L'Aigle peered through the window and waited. The only other exit to the house across the street was the back door, which opened up into a tiny courtyard enclosed by a tall stone wall, a portion of which had been demolished to allow access to those living in the next door apartment. Etienne had provided him with two men whom he had subsequently deployed at each door. The target was trapped.

The late afternoon was rapidly darkening to night, and the street was a bustling one. Through the window, he could hear the iron hoops of carriage wheels clattering across the cobblestones and the gruff voice of a Lyonese peddler, who had taken up residence beneath the sheltering overhang of L'Aigle's room, hawking coal. The Irishman was apparently going to stay the night. L'Aigle would make his move later, just before dawn, when the target was most likely heavy with slumber. He was accustomed to waiting. He was also meticulous, and while he trusted Etienne's judgment, he did not know these men who had been assigned to his service. Pulling the rim of his hat low over his brow, collar upturned to the chin, L'Aigle decided to make a last reconnoiter of the immediate vicinity. He would check the exits, check the roof-line, unobtrusively confirm the intelligence. Making his way down the rickety turret stairs, he emerged in the dark street, keeping, by habit, to the shadows.

It was then that he saw him—on the corner, where rue des Mauvais Garçons merged with rue de Réaumur. A darkly hunched figure in a broad-brimmed hat. The yellow light of the gas-lamp illuminated the greasy sheen of his coat but cast a deep shadow across his features. Fouché! What was he doing here? He appeared to be watching the wooden door across the street just as L'Aigle was doing, but why would the police commissioner be targeting a covert co-conspirator of Napoleon?

L'Aigle was aware of the chaos that pervaded the various policing agencies, remnants of the competing regulatory organizations established by the Committee of Public Safety under Robespierre during the Directorate. He also knew of Fouché's considerable authority and influence. Alliances were never clear or simple. Was Fouché intending to betray Napoleon? Blackmail him? Or was he simply collecting information to later be used at an opportune moment?

Then, in the gloom of a side street he saw another: a man slouched against the wall, hands buried deep in his pockets. And another there, on the other side of the house. Fouché's henchmen. As he was considering this new development, a gaunt drunk in a flaccid gray jacket staggered over, and, with one grimy fist, proceeded to bang on the door of 32 rue des Mauvais Garçons, hollering as he did so to the inhabitants within.

L'Aigle cursed under his breath. The situation was becoming entirely more complicated than he had anticipated and maintaining anonymity was of paramount importance. It was one thing to reveal his identity to Renault, who had no familiarity with aristocratic circles beyond those that frequented his café, and to Etienne who, however taciturn he might be, depended upon L'Aigle's frequent and generous custom. But Fouché was an individual most dangerous to L'Aigle, one who collected useless information for the power it could afford him—now or in the future. And he was tenacious. No, it would not pay to arouse his suspicions. He would have to wait, bide his time. The English contact would not be happy with the delay but that could not be helped. It seemed that it was time for Etienne's men again to earn their coin. They would take over the tracking of this Irishman and inform L'Aigle of his whereabouts, and then, when the time was right, he could step in and finish this infernal business.

# 65.

In the dim seclusion of Rumigny's living room, amidst the pastes and vials, the books and the boxes, Jeanne and Wolfe sat before a dying fire, heads bent together over the table between them, playing cards spread out upon its surface. Several candles illuminated the cards and cast a warm, yellow glow over the features of the players.

"Ah, Jeanne...I think you have me!" Wolfe exclaimed with a half-smile, tossing his hand on the table and rising to his feet with a languorous stretch.

"I believe I do!" Jeanne laughed triumphantly, turning her cards over to reveal a straight of five spades.

"I should've discarded the two," Wolfe remarked ruefully.

"Yes! And kept the queen, which would have prevented me from getting the straight." She tapped her winning hand, white teeth flashing in a delighted grin.

"Piquet is not my game, I'm afraid. I keep forgettin' the ace is high... Well, you don't need to rub it in," Wolfe protested, with a grin of his own.

"In fairness, to you, Monsieur Trant..."

"Wolfe," he interjected.

"Wolfe..." she amended with a smile. "I've had time to become acquainted with the new French way. While the ace in other parts of Europe is the lowest card and worth nothing, in France after the Revolution the elevation of the ace symbolized the removal of the nobility and the promotion of the common man...and, as you see, the traditional court cards," she gestured at the king and queen of hearts, "had their crowns removed so that they were more representative of democratic ideals..."

"'Tis interesting how everything is co-opted to the cause; makes you wonder how entrenched a notion really is if one must reiterate it in playing cards."

"A notion entrenched in the minds of the people, Wolfe, if not our imperial leader." Jeanne's smile faded and her face grew solemn as she gathered the playing cards together and slipped them in their case. "Of course, now that Napoleon has crowned himself emperor, he has re-instituted the crown upon the cards...and the ideals of the Revolution seem further away than ever before."

"The promotion of the common man," Wolfe mused, rubbing his stubbled chin between thumb and forefinger. "Which is all very grand, so long as the common man is worth promoting. Napoleon himself is a fine example: from Corsican son to Emperor of France. But you're seeking to restore the monarchy. Are you not afraid of replacing one tyrant with another?"

"Monarchy is the form of government most congenial to the French people; and what is needed now, more than anything, is stability. But the new king must make concessions; he must be bound by some form of constitution. What form of governance would you wish for in Ireland?"

"I would settle for Catholic emancipation and our right to take a seat in the legislative assembly. It would be a start, to be sure."

"And your United Irishmen? What do they want?"

"Everything. The end of monarchical rule. A sovereign independent Irish republic."

"But you desire this also?"

"Of course I do, but there's a saying in Ireland: 'A scholar's ink lasts longer than a martyr's blood.' I am starting to believe that there are better, more effective alternatives to battling and dying."

A quiet fell upon the room, each preoccupied with his or her own particular thoughts. Wolfe crouched down before the fire, added the last log to the smoldering pile, and attempted to coax a flame.

"What are you going to do now?" Jeanne asked. She pulled the blankets tightly around her shoulders as she drew her feet up on to the sofa, shivering slightly as a chill descended upon the room.

Wolfe jabbed at the logs with a poker, his broad shoulders silhouetted in a flurry of red sparks. For a moment, Jeanne thought he hadn't heard her. Then he rose, wiping the soot from his hands on his breeches before shifting his chair closer to the hearth.

"Nantes. I'll be going to Nantes," Wolfe answered finally, his voice gruff and quiet in the still room. "Come, sit yourself here. 'Tis warmer." Jeanne slid off the sofa in a bundle of blankets. She stretched her bare feet toward the fire and closed her eyes in silent appreciation as the growing warmth spread through her frozen toes. "How is it you've survived Parisian winters? You seem to have an uncommonly difficult time staying warm." He positioned himself in front of the fire, taking one of her icy feet in his large warm hands, rubbing the arch of her foot and massaging circulation back into her toes.

"A much easier time since I ran into you," she murmured with a half-smile, and both of them were reminded of the night in rue Demarest when they had each warmed the other. His hands tightened slightly around her foot, his gaze holding her own. The fire crackled and spit in its ashes; Rumigny's gurgling snore rattled across the room, his narrow chest rising and falling with gentle breath. "Why Nantes?" Jeanne asked, her voice husky, glancing away into the fire.

"There's a semaphore telegraph station there." His hands resumed their rhythmic kneading motion. "Napoleon intends to unite his naval forces in Boulogne. Admiral Latouche-Tréville commands the port with eleven ships-of-the-line." Wolfe relinquished one foot and began working on the second. "Ganteaume, stationed in Brest with nineteen vessels, will sail down to Boulogne—"

"That gives them thirty ships," Jeanne interjected with a start. "What...?"

"But still not *quite* enough to outmaneuver the thirty-three vessels the English maintain in the Channel. If, however, Admiral Villeneuve's twenty-one ships-of-the-line were able to make it to Boulogne from Malaga...well then, the French might just stand a chance."

"And *that* is Napoleon's plan?" Jeanne asked raptly, leaning forward, the blanket falling from her shoulders. "Mon dieu, I should have guessed! With Nelson in the Mediterranean...the timing is perfect!"

"Well, it would ha' been, to be sure," Wolfe affirmed, his mouth quirking in a crooked smile. "But I'm afraid that Admiral Villeneuve won't be able to make the rendezvous." He shook his head in mock regret. "He'll receive notice from Napoleon himself directing him to Cadiz, where he is to stay until further notice."

"And why would Napoleon do such a thing?"

"He isn't exactly renowned for his comprehension of nautical strategy, don't you know," Wolfe grinned, his teeth glinting whitely in the dim room.

"No, he isn't," Jeanne agreed with a muffled chuckle.

"And I do happen to have Napoleon's personal access codes."

"His codes?" Jeanne's mouth dropped open in disbelief. "His personal semaphore codes? We have been trying to get those for months!"

She referred to the sequence of nine numbers—Napoleon's numerical signature—that was affixed to the base of a telegraphed message. For obvious reasons, this information would have been of vital interest to the Resistance, but the numbers, and their particular sequence, were a closely guarded secret. Increasingly paranoid about infiltration, Napoleon altered the code every ten days, sending riders of his Imperial Guard out to the seven military commanders dispersed throughout France and beyond her borders with the updated version. It was an impressive expenditure of resources, but it had been effective. The Resistance had been unable to penetrate the guard or intercept the riders, and Napoleon had enjoyed a communication network of unprecedented alacrity.

"How much time do you have before they are changed?"

"Three days," Wolfe replied. "I will need to be leaving first thing in the morning."

"I know of someone who might be of use to you. A monk in Bourges. His brother operates the semaphore station in Limoges; it is closer than Nantes…"

They were interrupted by a strident banging and a boisterous voice, slurred and roughened by drink, at the front door. Jeanne leapt to her feet, waking Rumigny with an insistent shake of his shoulder. Wolfe moved swiftly to the door.

Rumigny roused himself reluctantly, stretching his arms to the ceiling and gathering his worn robe more closely about his thin frame. "Mon dieu, I hate that man," he grumbled with disgust, rubbing his eyes.

"Who is it?" Wolfe demanded.

Madeline scurried in from the kitchen, her round face drawn in lines of abject apology. She was a large, stout woman with thick red hair pulled back tightly from a pale, freckled face. Her large, unblinking brown eyes, flat nose, and wide, thick-lipped mouth gave her rather a bovine appearance, accentuated by the thick, stocky body encased in brown broadcloth beneath. She shrugged a shoulder, an eloquent gesture that bespoke years of helpless resignation and regret.

"Bouilly," Rumigny muttered contemptuously. "Madeline's drunken fool of a husband. He makes good shoes when he is sober but spends most of his time passed out on the floor of some tavern or another. I don't know why she tolerates him."

# 66.

*December 7, 1803*

Bouilly had been tucked in bed, Rumigny had retired, and Wolfe and Jeanne lay side by side on a lumpy bedroll that had been unfurled in front of a cold hearth. It was late, but neither of them slept. The moonlight streamed in through the window, bathing the room in a pool of pale light.

"Why are you doing this?" Jeanne asked Wolfe, feeling the hardness of the floor beneath her hip as she rolled on to her side to face him. He lay on his back, gazing up at the ceiling, his profile gilded in silver, arms folded across his chest. At her question, Wolfe closed his eyes, as if in pain, his large hands unconsciously tightening into fists. The anger emanated from every pore, evident in the long, rigid line of his body and the sudden tightness around his mouth. Then he inhaled deeply, slowly, deliberately; emptied his lungs through flaring nostrils, as if seeking to regain some semblance of control. When he finally spoke, his voice was flat and emotionless but inexpressibly weary.

"There was a battle," he began after a moment's hesitation, his eyes clouded with a pain that had never entirely gone away. "Seven years ago. At a little town called New Ross." His mouth twisted bitterly, his fingers tapping an agitated rhythm at his side. Despite his attempts to distance himself from his past, Jeanne could see that even now, seven years later, he had had little success; it continued to haunt him as her own haunted her. "'Twas an attempt to break out of the County Wexford, across the river Barrow, and to spread the rebellion into County Kilkenny and the province of Munster. I led a group of eight Irish lads who were trying to make a better world for themselves, for their families. Instead, they were butchered by English soldiers. I was stabbed in the chest…" His hand absently rubbed the scar that undoubtedly arced across his torso beneath the linen shirt. "And from my vantage point there in the dirt, lying in me own blood, I saw…"

Wolfe hesitated, jaw clenched in pained remembrance. He swallowed once before turning his head to face her, dark eyes smoldering with suppressed fury and despair, voice barely a whisper when he continued: "The soldiers…they locked all the townspeople in the barn, hundreds of them…women and babes too. And then they drew a bolt across the door and set it alight. I could hear the little ones screaming. I tried to get to them, but I couldn't help them." He was quiet for a moment before continuing, his gaze again on the ceiling, his voice huskily quiet in the still room.

"And after it was all over…after the doctors tended to me…" A bitter twist of his mouth suggested he would have preferred to have been left in the dirt to die. "Well, I didn't want to fight anymore. The soldier who stabbed me…he was just an English lad himself. I figured the battle was decided upon by English politicians and armchair generals, but it was the lads who fought and died. And these Irish lads I had brought into battle. They came because of me. Because they believed in me. And you know the worst of it?" He looked at Jeanne, mouth tight with anger, eyes flashing fire. "Nothing changed." He laughed sourly. "And everything changed. Their mothers couldn't look me in the eye. And I knew why, knew that I deserved their condemnation and more. I'd promised them a great world, a world where Ireland was free, where food and jobs were available for all who wanted 'em. You see, I believed that being free of the English yoke was the answer." Wolfe sunk down into the pillow, suddenly exhausted, his large body limp, as if the memory of this distant battle had deprived his being of life and light. "That once Ireland was an independent nation, we could engage in fair trade with England, with the continent," he said, enunciating the words with harsh emphasis.

There was a moment of silence. Wolfe stared moodily at the darkly scarred beams of the ceiling, his face drawn into lines of resentful anger.

"So what did you do?" Jeanne prompted, bringing Wolfe out of his reverie.

"Most of the past seven years, I spent fighting. Bare-knuckle boxing, actually. I crossed the continent, fought in Belgium, France before the Revolution, Germany…"

"Your penance?" Jeanne murmured, her voice soft in the dim room.

"I suppose it was," Wolfe admitted.

"And then?"

"I ended up in Russia. Bare-knuckle boxing had become greatly favored in St. Petersburg. To be sure, the vodka had something to do with it." Wolfe's mouth quirked in what might have been a grin. "The boxing was the same as everywhere else. Fists, blood, broken bones, and bruises...maybe a bit o' money at the end of the day, if you were lucky. Then, an pota óir, jackpot. I was invited to fight the Great Bogdan, Alexsei Klitschko. A hero of the people, a national icon. Bogdan meaning "given by God," ye see. The fight was to be out at the fort of Kronstadt, a two-hour trip by troika across a causeway of ice. The whole way there, I was warned to throw the fight. Probably would've been wise...but then, me ma always did say I was the stubborn one."

Wolfe closed his eyes, and he was there again: the fortress room made humid by the jostling pack of Cossacks wrapped in their long tunics. The czar, dignified and restrained, surrounded by his ministers, ambassadors, chamberlains, and young officers of every corps—Grodno Hussars in green; Hussars of the Guard with their short white dolmans slashed with gold and trimmed with a border of sable, their brave chests bestrewn with grand cordons of honor; all of them roaring in thundering accord as Klitschsko climbed into the ring: "Bogdan! Bogdan!" Wolfe remembered the adrenalin surging through his limbs; that telltale tingle in his fingertips; the dance; the weave; the chess game had begun.

"It seemed that the whole of Russia was there to watch," he continued quietly. "Even the czar. I barely survived the fight. Klitschsko was a bear of a man, but he could move like one half his size, and as I stood over him at the end of it all, hardly able to stand on me own feet as it was, they all went utterly silent—couldn't believe that an Irish upstart had defeated the great Bogdan. I left rather quickly, don't ye know." He gave a half-laugh, a soft brief sound in the back of his throat. "I may've been prideful, but ma taught me discretion...and I didn't know how long the hospitality might last, under the circumstances. I'd hired a driver to take me back after the fight, and at that instant of dusk on the ice, as the night was descending, the horizon seemed to have dissolved into the earth. 'Twas impossible to see where the sky ended or where the ice began. It felt like being trapped in an immense milky crystal. I remember staring pointedly at the horses, and they appeared to be flying in the ether like Pegasus or those chariots painted on the ceiling in churches. It seemed a wild rush through these desolate icy fields into Tirnan-Og itself. As if I had been touched by a sidhe and my strength was ebbing away and I was flying about as if in a living dream."

Wolfe was quiet for a moment, then continued: "If you spend any time in Russia you'll find 'tis a place that changes you... A place where a man meets his soul." Wolfe rolled on to his side to face her, propping his torso up on his elbow, his face pale in the lunar light, eyes downcast and shadowed, the long ridge line of scar tracing its way in shadow and light across his forehead and under his thick, tousled hair.

"We should've had plenty of time to get back, but one of the horses became lame. I knew I was in a bad way. I'd had enough injuries to know that this one was serious. When the horse collapsed... Well then, I knew that I, too, would die there on the ice. The driver dragged me, little more than a frozen corpse...the last thing I remember was this eerie clanging that echoed across the snow. 'Twas a house of refuge; they ring their bells during snowstorms to help guide lost souls. I thought it was the wail of a banshee summoning me to my death."

He looked at Jeanne then, and she felt the extent of his candid admission, realizing these were thoughts that he had never before expressed aloud. She lay utterly still, barely breathing, her gaze locked on his. "When I got back to St. Petersburg, I found the czar had been assassinated that very night of the fight. I didn't want to box anymore. So I took my years of modest winnings that were sitting uselessly in a bank and did the hardest thing I ever had to do. I went home."

"And you became a respectable merchant?" Jeanne asked softly, the corner of her mouth turning up in a smile. And the whispery spell of Russia faded, to be replaced by the warm green of Irish shores.

"Well, I don't know 'bout the respectable bit." He smiled. "I found meself at an auction in Carrickfergus. A grand old brick building, used to be a linen factory. I'll never forget it. The floor was crowded with workers...all hungry and dirty. They wanted to apply for work from the new owner as soon as the mill was transferred. But it had been a very long winter, and the mill had been failing for some time, with weavers being laid off."

"So you bought the mill?"

"I did," he said with a short laugh. "And I didn't know a damned thing about weaving! There was an old fella there having tea, just watching the proceedings like he didn't have a care in the world. I asked him how long it took to learn how to weave, and he replied, 'All your life, son, all your life.' But before I could think about it any further, I found I'd raised my hand, and all of a sudden, the mill was mine. And the look on those people's faces when I told them they all had jobs, double their previous wage with a week in advance. You can't imagine the way their faces changed—but it wasn't joy as you might expect, it was confusion. They didn't understand, you see; suffering and hardship was all they'd ever known."

He continued, his voice soft and resonant: "And I realized right there that boxing was all I had done for so long that I had forgotten there were other ways to make a difference. I wanted to try to make amends for the past. I wouldn't allow those boys to have died in vain. I still believe that to be strong we need to be free. So I made a deal wi' the devil to free Ireland, and if I lose my soul in the process…well, I think with the life I've led, 'twas lost long ago." Wolfe sat up restlessly, the blanket puddling around his middle. Their conversation had stirred up old ghosts.

"It wasn't your fault," Jeanne said softly, reaching out with a tentative touch. The corded muscles of his arm were rigid and unyielding under her fingers.

"And how the hell would you know that, then?" he countered harshly, his breath coming quick and heated in his chest. Then, after a moment, in a softer tone: "Forgive me. I am not looking for absolution, just a change of topic."

"We all make our own choices," she persisted, knowing that, despite his words, Wolfe did indeed need forgiveness—from himself. "Those boys did too. Where do you think your Irish heroes are born? From acts such as these, in times such as these…like you, those boys had the courage to take up arms in support of their convictions. They gave everything for their families, for their country. Don't you think for one moment their mothers aren't proud of their sacrifice," she continued fiercely. "These boys are heroes. Don't take that away from them."

Wolfe turned his head to look at her then, his face cast into darkness, the moon edging tufts of hair and the curve of an ear in white. He did not say anything but reached out with his left hand to cup the curve of her chin. There was gratitude in his gesture, a sense that despite the fierceness of his anger perhaps a redemption of sorts was possible after all. Nearly seven years had passed since that doomed battle and the heartbreaking losses that followed. Jeanne, however, lived with necessary deception and the fear of discovery on a daily basis. How did she do it? he wondered. How was it she was so strong?

He felt the softness of her mouth beneath his thumb, the heat of her breath on his skin, the smooth velvet of her cheek, and the hard curve of bone beneath. His fingertips brushed the small lobe of her ear and felt the short, silky strands of her hair. So strong and so soft. Wolfe trailed downwards, tracing the length of her slender neck, the hollow of her throat. Impulsively, he bent his head and kissed her there, where her pulse fluttered and trembled beneath pale white skin. Then he gathered her close, pulling her tighter against him, her head into his neck, her shoulders into his chest, her legs entangled with his own...

Later, he was jarred into wakefulness. What was it? Wolfe wasn't sure, but there was something wrong. He had little notion of Monsieur Rumigny's normal nocturnal routine, but something had roused him. Not only roused him but left him crouched in a fighter's stance, fists clenched and raised, eyes darting across the darkened room, Jeanne breathing deeply below him. What was it? Straining hard, head cocked to one side, he listened. Nothing. Had he imagined it? Instinctively, he felt not. And he had learned to trust his instincts. Reaching down with one hand, he gently shook Jeanne awake. "Time to leave," he whispered.

She did not question him but rose silently to her feet, her eyes searching the dark shadows that lengthened beyond the furniture and into the hallway. The gleaming edge of a blade materialized in her hand.

"I heard something," he muttered.

"If they have found us already, the exits will be watched," Jeanne whispered.

"So what do you suggest?"

"Upstairs," she whispered. "There is an attic window that opens on to the roof. A leap of about six feet over to the neighboring house, you should be able to make it."

"*Should* be able to make it?" Wolfe whispered. "Thanks very much!"

"Better go; you may not have much time."

"What about you?"

"Best that we part company for now. We need to divide their forces and maximize the chance that one of us gets out of this." He reached for her then, pressing his lips against her own with a brief but demanding insistence. And then he was gone like the memory of a dream upon waking.

# 67.

## Rue des Mauvais Garçons. Paris, France
*December 8, 1803*

The sun rose as a watery disc above rue des Mauvais Garçons, not that it made much difference to the residents of the Marais who, without the thick, warm coats and fur-lined wraps of the rich, tended to stay indoors. They clustered around the feeble heat of scantily fed hearths at local taverns and relied upon cheap brandy to warm them from the inside. None but the most hardy, or the most foolish, ventured out. Or the most dedicated, Fouché mused sourly, warming his frozen fingers under his armpits. Wolfe and Primrose would be undaunted by the weather conditions—so where were they? Certainly, they were not so imprudent as to spend more time than was absolutely necessary in one place? He had seen Bouilly's light in the window, two candles. The clear, moonlit night had rapidly deteriorated just after Notre Dame's resonant bells proclaimed the midnight hour. Dark masses of cumulus clouds brooded over eastern Paris. Snow menaced but did not materialize. Instead, a bracingly icy wind tugged and pulled at shutters and roof shingles.

*Where were they?*

Could the information have been wrong? No doubt it had been a mistake to rely upon an old drunk like Bouilly. But it had been an opportunity too good to pass up: a mole inside the safe-house. And all Bouilly had to do was confirm the presence of both parties. Fouché didn't want to move in until he was quite sure both Wolfe and Primrose were on the premises. If one eluded him, it might be weeks before he had the opportunity to apprehend the other. He needed them both at once, together.

Fouché, however, had expected them to emerge before now, before the light of dawn streaked across the eastern sky, before they could be seen and identified. He had expected a dark run, and his agents had been poised, watching the doors with a stoic patience even as the wind flattened their clothes against their bodies and froze their feet to the ground. But nothing. The house at 32 rue des Mauvais Garçons remained quiet and shuttered; the two candles had long since guttered to twin puddles of pooled wax.

*Where were they?*

Fouché fumbled in his pocket for a cigar. Merde! He had smoked the last one earlier that morning and had intended to send Chavert to replace them, but had forgotten to do so. Unlike him. He hunched under his dark coat, pulling the collar up to protect his face from the biting wind that howled and raged along the length of rue des Mauvais Garçons—the Street of the Bad Boys. Named after criminals who had resided here in the fourteenth century, or so Fouché understood. It seemed the brief halcyon days of the seventeenth and eighteenth centuries had been short-lived indeed, for the Marais was again the refuge of the felon.

Mon dieu, it was cold! He could not remember a winter this ferocious. The frozen corpse of a beggar had been removed from in front of the police department that morning, stiff and blue. There were hundreds of these desperate malcontents, or so it seemed, flocking to the capital in search of work, starving and miserable. The government had adopted a hard line on vagrancy that had placed a tremendous pressure on the reserve food supplies that were required to sustain the Parisian workforce during what promised to be a long and unimaginably harsh winter. The work-papers served to identify and differentiate the legal Parisian workers, who were eligible for food subsidies, from the tremendous influx of rural poor who had flooded the city in search of handouts. Migrant workers were one thing, Fouché thought, but these imbéciles did nothing but clog the city streets.

"Commissioner!" The leanly sallow face of a gendarme appeared beside him. "Alain was watching the back-street, and he saw someone climb out the garret window, over the far side of the roof, and down into rue de Masant." The man gestured over toward the gabled roof that perched like a witch's hat atop number thirty-two.

"When?" Fouché barked.

"Not two minutes ago," the man replied.

"One person or two? A man or woman?"

"One. A man."

Wolfe!

Fouché raised one hand in a quick gesture. It was mirrored by Chavert stationed across the street. The chief inspector had a total of eight men at his disposal, ample numbers to secure the house and the persons within—one of whom would be Primrose herself !

"Give this to the chief inspector," Fouché muttered, handing a quickly scrawled note to the waiting gendarme: *Secure the premises, allow none in or out, and under no circumstances move in until I return!*

Fouché had been pursuing this little French flower too long to allow anyone else the pleasure of her apprehension, but he did not trust these gendarmes with the crucial task of arresting Wolfe Trant—and he must have them both. The police commissioner scuttled rapidly down the street, under the darkly timbered overhang where the assassin had waited, and turned into rue de Masant.

# 68.

It was barely dawn outside; the roar and clamor of wind battered against the shutters and howled through cracks in the walls and under the door. Wolfe had made his stealthy departure over the rooftops five minutes ago or more. Jeanne had immediately roused Rumigny. Peering through cracks in the shutters, they counted eight gendarmes, shrouded in long coats against the weather, huddled against the walls of the neighboring houses, or lingering under gas-lamps in rue des Mauvais Garçons.

It was too late to escape across the rooftops as Wolfe had done— even in that short time the sun had emerged from its cloudbank to the east and sent a watery light across the skyline. Unless she could slither across the shingles, keeping her profile to a minimum. The gable roof, however, like others on the street, was sharply pitched, undoubtedly icy, and the increasing strength of the wind rendered it a rather unpalatable alternative. Besides which, Wolfe had left that way and the more divergent their paths from this point onwards, the better their respective chances of survival. Wolfe was too tall; together, they were too memorable. She needed a different route, a different direction, a different strategy.

But *what*?

Jeanne rubbed one gritty eye with the heel of her hand. Her thought process felt clouded, weighed down and hampered by a murky exhaustion. And again she kept coming back to the same questions. Why hadn't they stormed the house? What were they waiting for? Certainly, they had orders not to let anyone out—a disguise would be useless. But what else could she do? To stay, to make a stand here, would put Rumigny in danger. At least if she were able to create a diversion, force a pursuit, she might be able to draw the gendarmes away. The kind hairdresser was exposed, and the police commissioner would never forget. Rumigny would either be retrieved and interrogated or allowed to maintain his existing routine with the understanding that he was wedged and squirming on Fouché's hook—bait for more prestigious prey.

Jeanne rose wearily to her feet. It was time to go. The events of the previous few days had been compounded by two nights of very little sleep. And while fatigue slowed her movements and rendered her response sluggish, the fear and tension of flight would accelerate her heartbeat and quicken her step—at least for a short time. "Thank you, Monsieur Rumigny, for everything." Jeanne wrapped one of his coats tightly about her torso, her face largely obscured by a black hat pulled low over her brow. Now that her decision had been made, Jeanne was anxious to be gone.

"What are you doing?" Rumigny cried, alarmed. "Ma chère, you cannot be thinking of going out there like that?"

"And what choice do I have, monsieur?"

"They will be expecting you to try to run; they will be expecting a disguise." Rumigny reached over, enveloping her small hands in his own bony ones. "I have opened my home to you, have I not? Provided a refuge? However temporary it may seem?" he asked her fiercely, eyes bright behind his spectacles.

"Of course, and I am so grateful to you," Jeanne replied, gripping his hands tightly with her own. "But—"

"Then you will do this for me," Rumigny declared vehemently, his gaze and expression urgently compelling. "Jeanne, I need this. I need to feel useful again, do you understand? Certainly, royalties from my book sales keep me in food and firewood, but I am bored," he finished simply with a half-shrug, mouth curving in a tremulous smile. "Under the monarchy, I was sought after. I had access to the most powerful people in the nation, engaged in intimate conversations while I whirled and twirled, dusted, and pomaded. As you know, I was more than just a coiffeur; I was a confidant, a keeper of secrets, and now…" His hands fluttered expressively, his eyes blinking rapidly behind the glint and glimmer of lenses. "Let me do this, Jeanne. Let me do this for you. Please."

"Oh, Monsieur Rumigny, my dear old friend…" Jeanne stepped forward, enveloping the smaller man in her arms, hugging him tightly, herself blinking back tears. An image flashed through her mind: Rumigny's body dangling from the gallows, his hands so vital and fluid in life hanging limp and loose in death. Shuddering, the bile rising in the back

of her throat, she thrust the grim scenario from her mind. "Are you
sure?" Jeanne asked him quietly, her breath a whisper against his wiry
gray head. She had so few friends left, and having just re-discovered this
one—one who had known her for so long, before the Terror, before the
heaving change that had so dislocated her life—she was loath to let him
go. The beam that lit up his face, sending his cheeks and forehead into
a cascade of wrinkles, was her answer. "Very well," Jeanne conceded
wearily, leaning back against the wooden counter, suddenly exhausted.
She yanked the hat from her head and tossed it on the table.

"But now, ma chère, you must eat! You must keep up your strength.
We have ten minutes or so before we can start preparations."

So it was with a spirited élan and a barely contained skip to his step
that Rumigny bustled around the room preparing hot rolls accompanied
by preserved fruit compote. Coffee steamed and gurgled on the stove.

The kitchen, like the sitting room of the previous night, was a small
but convivial nook. Terracotta tiles covered the floor and a large fire
blazed merrily in the hearth, exuding a generous warmth that was welcome after the chill of the night. Copper pots and pans hung from racks
attached to the ceiling. The counters surrounding the central table were
strewn with baskets of dried vegetables and fruits. Madeline had spent
the previous evening cleaning out the cellar and replenishing its stock
for the coming winter. It was hard to believe that it was only early December and that the long winter months still stretched out before them;
the housekeeper's bustling preparations served as a bleak reminder that
the thaw of spring was distant indeed.

"Madeline!"

The housekeeper appeared in the doorway, wiping chapped red
hands on her apron.

"In about twenty minutes, I want you to slip past the gendarmes and
run to Monsieur Getaux. Tell him we want cab twenty-one rapidement.
Do you understand?"

Madeline glanced uncertainly at Jeanne, before turning her gaze back
to Monsieur Rumigny. The presence of the police outside unnerved
her, Jeanne saw. She was wavering between her allegiance to Rumigny,
who had not merely employed her as much as he had given her a home,
and her fear of Fouché and the silently hunched men who waited outside in the cold.

Monsieur Rumigny placed one hand on her shoulder and smiled into her doughy face. "You have your papers? They have been verified by Monsieur Berthier. You will not be troubled. I need you, Madeline."

"You can rely upon me, monsieur," Madeline replied, her voice a dry whisper in the quiet room.

"I know that I can." Rumigny patted her shoulder reassuringly.

"A cab?" Jeanne asked, sipping the last of the steaming coffee— more for something to occupy her hands than any desire for the wa-tered-down brew. She held the cup tightly between her palms, fingers clenched around the ceramic, in an attempt to still the trembling that seemed to have overtaken her limbs.

Suddenly, a sweet melodic trill broke the cold morning air: a woman singing scales—as startling as it was unexpected. Her voice ascended to a high C and was then joined by a graceful contralto, slightly deeper in weight than the first whose voice continued to trill in high melodic harmony. Lastly, a powerfully rich emotive voice joined them, one that emerged from deep within the abdomen. Their voices rose in a crescen-do of harmonious sound.

"My neighbors," Rumigny explained, his wrinkled visage breaking into a toothy grin. "Elbert, Louise, and Grizella are opera singers in *Echo et Narcisse*. They insist that my courtyard is perfect for their prac-tice. The sound is better than inside. So I had the wall knocked down so they could come and practice whenever they wish. They have the space, and I have the enjoyment of their voices. They are right on time," he finished with smug satisfaction, glancing at the carved clock that hung above the fireplace.

"On time for what?" Jeanne asked, but he had already hurried to the door and disappeared into the outdoor courtyard in an icy gust of wind.

# 69.

Wolfe hit the cobblestones with a grunt and was up almost immediately, moving quickly down rue de Masant. The wind was stronger now: it stirred the icy puddles to movement and swept fragments of street debris before it; it tugged and pulled at his coat, howled past his ears, and left his fingers and cheeks numb with cold. The clouds surged overhead in a leaden sky, partially obscured by the dark lodging houses that rose four or five stories on either side of the street. A deep gloom brooded in the overhanging hollows of balconied rooms and attics that, for lack of vertical space, careered out over the street and cast the cobblestones below into a perpetual twilight. A store-owner in a flaccid blue jacket was sponging warm water across his windows in an attempt to clear them of frost. But other than this ambitious proprietor, the streets were empty and quiet.

Glancing back towards rue des Mauvais Garçons, Wolfe tried to orient himself in the dim light of early dawn. What was it Jeanne had told him? Turn on to rue du Temple and then continue south to the Hotel de Martin. The manager, a Philippe Druillet, would arrange for his transportation to Bourges.

Wolfe turned left on rue du Temple, hugging the shuttered storefronts as he ran. The distant echo of pounding feet and the splash of quick movement through puddles alerted Wolfe to his pursuer. Darting into rue Berger, Wolfe found himself confronted by the towering solidity of the eastern walls of the Church of Saint-Eustache. A wrought-iron gate to his right led to the cemetery of Les Innocents, where even now laborers were toiling in the early morning light. An ancient wagon, in a state of near collapse, groaned under a gruesome burden. A black cloth had been flung across the back, but the grisly remains of several partially decomposed bodies could be seen emerging at the rear.

Without forethought, Wolfe raced through the gate, his mind a whirl of options, strategies, and possible routes. How many were there? Were they waiting for him? Positioned between Saint-Eustache and the Hotel de Martin? First and foremost, elude his tail.

Wolfe emerged within the cemetery compound, a large rectangular space enclosed by a narrow bricked building that edged the property. The front façade of this edifice was decorated with pointed arches, between which, in shadowy recesses, Wolfe could see ghoulish statuary of skeletal figures. But it was the cavity above the archways that stopped him in mid-stride; despite his own urgency, he gaped in horrified astonishment. Between vertical supports that connected the archways to the roof structure, and beneath the overhang of the shingled gabled roof were…bones. Scores and scores of mounded bones that filled the space like a macabre sort of building material. Long bones and short bones, their rounded joints gleaming whitely in the pale morning light. Some were neatly stacked, but most spilled in a haphazard fashion to the ground below. To his left, the roof had completely disintegrated, and he could see a tall pyramid of skulls that echoed precisely the shape of the absent roof.

My God, Wolfe thought, my God…and for a moment, he was paralyzed by the sheer number of dead: hundreds of thousands in bones, and untold more frozen and contorted in the ground.

In the center of the cemetery, ten or so laborers were engaged in the grisly work of transferring bodies to the cart Wolfe had seen outside. They were an ill-assorted bunch, united only by their extreme poverty. The bedraggled remnants of garments hung from bony shoulders, and the dark orbits of sunken eyes were not so dissimilar from those stacked within the roofs around them. They paused in their work to gape at the man who had arrived on the scene with such alacrity; usually Parisians moved rapidly in the opposite direction, if not from these poor then certainly from the putrid stench of the charnel house at Cimetière des Innocents.

"Fifty francs for each of you, if you'll hide me from the gendarmes!" Wolfe roared.

Needing no further encouragement, the men urged him into a crater they had been excavating and proceeded to cluster about him, resuming their work with an air of dazed bemusement. Crouching in the dank and putrid earth, Wolfe could imagine their mystification. Doubtless, from their dark and grimy habitations beneath the bridges, they had borne witness to the unbridled excesses of the new aristocrats: the extremities of fashion, the mania for dancing that had swept Paris after the Directory, the passion for haute cuisine—all of which must seem to be social proclivities of a race other than their own. The vast majority of Parisians were simply trying to survive. And these gravediggers represented the poorest of the lot. Few other than the truly desperate would undertake such a task with all the attendant horrors of infection, contagion, and poisonous miasmas that were believed to hover over the cemetery like a noxious cloud. Wolfe fervently hoped that these fears—ones he did not care to ponder too deeply himself—would serve to deter his shadow, or at least keep his search to a cursory one.

"Hé vous, là!" A short swarthy man swaddled in a greasy black overcoat hurried over, skirting fallen gravestones and crumbled masonry. He stopped six feet or so from the ditch where Wolfe was bent over fighting the bile that rose in the back of his throat. The pit had been hacked out of the frozen ground, and the walls and the floor of this trench were festooned with frozen body parts in various states of decomposition. The laborers pressed around him so densely that Wolfe felt a sudden claustrophobic panic, an inability to breath anything but the fetid stench of flesh-rot and decay that exhaled like a yawn from some monstrous mouth of the damned. "Did you see someone just run by here?" the man barked impatiently, his tone brusquely official but muffled, as if he spoke through a cloth pressed over his mouth. The workers stared dumbly; several shook their heads in a state of confused befuddlement. "Merde! Idiots!" And then he was gone, disappearing over the rocks and rubble with a panting curse.

Wolfe, having emptied his pockets to pay the gravediggers who accepted their reward with a solemn dignity, left by way of rue de la Ferronnerie.

The sun was higher in the sky now, and the streets were busier, which Wolfe was grateful for. He would be a more difficult target to locate. The streets rang with early calls of merchants and peddlers, the shouted warnings of carters and water-carriers, and the halting songs of street musicians warming up their lungs and fingers. The mingled aromas of baking bread and fragrant stews combined with the less pleasant tang of moldering fish bones and rotted vegetables that stewed and fermented in slowly thawing puddles. Women appeared in doorways, ragged children scampered the streets, and men busied themselves or loitered outside cafés. Ribald gossip, shared laughter, whispered threats. Paris was awake.

"Herrings, fresh last night!" a merchant bawled. Cursing under his breath, Wolfe leapt to one side, dodging a wagon weighed down with fish and oysters that careered through the street, the two wretched horses being urged on by a fishmonger anxious to get his wares to market before they spoiled.

Back on rue du Temple, Wolfe headed south. He didn't see anyone following him, at least no one who appeared particularly interested in his person or his destination. But who knew how many agents Fouché had on the street or where they would be waiting? For he knew now, the hunched man in black was Fouché. The gravediggers had known him—known of him anyway—which was doubtless why they had promptly escorted him to the gate and barred it against him after they had received their payment. Fouché was not one to be crossed.

Less than five minutes later, Wolfe found himself at the Hotel de Martin, a slightly disreputable establishment that rose pompously from the banks of the Seine. It overlooked the Place de Grève, where executions had been carried out since the fourteenth century and had lately served as the home of Madame la Guillotine during the recent Revolution. Despite the notoriety of its location, indeed perhaps because of it, the hotel was immensely popular. It offered cheap rooms, providing one was prepared to disregard the mold and the occasional weather that stained the ceilings and seeped down the walls.

Inside, Wolfe was directed to the manager's office, where Philippe Druillet was expecting him.

"I'm sorry…" were Druillet's first words upon Wolfe opening his door. "They were watching the hotel."

The hotel manager, a somber-looking gentleman in blue, was flanked by two gendarmes, a pistol at his back. Wolfe instinctively backed up but was brought up short by a gruff voice to his rear:

"Monsieur Trant, so nice of you to visit."

# 70.

The gendarmes rushed into Monsieur Rumigny's small house expecting to apprehend the infamous Primrose; perhaps they would find her tense and narrow-eyed over the barrel of a pistol, or perhaps, contrary to popular mythology, she would be cowering behind the sofa, tremulous and afraid. Instead, the four policemen who entered through the front door were greeted by a most unexpected sight.

Four women were lined up in a neat row, seated on high stools facing an empty hearth. They were dressed identically in wide-hooped gowns, their voluminous skirts bunched in a gorgeous profusion of green and gold taffeta and lace, the low-necklines embroidered in gold thread, a cascade of green lace spilling from the sleeve at each elbow. Their faces beneath elaborately powdered wigs were obscured by thick white stage paint, their cheeks circles of rouge, their lips painted over into identical cupid bows, their eyes heavy and dark with blue eye-shadow and rimmed with thick black kohl.

And—they were singing.

"A l'ombre de ces bois épais, dans une tranquille indolence…"

Their voices soared, rose in sweet melody, and filled the small room with a glorious harmony of sound. They turned in unison at the commotion, suddenly silent, mouths red Os of surprise.

Monsieur Rumigny paused in his attentions to the wig of one, turning irritably toward the gendarmes who now milled uncertainly by the door. "Yes? Yes? What do you want?" he barked, already turning his attention back to the blue-powdered hair before him, his fingers working fluidly and swiftly, creating a cascade of waves that supported a billowing tall ship that sat astride the woman's brow.

"We are looking for a woman—"

"One in particular, or would any of these suit?" Rumigny asked, with sudden gleeful good humor.

"Monsieur Rumigny!" A small woman in a magnificently towering red wig swatted his arm playfully. "You are too much!"

"Out of my way!" a voice bellowed. The owner, a slight man, emerged from the crowd of gendarmes that quickly parted to allow him access. His pale blue eyes narrowed in suspicion as he took in the four women, then rapidly scanned the room seeking places of concealment, noting exits and entrances. To his satisfaction, he saw the dark uniforms of the gendarmes bustling in the courtyard. They had surrounded the house and moved in upon his signal. The woman was here, he was certain of it, and Chavert was proud to have the responsibility of apprehending her personally. Fouché would claim credit, of course, but Chavert would have the infinite pleasure of the arrest.

He had been hesitant about moving in—under usual circumstances he would never dream of violating his superior's explicit instructions—but there was that woman. A heavy-set figure had fled from the rear of the house, brushing past one of his men to disappear into the shadows of the still-dark street. The gendarme had protested that the woman was a housekeeper on the premises, that he knew her family, that her papers had been signed by Monsieur Berthier himself . Perhaps so, but her abrupt departure made Chavert nervous. He could apprehend Primrose within and remain there until Fouché returned, the chief inspector reasoned. He felt an overwhelming need to assure himself that he had not just inadvertently allowed her to escape.

"We are looking for a fugitive, monsieur. We are here on very important police business," Chavert declared pompously, sharply gesturing to his men to search the house. Monsieur Rumigny heaved a deep sigh of what might have been exasperation, and, turning his back to Chavert, continued his ministrations. "Monsieur!" Chavert marched forward and yanked Rumigny's arm, twisting him around until his face was inches from his own. "We have reason to believe you are harboring Primrose," he spoke sharply, the mustache twitching and quivering on his upper lip, his pale round eyes boring into Rumigny's. The diminutive hairdresser stood, impassive. "If this is true, monsieur," Chavert hissed, "God help you, because the empire will not!"

"Monsieur—" Rumigny began.

"Chief Inspector Chavert!" Chavert interrupted with growing annoyance.

"Chief Inspector Chavert," Rumigny replied soothingly, ducking his head in a subservient manner. "I can assure you, we have every intention of assisting you. It is just that the emperor is expecting us at the Tuileries within the hour, and I am sure you are aware of his penchant for military precision in all things. I would hate to be the one to have to tell him we were delayed." Rumigny gripped Chavert by the arm in a friendly fashion. "The carriage is arriving any minute, and these girls are the opening chorus! Already, I am late! Oh, I am most terribly sorry!" Chavert glanced down to find a thick layer of beef lard smeared on the sleeve of his pristinely immaculate uniform. Rumigny's ineffectual attempts to wipe the grease with his cuff served only to enrage Chavert further.

"Get away from me!" he barked shrilly, his pale face suffused with a dull red. The guards were beginning to congregate in the sitting room now, having apparently searched the few rooms in the house and found nobody skulking in the cellar or hiding beneath the kitchen table. Leaning on their long muskets, they openly ogled the girls, grinning foolishly and elbowing each other for a glimpse of dainty ankle or shadowed cleavage. Primrose wasn't to be found, but there were other unexpected delights from this particular foray. The women had watched the performance between Rumigny and Chavert in open-mouthed astonishment but now, aware that they were the objects of interest, began their performance an hour early.

The red-wigged woman covered her mouth, stifling a laugh. She leaned over and whispered in the ear of the other seated to her left who also erupted into giggles. A taller woman, rendered diminutive only by the size of her monstrous green wig, fluttered her long lashes and smiled coyly at a young gendarme who blushed pink with delight. A heavy rapping sounded at the door, and Chavert, feeling as if he were rapidly losing control of the situation, moved to answer it.

"Carriage," a man wrapped in black pronounced in a bored tone.

"The cab is here, girls!" Rumigny called with restless anxiety. "Quick, let me inspect you before you go!" The women rose to their feet in a cacophony of giggles and shrill exclamations.

"I've never been in the Tuileries before," Blue-wig exclaimed, eyes dreamy under white stage makeup.

"Of course you haven't, Louise, you goose!"

"Didn't you know she was a confidant of Joséphine?" Green replied tartly.

"I have heard that the emperor's schlong is as long as he is tall," Red confided, eyes wide and dramatic in their heavy blue powder, eyebrows raised in conspiratorial mischief.

"Grizella, you are such a child." Green rolled her eyes, rouged mouth pursed in irritation.

"Better than being a bore, Matildé." Grizella stuck out her tongue, pink against her whitened cheeks. They appeared to have forgotten the presence of the soldiers in their excitement at the upcoming performance. Rumigny hovered above each in turn, righting a sleeve that had come askew, carefully greasing down a disobedient strand of hair, and removing a smear of white makeup from a dress with the sleeve of his coat.

"There!" he pronounced in satisfaction. "I believe you are ready!" Rumigny's face was a wrinkled vision of pride, his thick lips stretched in a toothy grin, his eyes suspiciously bright. "Remember, girls, be careful getting into the carriage, and don't forget to touch up after the second act. Matildé has the spare powder! Now, hurry, hurry!" Rumigny ushered them toward the door, hopping in excited agitation.

"They cannot leave," Chavert interjected suddenly, moving toward the door to stop the departing flurry of skirts and wigs. "They are suspects!"

"Suspects, Chief Inspector Chavert?" Rumigny repeated, wiping his flustered face with the edge of a now-grimy sleeve. "No, you don't understand. These girls are the chorus in *Echo et Narcisse*. The opera begins in less than an hour, Chief Inspector. I have had very strict instructions to have them at the Tuileries by ten. I understand it is an important performance." He moved closer to Chavert, murmuring in a conspiratorial manner, "Did you know Alexander I is attending? Yes, indeed, the czar of Russia!" Rumigny allowed himself a half-stifled giggle. "Forgive my overflowing enthusiasm, Chief Inspector, but it has been many years since I have had the privilege of preparing for such an illustrious audience, and I would shudder to disrupt such important proceedings by being late."

Chavert hesitated. The self-assurance he had felt only ten minutes before had evaporated into doubtful confusion. Napoleon's temper was legendary. To anger the emperor was unthinkable, but if one of these girls was in fact Primrose and he allowed her to slip through his grasp...? In truth, he feared Fouché's temper more than the emperor's.

One he had only heard about, but the other he had experienced first-hand and did not care to repeat. He shoved Rumigny aside, eying each girl with narrowed suspicion.

"You are opera singers?" he demanded. "Then sing! One at a time. First, you." He pointed at red-wig, who opened her mouth into a perfect red O and warbled her way through a series of beautifully pitched scales. The next began a saucy version of the opening score, smiling coquettishly at the gendarmes who milled behind Chavert. The third began where the second had left off: "Goute en paix le frais et le silence!" Her voice swelled with sweet strength, filling the small room in a cascade of sound. The last, Matildé, had a powerfully rich voice that emerged from her diaphragm with shuddering intensity. She sang with her eyes closed, as if in a trance, hands clasped at her breast.

"Enough," Chavert interjected furiously. "The girls can go…but you," he gestured in Rumigny's direction, "stay."

The girls hurried out in a swish of skirts and a flurry of excited conversation. "I don't know why she gets all the mezzo-soprano roles. It is so unfair! We contraltos are only allowed to play witches, bitches, or britches."

"Elbert!"

"It's true!"

Matildé cast an anxious glance back over her shoulder at Rumigny who gave her a quick grin.

# 71.

"You *idiot!*" Fouché hissed. He raised his hand and delivered a stinging slap to one side of Chavert's face with his grimy palm, leaving a crimson handprint on his pale cheek. "Napoleon *hates* the opera!"

Chavert chewed on the corner of his lip and said nothing, shoulders hunched, hat tucked beneath one arm, yellow hair slick against his narrow skull. He had learned the hard way that the best method for surviving Fouché's onslaughts was to hunker down and endure them in silence, much as one would brace oneself against a coming storm when caught in the open.

"How *could* you have been so stupid?" Fouché raged, stalking across the floor of his office. A flurry of papers, sent into motion by the violence of his gestures as well as the brisk winter wind that howled through the window, fluttered to the floor and were trampled underfoot by Fouché's muddy boots. "Do you know what this means?" he growled between clenched teeth. Chavert shook his head, a quick, furtive movement, eyes fixed on the scarred floorboards. "It *means* that you had better find Primrose, and quickly, or I will have you assigned to sewer duty for the rest of your miserable existence. Do you understand?" Chavert nodded. "Now get out of my sight!" Fouché spat, his mouth curling in distaste. Chavert donned his hat, the angle slightly less jaunty than previously, and left the office, the door closing softly behind him.

At least they had Wolfe in custody, Fouché thought, as he propped his feet up on the desk, his dark brows drawing together like sullen storm-clouds rolling over the ridges of his forehead. Mon dieu, how could he hope to accomplish anything when he was staffed with such incompetents? Chavert had let Primrose slip right through his fingers!

He had Wolfe, he reminded himself again. And certainly Wolfe knew where Primrose could be found. It was just a matter of making him talk, and he had just provided Chavert with an incentive for successfully retrieving such information. Then, of course, there was the matter of the duke: the prince of the blood who was seeking to reclaim the French throne. Fouché was quite certain of his identity now, but one small detail niggled at the back of his mind...

He had passed on the edited report of the carriage-bombing incident, detailing some aspects of the monarchist conspiracy to restore the Bourbons. Napoleon had skimmed through it in a superficial manner before tossing it to one side and dismissing the commissioner with an impatient flick of his wrist.

*Why* had Napoleon not pressed him for specifics, as was his custom?

*Why* was he so easily satisfied with the scanty platitudes that, more often than not, sent him into a rage? Particularly, when it was his own life that was at risk?

Fouché didn't like it. He felt instinctively that the emperor had acquired another, more primary, source of information: one that threatened his own supremacy...but *who*?

Under the circumstances, Fouché decided to remain silent about the identity of the duke. The time to divulge it would come, and when it did, when it best suited his own advantage, then he would reveal it. It always paid to have a scheme or two in reserve, he reflected with no small satisfaction.

# 72.

"So you are Wolfe Trant," Fouché remarked casually. He removed the tarnished glass cover to the gas-lamp and leaned forward, lighting his cigar in the naked flame. He sucked deeply, the tobacco igniting in a smoldering nest of yellowed wrappings. Fouché allowed the pungent smoke to fill his lungs before tilting his head back and exhaling a long plume toward the ceiling.

Wolfe said nothing. He tried to stop his teeth from chattering. He had been stripped naked and seated on a stool, arms bound tightly behind his back, ankles secured to two legs of the chair.

"An Irishman in the pay of the English? A most interesting arrangement. Tell me, Monsieur Trant, what is it that Pitt is giving you in exchange for betraying your country?" Wolfe said nothing. "What is it the Irish are fighting for these days? Independence? Religious freedom?" Fouché pulled a chair up close.

"What do ye want?" Wolfe asked stonily.

"Only what you want, monsieur. Peace for my country. But, from you, monsieur, I want to know the whereabouts of Primrose. Or is it Jeanne Recamier?"

"I don't know anyone of that name."

Fouché regarded him steadily from beneath shaggy brows. "I think you are an intelligent man, monsieur. You realize, I think, that I will obtain the information I want. But time is of the essence, so very strong persuasive methods must be applied. I am not a barbaric man, monsieur. I do not relish torture, regardless of what others might say. But I am fully prepared to do whatever is necessary to apprehend this conspirateur. Perhaps you will spare us both the ugly necessity of making you bleed?"

"I think we both know I won't be talking, so why don't we just get it over with, then?" Wolfe snarled, lip curling in distaste, eyes slits of cold fury, muscles bunching beneath his pale, scarred skin as he strained in futile effort against his constraints.

"Ah, shame." Fouché nodded toward a slight figure who loitered at the far end of the room. "Chavert."

Chavert moved forward into the pool of light that surrounded the prisoner. "Remember, Chavert," Fouché continued in low undertones, "you asked for this opportunity to rectify your monumental stupidity in allowing Primrose to escape. If you are caught torturing this man, I will wash my hands of you. I will claim I knew nothing of what went on here and, of course, will denounce you with all the suitable horror of one who is not only pledged to uphold the law but who is the law."

"I understand," Chavert replied, his eyes fixed almost greedily on Wolfe. "I will get the information from him, Commissioner. We will have Primrose before the day is out."

"See that we do," Fouché warned, holding Chavert's gaze for a moment before turning to leave, the door slamming heavily behind him.

"Do you remember me?" Chavert asked Wolfe almost eagerly, pulling a second chair toward the prisoner. He sat close, his knees almost touching Wolfe's bare ones, his pale blue eyes seeking Wolfe's darker ones.

"Can't say that I do," Wolfe replied steadily. "Your face is not a memorable one." Chavert's lips thinned in anger before he forced a laugh, a harsh, echoing sound that reverberated off the stone walls that enclosed them.

"Do you see that?" Chavert gestured toward a thick hook sunk into the ceiling above their heads. Wolfe realized that the rope that bound his wrists behind his back extended up through the hook and pooled on the floor beside a pulley system on the far side of the room "That is the infamous estrapade. It has not been employed in the prison system for over twenty years, but I thought we might reacquaint ourselves with its use."

He crossed to the thick wooden door and opened it, speaking softly to someone beyond. When Chavert turned back toward Wolfe, another man, in a coarse robe of dark blue canvas, had materialized behind him. He was barefoot, his face cast into shadow by the wide brim of his hood, a heavy canvas bag over one shoulder.

"This is Gargeud. He is a member of the Pénitents Bleus, and he knows more about the estrapade than any man alive." Chavert leaned toward Wolfe's ear, whispering with barely concealed smugness, "And do not try to plead with him for your life. He has taken a vow of silence."

"I wouldn't give you the satisfaction," Wolfe growled.

Gargeud moved silently around the room, gliding on pale feet gnarled and roughened by constant exposure to the elements. He pulled the rope through the pulley until Wolfe, with a grunt of discomfort, found his arms tautly outstretched behind his back. Gargeud then knelt at the foot of Wolfe's chair, removing heavy weights from the canvas bag he carried. Beneath the shadows of his hood, Gargeud's face was pale and sunken, the cheekbones and nose strongly prominent, his dark eyes red-rimmed as if from perpetual tears. His thin mouth formed a moue of discontent, suggesting the world was a constant source of disappointment to him. Gargeud untied Wolfe's ankles from the chair legs.

When he stood, Wolfe could see the left side of his robe was embroidered with the disturbing image of the penitent Saint Jerome, his body wasted by fasts, his breast torn by blows, his face drowned in tears.

"We are ready," Chavert whispered, a smile stretching across his mouth, his pale eyes shining. He moved closer to Wolfe. "I have waited a long time for this moment."

Wolfe struck. With his legs freed, he twisted in his chair and rapidly, before the chief inspector could react, landed a powerful kick smashing into Chavert's kneecap with his heel.

Chavert sank to the floor, crying out in pained surprise. Gargeud stood silent witness, making no move to assist Chavert who was moaning on the floor, clutching his knee as if he could hold bones and muscles together. When he looked up, his pale face contorted by pain, his washed-out eyes narrowed in fury, he spoke through gritted teeth: "You will regret that."

He gestured impatiently to Gargeud, who moved toward the pulley on the wall, his dark-robed figure melting into the shadows. Only his pale, gaunt face was visible as he turned the wheel of the pulley, the wooden teeth grinding into place with an audible crack. The rope tightened, and Wolfe felt his arms extend further behind his back. Chavert rose unsteadily to his feet and kicked the stool out from under Wolfe who, suddenly bereft of support, felt the full weight of his body applying pressure on his hyper-extended arms. With a grunt of pain, he stumbled to his feet.

Chavert nodded toward Gargeud, who advanced the pulley wheel another notch, the rope inching through the iron hook on the ceiling. Wolfe's arms were stretched further back, raising his body until his entire weight rested on the front pads of his feet. He could feel the searing pain travel from the rope cutting into his wrists to the muscles of his arms, quivering and tight under the strain, to explode with agonizing intensity in his shoulder joints. Wolfe tasted blood and realized he had bitten his own lip.

"The Pénitents Bleus believe that bodily suffering is a gift from God," Chavert spoke as he hobbled painfully across the room, looking up at Wolfe's face as he hung suspended just off the ground. "They believe that he punishes our bodies in this world in order to preserve our souls from eternal punishment."

"I know where your soul is going, and it sure as hell isn't to God," Wolfe bit out before the pulley again ground into action, and he was slowly, agonizingly, pulled off the floor. He sagged forward, his mind blinded by the searing heat of pain that enveloped his upper torso.

Chavert, moving closer, hissed, "Tell me what I want to know, and your suffering will be over. Where is Primrose?"

"Imigh sa diabhal. Fuck you!" Wolfe attempted to strike out with his leg, bellowing in pain as the momentum wrenched his body around, his fingers clenching convulsively around the rope above.

"It will only get worse, Monsieur Trant. I can promise you that," Chavert assured him triumphantly.

Gargeud knotted the rope into place at the wall and glided across the floor. Bending over, he attached one of the weights to Wolfe's feet, a thick iron lock snapping into place around each ankle.

A deep roar of pain erupted from Wolfe's throat as he felt his shoulder joints being wrenched from his sockets.

# 73.

"What the *hell* is this?" The door swung open to reveal a man clad in the regimentals of Napoleon's elite guard. He was accompanied by a second in the flowing, scarlet gown of an officer of the court, the braid specifying his rank as president à mortier. Wolfe hung from the ceiling, torso swinging slightly, dark head limp against his chest. "Cut him down!"

Gargeud obediently reversed the wheel, feeding the rope out until Wolfe hit the ground, legs crumpling beneath him. Chavert, frozen into pained immobility, was silent, his immaculate figure standing to rigid attention, his eyes fixed on the far wall as if there were something in the rough-hewn stones he found deeply engrossing. The president moved forward into the room, glanced down at Wolfe's naked form, then pinioned Chavert with an icy gaze, his lip curling in disgust. He was tall and elegant in appearance. His face, of swarthy complexion beneath a dark head of hair, was sharply defined by broad cheekbones and a pronounced chin. Deep-set eyes, a dark shade of gray, fixed Chavert in a cold glare.

"Torture may have been a legal recourse in the ancien régime, but the emperor has instituted more civilized forms of judicial punishment." He gestured sharply to his accompanying guard, who helped Wolfe to his feet. The prisoner was conscious, but barely, and his arms hung slightly hunched and extended out from his body in an unnatural manner. "What I would like to know, Chief Inspector Chavert," the president began, his voice harshly accusatory as he circled Chavert's rigidly unmoving figure, "is how this man came to be here? I have no documentation describing his incarceration, let alone the permission to conduct this manner of interrogation." He glanced scornfully at the weights and the thick ropes that were strewn across the floor. "You have been a privileged member of the police department for some years now, I understand. I should not have to explain formal procedure to you."

The president, in a deliberately derisive manner, continued, numbering each step of the legislative process out on long manicured fingers:

"The procureur should have formally notified the municipal judges of the crime. The accused should have been questioned by the capitoulat who would then have conducted interviews, issued witness subpoenas, and conducted a search of this man's lodgings and any other pertinent crime scenes. The results of this investigation should have been reviewed by the judges who would then recommend sentencing and pass the case on to the parlement for final deliberations." The president moved closer to Chavert, his undertone laced with steel and reinforced by the glacial ice in his eyes. "It is people like you, Chief Inspector, who make a mockery of our system of justice and undermine what I spend my life working for. It is for *you* that I would reserve the harshest of judgments."

He was young to have achieved such an illustrious position. The president à mortier supervised the judges within the various criminal courts that had survived the abolition of the parliaments during the Revolution. Like the police departments, the court system was in a state of confusion. On paper, the transformation could not have been more abrupt or sweeping: the Parlements had simply been replaced by the legislative fiat of the Constituent Assembly. But in practice, the last ten years had seen a massive expansion of elected officials that now staffed a variety of district and departmental courts, tribunals, and councils. Legislation was, generally, governed by coutume de Paris, literally the customs of Paris, that did not encompass a single set of laws but instead depended on local interpretation with the frequent employment of exemptions and special privileges. Which meant that, within the court system, the president à mortier enjoyed a relative immunity and power equivalent to that of Fouché. A dangerous foe.

And despite the president's professed disdain for torture, Chavert was well aware that this man could arrange any manner of punishment. A wide variety of torturing techniques had survived the philosophes' demands for abolition at the beginning of the Revolutionary period, as indeed the presence of Gargeud stood mute witness. Torture had been outlawed, but that is not to say it could not still be utilized...and looking at the sternly unyielding face of the president, the most chilling of possibilities flashed through Chavert's mind: the wheel, the rack, thumbscrews, branding, cutting off his nose and his ears. Or perhaps, the president would just toss him in a dark prison cell and throw away the key. Chavert, shuddering with fear and pain, stammered pleadingly: "Monsieur President...I was only following orders. I had no choice!"

For all his bluff and bluster, Chavert was not a brave man—which

was why he had become an officer of the law in the first place. It provided the very protection he yearned for after barely surviving the political instability of the Directorate. As a young man, he had assiduously
devoted himself to the policing arm of the Committee of Public Safety,
reporting to Robespierre himself. When his mentor was sent to the
guillotine, Chavert spent a week on the run—a time that haunted him
every time he closed his eyes. He had, since, worked tirelessly to present
the perfect façade, to become the ideal candidate for promotion—although not to rise too far. As ambitious as he was, he had come to
the conclusion that he never wanted to be the man on the top, just far
enough down so that he could claim ignorance, deflect responsibility,
hide under the skirts of procedural routine.

His doctored resume read like Fouché's carefully scripted fiction,
and perhaps accounted for why the commissioner had selected him as
chief inspector: he had taken up arms on all the correct occasions and
never missed guard duty, his two sons were serving the empire in the
army, his daughter was married to a defenseurs de la patrie and busily
engaged in making uniforms and bandages in Toulon—none of which
could be easily verified. Chavert paid his taxes punctually, had taken in
an aged patriotic pauper, denounced three royalists and five fanatiques,
had reported the hiding place of an émigré, and secured the arrest of a
counter- revolutionary living in a wardrobe.

Yes, he had succeeded in creating a political persona as pure as the
driven snow. It had survived inspection and accounted, Chavert was
certain, for his relatively meteoric rise through the lower echelons of
the gendarmerie. Until Fouché, that is. Joseph Fouché immediately
comprehended the nature of his deception. How he had surmised this,
Chavert had no idea. But instead of denouncing him, Fouché had raised
one dark brow and muttered sardonically: "Chavert, you are my man."
While he felt a certain loyalty to his sinister superior, Chavert was more
concerned with his own survival—political and otherwise. So, when the
president demanded the source of these orders, Chavert gave him up
without a second thought.

"Fouché...Police Commissioner Fouché!" Chavert cried, already
imagining himself being wrenched up to the ceiling in the hooks and
pulleys that coiled like fat snakes on the floor.

"Yes, I am aware," the president began sternly, his lip curled in distaste, "that you take orders from Fouché. This prison, and the customary laws of Paris, however, do not."

# 74.

TEMPLE PRISON. PARIS, FRANCE
*December 8, 1803*

Wolfe first became aware of the excruciating pain in his shoulders, then of the two who supported him to either side, both breathing heavily under his bulky weight. Jeanne, barely recognizable under a neatly trimmed mustache and goatee, nodded at him, a small smile curving her lips. A long passageway loomed ahead, the walls on either side divided by large stout doors identical to the one that had opened into Wolfe's torture chamber. Every twenty feet or so a light flickered within the sooty confines of a wall lantern. They were still in the lower levels of the Temple Prison. And then the walls themselves whirled, darkened in his peripheral vision, and finally disappeared altogether. His head lolled forward on his chest.

"Merde," Jeanne cursed, stumbling under his suddenly sagging weight.

"Through here, *quickly!*" Ducking back into the darkened alcove of a door-frame, they heard the metallic echo of nailed boots on stone. "Guards conducting their rounds," Casimir de Montrond whispered to Jeanne. "Two per floor, they will be back this way in approximately ten minutes. Ready to go?"

Jeanne gritted her teeth, yanked Wolfe's senseless arm more firmly around her neck, and nodded grimly in Montrond's direction. "Let's get out of here," she muttered. The Temple unnerved her. She had heard stories of the Devil's Pit—a yawning hole, the walls slick with damp and mold, impossible to climb, although apparently a countless number had tried and left their gouged scratches in the stone. A place where one was tossed and left to die, alone and abandoned with only the red-gleaming eyes of the rats for company—rats that would subsequently feast on one's corpse. These were the narratives of childhood, stories related with relish by the cook-master's son to scare her no doubt. But the horrifying image had remained, and rumor circulated after the storming of the Bastille of just such an abyss.

Jeanne shuddered and forced a faster pace, her back and shoulders aching with the effort of hauling Wolfe's inert body alongside. A small circular turret defined the corner ahead, with a steep stairwell disappearing upwards into the gloom. Branching to the right, the stone hallway appeared in receding pools of gaslight, each illuminating gray stonework and a prison door opposite.

"Mon dieu! How are we going to get him up the stairs?" Jeanne gasped, knees buckling under Wolfe's weight. Montrond hesitated, and in that moment, the relentlessly shrill clanging of the bell-tower sounded the alarm. Shouts and running feet could be heard on the floor above.

"Come on!" Montrond exclaimed. "This way!" Together, they stumbled down the right-hand passageway through each circle of gaslight until they heard the guards in the stairwell behind them. Pressing themselves back into the wall, in an interval where the light on each side grew dim, they waited, their breath harsh and quick in the stale prison air. The guards disappeared in a clatter of boots down the passageway toward Wolfe's cell. They were safe. For the moment.

"We can't get past the sentries now…even *with* the letter. If they hesitate, if they want verification…" Montrond panted, straining to hold Wolfe's limp body against the wall and out of the light.

"With the alarm raised, they'll undoubtedly want verification. We need to find another way out…" Jeanne managed. Her back felt like it was splintering apart under the strain. How much did this bloody man weigh?

"Our strategy was flung together in haste. What if one of them knows the real president à mortier by sight?" Montrond muttered. He paused a moment, gathering both his breath and his thoughts. "If we get up there and our exit visa is refused or delayed for whatever reason, we are all dead."

"Okay then," Jeanne impatiently agreed. "Any suggestions?"

"There may be." Montrond glanced down the stone hallway that disappeared into gray gloom to his right. "This prison was built by the Templars in the twelfth century and used as a residence for the Master of the Order after the fall of Acre."

"With all due respect, monsieur, this is hardly the time for a history lesson," Jeanne gasped. "I am assuming Chavert raised the alarm. When they find Wolfe's cell empty—"

"But the Templars, you see, were conservative in their architecture.

They utilized very similar floor-plans, employed the same secretive devices for moving treasure and escaping from enemies."

"*What* are you talking about?"

"A way out!" Montrond turned to her, and over Wolfe's drooping head, she saw his eyes gleam with hope.

"Lead the way, monsieur!" Jeanne urged him.

"Not far," he panted. They stumbled down the hallway, Wolfe seemingly heavier with each step they took, until Jeanne stumbled against the wall, lost her balance and fell. Wolfe crumpled beside her with a low, painful moan. "We are going to have to rouse him somehow; he has to walk...Monsieur Trant!" Montrond gently shook his chest. "Monsieur Trant!"

"Allow me." Jeanne slapped Wolfe hard across each cheek. "Get up, you bloody Irishman!" Wolfe's eyelids flickered.

"Who's there?" came the cry. Heart in her mouth, Jeanne turned to see a solitary guard moving cautiously down their hallway, pistol held high in front of him. He couldn't see them well, she realized, but he had been alerted by their efforts to get Wolfe on his feet.

"Stand on your own feet, *damn you!*" she cried, hauling Wolfe by his injured arms. With a heart-rending cry of pain, Wolfe's eyes opened as he struggled away from her. "Get up and move or we all *die!*" Jeanne hissed, her face close to his. Somehow he managed it, and the three staggered down the passageway, the sentry in their wake.

"Stop, or I will shoot!" the guard cried. A single shot rang out; the bullet hit the wall just to the right of Jeanne's head, the sharp staccato echoing through the prison.

"Where the hell are we going?" Wolfe rasped.

"Just up here...there's a door...on our left." Montrond eased out from under Wolfe's arm, gently pushed open the door and glanced inside, then with a quick motion urged the other two to follow.

It was a surprisingly spacious room with a barrel-vaulted ceiling that descended, in the form of massive support buttresses, to the floor on either side. The stone, like that of the passageways, was hundreds of years old, the masonry crumbling with damp and age. A sturdy table dominated the space, a deck of playing cards scattered across its surface. The remnants of a still-smoldering cigarito, and three skewed wooden chairs, one upturned, illustrated the haste with which their recent occupants had departed. A vast hearth occupied the far wall but now served as a storage space for a motley assortment of muskets, many of which appeared older than the stonework that housed them. An ornately carved lintel above the fireplace and the fading remnants of fresco painting on the ceiling proclaimed the building's more illustrious past.

Jeanne swiftly closed the door behind them, sliding the wooden bar into place. "Bought us some time. I hope you have a plan, Monsieur de Montrond, because now we are cornered."

"This was the kitchen!" Montrond exclaimed, releasing Wolfe's arm.

"Yes? Well, find me some muskets and ammunition that work, and I will be impressed," Jeanne snapped, turning to face him.

Undeterred by her tension, Montrond, running his hands over the carved masonry above the fireplace, continued, "The Templars, as you know, amassed great wealth with their interest in trade and letters of credit. Many were envious, and the Templars were attacked and persecuted for years before Guillaume de Nogaret led the arrests of all the High Dignitaries in 1307. They always built in strategic exits, secret passages that would enable them to escape. It was said that as the Great Master confessed to heresy while under torture, half his group fled through underground passages and continue the Templar legacy today, but in secret—"

"And this helps us *how*, precisely?" Wolfe rasped, swaying on his feet, arms held gingerly away from his body, his shoulders alarmingly swollen.

"Because it was *here* that the secret passage was located." Montrond gestured toward the fireplace.

"In the fireplace? That doesn't make any sense," Jeanne muttered, examining the blackened stonework.

"It concealed a passageway that often served two functions. It allowed the Templars to escape should that be required and a staircase that enabled the servants to deliver food to the Great Master and his entourage on the upper stories without having to inconvenience them by trailing up and down the main stairwells."

"All very interesting, to be sure, but where is it and how do we open it?" Wolfe growled. Montrond did not answer but ran his fingers over the intricately carved stone lintel that descended in a lip over the blackened hearthstones. A commotion of raised voices at the door announced the arrival of the Temple guards. The door shivered in its hinges as some solid object struck heavily from the other side. Another tremendous thud, and the wood around the lock began to splinter.

"We don't have much time!" Jeanne panted as she maneuvered the heavy table across the door-frame.

"Here!" Montrond exclaimed from within the fireplace, his head concealed behind the lintel. A small piece of stone projected slightly from its neighbors as Montrond pushed from the other side. "Need your help," he grunted. Jeanne added the force of her weight to his own. Wolfe, being unable to raise his arms, could only watch as the passageway was revealed. It was ingenious. The movable stone flap was self-replacing and finished externally so as to perfectly resemble the surrounding casing stones. Once the stone flap had projected fully, Montrond and Jeanne ducked under the lintel and applied their efforts to lifting it outwards from the face and up. "It operates on a pivot," Montrond panted, "with compensating weights fitted to counteract its heavy weight…inside the cavity…can you feel a lever, Wolfe?"

Behind them the wooden door began to give way with a splintering groan under the relentless pounding from the passageway. Wolfe raised one arm, supporting it with the other, as he felt within the cavity. With a grunt of agony, he wrenched the narrow rod to one side. An ancient scraping sounded in the fireplace, and a small opening revealed itself, exhaling the dark musty breath of a long-shuttered cellar.

"Go on!" Montrond cried. "We have barely a minute before the flap will swing back into place."

The passage was cramped and required them to crawl on all fours into the darkness. Wolfe followed, torso bent beneath the low ceiling, shuffling along on his knees in an effort to spare his agonized arms from bearing his weight. Montrond had barely made it before the stone door swung back with a resounding thud, and the passageway descended into a darkness so complete that it appeared to have swallowed the world.

"So where does this come out?" Jeanne's voice came out of the gloom as she moved tentatively forward.

"Not really sure," came Montrond's muffled voice from the rear. "But wherever it is has got to be an improvement over where we have come from, wouldn't you say?"

"As long as it gets us out of here," Jeanne muttered. From behind her came a groan of pain. "Wolfe?" Scuttling backwards, she felt his prone form with her feet. "Wolfe?"

"Gi' me a moment, will you?" came his growl in the dark. Wolfe's shoulders had spasmed, sending shooting pains down his arms and a numbing weakness in his upper torso. Fighting a dizzy nausea that seemed exacerbated by the ink-black oblivion that surrounded him, he laid his forehead on the cool stones and waited for the intensity of the pain to subside.

An hour later, knees scraped raw, they emerged, blinking, at a rusted grate overlooking the sluggishly thick waters of the Seine. The three— the president à mortier, his red garments slightly worse for the wear; Napoleon's elite guard, his goatee sprouting at rather an unusual angle; and a tall man holding a red cloak tightly about himself, arms held gingerly away from his body—clambered on to an adjacent quay. Within a few minutes, they had secured a covered cab and were making their way through the jostling crowd of carriages, nags, and peddlers.

"I have a cart waiting that will take Wolfe out of the city. A man by the name of Henri Dunant will be waiting in rue d'Esai. He has everything ready. We go there first. Monsieur de Montrond, I suggest you also leave Paris. While it is unlikely that you would be recognized, your role in today's events will not go unnoticed, and Fouché is relentless. Get word to Duc de Talleyrand if you can. But go dark, monsieur, go deep. Vous comprenez?" Jeanne spoke hurriedly, her voice hushed and furtive even within the confines of the cab.

Wolfe leaned against the back of the seat, eyes closed, his pale face clenched and tight against the pain in his shoulders, wincing involuntarily at each jerk and jolt as the cab rattled and lurched along the street. "What about you?" he asked, opening his eyes, his words a rigid enunciation that conveyed, more than any specific complaint might have done, the agonizing discomfort of his torso.

"I have something I need to do first," Jeanne replied tersely. "Then I will get out of Paris. Joseph will help me. Dunant will wrap your shoulders; it should help with the pain and accelerate healing." And then she gave him instructions, issued rapidly with curt efficiency. Wolfe had little time but to listen, for a moment later: "Quick, get out here. There is Dunant on the corner, do you see him? Bonne chance, mon ami!"

Montrond and Wolfe descended to the street, and she was gone, with a clatter of wheels, into the afternoon madness that was Paris.

# 75.

Wolfe lay in the back of the lumbering cart as it groaned and creaked its way down rue de Faubourg Saint Jacques. A bed had been manufactured for him beneath an artfully constructed arch of twigs and branches that, from the outside, resembled every other wood cart in the city. And there were thousands of them, more this year than the previous one due to the early severity of the winter weather. Wood carts cluttered every corner of the Parisian roadways with burly men throwing logs from the top of the carts, oblivious to pedestrian traffic beneath. The only particularly unusual feature of this one was that it was heading *out* of town. But the driver, a thick-bodied youth by the name of Henri Dunant, had that covered should he be questioned—which was unlikely, Jeanne had assured him.

Wolfe felt as if his arms had been ripped from his chest; with every jolting movement of the cart, he was reassured, with searing agony, that they were in fact attached. A compress of sorts had been wrapped around his upper torso, which minimized movement but did nothing to alleviate the fiery pain that burned through his shoulders and back. Blearily, through his physical misery, Wolfe wondered where they were. He had been in the back of this damned cart for what seemed hours now. Jeanne had said it would be forty-five minutes or so until they were through the city boundaries and he would be able to get out. She also said she had packed a bottle of whiskey for him—Bushmills single malt. How had she gotten that through the blockade? Uisce Beatha. The Water of Life. God knew, he could use a bit of that now, he thought, clenching his teeth to prevent himself from crying out as the cart lurched over a pothole. He heard, faintly at first, then with increasing intensity, the sound of shouting accompanied by intermittent gunfire.

Wolfe wedged his knee under a branch and, easing it up slightly, could see through a crack in the side of the cart. It had come to a standstill as the wood wagon was surrounded by a swiftly moving throng of people brandishing sticks and pikes. It was an enraged crowd, a group of rioters in full cry, screaming the litany: "A mort! A mort!" To the death. To one side he saw a cluster of blue uniforms: grim-faced soldiers moving quickly, muskets raised, protecting each other's flanks. Between them, stood the robust figure of General Moreau, his thick, dark hair and military brocade familiar to all on the streets of Paris. He was being escorted from the Temple to the Palais de Justice. Wolfe vaguely remembered Jeanne discussing it with Montrond as they dragged his prone, semi-conscious body up the tunnel of the Temple prison.

"He'll be transferred this afternoon!" she had panted, struggling under Wolfe's inert body.

"Surrounded by soldiers no doubt," Montrond had replied.

"But strong enough to deter a rescue attempt? We can try to infiltrate the escort. The general is very popular with the army, perhaps they can be persuaded to mutiny and rescue him?"

"You need to get out of Paris, madame," Montrond had told her curtly. "Let others try for General Moreau."

Suddenly, the throng took shape; it surged forward in one united movement, as if in response to an unseen signal. The cart jolted into movement once more, and as they turned a corner, Wolfe could see the soldiers hesitate uncertainly—fire into the crowd and be torn apart, or deliver up their beloved leader? Either option would not go unpunished. Wolfe did not envy them their decision.

Gradually, the cart left the narrow streets of Paris behind, and its injured occupant, snugly unobserved beneath his nest of limbs, fell into a fitful sleep. He awoke an hour later to find that the cart stopped beside a field, stubby with the stalks of last season's corn. Dunant had removed his overburden of twigs, and Wolfe could see the sun was low in a gray-washed sky. Grimacing with pain, he eased himself upright. The spires of Paris silhouetted the horizon, emerging from the rim of the basin in which she nested, and ahead, over the driver's slouched figure, he could see the rounded peaks and steep-sided valleys of the Massif Central.

"Where are we?" he muttered.

"Ah, you're awake!" Dunant twisted around in his seat, his round face ruddy in the setting sun. "Would you like some dinner?"

"I'll start with the whiskey, if you don't mind." Wolfe, cradling his arms to his chest, clambered unsteadily over the wood load and seated himself beside the driver.

"You look rough," Dunant commiserated, retrieving a small bottle from the satchel by his feet. "Primrose asked me to give you this." He said her name with a hushed reverence that one would reserve for the pure and sanctified—another disciple. Wolfe wondered whether any of these people actually knew her, whether any of them had witnessed her fear, her tears, or understood her humanity. It struck him again how difficult her path had become. To be the object of such worship, to inspire such fervor...how could anyone possibly live up to that ideal? No wonder she drew herself up so tightly. He took a long swig of the whiskey, feeling the burning heat trace a path down his throat and settle with satisfying fire in his gut. Nothing quite like Bushmills. Had Jeanne known it was his whiskey of choice? Somehow nothing about that woman would surprise him.

"Try this; it'll keep you warm, lad." He passed the bottle to Dunant who accepted it with alacrity. A gulp and he was coughing and wheezing over the reins. Wolfe grinned. "The best stuff will sear your throat and smolder in your belly. Makes the Irish winter shorter and a little bit warmer, but not for the faint o'heart, to be sure."

From here, they dispensed with the cart, saddled the horses, and galloped south along the banks of the Liong River. They emerged into an idyllic countryside of vineyards and rivers, with villages nestled amidst the forests of oak. At least it would have been idyllic, had it been summer. As it was, however, the vineyards consisted of knotted trunks and gout-swollen arms that had been frozen into contorted immobility; the rows between them consisted of parallel stretches of white frost and ice, glittering in the pale evening light. The Liong was flat and gray and did not flow so much as seeped sullenly, as if the winter had bleached it not only of color but also of all liveliness. The occasional houses they passed were closed and shuttered against the cold, wisps of dark smoke leaving soft trails against the sky. Unlike dwellers in the city, most rural farmers had fires; even when bread was in short supply, the trees and undergrowth supplied an abundance of wood. Whether due to the whiskey or the physical respite, Wolfe found his arms and shoulders feeling substantially better by the late afternoon. Dunant had gently manipulated his arms until they settled back into place with a heavy popping sound. From then on, the pain receded markedly, leaving only a residual heavy soreness that Wolfe, upon recalling his recent agony, found could be happily accommodated indeed.

The sun settled into late afternoon, and long shadows stretched across the landscape as they cantered into the city of Bourges; the town was defined by the confluence of the Rivers Yèvre and Auron on the one hand and the crumbling remains of the Gallo-Roman walls on the other. They entered the city beneath the St. Sulpice gateway via the narrow street of rue Gambon. It was a city of fading grandeur with timbered buildings lining the old Gallo-Roman road, now the city's central thoroughfare. The town had a neglected, forlorn appearance. The agricultural market, usually the bustling center of city life, consisted of three dusty stalls with paltry produce. Wolfe parted from Dunant with a warm handshake, leaving the Frenchman the quarter bottle of whiskey that remained. Perhaps the lad would acquire a taste for it.

Wolfe secured lodging at the Hotel du Central, which possessed the dubious advantage of overlooking the marshland to the south. Long fingers of land paralleled strips of water, gleaming orange in the dying light. The chatty barmaid, wiping work-roughened hands on her coarse linen apron, told him that they had been purchased by the Jesuits a hundred years before and were rented out to individuals who transformed them into garden plots. Not much gardening was being done at present, however, and the plots were bleak and barren under a mantle of gray snow and ice. A cold wind swept in across the marsh, rattling the shutters and howling its way through the cracks in the thinly timbered wall. But the hotel was cheap and Wolfe's supply of silver was dwindling faster than he had anticipated. After a bowl of hearty rabbit stew, he followed the directions of the barmaid to the house of Jacques Cujas, a cleric who dedicated himself not only to the congregation of Bourges but also administered to the body politic of France. He was a member of the French Resistance.

Cujas lived in the lower part of town, where merchants' shops clustered in tired proximity near the old wall. Trade seemed anything but brisk. An old man sat hunched in a dark doorway, knotted hands clenched over his knees, lips sucking rhythmically around the worn stem of a wood pipe. A small child kicked a pebble disconsolately against the timber side of a shuttered shop. Many of the shops were closed and from their general aura of dusty neglect, appeared to have been so for some time. From their midst emerged the colossal stone façade of Saint Etienne Cathedral like a giant griffin poised to take flight. Shrunk beneath the towering flanks, halfway down rue des Santine, was a modest building decorated in brick-and-diamond-shaped-lattice stonework. A lawn, neatly clipped but bare in patches, defined a courtyard in front.

The door was answered by a small wiry man dressed in a red woolen shirt and brown trousers secured around his waist by a black leather belt. A thick pelt of dark hair swept back from his forehead with a pronounced widow's peak. His narrow face had the swarthy complexion of a Spaniard and was framed by ears that stuck out almost perpendicularly to his head. Dark eyes narrowed suspiciously at Wolfe; a thick meaty hand, its fingernails neatly clipped, clenched around the side of the door.

"Yes?" he demanded, his voice well-modulated and pleasing to the ear despite his apparent hostility.

"Jacques Cujas?" Wolfe asked.

"Who are you?" the man challenged, his dark brows lowering to a frown.

"My name is Wolfe Trant. Primrose sent me."

"Primrose? Mon dieu! Come in, come in!" He opened the door and ushered Wolfe inside, casting a quick glance down the street. "Forgive me, Monsieur Trant. We have had difficult times in Bourges; one does not always know whom to trust."

Wolfe found himself in a small room, sparsely furnished with a table and several sturdy chairs. A wooden crucifix decorated one wall; a small painting of a severe-looking man in black with darkly hooded eyes and a bearded jaw hung on the other. Stout wooden doors ahead and to the left advertised the existence of at least two more rooms. The space, however, was dominated by books. Rows of books, their leather bindings neatly displayed, covered bookshelves that extended the length of the room. An open book and a quill wet with ink lay on the table. The gutted remains of numerous candles dripped in molten immobility from a tall wooden candlestick.

Over a sparse meal of slightly stale bread and cheese, washed down by a surprisingly fine wine, the two men talked. Cujas had been a Jesuit priest in Bourges for twenty years now and a contact within the Resistance for the last eight of those. The Revolution had wielded its scythe against the clergy as well as the aristocracy, and Cujas spoke darkly of times of turmoil and bloodshed, a time when those of the true faith went into hiding. Bourges had become a tired administrative center with a collapsed economy, inhabited by a population weakened by outbreaks of plague—a focal point of need and despair, and a cause to which Cujas had determined to administer. Bourges, like the majority of French towns in the early nineteenth century, was not without its history of violence.

"They took over the property of the church in the name of the Republic." Cujas spoke softly, leaning forward, his elbows on the table, dark hair gleaming in the flickering candlelight. "They abolished monastic vows and attempted to turn clerics into employees of the state with the civil constitution of 1790, murdering any who refused to sign it." Cujas slapped the wooden table with the palm of his massive hand in rhythmic counterpoint to each cataloged insult. "I lost many friends. And now, Napoleon, who has never been partial to religion and has little patience for those who preach its virtues, forces the Pope into a Concordat that reiterates the subservience of church to state, and he wonders why so many of the clergy take up arms in the Resistance?" Cujas's voice was soft but laced with a thread of steel. His strong hands gripped the table edge, knuckles white against the dark grain of the wood. Then he forcibly relaxed, uncurled his fingers, and exhaled sharply from his nose.

Cujas laughed, a deeply infectious chuckle that smoothed the lines from his brow and deepened those that had formed beside his eyes. "I do apologize, my friend." He slapped one hand on Wolfe's shoulder as he rose from the chair. Wolfe winced involuntarily. "There are few in Bourges now who have not heard my tirade. I became a little over-zealous at the prospect of a fresh listener. But let us move to the back courtyard; there is something I wish to show you."

Wolfe followed Cujas through a stout wooden door to a tiny brick patio. The house squeezed itself between the stone arches of two flying buttresses, the cathedral soaring above them to a dizzying height. Wolfe's attention, however, was caught by the stained glass window that was set into the gray stone and rose to a graceful apex forty feet above his head. It depicted the massive feathered breast of a pelican, her graceful neck curving above and around, bent to the young who nestled at her side. The sun was melting into the western horizon, and the dying light imbued the colors of the window with a deeply incandescent glow. The blue glass that formed the background was cast into various shades of shimmering azure, changing and shifting as the sunlight deepened and faded. The feathers, hues of brown and cream, shone as if with an inner light, endowing the bird with the warmth of muscle, sinew, and bone. Blood droplets that dripped from the pelican's breast to nourish her offspring glowed a deep ruby red. Then, a moment later, it was gone. The sun had slipped below the marshes, and the men were left in a rapidly darkening twilight.

"Magnificent," Wolfe breathed.

"Isn't it?" Cujas murmured. He sat on the stone bench adjacent, leaning his back against the wall of the house behind. "It is the original glass-work from the thirteenth century, and one of the few religious buildings that have survived. Most of them were pillaged when the city was in the hands of the Protestants during the Reformation. And, of course, again during the Revolution. This cathedral and three other small parish churches are all that remain of our religious heritage in Bourges. And it is why I bought the house. For a few minutes every night, it is cast in glorious living light. The pelican is a symbol of atonement. It reminds me of my purpose and helps instill in me the humility that I fear is not always there." Again came that rumbling laugh. "You see, I have the arrogance to entertain the notion that I can change the political landscape of our country." His eyes gleamed in the yellow gaslight. "But tell me of your purpose. Tell me why Primrose sent you to me."

"I want to send a message through the semaphore telegraph. A message from Napoleon redirecting Villeneuve's fleet to Cadiz. It has to be far enough away from Paris so that the officials will not be able to verify the command personally, but close enough so that the message will be sent, received, and passed on as quickly as possible. Primrose suggested the Limoges station. She said your brother is employed as the command officer there."

"Ah yes, my brother," Cujas mused, absently rubbing his jaw with one hand. "We have not spoken in some time…had a parting of ways after the Revolution. Nicolàs was determined to carve out a future for himself within the Napoleonic regime whereas I found myself consistently fighting against it. He will not help us." He regarded Wolfe steadily.

"If that order is not sent, Napoleon will combine his fleet in the Channel within the week. England will lie open to him. Once he establishes himself on English soil, he'll have an entrenched powerbase from which it will be enormously difficult to evict him. If you allow him that advantage, do you think you'll ever obtain true religious freedom in France?"

Cujas sighed, resting his elbows on the table, thick hands forming a steeple, mouth pursed thoughtfully against his fingertips. "Perhaps there is a way. I will accompany you to Limoges. I have skulked in Bourges long enough." He rose from the table with an air of decisive engagement.

# 76.

SHEFFIELD HOUSE. LONDON, ENGLAND
*December 8, 1803*

It was evident to Henry Eden, as well as to the other members of the Sheffield House clique, that though they were nominally the guests of Lord Sheffield, their real entertainer was her ladyship. In fact, she was not only lady paramount in the house but often insolently imperious toward her guests, whom, as one man wittily remarked, she treated like her *vassals*, though she was only a *Vassall* herself—alluding to her maiden name.

"The centurion," Eden remarked acidly from his vantage point across the drawing room, "did not keep his soldiers in better order than she keeps her guests." His voice rose in shrill mimicry: "To one it is: 'Go,' and he goes; and to another, 'Do this,' and it is done. 'Ring the bell, Mr. Macaulay.' 'Lay down the screen, Lord Russell, you will spoil it.' 'Mr. Allen, take a candle and show Mr. Cradock the pictures of Marie Antoinette.'"

His companion, Thomas Westin, a young man with curly hair the color and texture of greasy butter, chuckled, slapping Eden affably on the shoulder. "Never mind politics, Henry—you should have been on stage."

"Stagecraft seems a prerequisite to politics," Eden muttered, looking across to where Lady Sheffield was holding court at the far end of the room.

Her voice rose thin and acerbic above the muted conversations: "I am vexed, indeed!" she was saying. "Now that this Sir Richard Sheffield person is to become a baronet, there will be two Lady Sheffields in society." Lady Sheffield sniffed in disdain, her face pinched and pallid beneath the yellow silk hat that tilted precariously on a nest of wiry reddish hair. "I suppose it cannot be helped," she concluded waspishly, directing her comment pointedly in the direction of the Prince of Wales, who was huddled in conversation with her extravagantly beribboned husband, intimating, of course, that when his highness ascended the throne he could overturn this tiresome appointment that so inconvenienced her uniqueness in society. The prince, just as pointedly, ignored her but could not resist a jibe of his own:

"So I understand there are two Georges the Younger present this evening," he remarked gaily to his coterie, referring to himself and George Coleman, Junior, who was also of their party. "I should like to know, which of us is George the Youngest?"

"Oh!" replied Coleman with an ingratiating bow. "I would never have the rudeness to come into the world before Your Royal Highness."

The prince chortled and patted Coleman on the shoulder with his fan. "Very good, my dear fellow! Very good indeed!" He cast an imperious sideways glance at Lady Sheffield, then sniffed and turned away.

"Well!" she sniffed in her turn, mouth pinched in sour irritation.

All Whigs of import were gathered at Sheffield House this evening. Fox was hunched in candlelight, leaning forward in the upholstered green chair, the usual congregation of political neophytes clustered around him. Grenville was deep in animated conversation with Lord John Sackville, their heads enveloped in a cloud of pungent cigar smoke. The prince and Lord Sheffield presented mirror images of each other: both were extravagantly rotund beneath tightly stretched satin of garish hues, elaborately towering wigs falling in meticulous ringlets, the dust of face powder, and the slight hint of rouge on their lips.

They had dined on particularly extravagant fare—salmon poached in champagne, capons with a béchamel sauce, orange fromage bavarois followed by strawberry tartlettes—but Eden had tasted little of it. Like his hostess, he was also vexed. Wolfe Trant was still alive. L'Aigle was supposed to be the best. That Irishman had been in the French capital for three days now. Who knew what manner of mischief he had already accomplished? By now he must have met with Napoleon. Perhaps they were preparing the fleet for departure? Perhaps the Irish rebels were even now taking up arms to coincide with the French arrival?

Grenville was utterly disgusted with the entire affair and had accosted him at Carlton House the previous evening. Yanking Eden's lapels in one meaty fist, he shook him effortlessly until his teeth rattled—much as he would a recalcitrant child, Eden reflected sourly. "This was *your* idea, Henry. You fix this, do you understand?" Grenville's eyes bored into his. "If I lose my cattle lands as a result of this foolishness, I will hold *you* responsible!" Then, with a final shake, he disentangled his hand from Eden's crumpled cravat. "Fix it!" he reiterated in a hiss, cheeks red-blotched with fury, spittle gathering at the corners of his fleshy mouth. Then, with an admirable degree of control, he smoothed down his own satin coat-front and re-entered the festivities with a ready smile. If his eyes were cold, few noticed.

What, precisely, did Grenville expect him to do? Eden wondered. Ship off to Paris and challenge the Irishman to a duel? They had paid an outrageous sum to this assassin who had always met expectations before. Perhaps it was just a matter of biding time, Eden reflected, wiping the sudden sheen of perspiration from his brow with a linen handkerchief. Give L'Aigle a little more time, and hope Grenville would be patient just a little longer.

"Henry? Henry?" Westin nudged him good-naturedly. "I say, are you listening to me?"

Eden frowned. "What?"

"Henry, may I have a word?" Fox nodded amiably in Westin's direction. The latter, taking the hint, sauntered off to scrounge a cigar from Lord Sackville. "Did you hire an assassin to kill Wolfe Trant?" Fox began without preamble. Eden did not reply. He did not have to; his sallow face suffused with guilty color and then closed down. "Are you quite *mad*?" Fox exclaimed incredulously. "Do you realize the repercussions if this gets out? You witnessed the pamphlet wars between Pitt and Addington over the past few months. We are being scrutinized in the press to an unprecedented degree. Every detail of our policy, our campaign, is being examined by the electorate! Our success in the House of Lords and in the Commons is going to depend upon an untarnished reputation as the representatives of popular will."

"And what were you planning on doing? Exactly nothing!" Eden rejoined heatedly. "While Pitt conspired with an Irishman who would undoubtedly have betrayed us all!"

"This Irishman is the one man who can save us all," Fox replied steadily, his eyes fixed on Eden's. "Unable to gain Napoleon's confidence, he is, as we speak, making his way to Limoges to set wheels in motion that would divide and weaken Napoleon's fleet. *Prevent* them from uniting in the Channel. *Prevent* them from being able to invade *at all*," he finished. "Is this your definition of a traitor, Mr. Eden? Is this the man you have issued a death warrant against? The one man upon which all our hopes rest?" Fox glared at Eden, his narrowed gaze icy and penetrating, his pouchy cheeks wobbling slightly and flushed with angry heat. "We are making efforts to form a united administration," Fox hissed. "The *only* way in which Napoleon can effectively be opposed, and how are you contributing? By utterly tarnishing the reputation of the Whig party to which you are nothing but a petty recent addition! By attempting to assassinate the one man who can save us all? Let's hope to God your assassin fails, Mr. Eden, or believe me, *you* will be paying the price!"

Fox, normally so imperturbable, fairly shook with fury, and Eden, despite his cool bravado, quailed under the onslaught. But both knew that little could now be done. Wolfe's lot, and that of England, seemed to be irrevocably in the hands of Fate.

# 77.

## RUE DE LA VILLETTE. PARIS, FRANCE
### December 9, 1803

The young man was ill; that much was apparent. His pale cheeks were disfigured by livid red sores that clustered in angry profusion at the edge of his mouth. His gaze was glassy-eyed, his movements awkwardly jerky as if merely inhabiting his thin, shivering body was a discomfort to him. The few pedestrians awake at this icy hour, before the first feeble rays of the rising sun had appeared in the east, skirted around this sickly youth. Typhus? Plague? Didn't much matter...just don't get too close!

It wasn't just the wasted, feverish look of the boy that kept the early risers at bay; it was the cargo he was securing to the back of the cart: rough-hewn coffins of cheap pine. A stoic and silent old man sat tightly hunched on the front of an equally ancient wagon, holding the reins loosely between the thick fingers of one hand. His weathered cheek bulged with a wad of tobacco, his jaw moving in a slow, rhythmic motion like a cow chewing cud. The nag, as impassively patient as her master, stood, head bowed, her breath steamy plumes in the icy predawn air.

The inhabitants of these coffins were the unnamed victims of cold and hunger. There had been a grand movement, a sweeping gesture, initiated by the emperor to improve sanitation and hygiene in the overcrowded city of Paris. The cleansing of the Seine had been advertised, but the clandestine removal of bodies during the night was not. Remove the evidence. Napoleon was consumed by foreign affairs: Austria was growling on the northwestern frontier, the Third Coalition had reassembled a united opposition, and Russia was again intractable. Bonaparte could not afford internal dissent, and the bodies in the streets had an uncanny way of reminding Parisians that all was not well in Imperial France.

"Fini?" the old man grunted, half-turned toward the sickly youth in the rear. The boy nodded in assent, his bloodless mouth working

soundlessly as his frozen fingers fumbled with the last knot. He stood
for a moment, his breath a rattling wheeze, his face unnaturally flushed,
his trembling hand steadying himself against the cart. Then, body
straining with effort, he clambered over the coffins where he fell back
into a lethargic stupor.

The gruesome job was done. They had six bodies in various postures
of contorted rigidity squeezed into the coffins. Some of them had frozen with their eyes open and their arms outstretched in an eerily lifelike
manner, as if they were merely resting beneath their mantle of ice and
it was just a matter of thawing them out. Others were curled in tight
fetal positions in a last effort to conserve bodily warmth. They had had
to lop the arms off one in order to fit him into the coffin; the limbs
had fallen like tree branches, flesh crystallized into pink ice. There was
no blood, and the axe hitting the elbow sounded uncannily like a blade
biting into wood. But the boy preferred not to think about that. In fact,
this was only one more of many things he preferred not to think about.
Regardless, they had their quota, and his work was done.

The cart jostled and creaked toward the west Bellville gate. The sentries were cold and weary at their posts; they waited impatiently with
stomping feet, arms crossed tightly across their chests in an effort to
conserve body heat. The morning shift was late again.

"Papers!" a grizzled sentry by the name of Savoy demanded, his
florid face flushed with drink. He had found a way to keep warm. The
guingettes, or taverns, that operated just a few feet across the city limits
were not subject to the taxes that were levied on all Parisian wine merchants. Paris bottles were taxed at four sous for a wine barely worth
three. Beyond the boundaries of Paris, however, these taxes were not
applied, which accounted for the boisterous popularity of the infamous
Courtille guingette, to which Giscard Savoy was particularly susceptible.
It was the end of his shift and, after repeated forays across the border,
he was now pleasantly heated and sluggishly weary with wine—as the
sickly young man had known he would be.

"Papers!" Savoy repeated thickly, extending a meaty paw toward the
elderly driver.

"He thinks I am Primrose!" the old man cackled, to the amusement
of Savoy's fellow officers. His leathery cheeks pursed and, with surprising force, he spat the brown wad from his mouth.

Savoy's already flushed complexion darkened with anger. "Open up those coffins!" he ordered curtly, rapping the pine sides with his knuckles.

"The coffins?" the old man repeated. "Are you sure, Lieutenant? This winter's work is a fearful sight." Savoy stomped irritably around to the rear of the wagon and drew back in alarm as the feverish face of the young man, with its frightful array of lividly scarlet sores, appeared suddenly above the topmost coffin. "Just my grandson, Lieutenant. Let him alone now. He has the blood-fever, poor boy."

"Blood-fever?" Savoy drew back in horror. His meaty paw rose involuntarily before his face, as if to ward off the contagion that appeared to ooze and sweat from the boy's very pores. "Off with you! Get him out of here!" he hollered, waving the cart through as he gestured to his men to open the heavy wooden gates. The cart clattered forward, the crust of ice cracking beneath the stout wooden wheels.

Five miles beyond the city perimeter, shrouded within a copse of evergreens, Jeanne wiped her face of the meticulously applied makeup; from beneath the angry sores of the plague-ridden boy the pale face of a woman emerged. She clambered over the coffins to sit beside Joseph, who had similarly divested himself of makeup and wig. His brown cheeks wrinkled in a grin. "We did it!"

"We did indeed, mon ami," Jeanne replied, with a quick grin of her own. Then her face became abruptly shadowed, her voice more insistent: "And the courier, Joseph? He departed with all possible haste? You communicated to him the absolute urgency of the matter with which he has been entrusted?"

"Yes. He is most reliable. Have no fear." Sensing her trepidation, Joseph pressed her hand in reassurance. "He will prevail."

Jeanne shuddered, eyes closed momentarily as if in fervent prayer. Then, rubbing one grubby hand wearily across her face, she exhaled sharply before taking up the reins. "Now, we must make haste for Boulogne; we have some distance to cover yet."

They had managed to evade Fouché, they had escaped Paris, but the real challenge still lay ahead—Napoleon.

# 78.

PLACE D'ENFER. PARIS, FRANCE
*December 9, 1803*

The black-hooded priests shuffled through the bustling square of Place d'Enfer, their worn sandals scraping against gray crusts of ice that protruded between the broken flagstones. A Parisian abbot led the procession. Holding the chain of a metal censer between gnarled fingers, he swung it pendulously across the folds of his black robe; sweetish wisps of smoke trailed behind it through the air. A number of wagons followed with the dead, mounded and humped beneath black cloth. Last came the monks in their brown tunics, the lead monk ringing the obligatory bell, all of them chanting the deep hypnotic litany of the last rites: Miserére mei, Deus: secúndum magnam misericordiam tuam. Glora Patri, et Filii, et Spiritus Sancti.

This macabre convoy was a familiar yet feared sight in Paris as it wended its way from the Cimetière des Innocents to the catacombs. Together, bell and chant proclaimed a warning to inattentive pedestrians who—if caught in the path of such a morbid procession—scurried fearfully out the way, handkerchief pressed anxiously over mouth and nose. For noxious miasmas indubitably surrounded the dead and contaminated the living who foolishly ventured too close. And so it was that this dreary column passed, as it had done so often before, through the narrow streets without query or impediment—exactly as Duc de Talleyrand had hoped.

Having been ordained the bishop of Autun more than a decade before, Talleyrand had maintained contacts within the clergy, contacts that now served him well. A handsome donation to the Catholic church lubricated wheels and prompted allegiances. Talleyrand had discovered, half-buried in his last sack of coffee beans, a note from Montrond. It was concise and to the point: "Coffee beans increasingly difficult to acquire. Try tea." This served as a coded message previously established in case of utmost emergency: leave Paris immediately. And so Duc de

Talleyrand had called in a few favors, and now, just hours later, with jewels sewn into the lining of his habit, he was leaving his home behind. His staff had been instructed to inform any who enquired that he was making an extended visit to inspect and oversee renovations to his rural home of Château Haut-Brion in Bordeaux.

Upon arrival at the Barrière d'Enfer, the contents of the wagons were unceremoniously dumped into a well-like cavity in the yard behind, cascading in a gruesome waterfall to the dark belly of the catacombs beneath. Later, when the flesh had melted, thawed, and resolved itself into a dew, when nothing was left but the smooth yellowness of bone and the gaping cavities, then the remains would be shoveled, stacked, and classified by genre. And each would become yet another nameless relic, a random part that once belonged to one of the six million dead that now filled the walls and decorated the recesses.

Unnoticed, one priest peeled off from the convoy, slipped through the stone arch of the Barrière d'Enfer, and rapidly descended the spiral staircase that led to the opening room of the ossuary beneath. He hurried unheeded beneath the warning inscribed in stone above: Arrête! C'est ici l'empire de la mort—Stop! Here lies the empire of death. The light dimmed and the air became oppressively foul, the heavy stench of decaying flesh increasingly rancid and heavy. The fetid odor lessened as Talleyrand hurried from the open grave mounds, through the narrow passageways to the older sections of the catacombs. Ahead, he could see the flickering light of a gas-lamp held aloft. In a circular room, where the polished knobs of limb bones gleamed dully from floor to ceiling, Monsieur Marigny—son-in-law to Carême and quarryman in service of the state—waited.

"Here you are at last!" Marigny exclaimed, somewhat fretfully. "This way, please hurry!" A languid smile crossed Talleyrand's face at Marigny's obvious discomfort, but he merely inclined his head in a gesture of wry respect and followed his guide through the dark narrow passages of the catacombs. Progressively, the walls closed in, and the ceiling dripped wetly above to puddle underfoot. The air became increasingly dank and dark, with the yellow gaslight casting spectral shadows across the bone-filled walls.

They turned and twisted down various passageways, Marigny moving swiftly and confidently until they reached the Crypte de la Passion, a small circular room defined by pale blocks of limestone. The central feature of this space was the Rotonde des Tibias—the column comprised entirely of shinbones—behind which Talleyrand could see the heavy wooden door that marked the exit from the ossuary and the entrance into the old, disused tunnels of the stone quarries.

An hour later, having skirted collapsed passageways and negotiated cleared and shored-up channels, where timber posts groaned disconcertingly under a heavy burden of stone, the two men emerged into the dust-sprinkled quarry entrance. The soft morning light dazzled the men's eyes, and they blinked and breathed the sweet fresh air of the outlying township of Bagneaux. The air was as malodorous as anywhere else in Paris, with the stench of unwashed bodies and street-stewing offal, but to the two men who had surfaced from the depths of the Barrière d'Enfer, the morning breeze brought the perfume of life. Beyond the quarry lay the bustling mercantile district of Bagneaux and, most importantly for Talleyrand, a township outside of the Paris city gates that were, potentially, heavily guarded against him.

"Merci, Monsieur Marigny. I am in your debt." Talleyrand pressed several gold coins into Marigny's hand before he disappeared into the crowd, whistling a merry tune, his brown tunic quickly lost amongst the many others that thronged the city streets this early December morning.

# 79.

Most cities hummed with morning traffic: wagons and carts colliding in their haste to market, bustling shopkeepers intent on arranging their wares and preparing their inventory, and the ubiquitous throng of humankind—laborers and artisans, priests and laymen, the living and the dead—that swelled and shoved their way through narrow thoroughfares. Bourges, however, was strangely quiet, her streets curiously desolate and echoing, punctuated by a lonely impoverished figure here and there, but largely, it seemed, forsaken. Perhaps this is why his shadow had been so readily detected, Wolfe mused.

Wolfe strode swiftly down rue St. Marguerite, followed the street as it curved around the heavy walls of the cathedral, and ducked abruptly into a narrow lane that veered off to the right. Then he waited. A minute passed, and a green-cloaked figure emerged from behind the church, glancing quickly from the left to right. He was clearly an amateur. Not only had he allowed himself to be spotted, Wolfe thought grimly, but he was just about to be apprehended and questioned. Moving out from the alley at a run, Wolfe raced down rue St. Marguerite toward his tracker who hesitated uncertainly, clearly not expecting his target to turn so rapidly to the offensive.

The man turned and darted back the way he had come, cloak flying behind him, feet pounding the cobblestones. He was fast, but Cujas was ready for him. The priest materialized from a dark side street, drawing back a longbow with powerful precision. With a muted twang, the arrow shot through the air and embedded itself in the man's upper shoulder. With a cry of pain and surprise, he fell to his knees, the shaft of the arrow quivering in his flesh.

"A bow and arrow, is it?" Wolfe demanded, dark eyebrows raised in query. He stopped over the man writhing on the cobblestones.

"Our founder Saint Ignatius of Loyola was a soldier before he became a priest. He believed the bow and arrow to be the most civilized weapon of choice. I happen to agree with him," Cujas replied with equanimity as he replaced the bow in the leather holster slung over his shoulder. A single bedraggled spectator, mouth open in astonishment, paused over his roadside meal of turnips and fried onions.

"Time to go," Wolfe stated, pulling the wounded man to his feet. With the shadow's arms draped over their shoulders, Wolfe and the priest retraced their steps to Cujas's home. They had flushed the spy out. But who was he, and why was he here? Once within the small house, they roughly propped the wounded man against the wall. He was a skinny runt of a fellow, his frame small and narrow, his slender bones terminating in sharp points. He resembled nothing more than a small, dirty ferret, moaning piteously as he clutched his shoulder, the blood seeping scarlet beneath his gray woolen tunic.

"I'm dyin', can't you see? Fetch a doctor," he whimpered, slumping against the wall, tears squeezing out of the corner of his eyes. He was young, Wolfe realized, as he squatted down on his haunches to examine the wounded man more closely. Just a boy. Barely eighteen.

"Who are you, and why were you following me?" Wolfe demanded

"I dunno what you mean," the boy wailed fearfully. "I'm an apprentice to my uncle. I'm learning the roofing trade, just walking, and you shot me!" He directed an accusatory glare in Cujas's direction.

"Don't bother," Wolfe replied in a tight, steely tone. "I know you've been following me since I left Paris."

There was a moment's hesitation. The boy glanced at Cujas who, humming a cheerful tune, was studiously removing dirt from beneath one fingernail with the sharp edge of a knife. The transformation was as remarkable as it was instantaneous. The boy's features lost their soft vulnerability. The tears dried up, and his narrow face took on a crafty look. "And what if I have?" he said cocking his head to one side, his expression calculating, his eyes slitted and sly.

"If you're not prepared to talk, we'll just toss you into the marshes. Weighted bodies shouldn't surface until the spring thaw."

"I understand drowning is a rather unpleasant way to die," Cujas commented.

To their surprise, the boy threw his head back and laughed. A prominent Adam's apple jerked through the skin of a narrow neck ringed with grime. "You two are really something!" the boy finally said with a smirk. "I call the streets of Paris my home! It really don't matter what you do to me, Etienne knows where you…"

"Etienne?" Wolfe said sharply.

The boy's mouth dropped open in dismay and then shut just as quickly. His face took on a closed, stubborn expression, his mouth tight—as if by clamping his lips together he could forcibly prevent further words from escaping.

"Etienne," Cujas repeated slowly; his brow furrowed speculatively. "Etienne."

"You know of him?" Wolfe turned to the priest.

"Oh, indeed. He is the soul of the Parisian underworld. Controls numerous men, influences many more. Etienne is a powerful man, not to be crossed, not to be underestimated. Muscle-for-hire…into everything from prostitution to extortion. Politically, he is neutral; a mercenary in the truest sense of the word. The Resistance has hired him upon occasion. Through a third party, of course."

"So, most likely he's been hired by someone else to track me?"

"Undoubtedly."

"The assassin," Wolfe mused. The two men retreated to the far side of the room, conversing in low tones beneath the stern portrait of Saint Ignatius. The boy, his hand tight over his shoulder, regarded them with wary eyes that gleamed disconcertingly in the gaslight.

"Assassin?" Cujas inquired. Wolfe proceeded to fill him in on the attack that had taken place in the dingy house of rue de Vertbois and the mission which had been entrusted to him by William Pit. He felt an instinctive trust for the swarthy Frenchman. And it wasn't the God factor; Wolfe was too cynical to assume that a cleric was more holy than most. Talleyrand had been a man of the cloth himself, and there was none more adept at political survival. One did what one had to do, to survive, to prevail. It was the open directness in Cujas's dark eyes, the strength of his hands that one felt instinctively was used for good, his tone of quiet confidence. Whatever it was, Wolfe's instinct told him Cujas was to be trusted, and he made it a habit, when all else failed, to go with his gut.

"Sounds like there is someone who has a vested interest in your failure, mon ami."

"Aye," Wolfe agreed grimly. "Or when my mission was leaked, I became a political embarrassment for a prime minister who seeks to regain office. Which ever way 'tis, this message must be sent. We must leave immediately."

# 80.

Jacques Cujas procured a weather-beaten carriage and a tired nag from a sour-faced merchant who was, he said, washing his hands of Bourges. Cujas paid twice what the horse and conveyance were worth, but the two were pleased to have ready transportation. After a night of restless sleep, the men left for their two-day journey to Limoges. They left the wounded boy with the town doctor with private instruction to keep him confined to his room for a minimum of five days before releasing him. A few additional coins, furnished by Cujas, ensured their instructions would be carried out. The small spy would have no opportunity to report back to his employer.

They left as the sun was warming the River Loire valley, heading toward the peaks of the Massif Central to the south. The air was crisp and cold, and as they left the marshy land of Brenne and Sologne behind them, the bare oak trees gradually began to give way to spruce and fir that carpeted the lower slopes of the Massif. An hour out of Bourges, they passed a bedraggled train of people, their faces gaunt with hunger, toiling along with wretched carts and shapeless bundles. Cujas tossed several sacks from the back of the cart. The men, the women, the horde of half-naked children, watched them in silence.

"They do not even have hope left," Cujas muttered darkly as he urged the horses to a canter. "No one is prepared to help them. Every prefect just sends them foodless on their way, and then, when this ever-increasing army of want floods into Paris seeking work and food, the authorities round them up and drive them out." Behind them, Wolfe could see the men and women passing out bread to the children; they, at least, would eat. For much of the morning, the men were quiet; the plight of those they had passed haunted them both.

They made their way through U-shaped valleys, where villages nestled beneath thick folds of limestone cliffs and terracotta roof tiles glinted in the afternoon sun. By late afternoon, they arrived in Bour-ganouf; this small village, clinging to a rocky escarpment, commanded an imposing view of the silver-gleaming Taurion River as it meandered through the Plateaux de la Marche. A faded canopy in the village square shaded several tables of the only restaurant. Wolfe and Cujas seated themselves, intent on a quick meal before resuming their journey. A lone man, elderly and grizzled, sat in quiet contemplation of his coffee at another table, and several hens clucked and bustled underfoot. The square, defined by the stone-hewn wall of a Benedictine church and crumbling brick and mortar houses, was empty and quiet.

The waiter, a young man in his twenties, refilled the old man's cup. Wolfe wondered idly how he had escaped the vigilant officers of the draft, but when he approached their table, it became immediately apparent. Ridges of scar tissue twisted around the knuckles of his right hand where his fingers used to be.

"The most common form of self-mutilation," Cujas told him grimly as they shared a bottle of local kir, a tart combination of local black-currant liqueur, crème de cassis, and Bourgogne white wine. "Can you imagine a more eloquent expression of war-weariness than cutting off one's own fingers?"

Wolfe shook his head. "In Ireland we just keep fighting on and on till there are no more to fight…" He paused a moment, gazing out over the moss-bearded stones at the sweep and majesty of valley below. "But you see we're fighting for a cause that is the very bones and heart of us, whereas these poor soldiers are dragooned into endless foreign battles, the cause of which they don't understand and even less believe in."

"Yes, while Napoleon has his cadre of loyal battle-tested veterans, it is the baker's son and the rural farmer's boy, drafted against their will, who have most reason to dissent. And there are thousands and thousands of these deserters all across France, and untold more who will do anything to avoid conscription…including chopping off their own limbs."

After a steaming broth of game and a few indistinguishable vegeta-bles soaked up with hefty hunks of warm bread, Cujas and Wolfe set out with a renewed sense of urgency for Limoges.

# 81.

Unlike the lassitude of Bourges and the rural quiet of Bourganeuf, Limoges was bustling with activity. The city walls enclosed a network of cobblestone streets lined with narrow buildings of stone that, rosy and dove-toned in the shade, were imbued with warm rust and creams in the sun. The town's center was largely taken over by construction; many of the timber houses were being replaced by ones of stone. The skyline was punctuated by high lifting wheels wielding enormous quarried blocks, and the streets were thronged with workmen, laborers, and wagons transporting bulky loads of wood, stone, and sand.

Wolfe and Cujas had spent the previous night at a small inn on the outskirts of town, where they had exchanged their horse and carriage for two plodding mares. They wore the uniforms Cujas had been carrying in his pack and emerged loyal members of Napoleon's Imperial Guard in long dark-blue coats with white lapels and epaulettes. Red sashes crossed their chests and sabers hung at their sides. The most distinguishing feature of their attire, however, was the tall bearskin hats, each decorated with an engraved gold plate and a red plume that perched grandiosely above their brows.

"Is this really necessary?" Wolfe muttered, securing the leather strap beneath his chin. "I feel as if I have a dead beaver on my head."

"Probably the most necessary part of the uniform," Cujas replied, teeth flashing whitely in his swarthy complexion. "The hats will identify us as Imperial Guard which, as you may know, consists of the best veteran soldiers from every theatre of war: Egyptian Mameluks, Italians, Poles, Germans, Swiss and, of course, French. That will explain your atrocious accent." His grin widened at Wolfe's expression of mock dismay. "And serve to intimidate any who might oppose us." Cujas's smile faded as he cinched the saddle strap tightly around the gray flank of his horse. "Napoleon is not popular here, and the Guard are known as disciplined banditti. Depraved, reckless, and bloodthirsty, renowned for their skill in battle. No, the people of Limoges will let us alone, and in that attire, Nicolàs will trust that you do indeed come straight from the emperor himself."

"Makes sense," Wolfe replied, attaching his saddlebag to the rear pommel. For the third time, he checked the inside pocket of his coat. The letter was there: sealed beneath a glob of wax, scrawled in an elegant hand on the emperor's personal stationery—supplied by Talleyrand—with the bee insignia engraved in the upper left-hand corner. The personal access code was carefully printed at the bottom along with the words: *Avec toute la hâte possible!*—with all possible haste! Hard to believe that this small slip of paper could decide the fate of nations. Assuming all went according to plan.

"Do you think Villeneuve will delay?" he asked Cujas as they nudged their reluctant mares into a swaying walk. That was his greatest fear: that Villeneuve would not respond promptly enough for the plan to take effect, that he would linger in Malaga long enough to receive authentic orders that exposed the message in Wolfe's pocket as fraudulent. If the timetable was as close as Pitt believed it to be, if Napoleon had indeed scheduled an English invasion for three days hence, then surely the emperor would be sending a flurry of orders to ensure the timely arrival of his own fleet.

"No," Cujas replied. "Villeneuve has no reason to distrust the source of these orders. The emperor is known to be mercurial, willful. I think Villeneuve's only fear will be that he cannot comply quickly enough. I just hope the winds are in your favor, mon ami." The winds—of course. It all depended upon winds favorable in strength and direction that would allow the fleet to depart from Malaga. That, Wolfe mused grimly, would have to be left to Fate.

Skirting the chaos of the main square, the two men made their way through the back streets, slowing as their mares ambled through the human traffic. The houses here were of dark timber, warped and knotted with age, the joist beams sagging under the weight of upper stories. Wooden shutters were firmly closed against the cold, which did little, however, to deter pedestrians. Carpenters from Normandy congregated companionably on their way to work, leather aprons bulging beneath their coarse wool coats with the chisels, hatchets, and lathes of their trade. A roofer swore and cursed as he attempted to negotiate an unwieldy cart overflowing with wooden shingles through the rutted streets. Prostitutes in low-cut gowns loitered in the side streets, hoping to tempt some of the morning traffic. The shopkeepers had been up for hours; their street-fronts were swept, windows washed, wares laid out enticingly, and they themselves now hovered in anticipation of their first early customers.

The two men were making their way to the southern gate. From there it was a short distance to the semaphore station which was located on a rise overlooking the Vienne River. The day had dawned clear and crisp but piercingly cold, the sky streaked with long wisps of feathery clouds. Wolfe was conscious of dark glances; one laborer jostled him rudely, muttering insults and scowling over his beefy shoulder before disappearing into the crowd. Limoges was notoriously hostile to the Revolution and the empire that followed. They preferred to fight their own battles against their class enemies at home, in the streets of Paris and other towns, rather than revolutionizing the rest of Europe in threadbare uniforms.

Beyond the city walls, plowed fields lay fallow under a thin layer of frost. A flock of geese rose into the air with a cacophony of squawks, gray wings spreading powerfully in flight. A deeply pitted road, whose iced puddles had already been disturbed by morning wagons, forked just ahead. The left path had been taken by the majority of pedestrians that morning. Wolfe could see the brown homespun skirts of the porcelain workers as they made their way in clusters of four or five to the Baignol factory.

The right path led to the semaphore. The robust telegraph tower dominated the rise, the mortar still white and fresh between the newly hewn stones. Perched at the apex of this tower, about nine meters in height, was a mast from which a long crossbar extended parallel to the ground; that bar supported two additional rotating arms. The information, encoded by the positions of the arms and the angle of the crossbar relative to the ground, enabled a repertoire of one hundred ninety-six symbols. It was a new technology, but one which had been received by the French with excited acclaim. And none had been more fervent than Napoleon himself, who had envisioned a communication system that would enable the rapid centralization of intelligence. Less than a decade later, the crossbar-rod construction dotted the French countryside like the bony elbows of giant black beetles: from Paris to

Lille, Strasbourg to Boulogne, and now, freshly completed, to Toulouse via Limoges.

In 1794, the telegraph station in Lille brought news of the French capture of Condé-sur-l'Escaut from the Austrians less than an hour after it occurred. Now, with the addition of Napoleon's highly secret personal code, Wolfe would send instructions to Admiral Villeneuve in Malaga to make for Cadiz with all haste. It should take approximately thirty minutes to relay the signal through the fifteen intervening towers before arriving in Toulouse. From there, a waiting courier would ride for Malaga. The errand would be undertaken with even greater alacrity given the assumption that the message came from Napoleon's own portable semaphore.

"This is where I leave you, mon ami," Cujas said, enclosing Wolfe's hand in a strong grip. "Nicolàs will not recognize me at this distance, but to go any closer would not be wise. Godspeed, Monsieur Trant."

"Thank you, for everything. If you're ever weary of Bourges, you've a friend across the Channel."

Wolfe urged his mare into a canter, her breath a white mist in the frosty morning air. Upon arriving at the tower, Wolfe secured his mare and disappeared inside the telegraph station. Shortly thereafter, he re-appeared, right arm raised in quick salute—all was well. Cujas, whistling the La Marseillaise, tugged on the reins, and his horse settled into a steady trot. He skirted the city walls and turned north toward Bourges.

# 82.

L'Aigle moved from the shadows of rue Saint Martinique. The two men were on horseback and easy to see; they moved at a slow amble, inevitably detained by the morning laborers who stubbornly refused to make way for the Imperial Guard. A passive form of resistance, L'Aigle thought with some amusement. While deferring from open military opposition, unable or unwilling to risk life and limb, the inhabitants of Limoges were not averse to inflicting petty irritations. Whatever their intentions, the target and his friend would need the patience of saints just to make their way through the city streets.

Etienne's men had followed Wolfe through rue des Mauvais Garçons, lost him on rue du Temple, and then located him again as Fouché's men escorted him from the Hotel de Martin to the Temple Prison. L'Aigle had briefly contemplated an infiltration of the prison, weighing this rather unpalatable option against the consideration that Fouché might already have completed his work for him, when the mob had started to form. General Moreau had been arrested, and from the muttering of the crowd, L'Aigle understood that Moreau was scheduled to be transferred from the Temple to the Palais du Justice for trial. Crowds were reckless and easily swayed; they introduced an uncontrollable variable into the mix. While he appreciated the anonymity the rabble provided, L'Aigle didn't like to make mistakes.

As it turned out, Wolfe had escaped, and was later detected by one of Etienne's hirelings in a fully laden wood-cart heading *out* of town. L'Aigle appreciated this about Etienne's men: they were not merely brute muscles for hire but possessed intuitive intelligence that had, now and in the past, made all the difference. Wolfe had been trailed to Bourges by two of Etienne's lackeys and was subsequently overheard in conversation with a local priest formulating plans to travel to Limoges. Upon receipt of this information, the more seasoned operative returned to

Paris with due haste to inform their employer, leaving his apprentice in Bourges to shadow Wolfe in his absence. The young spy had been silent since, but L'Aigle had the information he required. Providing, of course, that the Limoges plans had not been a ruse intended to deceive an already-detected tail. Regardless, intelligence had not been forthcoming from any other quarter, and so it was here, in Limoges, that L'Aigle had spent the better part of the afternoon waiting for them.

Wolfe was a powerful adversary, even without the Jesuit warrior at his side, so L'Aigle determined to follow them until they separated. Moreover, he was undeniably curious about this target—where had he seen Wolfe before? L'Aigle followed the men to the city walls and, joining a crowd of brown-skirted porcelain workers, emerged on the rutted road that encircled Limoges. No one questioned him or even seemed to notice the addition to their party. They did not talk amongst themselves, just walked sturdily on, neither quickening their pace nor slowing it—just another day.

Porcelain was the real source of the city's wealth. Veins of kaolin, a rock rich in the fine, white clay required to make high-quality porcelain, had been discovered at Saint-Yrieix-la-Perche, eighteen miles to the southwest. The majority of the city's inhabitants found employment at the Baignol and Alluaud factories, either in the felling and transportation of wood required to fire the porcelain kilns, in the preparation of the molds, or the baking of the porcelain. The manufactured pieces used to be sent to Sevres to be painted, but after the death of Louis XVI and the disappearance of the royal monopoly and patronage, even that final stage was now completed in Limoges. Many of the workers were migratory, L'Aigle knew. He had seen Baignol pamphlets in Paris calling for wintertime employees.

The target had entered the semaphore station, emerged, and waved before again disappearing into the building. His friend responded in kind and then turned his horse toward the east, following the city walls. The Jesuit passed the workers and raised his hand to the rim of his bearskin hat in a polite salute. The porcelain workers stood in stony silence, watching him with dark, impenetrable eyes before resuming their early walk to work. Several minutes later, he had turned the corner of the city walls and disappeared. They had parted. Good. That would make his work easier.

L'Aigle stopped as the path branched off to the right. The workers continued onwards toward the factory, following the left path, the women's skirts trailing over the frozen puddles. He rummaged through his pack and withdrew a flintlock musket. Ramming a cartridge down the muzzle, he emptied gunpowder into the firing pan. L'Aigle crouched in the mud, sighting the dark open doorway to the telegraph station between his notched viewfinder. He remained there unmoving for several minutes, heedless of the alarmed murmurings and the rustle of skirts behind him as porcelain workers hurried past. Nobody bothered a man with a musket; instead, they hustled by as quiet as could be, fearful the weapon would be turned in their direction by its irate owner. L'Aigle did not feel the dampness of the earth soak through the fabric of his trousers or the discomfort of muscles held rigidly to attention but focused intently on the doorway. He put just enough pressure on the trigger until he could feel the firing mechanism tighten under his finger. Now, he just had to wait for the target.

As he waited in the dirt, L'Aigle's thoughts drifted to his uncle. He tried not to think of him; it served little purpose but to thrust him into an all-consuming rage, the anger seething out of every pore like smoke from a brazier. What was it his uncle called himself now? Ah, yes, *emperor* of Austria! In the face of Napoleonic posturing, Francis II had fearfully dissolved the Holy Roman Empire and abdicated not only his own rights to the empire but deprived his family, his children, of the honor that had been their birthright. What right did he have to dissolve an empire that had spanned the breadth of the Germanic territories and encompassed parts of France, Italy, Poland, Croatia, Belgium, and the Netherlands? An empire that had endured since the coronation of Charlemagne in 800 A.D.?

He had *no* right! He was afraid of that Corsican upstart, Napoleon. The Treaty of Campo Formio had been the beginning of the end. Francis had lost the Austrian Netherlands, Corfu, and other Venetian islands in the Adriatic, and agreed to recognize the Cisalpine and Ligurian Republics as independent powers—territory that had belonged to *their* family. Who knew what other republics Napoleon would feel like creating, and where, if ever, Francis would draw the line.

*Calm, calm!* L'Aigle felt his heartbeat accelerate, his breath coming quick in the back of his throat. His hands clenched and his finger tightened involuntarily on the trigger. *Calm...calm.* L'Aigle—or Antoine Albrecht Friedrich Rudolf Viscovitch, Prince Imperial and Archduke of Austria, Prince Royal of Hungary and Bohemia, Duke of Teschen, as he was known in Austrian society—had privately felt the conviction of his own rights to the imperial throne. His cousin Ferdinand, Francis II's son and heir, was a feeble-minded epileptic who had been recently married to Princess Maria Ann of Sardinia—a marriage which L'Aigle doubted would ever be consummated—in preparation for him to take the reins of government. His one coherent command thus far had been to his taster, who, in an effort to prevent him from eating dumplings due to a digestive sensitivity, had been imperiously told: "I am the heir to the empire, and I want dumplings!" So the son would continue the legacy of the father, and the proud remnants of the house of Habsburg-Lorraine would be obliterated.

Unless L'Aigle could prevent it.

Thinking of these things heated his blood and brought him to the quick, willful anger he prided himself in avoiding; a fury which, under normal circumstances, he managed to rein in before it affected him. He had learned early in his profession that a detached reserve was a critical prerequisite to success. But now, feeling that familiar rage course through him, he pulled the trigger a fraction earlier than he should have, and the figure that appeared in the doorway of the semaphore station froze as the masonry immediately to the left of him exploded with the impact of a bullet.

# 83.

*December 10, 1803*

Wolfe raced down the hillside, legs pumping, lungs working like bellows in his chest. He had emerged from the semaphore station quietly elated. The message had been sent. Nicolàs had accepted his story without demur. Mission accomplished. Or so he had thought. Until, in a spray of mortar and stone chips, a bullet had slammed into the masonry an inch from his head. Yelling at Nicolàs to remain in the tower, he raced down the hill, tracing a zigzag pattern he hoped would confuse any waiting snipers. In his peripheral vision, toward the factory, he caught sight of a sprinting figure in homespun—the assassin, he was sure of it: the same man who had attacked him in the stairwell in Paris.

It was time to find out who he was, once and for all. Was he another thug in Etienne's hire? Wolfe didn't think so. This man had the manner and bearing of an aristocrat. Certainly a wealthy one if his Hessian boots were any indication. Ahead, he could see the three-story brick façade of the Baignol porcelain factory. It had been constructed in a U-shaped configuration, opening up toward the Vienne River that wound through the fields behind. A fat, bottle-shaped kiln protruded from the tiled roof, belching dark smoke sixty feet into the sky. The rutted pathway gave way to stone pavers before a large wooden door painted a cheerful red. Wolfe hesitated, blood pounding in his ears, sweat beading on his brow despite the cool of the morning.

There was no sign of the assassin. All was rustic tranquility. To his right amidst the trees, a water mill churned away, driving overhead cables that powered the potters' wheels. The river behind was choked with massive logs from the forests of Limousin, the loggers trying to maximize their yield before winter stilled the river with an icy grip. Lumbermen balanced with nimble dexterity on the rolling logs, directing them with long pointed picks toward the banks where they were hauled up a rampart. The countryside, long denuded of timber, stretched away in shades of gray.

Wolfe ducked down the path to his right, where laborers were splitting logs. They paused in their work, tunics darkly ringed with sweat, mouths dropping in astonishment as a member of the Imperial Guard ran past, the plume on his hat bobbing in agitated accompaniment. A small door to Wolfe's left opened into a domed chamber dominated by a massive kiln thickly striped with iron bands that strengthened the structure during the expansion and contraction of firing. Brawny men, stripped from the waist up, skin darkened by soot, were throwing haunches of pine and oak into rounded alcoves that protruded from the base of the oven. The fires blazed like miniature mouths of hell, the timber quickly consumed in the inexhaustible hunger of the bottle kiln.

Wolfe blinked against the searing heat of the fires and the dark haze that permeated the room. The smoke, emerging sixty feet up from the central kiln, eddied and curled down into the building, entering the kiln chamber through ill-fitting windows and half-open doors.

No sign of the assassin. A door at the rear opened into a large central room, where potters, seated at their wheels, shaped the clay dexterously as it turned under their hands. Plates, bowls, and cups were emerging in various stages of completion, and a long, narrow table held the finished products, draped in damp cloth as they awaited their turn to be glazed and fired. At the far end of the room, Wolfe saw him—a figure in brown, a flash of a white face as he turned toward Wolfe—then he was gone.

Wolfe raced ahead, darted around wheels, and pushed open the door, knife in hand. He eased through into another room, bright and spacious with large windows set into brick walls. Rectangles of early morning sunlight streamed in the windowpanes, capturing sooty particles that swirled through the air. Numerous figures were bent over small boxes applying twenty-four-carat-gold ornamentation or polishing tiny metal hinges with agate tools. Several workers glanced up as Wolfe moved cautiously through the room, his gaze swiveling, muscles tensed.

Where had he gone? Wolfe calculated at least fifty workers occupied the space; a sea of dark heads, divided by a central aisle, bent attentively to their various tasks. A closed door to the far left served as the only other exit, but Wolfe was certain the assassin had not had the time to reach it undetected. He was here somewhere.

Wolfe's arrival had been noted, but there was little or no reaction to his presence. Cujas had told him a little of the porcelain factory as they had made their way into Limoges. The porcelain boxes that emerged from this region were a highly prized collector's item, all inscribed with the now-famous insignia *Peint main*. However, the French nobility was still a miniscule market, and the English blockade rendered any overseas trade virtually impossible. Constant wars limited the expansion of the porcelain industry. Jobs were few, and hungry workers clamored for the privilege; these employees had a quota to fill, or they would be replaced.

To Wolfe's right, the finished wares were being hand-dipped in a bath of clear enamel. He scrutinized the rows one at a time, searching for a movement that was out of place, a worker who was not what he seemed. There! A furtive movement. A man glancing sideways from his place at the enamel bath—a little less attentive to his task than his fellows. Dressed in brown homespun. It was he. Wolfe ran down the central aisle, skirting the workers as he approached the enamel bath. The assassin darted around the table, laden with delicate boxes. The men and women froze at their desks, their faces faintly dusted in fine particles of pale clay.

"Get out!" Wolfe bellowed, brandishing his knife menacingly. They remained immobilized at their stations like ice sculptures. L'Aigle raised his pistol casually with one hand, aimed at the brick ceiling high above their heads, and fired. A small but momentarily deafening explosion sounded in the enclosed room. The gunshot served to break the spell, and in a suddenly tumultuous clamor of pounding feet, the workers fled, leaving the growing quiet and a swirl of fine white kaolin dust in the air.

Wolfe cocked his head to one side, studying his enemy through narrowed eyes. "Because you're concerned for their safety, or because you didn't want any witnesses?"

"Both. I am not a monster, Monsieur Trant."

"Really? Considering that you've been attempting to kill me since I arrived in Paris, you'll forgive me if I find that hard to believe."

L'Aigle shrugged. "Usually it does not take me so long. It is to your credit as a worthy adversary. I am almost disappointed to have to kill you."

Wolfe grinned. "And yet here I am, so annoyingly alive." He moved slowly forward, arms loose at his sides, his gaze locked on the assassin.

"Indeed," L'Aigle admitted grimly.

"Well, for my part you've become as tiresome as you are tenacious."

"I am paid well to be tenacious."

"Oh, I'm sure you are. And what a noble profession it is, to be sure. A thug for hire. I'm sure your ma is so very proud."

L'Aigle's mouth tightened and then, by a visible force of will, relaxed. "I must compliment you on your own ingenuity. I can see that you have been well promoted for your efforts. Commander, is it?" He gestured with the barrel of his gun toward the epaulettes that decorated Wolfe's shoulders. "Napoleon is an ambitious man. Sooner or later, men of intelligence and ingenuity will run afoul of his self-aggrandizing schemes, and you will find yourself buried in an unmarked grave. Do you think the glorious emperor of the French has given a single thought to the plight of the Irish? You think he ponders, late at night in his map room, how he can free the Irish from their English oppressors? Is that what he has promised you?"

"What makes you think I've allied myself with Napoleon?"

"My sources have verified it."

"Then I suggest you re-examine your sources." L'Aigle raised his eyebrows, glancing pointedly at the Imperial Guard uniform. "How is it, then, that someone in your profession is so easily fooled by appearances?" Wolfe retorted.

A simultaneous crash of both doors announced the arrival of a number of gendarmes from ahead and behind. Wolfe counted six, three at each end of the room, all clad in the distinctive blue he had come to recognize, and avoid, in Paris.

"Messieurs, lay down your arms! I'm a member of the Imperial Guard and have specific orders to bring this man in!" Wolfe hollered, unrolling his letter to Villeneuve. Napoleon's personal seal and monogram were clearly visible.

"Stay where you are!" one of the gendarmes shouted. The door behind them opened again. A swarm of policemen spilled into the room, each clutching an antiquated musket that he raised, with relish, in the direction of the two men. Wolfe had the uncomfortable sensation that this cluster of restless boys had not seen much action and were willing to create some if it gave them something to boast about later.

"I am a member of the Imperial Guard!" he repeated more forcefully. Then, glancing at L'Aigle, he realized that both of them were covered in powdered clay. His hat had gone, his face was daubed in white, his uniform largely obscured. "I have Napoleon's personal orders right here! You are interfering with an imperial mandate!" A last-ditch attempt.

"I knew it," L'Aigle hissed, his face contorted by hatred. "You work for that tyrant!" Heedless of the bristling array of weaponry aimed in their direction, the assassin raised his own pistol, cocking the hammer as he did so. Wolfe froze. Dimly the thought occurred to him that the assassin had surreptitiously reloaded his pistol in the last few minutes without taking his gaze from his target. Impressive.

So his time had come to die in battle finally. Well, so be it. A single shot rang out. Wolfe tightened in expectation of the pain he knew was coming. When he felt...nothing, Wolfe opened his eyes without realizing he had closed them. The body of the assassin lay on the floor, blood pooling beneath his chest in a viscous scarlet puddle, turning the fine white dust to a deep pink.

Nicolàs, the officer from the semaphore tower, gripped him by the shoulder, his pistol still smoking in his other hand. "Are you hurt?" Wolfe shook his head, his gaze on the bearded man who lay still and pale on the factory floor. "I apologize for my lateness just now..." The explanation was obvious; the man had only one leg, a roughly carved wooden substitute fitted against his loose trouser where his left had once been. Wolfe had not noticed this in the telegraph tower where Nicolàs had been seated behind a table. "And these men are a little over-eager and under-trained. However, most of them are off for the front at the end of the week so both will be adequately addressed." Then, in a commanding bellow: "Lower your weapons! This man is from the Imperial Guard!"

# 84.

Nicolàs offered a horse cart for transportation back to Paris, which Wolfe accepted, and an escort, which he just as firmly declined. Anxious to put some distance between himself and Limoges before further questions were asked—ones to which he lacked adequate or appropriate answers—Wolfe, citing imperial duties as an imperative to haste, efficiently secured the wounded man within the cart.

"Thank you, for everything." Wolfe briefly clapped a hand upon Nicolàs's shoulder. There was an additional warmth in Wolfe's leave-taking, a gratitude to Cujas as well as his brother, and a pang for the fraternal divisions that kept them apart. Being estranged from one's brother was a sadness Wolfe knew much about. With a quick salute to the soldiers, silent now that the frisson of battle had passed, Wolfe directed his horse toward Paris; the cart and its unconscious passenger trundled behind. Once beyond the view of Limoges, he would turn his horse toward the coast and the transport that awaited him in Calais; the assassin he would leave with a doctor en route.

After ten minutes of eastward travel, the assassin's groans brought Wolfe to a stop. He carried the wounded man to the base of a nearby tree where the extent of his injuries could be more easily assessed. The pallid light of a watery sun cast the sky in shades of bone, the ground beneath whitely pristine with mounded snow. The wind whistled faintly amidst the branches of the trees, and the soft smudge of smoke from household fires in Limoges left trails against the sky to the west. Here, beneath the gnarled branches of an ancient fir, Wolfe laid L'Aigle gently down. Shrugging out of his coat, he roughly tore a strip from his shirt and bound it tightly around the assassin's chest. It was instantly suffused with a spreading crimson stain. The assassin's eyelids fluttered. He was regaining consciousness.

"I have to get you to a doctor."

"Why would you bother?" the assassin muttered heavily. "Napoleon will have me executed regardless…quite publicly, I should imagine. I would rather die here under the trees…" His eyes closed for a moment as his breathing became increasingly labored. A pinkish bubble of blood appeared at the corner of his mouth. "But then perhaps you desire credit for the kill…" he managed, opening his eyes again. They were dark eyes, deeply set in a narrow face, framed by heavy lids that seemed even heavier under their current burden of pain. An almost sculptural goatee defined the squareness of his jaw and the crisp lines of his mouth. It was a familiar face. A face he had seen before, he was sure of it.

"I do *not* work for Napoleon," Wolfe reiterated impatiently. "And if I'd intended to hand you over to the gendarmes, I would've done so already." *Where* had he seen this man? Those years spent boxing had often blurred under the influence of alcohol—his anesthetic of choice to dull the physical pain following a fight and to dissipate the mountain of guilt and regret that always seemed to linger in the back of his mind. He had learned that his memories could not always be trusted.

"You know me, don't you? Before this contract, I mean?" Wolfe asked him. The assassin did not reply but looked at Wolfe steadily. Something in his face confirmed Wolfe's suspicions. The blood seeped through the makeshift bandage, staining the snow like a brilliant flower opening to the sun. The assassin's face was pale. His lungs had been punctured, Wolfe knew. He would not last much longer. Around them, all was quiet, the landscape thickly shrouded in white. Something about the snow, the blood. Suddenly, it came to him—Russia.

"You were there!" Wolfe interjected suddenly. "In St. Petersburg, after the fight. You were with the czar the night he was assassinated."

He remembered that night vividly. The last fight of his notorious career. It had been after the dubious honors he had received as victor, through a dull fog of pain, one eye swollen shut, the other blinking back a river of blood that flowed from a cut on his temple; it was from then that he remembered this man—the thin face of an ascetic, the immaculately trimmed goatee that had never become fashionable in Russia. He had stood slightly aloof from the group, but Wolfe had remembered him because, amidst the frisson of post-battle adrenalin that infected combatants and spectators alike, this man had been unmoved. His interest had been directed not at the fight but at the czar, upon whom his dark gaze fixed with an unwavering intensity. At the time, Wolfe had assumed he was a bodyguard, but later, after he had learned about the czar's assassination, he had wondered. Now, years later, he knew for certain. "You killed him."

"Yes…I had a political imperative…just as you do," the assassin muttered darkly, eyes clouded by pain. "I am Prince Antoine Viscovitch, lately of the Austro-Hungarian Empire…which will now, it seems, die with me…seeking restitution…I wanted my country back, Monsieur Trant…just as you want yours…" His eyes closed; his breath came out in a soft wheeze.

"Who hired you to kill me?" Wolfe leaned close to his ear. "Who hired you?" he repeated more urgently.

Glazed eyes opened, seemed to fix on Wolfe's momentarily, and then closed again. "English…government….official…" he murmured. A thin trickle of blood spilled from the side of his mouth.

Wolfe's mind raced with the implications of the assassin's revelations. Czar Paul's assassination had allowed the rise of his son Alexander I, a Russian leader of more moderate, pro-English opinions, and initiated the collapse of Russia's coalition with France. Obviously, the prince was not above hiring himself out to the English if it coincided with his own personal mission. And it seemed his employers had yet again acquired a favored target.

Below him, the assassin's face tightened; his teeth bared in a grimace; his body convulsed slightly…and then he was limp. His expression relaxed; his hand fell open. And he was gone, lying over a spreading crimson flower in the snow with none left to mourn him.

# 85.

The *Bucentaure* was an eighty-gun ship-of-the-line and the flagship of Admiral Pierre-Charles Villeneuve, who cut an imposing figure on the stern deck in his long-tailed coat buttoned firmly to a somewhat pendulous chin. The morning sun, stretching its fingers across the timbered deck, lit the admiral's meticulously curled wig to brightness, gave a sheen to the golden epaulettes that decorated each shoulder, burnished the two-inch yellow stripe down each pant leg, and lent his sharp-toed half- boots an extra polish. His men, however, were utterly heedless of their admiral's fine turn of figure, and, despite his own care with his morning toilette, Villeneuve himself was stricken with his periodic bout of bilious colic—an ailment that often plagued him in times of stress. Sharp pains lanced through his abdomen as if he were being bored through by a gimlet. Misery tightened his features as he reached out to grasp the rear railing with one trembling hand; the other retrieved a handkerchief from his inside coat pocket and mopped the beads of sweat that collected on his brow and stained the green collar of his uniform. Villeneuve knew from experience that these attacks usually subsided after a few days of bed-rest and Dr. Bechamp's foul-smelling tonic. Bed-rest, under the circumstances, was out of the question, and he had already drained the last of the tonic earlier that morning to little effect. Surveying the bedraggled remnants of the fleet did little to encourage him. They were, again, pinned in Malaga by that infernal Nelson.

The afternoon before, under a brisk southeasterly, Villeneuve had ordered the squadron to sea. Only two English frigates darkly silhouetted the horizon, and so the admiral had obeyed standing orders to attempt to break the blockade. In a moment of bravado, he had the signal for the fleet to leave run up aboard the *Bucentaure*, and in the bustle that followed, he felt the ancestral pride of leading men into battle.

One of his predecessors had fallen at the side of Roland in the pass
of Roncesvalles; another had charged beside Richard Coeur-de-Lion in
Palestine. Admiral Villeneuve was himself a knight of Malta, the nine-
ty-first member of the family to belong to the order. This satisfaction
lasted until the fleet was just beyond the harbor pass, until they emerged
in chaotic disarray beyond the protection of the castles that flanked
the entrance and ventured forth into the Alboran Sea to do battle with
the two frigates. It was then that Nelson and his line of twenty-four
battleships appeared from behind the Cape of Fuengirola and Torre del
Mar, and the two had rapidly become twenty-six or more, taut of sail
and masterfully maneuvering across the swells.

The sea was often tempestuous between Gibraltar and Almerimar,
particularly in the winter months when the Poniente winds began their
annual appearance. The English ships hugged the coastline on either
side, preventing retreat. As the afternoon darkened into twilight and
the Pleiades appeared faintly in the eastern sky, Villeneuve had more
to fear from his own crew than those of the English. The French fleet
was populated by raw landsmen who, confined to harbor by the English
blockade, had little opportunity to gain experience or become trained
in managing a ship-of-the-line under sail. They were cluttered, in turn,
by an additional contingent of six thousand five hundred soldiers, all
seasick and wretched; these fierce veterans of terrestrial battles now
contributed masterfully to the chaos and rapidly falling morale of the
floundering fleet.

The Poniente winds, gusting when the French left harbor, had since
risen to gale-force strength. They rushed headlong through restricted
mountain gaps in the Sierra Almijara and exploded upon the coast like
demented furies, screaming through the rigging and driving the water
to white-crested swells. Buffeted and reflected by offshore islands and
the irregular coastline, the Poniente created the curious conflux of wind
and sea from one direction and swell from another. Many of the French
ships fell into wave troughs broadside to the wind, and the crews, green-
gilled and praying, gave up all attempt to manage the vessels. Through
the dark, cold night that followed, Villeneuve, hoarsely shrieking orders
that ill-trained men struggled to carry out, had little notion of broader
events other than his own immediate misery.

Daylight showed only seven ships remaining in company—struggling along with tattered sails, torn rigging, and broken spars. That left

four unaccounted for, with the only encouragement being the absence of Nelson's fleet, which had vanished as quickly as it had materialized. Evidently, Nelson had determined the few vessels that remained were incapacitated in one way or another, and hardly worth his attention. Villeneuve found himself in dismal agreement.

Further reconnoiter by *Bucentaure*'s first lieutenant determined that of the seven remaining vessels, one had lost her mainmast, another smashed her fore-yard, and the third had had one of her topmasts topple over the side. This, after venturing into the coastal waters for one night—waters that Nelson's fleet had spent the past ninety-four weeks patrolling! Surely that legendary figure was something more than human to have appeared like a wraith from their rear and then to have disappeared with the dawn. As far as Villeneuve was aware, the English had not even engaged; the storm had done Nelson's work for him. Or perhaps those missing four had fallen victim to that terrible fighter who must, even now, be poised a few leagues over the horizon. For with dawn came the hard-acquired wisdom: that Nelson would always be there, waiting, biding his time to spring the ultimate trap that would see Villeneuve and the *Bucentaure* at the bottom of the ocean.

"Admiral Villeneuve?" His capitaine de corvette, François Darlan, interrupted his dismal thoughts. Darlan was one of the few experienced men who had come up through the ranks in the heady burst of egalitarianism that had followed the Revolution. Schooling his features to hide his discomfort, Villeneuve turned and presented an impassive façade to his junior officer. It was a lonely position at the top, and Villeneuve felt that he was always teetering. "The courier has brought a telegram from the emperor." Darlan handed over the yellow envelope, nodded smartly, and left. He was overseeing repairs, Villeneuve knew—not that he would have much success.

While Malaga was home to shipbuilding yards, mathematical schools for marine artillerists, and manufacturers of sail cloth, French custom—without the cash to back it up—had become unwelcome indeed. Villeneuve was sorely lacking in funds. Upon first arriving in Malaga, he had requested cash to supply seventeen thousand men for fifty days, plus normal daily rations, but the French Agent General Le Roy had warned him that French credit in Malaga had already been exhausted. The inspector of artillery had refused to supply any powder or shot unless it was paid for in cash. And apart from providing ships with food, powder, and shot, there was the massive undertaking of getting them seaworthy.

Even before this recent fiasco with Nelson, he had been short-handed and overly encumbered with troops. The three-day run from Toulon had been plagued with difficulties. His ships seemed to lose their masts or sails at every puff of wind, and the fine weather found them constantly engaged in repairing damage. One battleship needed a new main-yard; another had lost her rudder-head; a third had a broken bowsprit; and a fourth had damaged sternworks in a collision. Two were leaking badly. Now, he was down to seven. Even if he miraculously managed to commandeer additional vessels, his crew had been decimated by illness. A little over seventeen hundred seamen were in hospital, and three hundred had deserted since his arrival in Malaga. Press-gangs roamed the streets looking for hardy fishermen but instead swept in a few luckless beggars, vagabonds, and common-law prisoners who didn't know a topsail from a mainsail.

The telegram from the emperor was, no doubt, more of the same: impossible expectations under equally impossible circumstances. Feeling an almost overwhelming anxiety, shards of pain stabbing through his belly, Villeneuve closed his eyes against the early Spanish sun, gripping the telegram convulsively. How did he come to be here? Villeneuve wondered frantically, his breath a quick, panted angst. He thought longingly of his wife in Provence, his home among the pine trees, the rhythmic song of the cicada, and the sun rising over the Alps that ripened the peaches and melons in his fields. Finally, the thought of home strengthening his resolve, he tore open the telegram and read the contents.

Cadiz. He was ordered to Cadiz with all possible haste. That was all very well, but with no ships fit for departure, no men to sail them, and no funds with which to rectify either? Napoleon expected miracles. It did not matter how they were achieved, just so long as they were.

"Capitaine Darlan!" Villeneuve barked, moving gingerly to the stern deck railing to look down upon his junior officer on the main deck. "Complete what repairs you can. We leave for Cadiz first thing tomorrow morning."

# 86.

HMS Victory. Twenty-five nautical miles to the
east of Malaga, Spain
*December 10, 1803*

"He lost his eye at the siege of Calvi, but 'twas at Santa Cruz where he lost his arm," First Mate Thomas Troubridge revealed, sandy hair falling in thick salty tangles over his darkly burnt face, meaty forearms crossed on the wooden mess table.

"And how?" breathed young seaman Mathew Gridley, wide-eyed and in awe of the legendary commander in whose ship he sailed. Various other seamen crowded around the mess table—many having heard this story before but all partial to Troubridge's telling of it, which had been perfected over the years.

"Well, his right arm was shattered and badly bleeding…and we rowed the commander back to the *Seahorse*, that bein' the closest vessel where he could get medical help, ye see. Anyway, Betsey Freemantle, newly married as she was, was waitin' there fer news of her husband, and we got to the *Seahorse*, and Nelson, half- unconscious, refused to board! When we told 'im his very life was in danger, he said: 'I would rather die than alarm Mrs. Freemantle by her seeing me in this state when I can give her no tidings of her husband.'"

A murmur of approval rippled through the sturdy men, sun-darkened and toughened to leathery strips of sinew and muscle. Regardless of age, rank or nationality, the crew of the HMS *Victory* were united by a fierce loyalty that surged through their veins with unbridled intensity; a devotion not to the English navy but to the cripple-gaited, one-eyed, one-armed, slight figure of their captain. With his boyish face furrowed with angst and pain, pouting mouth, and thickly disheveled hair, Horatio Nelson might have been mistaken for an overwrought poet. Earl St. Vincent had pompously pronounced him to be the "merest boy of a captain I have ever beheld!"

In battle, however, this delicate, emotionally erratic slip of a man was transformed into the ice-cold, steely-eyed, unswerving commander, one who thrived on the pitching deck of a ship in the midst of battle, whose cool imperturbability was only heightened by the deafening roar of cannon-fire and the blinding heat of gun-smoke. A glance from him could make the hardiest of men weep, not for any influence he maintained over their careers or their persons, but from his hold on their hearts—an effect only heightened by these mess-table tales that Troubridge related with such dramatic flair.

"And then what?" young Mathew Gridley asked, arms akimbo, round young face eager and expectant in the soft lamp flame that swung gently back and forth in the swell.

"Well'n we rowed him to 'is flagship *Theseus*, where I tried to 'elp him aboard, but he refused, ye see. 'I have got my legs left, and one arm,' he pronounced as proud as could be, and then he scrambled up the ship's side, face white as a sheet, uniform covered in blood, and 'is shattered arm roughly tied up. When he got on deck, he ordered the surgeon to bring the instruments. 'I know I must lose my right arm and the sooner the better,' says he. Half an hour later, he was back at battle, orderin' the men here and there…a sight I'll 'member till the last of me days." Troubridge shook his sandy locks in pensive admiration.

A deck above, Vice-Admiral of the White and Commander in Chief in the Mediterranean Horatio Nelson sat at his table in the day cabin, his thin frame bent laboriously over a parchment.

"Damnation!" he muttered, his quill puddling ink across the paper. Suddenly wracked by a coughing fit, he felt the sweetish heave of nausea that rose and swelled in the back of his throat like the surge of wave beyond the hull. With muscles knotted by rheumatism, recurring pain in his chest, and a perpetual sense of heated blood flaring up the left side of his head, Nelson had become accustomed to his particular bundle of frailties. The West India fever seemed to have taken up a permanent abode in his slight build, and other sicknesses of one kind or another appeared to find similarly ready welcome. Only a week before he had written to his Emma: "I have all the diseases there are, but there is not enough in my frame for them to fasten on."

Despite his physical misery, his thoughts were fixated upon one point: the position of the French fleet. After the encounter with Villeneuve off the coast of Malaga, Nelson had been intercepted by the HMS *Agamemnon* which had been tacking on the southward lee. Captain

Crawley had informed him that Villeneuve's fleet, which had departed from Toulon earlier in the week, had diverged into two: Villeneuve was heading to Malaga with eleven and a second fleet of ten was intending to revictual in Sardinia. Nelson had caught sight of Villeneuve off Valencia and tracked him south to Malaga, unaware of the remaining half of the French fleet somewhere in the Mediterranean behind him.

And so, leaving Villeneuve's crippled remnants licking their wounds in Malaga, Nelson had slowly fought his way east in the teeth of the gale which had dealt Villeneuve such a blow. But so far nothing: just the gray expanse of heaving swells and relentless driving rain that pitted the water and stung the eyes.

He had been given one imperative, and one imperative only: keep Villeneuve's fleet in the Mediterranean. And now there was this second squadron to contend with; one that must be found before it could be destroyed. Maps unfurled before him were covered with pencil lines and scrawlings in a tiny, slanted script: the estimated route (influenced by fluctuating wind strength in the Gulf of Genoa), currents, wave action, the inexperience of the French crew, the provisional options en route—calculations, in short, indicating the most probable locations of this elusive fleet. A raw irritation in the back of his throat announced a coughing fit that wracked his thin body and brought tears to his eyes. As the coughing subsided, Nelson re-read what he had written:

*I have neither ate, drunk, or slept with any comfort since Sunday. I consider the destruction of the enemy's fleet of so much consequence that I would willingly have half of mine burnt to effect their destruction. I am in a fever. God send I may find them!*

# 87.

The tubby fishing boat pitched sickeningly, yawing sideways as a heaving wave surged beneath the hull. It then rushed up eagerly on a rising wall of water, breasting the next swell, before plunging bow-first down in a plume of fine white spray. The sun had already started its descent into the western sky on this wind-whipped winter's day, sending soft shafts of light skittering across the giant swells of the English Channel. Wispy clouds streaked across the sky, their shadows chasing each other over the crests of water beneath, the Channel a patchwork of shadow and light imbued with shades of gray. Hulls of four or five ships-of-the-line lumbered and wallowed through the troughs, destined for the Thames for refit and repair before returning to the blockade.

Wolfe stood at the starboard gunwale, one hand gripping the railing, his back deliberately turned to the dour countenance of Monsieur Vierdieu, who glowered at him through the water-streaked window of the aft cabin. Despite its sometime clandestine operations on behalf of the Resistance, the wide-beamed vessel was a working one. Barrels of salt and bait were tightly secured with water-swollen knots. Forward of the cabin, the broad deck was occupied by the tar-furred ropes of the funnel net, opened to release a glistening mound of red-whiskered mullet and gray-spotted haddock; the catch intermingled with the usual bottom-dwelling crustaceans and shrimp that made their home on the Channel floor. Three men, rendered powerful by the hauling of nets, were gutting the fish, sorting them into different sizes, and packing them in barrels of salt. Seagulls wheeled, dipped, and hovered overhead; others, settling on the bow, fluffed their feathers in deprived agitation, screeching and squawking, their tiny marble-coal eyes fixed on the buffet that slid and jostled tantalizingly with each roll and dip of the boat.

Wolfe, gaze held by the misty horizon, breathed deeply; the tang of salt and sea was most welcome after the pungent, close streets of Paris. Vierdieu seemed to be under the impression that the identification and subsequent pursuit of Primrose was a matter entirely to be laid at Wolfe's door, and the Irishman feared Vierdieu might be right. This uneasiness was all that prevented him from tossing the man overboard.

"*You!*" Vierdieu had snarled when Wolfe boarded, the Frenchman's lips drawn back from his teeth in curled loathing. "I *knew* this would happen! Ce damné anglais send an amateur into Paris who endangers everything we have spent years working for…and now? Now, the French hope is gone. Napoleon maintains his grip." His pale complexion became red-blotched with anger, eyes flashing, and Wolfe was quite sure that if Vierdieu could have waved a hand and consigned him to the depths of hell he would have done so in an instant. Indeed, it appeared the Frenchman was tempted to lunge at Wolfe, beat him senseless, and toss him into a watery grave—anything to vent the steaming heat of his fury. Instead, with one shaking hand, he had combed his quivering mane back into place and, with great force of will, resumed his mask of sour complacency. Wolfe also worried about Jeanne. He had received word that she had safely escaped Fouché's net in Paris. But where was she? What was she doing now? He did not bother disputing Vierdieu's gloomy assessment of French politics, but Wolfe was certain that Jeanne would never admit defeat. As long as Napoleon held the French throne, she would oppose him. And she held the ace card, the prince of the blood, the Duke d'Enghien—unless Desant had already revealed his complicity.

As to his own loyalties, these were less clear. The assassin had been hired by an English government official. But *who?* It didn't seem Pitt's style, but then what did Wolfe really know? Pitt was determined and ruthless when it came to safe-guarding England from invasion; Wolfe knew that much. When the Napoleon infiltration scheme was revealed—and the part a renegade Irishman was to have played in it— Pitt's first instinct would be to publicly distance himself from it. And Wolfe, then, what would he be? A loose string? An inconvenient witness to a failed agenda—an agenda that would be as little understood in London as it would be in Dublin? He and Pitt would both be pariahs. But, of course, Wolfe was not seeking public office, and societal disapproval, however venomous, would not disturb him greatly. He was accustomed to a solitary kind of life where everything he had, he had fought bloody battles for. Pitt, on the other hand, was courting public opinion; he had assured Wolfe on several occasions that Dundas, Hester, Moore, and himself were the only individuals privy to the exact nature of the Irish agenda. So who could have betrayed him but Pitt himself ?

Within a few hours, they would be on English shores, and Wolfe would find Pitt. Usually, he would never have initiated a fight with one so unequal in strength and ability... Pitt was dying. But Wolfe, left with the bilious betrayal by an Englishman once again—one he should have known better than to trust—felt instinctively that the surging ferocity within him had little chance of being contained. And so, knuckles white-clenched over the railing, his face tight with a growing rage, Wolfe waited as the looming shores of England gradually distinguished themselves from the lighter gray of water and sky.

# 88.

Marcel Lavouse, a born-and-raised resident of Boulogne-sur-Mer, shuffled slowly down rue de Lille, past the thick walls of the Basilique Notre Dame, and eased his lanky frame painfully onto the wooden bench that overlooked the Liane estuary. Peering against the late-day sun, Marcel could see the brown alluvial waters of the river as they met the dark blue of the ocean that stretched out to the horizon in gentle rolling waves. A trio of screaming gulls circled high above him, to land with self-important fluffing at his feet. Usually he brought bread for them, but not today.

The city of Boulogne encircled him to the rear, occupying the summit and slopes of the ridge of hills that skirted the right bank of the Liane River. The rectangular shape of the city walls betrayed her origins as a Roman fort, the beach still dotted with Rome's characteristic red-slip ware. Marcel used to find shards as a child, smooth and red like pebbles in the surf. But that was many years ago now. So much had happened. He always sat this way, with the city behind him. Marcel preferred the water view. That at least remained unchanged from his childhood.

To his right, Marcel could see the harbor, which had been enlarged. It was now choked with gunboats and barges, bristling with armament where before there had been only fishing boats lying idyllically at anchor, the waves lapping at their sleek hulls, their owners sleeping in the warmth of the afternoon sun. The slopes had been leveled, access roads constructed, docks dug, quays built, and a lock dam manufactured to keep the vessels afloat during ebb tide. The hillside bustled with activity. Bird cry and wind rustle had been replaced by the roar and clamor of battle, with military exercises commencing at half-past four every morning. Cannon sent screaming iron across the hillside in black plumes of smoke, and cavalry, turning in quick unison, had long since reduced the fields of clover to dirt and mud. The fragrant scent of thyme and lavender that came in with the salty morning breeze was now tainted by gunpowder. Marcel could see the army encampment stretched out across the hillside, each unit divided into neat rows of huts, their perimeter divided by a regular grid. The Romans would have approved. Boulogne had been transformed into Napoleon's personal war-machine. And of course, there, across the wind-swept waters of the Channel, the English watched. And waited.

Not all of Boulogne was unhappy with the course of events. Monsieur Bardot was plumply smug: a merchant made wealthy by supplying the army with munitions procured from across the border. Marcel, however, missed the old days. He had heard a rumor that the invasion of England was imminent. He hoped it was true; he longed for the return of a quiet peace. He was too old for these carryings-on, he thought with some irritability.

A metallic clanking sound diverted him from his melancholy thoughts. A filthy old crone hobbled past, her back bent beneath a bundled burden. Her face, dominated by a sharply protruding nose and a patch over one eye, was framed by stringy clumps of black hair beneath a tattered bonnet. A wide leather strap worn across her chest sported a taonnelet, a small cask painted in red, white, and blue. Small tin cups jangled alongside and proclaimed her trade: she was a cantinière.

Like Monsieur Bardot, she served the needs of the army. But her product, no less necessary, was of a merrier sort. She supplied the soldiers with firewood, liquor, cheese, salami, sausages, coffee, and tobacco. The cantinière would also cook, wash laundry, and complete sewing for a fee. This old woman was followed by a cart, the rickety contraption hauled by a brawny man who walked with a peculiar side shuffle, one foot dragging behind the other, head bent to one side as if trying to scratch his ear with his shoulder. His mouth gaped vacantly. An *idiote*, Marcel thought as he squinted against the sun, shielding his eyes with fingers bent and swollen with arthritis. The two figures shuffled slowly past, the cart wheels clattering on the cobblestones behind. He had never seen her before, he was sure of it. Interesting.

He knew nearly all of the cantinières by name; the army had been camping on his doorstep for several years now, and the process of supply, and the individuals involved in it had become familiar to him. But then the Grande Armée received new recruits every day. Long lines of weary soldiers, slumped in their saddles, arrived from the Italian Alps or the northern frontier. More stomachs to feed. Still, for the rest of that afternoon, until the icy breath of winter began to seep through his woolen coat, chilling him to the bone, he wondered who she was and where she had come from.

"Stand aside, old woman!" a voice thundered from the road behind her. The cantinière shuffled to the road's edge, gesturing rapidly for her companion to follow. Eying the accumulating clouds, the man complied, his dragging foot leaving a slide mark behind in the freshly fallen snow.

A cavalry convoy passed, the soldiers' dark blue breeches and boots encrusted with weeks of dirt. The company's title was proclaimed in silver embroidery on their saddlecloths: Hussars of Death, a veteran contingent that had been fighting in the Italian Alps. Despite their obvious fatigue, the men were tightly wound; they scanned the snow-shrouded countryside, alert to any unexpected movement, cartridge boxes positioned at their hips for easy access. Others felt for the reassurance of bayonets holstered at their sides. They were almost at their destination, but battle tension remained like a humming in their blood, like a clash of steel in their ears, with visions of the dead and dying that would not be easily forgotten. Napoleon had taught them well. They passed the cantinière in a rhythmic thudding of horse-hoofs, splattering her dress and shawl with dark daubs of mud.

The cantinière grunted under her burden. The basket on her back was tightly packed with a fetid array of grimy socks, shirts, and breeches. It also contained—wrapped in a pair of soiled long johns—a bomb, much like the one that had been detonated in rue de Malte less than a week earlier, but smaller in size. Heavy enough that the cantinière was bent double. Joseph had suggested that they hide the bomb in the cart that trundled along behind, but Jeanne preferred to carry it. Limited the liability. Or so she hoped. If the bomb were discovered in her possession, there was the slimmest of chances that in the process she could create a sufficient distraction that would enable Joseph to escape.

Whatever remained of the Resistance had dispersed, its leadership fragmented. Desant had provided evidence implicating Pichegru, Cadoudal, and Moreau, all of whom had been taken into custody. Networks of informants and couriers that had taken years to establish had disintegrated overnight. Napoleon remained, with all his militaristic posturing, on the throne, seemingly more powerful than ever before. And while England beckoned tantalizingly across this brief stretch of water, she remained, it seemed, the last hope left. Jeanne had one last card to play.

# 89.

The officers' quarters were quiet, emptied of the raucous soldiers who had inhabited them only an hour earlier. The officers were all down in the grassy bowl by the sea, rigidly impeccable in blue regimentals, boots polished to a high gloss; Napoleon was in town. Jeanne could see him from her vantage point on the corner of avenue des Pyramides; he rode through the ranks on a spirited white stallion, closely encircled by generals and glittering aides-de-camp. It was the early inspection of the troops that had become customary while the emperor was in residence. He cut a fine figure, Jeanne had to admit. Napoleon held the reins indifferently in his right hand, utterly careless of the prancing, rearing horse beneath him. He rode like a man who was so adept at governing his animal when and as he desired that he did not consider it necessary to keep perpetually in order that which he knew he could subdue in a moment.

But Jeanne's work was not down there; it was up here, on the cliffs that overlooked the encampment, in a U-shaped wooden building painted a pale gray. The structure, erected in two days on a brick foundation, was approximately one hundred feet long, Twenty-three feet wide, with a central rotunda thirty feet in diameter that overlooked the harbor. Jeanne had studied the specifications; a copy of the blueprints had been acquired from the architects for a considerable sum. The central rotunda, or council chamber, served as Napoleon's office—and was where she intended to set the bomb.

Jeanne settled her cloth burden more comfortably across her back as she shuffled up rue de Valmy toward Napoleon's pavilion. All the streets in the Boulogne encampment bore the names of Napoleon's military victories over the Mamelukes in Cairo and over the Austrian and Prussian armies after the Revolution. Not a modest man, Jeanne mused, but certainly a shrewd move. These streets served to remind his men of their glorious past and the expectation of a similarly splendid future. She was surprised he had not named a street rue de Londres in his arrogant anticipation of conquering the English capital.

Breathing hard, the weight of the bomb heavy on her back, Jeanne finally emerged at the summit of the encampment where rue de Marengo widened to meet the lawns that surrounded the pavilion. Juvenile hazelnut trees lined the pathway, their bare limbs festooned with thousands of catkins that showered the snow-covered ground with yellow pollen. A formal pool, ice gathering around the edges, was home to pair of black swans, courtesy of the mayor of Amiens. Jeanne, however, was not interested in the grounds or even in the pavilion that rose in the center. It was the brick risings underneath that caught her attention. The sentries were stationed at the building's front and served as a ceremonial display of authority rather than fulfilling any real security needs. The Grenadiers à Pied de la Garde Impériale—which formed the most senior regiment in the Grande Armée—made their camp directly adjacent to the gray pavilion. During their campaigns in Poland, Napoleon had given them the nickname les grognards, the grumblers. It was this contingent of fiercely loyal infantrymen—some of whom had served with him in over twenty different campaigns—who formed his last line of defense and rendered any further protection superfluous. Napoleon, however, was galloping across the inspection grounds far below, and the Grenadiers, along with everyone else, were in rigid attendance. Regardless, a cantinière was out of place within Napoleon's manicured grounds; she served the needs of the Grenadiers, but the weekly supply wagon from Paris fulfilled the requirements of their emperor. Napoleon had little to do with the likes of her, and it would not do to be spotted in the vicinity.

Jeanne hastened around to the back of the building. There she paused, breathing hard, her cloth bundle deposited on the ground. Removing the layers of greasy underclothes, she gingerly grasped the bomb to her chest. Crouching down, Jeanne peered under the building. Brick columns, approximately ten feet apart, supported the structure and raised it a foot or so above the ground. This provided a certain grandiose aspect to the pavilion and enabled Napoleon a clear view across the Channel to where his enemy awaited him. It also allowed Jeanne the perfect place to plant the bomb.

She slithered under the house, the ground hard and cold beneath her layers of tattered rags, the bomb cradled to her chest like a newborn, the fuse an umbilical cord trailing behind. Ten feet or so under the house, she paused, trying to gauge her position. Approximately fifty feet of planking stretched out to either side; the central rotunda should be just overhead. Scooping out a shallow depression with frozen fingers, Jeanne deposited the hollow iron ball carefully in its snug nest of dirt. Then, running the fuse line through her fingers, she awkwardly shuffled her body backwards, retreating toward the pale light and the structure's edge. She could feel the ridge of thick twine under her fingers that spanned the fuse horizontally at thirty centimeter intervals. One. Two. Three…

What was it Pitt had written in his instructions? Thirty centimeters in sixty seconds. The Resistance had always used lightweight paper filled with gunpowder as a fuse, but earlier that year, an Englishman by the name of William Bickford had produced a startling prototype for the English government: a safety fuse which consisted of a hollow length of cord filled with gunpowder and coded in length according to its burn time. Thirty centimeters in sixty seconds. The paper fuse was, predictably, unreliable; it could not be used in wet or even damp conditions and was fragile, often tearing, spilling the powder, and breaking the line of fire. Pitt was a useful ally and his trust in her would now be vindicated. Sliding out from under the house, skirts damp and smeared with mud, she carefully concealed the fuse under an inconspicuous pile of leaves. Joseph would know where to find it. Napoleon would not die just yet—she had unfinished business with him first, and the emperor might require additional motivation to comply.

# 90.

BOULOGNE. FRANCE
*December 11, 1803*

"We caught her under the building, sir."

Initially, she resembled little more than a shuffling heap of dirty rags, her back humped with age, head bent to her chest. Black hair emerged, stringy and limp, from beneath her sagging bonnet, and her battered clogs scraped hollowly along the polished wooden floor. She could not have presented a more unfavorable contrast to the immaculately starched uniforms and gleaming leather boots of the soldiers who flanked her to either side or to the polished ostentation of the council chamber into which she was roughly propelled. The circular room was papered in silver-gray, the ceiling painted with golden clouds in an azure sky. An eagle soared overhead, directed in its flight toward England by a thunderbolt and a Napoleonic star. The imperial mission: to conquer the "nation of shopkeepers," as Napoleon had referred to them so derisively a month earlier. A map of the Channel hung on the wall, and at the large oval table covered by green baize was only one chair—for the emperor; officers were expected to stand in his presence. The chair was currently occupied, and the table strewn with papers. A dark, hunched figure in a greasy black overcoat stood to one side.

"She was caught with this, sir." One soldier came forward, a large bundle under his arm. He lay it gingerly on the table, the dirty blanket falling aside to reveal a bomb. For a moment, the men said nothing. Napoleon, seated comfortably behind his baize green desk, raised his eyebrows. The old woman kept her gaze fixed on the floor. Fouché could see the fleshy bridge of her nose below a stringy fringe of hair.

"What do you have to say for yourself, old woman?" Napoleon barked. "What possible reason have you to assassinate me?"

Suddenly, to their surprise, the woman erupted into a keening wail, falling to her knees. She was going to beg for forgiveness—how tiresome, Fouché thought.

"I think she must be mad, sir," the soldier offered. "Perhaps, some monarchist put her up to this—"

"Shut her up, would you?"

Fouché drew back his arm and slapped her hard, leaving the scarlet imprint of his hand across one cheek. The old woman subsided into muffled, gagging sounds, her thin shoulders heaving under the weight of some personal misery. "Did you find any money on her person?" Fouché asked. The soldier's involuntary wince told him they had not cared to look. The woman reeked; he doubted she had bathed since the Revolution. "Was she alone?"

"Yes, sir."

"Take her away!" Napoleon motioned irritably. The soldiers each took an arm and proceeded to drag the old woman out.

"Wait!" Fouché abruptly interjected, noticing a grayish smear coating the palm of his right hand. "Bring her back."

He yanked at her bonnet. The woman's hands flew to her head, emitting a shriek before hitting out at Fouché with mittened hands, screaming obscenities in hoarse, guttural tones.

"You are wasting my time, Commissioner," Napoleon spat irritably. "I have more pressing issues."

"You will want to see this." Fouché pulled hard on her hair until it came off in a matted heap in his hand. Beneath, shortly cropped dark hair was exposed. Grasping her roughly by the chin, Fouché forced her face upwards. There was a gasp of horror as the men realized half of her nose had gone. Fouché, undeterred, reached out with his other hand and proceeded to break off the chalky pieces of plaster that remained. Then, he wiped her cheek with the sleeve of his coat, smearing the thick makeup to reveal the pale, unblemished skin beneath. "Your Imperial Highness, meet Primrose."

# 91.

"Primrose!" Napoleon breathed in astonishment. "Mon dieu." The old woman straightened up, her figure, for the first time, erect, her hunchback, the dragging painful gait gone. More waif than woman, her shorn hair framed a narrow face, large dark eyes defiant. "Leave us!" Napoleon barked sharply, his narrowed gaze fixed on the woman before him. The soldiers, mouths agape, glanced back over their shoulders before moving reluctantly from the room. The infamous Primrose apprehended! And by themselves, no less! What a story this would be at mess…

"You, as well," Napoleon gestured impatiently toward Fouché, who started visibly, surprised at his unexpected eviction. The commissioner opened his mouth to protest; then, apparently thinking better of it, he inclined his head shortly and withdrew, eyes glittering, mouth tight with suppressed anger.

They were alone, the emperor of France and the leader of the French Resistance who had plagued him for so long. "How lovely to see you again," Napoleon began, his voice deliberately low. "Although, I must admit, your attire is somewhat less alluring than the last time we met."

"There are few cantinières clad in lace and muslin," she replied evenly.

"True," Napoleon mused, fingers drumming restlessly on the arm of his chair. His lips curved in a slight smile, but his eyes remained watchful and cold. "So you come to kill me yet again. I thought we had an agreement."

"You betrayed me," Jeanne said heatedly. "You told me that you would give me my brother in return for the name of the prince supported by the Resistance. I gave you the Duke d'Enghien. Now I have come for my brother; you will bring him to me, or the other bomb, that your soldiers did not find, will detonate and we will both die."

"You think you can threaten me? Here, in a camp surrounded by thousands of hardened, battle-tested soldiers sworn to protect me?" Napoleon rose from his chair, his sallow complexion darkening with anger. He stalked around the desk until he stood before Jeanne. "Do not forget, madame, that I am also a soldier. I will not hesitate to cut you down where you stand." His hand clenched convulsively around the hilt of the sword that nestled at his side.

"I have no doubt of it. But I am not afraid of it, mon empereur," Jeanne replied derisively. "And do not assume you will find me such an easy target. Death and I have become well-acquainted these three years past, but he has yet to call me in. When he does, it will be as part of the struggle to free this country from tyranny. But you..." she shook her head in mock sorrow. "Assassinated in a small bomb attack in your tent in Boulogne. Rather an innocuous end for such a great military commander, wouldn't you say? The English will be thrilled."

"You are bluffing. You could not have carried two such contraptions in here without being detected." He gestured at the bulky package wrapped in dirty rags that lay ominously still on the table.

Jeanne smiled slightly, her head dipping in acquiescence. "Assuming I am alone, of course," she murmured. "But then, your loyal battle-tested soldiers have sworn to it, so what do you have to worry about?" Napoleon held her gaze for a moment before moving rapidly to the door. He flung it open and barked orders at the soldiers waiting outside: instructions to disperse, find out whether Primrose had been seen with another agent, and search for a second bomb—most likely hidden on these very premises.

Shutting the door behind him, he returned. Leaning close, until his mouth was inches from her ear, he said quietly, deliberately: "Do you think I am stupid? Are you that enthralled with the monarchy that you would sacrifice your own brother to the cause?"

"What do you mean? I gave you what you wanted. Didn't you apprehend the Duke d'Enghien?"

"Oh, indeed, I did," Napoleon assured her, his voice smooth, his anger once again contained. He was entirely too glib; Jeanne didn't like it, and for the first time she felt a prickle of unease. "The duke was tried and executed at Château de Vincennes this morning for crimes against France." Jeanne blanched, unable to conceal her slight intake of breath. "The traitor was apprehended, despite your efforts to warn him." Napoleon withdrew a crumpled roll of parchment from the satchel that hung loosely on the back of his chair. Jeanne recognized the hasty note she had sent via horseback courier, alerting the Duke d'Enghien to his imminent danger.

"Napoleon Bonaparte seeks to end your life, hasten from France with all speed," Napoleon read flatly. "This," he stabbed the small sketch of a flower at the bottom of the note, "is your trademark, is it not? A primrose, is it? My men found this on his person when he was captured in Switzerland."

Jeanne swayed slightly on her feet, chest rising and falling with increasing agitation. So it had all been for naught. A prince of the blood, the hope of the Resistance…kidnapped and murdered. She was to blame. Michel Desant had given them all up—Moreau, Pichegru, Cadoudal. It was only a matter of time, Jeanne had concluded, before he named the Duke d'Enghien; she had hoped to pre-empt this seemingly inevitable disclosure by revealing the duke's identity to Napoleon in exchange for her brother, whom the emperor had confirmed was incarcerated. It had been agreed that when the duke had been secured, her brother would be released. Immediately thereafter, Jeanne had sent an urgent courier to warn the duke to flee France. In this manner, she had hoped to confirm her brother's whereabouts but also facilitate the duke's escape into Switzerland. He had made it across the border, but Napoleon's dogs had proved relentless. The Duke d'Enghien—the prince of the blood, heir to the throne of France, the last descendant of the House of Condé—had been brought back to Château de Vincennes where he was ignominiously shot, then buried in an unmarked grave.

Jeanne felt the world darken around her. All these years, she had fought for the overthrow of this Corsican tyrant and, in two days, she had succeeded in destroying the one man who could unify the opposition; a kind man, a good man. She felt the grief well up in her throat, tears trickle unheeded down her dirty cheeks.

"My brother?" she whispered hoarsely, clinging to a shred of hope that remained.

"You *presume* to ask about your brother? After betraying me?" Napoleon tossed the crumpled letter on the table behind him. He moved closer to Jeanne, grasping her jaw gently, running the tips of his fingers down the column of her throat until they paused and tightened slightly around her neck.

"Please…let me see Joachim," Jeanne pleaded, tears spilling freely down her cheeks. She felt that all her strength was gone. The discipline she had brought to bear in her training, and in every stratagem since, had evaporated. She felt as she did all those years ago, when she had first discovered her twin missing: lost and frightened, young and helpless.

"Joachim is dead. He was executed two years ago," Napoleon said flatly, his fingers tightening about her throat until Jeanne felt her windpipe constrict painfully.

"No!" she rasped, fighting to maintain focus, to remain alert as her vision blurred, blood thundering to a deafening crescendo in her ears. Not Joachim…please…mon dieu, not Joachim. It couldn't be true; she would have *felt* it. She would have known somehow, wouldn't she? And while Jeanne would feel the acute pain of the duke's death for the rest of her life, this man, *this monster*, had taken her brother from her. And from beneath the almost suffocating weight of her grief, the anger began to boil. Perhaps her life could still be employed usefully. Why should she die and leave him to live? It seemed that Death had finally called. She would not go alone; this much, at least, she could do right…

"Don't you realize," Jeanne rasped contemptuously, "however glad the nobility of the ancien régime may be to return to France, however willingly they might do lip service to the risen star, you could never be, for the true aristocracy or the peasants of La Vendée, the natural and legitimate ruler of France?" As she finished speaking, Jeanne flung her right arm upwards, slamming the heel of her palm against the side of Napoleon's nose.

He recoiled with a grunt of pain, blood flowing from his right nostril. "I'll kill you," he snarled, lips curling back from teeth washed pink with blood.

"Your Imperial Highness!" A sharp rap sounded at the door.

"Go away!" Napoleon roared, staunching the blood flow from his nose with the sleeve of his coat.

"A message from Admiral Villeneuve, sir! You said you wanted to be notified if any communication came from the fleet—"

The soldier's words were cut off abruptly as Napoleon flung open the door. Snatching the telegram from his hands, Napoleon rapidly scanned the contents, his face paling behind the starkly crimson smear of blood that decorated one cheek.

"Damnation!" he thundered, glaring ferociously at the messenger, who seemed to diminish into his boots with fearful dread.

"What the *hell* is Villeneuve doing in Cadiz?" Napoleon exploded, flinging the offending telegram at the cowering messenger. "Mon dieu, I will have his head for this! Get me Admiral Latouche! And get *her* out of my sight!"

As Jeanne was hustled out the door by two soldiers, each stumbling over each other in his haste to comply, she felt, amidst the immense weight of her grief and anger, a grim satisfaction that Wolfe's stratagem at least had been employed to good effect. The French fleet was divided. With Villeneuve in Cadiz, Napoleon could not hope to present a force sufficient to face the English on the Channel.

# 92.

"What did you think, Hazlitt? Quite a performance, eh?"

William Hazlitt, reporter for the *Morning Chronicle*, looked over his notebook at James Brighton, his colleague at the *London Times*. Hazlitt nodded perfunctorily and returned to his work, quill scratching rhythmically across the paper. Brighton, however, was not to be deterred.

"I thought Pitt quite astounding, myself…and to be cheered before he had even uttered a syllable! What do you think of that?" But evidently the question was rhetorical, for Brighton rambled on in a voluble display of Pitt-adulation that Hazlitt, a staunch Whig supporter, found most annoying.

"He exhibited strong marks of bad health, I thought," Hazlitt interjected ungraciously, determined to extricate himself from the conversation as soon as possible. "I would be surprised if he lasted the year."

Brighton blinked owlishly at him from behind iron-rimmed spectacles, a slightly hurt look on his face. "Perhaps, somewhat," he conceded reluctantly. "Pitt did seem to labor more than previously…in his lungs." Brighton worried a tuft of tweed that had unraveled from his pants leg. "But you must admit, overall, he was inspiring! The call to arms, the denunciation of France. How did he put it? 'The liquid fire of Jacobinical principals desolating the world!' There is little doubt, Hazlitt, who is best placed to fight this war; it certainly is not Addington. He cut a paltry figure in comparison!"

Hazlitt grunted noncommittally, head deliberately buried in his notebook. There was little he could say to refute Brighton's conclusions. Pitt was grudgingly acknowledged by his enemies, as well as by his friends, to be an orator of torrential eloquence, sweeping the masses along in the rushing noise and foam of a great enthusiasm.

Brighton, infused by Pitt's fiery oratory and eager to write his own account of the proceedings of the House, hurried away. Hazlitt, glancing up through the milling confusion of politicians and lawyers, caught sight of a lanky figure descending the stairs; a burly Scot flanked him to one side. Pitt! Hazlitt needed a quotation. Something to mitigate the damage done by today's thundering oration. Hazlitt hated to admit it, but Brighton was right. Pitt had always had a silver tongue; Addington appeared an ineffectual bumbler by comparison.

There was one curiosity that had caught Hazlitt's eye. He had been scanning the court records of the previous week's proceedings in the House of Commons and had come across a reference to legislation previously advocated, but this morning withdrawn, by Pitt. It referred specifically to the independence of Ireland and the emancipation of Catholics, a topic that had always served to isolate Pitt and unite his foes against him. Why, three years previously, would he insist upon the advance of this legislation, even when it forced him from office, only to withdraw it at the height of his popularity when the people were, Hazlitt reluctantly admitted, clamoring for his return? There was a story here, Hazlitt was certain of it. Something just didn't quite fit.

Dundas hovered attentively at Pitt's side as they made their way through the throng and press of bodies exiting the House. "Will, why don't we head to White's for some brandy? Or perhaps Drury Lane to see David Garrick? I have heard phenomenal reviews of his Hamlet."

"Thanks, Mal. But I'm really not in the mood." The session had gone as he had expected, but it left Pitt feeling dejected nonetheless.

"Or the Italian Opera House in Haymarket? Handel is playing—"

"Mr. Pitt! Mr. Pitt!" A reporter for the *Morning Chronicle* was shouldering his way through the milling crowd. With a sigh, Pitt recognized William Hazlitt, the militantly zealous reporter employed by a staunchly Whig paper. "What about Ireland, Mr. Pitt?" he called out. "Are you still advocating Catholic emancipation and independence for Ireland? Are you aware that many peers consider that treasonous?"

"Of course they do," Pitt snapped. "And these are the same peers who would like nothing better than to keep Ireland subjugated as long as England can profit by it." Mal laid a warning hand on his friend's arm, but Pitt would have his say. "To answer your question, Mr. Hazlitt, I have *always* advocated Irish independence and Catholic emancipation. It is not a question of prevailing political winds or economic convenience; it has become a matter of *morality*."

"But you withdrew the legislation in the House?"

"Yes," Pitt replied. "I did."

"May I ask why?" Hazlitt called.

"By all means, Mr. Hazlitt. I am as fierce a proponent of freedom of the press as I am of nations."

"Why, then?"

But Pitt had already gone, disappearing through the crowd with Mal Dundas at his side.

# 93.

"Will, 'tis cold; let me call you a cab at least."

"Dammit, Mal, stop treating me like an invalid! I am going to walk. By myself !"

Pitt glared at Dundas, then turned and stalked down Victoria Street, his shoulders hunched against the cold. He turned left on Marsham, intending to stop at Fuller's pub on Horseferry Lane—he hadn't been there since his student days, and a hot brandy sounded just right.

Pitt had been ill all the previous afternoon. Doctor Canning had busied himself over his prostrate form with fidgeting fastidiousness. Canning prescribed a two-week spa trip to Bath for the waters that Pitt refused to take, a new concoction of magnesium bitters that Pitt refused to swallow, and an injunction to remove his mind from public business, whereupon Pitt merely raised his eyebrows with amused disbelief.

"I believe I have at last baffled the art of medicine, and that the expedients to rescue me are, thankfully, at an end," Pitt had remarked with his usual good humor. The former prime minister, despite his feeble frame, had been endowed with a jovial temperament; he possessed a mental Midas-touch, which transformed all the quotidian tedium of life into the bright gold of amusement—a quality that was as endearing as it was frustrating, particularly for those that insisted upon, and continued to hope for, medical restitution.

As the afternoon had faded into early evening, Dundas had poked his head around the door of Pitt's bedchamber. "How is he, Hester?"

"He is bloody miserable! He can keep nothing on his stomach, nor can he sit down to dinner without being sick!" Hester had hissed, hands on her hips, face clenched in worry. She sighed and rubbed her forehead with the heel of one hand. "He was roused from sleep yesterday morning with some dispatch or another, then went down to Windsor. Mr. Adams arrives with a paper, Mr. Long with another, then Mr. Rose… I manage to convince him to take a little bottle of cordial confection in his pocket before he is off to meet with the king, and then the House until three or four in the morning. Home for supper and closeted for another two hours or more reviewing papers and agendas...and wine and wine! Scarcely up this morning, when rat-a-tat-tat—twenty or thirty people, one after another, and the horses walking before the door from two till sunset, waiting for him. It is enough to kill a man—it is murder!" Pitt had always been notoriously feverish in his devotion to political duty, but this was unprecedented, even for him. With the French preparations escalating for imminent invasion, Pitt thought it worthwhile to make one last attempt to force the Addington administration to any coherent defensive action. When this proved to little effect, he had again begun to dominate affairs through sheer merit, speaking with violent passion against weak or pernicious half-measures. His lanky frame, despite wracking coughs and an increasingly alarming pallor, was the personification of activity and purpose.

"To what end?" Dundas asked, his expressive countenance reflecting sinking dread, fear, and worry.

"No bloody end! It is all *useless*!" Hester exclaimed with tearful fury. "Addington has truly befuddled the situation, damn him! And it seems Will must pay the price!" Angrily wiping the tears from her cheeks, Hester glanced toward Pitt's prone figure, a slight mound under the bedcovers.

Eventually, a tepid bath and a strong night draft appeared to produce a surprisingly sudden recovery. Against the vigilant objections of both Hester and the doctor (Dundas remained silent, knowing Pitt's stubborn intractability), Pitt insisted on keeping a further appointment with the king, and then on going to Parliament that very night.

A dank stench pervaded the backstreets of Westminster. Faded advertisements plastered chipped and mildewed masonry; yellowed and torn, they advertised the legendary tricks of the conjurer Breslay and the uncanny bird imitations of Italy's Gaietano. In these narrow lanes— between last year's entertainments, the detritus of rotted vegetables and the occasional maggot-breeding carcass—the poor and downtrodden skulked. Pitt had forgotten: the smells, the dark labyrinth-like architecture, the tiny slipways and hidden courtyards. It had been years since he had revisited this part of town, on foot, that is. Despite constantly being in Parliament, he had always taken the carriage to Holwood or Downing Street.

Fending off the occasional hawker, Pitt made his way to the river, an unremarkable figure in his faded black overcoat buttoned to the neck and the old-fashioned top-hat that had seen several seasons. Pitt was, if nothing else, frugal by inclination as well as by necessity, and this somewhat patched appearance served him well in the backstreets of London. From the shuttered windows of a grubby tenement, a mother's hoarse voice could be heard singing a lullaby, her tired melody interspersed with the persistent wails of a colicky infant:

*Baby, baby, naughty baby,*
*Hush, you squalling thing, I say.*
*Peace this moment, peace, or maybe*
*Bonaparte will pass this way.*
*Baby, baby, he's a giant,*
*Tall and black as Roen's steeple,*
*And he breakfasts, dines, rely on't,*
*Every day on naughty people…*

Pitt shook his head wearily as he listened, pausing momentarily before her window. While English caricature strove to cut the Little Corporal down to size, he loomed ever-ominous in the people's imaginations—a dark shade poised to gnaw on the bones of disobedient children. Not unlike the giants that inhabited Jack's beanstalk, mused Pitt; didn't they eat Englishmen too? *Fee-fi-fo-fum! I smell the blood of an Englishmen, be he alive or be he dead, I'll grind his bones to make my bread.* What was it with cannibalism and nursery rhymes? Perhaps it was about raising children ready to do battle? The small boys in Walmer, marching proudly behind Colonel Pickford, came to mind. The thought depressed him, and he strode deliberately onwards, booted feet splashing through the muddy pools left from last night's rain.

The pub was situated on the Thames. The river gleamed with an oily sheen in the light of a yellow moon, exuding a vaporous gas that hung over the surface like a shroud. Pitt was reminded of the legislation he had planned to push through in his last years in office, a proposal by— what was his name? Martin, John Martin—to construct eighty-three miles of subterranean sewers, brick channels that would contain the noxious discharge that currently choked the Thames, killed the fish, and flowed freely through the streets and thoroughfares of London. Mal was right. He had to get back into office. Addington was a failure.

Pitt paused in mid-stride, feeling the familiar knife-blade in his belly.

The pain surged and intensified until Pitt, immobilized by it, thought the end had come. He wished momentarily that he was delivering a thundering oration in Parliament, as his father had been when he died. Instead, he thought with wry humor, they would find him face-down in a puddle of sewage in a dingy alley in the old part of Westminster; this vision was followed by a simple regret for all the things he had left unaccomplished. Just give me a year, or six months even; there was so much left to do.

A dark figure emerged from the shadows, blocking his path.

"I was just wondering, Mr. Pitt. Were you intending to betray me all along, or did the commitment to Irish independence just become a bit inconvenient?"

Wolfe Trant. Pitt did not reply—he had not yet the breath for it. The pain lessened slightly. Perhaps he was not to die today after all. Or perhaps that fate would now be fulfilled by an irate Irishman instead of a bellyache.

"And why, after all, should a prestigious politician such as yourself be required to keep his word to an Irish knockabout?" His voice was dangerously soft, his tone scathing.

"You do not trust me, Mr. Trant. I do not blame you for that; you do not know me," he managed.

Wolfe laughed mirthlessly, his hands clenched. "Know you? Aye, I know you well enough, Mr. Pitt. You're another Englishman full o' empty promises. Hanam 'on diabhal, I trusted you!" he ground out. "More fool I."

Pitt reached inside his coat but before he could retrieve what he was looking for, he found the sharp point of a blade pressed against the column of his throat.

"I'd think a bit more about that, if I were you," Wolfe growled. "Someone in the English government wants me dead, Mr. Pitt, and I am not entirely sure that isn't you."

"Papers, Mr. Trant…I want to show you papers…"

Wolfe stiffly nodded his assent, and Pitt withdrew a creamy roll of parchment that he unfurled. Small neat lines of dense script covered the page, which was embossed at the bottom not only by the royal seal but also by the extravagantly flourished signature of the king himself.

"What's this, then?" Wolfe glanced up, suspicion and distrust etched in every line of his face.

Pitt recited the first paragraph without glancing at the paper, his eyes fixed on Wolfe's: "Herein contains the solemn commitment of His Royal Majesty, King George III, to support, and enlist support within the highest level of the peerage, the independence of Ireland and religious freedom for the Catholics."

"So why, then, did you withdraw the legislation in the House?"

"Because the king is not yet prepared to support it. This," Pitt gestured toward the parchment in Wolfe's hand, "depends upon two factors."

"Which are?" Wolfe growled.

"My resumption of the office of prime minister and the containment of the French threat."

"The *containment* of the French threat?" Wolfe asked incredulously. "Sure, England has been at war with France on and off again for the past five hundred years; who's to say when France is *contained*?"

"Napoleon's army of invasion, Mr. Trant. Just the invasion threat to England. I know you are impatient; you have every right to be. You have been an advocate for Irish independence for decades now, as have I. But we have to bide our time if we want this to work. Even with the king's support, legislation supporting independence in Ireland will not pass now. The Houses are focusing on one thing and one thing only: the French. We need to establish a strong coalition government to deal with Napoleon. Then, and only then, will I be able to push forward the Irish legislation."

Wolfe continued to look suspicious.

"As you can imagine, Mr. Trant, this document was obtained with no little effort, and I hope satisfactorily illustrates my commitment to Ireland, as well as to the terms of our own agreement."

"And the assassin hounding me ever since my arrival in Paris? Do you have any knowledge of that, then, Mr. Pitt?"

"Somehow, the opposition discovered our meeting at Newgate. They will do anything to thwart Irish independence and my return to power."

Wolfe said nothing for a moment, then, realizing that he was still holding a knife to Pitt's throat, dropped his arm. "I apologize, Mr. Pitt," he said gruffly, "for doubting you. I've had little experience of honest Englishmen."

"In politics, Mr. Trant, neither have I..."

# 94.

"We must hit Boulogne with *everything* we've got," General John Moore stated emphatically, leaning over the table toward Pitt. "We've little choice. We don't know where Napoleon intends to land. We cannot even muster adequate defenses to protect London."

Pitt sighed, his breath a sharp exhalation in the cold morning air. "What do you think, Mal?"

"'Tis the age-old tenet of English naval strategy, as ye know," Dundas mused. "In a crisis, you must concentrate on the point of greatest danger. As at the time of the Spanish Armada, so now with the French. The western approaches to the Channel are the most vulnerable. The best defense may verra well be an offensive action."

The wooden picnic bench was snugly situated beneath an ancient yew and teetered slightly atop the massive gnarled roots that extended out from the mottled trunk like thick weathered arms. The damp remains of last year's canopy formed a pungently earthy carpet underfoot, and the thin needle-like leaves in the dappled branches above glistened with dew in the lackluster warmth of a pale early sun. While the pewter sky was free of clouds, gusts of wind blew down from the north, stirred the leaves, tugged at the coats of the men, and rattled the edges of the map that was unfurled across the table. Pitt, however, had insisted upon being outside.

"The sun is out, and so must we be!" he had declared with determined joviality. Hester had brought tea and scones. The scattered remnants of crumbs and jam dotted the map; the teapot anchored one corner, while the cups and saucers did service to the other three. Pitt himself appeared the picture of rural tranquility, his long figure sprawled casually in his seat.

Difficult to believe they were planning a daring midnight raid upon which their very survival as a nation depended, Dundas pondered, examining the map again through bleary eyes. "Our defenses are pitiful, that much seems clear. But how bad is it really?" he asked.

"Our defensive force is concentrated in Chelmsforth, to the north," Moore answered, his finger tracing an arc on the map before them.

Pitt and Dundas were heavy with a gritty weariness that shadowed the hollows of their faces and rumpled both hair and clothing. Having snatched an hour or two of rest here or there, in a stiffly upright arm-chair or slumped across a sofa, they had emerged in much need of the tar-black tea Hester had provided. The long stretch of night—poring over maps, forming and discarding strategy, planning and preparing— had left them drained and exhausted. General Moore, however, seemed impervious to the general air of overnight dishevelment. His uniform was crisp; his hair, neat and gleaming; his swarthy face intent; his dark eyes probing and alert. He was the epitome of professional vigilance.

"Batteries," the general said, "have been established in the Thames and at Chatham, to the south and the east. Should Chatham fall, the main line of defense for London will be along the heights from Black-heath, Battersea, and Wandsworth. To the south, we will make a stand along Sussex Downs, a particular vulnerability being the Dorking Gap, the deep valley formed by the river Mole that extends between West Humble and Mickleham."

There was a silence as the men pondered the map before them. They were all painfully aware of the inadequacy of the defenses, and the ease with which Napoleon, with his formidable army, would be able to penetrate them. Once the French emperor managed to get his troops on English soil, London would be his. It was just a matter of time.

"And at sea?" Dundas asked.

"At last word," Pitt spoke, smoothing down a corner of the map the wind had tugged free, "Napoleon's Mediterranean fleet had divided in two, Villeneuve heading for the south of Spain and the other squadron sailing, apparently, to Sardinia for provisioning. We have since received word from our agent in Cadiz confirming Villeneuve's arrival; it seems Wolfe was successful in diverting him."

"And the other fleet?" Dundas asked. "Do we know where it is? Has it been confirmed in Sardinia?"

"Captain Calgrave of the *Agamemnon* intercepted Nelson, who is currently attempting to locate the other squadron, but the weather is hell in the Med at the moment…"

"So…we don't know where it is, precisely?" Moore interjected somberly.

"No," Pitt sighed. "Which leaves a fleet of ten unaccounted for."

There was a moment's silence as the men contemplated the likelihood of this second squadron eluding Nelson and making it through the Straits of Gibraltar.

"And with St. Vincent's fleet out of commission…" Dundas muttered.

Pitt had received notification less than an hour before of repair delays in Southampton where St. Vincent's fleet had been berthed. The missive from Pitt's contact had been terse: sabotage was suspected, but culprits had yet to be apprehended; the situation was being further exacerbated by escalating tensions between officers and sailors. It was unclear, at this stage, how many of the twenty ships-of-the-line were affected, or whether any could be mustered to sea within the next twenty-four hours.

"Gentlemen," General Moore began forcefully, rising to his feet in a decisive manner. "We have no choice. With the Channel Fleet thus diminished, with a second French squadron unaccounted for, and Nelson days away from Gibraltar, we must attack Boulogne, and we must do it *now.*"

"I agree," Dundas pronounced firmly. "We *cannot* trust the country to Addington. We need to take the offensive and, perhaps, with Fulton's contraptions, we can secure the advantage."

"What will we be up against?" Pitt asked.

"There is a cordon here." General Moore held down one end of the map with a   beefy hand and traced a curve around Boulogne harbor with the other. "A line of twenty-four brigs and gunboats have been anchored across the harbor mouth. Their defense is further strengthened by the presence of three stone forts, here, here, and here." A thick finger stabbed a trio of points that defined the harbor edge. "They command a total of ten batteries of heavy guns."

"A night attack seems the most sensible option," Pitt reflected. "If we must grapple with the line, best to do so in the dark when the shore batteries might not dare to fire blindly at gun-flashes for fear of hitting their own ships."

"Exactly." Moore nodded in affirmation. "I propose four attacking divisions, each commanding fifteen gunboats, led by Captains Somerville,

Parker, Cotgrave, and Jones; Conn, leading a fifth defensive contingent of eight flatboats, will provide supporting fire with eight-inch mortars. Each of the four assaulting divisions will have, in addition, two boats equipped with axes and grappling irons to penetrate the enemy line. They will cut the moorings and tow any that can be captured out to sea. They will also be equipped with a bomb-ship, from which four rowed boats will deploy to release Fulton's underwater incendiary devices." He looked at each of them in turn, his expression intent. "I do not need to explain to you the futility of a land assault against Napoleon's army. This, gentlemen, is our only hope."

"So when do we do this?" Dundas asked bluntly, turning to Pitt.

"Tomorrow night," Pitt replied. "Can you have the men ready by then, General?"

Moore nodded, his face grim and set.

Wolfe crossed the lawn. The frost-stiffened grass crunched under his boots and the icy breath of the wind bent the shrubbery and battered the wiry stems of cyclamens. The gusts had risen in intensity since the men had come in from the garden, emitting a low, keening whistle as it swept and raced its way from the shingle beach below—as if in irritable discovery of newly encountered impediments in its path. Beneath the limbs of the yew, still dark against an early leaden sky, Pitt remained; his dark figure sprawled across the picnic bench, one arm resting languidly across the table, his tea, cold now, untouched, just beyond reach of his still fingers. For a moment, there appeared something terrible in the stillness of the man, made more poignant by the wind-thrashed landscape that surrounded him, and Wolfe's stride faltered momentarily.

"Mr. Pitt?"

Pitt turned, one dark eyebrow raised, mirrored by the upturn of his mouth into a crooked smile. "Mr. Trant." His gaze was sharp and keen in his pale face, dark hair tousled and wind-whipped around the high collar of his coat. "Don't you think it is time that we dispensed with formalities? I would like to think that we are becoming friends as well as allies. Try Will."

"Will," Wolfe acknowledged, somewhat awkwardly, as he lowered himself to the bench opposite Pitt. This level of intimacy, and the strengthening bonds implied by it, still unnerved him. While he had at last accepted and understood Pitt's commitment to Irish mercantile and religious freedom, he was unaccustomed to trusting another quite so implicitly—let alone an Englishman.

"This came for you, from London." Wolfe held out the sealed note that had arrived moments before by courier. He watched as Pitt slid one finger under the seal and read the note which fluttered in the wind.

"It is from Dragonfly, requesting a meet." He looked up at Wolfe. "What do you know of your brother's activities?"

"Egan? I haven't seen him in years."

Pitt acknowledged Wolfe's evasiveness with a slight smile. "As I am sure you are aware, he has become the head of the London cell for the United Irishmen, who are planning a revolutionary uprising to coincide with the anticipated arrival of the French fleet. Dragonfly is our mole."

Wolfe was silent for a moment, looking past Pitt at the oblique patch of gray sea visible through the bent shrubbery. His relationship with his brother was complicated, and while he did not agree with Egan's methods or his more extreme politics, they had been allies once, allies in the battle against the English. While Wolfe knew Egan would have little hesitation in executing his own brother for what he perceived as the worst kind of treason, he refused to be responsible for turning Egan over to the English. Pitt, looking into Wolfe's set features, knew as much and would not have asked it of him.

"I will meet with Dragonfly, or rather a trusted proxy will. I am hoping he will be able to give us details of the planned insurrection—"

"Let *me* go," Wolfe interrupted forcefully, leaning forward. "Let me meet with Dragonfly."

Pitt rose to his feet, stretching his arms languidly over his head as if he had just risen from a much-needed nap. The wind, whining through the limbs above his head, tugged and pulled at his lapels and cravat and flattened his coat-tails against his long legs.

"Why?" he asked Wolfe, the casual manner of his inquiry belied by the quick intensity of his silver-bright gaze that scrutinized every nuance and shadow of the Irishman's expression.

"Don't fret," Wolfe muttered, also rising to his feet. "It isn't 'cause I want to warn Egan about your involvement. He's made his bed and has every desire of now lying in it. In all truth, I probably can't stop him from that, although, I damned well mean to try. There's been too much blood in the streets already."

Pitt handed him the courier's note. "Black House, Drury Lane.

Tomorrow evening at nine. Wear a red band on your hat and Dragonfly will find you. Oh, and, Wolfe?"

Wolfe, already turning to go back to the house, paused, glancing back at Pitt.

"I thought you might like to know," Pitt continued, "I filed an official complaint with Warden Brunskill at Newgate Prison regarding your treatment while you were incarcerated. I received word this morning that your old nemesis Jack Manning has been convicted of abuse and battery and admitted to Newgate as an inmate due to serve ten years."

Wolfe stared at him in silence for a moment, a muscle twitching in his tightly clenched jaw.

"I apologize if I overstepped my bounds in this regard," Pitt began, hunching his shoulders against the cold, hands buried in his coat pockets. "But I had hoped it might save you from issuing a retaliatory beating, one that might end up putting you back in Newgate. And can you think of a more apt punishment for Mr. Manning than imprisonment in the company of men that he himself has so abused?"

"To be sure, I can't think of any punishment I could've inflicted that would be quite so effective as that," Wolfe admitted, his voice low. He reached out with an open palm, and Pitt grasped it in his own. "Thank you."

# 95.

Nick O'Connor leaned back against the brick wall of a haberdashery shop and watched the bustling thoroughfare where Lombard Street intersected with King William and Threadneedle. The imposing edifice of the Bank of England dominated the junction, and, O'Connor took careful note, the stiff figures of four constables lingered in the Grecian-style colonnade beneath the central rotunda. To the right of the great financial institution, was the Stock Exchange, known affectionately as the Old Lady of Threadneedle Street. To its left, the green sign of the prancing mare announced Lloyds Bank. Squeezed in-between and around these relatively grand façades were the more modest frontshops of various moneylenders and pawnbrokers who catered to the immediately needy.

The location of the post office was indeed unfortunate. Situated across from the Bank of England, spanning the triangular projection between Lombard and King William, it consisted of a spacious brick building of unremarkable yet sturdy construction. Long rectangular windows graced the three upper floors, with the ground level entrance defined by a trio of archways. Being, as it was, in the financial heart of the city, where bullion reserves gleamed in the dark belly of the bank and where silver stocks were maintained in various amounts, security was vigilant. In addition to the four constables outside the Bank of England, there were at least eight more within. Lloyds possessed a similar battery. It was crucial then not only to occupy the post office and prevent the mail coaches from leaving, but to do so discreetly. They had to maintain control of the facility for at least two hours, and early suspicions could jeopardize the entire enterprise.

It was already dark, and the gas-lamps, frequent in this part of the city, illuminated the streets in pools of yellowish light. The junction was a busy one, with bank clerks in somber clusters of gray and black hastening home like flocks of crows. Street-sweepers dodged clattering carts and wagons. Grubby children scampered around the skirts of herb-wives and turnip-maids hustling to the evening market at Cheapside. The ever-present drunks, vagabonds, prostitutes, and beggars skulked in adjacent alleyways but rarely ventured into the brightly lit square where constables frowned beneath the rims of their dark felt hats.

Some peddlers, however, eschewed Cheapside, hoping to snare more studious prey. The pale-faced man outside Lloyds, with his top-hat and black velvet bag, was a recently recruited member of the United Irishmen. "Mister, will ye buy a fine felt hat? Or spectacles ta read?" he cried out as various banking officials hurried past. A "competitor," also catering to those who poured diligently over finely scrawled accounts, had an array of spectacles laid out on a dingy cloth nearby—another Irishman ready to make a difference. O'Connor had fourteen men in all, waiting at various posts, ready to make their move when he gave the word.

Go mbeire muid beo ar an am seo aris! May we be alive at this time next year, he thought. Pulling his dark coat tightly around his narrow frame, O'Connor strode into the street. Raising one arm above his head in a quick salute, he sent the signal to the diminutive figure that waited on Threadneedle Street.

"Git away wi' ye!" a deeply hoarse voice hollered as two figures struggled and swore in the yellow gaslight directly in front of the bank. Tatty would provide the requisite diversion. Sparing a sideways glance, O'Connor noted the constables had descended the great steps of the Old Lady to establish the cause of the disturbance. Tatty was a showman by nature; he had lost his legs in the Gordon Riots and now propelled himself along the pavements of London on a wheeled wooden platform. He had the florid expression of a sailor and the robust brawn of half a Hercules—his upper torso had acquired all the strength and musculature that should have dwelt in his legs. His opponent, known only as 'Ol Tom, was a darkly wrinkled mass of rags, stained the color of the cheap ale that formed his primary diet. From beneath a twisted mess of black hair, the whites of his eyes glimmered in taunting insolence. A scuffle ensued, a crowd gathering to cheer and hoot as the two Irishmen battled and swore. One wheeling deftly, the other staggering ineptly, both yelling obscenities. It was a show worthy of Barnum himself and attracted the desired attention.

Walking swiftly, O'Connor entered the post office, the wooden door

swinging to a thudding close behind him. A single spacious room defined the lower floor, divided by a high counter-top with an iron-bar
barrier. Beyond the bars, he could see the bustle and murmur of clerks
as they sorted, divided, and stacked the mail. Several elegantly dressed
women and men milled about and sat in chairs as they awaited the departure of the mail coach. Posing as a potential passenger himself, he
nodded politely at them as the coach guard, clad in the signature uniform of scarlet and gold, locked the door behind him. Just in time. The
mail coaches departed at eight p.m. sharp. In order to keep this schedule
the post office closed by seven p.m., allowing time to finalize passenger
arrangements and deposit the mails in their respective coaches.

"Yes?" A gaunt lady in dark blue had appeared at the counter, her
finely penciled brows rising into her wrinkled forehead, mouth pursed
in distaste as she disapprovingly scanned his threadbare coat and faded
breeches.

"I'd like a ticket to Bristol, ma'am," O'Connor replied.

Her meticulous eyebrows raised even higher, her small dark eyes
narrowing in suspicion beneath her neat coiffure of tight gray hair.
"Outside, I presume?" An outside seat cost half as much. O'Connor's
hands clenched by his side, his mouth tightening in displeasure.

"Inside, if ye please," he snapped, shoving a guinea across the counter. Careful, Nick, careful. He forced himself to exhale. The situation
was tense and charged as it was, without allowing some old crabbie to
rile him further. The seats inside a Royal Mail coach weren't cheap; they
cost about a penny a mile more than a privately owned stagecoach, but
provided the added luxury of travel unencumbered by odors of vomit,
urine, and musty carpets, and a happy absence of the biting vermin that
invariably hitched a ride on more economical forms of transport.

And so it was that mail travelers tended to be of a more affluent sort,
O'Connor acknowledged, glancing down at his workingman's garments.
Not that it mattered—he would not be traveling in the Royal Mail coach
this evening, and neither would they; he glanced across at the waiting
passengers.

Another minute, a scurried motion, and cries of surprise and alarm
indicated Finney's arrival. He came through the back doors into the
clerk's sorting room like a behemoth, an Irish giant with orange hair
blazing and his freckled face split in a grin. In each hand he brandished
a pistol. Just before the double doors closed behind him, O'Connor
could see the row of distinctive black-painted coaches with scarlet

wheels. Snatching a pistol from his waistband, he swiveled on his heel and struck the guard to his rear a knockout blow to the side of his head. O'Connor watched in satisfaction as the man crumpled to the floor. The passengers beside him squawked in alarm, the women clustering together like frightened hens.

"I say! What is the meaning of this?" A portly gentleman separated himself from his ladies in a show of bravado.

"Just stay where ye are, good sir, and none will get hurt."

A side door opened, and Arthur McCourk's eager young face appeared, flushed with excitement. "'Tis done," he announced breathlessly. Eight Royal Mail coaches were scheduled to depart this evening, which meant that eight guards, employed by the post office to accompany and safeguard the mail (passengers were on their own), had been lounging in the upstairs room awaiting the departure time. McCourk's appearance confirmed that the six Irishmen, entering the post office from the rear entrance in Clement's Lane, had contained the guards and secured the upstairs floors. Thus far, everything had proceeded smoothly. Upon taking up their position on their respective coaches, each guard would have been issued a blunderbuss, two horse pistols, and a cutlass; these, however, were secured in the downstairs munitions room until just before eight p.m., and dispensed by the manager—who even now cowered under a clerk's desk. And the guard, who had closed the door behind O'Connor, had been bribed to "cooperate" with a sluggish response to the subsequent upheaval. Good jobs were scarce and coach guards were paid handsomely. This one had been reluctantly bribed only with the assurance that his complicity would never be detected.

"The door is locked there, Finney?" O'Connor called through the bars.

"'Tis indeed, Nick. Nobody is comin' or goin'," Finney hollered back cheerfully.

O'Connor glanced at the massive clock that hung on the far wall. Seven minutes past seven. They had just under an hour before the coaches were due to depart. It was only after eight p.m. that the stationary coaches, usually en route at that time, might begin to attract attention. Departure delayed by an hour or so would suffice to convey the signal to the waiting insurgents in Bristol and Manchester. Sixteen hours until the Uprising. He felt his stomach clench in fear and exhilaration.

# 96.

BLACK HOUSE. LONDON, ENGLAND
*December 14, 1803*

Black House was situated on the corner of Little Wild and Long Acre Lane, just east of Covent Garden and south of the newly refurbished Royal Theatre in Drury Lane. Its clientele consisted predominately of the usual mix of rough-and-ready characters, peppered with out-of-work actors, coachmen, and carpenters. Tonight, however, it was dominated by a knot of Irish veterans clustered around the bar, raising their tankards in sloshing toasts and clapping each other with resounding force on the back. These men were now too old or too disfigured for mercenary work; their shabby coats, brawny chests, and thickly muscled arms, all darkly dusted and begrimed with the powder of their trade, pronounced them coal-heavers. With typical Irish gallows-humor they belted out a ballad with booming enthusiasm of the horrors of San Sebastián, a massacre of the Revolutionary Wars where the French decimated the Irish force, leaving a tangled mass of ruined bodies behind them.

*You haven't an arm and ye haven't a leg*
*Hurroo! Hurroo!*
*You haven't an arm and ye haven't a leg*
*Hurroo! Hurroo!*
*Yer an eyeless, noseless, chickenless egg*
*Ye'll have to put with a bowl to beg:*
*Och, Johnny, I hardly knew ye!*

With whoops and hollering and a wayward jig or two, another round was ordered and a sole baritone began a keening ballad about lost love which momentarily subdued the men into a blurry melancholy.

Wolfe, seated at a table in the shadowed rear of the establishment, raised his mug to his lips and took a deep swallow of the dark, frothy ale. It swirled across his tongue in a pleasant combination of hops and wheat, and filled his belly with a satisfying if insubstantial warmth. We

Irish might be down, he mused, we might be trodden into political and economic obscurity, we might be beaten, flogged, and ultimately hung, but we will be defiant until the end, and thus never truly beaten.

"Wolfe Trant? Blessed be!" The immediate environment reasserted itself, and Wolfe looked up as a man entirely nondescript in appearance approached his table. He was of medium build with dark hair and brown eyes that glimmered with intelligence. A ready smile, and Wolfe found his hand being pumped with unabashed enthusiasm. It took him a moment to place the man before him. "It has been many a year!"

"It has," Wolfe affirmed, his smile a little more strained than that of his companion. He had several hours before his meeting with Dragonfly and was seeking a comfortable anonymity to unwind and think things through. The last thing he wanted right now was to rehash childhood memories with Nick O'Connor, not that they had many in common. Nick was the son of a wealthy Protestant farmer, and Wolfe, well, he was a Catholic scrapper from the less affluent side of town. "What brings you to London?"

"Your brother, for one," O'Connor muttered, glancing around him as he pushed a folded piece of paper across the table. Wolfe unfolded it and read the contents aloud: "How long will you quietly and cowardly suffer yourselves to be imposed upon, and half-starved by a set of mercenary slaves and Government hirelings? We are the sovereignty, rise then from your lethargy. Be at Tower Hill tomorrow." He raised his eyes to O'Connor and asked quietly "What's this about, Nick?"

O'Connor leaned forward on his elbows and rubbed the bridge of his nose with thumb and forefinger. He was the picture of disheveled weariness—sharp lines edged his mouth and furrowed his brow, and his eyes were red-rimmed with fatigue. His coat, drawn tightly around his narrow frame, was two weeks short of a wash, and concentric stains of sweat decorated each armpit.

"It's Egan," O'Connor began, raising his gaze to Wolfe's. "I wouldn't talk about this wi' anyone else...but your his brother, man."

Wolfe signaled to the barmaid, who made her way lethargically in his direction. "An ale for my friend." When she had departed, wending her way back to the bar in a desultory fashion, Wolfe turned his attention back to O'Connor who needed little prompting to resume his explanation. Indeed, the account spilled out over the course of a late dinner— Black House's dubious fare of chicken pie that appeared in a congealing

lump of greasy meat, a stale bread roll on the side. After several more
ales, neither man minded. Wolfe leaned forward on his arms, his dark
head close to O'Connor's. "Start by telling me everything, Nick."

"That there is the problem, Wolfe, I dunno everything...just my
own bit o' things, Egan keeps it all to himself. I took the post office
tonight, prevented the eight p.m. coaches from leaving. This sent the
signal for the uprisings in Bristol and Manchester tomorrow, and began
the countdown to the London Uprising which will take place tomorrow
night. Tom Dildin and his men will take the Tower of London and
raid the munitions store...Finney has fifty with him who will start riots
all over London. I'm guessing there are close to fifteen thousand men
altogether, and who knows how many more will join once the mob gets
going."

"Óinseach," Wolfe breathed, his face pale with shock. While Pitt
had informed him of the intended Irish insurrection he had had little
conception of the scope of the operation. "Do you know the targets
of these riots?"

"I don't. Your brother doesn't exactly trust any of us. He keeps the
agents and actions apart, so none of us really know what the other is
doing. These are my guesses, to be sure, based on the meetings we've
had. There's also a naval captain who's been paid to start a mutiny. Sailors were stirring and angry anyway... The captain is organizing them to
take over the docked ships-of-the-line. The time exactly I don't know,
but you can be certain 'tis all happening tomorrow night."

"And where will you be, then?"

"I am to meet Egan later tonight. Warwick Lane at two in the morning. He'll have instructions for me."

Wolfe stared intently into O'Connor's face, his gaze twin points of
blue fire, his large hands clenched on either side of his plate. "'Tis idio-
cy, Nick. Can't you see that? They'll be cut to ribbons, just like before."
The image of a night consumed by fire and heat flashed across the
inside of his mind. The sharp tang of blood and soot, a young lad lying
dead in a pool of his own blood...

"Are you all right, Wolfe?"

"I am." With a force of will, Wolfe thrust the images of New Ross
from his mind. "We've got to stop him, Nick."

"'Tis too late, Wolfe, it's all in motion now, and as scairt as I am..."
He shrugged, his face suddenly very young beneath the lines and

furrows. "Well, to be doing something to change things. To make things better…" O'Connor leaned forward, his eyes searchingly intent, his voice low enough to reach Wolfe's ears alone. "It's just I get the feeling that Egan has crossed over somehow. He's different from when we were young. He doesn't seem to care for *people* anymore but is driven by this political ideal over the edge of reason." O'Connor shrugged. "And 'tis important, of course 'tis, but how much blood is too much?"

"New Ross was too much, Nick," Wolfe replied grimly.

"Well, what do ye think should be done then, Wolfe?"

Wolfe rubbed the back of one hand wearily across his eyes. He didn't want to run the risk of alienating O'Connor by revealing his collaboration with Pitt, and he could not inform him of the mole in the UI without divulging where the information had come from. Nick O'Connor was a thoughtful man, already disillusioned with Egan's extremism but not necessarily with the United Irishmen, nor was he reluctant to take up arms on its behalf. While Wolfe thought he could make him understand the importance of gaining independence for Ireland with England as an ally rather than a foe, there was, as of yet, not the time. And it was doubtful, should the conversation extend to the bar as a whole, that there would be much understanding for an Irishman with English leanings. And O'Connor's perspective, Wolfe reminded himself, was one of confiding his fears to a fellow Irishman and the brother of his unit leader, certainly not one in league with William Pitt, ex-prime minister and covert spy-master.

"I'll talk to Egan, Nick. See if I can make him see reason. The English, as you are well aware, are always ready for the Irish uprising and will pay for it with the blood of those who oppose them. I think with Napoleon loitering in Boulogne, with the pressure of invasion, the time is ripe to come to some agreement. Addington can't afford enemies on both fronts, to be sure. I think there has to be a better alternative to blood in the streets, Nick."

"Aye, well, I hope your right, Wolfe." O'Connor leaned forward, his voice low. "I can't lie to ye, taking the post office 'twas exciting. It felt grand to be doing something other than sitting on me arse. I wasn't involved in the fight in Ireland; my ma kept me out o' it. And to see all that suffering and to finally be able to do something … Well, it felt grand."

"It felt grand, my fine friend, 'cause you didn't have to kill anyone,"

Wolfe replied grimly. "But this battle that Egan is planning …that'll be a whole 'nother story. And the tragedy will be that it will all be for naught, and we'll be worse off than afore we started. There are better ways." He paused slightly, appearing to mull something over in his mind; then, leaning forward, his gaze intently holding Nick's, he spoke, his voice hoarsely fervent: "Do you trust me, young Nick? Do you believe that I am Irish to the heart and soul of me?"

O'Connor, eyes widening slightly, stammered, "O' course I do, Wolfe; I've known you since we were lads…"

"Well'n then, there's something you need to know…"

For the next few hours, the patrons of Black House ebbed and flowed about the quiet man that occupied a table in the dim recesses. The Irish balladeers had been hustled out when one back-slap too hard or too many had erupted into cursing fist-falls and crashing bodies. Three lads, encouraged by the owner's promise of a free round—and rendered successful only by their relative sobriety—herded the mass of stumbling, disgruntled Irishmen, with their torn coats and bloodied cheeks, out the door. In the process of finding themselves evicted, they rediscovered their camaraderie and, arms wrapped around each other's necks, belted out a jubilantly slurred ballad as they staggered off into the dark night.

After the group had turned the corner into Long Acre, stumbling through stagnant puddles and tripping on the flagstones, a man emerged from the shadows opposite Black House. He pushed open the tavern door and paused on the threshold, surveying the warmly inebriated interior from beneath the broad rim of his black hat. Catching the eye of the solitary man in the rear, he made his way over to the table where Wolfe waited, a red band in his cap.

# 97.

In the shadowy retreat of Warwick Lane, Egan Trant waited on horseback. A steady throng of population weaved past and around him, intent on their own purposes this raw winter's night. Splashing through puddles of debris, the late-night idlers emerged: pick-pockets, prostitutes, drunks, beggars, and vagabonds of every description. Several of them cast a sly glance his way. One vacant-eyed miss offered him a night of pleasure for a sixpence only to be kicked in the teeth—or she would have been, if she hadn't been so quick on her feet. She withdrew back into the darkness with a scowl and a shrill cascade of cursing.

Egan glanced at his pocket watch. Two a.m. The post office had been secured, the coaches delayed, the message sent. The Uprising had begun. Finney had made contact and now it was just a matter of providing O'Connor with his instructions. His horse stamped his hooves impatiently and whinnied, tossing his head to one side. "Be still!" Egan cursed the animal, giving the bit a sudden and painful yank that succeeded in momentarily subduing his mount.

"What the hell are you playing at?" A dark figure appeared at Egan's foot, grasping the bit with one firm hand. Wolfe's upturned face was caught in dim gaslight, set in lines of stern disapproval. A turbulent anger raged beneath the surface of his skin like a torrential surge beneath the winter ice, suggested by a tremor or twitch here and there. Egan knew that look well. Despite himself, for just a moment, he withered beneath that fraternal onslaught, and then, straightening his back, he cast his brother a wilting stare.

"I'm playing to win," Egan replied icily. "And you, Wolfe? Why are you back in the game? Getting a little long in the teeth fer boxing? Finding linen production a bit tedious, are you?" he sneered, attempting to wrench the reins from Wolfe's grasp.

"That's just the problem, little brother, this has always been a game to you. Do you really think Napoleon cares one bit about Ireland?"

"Ireland, no. England, yes. Napoleon drools at the thought of crushing the English beneath his heel. I'll use that to liberate Ireland."

Wolfe laughed, a bitter sound threaded with disbelief. "God," he snorted. "I'd no idea you were this naïve. So, what's the plan, then? Let me guess. An uprising in London timed to coincide with the arrival of the French? Overwhelming odds?" He inadvertently pulled on the bit and the horse whinnied in protest. Absently, Wolfe rubbed her nose, his narrowed gaze focused on his brother. "Just like New Ross?" he demanded, his voice barely more than a hoarse whisper. "We had overwhelming odds there, didn't we, brother?"

Egan leaned down, pulling viciously on the reins until they were free. "This is different," he hissed. "We have the French."

"Do you now?" Wolfe raised a skeptical eyebrow. "Well then, good for you, brother. I s'pose I can rest easy. Tá na Francaigh teacht thar sáile!" His tone was heavy with sarcasm. The French Are On the Sea! "I can't believe you're so deluded. 'Tis some messianic hope that a great external power is on its way to deliver us from our enemies. You play the messiah do you now, Egan? And the London recruits, let me guess: farmers and apprentices? To be sure, you have a soldier or two among them? Trained in the manner of war?"

Egan did not reply immediately, but his tightened mouth and flaring nostrils said it all. Then, quelling his anger, he spoke sharply: "They have the passion and the drive just like Napoleon's army under the Republic!"

"Aye, but the republican army was fighting within the borders of a nationally recognized country, were they not? You expect these boys to rise up against the London forces? You must be out of your mind! They'll be slaughtered in hours…" A pained look crossed Wolfe's face as realization dawned. He whispered: "But that is what you're expecting, isn't it?"

"They'll provide the essential diversion that'll engage the attention of the English troops, while the naval mutiny will allow the French forces to penetrate the blockade. They'll be sacrificed in good cause. Ireland will be free as a result of their efforts."

"You're rather free and easy with other men's lives, brother," Wolfe growled. "Where are you going to be during this grand revolution?"

"Where my presence is most needed," Egan replied stiffly.

"And assuming you can achieve independence, Egan, what will you do about the Protestants? Do you think they'll welcome you? They've lined themselves up with the big landlords and the English government and live in fear of the hungry Catholic hordes." His face twisted in anger, his voice scathing. They had numbered among those hungry Catholics themselves. Wolfe exhaled sharply, before turning to look at his brother. "Egan, I know what you're trying to do, I understand, but you're going about it in the wrong way. Ireland won't be free this way, little brother. She'll turn on herself, Protestants against Catholics. You are condemning us all to a civil war."

"Once independence is achieved, we can work on our own problems without interference. We, the Catholics, that is, will be free to vote, they'll be free to worship—"

Wolfe laughed in disbelief. "You think that will end the strife? 'Tis more than political equality that is needed, Egan. Do ye not remember what was most important to Ma? *Land.* She was always so afraid of being evicted. You were young when you went to live with Uncle Dougal, mayhap you don't remember so well. Catholics want, more than anything, nothing short of a social revolution where the land is distributed equally. Now surely you don't think the Protestants will politely agree to such a plan?"

"And what is your plan then? What has your plan ever been?" Egan retorted scornfully. "You're up here selling your fancy linen on the backbreaking labor of poor Catholic workers—"

"I'm not selling anything, Egan," Wolfe ground out, his face dark with suppressed fury, "other than a realistic perspective. Ireland will never be free with a hostile England at her doorstep. Whether you like it or no, we can't reconcile the Catholics and Protestants in Ireland without English support…"

"Jesu! 'Tis *you*, isn't it?" Egan's face paled with shock. "*You're* the Irishman workin' with Pitt? It's been in all the broadsheets—"

"Egan—"

"You *traitor!*" Egan hissed, almost spitting with the force of his rage. "I should shoot you where you stand!"

Wolfe released the horse's bridle in a casual movement; his hands uncurling by his side, his gaze fixed on his brother: "Go ahead, lil' brother." Egan had pulled a pistol from beneath his coat and held it down towards Wolfe's chest. "Éirinn go Brách."

"What's goin' on 'ere?" an authoritative voice demanded. The upright form of a blue-clad constable approached them, gas-lamp held aloft. Egan cursed under his breath and viciously kicked the flanks of his mount who reared in protest, the whites of her eyes gleaming wildly in the yellow light. She raced forward, the cape of the man on her back flying out behind them. The constable fell back with a cry of alarm and Wolfe took the opportunity to melt into the deep shadows of Warwick Lane.

# 98.

Pitt's face was ashen. The paper fluttered from his suddenly lifeless fingers. He stumbled slightly and sank into his chair; an almost involuntary movement, as if his weight had suddenly increased to the point where it was more than he could bear. "My God," he muttered. "My God."

"What is it?" Wolfe demanded impatiently.

Dundas retrieved the letter from the floor. It had arrived by urgent courier minutes before and been brought to the study at Walmer where Pitt, Dundas, and Wolfe were reviewing the plans for the night assault on Boulogne. He scanned it rapidly then raised a pale, shocked face to meet Pitt's. "The duke," Dundas managed, his voice hollow with mingled horror and disbelief. "The Duke d'Enghien has been murdered."

"Murdered? When?" The Duke d'Enghien was instrumental to the formation of peaceful government after the overthrow of Napoleon. He was one of the very few candidates to find unqualified support among the French, as well as from their continental neighbors who were singularly anxious for France to return to the monarchical bosom. The duke had inspired loyalty not only for his honorable nature and handsome personage but also for his unblemished pedigree: he was a prince of the blood, a legitimate successor to the throne. Wolfe thought of Primrose. Did she know? It would devastate her...

"Two nights ago, dragged from his fiancée's in Switzerland...brought over the French border to Vincennes where he was shot like a dog by Napoleon's henchmen," Pitt finally managed.

"Napoleon?" Wolfe asked. "But how?"

"Primrose," a languid voice uttered behind him. Wolfe turned to see Talleyrand lounging against the door-frame.

"The Duc de Talleyrand, Prime Minister. I apologize. He would not wait to be announced." James hovered indignantly behind the resplendent figure of Napoleon's foreign minister.

"That is quite all right, James." Pitt rose unsteadily to his feet, his face still starkly pale, hands trembling slightly in tight fists behind his back. "Duc de Talleyrand…you are indeed welcome, sir. You follow hard upon bad news, I fear." James efficiently helped the duke out of his traveling greatcoat and took his hat, before disappearing down the hallway. Dundas handed Talleyrand a glass of whiskey, which he accepted with a gracious nod.

"*No,*" Wolfe stated emphatically, his gaze sternly fixed on Talleyrand.

"She has betrayed us," Talleyrand replied. "Primrose is Napoleon's agent, after all." Pitt rubbed the bridge of his nose between thumb and forefinger. He did not refute Talleyrand's assertion.

Wolfe glared from one man to the other. "What do you mean?" he growled. He knew what Talleyrand meant but needed to hear the words, the verbal confirmation of a sudden painful grip in his guts. "How do you know this?"

"An aide-de-camp working for me at the Tuileries informed me of her visit to the palace several days ago, that she was closeted privately with Napoleon. Less than two hours later, four of Napoleon's Chasseurs à Cheval rode east out of Porte Saint-Victor. I assumed the worst and immediately sent a trusted agent north in an effort to warn the duke. I was too late; by the time the agent arrived, the duke had already been tried by a military tribunal and shot. Shortly thereafter, I received a note from Casimir de Montrond, with whom I understand you are acquainted, Monsieur Pitt? He suggested a timely vacation from Paris might be beneficial…and I preferred to tell you in person. However, I see the regrettable news has preceded me."

"If she was working with Napoleon, *why* didn't she turn me in when I first arrived in Paris? There were many opportunities where she could've handed me over, but didn't. *Why* rescue me from Temple Prison? *Why* put me in contact with the Resistance in Bourges?" Wolfe shook his head. "No, it doesn't make any sense…"

"Perhaps she has not always been Napoleon's agent; perhaps it is a recent conversion," Dundas contributed gravely.

"Napoleon's plan consisted of uniting the fleet in Boulogne to invade England. He would never have sanctioned dividing the fleet and sending Villeneuve to Cadiz," Pitt said wearily. "No, Primrose must have turned after helping Wolfe. Whatever the circumstances, it seems clear that she has betrayed the Duke d'Enghien and he has been shot as a result."

"Who is the next heir apparent?" Dundas asked.

"Potentially, Louis Stanislas Xavier, Count of Provence," Talleyrand replied. "Brother to the late King Louis XVI, currently in exile in Latvia. He is not as popular with the people of France, drowning in debt, and no doubt a harder sell than the Duke d'Enghien."

"What did Primrose know of the invasion plans? How compromised are we?" Dundas asked.

"She knew nothing of the planned assault on Boulogne," Pitt replied with a dismal shake of his head. "But, of course, Duc de Talleyrand, she knew of your involvement with the Resistance and with myself."

"Yes, I thought it a fortuitous time to travel," Talleyrand acknowledged with his usual wry understatement. "As far as I am aware, she has not betrayed me. If she had told Napoleon of my association, he would have immediately sent dragoons to arrest me as he sent them out against the Duke d'Enghien. No, for whatever reason, that bit of information Primrose is keeping to herself, for the time being."

"Where is she now, then?" Wolfe demanded.

"She has joined Napoleon at Boulogne."

Striding furiously through the icy undergrowth, Wolfe was oblivious to the wet and the cold. His mind whirled at the implications of Talleyrand's revelations. The rage smoldered in his chest and left a sour taste at the back of his throat; his fingers curled into fists at his side. He felt a blind need to move and keep moving. She was a double agent!

With every fiber of his being he wanted to deny it—a horrible mistake. But somewhere, deep inside, he recognized the truth of it. Jeanne's visible attacks of stress and anxiety came not from evading Napoleon's secret police but from the fear the Resistance would find out she was in league with them! He wanted to hear her admission of guilt. Let her try to justify her actions, let her plead her case. But she would not; he knew her well enough to know that. She would be silent and proud, wouldn't she? What did he really know of her after all? Her convictions had been expressed with such fierce passion. How could he have been so wrong? How could she have fooled him so completely? She was an actress; that was her job. He had been impressed with her impersonations of whore and fishwife, aristocrat and countess— each one seemingly more authentic than the last. But if the truth be told, he had no idea of the true extent of her talents. Her deception had been practiced with such consummate skill.

Something yanked at his coat as he charged headlong through the undergrowth. Impatiently, he reached down to disengage a long trailing branch that had snagged him, and a thorn stabbed into the fleshy base of his thumb.

"Hanam 'on diabhal!" he bellowed, brutally yanking the branch from the gnarled trunk. The red-misted rage coursed through him, rising from within, heated and ungoverned, obliterating reason and logic; it was as if he were merely a vehicle, a solid mass of flesh and bone, directed to violence by some uncoiling serpent of wicked intent. The strength of his fury tightened his muscles, accelerated his heartbeat to a thundering crescendo, and brought his breath quick and hot in his throat. He could not think, could barely feel, but was consumed by the unmitigated need to strike out, to smash, pound, or beat whatever happened to be in the vicinity.

"Bualadh craicinn!" Wolfe, heedless of the thorns, jerked the branch with such force that the small bush came free in his hands.

"Crab suas!" He wrenched at the dense tangles of short twiggy branches, the coral-bright berries smashed to a pulp beneath his boots.

Wolfe had always had a wellspring of rage stored up tightly inside, which had contributed to his success as a bare-knuckle boxer. He could access it almost at will and it lent him speed and impact powered by an admixture of fury and adrenalin. It had been years, however, since he had felt the effects of unbridled temper—years since he had allowed it to overcome him so completely. And so he bellowed like some wounded beast, thrashing through the shrubbery, yanking and pummeling, thundering against the bitter gall of betrayal and deceit—like a fire, his rage must needs burn itself out.

Finally, his anger spent, he leaned forward, hands on his thighs, the pyracantha bush a mangled corpse at his feet. It would have produced an abundant display of creamy blossoms in the spring. His breath coming in harsh pants, Wolfe recalled Pitt pointing the fact out during a garden tour. He inhaled deeply, held the crisp air in his lungs for a moment, and then exhaled in a plume of warmth. Feeling his heartbeat begin to slow, he bent to his knees in the dirt, and gently repositioned the root-ball, scraping dirt around the base of the plant.

Who was he kidding? He didn't want to mangle a bush that bore blossoms in the spring. He wanted to kill a small roadside flower that was as poisonous as it was pretty. And he would do it himself—with his bare hands.

# 99.

"The great evil of our navy is that the men who command it are unused to the risks of command! What is to be done with admirals who allow their spirits to sink, their resolve to be beaten home at the first damage they suffer? Is this what Villeneuve will tell me? He will blame this fiasco on Nelson? Is *this* what the French martial spirit amounts to?" Napoleon demanded, bearing down upon Vice-Admiral Latouche, who stood impassively in his black military greatcoat.

A portly man with white curls that fringed a fleshy dome of a head, Latouche had reached fifty-nine years, was suffering intermittent chest pains, and was increasingly weary of his military responsibilities. He was one of the few battle-tested naval commanders of ability upon whom Napoleon could rely, having successfully repelled several attacks by Horatio Nelson the previous year, subdued the slave uprisings in Saint-Domingue, and, at this point in time, had no fewer than three ships named after him.

Napoleon, however, was utterly careless of Latouche's credentials or achievements; he was merely another naval subordinate who would bear the brunt of the ferocity that could not, at this time, be vented upon the head of Villeneuve. General Morand, Marshal Masséna, and several other officers were present, having been summoned to the emergency meeting. They stood silently, gazes deliberately downcast, while their emperor, face suffused with fury, issued a torrent of camp-fire oaths, stamped, and raged about the room.

"*Why?* Mon dieu! *Why* would Villeneuve put in at Cadiz when I sent specific orders to rendezvous at Boulogne? Can you answer me that, Admiral Latouche?" Napoleon shrieked, spitting and bristling, his short, gray-coated figure shuddering with the force of his wrath. "*How* did I end up with such incompetents? *How* can we possibly break the English blockade without Villeneuve's ships-of-the-line?"

They could not, as all the men knew. They also knew that during these tirades Napoleon's questions were entirely rhetorical, and that, indeed, from his lofty perspective they might all have been but articles of furniture. So they stood steadfast and silent, bracing themselves against the onslaught like lashed trees in the face of a hurricane. Napoleon thrived upon these public reproaches, from which none in his entourage, from wife to cook, were immune; all lived in dread of being derided before a simpering crowd—the amusement, however, was mitigated by the understanding that each of them might be the next to endure the same ridicule.

Sweat beaded on Admiral Latouche's brow.

In one vicious movement, Napoleon ripped the Channel map from the wall and, turning to glare at his generals, barked: "We go to Austria. Admiral Latouche, you will remain and oversee the decampment. Dismissed!" The men filed from the room, leaving Fouché alone in the Council Chamber with the emperor.

"Your Excellency," Fouché murmured, inclining his head respectfully. "If you will permit me, I would like to speak with you regarding the Duke d'Enghien."

"What is it?" Napoleon growled irritably, glaring at his police commissioner, as he proceeded to shove rumpled papers into pockets of a large satchel.

"If I may ask, Your Excellency, from where did you receive such intelligence regarding the duke's involvement in the Resistance?"

Napoleon laughed bitterly, his full lips drew back in scorn. "Do I have this right, monsieur? Is my commissioner of police asking me to clarify the source of intelligence?"

Fouché bowed stiffly from the waist. "My sole concern is to maintain Your Excellency's personal safety," he murmured.

"And the fact that it was not *you* who brought this information to my notice leads me to question the value of *your* services!" Napoleon snapped. "Now get out, I have much to do!"

Fouché bowed again, adding a slight flourish with his right hand for good measure. He had endured and survived tirades before, and had little doubt he would persevere through this one. The function he fulfilled was too critical, and the intelligence he had gathered too extensive, to be easily dismissed. Napoleon needed him as much as Fouché needed the emperor. But the timing was unfortunate. With Villeneuve blockaded in Cadiz there was no hope of uniting the French fleet in the Channel as Napoleon had planned. The English invasion was, once and for all, off the table. Understandably, the emperor was enraged, but Fouché personally thought the Channel crossing would have stood little chance of success against the English navy. Terrestrial warfare was where Napoleon Bonaparte's true genius lay. Certainly, they would have more luck in Austria—another Marengo, perhaps.

Fouché mused on these thoughts as he left the Council Chamber, making his way out to the frost-lined driveway. What most concerned him, however, was the fact that someone else was obtaining intelligence and supplying it to the emperor. Napoleon, increasingly paranoid and distrustful of even his closest staff, had lately decided to keep sources to himself and thus undermine and even potentially supplant Fouché's role as the commissioner of police.

Fouché wondered idly whether Chief Inspector Chavert might have decided to sidestep his superior and make a play for the emperor. It was something that Fouché would have done in his younger days, but somehow he doubted Chavert had the requisite spine. He was wily enough, but wholly inexperienced and ultimately stricken by cowardice. Face the emperor and his legendary wrath? No, Fouché thought not. Despite the fact that Chavert's utter disgrace at the Temple Prison was only known to the two of them (having, according to his usual procedure, ensured complete discretion in the event that something went wrong), it had so unmanned the chief inspector that Fouché doubted he would be ready for active duty for some time. And when he was, Fouché would have the perpetual leverage of the Temple to hand. Yes, that had gone quite satisfactorily indeed. Since Wolfe Trant would not, in any event, have cracked under torture, Fouché had been quite sure of that before they began. While the incident had given Chavert the illusion of temporary power, in reality it had provided his superior a long-term stick with which to beat him, should such a thing be required. One never knew when that quick retreat down a dark alley or across the shifting sea might become necessary; and, when it came to matters of self-protection, Fouché felt he could never have too many indebted individuals upon whom he could rely.

Fouché dug into his pocket and withdrew a crumpled cigar. He opened the smoky latch of a gas-lamp, one of two that framed the entrance to the Council Chamber, reached in, and lit one end of his cigar.

Raising it to his mouth, he gratefully inhaled, filling his lungs with the acrid smoke, and then, eyes narrowed above the plume which issued out between thin lips, he contemplated his next move. The assassination of the Duke d'Enghien would utterly alienate the European monarchy, who already had qualms about welcoming the Corsican upstart to their collective bosoms. Fouché wondered whether Napoleon's glorious ascendancy might be coming to a close. England, unbroken upon the seas, yet maintained the blockades.

Above all, the police commissioner knew how to ensure his own political and personal survival; with this in mind, he strode down the hill through the encampment to the older section of Boulogne.

Perhaps, he would pay a visit to the prisoner in the morning.

# 100.

Icicles hung thickly from the pines, and the air was cold and raw in Wolfe's lungs. He crouched beneath the dripping foliage while fat drops gathered wetly on the back of his neck, formed icy rivulets down each side, and disappeared into his thick coat. The only sound was the occasional plaintive cry of the pomarine skuas as they tracked their southern migration route, winging their way in effortless formation high above his head. The earth beneath was still and silent.

Having acquired passage on a late-night trawler, Wolfe had crossed the dark, heaving waters of the Channel and been deposited ashore near a cluster of fishing cottages several miles south of Boulogne-sur-Mer. He had carefully selected his hiding place. Through the icy branches, he could see the curve of the road ahead as it disappeared between the trees, winding its way north to Boulogne; it had been reduced to muddy ruts, offering little traction for horse or wagon. Dangerous travel at this time of year, Wolfe mused. It was bitterly cold, the world blanketed in white—easy for a man to lose his bearings; easy to hide a body.

Napoleon would hear no excuses, and his personal supply convoy would know better than to offer them. They left Paris every Monday morning, regardless of the weather; the wagons groaned under cases of Montegnard brandy, cured trout, and cages of feathered hens while, usually, a goat or two trotted along behind. There were always four soldiers, one riding a horse up ahead, two on the wagon driving the donkeys, and one bringing up the rear on a second horse.

An hour or so later, Wolfe heard the voices of the guards. They were singing. Drunk. Good, he thought grimly; his job would be easier. Shortly thereafter, the small cavalcade ventured beyond the hill, the horses whiskered in ice, the men huddled beneath their thick red regimentals. The lead soldier wove slightly in his saddle. Wolfe, hidden and still beneath his snow-covered canopy, could see the brown flank of his mount as he passed, a black-booted foot encrusted in mud, the snorting breath of the laboring donkeys that followed, and the creaking wheels of the wagon, slipping and sliding in the sludge.

When the last soldier was slightly ahead of Wolfe on the path, he leapt from his concealment, cut the saddle straps, and yanked the guard sideways into the snow.

"Waaaa…?" the soldier began in bewilderment as he lurched sideways, landing heavily in the embankment beside the road.

The horse slowed to a stop. The soldier began to rise unsteadily to his feet. Wolfe landed a powerful punch to his stomach and a second to the side of his jaw that, combined with the wine, sent the soldier reeling backwards into the snow. It was all about speed now. Had the convoy noticed their rear guard had disappeared? If so, his mission would be over before it had begun. He could always wave them on in a befuddled manner, hoping they assumed he had stopped to relieve himself. His countenance was largely obscured beneath the shadowed overhang of his hat and the strategically adjusted collar of his coat. In an outer pocket of the guard's regimentals, Wolfe discovered a black scarf which he wrapped around the lower portion of his face. The danger lay in prolonged conversation; his accent alone would provide glaring evidence of his deception. He could mumble a few words in French and probably get away with it. The other men were drunk, the air was bitingly cold. Nobody would want to linger.

Wolfe rapidly traded his outer garments for those of the unconscious guard and dragged the prone body to the bushes. The cold would get him, and, even if it didn't, by the time the soldier recovered consciousness and raised the alarm, Wolfe's work would already be done. He dressed quickly, gathered the horse, and was soon trotting after the convoy, swaying slightly in the saddle as his carefully slurred voice joined theirs in song. They had noticed nothing; Wolfe breathed a little easier.

An hour later, they passed through the inspection gates and proceeded into the military encampment. The convoy was a weekly routine, and one masculine face, buried in swathes of coat and hat, was much the same as another. They were waved through with little fanfare; the Grande Armée of Napoleon Bonaparte was hardly expecting an infiltrator.

The supply convoy threaded its way through the camp, the soldiers calling out boisterously to friends en route as they made their way toward Napoleon's pavilion. Then, as the group rounded a corner, Wolfe urged his horse to a stop and slid to the ground. Crouching by the horse's side, he pretended to adjust the stirrup until the convoy was out of sight. The settlement was laid out with impeccable military precision; the main thoroughfare, intersected at regular intervals with narrow roads, traversed the length of the camp, and, unlike the muddy route from Paris, was immaculately maintained. Adjusting his collar to hide his face, Wolfe stuck his hands deep in his pockets and, leaving the horse tethered to a post, strode purposefully down the nearest side street.

# 101.

The people had begun to gather. They came from all parts of London: the dregs and the downtrodden, rising from their lethargy to answer Egan's call. His memorandum had found its way from the winding lanes of Whitechapel to the crowded thoroughfares of Spitalfields, from Blackfriars and St. Giles to Bethnal Green and Drury Lane. Copies were passed from one work-roughened hand to another, tucked between pages of the penny press, beneath meager loaves of bread, and wrapped up in cheap packets of innards and offal. The contents, read in stifled whispers, reminded these ragged inhabitants of what had been accomplished across the Channel, of the death of a king, and the latent power that resided in the humblest of people.

And so they came, trudging a circuitous route through the darkening city, gathering in numbers until they resembled some kind of matted creature that had ventured forth from its subterranean lair. The learned bystander, peeking apprehensively from behind shuttered windows, might have thought of Comte de Buffon's recent treatise, particularly of his theories concerning the aggregation of organic molecules (prompted by some inexplicable force) that resulted in the formation of gentle quadrupeds of yore. The coal-heavers and scullery-maids, the weavers and the shoemakers: all molecules that combined to create a larger whole, with Egan's memorandum and their own dearth and desire providing the requisite force. This beast, however, threading its way through the London streets, was something quite different from those of Buffon's menagerie; a Hecatoncheir with heads and hands enough, and marching feet to match. And, unlike the gentle grass-chewers of old, the lumbering giants of antiquity, this guard of Tartarus had fangs.

In a body, they emptied themselves on to the Great Tower Hill. The murmur grew to a rumble as the beast expanded in size until it swelled and filled the dirt expanse beneath the broad stone shoulders of the implacable Tower prison. Opportunists came, attracted by the noise and numbers. Ballad mongers and tale-tellers hawked "Last Speeches and Dying Confessions" of the recently executed, while others dealt in the deceased's severed extremities: the dead hand of a hanged man—a certain cure for scrofula. Tripe dealers and orange-girls set up shop on the peripheries, battling for vocal supremacy over the hollering advertisements of Dr. Newman's anti-venereal pills: "If ye've nodes, buboes, or broke out in blotches—all will be well! Sold at so easy a' price, only two shillin's each!"

A neighbor diligently sought customers for little blue pills that "restored vitalism," while another attracted a crowd with dramatic demonstrations of nitrous oxide "which bestowed all the benefits of alcohol but none of its flaws!"

These industrious proprietors of newly invented commodities jostled alongside fencers and jugglers, clowns and acrobats; they rubbed shoulders with buffoons and charlatans, all seeking the attention and coin of the gathering crowd. Hocus-pocus men drew awed disbelievers; minstrels and tumblers entertained; puppeteers and rope-dancers performed to enthusiastic applause. And every manner of rag merchant was there, selling fruit, games, potions, medicines, toys, and buttons.

The medley had all the appearance of a carnival, with hollowed cheeks well- rouged and "silks" strategically patched. The darkness did justice to them all: every pockmarked consumptive was a beauty, every squinting thief a "genl'man" with slippery fingers sliding artfully into pockets and with desperation hovering on the edge of conviviality— there are none who know how to savor the moment like those who understand there are not so many left. Moreover, there was warmth in numbers and little to do within doors but contemplate the misery of the morrow. London, with all its fear of the "Frenchies o'er the pond," needed a distraction; Egan, via his countless contacts, had provided it.

A gaunt man in black, white hair disheveled about his shoulders, began to prepare his hurdy-gurdy, blowing on his frozen fingers before settling the instrument upon his lap. His fellow musicians began to congregate: the barrel organist settled in beside him; a robust red-scarved woman with a tambourine grinned in toothless display. And the clustered crowd, in anticipation of the musical entertainment to come, stomped their feet in festive impatience. Unkempt though they were, with grime beneath their fingernails and lining the creases of their necks, their faces were fiercely aglow with a bright enthusiasm.

And so it was that the fangs were temporarily retracted.

"Where *are* they?" Finney muttered anxiously, his gaze fixed beyond the black water of the Thames and the solid barrier of Byward Tower. Dildin was supposed to have docked at Billingsgate a half hour ago—he, his men, and a boatload of weaponry scavenged from the munitions store beneath the Tower. But the waters, beyond the clamor and roar of festival behind him, were black and still.

# 102.

"Through there, do ye see?"

The boat tipped precariously as Dildin pointed out the Waterman Stairs that led up to the darkened salt-tanged boards of St. Katherine's Dock. Beyond the stairs that rose from the murky blackness of the Thames, the men could see the formidable stone wall of Develin Tower and the dark alcove that comprised the Iron Gate.

Theirs was the first boat of three. Each accommodated twenty men armed with muskets, pistols, pikes, blunderbusses, and whatever other weapon of convenience they had managed to snatch up or steal. It was not without trepidation that these men made their way across the placid blackness of the Thames on this moonless night in December. Dildin felt it too—the fearful awe when confronted with the powerful solidity of the Tower of London, and the tales of torture and execution that went on within the walls.

"Here we go, lads…Éirinn go Brách." Dildin leapt from the boat, his men following in a stealthy series of black shadows.

"Éirinn go Brách," they murmured under their breath—their prayer before dying.

Dildin's crew was to go first, open the Iron Gate, and then signal to the remaining men that the way was clear. Within, between the bars, the men could see the steady glow of gaslight but no sign of life. The Iron Gate comprised a sturdy series of iron bars, crosshatched at one foot intervals. The lock itself consisted of a simple sliding-bar construction that slid into a cavity in the stone. If they could cut the locking bar in two, the gate would swing easily open. While the process was relatively straightforward, it was also a time-consuming method that not only would require several saws, but would also produce a disconcertingly shrill grating of metal grinding down metal.

"Got the hacksaw?" Dildin whispered to Shaun. He barely recognized the apprentice carpenter he had recruited from Long Acre several weeks before. The thatch of unruly dark hair was confined beneath a formally curled, powdered wig and black velvet ceremonial bonnet. He, like Dildin, wore the splendid regalia of the yeoman of the guard, with crimson dress coats lined and edged with gold lace, detailed with a rose, thistle, and crown, and the letters G. R. embroidered on the back and breast of each. Crimson cloth breeches and gray worsted stockings completed their attire. The Yeoman of the Guard were issued new uniforms annually, the old ones becoming that individual's property to dispose of as he wished. Numerous uniforms ended up in the theaters of Drury Lane and Bow Street, and it was there that Dildin had purchased them. Black cross-belts supported ponderous matchlock rifles, and swords slept in black leather scabbards on their left hips. If all went according to plan, neither would be required.

Shaun motioned to a man behind, a blacksmith from Spitalfields, who brought forward a long, serrated blade. They crouched in the gloom, waiting. Behind them, the other two boats were now secured to the docks; their men, dressed in the somber shades of black and gray, waited for the signal to move in.

After the assassination attempt on the king's life at the Royal Theater four years before, the Yeoman of the Guard were redeployed in greater concentration around the Royal Residence, which, at this time, was Kew Palace. Those yeoman who remained at the Tower of London fulfilled duties that were largely ceremonial. The Crown Jewels had been removed to allow for the refurbishing of the Jewel House. There were, as far as Dildin knew, no illustrious personages inhabiting the Bloody Tower that would require additional security. All of these circumstances would work in favor of an easy infiltration. Once inside, they could subdue each yeoman that remained, and the Tower would be theirs.

"They should be playin' already?" Shaun whispered, his face as white as his wig in the dim light. Dildin did not reply, but stood with his head cocked to one side, his ears straining to hear the expected cacophony. A moment later, it came: the strident caper of the hurdy-gurdy combined with a raucous scale upon the organ and, if that didn't create enough of a piercing racket, the triangle and tambourine joined in—each striving to outperform the other and winning, by their united exertions, the stomping and hollering applause of all bystanders. And Egan had arranged for a large audience. The din from New Tower Street would, at the very least, cover the rasping of saw on iron.

Dildin flicked his hand forward, beckoning the blacksmith, and, with a rhythmic grating that made the men wince for fear of discovery despite the carnival street-side, he set to work on the lock bar. Half an hour later, the second saw discarded in the Thames, their brows dripping with sweat, the men edged through the Iron Gate into the courtyard beyond. With Dildin leading, they entered noiselessly through a stout wooden door at the base of the Bloody Tower; one by one, they filed in, until all eight men were pressed against the shadows of the Queen's House, the gloomy expanse of the Tower Green before them.

"Where is everybody?" Shaun muttered, glancing around him uneasily. The street-side carnival reached their ears as a dull, muffled sound much diminished by the thick solidity of stone around them. Within the keep, the occasional gas-lamp illuminated the white stone and the gleam from squared glass windows between iron brackets. The men moved forward, staying in the shadows. The White Tower was their destination—its basement being the home of the Office of Ordnance and of all the various munitions and explosives that formed the artillery store.

"Back!" Dildin hissed as several Beefeaters came into view, crossing the grounds in front of the Waterloo Block. From their shuffling gait, it quickly became apparent that these were the old men war had left behind. "We split up. We are far less noticeable in groups of two or three—"

Dildin was interrupted by a most unexpected sound. It started soft and low and escalated into a high-energy, full-throated roar that the men could feel vibrating through their bones. The men froze.

"What t'hell is that?" Shaun whispered stricken, the whites of his eyes wide in the dark.

"God between us and all harm," another muttered fervently under his breath.

"'Tis the Royal Menagerie," a third offered. "The animals are kept 'ere at the Tower. Lions, tigers, monkeys, and snakes, an' even a polar bear that fishes in the Thames. I read ta'boot it." The roar subsided into a series of staccato grunts, a *huh huh huh* that echoed disconcertingly around the interior keep.

"S'long as they stay in their bloody cages," another muttered. "Let's git on wi' this damn thing, then."

Half an hour later, the men had incapacitated the few yeomen that remained in the Tower, taking their place in full regalia, and had breached the munitions store beneath the White Tower. There were a few crates of rusty sabers, muskets, and pikes, but none of the gleaming stacks of well-oiled and maintained supplies the men had expected.

"We've been had," Shaun muttered as they glanced dismally around the shadowed cobwebbed basement. "Well, given the fact that Ol' Boney is prac'lly on our shores... makes sense the guns would've been sent out fer defense, right?"

"That would be right, indeed," a voice rang out, the owner of which cautiously pushed open the wooden door with one foot, his musket aimed at Dildin's head. "I suggest you put your weapons down, or your leader will be the first to fall."

A group of grim-faced English soldiers, clad in the red and white regimentals of the King's Guard, filed into the room and silently surrounded the Irishmen.

"Your men waiting in the boats have already been apprehended. You are alone, and you are outnumbered. I say again, throw down your weapons!"

"I had a feelin' 'twas all too easy-like," one mumbled under his breath.

For a moment, the men stood in an uneasy standoff; the English troops glared over the barrels of their muskets; the Irish clenched their fingers around pistols they held by their sides...not yet daring to raise them.

"Drop yer guns," came Dildin's voice, low and husky.

"But..." Shaun protested in a sideways mutter, his gaze firmly fixed on the English dragoon opposite. "Ought'nt we ta put up a fight?"

"Not if we all die needlessly," was Dildin's harsh retort. The clatter of steel on stone announced the Irish surrender. "Don't harm my men, or ye'll answer fer it!" he called out, his voice ringing with command, despite his strategically inferior position.

"There ye go, young Tom, give 'em hell!"

Various mutterings of approval came from his men. If one was going down, it became all about how it was done. Dildin, however, unbeknownst to his men, had had the advantage of practicing his surrender, and so, when it resounded through that stone basement, it was imbued with a confident bravado that found ready endorsement the effect of which pleased Dildin quite nicely.

# 103.

"Well, Finney? Any sign o' them?"

Eight or so Irishmen hovered behind Finney, agitated in their impatience. Dildin was now an hour late. A dark kernel of dread gathered and knotted in the depths of Finney's belly. Something had gone dreadfully wrong.

"Not yet," Finney muttered anxiously.

"We have naught but kitchen knives." Patrick O'Neal came up beside him. "We can't rise against the English so under-armed…"

"We can fight wi' our bare hands, but we won't git so very far," another remarked despondently.

"I promised my men arms the equal of the English."

"Well, you'll bloody well have to fight without 'em!" Egan Trant's voice cut through the milling disquiet as he cantered in on a black stallion and, slinging his reins aside in one careless movement, swung down from his horse. Pinioning Finney in an icy glare, he demanded, "What the hell is going on?"

"No sign o' Dildin, nor the four boatloads o' men. 'Tis like they disappeared," Finney confided grimly, genuinely at a loss to explain the lack of eighty men that had so recently been accounted for.

"Well then, we go ahead without 'em," Egan barked.

"But 'twill be suicide," a man bravely protested. "Already, we seen redcoats on Cannon and again on Blackwell Street. Almost like they was expectin' us… We've no means to fight 'em!"

Egan turned on the man with an expression of utter ferocity, grabbed him by the collar, and, hauling his face close to his own, hissed, "Well then, ye pick up a bloody kitchen knife, you coward, and you charge forward in the name of Ireland, do you understand?" Egan felt the heat of unmitigated rage rise to his cheeks, his breath quick and hot in the back of his throat. Things were slipping beyond his control. Egan

flung the offender to the ground. The clustered crowd shifted their feet
uncertainly, muttering under their breath. If he was to win them, the
time was now, Egan knew. Placing one foot in the stirrup of his mount,
he swung himself back into the saddle.

"The signal has been sent to Bristol, to Manchester, and to Ireland!"
Egan raised his voice so all could hear him. "Even now your brothers
are rising up against the oppressors. Will ye stand by idly while they
fight your battles for you? Are ye that kind of men? Will you let your
wives and chil'ren starve in their garrets, or will you fight for the rights
that will set them free? I mean to fight with my bare hands if need be,
because over there," Egan pointed with his dagger across the Thames
to the Channel, "over there, Napoleon is readying his boats for battle.
And Ireland will finally be free of the tyranny the English have imposed
upon her. Are ye with me?"

The men and women responded in thunderous accord, a roar that
erupted from all throats simultaneously to produce a single voice—
one imbued with the deep and dark anger of generations, fueled by
hatred, whiskey, and hope. All souls armed with whatever weapons
they could find: broken pitch-forks, rusted muskets, chipped scythes,
and old daggers. The carnival, with enough disgruntlement simmering
under the surface, required merely a slight push to shift from heedless
frivolity to a contentious offensive. From within the thick stone keep
of the Tower, Dildin and his men could hear the change in the crowd:
the high-pitched laughter, the music, deepened into something darker.
The bellowing curses, shouts, and cries of complaint, each protesting
its own particular slights—the incalculable hardships of poverty and
neglect, the lack of a working wage, or simply the plight of the have-
nots who were inclined, that night, to finally have. The recruited Irish
would then, in turn, be joined by thousands of those who felt similarly
denied, who would not stop to ask the cause, but who would riot, rage,
and loot.

The belligerent pressed forward, the hot press of bodies pushing
and shoving like the pulsating membrane of a monstrous skin. The
purveyors of assorted goods scuttled aside, daring life and limb in the
rescue of cart and wares from the heedless onward rush. Many joined
the fray, scrawny arms brandishing makeshift weapons, seeking recom-
pense from the "mercenary slaves and government hirelings" who conspired to keep them oppressed. Others waited, quiet, on the outskirts,

teetering on barrels, and perched on window ledges, craning to see the man at the center of it all.

Egan, from horseback, felt with exhilaration the rising fury of the crowd, and knew that he could manipulate that emotion to maximum effect. These poor sods would buy the time that was needed, engage the English dragoons in the streets of London, so Napoleon, unopposed, could disembark and move to occupy the city.

"Wait!" a man hollered, climbing on the upturned end of a barrel.

"O'Connor, a fine fighting man to have at our side!" Egan shouted.

"No!" O'Connor yelled. And again: "No!" into the diminishing murmur of the crowd that now hesitated uncertainly. "The English know we are rising. They've been forewarned. To riot now is suicide! What good will it do for blood to run again in the streets? The soldiers are even now waiting fer us, waiting with their bayonets and their muskets to shoot us down where we stand! And what of your wives, your chil'ren? What will happen to them after your dead?"

"You damned traitor! You've betrayed us to the bloody English!"

With a face contorted by fury, Egan inadvertently yanked on his reins, his mare rearing up in protest, her eyes wild and rolling. Sliding off his horse, Egan stalked over to where O'Connor was standing and kicked the barrel out from beneath him. Stumbling, O'Connor was on his knees in the dirt when Egan reached down with one hand and hauled him unceremoniously to his feet.

"I trusted you!" he hissed, eyes narrow slits of rage, lip curled back from teeth in a primal snarl. "We have our traitor!" Egan shouted, pulling his pistol out of his waistband, cocking the hammer as he raised it to O'Connor's head.

A dark muttering rose through the crowd, like the sound of a rising storm on the distant horizon, like the ferocity of an ancient beast preparing for battle. The concurrence of only a few minutes ago had now become threaded with doubt. O'Connor, for them, was the face of the movement—the linchpin behind the rebellion. He was the one who had recruited them, exhorted them, and drunk with them. His was the face they trusted; Egan's they knew naught of. While they were aware of Egan's existence and his role within the United Irishmen, it was not with him that the bond had become established.

"Are ye a traitor, O'Connor?" a hoarse voice called out. The crowd fell into a hushed quiet as they all awaited O'Connor's answer.

"I am not!" O'Connor cried, his voice strong and sure. "I give you my word! I came across this information only by happenstance. I am an Irishman and would die for my country, but this is not the time. There are men in Parliament, powerful men, who are even now backing Catholic emancipation and independence for Ireland. I know that I recruited many of you, and I know I've pushed you to battle on this day, but I won't have you die for nothing! And if you die today, then it will be in vain! I ask you one last time to trust me. Let's give Parliament the chance to do right by us afore we make widows of our wives and beggars of our chil'ren."

"God damn you to hell!" Egan roared. As he squeezed the trigger, a burly man in the crowd leapt forward, grappling Egan about the shoulders and knocking him to the ground. The bullet, instead of penetrating O'Connor's skull, lodged in his right shoulder, which he felt as a burning trail of heat mitigated and dulled by his feverish agitation. One hand to his wound, blood seeping scarlet between his fingers, O'Connor again climbed on to the barrel that enabled him to look out across the sea of upturned faces. Egan continued to spit and scream, but nobody paid him any mind.

"The French are not coming. The English soldiers are waiting with arms and munitions, much more effective than ours. We have two choices—we can go into the streets, and fight, and die; or we can live, and continue to fight for Ireland in a way which will be truly useful! Éirinn go Brách!"

"Éirinn go Brách!" the crowd roared in response.

"We've much to be grateful for this night!" O'Connor hollered. "We have an advocate in Parliament, we have our very lives, and that of our families…also, we have the good Irish whiskey" (a howl of approval erupted from the crowd) "and Ann, at the Green Dragon, is serving free ale to all Irishmen tonight!"

And the crowds began to disperse, arms around each other's shoulders. In their giddy camaraderie, most did not notice the redcoats, disconcertingly abundant in number, as they stood in flanking formation down the narrow alleys that intersected with Tower Hill. The English soldiers watched with steely, narrow-eyed countenances behind bristling bayonet points as the men and women began to disperse; and so it was that the tinkle of the hurdy-gurdy, and the raucous laughter of the soon-to-be-drunk, replaced the aggressive fury of a people denied and a battle ready to begin. Taverns in Butler's Wharf and Little Eastcheap did a roaring trade that night, as did the whores in Rosemary Lane. The redcoats emerged in twos or threes, bayonets slung deliberately behind their backs. They had orders to take Egan in, and by the time he was hustled to his feet and marched, flanked by soldiers in red, to the Tower, the crowd had already gone.

O'Connor watched him go, feeling a relief at the avoidance of bloodshed, but also an inextricable sadness that Ireland was, yet again, at the mercy of politicians. Wolfe Trant had been so insistent: "Trust me, Nick," he had said, his blue gaze holding O'Connor's, his intensity compelling, his tone low and forceful. And so O'Connor had transferred his faith from one brother to the other, and in so doing had felt, in the deepest parts of himself, a confident assurance that the London Irish would indeed be better served.

# 104.

So this was how it was going to end: in a damp dungeon in Boulogne. Jeanne felt curiously calm about it. Shock, she assumed. But there was also a sense of liberation. A relief that she did not have to pretend anymore, that all those years of lies and deceit were behind her. At least she could die as herself.

Her deep and lasting regret was for the Duke d'Enghien and Joachim…dear Joachim. Even now she found it hard to believe that he was dead. All through the past years she had kept expecting to see him and, indeed, often imagined that she had: glancing after a stranger in the street because his profile looked familiar; watching another who had a shock of hair that tufted up in the front, just as Joachim's had; staring after a man who walked with the same swinging, carefree kind of gait. Each time, her heart had leapt, tugged, and died. At least, she wouldn't have to hope anymore. And she would be joining him soon, wherever he was, of that she could be certain.

Her cell was small and featured walls of damp stone and crumbling masonry. A patch of vividly green lichen edged the ceiling, and had, curiously, frozen within a thin layer of ice. The water that had given the lichen life seeped over the stones from some unknown source and dripped periodically from the low ceiling. Cross-hatched iron bars constituted a doorway that offered a dismal view of dark shadows and grimy flagstones. She had emptied herself of all tears and felt hollowly calm. Where the chaos and humanity of the world had once moved her, where the cause for which she had fought so long and so vigilantly had once meant everything, now, there was nothing—just an empty diffidence. Vaguely, in the back of her mind, Jeanne realized she was in shock…but what did it matter now?

Her damp solitude was interrupted by the rhythmic sound of footsteps, muted voices, and the clanking of keys.

"In here," a voice mumbled. A guard, pocketing a handful of coins, gestured toward the cell and left, his echoing footsteps retreating back down the passageway. Out of the shadows, the small, dingy figure of Fouché moved forward, closing his hands around the thick, rusted bars of her cell door.

"Primrose," Fouché said, his voice deep and surprisingly resonant in the small cell. "I am honored to make your acquaintance at last. You have proved a most able adversary."

Jeanne did not reply. She felt the cold wetness of the drip at the back of her neck, a substitute tear for the ones she could no longer shed. She waited for it…ten seconds, then another fat drop splashed against her skin and trickled in a river of gray makeup down the back of her neck. Curiously, she felt as if this wet droplet were the only thread that connected her to reality; the rest transpired before her as if in a vaguely understood passing dream. Was she going mad? she wondered. Either that or she was about to scream until she shattered into innumerable pieces.

"Primrose… Perhaps, you would prefer I called you Madame Recamier?" Fouché asked pleasantly, not seeming to mind her lack of response. "After all, there are no pretenses between us now, are there?"

Jeanne closed her eyes. *Drop…drop…drop.*

"Napoleon has left Boulogne," Fouché continued, digging with grimy fingers in the pocket of his overcoat. "Merde!" he muttered under his breath upon finding it empty. "Before departing, he left orders for your execution tomorrow at dawn. Admiral Latouche-Treville has been instructed to begin breaking camp and to follow to Dieppe within the week. It seems the nation of shopkeepers will open their doors tomorrow for business as usual." He grinned, a grim flash of large, yellow teeth. There was a moment's silence in the damp cell. "I come with an offer regarding Joachim," Fouché continued in quietly measured tones.

Joachim? Jeanne's eyes flew open and she turned toward Fouché, her mouth parting in question.

"Two years ago, he was sent to Île du Diable."

Devil's Island, the smallest of the three islands that made up the Illes du Salut off the coast of French Guiana. Its name had imprinted itself upon the French consciousness as a tropical Hades, complete with spear-bearing natives and horrible wasting diseases. A remote prison for the most dangerous of men.

"Is he alive...do you know?" Jeanne whispered, scrambling to her feet. Her ears were suddenly filled with a rushing noise: the sound of her heartbeat as it raced frantic and heavy within her chest.

"As of six months ago, yes," Fouché replied.

Joachim, alive! Was it really possible? If it was possible, then there was work to be done. Shaking off her lethargy with a concerted effort of will, Jeanne moved to the door, imbued with renewed energy and purpose. "What do you want?" she asked, feeling a measure of her old vibrancy return.

"My aim, Madame Recamier, is to prepare for all eventualities. No matter how long his luck runs, Napoleon is eventually going to be ousted or killed. If, at that eventuality, a Bourbon prince claims the throne, I want Pitt's personal assurance that London will accommodate me if the Bourbons cannot reconcile themselves to my...past activities."

"And you want me to acquire that assurance for you?" Jeanne asked carefully. He didn't know, she realized. Fouché didn't know that she was the one who had betrayed the Duke d'Enghien. He didn't know that by her actions she had betrayed whatever trust Pitt might once have held in her. As far as the police commissioner was concerned, she had been caught in an assassination attempt and was to be executed as a result. Perhaps she could encourage this belief long enough to free herself. "I cannot speak for Pitt, let alone whether he will resume the prime minister-ship..." Jeanne began warily, her instinctive distrust of Fouché manifesting itself. What if he was lying? What proof did she have that Joachim had really been sent to Île du Diable? And certainly Fouché wouldn't trust her if she conceded too readily.

"Do not attempt to mislead me, madame. I know of your close friendship with the English Pitt. You would be unwise to assume that my agents are confined to this continent."

"And what proof do I have that what you say is true?" Jeanne asked, hands grasping the bars, her gaze intent on Fouché's.

"In Paris. I have a lettre de jurrispri directing one Joachim d'Agin to be shipped to Île du Diable on the next available tide. Sentenced to life. Dated two years and ten days ago."

Lettres de jurrispri were the Napoleonic cousin to the lettres de cachet that had preceded them; these referred to documents signed by the king of France, counter-signed by one of his ministers, and closed with the royal seal or cachet. They contained orders directly from the king—often to enforce arbitrary actions and judgments that could not be appealed. Under the ancien régime, they had been utilized by unscrupulous aristocrats to dispose of unwanted individuals who were subsequently confined to a hospital, imprisoned, or transported to the colonies. During the Revolution, these lettres de cachet had been publicly denounced as prominent symbols of old abuses—their suppression lasting until Napoleon quietly resurrected their penal equivalent.

Jeanne bit her lip, her mouth dry with the fear of false hope—and the kind Fouché offered seemed tantalizingly authentic. He exerted his shadowy influence in every segment of Parisian society; he could have conceivably obtained a forgery, although this would have been monumentally difficult, even for a man as wily as Fouché. He would have to obtain Napoleon's personal stationary—the heavy parchment, the personal insignia of the bee, the distinctive flourish of his signature at the bottom—all identical to the forged order that Wolfe had procured with such effort; one that Talleyrand had supplied from the emperor's own study, an inner sanctum denied to such as Fouché.

It *had* to be authentic. The lettre would explain his sudden disappearance, and the complete lack of information regarding his subsequent incarceration. Lettres de jurrispri were used rarely and conducted with the greatest of secrecy. Joachim could have been taken from his bed and deposited, manacled, in a ship's hold within hours…with only this document testifying to his fate.

"Very well," Jeanne conceded finally. "I will use my influence with Pitt in your favor. When I have my brother, you will have your document."

Fouché nodded perfunctorily, a ghost of a smile playing around his thin lips. "Until we meet again, madame." And he was gone, carelessly dropping the keys on the floor behind him.

# 105.

At General Moore's signal, the vessels extinguished their lights as they approached the harbor of Boulogne. The strengthening wind moaned in their rigging, and the black sea sluiced between their hulls. The flotilla was comprised of heavily built gunboats belligerently named *Boxer*, *Flamer*, *Attack*, *Bruiser*, *Conflict*, *Archer*, *Bold*, and *Charger*, their gun-brig counterparts included *Hasty*, *Biter*, and *Bouncer*. These were shallow-drafted sailing vessels, sixty feet in length and twelve in beam. Twenty-four-pounder guns were positioned at the bow, with three thirty-two-pounder carronades amidships—all bristling with armament and ready for battle. The *Boxer*, captained by Moore himself, led the convoy, and it was upon his next signal that they separated into five attacking divisions.

The dark sky was dotted with pinpricks of light, intermittently obscured by gust-driven cloudbanks. Dark cumuli scudded across the last quarter of a waning moon which shone like a bright half-penny in the black sky. Moonlight illuminated their wooden decks in a flash of clear light, then was gone just as suddenly. What worked against them also worked in their favor. The cordoned vessels of the French were lit as brightly as their own, the forts behind them darkly silhouetted against the sky.

"God be with us," Moore muttered to himself from his position at amidships. "And a little luck."

Silently, the vessels glided toward the harbor, their sails stowed, their oars dipping in unison through the dark water.

"Ready, General Moore?" His second waited behind him, a young redhead, freckles stark on his pale face in the sudden shaft of moonlight. Moore winced.

"Wait...wait..." A bulky cloudbank moved across the sky; again, the deck of the *Boxer* descended into darkness. "Now."

The young man raised a horn to his lips, giving one clear sound that more closely resembled a goose than an instrument manufactured by man. This signaled the deployment of the small rowed boats from the bomb ships. Moore watched as the *Bruiser*, situated alongside, lowered its first boat into the water. The vessel had been ballasted to lie just under the surface and was manned by a crew clad in black, their faces smeared with pitch. They silently took up paddles, the ends muffled with sacking, and rowed through the cold waters into the harbor. It was a peculiar sight—only the men's heads and shoulders were visible above the water, and, then, only if you knew when and where to look; otherwise, their figures were indistinguishable from the blackness of the swelling sea.

Trailing behind these boats like a tether that had come untied was a line buoyed by corks along its length but tugged down at each end by some mysterious weight. In the black depths, gently carried along by the power of the men above, hollow copper spheres carried a murderous charge of black powder. Up current of the target, these boats would drop one sphere or carcasse and when the line had been fully extended, the other—both having been carefully primed and set to time—would be slipped into the water. The line would drift until it struck the cable of the target vessel, propelling the carcasses to either side of the bilge where they would explode upon impact, shattering the hull and rapidly scuttling the ship.

At least that was what Fulton had confidently predicted.

He better bloody well be right, Moore thought grimly, his gaze focused on the bobbing torsos of his men as they paddled through the silently heaving seas. *Flamer, Bold, Archer,* and *Conflict* were breaking away in turn as they lowered their individual boats, each carefully loaded with grappling irons, into the dark water.

Boarding parties buckled on white belts to distinguish themselves from the enemy in the dark. If that failed, the password was *Nelson*, and the appropriate response *Brontë*. Freshly sharpened cutlasses, pikes, and tomahawks were being handed out to the waiting soldiers; pistols and muskets were prepped and loaded. Moore could see the men lined up along the gunwale and between the rowers, taut with battle readiness, gripping axes and grappling irons. This miniature army of soldiers, spread out between the eleven boats, was loosely linked with tow ropes so as not to be separated by the powerful tidal currents.

He sent a silent prayer that they would return victorious.

# 106.

The city of Boulogne was comparatively small in size but had served as the base for several successful campaigns into Britain—Julius Caesar's in 55 B.C., and Claudius's a generation or two later. Napoleon had hoped to continue the tradition, aspiring to the classical greatness that all acknowledged to be the legacy of Rome. The muted thunder of artillery fire in the harbor below sounded Moore's assault—Napoleon would have his Vercingetorix. The old defensive walls of a now-crumbling Roman fortification defined the parallelogram that formed the city limits; ancient arched gateways allowed entrance at each end. The castle, where Jeanne was being held, had been built in the thirteenth century on the foundations of earlier Roman walls and served to strengthen the weakest landward-facing corner.

Wolfe entered beneath the Porte des Dunes and raced down rue de Lille, his gray military-issue cape flapping behind him. Since infiltrating the camp, he had learned that the infamous Primrose had been apprehended and was scheduled for execution the following morning. It didn't make sense; obviously she had fallen afoul of Napoleon's legendary temper. Whatever the case, he had his own pound of flesh to extract.

The men were in the process of dismantling the military huts. Napoleon had tired of gazing in idle impotence at the white cliffs of England; Austria had delivered an ultimatum; war with Austria now suited Napoleon's purpose perfectly. So, turning his back on the Channel, Napoleon had begun his march resolutely eastwards across Europe—leaving chaos in his wake.

Entering the tower through a wooden door in the base, Wolfe hesitated a moment before descending the narrow stone stairwell into the darkness. Deliberately thrusting thoughts of the Temple Prison from his mind, Wolfe found himself in a dark hallway with cell doors lining the walls to each side. Hearing a scraping sound from his right, he moved rapidly in that direction just in time to see a slender arm reaching through the base of an iron-grille door, fingers desperately seeking the keys that lay just beyond reach.

Moving forward, he stepped deliberately on the keys and crouched down, pistol extended in front of him, so that he and Jeanne were eye to eye through the rusted iron grillwork. She was lying within the cell on her stomach, arm extended through the door grill up to her shoulder.

"Wolfe!" she gasped upon seeing him, her eyes widened; a momentary pleasure crossed her face, and then a stillness as his weapon registered. Scrambling to her feet, she eyed him cautiously through the grill.

"What the hell have you done?" Wolfe growled, his face taut with suppressed fury as he moved closer to her. "Talk to me, dammit!" he demanded, fist curled into rigid whiteness around the pistol, forefinger poised on the trigger. She flinched slightly.

"What do you want me to say?" she said, her voice a parched whisper.

"So 'tis all true, then?" He inhaled sharply through his nose, looking at her with horrified disbelief. "You betrayed your country, your friends, your cause...for what?"

"I don't expect you to understand."

"Well I don't, Goddammit!"

"Why do you want to?"

He stared at her a moment. "Hell if I know," he said angrily. "But I do."

"Why don't you just kill me?" she asked wearily. "It's what you really want to do, isn't it?" She raised her chin proudly, exposing the long column of her neck; a pulse fluttered under the curve of her jaw.

"Aye," he whispered fiercely. "Just tell me why you did it." For a moment she didn't reply. "Is that why you took me to your bed? So I would trust you?"

"No," she stated with some vehemence. "I took you to my bed because I wanted to. You came from some other world, and I had every expectation you would soon be returning to it. It was a moment I wanted for myself, a rare moment without risk or fear, one for which I have no regret. As for the rest, well, I did what I had to do. I tried, you see, to save them both."

"Both?"

"I went to see Napoleon, after you left Paris, and he told me the truth…that he had my brother. He was prepared to exchange him for the identity of the Bourbon prince. I didn't hesitate." She raised her head to meet his gaze, eyes bright with unshed tears, her voice twisted with anguish.

There was a long moment of silence. Both Jeanne and Wolfe were stalled in a frozen tableau, the gun fixed unswervingly at her head. Then, struggling to maintain a composure that was rapidly crumbling, Jeanne continued, her voice a husky whisper in the dim room: "Fouché had Michel Desant in custody…Desant had already betrayed Cadoudal, Moreau, and myself… I assumed the Duke d'Enghien would be next…I…I hoped…" her voice struggled and stalled over that word, "that I would be able to… to…use…" Again, she faltered, and fresh tears appeared in her eyes and ran in rivulets down her dirty cheeks. She gulped in air as one mortally deprived, her chest rising and falling in anxious agitation, and then she continued: "I hoped that I would be able to free my brother…that I might use intelligence that I had every expectation would be disclosed anyway."

"He was your brother," Wolfe acknowledged reluctantly, a man who understood the enduring strength and power of family bonds. He was from a place where three-quarters of the population lived in poverty, and caring kin might be the difference between life and death.

"He was sent to Île du Diable. I don't know if he is still alive."

"I am sorry."

"No," Jeanne said fiercely, drawing back from the grilled door. "I am sorry. I killed the duke myself. I turned him in—a good man, a man destined to lead France out of this imperial tyranny—a prince of the blood. I sent a runner to warn him…told him Napoleon knew of his involvement in the Resistance." Tears flooded her eyes and spilled in twin streams down her cheeks.

In her face, he saw written the exhausted despair of a generation, a generation that had survived the Revolution, the political purges of the Directory, the bloody assassinations of the White Terror, the wars, the losses, and the perpetual scarcity of common essentials—the desperation of a people haunted by a past they could not escape, yearning for a small patch of stability and sufficiency. And particularly, he saw the face of a woman who had fought tirelessly for an idea, for a cause that was intended to have healed the pain of a nation, only to realize the inestimable grief of bringing about its own destruction. And in that moment, he knew he could not kill her. Not matter who she was or what she had become.

Jeanne turned from him, steadying herself against the cell wall as she attempted to quell the emotional tide. "I told him to get out of France…" Her voice roughened, filled with a grief and regret that he knew only too well. "But…I was too late."

"You did all you could." Wolfe lowered his gun, gripping the bars that divided them with his other hand. In the dim cell he could see only her narrow back, shuddering slightly, and the pale nape of her neck beneath the darkness of her hair.

"Jeanne," he said, his own voice gruff with emotion. "The duke would've been discovered. Desant would've betrayed him; 'twas only a matter of time. You cannot condemn yourself for trying to save Joachim out of the mess of it all. You didn't kill the duke—Napoleon did."

"You will not forgive me, do you hear?" she interjected sharply, her voice breaking with anguish. Jeanne would not forgive herself and could not abide his absolution. In a moment, he had opened the door and caught her in his arms. She trembled like a trapped bird, head against his chest, tears wetting the red fabric of his surcoat. "A mhàin Dia bhitheas breith orm," he whispered into her hair. What right did he have to pass judgment on this woman? He, who carried the bloodstain of murdered youths on his soul? He was as guilty as she.

A volley of musket fire shattered the stillness of the night.

"What's going on?" Jeanne raised her face to his.

"Pitt has attacked. Should buy us some time to get the hell out of here."

# 107.

Emerging from the castle prison, Jeanne and Wolfe were immediately confronted by the ordered turmoil of soldiers hastening to duty with their misbuttoned coats and sleep-rumpled hair, hollering for horse and saber. The contingents on night-watch had already engaged; thick columns of smoke obscured the shoreline, lit beneath by the periodic flare of cannonfire, and above by a quietly incandescent moon. Ordered volleys of musket fire sounded from the French ranks, which were answered sporadically by the encroaching English divisions.

Amidst the tumult, the two fugitives were utterly unnoticed. Regiments of infantry hustled past them in their blue coats and red lapels, the soldiers tightly gripping muskets, their faces set and tense. Commanders, mounted on skittish horses, waved their swords and bellowed orders. The camp had been partially disassembled the previous afternoon, and mounded wagons, stacks of folded canvas, barrels and carts formed darkly shrouded humps by the roadside. Between them, the regiments shuffled through to the steady rat-a-tat-tat of drums, white sashes across their chests a dull gleam in the lantern-light. Sharp ranks of bayonets rested upon their shoulders as they advanced relentlessly forward in a steady stream of booted feet, like some monstrous bristling centipede.

Ducking and weaving between gun teams and foot artillerymen, around the stomping hoofs of cantering cavalry, Jeanne and Wolfe made their way to the eastern gate—the one through which Wolfe had entered less than an hour before. They were brought to a sliding halt by the rearing horse of a general, a congregation of cavalry behind him, their horses nickering in fright at the deafening crescendo of cannonfire. The cavalry had been deployed to the camp perimeter, Wolfe realized, in the event that the port attack served as a prelude to an English military landing. The gate, their only feasible route to freedom, was barred by the muscled flanks of horseflesh and the gleaming boots of heavily armed cuirassiers, straight-bladed cavalry swords clanking at their sides.

"Marshal Masséna!" the general thundered. "Where are you?"

"Yes, General?" An officer separated himself from the ranks.

"General! General!" They were interrupted by a lieutenant pushing his way through the thick stream of infantrymen: "Boatloads of English soldiers are heading for the harbor breakwater!"

"Take a message to the officer in charge of the *Lanterne*," the general barked, reining in his skittish mount, "and instruct him to direct all his efforts on the approaching English brigs." The lieutenant nodded a rapid affirmative, already turning back toward the dock. "Marshal Masséna," the general shouted, "Take this infantry unit and—"

"Explosives...incoming!" a hoarse voice yelled.

And at that very moment, in the dreadful quiet that followed, the shell could be heard winging its way overhead in the black sky—a high-pitched whine that intensified to a metallic shriek before it hit the crowded square. It exploded with a deafening roar, freezing, for an instant, the general expression of horror and confusion in its white light. Afterwards, there was a complete and utter darkness.

When Wolfe rose, dazed, from the ground where he found himself after the explosion, he looked for Jeanne. There had been casualties; the bodies of soldiers and horses materialized as the haze of gunpowder dissipated.

"Jeanne!" He frantically pushed past men who had lurched to their feet, tripping over others, who lay bloodied on the ground.

"Jeanne!" Wolfe staggered through the wounded, disorientated by the persistent ringing in his ears; he could see the pandemonium in the haphazard motion of figures through the haze, the screams of the maimed, and the wild rolling eyes of a bolted horse, its reins flapping loosely against its bloody flank. He could see it, but he could hear nothing above the shrill cadence that echoed through his head. It was like some macabre mime played out to a hurdy gurdy with a stuck wheel.

Then he saw her—a part of her anyway: her stockinged feet, one missing a clog, and the lower portion of her tattered dress, visible beneath the rotund figure of a prostrate soldier.

"Jeanne!" Wolfe shoved the body of the soldier aside and helped her to her feet.

"Wolfe..." she murmured, stumbling against him. It was then he realized that she was bleeding—heavily. The front of her dress was saturated with blood, her eyes glazed and unfocused in an ashen face.

"Hush now, a ghaoil…I'm taking ye home." He gathered her unresisting body to his chest, her head lolling over his arm; she had lost consciousness. There was so much blood.

Gradually, the buzzing in his ears subsided, and he became aware of the cries of wounded men and the authoritative voice of the general directing offensive efforts. The whistle and whine of cannon continued in the harbor, along with the intermittent flashes of detonation and the perpetual staccato of musket fire. Wolfe blinked against the acrid gunpowder that lingered in the air.

Which way was the gate?

He felt a panicked disorientation, the woman limp and heavy in his arms.

Then, through the veil of smoke, he saw the parapet above each side of the gate. Resolutely ignoring the mayhem that surrounded him, he shouldered his way through

the gathering crowd of soldiers, stepping over the dead and the wounded, until he reached the gate. Wolfe shoved it open with one shoulder and began the long trek to the beach.

# 108.

"I have a letter I would like to read to you, if you don't mind," William Pitt began from his place at the pulpit. "It was written to me several weeks ago by a Mr. George Cooper, Barrister-at-Law, unaffiliated with any particular party or interest. I asked him to travel to Ireland and provide me with his frank appraisal of the situation and condition of the people who reside there. While remote corners of the Hebrides have been often explored and the name of Ireland is most familiar to our ears, yet both the kingdom and its inhabitants have been as little described as if the Atlantic flowed between us. There is a reason for this. Quite simply, the Whigs do not want you to know."

A murmur rippled through the audience. From his vantage point at the back of the hall, Wolfe could see the opposition stir uneasily. Adjusting the spectacles upon his narrow aquiline nose, Pitt began to read, his voice clear and sonorous even to those jammed in the back of the crowded hall:

"'Here, I will be bold enough to assert that the peculiarity which most strikes every stranger upon landing in Ireland, and of which I myself felt the full force, is that face of beggary, misery, and starvation which everywhere presents itself...'" Pitt glanced up at his audience who sat silent and attentive before him.

"Beggary...misery...starvation..." he reiterated over his spectacles before continuing to read: "'I cannot conceive of any other situation of slave or vassal alike to be so miserable as that of the Irish peasantry, who live in a state of squalid savagery feeding upon milk and roots.'" Pitt folded the letter in half and removed his glasses, his breath exhaled upon a heavy sigh. He placed his hands carefully on each side of the podium, as he had been known to do when addressing a topic about which he was particularly passionate. The audience leaned forward almost imperceptibly in their long wooden benches.

"I have felt the profound dignity of human nature," Pitt began, his voice deep and resonant, his silvery-bright gaze so compelling that every gentleman was convinced Pitt was addressing him and him alone, "when I have beheld a race of men, in form and motion, in stature and countenance, who were the pride of the species, on whose persons heaven had lavished all its favors…who are gifted with courage and generosity, indeed with all the heroic virtues—as many believe the English to be so described." He smiled slightly, and a ripple of amusement ran through the audience. "But to see a neighboring nation humiliated and degraded to so wretched a condition…" His voice broke slightly, and he looked down at his papers, blinking furiously as if to hold back tears. A murmur threaded its way through the attendant grandees, accustomed to the machinations of politics but to whom genuine distress on the podium was somewhat foreign.

"I speak not as an advocate of rebellion," Pitt continued with renewed force, "but this I *must* say; if such men as these are to be made helots, to be chained to the cultivation of the soil, without partaking of any of its fruits, their lords and rulers must expect that the avenging thunder will sometimes *burst* upon their heads! Having seen for ourselves the effects of revolution, and suffered the chaos and misery that is provoked for subsequent generations, *why* do we not extend the hand of love and affection? Gentlemen of the House, I intend to unequivocally support Catholic emancipation in Ireland and the guarantee of trading rights that respect Irish sovereignty. I expect you to stand with me."

In the thunderous applause that followed, Wolfe slipped through the door. He descended the steps outside the Houses of Parliament to a carriage, a lady, and a dog that waited for him.

# Epilogue

## The Historical Record

This is a work of fiction. While I sought to maintain a high degree of historical accuracy throughout the course of this novel—from plants and architectural façades, to fashions, and foodstuffs—details of the historical record were utilized in service of what I hoped would be a compelling fictional narrative.

Many of the characters contained herein are historical figures, and their depicted appearance and personalities were also based upon extensive research. Historical accounts refer to Napoleon Bonaparte seeking an English captain to guide his invading flotilla through the treacherous Goodwin Sands, and certainly it was hoped among the Irish that the French invasion would support and coincide with their own bid for constitutional and religious freedom. A fictional tweak I allowed myself was placing Napoleon's self-coronation as emperor a year prior to its actual occurrence in 1804.

The Prince of Wales: The Houses of Parliament met at the end of 1810 to review a report by the king's physicians. It was decided that due to the king's ongoing and debilitating mental concerns, the Prince of Wales should become Regent. The ceremony of conferring the regency on the prince took place at Carlton House with great pomp in early February of the following year. In his usual ostentatious style, the soon-to-be King George IV gave a grand supper to two thousand guests upon a marble table—through the center of which in a shallow canal flowed a stream inhabited by gold and silver fish.

The Duc de Talleyrand resigned as minister of foreign affairs in 1807. He opposed the harsh treatment of Austria after the War of the Fifth Coalition in 1809 and was a critic of the French Invasion of Russia in 1812. In April 1814, he led the French senate in establishing a provisional government in Paris, of which he was elected president. On the second day of April, the senate officially deposed Napoleon and a created a new constitution to re-establish the Bourbons as the monarchs of France. Talleyrand died in May 1838, having outlived many of the men who accompanied him in political power, and was buried in Notre-Dame. Today, when speaking of the art of diplomacy, the phrase "He is a Talleyrand" is used to denote a statesman of great resource and ability.

Joseph Fouché was dismissed from Napoleon's service in 1810; he kept significant documents hidden from his former ministry and undertook secret negotiations with the English cabinet. He attempted to flee to the United States but was compelled to return to port due to inclement weather. Fouché cleared his name and urged Napoleon to democratize his rule: "the sovereignty resides in the people—it is the source of power." When Napoleon refused, Fouché joined the invading allies and conspired against Napoleon, but again allied himself with Napoleon during the short-lived Hundred Days. After Napoleon's final fall, he joined the provisional government and tried to negotiate with the allies. Fouché, once a revolutionary using extreme terror against the Bourbon supporters, now initiated a campaign of White Terror against real and imaginary enemies of the Royalist restoration. He was dismissed to the post of French ambassador to Saxony in 1815, and died in exile in Trieste in 1820.

William Pitt returned to the premiership in May of 1803 and joined the Third Coalition of Great Britain, Austria, Russia, and Sweden, against Napoleon's armies. Horatio Nelson won a crushing victory in the Battle of Trafalgar against Villeneuve's forces as they emerged from Cadiz, ensuring English naval supremacy for the remainder of the war. The annual Lord Mayor's Banquet toasted him as "the Savior of Europe"; Pitt responded, "I return you many thanks for the honor you have done me, but Europe is not to be saved by any single man. England has saved herself by her exertions, and will, as I trust, save Europe by her example." He died in 1806, his poor health worsened by a fondness for port that began when he was advised to drink the wine to deal with his ill-health. His last words: "Oh, my country! How I leave my country!"

Primrose exists in the historical records as a shadowy figure; a charismatic woman who led the Resistance movement against Napoleon Bonaparte. Little is known of her, other than the mythology that embellished her person and grew up surrounding her exploits.

Admiral Pierre-Charles Villeneuve received orders from Napoleon to join the French fleet at Brest, with the intention of combining the ships-of-the-line and breaking the English blockade. Villeneuve, however, inexplicably sailed to Cadiz, and the French opportunity to competitively engage the English at sea was lost. Admiral Villeneuve was subsequently defeated by Admiral Lord Nelson at the Battle of Trafalgar.

Irish Independence: After Pitt's death, Irish independence was still over one hundred years in coming. In 1919, Irish nationalist parliamentarians supported the establishment of the Irish Republic and formed a secessionist parliament; the Irish Republican Army launched a guerrilla war to realize independence. The Anglo-Irish Treaty of 1922 concluded that war and established the Irish Free State as a self-governing dominion within the English Commonwealth. Northern Ireland chose to remain as part of the United Kingdom. A new constitution, introduced in 1937, declared the Irish Free State a sovereign state named Ireland (Éire). The Republic of Ireland Act proclaimed Ireland a republic in 1949 by removing the remaining duties of the monarch.

# Acknowledgements

The path of composition was a lengthy one; I spent ten years researching and writing this novel. In the course of that time, I received support and encouragement from many quarters. Thanks to my parents for their unstinting support of my writing career—from my earliest of days. Next to Megan and Ben, my much-beloved siblings, who have always been there for me, reading rough drafts or seeking out potential marketing opportunities; gratitude, with loving remembrance, to my dear uncle Ernie, who first introduced me to Gogol, and whose unfailing good humor will always be an inspiration. And to dearest Pat, my familial cohort in writing and painting.

Writing can be a lonely endeavor, and my tendency to professional hermit-hood would have been complete, indeed, if it had not been for several special fellow writers who obligingly read "the beast," offering critical feedback and suggestions for improvement. The focused solitude, the obsession with the stringing together of words, of painting a picture, vivid and visceral, in one's mind's eye, is all the more delightful when you can share it with those who are similarly engaged. A special thank you to Roderick Mackenzie—an early reader of *Killing the Bee King* and himself a simply marvelous writer—whose generous praise served as critical propellant for onward momentum; a depth of gratitude to Pim Wiersinga, who has provided unfailing support from across the Atlantic, and whose own works of historical fiction serve as perpetual inspiration. Thanks to Rosalind Brackenbury for her invaluable assistance with my French, and to Philip Tisseyre for similar aid most kindly provided.

I am grateful, indeed, to Camille Wiley, a genius of the poetical phrase, for her steadfast encouragement and for our coffee/wine hours that have been a bastion of all things literary. Thanks to my sister-of-the-heart, Julie Polzer, who is there through thick and thin; to Tania Keller for her ongoing friendship and perpetual encouragement; and to the marvelous Literary Endeavor group on Linkedin, who have demonstrated, in twenty-first-century style, the heart-felt support that can also be offered via virtual community.

The editing task has been a monumental one. Oscar Wilde put it brilliantly: "I'm exhausted. I spent all morning putting in a comma and all afternoon taking it out." While I am delighted under any pretext to associate myself with the great and witty Irish writer, my novel has benefited from the tireless efforts of Charity King Tirado who spent many a month rectifying my grammatical errors. A debt of gratitude to Ruth Feiertag, the editorial genius par excellence and the best of Shakespearean cohorts, who has bailed me out of many a grammatical fix at three in the morning—and to whom I owe more than I can ever begin to express.

As is customary, my greatest debt is acknowledged last. If the writing process was, at times, an obsessive one in which eating, sleeping, and the maintenance of good temper were often in short supply, then I owe more than I can say to my children who have loved and supported me throughout: Chiana, Talin, and Brax. And if life with a writer can be fraught with emotional outbursts and long stints of unsociability, then Jeff has nobly put his shoulder to the wheel. This book is for him.